THE WITNESS

THE WITNESS

A NOVEL

Naomi Kryske

DUNHAM
books

Dunham Books
63 Music Square East
Nashville, Tennessee 37203
www.dunhamgroupinc.com

This book is a work of fiction and, as such, is a product of the author's imagination, experience, and research. No resemblance to anyone living is intended. The reader will note that the British characters reflect their culture through their use of common British expressions and spelling for the words they say or think. The American characters use American expressions and spelling.

Trade Paperback ISBN: 978-0-9851359-2-8
Ebook ISBN: 978-0-9851359-3-5

Library of Congress Number: 2012941148

Printed in the United States of America

To the one
Who believed in me before I believed in myself
And who still does

PROLOGUE

Detective Chief Inspector Colin Sinclair was dog tired. Sleep had been a stranger to him since early Tuesday morning, when the girl's body had been found. Victim, he corrected himself. She was still alive, although the first officer on the scene had not thought so. Young and inexperienced, he'd seen the blood and the pasty white skin of her nude body and had concluded that the young woman rolled up in the rug was dead. Never checked. Fortunately his supervising officer had not been deterred by her condition or the squalor in the alley off Liverpool Road. He had lifted her out of the rubbish in the skip and found a very faint pulse.

At that point things had begun to happen very quickly. An ambulance had arrived. Islington was his borough, and he had been called. He and his sergeant, David Andrews, had gone first to the alley to view the deposition site and then to University College Hospital's casualty department and operating theatre. The ambulance, a crime scene now, had been isolated. A forensic doctor had worked with the UCH staff to supervise the collection of evidence from the victim—also considered a crime scene—a delicate procedure since it was of paramount importance not to endanger her life.

He ran his hand through his hair. At first the doctors wouldn't give him any odds on her survival. They were brusque. "It's too soon for a diagnosis," he'd been told. "We'll know more in seventy-two hours." When he'd heard the catalogue of her injuries, he understood why. The only things she had going for her were her age and a strong heart. She was unconscious and heavily sedated. It had taken all his considerable powers of persuasion to convince Doctor Walsh to let them see her.

The doctor's face had registered his displeasure, but he hadn't wanted Sinclair's arguments to deplete his time any further. He had donned a surgical mask and given Sinclair and Andrews masks as well before taking them onto the intensive care ward, each bed with just a curtain for privacy. The only sounds came from life support and other medical equipment. "She was bleeding internally," Walsh said in response to their surprise at the masks. "Her spleen had ruptured. We had to remove it. As a result her immune system has been compromised. If she lives, she'll be more susceptible to infection the rest of her life."

Dr. Walsh's movements were smooth and precise. He pulled back her hospital gown with slim, gloved fingers and described the injuries covered by surgical dressings. One of the victim's arms was in a cast. "She was also severely dehydrated when she was admitted. She has several cracked and bruised ribs. Broken ribs—here and here—punctured her lung and caused bleeding in her chest. We're draining that." He pointed to a tube stitched to the skin beneath and to the side of her left breast, and Sinclair winced.

"She's not breathing on her own," the doctor added, gesturing to another tube which ran from her mouth to a machine on the floor. "We sutured multiple lacerations. There are too many contusions to name. The worst, aside from those on her abdomen, are on her right shoulder and left thigh. If haematoma develops in the thigh—blood collecting in the tissues—we'll have to open it and drain it surgically. The leg is elevated to reduce the danger of a clot. The man who did this didn't hold back his rage, and he didn't miss much."

It was always difficult for Sinclair to see the damage done by brutal men to innocent women. This young woman was clinging to life. If she regained consciousness, at some point she'd know that others had seen her without her permission. It struck him that that would be another assault, an assault on her soul.

Walsh was still speaking. "Her liver was bleeding and needed repair, and there are some unusual marks on her thighs." He lifted one of her legs slightly to show them. "Her concussion wasn't severe, but there's something else you need to know: She was a virgin when this bloody attack took place. The complete details will appear in her medical record." The anger in his voice had been unexpected. "I have a daughter," Walsh explained. "It's not possible to be equally objective with all patients." He covered her, removed his latex gloves, and led them into the corridor.

"When can we speak with her?" Sinclair asked.

Walsh looked as tired as Sinclair felt. "It's Tuesday. We won't begin to ease up on the sedation until Friday. She should regain consciousness later that day, assuming no complications develop. She won't be able to talk to you, though. We won't start weaning her from the respirator until Saturday, and the endotracheal tube will have to remain in place until we do."

"I understand," Sinclair said, but Walsh gave a further warning.

"It's going to be difficult. Even after the tube comes out, she'll be in significant pain for some time. Your sessions will have to be very brief." He'd given Sinclair a sharp nod of dismissal and moved quickly toward the nurses' station.

So Sinclair had waited, visiting the hospital regularly. Each day the nurses reported no change, but Sinclair still spent a few minutes by her bed, brooding over her broken, battered, and ravaged body. It was hard to imagine this frail, still form having a life, laughing, loving. The end of a life usually meant, for him, the beginning of an investigation. This life-in-stasis meant that he could not advance. He had never been one for marking time, always preferring forward motion with reason dictating each step.

Their lack of progress on the case ate at him. They still didn't know who she was. A missing persons report had been filed by a central London hotel and was being investigated, but no determination had been made. According to the hotel manager, a white female, American, had not returned to her room. She was described as short and slim, with dark hair and eyes, probably in her early twenties. Police had spoken to her family briefly to inquire about her possible movements. Did she have a friend she might be visiting? Was she planning to travel somewhere outside London during this time? Had they heard from her? A photograph had been requested but not yet received. The unidentified female in hospital had not been mentioned.

This young woman had not been the first victim; six others had preceded her. When London's Metropolitan Police had realised they were dealing with a serial killer, the pressure to get things done had escalated exponentially, and the Special Homicide Squad had been created at New Scotland Yard. It stood to reason: They had the space to accommodate all the personnel and specialist functions required by a major investigation.

Sinclair and his sergeant had just recently been seconded to the squad. Andrews had rearranged the letters and called it, SSH, the Library Squad, and Sinclair appreciated his sense of humour. He was surprised, however, that the summons had come so quickly, before forensic evidence had been processed that would establish substantive links to the other crimes. It was an indication, he supposed, of the Yard's desire to commit their full resources to solving the case. Crimes committed by strangers were the most difficult to solve. Evidence collected in this woman's case could provide new avenues of investigation for the others. "Operation No Mercy," it was called, and indeed the villain who had murdered six women and nearly killed a seventh had shown none and deserved none.

It was now Friday, and the first newspaper story—"Newest Victim of Carpet Killer?"—had appeared two days earlier. The man who had tried to kill this girl knew he had not been successful. He also knew where she was, hence the uniformed officer assigned to guard her. She looked tiny and completely defenceless in the big hospital bed. She had a straight nose, arched brows over long lashes and a small mouth, still closed over the tube that helped her breathe. A bandage covered one cheek. Her skin—where it wasn't bruised—was unnaturally pale, and it made her short brown hair look particularly dark against the pillow.

He wanted very much to speak with her. Would she be coherent? What would she be able to tell them about her attacker? If her memory were intact, she would awaken to a nightmare. The injuries to her body were appalling, and he knew from experience that her mind had been raped as well. At the moment she was blissfully unaware of the challenges that lay before her. Soon, he hoped, she'd be reassured by the sheer number of people working on her case. The Yard was like a huge lion, crouching in the shadows and ready to spring upon the monster who had caused such heartache to so many. All they needed was a description, and they would find him and sink their teeth into him.

PART ONE

SEPTEMBER, 1998

Truth will come to light;
murder cannot be hid long.

— William Shakespeare

CHAPTER 1

The room was dim, but the pain was not. The woman without a name remembered the pain, and she felt it now, as sharp, constant, and deep as her fear, commanding her attention and making it difficult to think. My God, there was something in her throat! She reached for it, her shoulder throbbing, and heard a man's voice say, "That must be uncomfortable, but you need it just now." She wanted to scream, but she couldn't even make a sound. She struggled against the firm hand restraining her weak, slow one. When he moved into her field of view, she saw a wide face drawn in fatigue. The eyes above the mask were startlingly blue.

"Don't be afraid," he said. "You're in hospital."

Curtains instead of walls. Sheets covering her. Light pulsing across a screen. She could hear the bleep of a monitor. Other buzzes and clicks. Was he a doctor? He had dark brown hair, mussed as if he had run his hand through it one time too many, but—a tweed coat? Was he a minister? Was she dying?

"You're safe now."

She would never be safe.

"I'm a policeman. I'm here to help. Are you in pain?"

She dipped her chin. Even that motion hurt, and tears she couldn't wipe welled up.

He took her hand. "I'm Colin Sinclair. I want very much to know your name." He put a pen in her fingers and held a small notebook against them.

She wrote *Jenny* before her grip weakened and the pen fell. She closed her eyes.

Very quietly he retrieved his pen. She knew who she was, so she had memory. That was positive for the investigation but perhaps not merciful for her. On his way out he reported her brief period of consciousness to the nurses.

CHAPTER 2

Saturday morning a nurse woke Jenny. She'd just received her pain medication when a doctor came in, holding her chin still while he shone his light in her eyes. Then he suctioned her mouth and the tube in her throat. A second nurse pushed her upright, causing a stabbing pain in her ribs. The first nurse said something, but her accent was thick, and Jenny couldn't understand her. Her heart pounded.

"Breathe out," the doctor said.

It hurt to do that! Didn't they know?

"Harder!" the nurse behind her said.

The tube was long, and its movement made her gag.

"All done now," the doctor said briskly.

Jenny coughed, the pain from her ribs making her dizzy. One of the nurses slipped an oxygen mask over her nose briefly.

"Hurts," Jenny said in a voice so raspy that she didn't recognize it.

"Silly cow," the nurse said, not unkindly. "Sore throat's normal after extubation. Some water will soothe it and your dry mouth. You can rest then."

- -

On Saturday evening, Sinclair checked in at the nurses' station before heading to Jenny's space. "She had a rough time today," he was told. "She's breathing on her own now, but it's painful, and she's exhausted. You'll have better luck tomorrow if you want to have a word with her." Still, he felt compelled to look in. Her breathing was laboured and shallow without the help of the ventilator, but he was relieved to see that the tube had been removed from her throat. He couldn't imagine how helpless and frightened she must have felt, with something foreign inside her body. Tonight only the light on the headboard was illuminated; subdued light for a subdued spirit. He took her hand and squeezed gently, but unlike the cinema, she did not squeeze back. Taking the nurse's advice, he headed home.

When he arrived at the hospital on Sunday afternoon, a nurse was holding Jenny in a sitting position. Jenny's right arm was around the nurse's shoulders, and her legs were dangling over the edge of the bed. Her head was bowed, and tears were streaming down her cheeks. He found himself unable to watch, so he waited outside with the officer on duty until the nurse finished.

"Jenny," he said, "I'm a detective with New Scotland Yard. Colin Sinclair." He opened a black leather-bound folder and held out his warrant card.

He was tall, lanky. Sans the accent, he could have been a Texan. She gripped the blanket, trying to regulate her breathing to control the pain.

"I need to know your full name."

She breathed out slowly. Her hoarse whisper was weak. "Jennifer Catherine Jeffries."

The young woman reported missing by the Hotel La Place—they had insisted that they knew their guests, and they had been correct. He'd send a policewoman round to collect her things. "You're an American?"

"Yes. Texas."

Her fist was still clenched. Perhaps if he used a more formal form of address, she'd relax a bit. "Miss Jeffries, I know this is hard. Can you give me just a few more minutes? Do you know what happened to you?"

She made a writing motion in the air with her fingers. He took out his notebook and pen and held them for her.

Hurting. Stop.

Respecting a victim's wishes was critically important. Further questions would have to wait. "Sorry," he said. "I'll let you rest."

When he came back in the evening, he used a gentler approach. "I want to have a word with you, but I'll stop whenever you want me to do. I need to notify your next of kin. Can you write the information down for me?" He handed her his notebook and pen.

Bill and Peggy Jeffries, he read. *Houston, Texas.* There was a series of numbers. "Your parents?"

She nodded.

"Thank you. I'll ring them tonight." He wanted desperately to know the Who, What, When, and Where, but he was constrained by the lack of privacy in the intensive care unit. He tried to keep the frustration out of his voice. "Miss Jeffries, why were you in London? Were you on holiday?"

Graduate school, she wrote.

"Are you a student?"

Not yet, she penned.

"How old are you?"

23.

"No more questions for now. You've done very well. I want you to know that you're safe here. We have a PC just outside."

Her brows furrowed.

"A police constable," he explained. "Round the clock. You don't have to be afraid. Do you have any questions for me?"

How did I get here?

He waited until she looked up at him. "By ambulance. You were found in an alley, wrapped in a rug."

Her face crumpled, and her penmanship deteriorated. *He threw me away*

"Who, Miss Jeffries? Can you tell me who did that to you?"

Tears came, but they were silent, and she was still. She had learnt to cry without moving. It made him angry that she couldn't even cry without pain.

"Sorry," he said. "I'm meant to be answering your questions." He collected his notebook. "You're going to be all right, you know. It will take some time, but you're going to be all right. I'll tell your parents that when I speak with them."

"Wait—"

Her voice was so faint he wasn't certain she'd spoken.

"Don't—tell—"

"What don't you want them to know?"

"Not—"

He followed the direction of her eyes. "I understand. I won't mention the sexual assault."

He went back to the Yard to bring his partner up to date. Perhaps if he waited until later in the evening to ring the Jeffries, he'd find the words he needed. He dreaded the news he'd have to give them, but Jenny was lucky: She was alive.

CHAPTER 3

Sinclair waited until it was almost 1 a.m. London time before dialling the numbers Jenny had given him. He had returned to the Yard earlier in the evening, only to find his desk littered with the latest editions of the newspapers, all with headlines concerning what they called the "Carpet Killer" cases. He didn't read them, though he was sure Andrews had.

Fortunately Jenny was insulated from the media frenzy while she was in hospital. The officers on duty had been briefed; they would keep even the most persistent reporters away. But there was so much she needed protecting from! The attack had been invasive; the emergency treatment also invasive; and the interview questions—when she was able to handle them—would be invasive as well. It was a distasteful process, asking distressed strangers to disclose so much painful, personal information.

And police interviews were only the first step: Jenny would have to deal with legal counsel, a solicitor pretrial and barristers on both sides of the case when her testimony began. It was no wonder that so many victims lost their resolve to see it through. Justice could be cruel, even to those who least deserved cruelty. He shook his head at himself. He could not ring Jenny's parents while he was in this mood.

He decided to pay a visit to the Tank. Having a gym on the premises of the Yard offered a more constructive way for officers to deal with their stress than drinking at the bar it had previously been. He worked himself to exhaustion on the rowing machine. After a quick shower and change of clothes, he headed back to his office. He hoped Mr. Jeffries would be at home. In his experience it was easier breaking bad news to fathers than to mothers, although only marginally so.

It was a difficult phone call. Mr. Jeffries had been frantic for news about his daughter but faltered upon hearing that she had been assaulted and was in intensive care. No matter how clear and simple the words, a parent's initial reaction was confusion and disbelief. In a perverse sort of reassurance, Sinclair repeated the information and heard the transition from shock to horror. He had heard it before, in the voices of other parents, and the long distance connection only made the sound more poignant. It was rare for a crime to affect the victim only; most had families and friends who felt the repercussions as well. Hence Sinclair preferred to notify loved ones in person with a family liaison officer present, but that was not possible in this case.

Unfortunately it would be some time before Jenny's parents could travel to London: Their passports weren't current. In the face of Mr. Jeffries' agitation, Sinclair kept his voice calm. He had learnt early in his career to do nothing that would escalate a situation. He assured Mr. Jeffries that Jenny was safe and receiving the best medical care. He promised to ring again in the next day or two. It had not been difficult to avoid disclosing the exact nature of her attack.

CHAPTER 4

Monday morning found Sinclair on his way back to the hospital. He had just greeted Jenny when Dr. Walsh pushed the curtain aside. "I'd like to have a look at you," he told her.

Feeling a traitor, Sinclair stepped outside. In a few minutes he heard a rasping cry. The privacy provided by the curtain didn't seem sufficient. There were several more cries, muffled, a few minutes apart. How did doctors continue their treatment when what they did was hurting someone? The same way coppers did, he guessed: by focussing on the outcome. In Jenny's case, that would mean taking a very long term view indeed.

When Dr. Walsh came out, he was smiling. "I removed the chest tube and the sutures the plastic surgeon put in. Miss Jeffries is healing beautifully. You can go in now."

"I heard her cry out."

"There's a sharp pain when the chest tube is removed," Dr. Walsh explained. "And the incision site will be tender for some time. But she's doing well, and we'll be transferring her out of intensive care this afternoon."

"Not to a ward," Sinclair said quickly. "And not on the ground floor."

Dr. Walsh thought for a moment. "I'll see if there's a barrier nursing room available. That's an isolation area—it should suit."

Sinclair spoke with the PC on duty before rejoining Jenny. "She's going to be moved. Stay with her. I'll have backup for you by the start of the next shift." The curtain was partly open, and he could see the nurse arranging Jenny's bed. Jenny was lying flat, and she was taking careful, shallow breaths, her face tight with pain. The bandages had been removed from her face, and the intravenous drip was out also.

"Miss Jeffries, I have some good news for you. I rang your parents last night and had a word with your father. He asked me to give you a message." He recited the lines. "It's a bit cryptic."

"No, they're lines from a poem by Robert Frost. 'But I have promises to keep, And miles to go before I sleep...' He's coming; I bet both of them are coming." She tried unsuccessfully to clear her throat.

"Miss Jeffries, Dr. Walsh says you're healing beautifully."

He was so austere in his dark three-piece suit and tie, and the stilted way he spoke—and his clipped speech—seemed to belie his comforting words. “That’s just an expression doctors use,” she whispered. “There can’t be anything beautiful about it.”

“They did their best for you. A plastic surgeon put the stitches in your cheek. Didn’t they show you?”

“Is that supposed to be a good thing? That I had a plastic surgeon?”

The hoarseness in her voice made it sound like there was something broken inside. “It’s not bad at all,” he told her. “It’s like a wrinkle, a pink wrinkle. There’s a clear adhesive strip over it.”

She searched his face for signs of revulsion but found none.

“You’ll be pleasantly surprised,” he insisted. “And what you see now will fade and improve over time.”

She was quiet. She wanted more than speeches. She wanted the endless succession of interruptions by strangers to stop. She wanted the pain to stop. She wanted her sentence in this beneficent prison to be over.

“And there’s more,” he added. “You’re going to be moved out of intensive care this afternoon. When I see you later today, you’ll be in your own room.”

No, she thought after he left, it wouldn’t be her room. Her room was in a house in Houston, with faces she knew and voices she recognized, a place where her privacy was respected and she could shut everyone out if she wanted to.

It was late afternoon before Sinclair and Andrews made their way to Middlesex Hospital, where they introduced themselves to Jenny’s new doctor, Dr. Adams, a neat trim man with a pepper-and-salt beard. Then they located her room. Sinclair was glad to see that the backup had arrived: There were now two PCs seated outside, one of them female. “You know the drill,” he said. “Check IDs on all medical personnel until you know them. I’ll be supplying you with a list of approved providers. Until then, err on the side of caution. I don’t care if someone’s offended. This girl has been through too much already for us to take any sort of chance.”

“Sir, the move from UCH was hard on her,” the WPC reported.

“I expected that,” Sinclair replied. He knocked lightly, and he and Andrews entered. “Miss Jeffries,” he began, “I’d like you to meet David Andrews. He’s a detective sergeant and will be working with me on your case.”

Sergeant Andrews opened his warrant card. He was broad, even without a uniform. Despite his friendly face, she was glad when he chose to sit in the background, letting the taller man—what was his name?—Mr. Sinclair?—take the chair next to the bed.

“Congratulations on your new address,” he said. “Are you able to answer a few preliminary questions for us?" He knew from her medical report what had happened to her; he also had a general idea of when, based on her admission to hospital. He decided to enquire only about the Who and the Where.

She saw the sergeant take out his notebook.

"We know that someone hurt you," Sinclair said gently. "Do you know who it was?"

She shook her head.

"Can you give us a description?"

Her voice was still hoarse. "He was tall and slim. I don't know how tall. I was on the floor, and he was standing." A shadow crossed her face.

"What else?"

"Blond hair. Cheekbones—high. Nose—long and narrow. Lips—thin." She stole a quick glance at the young sergeant. He was recording everything. He looked up at her, an attentive expression on his face.

"Can you tell us anything more?" Sinclair wasn't using his notebook.

"He had a gaunt, weathered face. Ranchers in Texas look like that, because they've spent so much time in the sun. And crow's feet, maybe from squinting at the sun."

"What colour were his eyes?"

"Gray." She shivered. "When I close mine, I can still see him."

"Miss Jeffries, was he alone?"

"Yes—no—there were two other men," she stammered, "but they weren't—I mean—they didn't—"

Not a single assailant then. Until this moment no one had known how many evildoers they were seeking. Forensic had been able to demonstrate the involvement of just one, but detectives had wondered how a single individual had managed to dispose of the bodies. "Miss Jeffries, I know this is upsetting. I'd like to hear about those men, but I'm willing to do this at your pace. I don't want you to feel any undue pressure."

"Are you kidding? It's all pressure. You want me to remember, and all I want to do is go home and forget."

"Miss Jeffries, speaking with us does not obligate you in any way, although I do hope you'll continue to help us."

She stared at him. Didn't he know how out of control she felt? No matter how courteously he spoke, she was still at his mercy—at the mercy of whoever walked through her door. "What did you ask?"

"Can you describe the other men?"

"I only saw them for a couple minutes. One man was stocky. Muscular. No neck. Shaved head. The other was taller and thinner."

Sinclair saw her wince as she tried to shift her weight. "The shorter man: What was his ethnicity?"

She matched his politically-correct language. "Caucasian."

"What was he wearing?"

"A tight t-shirt and dark pants."

"And the man with him?"

"I can't remember his clothes. Just his face—thick black eyebrows and mustache. Hair slicked back."

"Accents of any kind?"

"They didn't say anything."

"Did they injure you in any way?"

She was so tired. "I couldn't get away."

"Miss Jeffries, you have to help us here. What did they do?"

"They—they were *there.* When the light went on. Near the door. Just a few feet away. They locked me in. Isn't that enough?"

"Where?"

She shook her head. Her voice was giving out.

"Miss Jeffries," Sinclair said, "I have just one more question. When you were admitted to hospital, forensic samples were collected that could provide important evidence in your case. Do we have your permission to process this material?"

"I don't understand. Why are you asking me?"

"Miss Jeffries, the samples were taken from your body. Had you been conscious, we would have asked your permission to procure them. Your consent is very important to us."

Consent: What a concept. The monster didn't ask for her consent. Even the doctors and nurses didn't. Amazing that the police did. "Yes."

There was a knock on the door. One of the PCs pushed it open. A nurse was bringing Jenny's dinner. "Time to sit up, lamb," she said.

"What's on the menu tonight?" Sinclair asked. There wasn't a plate on the tray. Everything was in polystyrene cups.

"Chicken bouillon, gelatin, apple juice, and tea," the nurse answered. "And pain medication prescribed by Dr. Adams."

"Yum," Jenny said. Her hand was shaking as she reached for the pills.

CHAPTER 5

Sinclair had asked the police sketch artist to meet Andrews and himself outside Jenny's room on Tuesday. As usual, Sinclair was early and impatient for the others to arrive.

"Quiet night, sir," one of the PCs reported.

Andrews arrived next. Sinclair checked his watch. It was late, even for Sutton. He saw a slim young man with a boyish face and curly black hair hurrying down the passage. "Sorry, sir," he said. "I've never liked coming to hospital. Are you sure you need me to go in? Couldn't I wait outside while you get the details? Hearing them from you would do just as well, wouldn't it?"

"I'll let him know what to expect, sir," Andrews said.

Sutton couldn't seem to stand still; he transferred his weight from one foot to the other and back again.

When Sinclair entered, Jenny turned toward him.

"Are you up to a chat?" He stood beside the bed. "The description you gave me of your attacker was a good one. Do you think you could add to it if you saw it on paper?"

"I'll try."

"Andrews," he called. The sergeant pushed the door open and stepped inside, Sutton hanging back behind him, clutching his sketch pad to his chest like a shield.

"Miss Jeffries, do you remember my partner, Sergeant Andrews? And this is Jamie Sutton. He's a sketch artist. Sutton, show Miss Jeffries what you have so far."

Sutton opened his pad. At Sinclair's insistence, he came a bit closer. The drawing was life size, light pencil strokes marking the features she had described.

"How old a man was your attacker?" Sinclair asked.

Jenny shrugged. "I don't really know," she said. "How old are you?"

"Thirty-six."

"A little older," she concluded. "Rugged looking."

"Is his face the right shape?" Sutton asked.

"Long and thin face," she remembered.

The artist drew quickly then turned the pad in her direction.

"His hair fell part way over his forehead. It was wavy, like Sergeant Andrews'. His eyes were more recessed."

Sinclair watched and listened. Sutton didn't have the rapport with witnesses that he would have liked. Still uncomfortable himself, he had made no attempt to put Jenny at ease. He was, however, skilled at eliciting descriptive details, adjusting the size of the attacker's eyes, nose, and mouth as she directed.

"Any facial hair?" Sutton asked.

"No," she said slowly. She considered the picture. "The eyebrows aren't quite right."

"I can do long—thin—full—heavy," Sutton said, demonstrating each type. He was more comfortable looking at his work than at her.

"They weren't thin," she said, "but he was blond, so they didn't dominate."

"Any distinguishing marks?" Sutton asked. "Moles, blemishes, maybe a scar? Oh, sorry! I shouldn't have said—I didn't mean—"

Her eyes filled, and she put her hand over her cheek. "It *is* a distinguishing mark, isn't it? I knew it—it looks bad, doesn't it?"

"It's not bad at all, Miss," Andrews responded, feeling the need to cut through Sutton's distress and his boss' displeasure.

"What's left?" Sinclair asked Sutton.

"Just the chin, I think," Sutton said quickly. "Rounded? Pointed? Or square, like this?"

"Square," she answered.

Again the artist corrected his drawing.

"Not—cruel enough," she faltered. "More lines of cruelty around the mouth." When the artist had added the final details, she began to cry. "That's him."

A look passed between Sinclair and Andrews. The face bore a striking resemblance to someone they both recognised. "Out," Sinclair said. "Cover that picture. Wait for me." Sutton was out of the room in a flash. Andrews followed.

"Miss Jeffries, thank you. Our combined efforts can accomplish a good deal."

The phone rang, startling both of them. "I'll answer for you," he said, knowing she couldn't reach it. He heard a female voice, American, ask for Jenny. He had just transmitted the number to the Jeffries the evening before. What time was it in Texas? Jenny's mother must have risen early. "Stand by," he said, handing the receiver to Jenny.

Jenny's eyes were eager with anticipation, but when she heard her mother's words, she looked shocked and then broke down. Sinclair could hear Mrs. Jeffries assuring her daughter that they'd be there as soon as they could, and they were so, so sorry for the delay. Jenny was sobbing. He took the phone from her. "Mrs. Jeffries? DCI Sinclair here," he said. "Yes, Jenny's all right, she's just happy to hear your voice. Let me see if I can help her settle a bit. Hold on, please." He sat down on the bed.

"Miss Jeffries, focus on something neutral," he suggested.

She looked at his tie—stripes of silver alternating with several shades of blue. Was that supposed to help? Her parents weren't coming soon; she was stuck here. Nothing was going to help.

"Mrs. Jeffries? We're not making much progress here. I know this is upsetting, but she's really all right." He listened for a moment. "I'll do that," he said. "Give my regards to your husband." He ended the call. "Miss Jeffries, your family loves you. They'll ring again."

He held out his handkerchief, but she gripped his hand instead. He was surprised and strangely touched. "Sshh," he soothed. "I know it's difficult for you to be separated from your family right now, but you're not alone."

He had a deep resonant voice that reminded her slightly of her father's, but he was not her father. He wasn't any part of her family. She realized that she was still holding his hand. She dropped it quickly, embarrassed that a stranger had witnessed her distress.

CHAPTER 6

Detective Superintendent Jeremy Graves was a spare, restless man with a seemingly endless reserve of nervous energy. Sinclair had worked with him before, when the Regional Crime Squad was investigating a case with Islington connections. Most coppers were accustomed to pressure on the Job, but Graves never ran out of expectations. He pressed hard—sometimes too hard, Sinclair thought—for a good result.

"How's our witness?" Graves asked. "Feeling any better?"

"Still weak and in significant pain, sir, but we do have a description of her attacker." He held out the drawing.

When Graves saw the artist's sketch of the suspect, he snapped, "Damn! Looks like Cecil Scott."

"That's what I thought, sir."

"Colin, is this witness credible? Coherent? Do you believe her?"

That was typical of the D/S; he never fired just one shot. "She's intelligent, sir. Her description was clear and to the point."

"Does he have form? Have you checked?"

Sinclair knew Graves was thinking of the psychological profile. According to the psychologist, sadistic killers didn't develop overnight. Scott should have previous offences, escalating in severity. "He's clean, sir, but he has travelled extensively."

Graves nodded: possible victims in other countries. "Do you know this man socially? Personally?"

"No, sir. We've met once or twice but not recently, and I wouldn't say that I know him personally at all."

"Impressions?"

"Superficially charming. Impatient. Unusually self-centred. The sort of man who's used to getting what he wants."

That fit the profile. "Any evidence of previous anti-social behaviour?"

"No, sir."

The D/S frowned and drummed his fingers on the desk. "I take it our witness can't appear at an identity parade? Then it'll have to be photographic. Don't make it easy! Make each snap as similar as possible in dress as well as in appearance. We have to be certain. If she identifies Scott, proceed as you would in any other case. Keep me informed. Does she have protection?"

"Yes, sir. And I doubled the detail when she came out of intensive care."

Graves leant forward. "Colin, will she follow it through? It's your job to ensure that she does."

"Yes, sir. I'll see to it."

"Family here?"

"There's been a delay, but they'll want to take her home."

"Can't blame them, but we'll have to move quickly then. Tell her the full resources of this force are with her. Until now we've been at least one step behind this bastard. I'd rather be one step ahead."

"She's been cooperative so far. She's given her approval for the forensics to be tested. Could you prod the lab for us?"

"Consider it done. And his accomplices?"

"We have insufficient information for an ID."

"The artist understands his role in this?"

"Yes, sir."

"You'll control Andrews? As of yet this ident is unconfirmed."

Sinclair smiled. "Yes, sir."

"Carry on."

Sinclair headed to his office to find someone to prepare the photo array. Andrews would be at the hospital, assisting Hartley in her interview of Jenny. Both were delicate assignments. The Sexual Offences Investigative Training officer would need to treat Jenny with kid gloves, and Scott was an ambassador's son. The rules might be the same for all suspects regardless of heritage, but in his case they would be more politely applied.

CHAPTER 7

Sergeant Andrews and the SOIT officer, Sergeant Hartley, identified themselves to the officers on duty. "There's a physiotherapist in there," they were told. Jenny was sitting up, and the therapist was replacing the sling over her neck. They saw relief come over her face when her shoulder didn't have to bear the weight of the cast.

"I'm Sergeant Hartley," the female officer said, extending her warrant card for Jenny to see. "Sergeant Summer Hartley." She smiled at Jenny's expression. "It's okay; everyone's curious about my name. May I sit down?"

Jenny nodded at the chair next to the bed. She thought the officer's name fit her—her hair was the hue of summer wheat, and Jenny could picture her walking outside, the wind rippling through it and the sun spotlighting her fresh face. Jenny couldn't see any evidence of makeup, yet her complexion was smooth and clean. She wasn't wearing a uniform; her clothes were varying shades of autumn browns and golds. Jenny felt drab in her hospital gown.

Hartley was trying not to react to Jenny's battered appearance. She'd been told what her medical condition was, but seeing such extensive injuries firsthand was difficult. She felt a bit queasy and was glad she was seated. "I was a summer baby," she continued, "and since my parents' lifestyle was unconventional, to say the least, they decided that I would be a remembrance of the season."

"Is there such a thing as summer in England?" Jenny asked.

Hartley gave what she hoped was a relaxed laugh. "I know we've got nothing that compares to your Texas temperatures, but the mercury only has to rise a bit, and we're outdoors making the most of it." She smiled again. "Do you have any brothers or sisters?"

"Two brothers, both younger."

"I have a younger sister," Hartley said. "When she was born, my parents were in their spiritual phase—her name is Grace."

Hartley's hair was long enough for a pony tail, but she wore it loose. Jenny wished she'd at least been able to wash hers.

"Sergeant Andrews and I want to have a chat about what happened to you," she said. "You needn't be afraid; we can stop at any time. Our goal is to achieve the best evidence we can, but we're not going to do anything without your consent. We'd like you to use your own words. Do you have any objection to being taped?"

Jenny hadn't seen a camera. "It's not a video, is it?"

"No, Sergeant Andrews has brought a tape recorder."

"Interview with Jennifer Jeffries, Middlesex Hospital, London.

Sergeants David Andrews and Summer Hartley present." Andrews gave the date and time. "Your statement is really important to us," he said. "It will help in our investigation and provide the basis for legal prosecution later, should you decide to participate in the criminal justice process."

"Do I really have a choice?" Jenny asked, surprised.

"Jenny," Hartley responded, "this interview is just the first step. And we will not proceed with it unless we have your permission. At each stage you are the one who will determine if we go on."

"I don't understand," Jenny said, her voice rising. "I described somebody. You have a drawing. Didn't the other detective tell you? Haven't you identified him?"

"Jenny," Hartley said patiently, "there are a large number of people working on this investigation. Each of us will play his or her part. We have many avenues to pursue, and we follow established procedures."

"Oh, God," Jenny cried, "you have to find him and arrest him. He'll do this to someone else if you don't! You can't let that happen!"

Andrews and Hartley exchanged glances.

"You don't even know how badly it hurt!" Jenny continued, her sobs distorting her words. "And it still does! You have to help me!"

Hartley stood up. "That's just what we're going to do. Sergeant Andrews is going to call the nurse, and we're going to make sure she looks after you. You don't have to do this when you're so upset."

Andrews spoke into the machine, reporting the time the interview was suspended.

During the afternoon interview, Jenny was frustrated with the small talk and impatient with Sergeant Hartley's careful adherence to procedure. She hurried through the background questions Hartley asked and tried to ignore the neutral expression the trim sergeant wore. Jenny hadn't forgotten the shock Hartley had struggled to conceal in the morning, and it made her wonder how her mother would react when she saw her.

Hartley's skin was flawless, and she was graceful, crossing her legs with unconscious ease. Jenny's left leg still throbbed from the vicious kicks it had received. In fact, her whole body looked and felt like someone had taken a jackhammer to it. Her throat was tight, but the tape recorder was running, so she tried to focus on describing the sights she had seen her first few days in London.

Her last glimpse of her normal self had been in the mirror in the hotel lobby. She had given a carefree wave to the manager and headed toward the bus stop, her feet light on the sidewalk, her heart full of anticipation for the day's events: touring as many galleries of the British Museum as she could.

There had been no gallery tours, no examination of relics, art, or literary works. She had been taken, stripped, beaten. She remembered the monster's hand striking her cheek and his body poised to impale her. The tightness in her throat spread to her chest. She couldn't possibly detail the monster's actions to the sergeant with the pristine features. Hartley's reassurance didn't assuage her dismay, and she began to cry.

She heard Andrews' voice: "Interview with Jennifer Jeffries terminated."

CHAPTER 8

At the Yard Andrews and Hartley were reporting their two failed attempts to interview Jenny. "Sir, I don't know how to explain it," Hartley said. "In the morning we stopped when she became upset. Often that happens, but usually it's better the second time round. In the afternoon she seemed determined to talk to us, but she just couldn't do. Perhaps the trauma is still too recent, or the absence of her family makes the attack too difficult to discuss."

"Sergeant Hartley did it by the book," Andrews added, "but Jenny lost control long before we reached any sensitive areas."

"Is it worth another go?" Sinclair asked.

"Not by me," Hartley said.

"Can't you set your feelings aside?"

"Of course, sir, but my feelings aren't the issue. Hers are. She knows her appearance has been compromised. She kept staring at me. I think she'd do better with a different officer."

He dismissed Andrews and Hartley and then settled back to listen to the tape. Pain may have been a factor, but he thought that fear was the reason the first interview had failed. She knew her attacker was still at large, and remembering the attack resurrected the fear.

He listened to the second session twice but came no closer to understanding what had gone wrong. However, Hartley had acquitted herself well. Terminating the interview had been the only course. And her appraisal of Jenny was probably correct. He closed his office for the night.

On his way home he stopped by the hospital. There was a stillness in Jenny's room he couldn't identify. Her eyes were red and puffy. More tears then. God knew she had a right to them. "You had a rough time today. Care to tell me about it?"

She looked at him, wondering what was wrong with her. She'd been glad at first that the police were there, but now she just wanted them to go away and take their questions with them. "No," she said. "I'll cry, and it hurts to cry."

"Take a deep breath and steady yourself," he suggested. "Then talk to me."

She shook her head slowly. "It hurts to breathe."

"Do you need medication for pain? I'll get the nurse for you."

"I've had it already," she whispered. "There's nothing they can do."

"Miss Jeffries, I'm just a policeman, and I understand that you don't know me very well, but I'm not going to desert you. How can I help?"

"The doctors and nurses call me 'Miss Jeffries,' and then they do things that hurt. Could—could you please call me 'Jenny'?"

"Jenny, what hurt you today?"

"I'm scarred. It's awful! They're everywhere! I should have died!"

Of course. According to the nurses, Jenny hadn't watched the doctor remove her chest tube. This morning, however, before the first interview, they had cleansed the sutures and changed the dressing. She had seen the surgical incision and more. He stepped closer to the bed. "The only scar I see isn't awful at all," he said softly.

She gave no sign of acknowledgement.

"You've still not seen the one on your face?"

She shook her head.

"Shearson!" he called.

"Sir?" The constable pushed the door open slightly.

"Borrow a mirror from one of the nurses and bring it to me." He saw what little colour there was in Jenny's face drain away. "We're partners," he told her. "That means we look out for each other, trust each other. And this is the first step. Thank you, Shearson," he said when the mirror was provided. "I'm not going to make you look, Jenny, but you're going to feel better when you do. Knowing is always better than not knowing."

She held the mirror face down in her lap. There was a long silence.

"You're still pretty, Jenny." All Scott's victims had been pretty. He had seen snaps of them, keepsakes their families treasured, pictures of special occasions when everyone was smiling.

"I've seen enough scars for one day," she whispered. "I just can't do it. Please don't be mad."

Mad? Oh—culture gap: She means angry. "A scar is a sign of healing," he pointed out.

"Not to me."

"You're going to get better, Jenny. It's early days yet."

"Is it bad? Will people stare, like they do at crippled people?"

"Not a chance," he assured her.

"It's not like having freckles," she insisted. "This is different—you know it is."

"No, Jenny, it's not. We're all more than a single feature." He changed the subject. "About today—"

"I lost it today," Jenny whispered. "I wish I didn't remember what happened to me. Then I wouldn't disappoint anybody."

"You didn't disappoint," he said quietly. "Nothing of the sort. May I prove it to you?" He held out his hand. "You don't have to take it. My feelings won't be hurt if you don't. All the books say I shouldn't offer it. But sometimes human need goes beyond words."

She did take his hand. His long, slim fingers swallowed hers. "Will you give me another chance?"

"Dozens of them," he assured her. "We'll all start with a clean slate tomorrow."

CHAPTER 9

Sinclair hadn't visited anyone in the hospital on such a frequent basis since his father's illness. It struck him how vastly different the two experiences were, his father with a negative prognosis, Jenny with a positive one. But his father had not been isolated. His mother had been with him almost round the clock. He had visited regularly, his sister had, and there had been other family members and friends. Jenny's family was still an ocean away.

They had kept his father company, adjusted his pillows, refilled his water, brought treats. They had encouraged him, entertained him, reminisced with him, been with him when the doctors made their rounds. Jenny had no visitors except medical personnel and police. When the doctor's treatments were painful, there was no one to lend support. He and Andrews came with questions, not comfort.

Over time, his mother had brought things from home to cheer his father: family photos, a favourite book, music that soothed and relaxed him. Near the end, she had read to him, short humourous pieces, poetry, verses from the Bible. He could still recall her light, expressive voice. It had distracted his father temporarily from the deteriorating condition of his body and the rest of them from their impending loss.

Jenny's room was bare, but he could do something about that. Perhaps flowers could help bridge the gap until her parents arrived. He managed to talk the florist out of a formal arrangement with lilies, thinking her samples looked funereal, and selected instead miniature roses, sweet peas, and the delicate *de rigeur* baby's breath. He didn't know what would appeal to a young wounded Texan, but the gentle colours pleased him.

She looked up and smiled when she saw the flowers. "Is there a card?"

"I'm the card," he told her. "They're from me. I thought you could use a bit of encouragement."

"They're beautiful. Thank you. My parents called last night after you left," she continued. "I cried, so my dad did most of the talking at first. When I calmed down, my mom had questions—how was I feeling, what was the hospital like, did I like my doctor—parent stuff. I never thought that parent stuff would sound so good, but it did. I didn't want to hang up."

"Jenny, they're lovely people. I've spoken with them several times." He realised that it was the first time he'd heard her speak without tension. There was warmth in her voice. He'd heard other Americans speak, so it must be the Texas accent that broadened her vowels and softened her consonants. His voice must sound cold. She was used to hearing a slow drawl.

The food on her breakfast tray was virtually untouched. "I see you're not sold on our British cuisine," he said.

She tried to respond to his lighter tone. "What is British cuisine, exactly?"

"Why, we have very upmarket items," he told her. "You haven't experienced the wonders of fish and chips, or bangers and mash, or spaghetti on toast?"

"No, I have been culturally deprived," she said, "and I'm not sure I want to assimilate. Didn't George Bernard Shaw say that we were 'two people separated by a common language'? I think we're separated by lots more than the way we speak."

"Our legal systems differ also, but there are many common factors. In both our countries police depend on the willingness and goodwill of witnesses to help them stem the tide of crime."

"Are you asking me if I'm willing to be a witness?"

"For now I'd just like you to think about your readiness to participate in the interview process," he said. "If the events are still too traumatic for you to speak of, I need to know."

"Will Sergeant Hartley be coming back?"

"No, I'll be assigning another officer, either a male or a female, whichever you prefer."

"Why do I have to do this at all? You'll have scientific evidence."

"Jenny, we have only your description of the man who assaulted you. We need to identify him and locate him. And before we interrogate him, we need to know from you everything that happened."

"It's hard to think about telling everything to a stranger," she said slowly.

Victims of sexual violence were usually interviewed by specialists, but it wasn't easy to establish rapport with people who were frightened or in pain. Jenny was both. How long would it take a new officer to gain her trust? A witness had to have confidence in the police. They were the first representatives of the criminal justice system they encountered.

"Then talk to me," he said.

"Now?"

"No, after lunch. I'll bring another officer with me, and we'll make an official record of what you say."

She felt cornered. She hadn't been able to get away from the monster, and now it appeared she couldn't get away from the police. But maybe if she gave them the information they wanted, they'd leave her alone for a while. "After lunch," she confirmed.

CHAPTER 10

Sinclair returned to the hospital in early afternoon to show Jenny the photo display that included Scott's picture. "As you know, we have a sketch based on your description of your attacker. We've tried to match the sketch with photographs. We need to see if you can identify your attacker's photograph when compared with other similar ones. If his picture isn't here, please say so. We want to be certain before we arrest someone."

He handed her twelve photos. It had taken some time to compile them, since the only photographs they had of the man they suspected showed him in evening wear or some other type of specialised clothing. Sinclair didn't want her choice to be affected by differences in dress. Facial features alone needed to be the determining factor.

"He's the one," she said shakily when she saw the twelfth picture. Seeing her attacker—even smiling, as he was in the photo she held—made her dizzy with fear. "There's no doubt."

She had pointed to the photo of Cecil Scott. "Are you willing to testify in court to that effect?" he asked, trying to conceal the excitement he felt.

"Testify? I can't face that! I can hardly stand up."

"Jenny, he needs to be in prison, and you can help us accomplish that. May I count on your cooperation?"

"What do you think I've been doing?"

"I'd like to encourage you to consider taking a further step."

"Why? Why do I have to be the one?"

"Because there's no one else. Are you aware that there were other victims? What you may not know is that none of them survived."

"Into the valley of death rode the six hundred," she said bitterly.

He recognised the Tennyson quote. "Jenny, this isn't a suicide mission. The Metropolitan Police have a world-wide reputation for excellence and integrity, and we can protect you from any threat. We've provided protection for you since you were found, one officer while you were in intensive care and now two. I understand that it's difficult for you to trust anyone just now, but that's rather compelling evidence of our commitment to you."

"But—my family—I want to go home. I want to see London in my rear-view mirror."

"Each case, each witness is different. We are more than capable of responding to your individual needs." He decided not to appeal to her sense of civic duty. London wasn't her city. In the short time since they'd met, he'd seen fear, pain, and despair cross her face. Occasionally she'd expressed frustration, but not anger. Some victims wanted revenge; fuel their anger a bit and they'd agree to testify to anything. He didn't see that in Jenny. He'd been struck by her helplessness, so he decided to emphasise the empowering nature of what he was asking her to do. "Jenny, there's power in speaking the truth. I know your feelings overwhelm you sometimes, but you seem to right yourself. It takes a special sort of strength to face someone who has hurt you, and I believe you have it." He smiled. "You're the spark that will ignite this case."

"No, I'm the kindling. I'll be consumed."

"It's your choice to make, Jenny."

"Do I have to decide now?"

"No, although I'd like to suggest that you'll feel more at peace when you do. Jenny, I'm offering you the opportunity to take back the part of your life that your attacker took away. Asserting yourself will make you feel stronger."

She looked down. The suspect photos were still on her lap, the one of Scott on top. Her strength had bled out of her; the surgeon had stitched up an empty shell.

He collected the photos. "I'll be back shortly," he said.

Andrews and the new SOIT officer were approaching. Sinclair gave Andrews the envelope of suspect snaps. "We've got him!" he said. "Take this back to Graves. The high-profile nature of this case has just escalated. And Andrews—the fewer people who know about this, the better."

CHAPTER 11

At the sound of the knock, Jenny turned toward the door. Mr. Sinclair had a tape recorder in his hand, and there was someone with him, a man with sandy-colored hair receding slightly at the temples and a boyish, easy smile. He was wearing jeans and an open-neck shirt under a pullover sweater. He reminded her of her brother, Matt, who was lean and wiry and wished he were taller.

"Jenny, this is PC Bridges." He didn't mention Bridges' specialist training.

She blinked. "You don't look like a policeman."

Bridges laughed. "I'll take that as a compliment, but the name's Barry." His eyes twinkled. "I'm afraid to ask—what do I look like?"

"A teenager."

"My wife would agree that I act like one sometimes," Bridges smiled, "but I've seen sweet sixteen twice." He and Sinclair pulled chairs next to the bed and sat down.

Jenny realized that the side of her face with the scar was next to him, and she covered her cheek quickly.

"You needn't do that, Jenny. May I call you Jenny? We all have scars. Want to see mine?" He stood up, propped his foot on the bed, and pushed his sock down.

"I can hardly see anything," she said.

"That's just what people are going to say about you before long."

"How did it happen?"

"Poor quality shin guard." He rearranged his sock and sat down.

"What can I tell people about my scar?"

"Tell them it's from a sport injury," Bridges joked.

"Do you play soccer?" she asked Bridges.

"Football, we call it," he answered. "I used to. Now I coach it—seven- and eight-year-olds."

Sinclair was enjoying this exchange. He'd wondered what Bridges would do. Many SOIT officers watched popular TV shows to help them develop rapport with a victim, but Jenny was from a different culture and wouldn't have been familiar with British fare.

"Both my brothers play," she said. "When they started, their coaches had a terrible time getting them to do the drills. How do you get kids that young to do them?"

"I participate with them, and sometimes I even give one of them the whistle so he can start and stop the play. And I'm going to do the same thing with you, when you're ready."

She turned to Sinclair. "I thought you were going to question me."

"You seem to be getting on with Bridges."

"I like helping people," Bridges said. "I want to help the investigation, of course, but more important, I want to help you. If you can trust me enough to tell me what happened, you'll have made an important first step." Like other SOIT officers, he had been trained to place the needs of the victim first. Doing so not only yielded better evidence but also established a strong relationship that encouraged victims to follow through.

She looked down at her lap. "Talking about it makes it seem like it's happening all over again."

"Then it's time you left the defence to us. We have the best defence in the world right outside your door." He stood and summoned the two uniformed police. "We're having show and tell, gentlemen. Please introduce yourselves."

"PC Denton, Miss," the first man said. He looked like an NFL linebacker, broad and solid, but he was not armed.

"PC Bolton," the second, slimmer man said.

"This is not my area of expertise," Bridges continued, "so we won't cover everything. However, even I know that you have radios, in case you need backup. And clearly you both carry truncheons. Would you like to tell us why you're here?"

"To protect this young lady," Denton answered. He looked in Jenny's direction.

"How can you do that without guns?" she asked.

"We don't need firearms to protect you, Miss. If you need us, all you have to do is call." He nodded at the DCI.

As Denton and Bolton left, Bridges continued. "They check everyone's identification, Jenny, every time. When the Chief Inspector and I arrived this afternoon, we both had to show our warrant cards. They have a list of approved medical personnel. DCI Sinclair has given very specific instructions to ensure your safety."

She was seeing only a small part of the picture. "Will you help me?" she asked Bridges. "Yesterday I was—offsides."

Bridges smiled. "My kids do that when they're trying to win the game all by themselves. You don't have to. With your permission, we'll record what you say so you won't have to relate everything more than once. We may have follow-on questions, but those can be asked at a later time."

"I didn't do anything wrong," Jenny said in a strained voice. She watched Bridges' face very carefully, but there was no sign of censure in his expression when he replied.

"Of course you didn't. The man who hurt you was in the wrong, not you. Do you want to tell us about it now?" He saw her face turn pale. "You can begin with your arrival in London," he said quickly. "Was this your first trip across the pond?" He turned toward Sinclair. "Sir, if it's no bother—"

She heard Mr. Sinclair recording the introductory information.

She nodded. "I'd never gone through customs before. When the official asked if I were entering the country for business or pleasure, I didn't know what to say. I took the train into the city. Seeing London's landscape for the first time—Texas is a horizontal landscape, but it seems like everything here is vertical."

"Were you tired at that point?" Bridges asked.

"Yes, tired of lugging my bags. I'd been too excited to sleep on the plane, so I had to nap when I finally got to the hotel. The owners lived in Texas for a while, isn't that crazy? They recommended places in the neighborhood to eat and gave me directions. I found a chocolate shop. Everyone was so courteous. I thought I was off to a good start."

"You are," Bridges said.

"The next day—Thursday—I went to the planetarium. It's near the hotel. And I walked through the Wallace Collection. That was amazing! Museums in the southwest are in new, contemporary buildings for the most part. The mansion where the Wallace Collection is displayed is so magnificent, it's a work of art in itself." She looked at Sinclair. "Do you really want to know all this?"

"We want to know everything you're willing to tell us—where you went, what you did, what your impressions were. It may help us to establish when you were targeted by your attacker." If he prolonged the conversational nature of the interview, perhaps she'd be able to maintain her relaxed tone. "Which part of the Wallace exhibit did you like the most?"

"The room with the knights and the armor. Cowboys in Texas wear spurs on the back of their boots, but the knights' boots had points on the front, too. And their armor was so small! Some of it would have fit me, I think. I should have taken some." Her voice choked. "I could have used it."

"Just dribble the ball, Jenny," Bridges said gently. "One touch at a time."

The pained look left her face for a moment. "Friday—the Changing of the Guard and Trafalgar Square. The National Gallery. Saturday—Westminster Abbey and Big Ben. Texas doesn't have much history compared to you. Sunday—I went shopping. I was told that Marks and Spencer would be cheaper, so I went there first." She blushed. "I never saw so many bras and panties in all my life! I didn't buy any—there were too many to choose from, and the sizes weren't the same as at home. Then I went to Selfridge's. That took more time than I thought it would, because they sell books. Department stores in Texas don't."

When she didn't continue, Sinclair spoke. "What did you plan for the Monday?"

"The British Museum. It didn't open until 10, but I was really eager. I started out early, because I was going to take the bus, and I didn't know how long I'd have to wait for the right one or how long the ride would be. I figured I could find a coffee shop near the Museum if I needed to wait. The staff at the hotel—they were so friendly—told me to walk down to Oxford Street and wait at the bus stop on the north side of the street, just outside Selfridge's. Selfridge's," she whispered. "I was so confident, because I knew how to get there. I had just been there the day before."

"Keep your eyes on the ball, Jenny," Bridges said.

"I was trying to figure out how to use the ticket machine when someone behind me bumped into me, hard. I lost my balance, then I felt a stick. Someone put his arm around my waist. I was dizzy. I must have passed out. On the street. Near Selfridge's." She stopped and swallowed hard.

Possible CCTV footage. Sinclair made a mental note to check.

"I woke up," she gasped. "It was dark, like a cave. I couldn't see a thing! I was shaking with cold. I didn't have any clothes on! Oh, God, who would strip me and leave me naked in the dark?"

Not only did Sinclair want the answer to that question, he wanted to be able to prove it.

"I was too nauseated to move. I didn't know where I was. I wanted light! Somebody to help me!"

Not for the first time, it struck Bridges how much help trauma victims needed and how limited the police response could be. He didn't know which was worse, losing a loved one to death or losing a loved one to trauma. Trauma had a long life.

"It was so quiet. My heart was beating really fast, and my mouth was dry. Then I heard a door open, and a light came on. Two men were standing just inside the door." Her voice faltered. "Two men! And I was naked! I was so scared! I tried to cover myself with my hands. But they just eyed me and left. I heard them lock the door. I saw a chest of drawers on one wall, and I crawled over to it, but my clothes weren't in it. Just some women's jewelry."

Bridges moved his chair marginally closer to the bed and nodded to Sinclair to do the same. He didn't want to make her repeat herself, and he wanted to be sure the tape recorder could pick up even her muffled words.

"I know I said I would—" she whispered—"but do I have to tell you everything? Can't you figure it out from the evidence?"

Sinclair responded. "I'm afraid not, Jenny. Without your statement, we have only a skeleton to work with. We don't do this because we want to invade your privacy or cause you embarrassment. We do it because we can't guarantee justice without it."

"Please continue," Bridges said.

"The door opened," she breathed. "Another man came in. Oh, God, what was he going to do to me?"

There was a light knock, the door swung open, and the nurse trilled, "Time to check vital signs, dear."

Jenny jumped and cried out.

Sinclair stopped the tape and shouted, "Not now! Damn it!"

Jenny's hands flew up to shield her face.

Bridges ushered the startled nurse out of the room. He gave hurried instructions to the two PCs. Sinclair stood, took a deep breath, and ran his hand through his hair.

Bridges returned. "Half-time, Jenny. Even the best athletes need to rest and recharge. Wouldn't you like something to drink?"

She leaned back and watched them go. Her heart was racing as if she'd run a marathon, and she'd barely begun. She remembered her father's quote: "Miles to go before I sleep." The miles ahead of her weren't measured in physical feet but in yards of pain and fear. She wished she were a little girl again, with a child's faith that bumps and bruises go away.

CHAPTER 12

Sinclair and Bridges returned shortly with tea and biscuits. The hot tea was soothing, but it failed to quiet her nerves completely or calm her unsettled stomach, so she didn't eat anything. None of them spoke about the interview. Bridges told humourous stories about misadventures of players on his son's football team, and Jenny was reminded of similar events on her brothers' teams. It was only a partial distraction, however, because she knew what lay ahead. "I think I need a pep talk," she said.

Bridges smiled, hoping to dispel her fearful expression. "Then I'll remind you that you're the most important person connected to this case. You're in charge. We're here to encourage and support you."

She heard Mr. Sinclair give the introductory information. The tape recorder was running, and she realized that others would hear it. "No—wait—I don't want everyone to know."

Bridges nodded at Sinclair to stop the recording. "Jenny, it's time for you to pass the ball to us. I know it's very difficult for you to trust anyone just now, but this is a team effort."

"But I just want to forget," she whispered.

"Jenny," he said quietly, "I'm sorry to tell you that's not likely to happen. No one I've interviewed has ever forgot what happened to them, but many have been able to let it go. It's a process, and it begins with your willingness to work with us." Patience showed respect, so Bridges waited. In his experience the best victim statements came from those who didn't feel rushed.

"He was a monster," she said finally.

Sinclair pressed the record button. He was ready to move on. As a detective, his focus was on gathering evidence. Quickly, if possible. "What did he do, Jenny?" he asked. "What happened when the third man came into the room?"

"He—he meant to kill me. I know he did, because he told someone outside the room to get rid of me!" Tears began to clog her throat, and she had to force the words out. "'When I'm through in here, dispose of it,' that's what he said!"

Sinclair wondered if the other women had been similarly terrorised, or if Scott's methods had become more extreme with each offence.

"He slammed the door like he was angry! I was huddled next to the wall, and he grabbed my arm and dragged me to the middle of the room. My knees were so weak I could hardly stand, and he hit me in the stomach with his fist, and I fell down, and all the time he was making a terrible noise in his throat, and I couldn't get up!"

The interview itself could be a trauma for many victims. "It's okay to cry, Jenny," Bridges said.

Again both men waited, Sinclair with less ease. He did not want her to fail this time, and he needed the evidence from her mind as well as from her body. "Tell us why you couldn't get up."

"Because my legs wouldn't support me. He beat me while I lay there on the rug. He kicked me, and he hit me, and he had a large ring that cut me open! He—he—slashed me!"

He had—Sinclair had seen the pictures. Her DNA would be on Scott's shoes and ring.

"I couldn't react quickly enough to get away," she wailed. "He kept on and on, until I was bleeding all over! I was afraid I'd bleed to death! I wanted to hold myself together—it was my life pouring out on that rug! I screamed and screamed, and then I wanted it to be over with, I didn't care how! I hurt everywhere, and I still hurt everywhere, and I wish God had let me die in that room like the others!"

She was on the edge of hysteria, but her statement was critical. Her descriptions were the only guide they would have as to what the other women had experienced. "We'll take a short break," Sinclair said, motioning for Bridges to stop the tape. He had to find the right blend of pressure and empathy. Too little empathy and she'd clam up. Too much, and she'd spiral out of control. "You're right, Jenny. You should have died in that room, but God didn't let you. You know what your purpose is in this, and you're strong enough to do it, because you don't have to do it by yourself." He spoke slowly, hoping his pace would affect hers. "I know something else also: It's only real once. Did you hear that? It may seem real, but it isn't. *It's—only—real—once.*"

Bridges watched Jenny look up at Sinclair, her face streaked with tears.

"Let's finish this, shall we?" Sinclair suggested.

Bridges punched the record button. "Interview resumed," he said, taking Sinclair's seat near the machine.

"I thought he just meant to beat me to death," she whispered. "When he started to undo his belt, I thought he was going to beat me with it. I was naked when he came in the room—if he wanted sex, why didn't he do it then?"

Bridges could see her chest rising and falling, and he knew she was crying again. "Jenny, please tell us about it," he said.

She took a breath. "He unzipped and dropped his pants, then his underwear. And I couldn't even move! But he could. He did." She shook her head. "You don't respect me now, do you? I didn't defend myself. I won't be a good witness."

"That's shame talking," Bridges said gently. "You're afraid we'll think less of you because you were attacked, but that's not going to happen. Jenny, fear can paralyse people. The shock—the suddenness of an attack—factors like these keep many people from defending themselves effectively. In your case it's likely the drug you were given reduced your ability to resist. You did the best you could. I know it's difficult for you to speak about this, but the more you do, the more I respect you." He paused. "When you can—what did he do next?"

"I saw his—it—he was ready for sex. He knelt down and ripped off my necklace. I didn't look after that. He pried my legs apart and tried to push inside. It hurt so much! He held my legs—he was enraged—he couldn't push all the way in at first..."

Dear God, no. Bridges struggled to set his horror aside as interviewers had to do: If victims saw or heard any trace of distress, they would assume judgement and refuse to speak.

"Because I'd never—I'd never—he dug his fingers into my thighs for leverage, and then he was all the way in. He rammed me again and again! Oh, God—he was tearing me in half, and I couldn't even move..."

Bridges could barely hear her. He adjusted the volume on the tape recorder.

"I thought it was all over...he stopped pushing..."

Sinclair prompted her. "But it wasn't over, was it? Tell me what he did next."

"I can't," she whispered.

"I need to hear it from you," Sinclair said quietly. "Tell me, Jenny."

"He rolled me over," she sobbed. "He was so rough! Punching my shoulder and the side of my hip to make me turn—it hurt even more, lying on my chest—I couldn't scream any more, I could hardly breathe—No! No! No..."

There was a low point in each victim's statement, but Sinclair did not soften his approach. "What did he do, Jenny?" he asked. "Can you tell me anything? A fragment?"

Bridges could hear her laboured breathing. "Sir..."

Sinclair glanced at him. "Right." He took a step away from the bed and sat down. "Jenny, did the other two men come back?"

It was a minute before she responded. "I don't know. The monster kicked me in the head. That's the last thing I remember. When I woke up, I was in the hospital, and you were there. That's all."

Sinclair nodded for Bridges to give the closing remarks and stop the recording.

The room was quiet. Bridges stood and slowly stretched his stiff legs. "You did brilliantly, Jenny," he said. "Memory is power. You've just done a very powerful thing. Your statement will help us nail this guy. I'm proud of you." He turned to Sinclair. "Sir, I'll wait outside for you."

"Well done, Jenny," Sinclair added. "Thank you."

She felt like the clown after the parade, the freak picking his way through the empty candy wrappers and spent balloons. His antics and painted-on sad face had made others happy, but the clown could wash his despair away and she couldn't, no matter how hard she scrubbed. She watched Sinclair go.

Bridges was still in the corridor, leaning against the wall, his arms at his sides, his head bowed, no longer concealing his stricken face. Often in his job he was confronted with the injustices of life, and an injustice this was, for an eager young visitor to his country to be given such a sadistic welcome. "Did you know, sir? That she was a virgin?"

Sinclair nodded. "The doctor told us, early on."

"She had the stuffing beat out of her. Then he tore her up, inside and out. Some world we live in." He sighed. "When do you want to conduct the next interview?"

"Tomorrow afternoon. We'll review the transcript of today's interview in the morning. Go home to your family."

"Thank you, sir. I'd like to hug my wife and hear my children laugh. I particularly need to hear my daughter laugh." He straightened. "But first I'll handle the cool-down with Jenny."

Sinclair knew he was referring to returning to the part of the interview which covered lighter topics. Proper interview procedure recommended against leaving any victim with traumatic images fresh in her mind. He headed for the lift.

CHAPTER 13

When Sinclair and Bridges returned to the hospital, the two PCs on duty reported that Jenny had had a rough morning. "She cries when the physiotherapist makes her stand up. I suppose it's necessary, but it's hard to hear. Then the nurse takes her pulse and wonders why it's high. Hospitals can be unforgiving places, sir."

"They can indeed."

Jenny tried to smile when she saw Bridges.

"Did you enjoy the chocolate?" he asked.

"Barry brought me a Penguin bar last night," she explained to Sinclair. "I'd never seen one, but the nurse wouldn't let me eat it. She said the chocolate would be too hard to digest."

Damn. We work so hard to give control back to a victim, and in hospital they take it away. "I'll bring you another," Bridges promised.

"I'd like to thank you for your statement yesterday," Sinclair said. "Having heard it, I'm even more resolved to proceed against your attacker, but I need your help, your testimony, to tie it all together."

Bridges wasn't surprised by Sinclair's agenda. It was a big case, and he knew the DCI had been instructed to move quickly to secure her commitment to testify.

"But I'm going home," she said.

"We can be in contact with you," Sinclair said.

"Jenny," Bridges added, "my job is to look after your needs. That means I'll keep you informed about what's going on with the case and when the trial has been scheduled."

"I don't want to come back here. And I don't want to see the monster again, ever."

"You'll only have to see him in court," Sinclair encouraged, "in very controlled circumstances. You won't be a victim then or even a survivor. You'll be a witness, and that's a rather significant shift in the balance of power." She was showing no sign of agreement. He leant forward. "Jenny, I am very, very angry at the man who hurt you. I intend to get him. Your cooperation will help me, but I believe it will also help you—help you to have a purpose."

Barry had teased her gently the evening before about her sweet tooth. Neither he nor Mr. Sinclair was smiling now. Why did police always work in pairs? Where was her backup?

"That's true," Bridges said. "In my experience victims who follow through, who participate in the system, make a better recovery."

"It's the right thing to do, Jenny." Sinclair held his breath.

"That's what my daddy would say," she said slowly. "But I haven't always wanted to do the right thing."

"Jenny, I don't want another woman to be hurt the way you have been," Sinclair responded. "You can make a difference."

"I'm not sure I can do it at all," she said. "I'm all beat up."

"You'll have time to heal. Jenny, a commitment from you—some follow-on sessions—then you'll have seen the last of us for a while. Will you testify to your offender's actions in a court of law?"

She shrugged her shoulder, like a butterfly fluttering a wing. It struck Sinclair how exposed she was—with her left limbs elevated, she couldn't even turn on her side for privacy. In court she would have to stand in the witness-box with her experience laid bare to the scrutiny of others. The tension level in the room rose.

"I can't think about that today," she said finally.

Sinclair sighed and handed the tape recorder to Bridges, who introduced the interview. She appeared to relax slightly as he questioned her about her clothing on the day of the attack, her handbag, and its contents. "Was the pavement busy?"

"Pavement? You want to know how many cars there were?"

Bridges realised he'd have to clarify the word. "The area where pedestrians walk."

"The sidewalk—sorry," she said with a smile. "No, not very—it was early."

"At the bus shelter," Sinclair said, "you mentioned someone coming up behind you. Man or woman?"

"It was a man's hand. A man's arm."

"Jenny, you identified the man who attacked you. Was it his arm?"

"I—I don't know. I just remember seeing the sleeve of a dark jacket."

"Can you remember anything at all between the bus shelter and the time you woke in the little room?"

"It's a complete blank."

"How long were you alone in the dark?"

"I don't know."

Bridges took up the questioning again. "What time was it when the two men came in?"

"I don't know."

"Weren't you wearing a watch?"

"I had my watch on when I left the hotel," she said slowly. "I didn't have it later."

"What did it look like?"

"Gold, with an oval face and a black leather band."

"Was there a clock in the room or a window? Were you hungry?"

Bridges stopped. "Sorry—one at a time is hard enough, isn't it? Can you give us any clue about the time?"

"No windows. No clock. I was empty. Sick. Terribly thirsty. And cold."

Sinclair asked the next question. "What did the room look like?"

It was an elaborate game. First one man carried the ball and then the other. They could pass it back and forth, but she couldn't. "Small and plain. There were moisture stains on the walls, dirty white cinder-block walls. Concrete floor."

"Were there furnishings of any sort?"

"Just the chest of drawers with a mirror over it. There was no place to hide."

"How long were you there with the light on before your attacker came in?"

"I have no idea," she said, shrugging.

"Can you describe the jewellery you saw?"

"I remember a charm bracelet; a watch, silver, I think; and—a necklace, a gold chain. Maybe some smaller things, I'm not sure."

"What did your necklace look like, Jenny?" Sinclair continued.

"It was gold, with an amethyst cross on it. My parents gave it to me when I was confirmed in the church."

"You mentioned a rug," Bridges reminded her. "Can you describe it?"

"Mostly red, when he was through with me." She was upset by the memory. "Sorry—that isn't what you want to know." She paused. "It was round and braided, with lots of colors. It wasn't very soft. Think, rug burns. The braids made it lumpy."

"You said the first blow was a fist to the stomach which knocked you down. Did you fall all the way down?"

"No, I fell to my knees. He hit me on the shoulder next, and I landed on my side."

"Left or right side?"

"Left."

"Then what?"

"He kicked me—all over. My arms and legs, my stomach, my chest, my back. I was hurt pretty badly pretty quickly."

"He used his hands as well, is that correct?" asked Bridges.

"Yes, his fists mostly, but his ring—that sharp ring—that was awful."

"Left or right hand?" Bridges continued.

She closed her eyes for a moment, remembering. "Fists—both hands. When he used the back of his hand, it was his right hand. His ring was on his right hand."

"Did he hit you with anything other than his hands and feet?"

"Like the proverbial blunt object, you mean?" she asked. "No. It was all very personal. At least, it seemed that way."

"He didn't have a weapon of any sort?" Sinclair asked.

"*He* was the weapon," she replied.

"How long did the beating last?"

"Too long."

"You were lying on your side."

"Yes. He bent over and pushed me onto my back. That's why I remember seeing him undo his belt. My left arm hurt too badly, but I put my right arm up to push him away. That's when he struck me across the face with the back of his hand. It was humiliating. Why did he want to destroy my appearance when he was going to kill me? And it hurt so badly."

"Because of the ring he wore," Bridges clarified.

"Yes. Isn't that stupid? I was bleeding in so many places, more life-threatening ones, and I was trying to protect my face."

She was tiring, but Sinclair had other questions for her, things he wanted very badly to know before they arrested Scott. "What did he do with your necklace—the one you mentioned with the cross on it?"

She thought for a moment. "He held it in his hand, I think. I don't remember seeing him put it down anywhere."

"So when he gripped your thighs, he had it in his hand?" Bridges asked.

"Yes," she confirmed.

That explained her unusual bruises. Many rape victims had bruises on the inside of their thighs. Jenny had cross-shaped bruises as well. "Jenny, do you have any idea how long the rape lasted?"

"That's sick!" she cried. "Why would you ask such a thing?"

"To establish a timeline," explained Bridges.

"Oh. No. It hurt so much that it seemed like it took forever, but I really have no idea how long it was."

"Did he use a condom?"

Her eyes widened. "I didn't see—oh my God—unprotected sex—I need to know!"

Bridges looked at Sinclair. You field this one, boss.

"The forensic data should tell us. Let's move on," Sinclair said.

"Did he lie down on top of you?" asked Bridges.

"No, thank God; I think I would have suffocated."

Broken ribs, collapsed lung: It was possible. "Did he caress you in any way?" Sinclair asked.

"All his touches hurt," she said. "He wanted blood, not affection."

"Did he want oral sex?"

She recoiled and did not reply.

"For the benefit of the tape, Miss Jeffries answered with a negative gesture," Bridges said after a minute.

"Jenny," Sinclair asked quietly, "did he complete the sexual act?"

"He stopped, if that's what you mean."

"Did he ejaculate inside you?"

"I don't know! I'd never had sex before. I don't know how to tell!"

Sinclair sighed. He didn't know exactly how to word the next question. He didn't know if she would understand the criminal term. He decided against it. "Jenny, I have to ask you very specifically. What was the final act of abuse committed against you?"

She shuddered. "I can't talk about it," she whispered. "I can't. It's too horrible."

Finally Bridges spoke. "Let the record show that Miss Jeffries was unable to answer fully," he said quietly.

"Jenny, I have one more question." She was crying, and Sinclair waited for her to collect herself slightly. "Did you give your consent?"

That was the end of her even partial composure. "Are you kidding?" she cried. "Consent to *this*?"

"I need an unequivocal answer," he said heavily. "Yes or no."

"No!" she screamed. "The answer is no!"

"Interview with Miss Jeffries terminated," said Bridges in a subdued voice, adding the other pertinent information before stopping the tape. He stood. "Jenny, our purpose isn't to dispute anything. We weren't there, that's all, and we need the clearest picture of what happened in that room." She still looked upset. "I wish I had half your courage," he said. "You're quite a girl, and getting stronger all the time. If that bastard had any idea what he's up against, he'd chuck in the towel now."

"I'm sorry," Sinclair said. "Consent is a legal issue."

She looked at him. He was wearing cufflinks, silver rectangles with a stone in the center that matched his tie. Her father wore cufflinks sometimes. The memory made the pain in her chest almost palpable. Her father wouldn't have treated her the way Mr. Sinclair had, law or no law. "Go away," she said.

CHAPTER 14

"That was rough, sir," Bridges commented to Sinclair in the corridor. "The hospital environment hasn't been kind to her, and having no family with her—I'm surprised she's doing as well as she is."

Sinclair's focus was on the case. "DNA evidence will be important. Scott may ditch his shoes, but he'll never get it off his ring, no matter how he washes it. And if he left some inside Jenny, the way he did with the others, the rape kit will tell us."

"Sir, why would he leave evidence like that behind?"

"Arrogance, according to the psychological profile."

"It's going to give some prosecutor a conviction on a silver platter."

"Let's hope we get that far," Sinclair replied. "I'm off to the Yard. Scott's been placed under surveillance, his arrest warrant is in, and we have some planning to do."

"I'll stay on here for a bit."

Jenny looked up but didn't smile when Bridges returned. "Is he gone?"

"Back to his office. His work on the case is ongoing."

"Are you going to defend him?"

"No, he can look after himself. My job is to look after you."

"I just want to go home."

"Home's the best place for you. It's good to have loved ones close. Give your body time to heal. Trust us to keep you safe when you come back."

"So you can get justice?" she asked bitterly.

"Justice is good," Bridges said. "I believe in it. I work for it. But in my experience victims are usually motivated by something more personal. I think you'll agree to testify because you need to do it—to fight back, to keep other women from suffering—however you define it, that need won't go away, even when you go home." He paused. "Jenny, my son's the goalkeeper on his football team. If he's been scored on quite a bit in a game, he loses confidence. I put him up front for a while to give him a chance to take the offensive. That's what I want for you—after a long halftime at home, to finish strong."

CHAPTER 15

By nine o'clock in the evening most of the hospital visitors had left, and the passages were quiet. The two policemen outside Jenny's room had been on duty since four with only routine responsibilities. A balding, heavyset man approached them, wearing tan trousers, a blue shirt, and a dark tie under his white coat. His hospital ID card was pinned to his pocket, and his stethoscope draped around his neck. He stopped in front of the PCs and gave them his name, telling them in an overly hearty voice that he was a psychiatrist and had been asked to stop in. Neither man had seen him before, but his name was on their list, so they permitted him to enter her room.

PC Sullivan had a strange feeling about the man that he couldn't explain, so he followed the psychiatrist into the room and rested his hand on his truncheon. When the psychiatrist turned toward him and told him to step outside, he didn't. Most doctors didn't like their authority questioned, but Sullivan was uneasy. He planned to wait where he was until he was sure Jenny was comfortable with the session. So far she wasn't.

"I have something here that will help you relax," the doctor said. Jenny screamed as he took something out of his trouser pocket, something that looked small in his thick fingers. Sullivan was young, and his reflexes were quick. He stepped forward, swinging his truncheon as hard as he could at the arm that held the syringe. There was a loud crack as the truncheon connected with his elbow, the doctor bellowed with pain, and the syringe fell from his fingers and slid across the floor.

The doctor lunged at her with his good arm, and she felt his thumb and index finger around her throat, squeezing. The weight was crushing, forcing her head into the pillow and strangling her second scream. It was sudden, and it took her a moment to react. She put her hand on his hand, but there was no strength in her grip, and she couldn't pry his hand away. His face loomed over her, not slack and affable now. She could see the young officer behind him, his arm around the man's neck. He was yelling for his partner. Sudden pinpoints of light burst before her eyes, and she thought the tiny sparklers and a man's contorted face would be the last things she would ever see.

In the meantime the PC outside had heard the commotion. Together he and Sullivan tackled the man, who cursed loudly and struggled wildly against them. "You've broken my arm!" he howled. Privately Sullivan hoped so. Because of the man's frantic resistance, it took both of them to pin him to the floor and handcuff him.

"Are you all right, Miss?" asked Sullivan, as soon as he could catch his breath. She was gasping and coughing.

PC Wilson dragged the assailant outside the room and called a nurse for Jenny.

Sullivan radioed for backup and then for the Chief Inspector.

Jenny was sobbing and shaking.

"Try to take it easy," Sullivan told her.

In a few minutes they could hear other voices outside. When the door opened, Jenny inhaled sharply, but it was PC Wilson notifying them that the additional police had arrived.

In the meantime the nurse returned with Dr. Patel, the doctor on call. She found Jenny's pulse elevated and deep bruises already appearing on her neck, but no physical injuries that required treatment.

Sinclair arrived and held up his warrant card. "What's going on here?"

"She needs a sedative, but she's too distressed to swallow it. When I ordered an injection, she became more upset. And your policeman won't allow me to give it."

"Is she physically all right?"

"Yes," reported Dr. Patel, "but she needs something to calm her down."

"Not until she's spoken with the Chief Inspector," Sullivan insisted.

"Doctor, I appreciate what you're trying to do, but could you give us a few minutes, please?"

"Certainly," said the doctor.

Sinclair nodded at Sullivan, and he stepped out as well.

"I thought I was in a cocoon," she sobbed. "I wasn't—I'm a sitting duck. What am I going to do?"

Sinclair put a hand on her shoulder. "Jenny, stay with me. I know you're frightened, but I need to know what happened. Can you do this for me?"

"A man—a doctor!—tried to kill me."

"How?" Sinclair didn't relax his grip on her shoulder.

"He had a syringe. I saw it. Then he grabbed my neck." She tried to clear her throat, but it didn't help. "He said he was a psychiatrist, but he came too close, and I screamed, and one of your men was here, and he saved my life."

"Jenny, I want you to know that you're safe now." He released her shoulder. "I'll be just outside. Wilson!"

"Sir?"

"Stay with Miss Jeffries while I have a word with Sullivan."

Sullivan was waiting to be interviewed.

"Tell me what happened here," ordered Sinclair.

"Sir, the man's name was on the list. He had a hospital ID, but I had a bad feeling about him so I followed him into Miss Jeffries' room. I thought I'd back off a bit when I could see that they were getting on okay. When he took the syringe out of his pocket, I hit him with my truncheon."

"Sullivan, what was odd about a doctor with a syringe?"

"Sir—maybe it was the stethoscope. Why would a shrink need a stethoscope? And why would a doctor carry a syringe in his trouser pocket?"

"Did Miss Jeffries see the syringe? Is that why she screamed?"

"No, sir, she screamed first. I don't think she saw the syringe until after I did. Of course, Will heard her from outside and was with me straightaway, which was a good thing, because it took both of us to bring him down. We slammed him down pretty hard, sir."

Good. "Did he touch anything in the room?"

"No, sir, not that I saw."

"So you saw the syringe and hit him. Why does Miss Jeffries have bruises on her neck?"

"Because he lunged at her with his other arm. Sir, she couldn't get away, and she only ever had the one hand to defend herself with."

"What did you do next?"

"We wrestled him to the floor and cuffed him. Will called the nurse, and she paged the doctor. I radioed for backup and then for you. That's it, sir."

"Where is the syringe?"

"In the corner of her room, on the floor. We didn't touch it."

"We'll wait for the SOCOs to bag it," Sinclair nodded. "We'll need a formal statement from you later. For now, relieve Wilson inside."

When PC Wilson came outside, Sinclair took his initial statement. It corroborated Sullivan's. He had heard Miss Jeffries' screams and Sullivan's shout and had entered her room immediately to assist. "The scum's being x-rayed downstairs, sir. He'll be taken to the custody cells at Paddington Green."

Sinclair stepped back inside. "Thank you, Sullivan," he said. As he left, Sinclair brought Jenny a glass of water and watched while she took a sip. "PC Sullivan said that you screamed before he hit the man with his truncheon. Why was that?"

"I saw his eyes," she said in a pinched voice. "They were cold." She coughed and then swallowed. "I didn't think a psychiatrist would have cold eyes." She touched her neck gingerly. "I didn't see the syringe at first. I wasn't looking at his hands until he moved. Then the policeman knocked it out of his hand."

A shiver went down Sinclair's spine. Had Scott intended to have her killed before she gave her statement to police? If so, he had nearly succeeded. He stepped outside. He asked Dr. Patel if Jenny could be given the oral sedative when the investigation in her room was complete. In spite of her less troubled demeanor, he wanted her to receive something strong enough to help her sleep. The doctor concurred.

When the Scenes-of-Crime Officers arrived, Sinclair accompanied them into her room. They were clad in white overalls, and the bulges from the clothes they wore underneath made them look to Jenny like white inner tubes in varying degrees of inflation. The one with the round face, who most resembled the Michelin man, approached the bed. "If you'll permit me," he said. The bedside rail was then dusted for fingerprints, although she couldn't remember the strangler touching it, and the hospital blanket was removed from the top of her bed.

The photographer was there. "With your permission, Miss," he said, and she realized that he wanted to take pictures of her neck. Very gently he positioned her chin. She covered her scarred cheek with her hand and closed her eyes against the camera's prying one.

She heard Mr. Sinclair's voice. "They'll want to examine your fingernails, Jenny." She didn't know why—she hadn't clawed at her attacker. She should have, but she hadn't thought of it. She had wanted only to pull his hand away from her throat. She lowered her hand from her cheek and watched while scrapings were taken and each nail was carefully trimmed.

The syringe had been collected and bagged. With a nod to Sinclair, the forensic officers withdrew. Sinclair then spoke to her. "Much as I'd like to," he said, "I can't stay. I'd like you to take the medicine the doctor has for you. I'll be back first thing in the morning."

Her chest was tight, and she was weak with exhaustion. She looked down and started to cry. "I wish I'd never come here! I'm in a hospital in a foreign country. I'm not safe anywhere. I should never have let my guard down. I shouldn't have hoped."

He watched the tears roll over the adhesive strips on her cheek and down her neck, dampening the hospital gown she wore. It was a cry for help. Not a commitment to testify but perhaps his response to the one could lead to the other. "I'll have PC Sullivan sit with you until you fall asleep." He summoned the young constable, then stopped by the nurses' station to report that they could give Jenny the sedative the doctor had prescribed. He also asked for a description of the real hospital psychiatrist and told the SOCOs to check his office. Then, while the nurses were away from their post, he rang the D/S. "Sir," he said, "there's been an attack on our witness."

"Is she alive?" Graves asked sharply.

"She survived, yes, and we have the assailant in custody, but we need to move her straightaway."

"Witness Protection should handle it," Graves said.

"Sir, we can't wait for their careful planning. She's a soft target as long as she's in hospital. We have an obligation to remove her ASAP. A duty of care."

"A hotel then."

"A hotel will require a larger team and be less covert. She needs to drop off the radar screen. A flat has just been vacated in my block. I don't know if it'll suit, but I'll find out in the morning. We still need access to her."

"Colin, that's amateurish," Graves objected. "It's not the way we do it."

"Sir, I know it's irregular, but it's an emergency, and it's temporary," Sinclair argued.

"Then place her in a safe house with a WPC and a panic button."

"She needs medical assistance. She's still too badly injured to look after herself."

"Then get her a nurse!"

"Sir, I'll not ask civilians to place themselves at risk. Don't we have anyone who's been a paramedic? I want round-the-clock protection. Just three men to start—the fewer officers involved, the less chance of discovery."

"You mean, three per shift—two teams with changeover every twelve hours is standard."

"Sir, I want one small, stable team. She's in a bad way. She can't handle anything more."

"Colin, we can't ask for a twenty-four hour commitment from our men."

"If you'll excuse me, sir—we bloody well can, on a short-term basis at least. Are you willing to lose this witness? Scott will never confess, and without Miss Jeffries' testimony, we can't link any forensic evidence to him. The more control we have over her, the better it is for us. And sir—I want these officers to be armed."

"Armed officers? Is that necessary?"

"Sir, Scott is determined and desperate. I believe his methods will escalate."

"Recruiting's down on the specialist units. Don't know if I can get support from them, but a smaller team may be an easier sell. Anything else?"

"A young PC here—Sullivan—was on the spot tonight. If he's firearms qualified, he should be considered."

"What's your timeline?"

"Forty-eight hours, if I can convince the doctor to discharge her."

"We'll need to brief the team tomorrow then," Graves concluded. "Give us a bell in the morning." He put the phone down.

Sinclair breathed a sigh of relief. He had seen to Jenny's immediate safety. He notified Bridges of the incident then rang Andrews at home and told him to meet him at Paddington Green. He hadn't even left the hospital when the SOCOs called him back. They'd found a man unconscious in the psychiatrist's office who matched the description given by the nurses. Sinclair headed downstairs at the double.

CHAPTER 16

Thursday night stretched into Friday morning. Marcus Bates, the hospital assailant, required medical treatment, causing the preliminary interview to be delayed. When Sinclair saw him, however, he didn't think that Bates' pale face and nervous manner were the result of his injury. Cecil Scott was the only man Sinclair knew who wanted Jenny dead, and this man, Bates, had failed in his effort to please his employer. An attempted killer in pain with a cast like Jenny's—to Sinclair's eyes it was a welcome sight. Mr. Bates' request for a brief was not.

He pressed his thumb and forefinger against his forehead in a futile attempt to settle his thoughts. The attack on Jenny in hospital changed everything. He had known from the outset that Scott had the money to go after her. Bates was proof that Scott had the intent.

He snatched only a few hours' sleep before accompanying Graves and uniformed police to Scott's flat. No one responded well to an early morning arrest, but Sinclair was still surprised that Scott's breeding did not moderate his outrage. He cursed at the intrusion and at the officers watching him dress, not heeding their courteous warnings to watch his language. He cursed Sinclair when he recognised him and threatened legal action against all of them. When the handcuffs were applied, Sinclair saw his own grim satisfaction reflected on Graves' face.

The detectives on the cases of the six murdered women—and there were scores of them—had a wealth of forensic data, but contrary to the popular view of crime solving, scientific evidence didn't generally break a case. It took old-fashioned policing: thorough, painstaking, often tedious work. Yet despite their best efforts, they had been unable to locate any witnesses or find a common thread amongst the victims. Deposition sites had varied, and there were no CCTV cameras in the areas where the bodies had been found. Appeals to the public had yielded nothing of use. Jenny's identification of Scott had been the breakthrough they'd needed to breathe new life into their investigations, and they had been elated. Copies of her initial statement had them all champing at the bit, but they had been ordered to temper their eagerness. Impatience could tip off the very individual they planned to arrest. Now that Scott was in police custody, there would be plenty of time to gather supporting evidence of his guilt in the other crimes.

He rang the lease agent as early as he dared and was informed that the flat wasn't ready for occupancy, having not been refitted after the departure of the last tenant. He pulled rank and made a late morning appointment to tour the premises anyway.

When he arrived at the hospital, he was glad to see that the additional men he had requested were already by the stairwell and the lift. The armed PCs outside Jenny's room stood as he approached. They were smiling broadly. "Congratulations, sir!"

Sinclair raised his eyebrows.

"The news got round," one of them reported, "about the arrest. Well done."

Those highs didn't come often enough in policing, so Sinclair accepted the compliment, recognising as he did so the part that Jenny had played in it. "The young woman you're protecting did all the work," he replied. "I hope you know—and will pass it on to the next shift—that the danger to her has not diminished. I'm counting on you. More important, *she's* counting on you."

He went in. He was surprised to see Sullivan still with her, but even more surprised—shocked, even—by her appearance. She looked as frail and weak as she had in intensive care.

Sullivan rose to his feet immediately, his hat in his hands, his dark eyes sober, his dark hair dishevelled. "She had a bad night, sir," he said. "The sedative didn't work very effectively. I didn't like to leave her alone."

Her eyes filled. When bad dreams had fractured her sleep, he had encouraged her to keep at it until she got a good one. When the dragon lady had swept in to take her vital signs—the night nurse whose swift, abrupt movements startled her in the dark—he had called her an old bat and insisted he was scared also. When she had cried from exhaustion and despair, he had distracted her with tea and stories about growing up with too many sisters. He was the first officer who'd talked to her about anything other than police matters.

"I kept it as light as I could, sir."

"Well done, Sullivan."

"I'll just push off then." He put his hat on. "Time to look like the real thing," he grinned, giving Jenny a jaunty salute as he left.

"I'd be dead if it weren't for him," she told Sinclair, her voice flagging. "I've been here—two weeks? three?—and I've almost died twice. I wish I were somewhere else; I wish I were someone else."

She was emotionally overwrought and physically exhausted. Dr. Adams would never agree to release her in this condition, nor would she be able to maintain focus during the next round of questioning. "Jenny, I can't grant those wishes, but I can promise you a better day, beginning right now. Denton!"

The officer with the rugby physique answered Sinclair's summons. "Sir?"

"I don't want Miss Jeffries left alone," Sinclair told him. "Take a seat and stay with her until I relieve you." He headed to the nurses' station to inform them that there would be no physiotherapist visits to Jenny today. If any nursing functions needed to be performed, they should be done immediately. His men were going to guarantee her a three-hour rest period. He moved one of the PCs from the stairwell to maintain the force level at Jenny's door. "Your instructions are to bar everyone—medical personnel included—from entering this room until noon today. No exceptions." It was probably outside the scope of his authority, but the officers on duty now were armed, and that should be sufficient for the short term. "I'll be back at noon to deal with any malcontents."

On his way to meet the lease agent, he rang the Yard. Graves had scheduled a briefing for five p.m., Andrews reported. "Tell Bridges to meet me at the hospital at noon," Sinclair ordered. "Jenny's at the end of her tether, and we need to find a way to improve her frame of mind."

When he reached his block in Hampstead, the agent was waiting. Sinclair found the flat sufficient, and he convinced the man that cooperating with the police would be in his best interest. He was allowed to sign a month-to-month lease agreement without a deposit, and he took the keys with him. He walked downstairs to his own flat and retrieved his Bible. Perhaps some spiritual encouragement would not be out of order. He took the tube back to central London and purchased takeaway from a sandwich shop.

Bridges was waiting for him outside Jenny's door. "The *Do Not Disturb* order is lifted," Sinclair told the officers. He went in first. She was asleep.

"She rested, sir," Denton said quietly.

"No upsets?"

"One, but I spoke to her, and she settled."

She stirred and woke.

"I have some things for you." He set the Bible down on her bed. "It's worn, because it's been in my family for generations. It has guided and comforted many people over the years, and I hope it will help you. Also, the hospital chaplain should stop round today." He turned to Denton. "Tell Bridges I'm ready for him."

Bridges came in with a teddy bear. "For you," he said.

"He's dressed like a policeman."

"A London policeman," Bridges corrected. "He's a bobby bear."

"Then I'll call him Bobby," she smiled, catching the joke. "He'll be my personal bodyguard." She set the bear in her lap.

"Next, we're going to have an indoor picnic," Sinclair told her as he spread the food on her tray. "You choose first. We have turkey, beef, and ham sandwiches, fruit, crisps, and tea."

She was surprised at his informality. "I'd like the turkey. Do you have iced tea, or is that just an American thing?"

"All good tea is hot, don't you know that?" Sinclair teased. When they finished their sandwiches, he served the pudding.

"It doesn't look like pudding," she said.

"I'll translate," Bridges offered. "Pudding is a general term for dessert."

"I thought my hearing was bad, or my eyesight, or both," she smiled.

Bridges finished in two bites. Sinclair took his time, using his considerable charm as he chatted with her. "I have good news for you, Jenny," he said when he set his plate aside. "The man you identified as your attacker, William Cecil Crighton Scott, was arrested early this morning." She closed her eyes for a moment in relief but showed no reaction to the name. He considered briefly making another request for her testimony but thought better of it. "I can't thank you enough for your assistance. We do, however, have a few more questions for you, if you're willing to help us."

"About the man from last night?"

"No, about your initial attack."

She closed her fingers around the teddy bear. "What else do you need to ask me? Will it be bad?"

"Jenny," Sinclair replied, "this is a trust relationship, and that means truth is required from both sides. It'll be a shorter session and not as difficult for you."

Bridges started the recording. "The procedure is a bit different today," he said. "Take a moment to clear your mind. Then close your eyes and imagine that you are in the little room you described. Use your senses and tell me what impressions you have." He saw her shoulders stiffen. "What do you see?"

"His anger. His hands on his belt, a black leather belt." She trembled. "Oh, God, I didn't know whether he was going to hit me with the buckle or the strap. I was already in so much pain, but he had something else in mind, something worse."

"Jenny," Bridges said softly, "I'm here. The chief inspector is here. Denton is outside. You're in a protected and caring environment. Try to focus on the little room and what you saw there."

His face. His fists. His body. When she closed her eyes, she saw his savage silhouette, the bare bulb in the ceiling illuminating him. "I don't want to see it," she sobbed.

She was too upset to maintain the mental image. "You don't have to do this, Jenny," Bridges soothed. "Take a moment to collect yourself. We'll continue in the regular way."

She looked up, her relief clear.

"Tell us again why you were in England," Sinclair requested.

"To visit graduate schools," she answered. "To study English lit."

"If that was the purpose of your trip, why didn't you visit any universities?"

"I came to evaluate the environment as well as the educational opportunities," she explained. "If I didn't like London, or England, then I probably wouldn't want to attend school here, regardless of the quality of the curriculum. So I explored London first. My second week I would have visited universities in London, and after that, outside London."

"During your first days here, did anyone approach you? Bother you? Speak to you in an unusual manner?" Bridges asked.

She shook her head then realized she needed to answer orally. "Not that I can remember."

"Where did you eat?"

"Café Rouge is the only restaurant name I can recall," she said. "They had wonderful soup. There were a number of French bakeries in the neighborhood that had sandwiches. I bought snack items at a grocery store. There were some interesting looking Italian restaurants in the area, but they were expensive, and I didn't think I'd feel comfortable eating there by myself."

"Did you go into Regent's Park?" Bridges was still the questioner.

"I didn't know if it would be safe. Some city parks in the U.S. aren't."

"Did you go to the theatre or visit any night clubs?"

"No. I didn't want to be out by myself after dark."

"Did you take the tube?"

"No, I took taxis or walked."

"Jenny," Sinclair asked, "did you plan your itinerary ahead of time?"

She smiled. "Well, I knew where I wanted to go before I went there," she said. "If you mean, was my itinerary known by anyone else ahead of time, the answer is no."

"Your passport was found in your room, but where is your hotel key?"

"In my purse."

"Have you ever heard of Special K or Vitamin K?"

"Special K is a breakfast cereal. Vitamin K has something to do with healthy blood, but I'm not sure what."

"Super K?"

"Is that a discount store?"

"They are street names for a drug called ketamine hydrochloride. Traces of it were found in your blood. Amongst other things, ketamine causes nausea and temporary loss of coordination."

She shivered. She didn't belong to herself anymore. He knew things about her that she didn't know. They both did.

Sinclair knew she felt exposed. "Jenny, have you ever heard of that drug?"

"No."

"Do you know where the room was, the one you described?"

"I have no idea."

"Jenny, what happened to your clothes?"

"I don't know," she answered. "I didn't find them in the little room."

"Were you wearing any jewellery?" Bridges asked. "Besides your watch and your necklace, I mean."

She ran her fingers over her ears. "I had a pair of pierced earrings. They're not on now. And a pearl ring. A friendship ring."

"You were wearing the earrings when you were admitted to hospital," Sinclair informed her. "They'll be returned to you when you check out.

What did the ring look like?"

She was looking at her bare finger with dismay. Someone special must have given her that ring. "It was a pearl ring?" he prompted.

"Yes," she said slowly. "There were small pearls across the top. A plain gold band on the bottom."

"Jenny, the two men you mentioned—were they wearing any jewellery?" Bridges asked, hoping to get her back on track.

"I don't think so," she answered after a moment. "I don't remember."

"When they turned the light on, did they speak to you?"

"They didn't say anything to me."

"Did they speak to each other? Address each other by name, for example?"

"No, they didn't speak at all."

"When Scott came in," Sinclair asked, "what was he wearing?"

"Gray slacks," she remembered. "Dark shirt, with the sleeves rolled part way up."

Sinclair paused. "Jenny—Scott's final attack. Can you tell us about it now?"

"He kicked me in the head. He knocked me out."

"Jenny," he said gently, "that's not the final attack I was referring to. Scott's final *sexual* attack—we need you to name it. For the record."

The colour left her face.

Damn it, sir, she can't face that yet. Rape is a violation, and Scott's final act had been one of total degradation.

Her fingers gripped the bedclothes. "I—I feel like I'm falling," she said.

"Lean forward, Jenny. As far forward as you can. You'll feel less faint in a moment."

She couldn't. Her cast was in the way, and the pain in her ribs made her cry out.

Bridges reclined the bed and put a pillow under her feet.

"Stop. Make him stop," she said to him.

The tape recorder was still running. Sinclair spoke quickly into the machine then stopped it. He shouldn't have pushed her so hard. It might have been easier if he had scheduled more, shorter sessions.

"I have a surprise for you," Bridges said, taking a box from his jacket pocket. "Don't mind the label—it's not soap." He opened one end so she could see inside. "Another Penguin bar, cleverly disguised so the nurses won't nick it." He closed the box and put it in her limp hand. "Reward for a job well done."

"Jenny, I'm proud of you also," Sinclair said. "The information you've given us—I can't overemphasise its importance. Thank you."

"Is it over?" she asked, finally turning in his direction.

"For now."

CHAPTER 17

Sinclair and Andrews arrived at the D/S's office a few minutes ahead of schedule. "Andrews, we're in the conference room," Graves said. The sergeant took the hint and left. Graves then turned to Sinclair. "Have you secured Miss Jeffries' cooperation yet?"

"I'll be reintroducing that subject soon, sir." Graves liked to take charge; Sinclair was surprised that he hadn't been by the hospital himself to press the case.

"Also, we know now that she wasn't attacked in Scott's flat. How confident are you in her identification of him? His solicitor won't allow a video ID."

"Confident enough to follow it through, sir. We'll need a warrant to examine the ambassador's residence. The surveillance team reported him visiting there."

"Take a videographer in addition to the usual team. Colin, we'd best not be wrong about this." Graves handed him a set of files. "We hit the jackpot in our paramedic search: a former Royal Marine Commando medic. He's more than qualified but none too pleased with the assignment, and I expect you'll have to persuade him to comply."

Andrews and the three other men stood when Graves and Sinclair entered the conference room. "As you were," Graves said. He remained standing. "We arrested a suspect in the 'Carpet Killer' case this morning. His name is William Cecil Scott, eldest son of Ambassador Sir Edward Cullen Scott. You are here because our witness in this case was attacked last night in hospital. As a result, we are planning to transfer her on an emergency basis to a safer location. You are her interim protection team.

"Sergeant Casey received his initial medical training from the Royal Marines and was a member of our special forces until an injury forced him to retire. After joining the Metropolitan Police Service, he qualified for our tactical firearms unit. He will report directly to her medical team at hospital, where he will be provided with instructions and whatever medications they feel she may require.

"PC Davies is also firearms qualified. He's rather new to the unit but has performed adequately so far. PC Sullivan is the reason we still have a witness to protect. Sullivan, I commend you for your quick thinking.

"One more thing: Your job is to keep this witness safe. Scott's a nasty piece of work. She is the only one who survived. Her cooperation is essential. Don't screw it up."

Graves moved toward the door. "Firearms are authorised for this assignment. Sinclair, carry on. I'll send the SOIT officer along when he arrives."

"I don't treat women," Casey said when the door closed.

"You treat injuries, don't you?" Sinclair retorted. "Our witness is an American. Her name is Jennifer Jeffries."

"He wants us to mind a spoilt Yank," Casey muttered to himself, shaking his head.

"Damn it, Casey!" Sinclair erupted, slamming his fist on the table. "That bloody bastard raped and brutalised her, and he did it on our watch! Spoilt? I don't think so. She was a virgin before this!" He drew copies of the police photographer's pictures from one of the files on the table and threw them onto the table. He saw Davies' jaw tighten. Sullivan paled. Casey studied each one, his frown deepening.

"In case those photos don't make it clear," Sinclair continued grimly, "Scott did a job on her. Modern medicine notwithstanding, some of her injuries are going to take a long time to heal. If any of you feels that he can't be committed to this assignment, I'd like to know straightaway. I will replace you with prejudice." He directed his gaze at Casey.

"I'm on board, sir," Casey replied.

There was still an edge to Sinclair's voice. "As Superintendent Graves said, it's our job to preserve her life. Andrews, distribute the files."

The files given to Davies and Sullivan contained a fact sheet about Jenny, a record of her taped interviews, and a summary of her medical condition. Casey's file had the fact sheet and ROTI as well as a copy of her medical record. All three had been given the address of the safe house and a key. Each carried his own pink authority-to-draw-firearms card.

Sinclair had personnel files for each man. Casey was qualified medically, as Graves had said, but he was ex-Special Boat Service. He had a take-no-prisoners expression. What would his bedside manner be like? Forbidding? Davies wasn't as experienced with firearms as Casey; it was evident that the specialist squad had sent an officer with low seniority.

"Now for what's not in the file," Sinclair said in a slightly more even tone. "She's in pain. She's frightened of men she doesn't know, and she's not going to trust you automatically just because you're coppers. Don't take it personally. She is young, single, and emotionally fragile. You'll be living in rather close quarters. Must I define what integrity means?" No one responded. He heard a knock. "Gentlemen, PC Bridges is the SOIT officer who facilitated the interviews. I've asked him to brief you on Jenny's psychological condition."

Bridges shrugged out of his jacket. He was the only one present who was informally dressed, Sinclair and Andrews still wearing suits and the three officers assigned to the protective team in uniform. He was also the shortest, but he did not bother to stand. "Jenny's trauma isn't over just because the attack is over," he said. "In some respects, it's just beginning. She's broken. There's an empty place where trust used to be. Rape changes everything about a woman's world. Whatever Jenny knew to be true about herself has been shaken. How you respond to her will tell her who she is and what the world is. She needs very badly to feel she's in control."

"She's not," Casey said.

"I realise that," Bridges replied, "but it's a matter of perception, isn't it? There are bound to be small issues over which her preferences can be respected." He paused. "Usually I encourage the victims I interview to speak freely, to tell me everything in one go, and I don't interrupt or ask for more detail until the follow-on interview. Jenny couldn't do that. She could only face one bit at a time. Both the chief inspector and I had to prompt her repeatedly. And even with help, she couldn't relate everything."

Sullivan remembered how Jenny had looked when he'd left the hospital in the morning: fearful, distraught.

"Don't push her to get over it—you'll wound her again. No matter what she says, believe her. Show no doubt. She looks a mess, and she knows it. She'll have mood swings, be numb, depressed, ashamed, embarrassed, upset. That's all normal. *She's* normal; it's what happened to her that wasn't. The problem is, she has to live with the consequences."

Bridges was drawing the box. Casey had used the same briefing method on occasion.

"Don't get too close. She may be afraid to be touched. And make sure she eats—she may lose interest in food." He smiled briefly. "Except for chocolate." He glanced at Sinclair. "In normal circumstances, I'd keep in contact with her, provide encouragement and reassurance. Sir, will that be possible?"

Sinclair shook his head.

"Will a liaison officer be assigned to her?"

"I'll fill that role."

"Sir, she was—desecrated. She'll need very sensitive treatment."

"Questions?" Sinclair asked.

Davies' face was sombre. "Sir, the hospital attack isn't described here. What form did it take?"

"The attacker posed as a psychiatrist. He intended to inject her with a syringe which we believe was filled with a toxic substance. When that failed, he attempted to strangle her."

"Was she injured further?"

Sinclair responded. "No permanent injuries, but it was a close shave. He got his hand on her neck. I should add that she also suspected that he was an imposter, but she could not defend herself."

Casey had resumed his reading of Jenny's medical record and was cursing intensely under his breath, a continual stream of colourful expletives. "I'm surprised she lived, sir."

"We were fortunate," Sinclair said, glad that Casey was finally angry for the right reasons.

"She can't walk, can she?" Casey continued.

"Not by herself, no. Also, the three of you will have to take on the cooking and cleaning responsibilities. She's not mended enough to assist. Regarding the flat: It's in Hampstead. She's not to know the location. My side of the block has a private front and rear entry. There are only three tenants. The elderly couple on the ground floor will be told that you're internet web designers with a combination home/office. I'm on the first floor. You'll be on the second. There's a small car park round the back. Casey, I'd like you to set the watches."

"I'll take the first. We'll rotate every eight hours. I'll reevaluate when I've assessed her condition and the security status of the flat. And we'll need a locker for our firearms."

"Anything else?"

"Sir, why aren't there more of us?" It was Davies.

"To reduce activity in and about the block and to minimise the trauma to our witness," Sinclair shot back. "I realise I'm asking a good deal of you, but this is a temporary assignment. Be at the hospital tomorrow night at eight o'clock. No uniforms. Have your belongings prepositioned. Come armed. I'll brief you on the transfer procedure then. Other questions, call my mobile. Andrews, you and I are going to the supermarket. Thank you, gentlemen."

CHAPTER 18

Jenny looked up in alarm when she saw Sinclair Friday evening. "More questions?"

"Not the sort you're expecting." He smiled. "How was your afternoon?"

"The chaplain came by. I was a little nervous at first, but one of your men stayed, and that helped. I had a question for him: Where was God when I was being attacked?"

"That's a tough one," Sinclair commented.

"Not for this chaplain! He was what Texans call a straight shooter. According to him, if God hadn't been there, I would have died. And he said something that really touched me: that God's a gentleman, that He doesn't force His will on us. Then he delivered the punch line: God is a God of justice, and He chose me to see this through. He seemed so sure." She sighed. "Also, Barry came by, and your Sergeant Andrews, to question me about the strangler."

"I have a bit of business for you as well. I need your signature on your formal statement." He handed her the printed copy and a pen. "Read it before you autograph it."

"I'd rather not," she said slowly. "There's something frightening about seeing things in black and white."

"Jenny, you must. If you need to make any changes or corrections, you should do so now. This is a legal document, and any deviance from it in court will cast doubt on its accuracy as a whole."

The statement was verbatim, and it was long. It was an alien document, with her words rendered according to the British rules of spelling, yet the events it described were part of her now, an irrevocable part. As she read, Mr. Sinclair and Barry's questions receded, and she heard only her own voice, describing the monster's blows. She felt the slash on her cheek, so real that she half expected to see blood on her fingers after she touched it.

He watched her. When he'd told the protective team that she was fragile, he hadn't misrepresented the situation. He hoped they were the right men for the job. On paper they were sufficiently qualified to protect her, but what were their personalities like? Could they live with her, even for a short period of time, and not drive her round the bend? The thirty-two-year-old Casey had been in the special forces. All warriors had an aggressive edge. Had that mentality moderated since he joined the police? As a medic, he might not be unsympathetic, but he looked it. Both Casey and Davies were accustomed to working primarily with men. He realised with sudden clarity that this sort of protection could be very difficult for her. He'd have to observe closely.

The more she read, the more upset she became. Her hand shook, and she crushed the edge of the page in an attempt to steady herself. Mr. Sinclair's hand on hers startled her.

"Take it easy, Jenny."

"Mr. Sinclair, I have to stop him."

"You have, Jenny. Your identification and statement led to his arrest."

"No, I mean stop him for good. I'm scared to death of him, and I don't know how I'll be able to do it, but I have to. Go to court. Testify. Whatever it takes. I can't let him do this to anyone else."

He couldn't restrain a smile. "Brilliant! Well done. Jenny, with your help, we'll prevail. *You'll* prevail. You'll see this nightmare end."

Finally she finished her reading, signed where indicated, and handed the pages back to him.

He thanked her again before departing. As he headed home, he thought about how bruised and scarred she was. Somehow she had survived Scott's onslaught. Six others hadn't, leaving their families devastated. The lack of progress in the investigation had dispirited them and frustrated Met officers. Now this tiny Texas tourist had made a powerful decision that could begin to set it right.

CHAPTER 19

"It's a bit imposing, sir," Andrews said. He and Sinclair were outside Ambassador Scott's private dwelling in Kensington Gardens early Saturday morning. The residence itself was immense, and the metal railings surrounding it were as polished as a Royal Marine's boots.

"It's meant to be," Sinclair answered.

When the other officers arrived, he assigned one lot to establish the perimeter and instructed the forensic team to stand by. The rest of them walked down the driveway to the rear entrance. "Start the video," Sinclair said. He gave the standard introduction, then stood back to give the locksmith room to work.

"We're in, sir," he reported.

"Police!" Sinclair called. "Police!" He didn't expect an answer; the ambassador was still abroad. He stationed a PC by the back door. He, Andrews, and the videographer entered first. "The room we're looking for will be downstairs," he said. "Access to it will be from the back of the house." They located a door behind the kitchen, but it was locked, and Sinclair again required the locksmith's services.

The light switch at the top of the stairs revealed one flight of plain wooden steps leading down to a short hallway. There were two doors off each side of the hall. The first room on the right appeared to be a small storeroom, but just a few tins remained on the shelves. The second room on the right was the one they had been looking for. It fit Jenny's description exactly, from the concrete floor to the chest of drawers and the mirror on the dirty white wall. The other women had been here; Sinclair could feel it. He hoped they could prove it. The Scenes-of-Crime Officers were waiting outside. "Call the SOCOs," he said.

"He brought her to his father's house? Why?" Andrews asked when he returned.

"To emulate him? To embarrass him? Because he thought it was safe territory? We may never know." Both men donned latex gloves. Sinclair opened the drawers, one at a time, wanting further confirmation of Jenny's statement. Two were empty, but they saw several items of women's jewellery, including an amethyst cross, in the third. "That's as far as I dare go," he commented, knowing any more interference would incur the wrath of the SOCOs.

Sinclair made a cursory inspection of the rooms on the left side of the hall. Neither looked as if it had been used in some time, but forensic would have to examine them nevertheless. Glancing behind him to be sure the officer with the camera was still with him, he said, "We'll move upstairs next. There may be something there that will tie Scott to the other victims."

The formal rooms on the ground floor had dust on the floor and dust sheets over the furniture. The same was true for the private sitting rooms, bedrooms, and baths on the first floor. The attack on Jenny was only the most recent. Evidence relating to the other women could still be present, even under the dust. All spaces would be searched eventually, but Sinclair's focus was on Jenny's case. On the second floor one of the bedrooms was in disarray, and the towels in the adjoining bathroom had been hastily hung. Every drawer, every cabinet would have to be opened and inspected, and every surface tested. There were a number of items to be collected and bagged, including several pairs of shoes and what appeared to be drugs and drug paraphernalia.

Sinclair removed his gloves and returned to the scene of the attack downstairs. The forensic team had discovered that what Jenny had thought was a mirror in the little room was actually a window from the storeroom next door. Anyone standing in the storeroom could see the other room totally and clearly. Sinclair had a sudden vision of Scott's accomplices, watching and waiting while he destroyed a young woman's life. "Test this area for fingerprints also," he said in a thick voice, turning away to conceal his anger. He wanted more than ever to identify them.

Stepping back into the room where the attack had taken place, he called for an officer to stand by the door. "Close the door and turn off the light." The darkness covered them like a shroud. The dank smell was more evident in the dark, and he could feel a warped malevolence seeping into his pores. Fear was one of the few things that you could see in the dark—and dear God, how frightening it must have been, for a young woman to find herself naked in this evil pit! He was wearing a three-piece suit, as usual, and still he shivered. "Thank you," he said, and the light was flipped on. His anger had not dissipated.

Sinclair waited while the other men worked. Plastic evidence bags were labelled and sealed. Fingerprint powder covered everything, like a light dusting of sinister snow. When the SOCOs finished in the little room, he turned off the light and closed the door. Forensic had finished in the room next to it also, but Sinclair hadn't. The window still haunted him. Andrews had started up the flight of stairs when he heard glass shattering and rushed back down.

"Bastards won't be using this any more," Sinclair said through clenched teeth.

"Sir," Andrews stammered, "your hand is bleeding." He could see his words hadn't registered. "Sir! Your hand!"

Sinclair's face was still dark when he tore his eyes away from the shards on the floor. He wrapped a handkerchief around his fist and put it in his pocket. He was surprised and vaguely pleased with himself. He led the way up the stairs. "I'd best ring Graves. He'll need to report the search to the Foreign and Commonwealth Office." He and Andrews stepped into the kitchen. "You'll continue on here? I'll meet you at the hospital tonight. I need to collect a few more items for the flat."

"Sir, stop in at hospital first."

CHAPTER 20

It would have surprised his sergeant, but Sinclair took his advice and made hospital his next stop. He had Sergeant Casey paged, and as he waited, his mind travelled back to the little room and Jenny's experience there. He found it hard to shake the weight he felt on his shoulders, and his encounter with the concealed window had only temporarily eased his anger.

"Sir?"

Casey's voice startled him. "Sergeant, is there a treatment room available?"

"Yes, sir, this way." He led Sinclair down a corridor and pushed open a door.

Sinclair took his hand out of his pocket and removed the handkerchief. "Can you clean this up for me?"

"Yes, sir." He washed his hands and then cleansed Sinclair's. "No sutures necessary," he reported. He applied an antiseptic cream to the lacerations and wrapped the hand in a gauze bandage. "You're good to go, sir."

Sinclair opened and closed his fist a few times. He appreciated Casey's apparent lack of curiosity. "Thank you, Sergeant. Are you getting on well with Dr. Adams?"

"Yes, sir. I'll be ready."

"Tonight then," Sinclair said. His next stop was the supermarket, followed by a trip to the flat. He and Andrews had already stocked the pantry and refrigerator with the basics, including dry goods, tinned soups, spices, and the usual breakfast and lunch items. This time he purchased a variety of meats, fresh vegetables, and fruits. He hoped the protection team would know what to do with them.

He walked through the rest of the flat, noting the extra pillows Andrews had provided for Jenny's bed. There seemed to be sufficient sheets and towels for four people, but nothing for entertainment besides the TV. The rooms were not large, but it was still the nicest safe house he'd seen in his years on the force. The 6'5" Davies would have to bend down to get through the doorways, but he was probably used to that.

He walked back into Jenny's room. There were several drab prints in the sitting room and dining room, but none in here. What sort of surroundings was she used to? Even with the carpet and regular bed, this room was almost as stale and sterile as her hospital room. Into this setting he was going to place a young woman who had studied literature, who remembered and quoted some of the most beautiful words in the English language, who had seen the ugliest side of man. Could she heal here?

He headed back to the Yard, stopping for a quick bite to eat on the way. That would have to be his lunch and dinner. At his desk he marvelled at the size of Jenny's file: at first so slim, and now that she had identified Scott and potentially linked him to six other cases, voluminous in scope and detail. A field day for the Crown Prosecution Service. The results of the rape kit were not back from the lab. Scott's DNA had just been collected. The reports by the SOCOs would take days to complete. He sighed. He was still haunted by that little room. He did not suffer from claustrophobia, but he had felt the blackness closing in even during his brief time in the dark. He ran his hand through his hair. Was it too early to go back to the hospital? No matter; he'd spend a bit of extra time with Jenny before reviewing the transfer procedures with Andrews and the others. He collected his raincoat on the way out.

CHAPTER 21

When Sinclair entered Jenny's room, she greeted him with a tentative smile and a question about his bandaged hand. "Policing is a dangerous job sometimes." He sat down next to the bed. "What does the song say? 'A policeman's lot is not an 'appy one.'"

"Gilbert and Sullivan," she said, recognizing the reference. "As I recall, the police won in that operetta."

He was surprised she knew it. "Yes, they invoked the name of the Queen, and the pirates yielded."

"Will the monster yield? Plead guilty, I mean. If he did, I wouldn't have to tell everyone what happened to me."

"It's too soon to know," he said, although he didn't think submission was a part of Scott's character. "Tell me about your day."

"The chaplain came by again. My behavior yesterday didn't scare him away! He left the Scripture reference in your Bible but said that he just had two words for me today: 'Choose life.'"

That struck Sinclair. In other circumstances he had urged men—desperate men—to surrender peacefully, to choose life over death, and it was a spiritual choice everyone had to make at one time or another. "I hope he was able to shed some light."

"He didn't know what it meant for me exactly. Perhaps choosing trust over fear and shame, or choosing to look ahead and not back. He thinks of himself as a farmer, because when he visits patients in the hospital, he just plants seeds. He doesn't get to see if they grow or not."

"That's a good analogy. The seeds of justice are already growing in you."

"Then I must be the dirt," she said with a rueful smile. "That's how I feel most of the time, so if something good could come out of all this, it would make a big difference."

"It will," he assured her. "How are you otherwise?"

"I should be asking you that," she replied, glancing at his hand.

"It doesn't bother me." He handed her a copy of her statement about the hospital attack.

"I know—read and sign," she said. It didn't take long.

There was a knock at the door. "Time for a wash," the nurse said.

"Already?" Jenny's face was suddenly tense.

"I'll step outside." He walked down to the nurses' station. Andrews and Casey were both there. Andrews had probably given Casey all the details of his bout with the window. He took the opportunity to review the transfer plans with Casey. "Andrews, give me about ten minutes," he said, when he saw the nurse leave Jenny's room.

Jenny looked like she'd had the wind knocked out of her sails. Her arm clutched her teddy bear. "Are you all right?" he asked.

"It still hurts to move. The nurse did her best, but…"

"But?" he prompted, wondering if she could weather what he had planned.

She was a little disconcerted by his attentiveness. "I'm shy," she said slowly. "I know she's given baths to hundreds of people, but I'm such a mess. I don't like people looking at me." She missed the pained expression that crossed his face.

"Jenny," he said, stepping closer to the bed, "we'll be moving you tonight."

"Home? Are you sending me home?"

"No, but we've found a safe place for you, and I'd like to take you there."

They heard a knock. "Sir, we're ready." Andrews was accompanied by Dr. Adams and a tough, stern-looking man. "Sergeant Casey will be looking after you when you leave hospital," Dr. Adams informed her.

She stared at Sergeant Casey. He wasn't in uniform; what kind of sergeant was he? He was wearing dark trousers and a dark turtleneck shirt. His jacket wasn't buttoned, and she could see a gun strapped to his belt. He was younger than the chief inspector and not quite as tall. His ginger hair was cut short, his eyes were icy blue, and he didn't have an ounce of spare fat anywhere. Her stomach turned over. What did "looking after her" mean exactly? "Where am I going? Is he going, too? Don't you have to ask me? He doesn't even look like a policeman!"

"Before I joined the police, I was in the military," Casey said.

"I don't understand any of this!"

Sinclair didn't intervene. He wanted to see how Casey would respond to her.

"Miss, I've seen your file. I know what was done to you, and you have every right to be afraid of men you don't know. You need to know some things about me. In my work I had a mission. Amongst other things, I was what you Yanks call a combat medic."

Her eyes widened. "Why do I need you?"

"Because I know how to treat the wounds you have, and I can protect you at the same time."

"Will you understand that I'll be afraid sometimes?" she asked in a low voice.

He'd seen the forensic photos. He noted the recent bruises on her neck. "Love, we're all afraid sometimes."

Sinclair heard a new gentleness in his voice. Casey adapts fast.

Good.

"Miss Jeffries, I need to show him where you've been hurt and tell him what treatment to provide," said Dr. Adams.

"No, please." She clutched her hospital gown tightly, holding it closed with her fingers. "Can't he just look at my chart or something?"

"He needs to have a look at you," Dr. Adams insisted.

"Are you all going to watch?" she asked, her tension mounting.

"I'll step out." Andrews handed his boss a small envelope, containing all the personal belongings Jenny had had when she was admitted to hospital: two tiny earrings.

Sinclair decided not to give them to her just yet. He put the envelope in his pocket. The door closed behind Andrews, but Sinclair did not budge. He wanted to watch Casey.

The sergeant moved closer to the bed. "Dr. Adams is right, love. I need to see where you've been hurt and where you're still hurting. I'd rather do it with your permission." He let his hand rest on her hand, very lightly.

She didn't miss the implication, and she began to cry.

"Here's what we're going to do," Casey continued. "I'm going to move my hand, and then you're going to move your hand. Then Dr. Adams is going to show me what to do. I won't touch you unless I have to."

Her hand was shaking, but she did as he suggested. She saw anger cross his face after Dr. Adams opened her hospital gown and exposed her injuries. Sinclair saw it as well. There was no sign of Casey's initial resentment. When Adams finished, Casey covered her.

"Gentlemen, I need a few minutes alone with my patient," Adams informed the two policemen. When they had left, he sat down next to the bed. "Miss Jeffries, you're leaving hospital a bit ahead of schedule, but Sergeant Casey is a good man."

"Dr. Adams, he's so scary looking! That stony face!"

"He's been well trained. However, I want you to promise me that you'll make him contact me if any problems develop that you feel he can't handle. You're too important for him to refuse you. You know your body, and if you don't feel right about something, stand your ground and insist. Will you do that?"

She swallowed hard. Dr. Adams' face softened, and he dropped his professional manner for a moment. "You're recovering well, you know. You're going to be completely all right." He patted her hand, not expecting a reply, and summoned Sinclair and Casey.

"The passages are clear. It's time to go," Sinclair said.

"Miss Jeffries, Sergeant Casey is going to give you a strong sedative," Dr. Adams said. "When you wake up, you'll be in your new surroundings."

She saw the syringe in the sergeant's hands, and she paled. "Do I have to have a shot? Does he have to do it? Is it safe? Who's going to protect me from him?"

"It's best," the doctor assured her. "It takes effect quickly, and your escorts are in a hurry. The trip would be too painful for you otherwise."

Sinclair moved to the other side of the bed and took her hand. He nodded to Adams and Casey.

Dr. Adams turned Jenny on her side slightly and pushed her hospital gown out of the way.

"What are you doing? Cover me up!" she cried, trying to pull her hand free from Sinclair's grip.

"Miss Jeffries, the injection goes in your hip," Adams explained.

"No! No..." she wailed, but Mr. Sinclair did not release her hand. Oh, she hated them all—Mr. Sinclair, who talked about consent but didn't practice it; Sergeant Casey with his hard face; even Dr. Adams and his matter-of-fact tone. She felt cold alcohol, then the sting of the injection. Sergeant Casey was quick, at least.

Casey watched her blink rapidly, fighting the effect of the drug. Sinclair held her hand until her eyes closed and her breathing became relaxed and even. "Let's move," he told Casey and called for Andrews, Davies, and the officers outside. Dr. Adams and Sergeant Casey shifted her to the stretcher that Davies and Sullivan brought, Sinclair shook hands with Dr. Adams, and in a few minutes they had wheeled her down the passage and out of sight.

PART TWO

We look before and after;
We pine for what is not;
Our sincerest laughter
With some pain is fraught;
Our sweetest songs are those
That tell of saddest thought.

— Percy Bysshe Shelley

CHAPTER 1

In the half light of dawn, the pain was bright and strong. Fearing any movement would aggravate it, Jenny tried not to breathe. And failed. Someone pressed two pills into her palm. An arm behind her back forced her forward, causing additional pain in her ribs. A glass appeared at her lips.

"Drink," a rough voice said. She was at his mercy. She obeyed. He allowed her to sink back. "She's awake, sir," the voice continued. "See you in five."

When she opened her eyes next, Mr. Sinclair was sitting next to the bed, concern filling his blue eyes. "I know this is hard," he said. "That's why I'm here. You're in a safe place now. I want to do my best for you, and Casey does as well."

She felt disoriented. She'd gone to sleep in one place and awakened in another: the Wizard of Oz syndrome. The pain retreated slightly, and her mind began to focus. No harsh hospital sheets here—and a real comforter covered her. She was in a room with cream-colored walls and pale print wallpaper. Heavy curtains kept the light out.

Casey stepped forward. "I expect you'd like to get up. Can you swing your legs to the edge of the bed?"

"No, sir—yes, sir—"

"You don't have to call me sir. Put your arm on my shoulder, and slide onto your feet."

She leaned against him, all her weight on her right leg.

"Try to use your left leg a bit," Casey advised. "Now, to the loo."

She shuddered. Was this man going into the bathroom with her? The carpet felt soft on her feet, but her leg throbbed, and it was slow going. The bathroom was small, at least by Texas standards. No room for him, thank God. "I can manage," she said through clenched teeth, hoping it was true.

"Call me," he said and closed the door behind him.

She did what she needed to do and then gripped the sink for support. Without thinking, she looked up. What she saw in the mirror shouldn't have shocked her. Of course the gash, even patched up, was more than readily visible—it was smack dab in the middle of her cheek.

Mr. Sinclair had been kind to describe it as a wrinkle. Of course there would be bruises, making her skin look sallow. But still she felt shaken. She wanted to get back in bed and pull the covers over herself, but Mr. Sinclair had other ideas.

"I'd like you to see the rest of the flat and meet the men who are guarding you."

"I can't face anyone now," she objected. "Not looking like this."

"Your bruises have faded, and your wound is healing. You'll be fine. Sullivan's here, Jenny. There's just one new officer."

She tried another approach. "I'm not dressed! I'm naked under this hospital thing."

"Jenny," he said in a lighter tone, "we're all naked under our clothing."

She couldn't appreciate his humor. "I'm not covered enough," she insisted.

"Then use this for the time being," he suggested, handing her the hospital dressing gown.

Again she put her arm on Casey's shoulder, but his support wasn't sufficient. She sagged against the sofa when they reached the living room.

Sinclair frowned. He should have realized how weak she would be. Pain from her ribs, incision, and leg had kept her physiotherapist sessions short. Even with assistance, she hadn't taken more than a few steps at a time. "You'll have to pick her up, Sergeant."

"I've carried packs heavier than you," Casey told her.

Danny pulled out a chair for her at the kitchen table, but she didn't greet him—she was shaken by the sight of a huge man with hair the color of rye toast. Her mouth went dry, and she angled her injured cheek away from him

"I'm PC Davies," the stranger said, rising to his feet, "but you can call me Brian if you like." He didn't react to her appearance.

"The tea's wet—do you fancy some?" Danny asked.

"Yes, thanks," she whispered. "I can't make it myself yet."

"Not to worry," Danny said. "We're your slaves! We'll do it all. Milk and sugar?"

"Ugh. No milk."

"So American!" teased Danny. "Cereal? Eggs? You're too thin! We need to feed you up."

"I don't feel hungry." She took only a sip of the tea. "How large is this place?"

"Three bedrooms and two bathrooms," Sinclair replied. "You've already seen the sitting room and dining room. There's a utility area off the kitchen."

"Why so much space?"

"Because Sergeant Casey and the other two men will be living here with you."

"I want my parents to take care of me. Can't I go home?"

“You haven’t healed enough to travel. You’ll have to be our guest for a bit.”

She tried to focus on Mr. Sinclair and not the dark shapes looming behind him. “Please, could I go back to the hospital?”

“You’ll be much safer here. Our goal is total protection, nothing less.”

“In an apartment with three men? Is this a cruel joke? Don’t you have any policewomen?”

“Jenny, police officers protected you while you were in hospital.”

“Yes, but that was a public place with lots of people around. And this is so sudden!”

“It was felt that your circumstances warranted a rapid response.”

She swallowed hard but did not reply.

She’s frightened, Davies thought. Of us. Of me. He knelt down and spoke to the wary eyes. “It’s a bit overwhelming, isn’t it? I’d like to help if I can.” He noted the thin hospital gown, the bruises it did not cover. “Sir, she’s cold.”

Sinclair shrugged out of his coat and draped it over her shoulders. “Jenny,” he said gently, “we would be remiss if we didn’t prepare for every sort of threat.”

Davies straightened and stepped back.

“Serial murder is rare in England,” Sinclair continued. “This is a big case, and there is enormous pressure to get things done. Your testimony against Scott is the most powerful evidence we will have. All I’m asking of you is to give these men a chance to prove they are trustworthy.”

She was tired already. Her chin drooped.

Sinclair gestured to Casey to take her back to her room.

She paled. And strained to keep her eyes open until Casey had settled her in bed and left.

CHAPTER 2

When Sergeant Casey looked in on Jenny, she was already awake. The men brought her lunch on a tray. Hot soup. More tea. Danny was the most outgoing, and he kept the conversation lively, even from his position on the floor. "Rank has its privileges—and so does size," he joked as Casey and Davies took the chairs. They all had some rank—someone had acknowledged their value. In the hospital she'd been the "fractured ribs" or the "police patient" or worse. What was she now?

A coward. She didn't want to know these men; she wanted to hide. And to sleep—the smallest movements wore her out.

The flat was very quiet. There had been so much going on at the hospital, nurses or other personnel in and out of her room day and night. She hadn't thought she'd miss the interruptions, but now her world had been reduced to four beige walls, three strange men, and one pathetic set of clothes.

Danny escorted her to dinner. The men had laid the table for four people. "Where's Mr. Sinclair?" she asked.

"He'll call by later," Sergeant Casey said. "He's got a lot on."

Call by? What did that mean? Was he calling or coming over? "He's left me with the men in black," she said despairingly. "If you're the good guys, shouldn't you be wearing white?"

"Good film!" Danny responded with a laugh.

Someone had made roast chicken, vegetables, and tossed salad, but her stomach felt unsettled, and she didn't eat much. After dinner, Brian invited her to watch television with them, but it was hard to stay awake. She wanted to climb into bed and pull the covers over herself, to shut out this alternate universe with its uniformed men and their accented, archaic language.

Sergeant Casey helped her into the bedroom, where he explained that he would be on watch again that night.

"What's that?" she asked, tensing at a sound.

"The furnace. There's a click before the air begins to flow."

My God. She was afraid of the *appliances.*

When he brought her pain tablets, he had some medical supplies on the tray. He removed the steristrips from her cheek. "I'll cleanse the sutures from your chest tube and replace the dressing," he said. "It won't hurt." He folded back one side of her hospital gown.

"No—wait—" She tried to cover herself.

No one in the Royal Marines had been shy, and it was a moment before he understood what her concern was. He covered her breast with the top of the gown, but her long abdominal scar was still exposed, and she began to cry, slow, silent tears that leaked from the corners of her eyes and ran down the sides of her face. She knew that she should feel grateful for his care, but she didn't. She was afraid of him, of his closeness, his hands on her body, the crease between his brows that made him look like he was frowning all the time.

When he finished, he looked up. "You're going through a rough patch, but you'll make it." He reached down and turned off the light by her bed.

The dark—the little room—the monster—fear gripped her like a glove, and she couldn't keep from crying out. "Sergeant Casey," she begged, "please don't leave me in the dark."

He switched on the lamp. "I'll not do that."

"Promise?" she gasped. "You won't decide I have to sink or swim?"

"No, love. That's a judgement only you can make. Now, let's calm you down. Watch me breathe, and breathe with me." He matched her frantic breaths and then gradually slowed them.

The effort exhausted her. Her eyes were too heavy to focus on the light.

When Sinclair arrived, the men reported that they'd hardly seen her during the day. She had stayed in her room except for dinner and a brief stint in the sitting room. She'd slept a good deal. At mealtimes she'd been quiet and hadn't had much appetite. He went with Casey to her room. "You left the light on?"

"She's afraid of the dark, sir," Casey answered.

Sinclair approached the bed. The lamp on the nightstand cast an amber glow on her face but did nothing to mask her bruises. The teddy bear Bridges had given her was next to her. Afraid of the dark—he should have anticipated that. What else had he missed in this precipitous move?

CHAPTER 3

After her medicine and morning tea, Jenny wanted to get dressed, to cover herself with layer upon layer of clothing. The chest of drawers wasn't far from the bed; she could get there. Big mistake—her legs didn't support her, and she hit hard, jarring her ribs. She bit back a sob and waited for the pain to subside before opening the drawers. None of her slacks or jeans looked loose enough to fit comfortably over her bruised and sore leg. She hadn't packed any dresses for her trip abroad, planning to wear slacks, jeans, or skirts with a variety of blouses, and her blouses wouldn't fit over the cast on her arm.

The bed looked very high. She hadn't thought about how to get back in it, but now she realized she might as well have tried to climb Mt. Everest. She was useless. "Hello?" she called. "Hello?"

She heard heavy footsteps approaching, and her heart started to pound. It was Constable Davies. Mt. Everest was coming to her.

"Are you all right?" he asked. "Did you fall?"

"No, but I can't get back in bed. Could you call Danny, please?"

"No, I'm here. It's no bother."

"No, please," she pleaded, but he bent down and easily scooped her up.

"Better?"

She nodded so he would not stay.

The morning dragged on. She asked Sergeant Casey how long her cast would have to stay on, and he replied that it would be another four to six weeks. That was a blow. She had only hospital attire. Would she have to dress like an invalid for another month? She couldn't parade around the apartment in her nightclothes! And how could she get home if she had nothing to wear?

Danny was in the kitchen washing up from the lunch she'd barely touched. She was left with the two silent types, and she wished they were sitting farther away. "People are people, Jennifer. Go the extra mile," her mother had said when she was shy. She felt a deep ache. It was so awkward. They were strangers—she certainly didn't want to talk to them about what had happened to her. And they weren't even American! If she mentioned sports, they wouldn't know the names of the players. If they told her where they were from, she wouldn't recognize the places. But she had to try. She was stuck here. "Why did you become a policeman?" she asked Brian.

He leant back in his chair and put his feet on the coffee table. "I grew up on a farm, with a sister and two brothers, but I didn't want to be a farmer, and I wasn't clever enough for university. After I took my exams, I worked for a couple years, mostly unskilled labour jobs because of my size."

His size. She didn't need reminding of what someone his size could do.

"I wanted to do more than that, so when I was old enough, I applied to the police."

"Do you like having a gun?" she asked, realizing too late what a stupid question it was.

"I've been with the Met almost ten years, and for a good portion of that time I didn't carry a firearm. And I've yet to fire it on a mission."

She could feel the tension in her chest, but she pushed herself to continue. "What about you, Sergeant Casey?"

"I don't discuss weapons with civilians."

"Throttle back, mate," Brian advised. "She's not asking that. Tell about your family."

"There's just my mum and my brother."

"Why'd you join the Royal Marines?" Danny asked.

"A judge's recommendation. I was a bit of a tearaway, and he thought military structure might teach me discipline and respect for authority."

"Did it?" A disciplined Sergeant Casey was scary enough. She didn't want to imagine what an undisciplined sergeant would be like.

"Not straightaway," he admitted. "There was a certain sergeant major who had to teach me the facts of life all by himself."

Danny chuckled, but Jenny didn't understand.

"I was supposed to maintain a certain attitude while in uniform," Casey explained. "Before his instruction, I wasn't doing it. After his instruction, I was. Let's just say that his instruction was rather physical."

"Did he hurt you?" she asked, her voice rising.

Casey paused. "He made his point. He taught me a valuable lesson. I was a better Marine after."

She paled. "Are you going to do that to me? Teach me a 'valuable lesson' so I'll measure up?"

He could hear the panic. He checked his watch. She was overdue on her pain meds. "Sullivan, my kit. Davies, a glass of milk for the lady." Fear and pain—a bad combination.

She took the milk and swallowed the tablets quickly.

Brian and Danny were looking on, silent specters, but she could not keep an eye on them and watch Sergeant Casey, too. When the pain eased, she leaned back on the sofa. Her eyes grew heavy, and her breathing slowed.

"We should move her to her room, shouldn't we?" Sullivan asked quietly.

"I'll do it," Davies said. He gathered her up, shaking his head at the multitude of deep bruises he saw. He set her gently on the bed and covered her bare feet and legs with the blanket. He stood for a moment watching her then turned on the light before leaving the room.

CHAPTER 4

At the Yard, Sinclair was having a constructive day. Fingerprints at the crime scene had confirmed Scott's presence and identified two other men. Leonard "The Brute" Stark, 38, was an American, an ex-boxer and bodybuilder whose physical services were now on a different sort of market. The Met's counterparts in Las Vegas, Nevada, were well acquainted with him, having arrested him several times on suspicion of assault. No convictions had resulted, however. The other fingerprints belonged to Anthony Michalopolous, 43, a petty thief and drugs user. Photo arrays were being prepared for friends and families of the six murder victims to see as well as for Jenny.

On his way home he stopped in at the protection flat. He watched Jenny pick at her food while the men devoured theirs. When the dishes had been cleared away, he had a word with her. "Are you having difficulty here? You're safe, you know. Only a handful of people have been made aware of this location."

"You dumped me here with King Kong and the Terminator. I didn't want to come," she stammered.

He hadn't prepared her; that was true. "It's not easy being in an unfamiliar place, is it? Even for a short period of time. Tell me how I can help."

Something in his gentle tone touched her, and she began to cry. "I'm a freak. I'm crippled. I can't do anything. I can't even get dressed."

He handed her his handkerchief. "I need to know more, Jenny."

"None of my clothes will fit over my cast. And I'm scared of your men. I'm defenseless."

"Have they done anything to frighten you?"

"I'm okay with Danny—he helped me in the hospital, so I don't think he'd hurt me here, but I don't know Constable Davies. I don't want Sergeant Casey, either—I want a real nurse. And I want to go home, and you're not letting me."

"Davies won't harm you, Jenny. He's the one who took you from the van and brought you up the stairs to this flat."

She was appalled. "You let him touch me when I was asleep?"

"I allowed him to carry you, yes. Casey, Sullivan, and I were there. You were perfectly safe. Shall I tell you about Sergeant Casey?"

"I'm not sure I want to know."

"We'd be dead in the water without him. Do you realise what being a combat medic means? He went into combat with a medical kit."

"He had a gun, too—you can't tell me he didn't! He was probably born with one."

"Jenny, I'm speaking of priorities."

"But he looks—like a hit man!"

"He was in the special forces. He has seen things no man should have to see."

"Haven't you?"

"Yes, but he saw them happening. When a man died, he took the loss personally. I see things after the fact. There's a big difference, believe me. Jenny, he is a dedicated officer. He will put your needs ahead of his every time."

Her cheeks burned. "I'm so sorry."

"It's my mistake. I should have briefed you about them." He paused. "I'll see what I can do about the clothes problem. And Jenny—about going home—at the moment you're not well enough for travel. You don't have the stamina. And you're not eating enough to regain your strength." He called for Davies to bring her a sandwich.

Sergeant Casey watched her carefully.

"Are you counting my bites?"

"Something like that." He watched her head turn, like a startled animal's. A motorcycle was going down the street, and she had reacted to the noise. "A lad delivering pizza, most likely," he said.

When Sinclair left, Casey helped her into the bathroom and then into bed. "I'm going to give you a bit of a cleanup. Your sutures."

"Do you have to? I don't want you to see."

"I've seen worse."

"But I haven't!"

"Best to get it over."

She held her breath and tried to think of something besides what he was doing. "Where did you learn all this?"

"As part of my training, I spent some time each year in the casualty ward of a civilian hospital."

"You're overqualified for this job."

"I expect so."

"What day is it?"

"28 September."

"What day of the week?"

"Monday."

"Two weeks ago today," she whispered and then couldn't keep the tears from coming. "Two weeks ago today, I had a life. Now I can't tell the good guys from the bad guys."

He sat down on the edge of the bed and took her hand, running his thumb up and down her small, slim fingers. "You're cold. You should have told me."

"I wasn't sure it had anything to do with the temperature."

She's sad-on, cold in her soul, he thought.

CHAPTER 5

In the morning Casey came in with jog pants and a t-shirt on and a towel around his neck. He was carrying a radio. "Shall I help you up? You can do it yourself, but your ribs will hurt."

She didn't want to need this man, but in the alien world that was her new life, she did. She took the glass of milk and her morning medicine. "Have you been exercising?"

"Running. Davies and I go in turn, early, before you wake up."

"What's the radio for?"

"To make vibrations against the window so people can't eavesdrop." He plugged it in. "It has to stay on all the time."

"But it will keep me from hearing things," she argued. "I won't have any warning."

"That's what we're here for, love."

Then it was time for the long march to the kitchen. Brian made her a cup of tea and offered his short-order cooking skills, but she wasn't hungry. "Where's Danny?"

"Sleeping." Casey helped her into the sitting room, and she discovered that daytime TV in England was just as bad as daytime TV at home, if not worse. The monster wouldn't have to shoot her. She'd be assaulted by boredom and die a lingering death. It was all very strange—strange not knowing where she was, strange being with policemen, strange not being able to take care of herself, and strangest of all, hardly recognizing herself, with the landscape of her body altered, as if someone had taken it apart and then put it back together without the directions. Even these thoughts were strange: She'd never been this melancholy. She used to be able to connect with people. She remembered the lines from *Macbeth* and wondered if all the tomorrows she spent here would "creep in this petty pace from day to day." The rest of that speech was depressing, too. The lines about sound and fury reminded her of the monster, and others implied that life had no meaning.

Danny woke after lunch, made himself a sandwich, and brought her a dish of ice cream. "I've got two older sisters," he told her while they ate. "Samantha's a hairdresser, and Gemma's learning to be a secretary. If she can type as fast as she talks, she'll do fine." He laughed. "I also have a younger sister still in secondary school. It's secondary school, all right—boys are primary!"

After dinner, the men heard the chief inspector's knock on the door. When both Danny and Sergeant Casey went, she asked Brian, "Why does it take two of you to answer the door?"

"One to open it and one for backup," he explained. "We like to err on the side of caution. And the chief always phones ahead so we know when to expect him."

Sinclair quickly briefed Casey. "You're in charge of this mobile phone. Jenny's only authorised calls are to her parents or to me. The numbers are preprogrammed. I don't expect her to like it."

"I have some surprises for you," he told Jenny, holding out two carrier-bags. Andrews' wife, Susie, had done the shopping.

"I always thought caftans were for older women, but these are gorgeous," she said, holding up the contents. One was kelly green with gold embroidery around the sleeves, v-neck, and leg slits; the other, a deep blue with white satin trim. They would cover her completely. The nightgown was long, a Lanz with the signature small print and eyelet trim, and it looked warm, as did the nightshirt. The soap had a lavender scent.

Sinclair was relieved. They'd looked like two shapeless dresses to him. He hadn't realised women wore such things. He took the hospital envelope from his pocket and handed it to her.

"My earrings! I wondered what had happened to them."

He watched her put them on, entirely by feel. "Lovely."

"Mr. Sinclair, thank you so much. How can I repay you?"

"Tell us about growing up in Texas," Sullivan prompted.

"Sounds a fair trade to me," Sinclair said.

She shifted her weight to make herself more comfortable. "I grew up in Houston. My dad's a college professor. He teaches American history. My mom's just a mom. I have two younger brothers. I miss all of them."

She paused and took a deep breath, wincing when her ribs reminded her that they had not healed. "I liked growing up in Texas. I didn't mind the heat and humidity. And it's a modern state. Don't believe the stereotype! There are universities, sports arenas, symphonies, and shopping malls. There aren't as many ranches as there used to be, but there are still cowboys, and some cities have rodeos in the summer. I can't remember when the last Indian raid was exactly, but it was much later than you would think—1917 or 1918, maybe. Texas was the biggest state in the U.S. until Alaska came in. Texans swagger, though, as if it's still the biggest."

"How far is it from Houston to Dallas?" asked Sullivan. "And who shot J.R.?"

She laughed. "Is that program still showing over here? It's so fake!

I've seen the set, and that swimming pool is tiny. The corral isn't real, either—no working corral would be that small or that clean."

"Davies, Sullivan, it's time I had a word with Jenny," Sinclair said. "Casey, stand by."

She watched them leave.

"Jenny, you need to have a wash."

"A bath?" Was that why he'd brought soap? And she'd thought that having scented soap was such a luxury.

"Yes, the sergeant and I will help you."

"Two against one isn't fair."

"One of us then. It's your choice."

"I don't like those choices," she said, trying to be brave. "Can I have two more choices?"

That made both men smile, and she noticed that Casey didn't look quite as fierce when he smiled. It didn't make any difference, though. She tried another tack. "Mañana!"

Sinclair gave her a questioning look.

"That's the Spanish word for tomorrow. But sometimes it can be used to mean a tomorrow you hope never comes."

"Jenny," Sinclair said softly, "you must let someone help you. You can't take a real bath or shower until your cast has been removed."

"It'll be like last night," Casey said, "with you in bed. Only more thorough." She was looking at him like he was the enemy. Damn. This assignment was turning into a hearts-and-minds op. "Jenny."

It was the first time Casey had used her name, so she paid attention.

"We'll do it in turn. There are some places I am not going to touch you."

Her heart pounded, and the dread stretched her muscles tight, making each injury throb with new intensity.

"I'll deal, sir," Casey said.

"I'll leave you to it then," Sinclair said and departed.

Sergeant Casey helped her into the bedroom. He brought a bowl of warm water, a bar of soap, a face cloth, and several bath sheets. He removed the sling from her left arm.

The preparations did nothing to ease her anxiety. "Will Danny and Brian come in?"

"No, they've been briefed."

Was that good or bad? They wouldn't watch, but what if she needed them? "I wish my mother were here."

"I don't want to do this any more than you do," he said. "Can we agree to make the best of it?"

Her look of despair told him she wouldn't. He proceeded by degrees, uncovering only one part of her body at a time. She must have worn a bikini in Texas—the strap lines were evident on her tan skin. There were still marks of the attack everywhere as well, and he kept his movements economical, working as quickly as he could. From time to time he brushed the face cloth across her cheeks to clear the tears away.

He cleansed both feet and legs, being particularly careful with the angry contusions on her left leg. She was the shapeliest patient he'd treated; most had been soldiers with legs as hairy as his own, not with this small waist and soft skin. And those same soldiers would think he was playing without a full pack if they saw him now—alone in a bedroom with a half naked woman and not pushing the envelope, not even a little bit. "No totally unnecessary breast examination? I'm disappointed in you, Doc!" But he was on duty, and besides, he didn't get off on battered women. After he rinsed the face cloth in the bathroom, he handed it to her. "Your turn now. I'll close your door and give you about ten minutes."

She did her best to clean her front. Even with no one present, it was mortifying, but at least the worst part was over. She pulled the sheet over herself and waited.

"I'll take your dirty clothes away."

She didn't move.

"Where are they?"

"I'm wearing them," she said, clutching the sheet tighter.

"You're still wearing your knickers? Did you wash?"

"Above the waist," she whispered. "I didn't take my panties off. I didn't want to be naked."

He thought for a moment. "What would you like to sleep in?"

"The nightshirt," she answered, but she couldn't get it on. The cast on her left arm wouldn't fit through the sleeve.

While she struggled with it, he bent down. When he straightened, he had a vicious-looking knife in his hand.

"What are you going to do with that?" she gasped.

"Help you dress," he said and sliced through the shoulder seam of the nightshirt. He replaced the knife in its calf holster and helped her adjust the nightshirt. "You're not naked now. It's time to finish the job. One of us has bloody well got to do it. Who's it going to be, Jenny?"

She decided she didn't like it when he said her name. It was his way of telling her that he meant business.

"I'm back in ten," he said. He handed her the face cloth and left.

She cried as she wriggled out of her panties. She had heard the *or else* he hadn't said aloud. She thought of him waiting outside her door, knowing what she was doing, and her whole body shook. What if he didn't believe she'd done it? What then? She was still trembling when he came back in.

He put the bath items and clothes away. He replaced the sling and adjusted her pillows. His mobile rang. He stepped outside her room and spoke to the chief inspector. "She didn't do well, sir."

"I'm on my way," Sinclair answered. When Davies and Sullivan let him in, he went straight to her room.

"I'm surprised he checks on her so much," Sullivan said.

"Don't be fooled," Davies warned. "He's checking on more than Jenny."

Casey stood when Sinclair knocked and entered her room.

"Thank you, Sergeant." Sinclair saw her red eyes and sat down on the edge of the bed. "What happened to your nightshirt?" Her left shoulder was bare.

He didn't sound mad—just curious—but she was afraid that if she mentioned the knife, he and Casey would both be angry. "Sergeant Casey fixed it so I could get it over my cast."

"Did he hurt you?"

"He—everything he does is frightening, but he didn't hurt me. The—the monster—hurt me, and I'm afraid I'll never be the person I was."

She was right. Experiencing violence—particularly rape—changed a person, but he didn't intend to tell her that. "I admit I don't know what you were like before all this happened, but I'm rather impressed with what I see now. Under your tears are determination and courage."

"There's no courage," she said. "It's all fear."

"I disagree. Fear may be what you're feeling, but courage is what you're doing. You're here because you're planning to do a very courageous thing. From the time I met you in hospital, you've done one courageous thing after another. You trusted me, you identified Scott, and you agreed to testify. You sit and walk in spite of the pain. When these tears have washed the dust off your wheels, you're really going to get moving. None of us will be able to keep up with you."

In spite of herself she had to smile.

"I'll tell you something else I've learnt about you. You have very high expectations of yourself. That's good, but there are times in life when you have to accept the help of others. It's not weakness to do that; it's a matter of perspective, of knowing when that extra boost will give you the edge you need." He wanted very badly to retain her cooperation. He recalled a tactic a previous chief had used when he wanted to keep a witness sweet. "Would you do something for me? I'd like you to consider calling me Colin."

"C-O-L-L-I-N?" she spelled.

"One L," he corrected, "but it's pronounced as if there were two."

"I haven't known what to call you," she admitted.

"Detective Chief Inspector is a mouthful, isn't it? Hearing 'Mr. Sinclair' makes me feel ancient. And there are plenty of sergeants and constables to call me sir. Will you give it a go?"

She looked at him and wondered if she could. His face wasn't lined. Was it his air of authority that made him seem older, or his immaculate, tailored style of dress? She came from the land of denim—jeans, jackets, skirts—she even had a denim dress at home.

"Everything's so impersonal," she said slowly. "I wear a lot of labels—a patient, a witness—a pain in the neck, I think—I don't feel like I belong to myself any more."

He smiled. A sense of humour in the wake of despair was a good sign. "Perhaps our being on a first-name basis will help."

CHAPTER 6

The incident room was crowded. Investigative teams on the cases of the six murdered women were present, the detectives in charge as well as the scores of officers tasked with detailing the criminal histories and recent movements of Leonard Stark and Anthony Michalopolous, more familiarly called the S&M duo. The news was not good. Both had kept low profiles since entering the UK. Stark had not been in the country when the first two murders were committed. CCTV footage from cameras near Jenny's kidnap site had yielded nothing of use. Without her ident, there were not sufficient grounds for arrest. Sinclair planned to show her the photo arrays that evening. Further, it was unlikely that either would be remanded unless they could prove they had a larger role in Jenny's assault or could be linked to the deaths of any of the other women.

"Cursed with a paucity of evidence," Graves grumbled.

"Nothing from Scott?" an officer inquired.

"No, the family solicitor was summoned immediately and has been present at every interview."

"How were the bodies disposed of?" a second officer asked.

"Not in Scott's car," a forensic tech replied. "It was clean. Neither Stark nor Michalopolous own vehicles."

"In some sections of our fair city, they could have used public transport and no one would have noticed," another officer lamented.

Sinclair stood. "The ambassador and his wife are on their way back to London. Scott himself has travelled extensively. Not just to Europe and the sites of his father's postings but also frequently to the States. We believe that's where he met Stark. Both may have considerable contacts there."

Graves gave him a sharp look. "That doesn't bode well for our witness."

Sinclair agreed. Jenny's Texas home was half a world away from the site of her attack but an easy destination for anyone accustomed to international travel.

"How are you getting on with her parents?" Graves asked.

"Every conversation is difficult."

"Still awaiting passports?" He saw Sinclair's nod. "Good. That gives us time to take permanent charge of her protection."

"She's expecting to return home with her family when she's well enough."

"Return to the States, where every weapon known to man is readily available? For her own safety, we can't allow it. Not until this thing is concluded. Have a word with her parents. Arrange for someone from the witness protection unit to meet with her. Let's get it done."

CHAPTER 7

While Sinclair was receiving Graves' instruction, Jenny was beginning her first set of exercises with Sergeant Casey. He wanted her to be on her feet more to improve strength and circulation, particularly in her left leg, where the contusions had been the most severe. First he asked her to stand up straight, putting her weight on both legs equally.

"I'll fall," she objected.

"You'll not fall. Your leg will hurt, but it will support you." He nodded to Davies to stand next to her. "Tense the muscles in your left leg and then relax them." To be sure she was following his instructions, he knelt down beside her and slid his hands under the caftan, resting one on her calf and one on her thigh.

She gasped and pulled away.

Casey looked up. "Sorry," he said. "Let's try it again."

She watched him place his hands on top of the fabric. She held onto Brian, squeezing his arm reflexively each time she felt the pain from tensing her leg.

"Now put a bit more weight on your left leg."

She responded.

"That's it," Casey said. "Can you tell now that it isn't going to give way?"

"No, the only thing I'm sure of is that Brian isn't going to give way."

Casey smiled. He directed her through the routine over and over, monitoring her leg but not noticing how pale her face was becoming.

"Time out," she panted. Her legs went rubbery, and she sagged against Brian, who lowered her to the sofa. "How'd you become the world expert on legs anyway?" she asked Casey.

He didn't answer, just sat down and pushed his camouflage fatigues above his right knee. When she was able to tear her eyes away from the knife strapped to his calf, she saw a wide scar that ran from the middle of his thigh to the kneecap. She felt a sudden kinship with him. "You're scarred, too! And you run in the mornings? How do you do that?"

"The same way you will, when I get through with you."

"Is that a promise or a threat?"

"Bit of both. Now I'll do the work for you. Gather your dress above your knees."

She hesitated. He was not going to tolerate insubordination, but her legs looked like they'd been trampled by a bull.

Casey saw the direction of her gaze. Jog pants would help her; he'd ask the boss. He held first one foot, then the other, and asked her to push against his hand gently, then more firmly. It was easier at the beginning than supporting her own weight, but as he increased his pressure, she had to clench her teeth against the pain.

"Whoa!" she cried.

"That'll do then," he said. "Now for the ankle exercises." After a few minutes he sat beside her on the sofa. "Now the shoulder." The cast was heavy, but she had done shoulder exercises with the physical therapist in the hospital, and they weren't as uncomfortable as the leg exercises had been.

"You have to keep your joints moving," Casey explained, "or they'll stiffen."

"Good cover story." She leaned her head back on the sofa. "Actually, it's the Genghis Khan approach to fitness—exercise until it hurts."

When Sinclair's long day at the Yard concluded, he stopped by the protection flat.

"Jenny's fast off," Davies told him. "Casey's exercises wore her out."

"I'll wake her." He knocked lightly on her door.

She stirred and opened her eyes.

"Are you up to a bit of police business?" He handed her the collections of photos which included Stark and Michalopolous's. "Do you recognise anyone?"

"This one," she said. "The others on this page don't look as menacing."

She had identified Michalopolous. It took her longer to isolate Stark. "The other man—his eyes were the only small thing about him."

Sinclair felt a rush of relief. The arrest of these two and subsequent search of their flats could strengthen their case. He sat down. "I spoke with your mother this afternoon. They're expecting their passports any day now."

"She called me. Sergeant Casey brought me the phone, but when I was through, he took it away. 'I'll have it back now,' was how he put it. Why can't I keep it?"

"I want an officer screening any incoming calls on your line."

"Can't I call my friends?"

"I'd prefer it if you corresponded with your friends. There are a few rules I'd like you to follow when you do—don't mention the men's names, and don't seal the envelopes."

"You're going to read my mail? Isn't that a crime?"

Sinclair aimed for a light tone. "Jenny, if we allowed you to reveal details, it would rather defeat the purpose, wouldn't it?"

"That's not fair! What gives you the right to know everything about me? Even the thoughts I express to friends?"

"Jenny, I am responsible for your life. I don't intend to take any chances with it." He discarded the idea of telling her now they wanted to keep her until after Scott's trial. He collected the photos and departed.

The men were quiet during dinner. They were concentrating on their food, and she became curious about their use of utensils. They held the fork in their left hand and the knife in their right. The fork was always upside down. Sometimes they used the knife to mash the food onto the fork. "Do you all eat like that?" she asked. She had switched her fork to her right hand and was using it to scoop up the potatoes.

"We like to get on with it," Brian answered.

"Changing hands all the time like you do would slow us down," Danny added.

She looked at her plate. They did eat faster. Brian cleared the table, Danny began to wash up, and Casey helped her to the bedroom.

He removed the sutures from her chest tube. "The surgeon did nice work."

"He left me another scar."

"He left you breathing." Then he began her bath, using the same format as the night before.

It was still frightening, but this time she didn't have to be told twice when it was her turn to do the washing. She cried when she saw him return.

Rita had cried when he left on missions. Jenny was the first woman he'd known who cried when she saw him coming. When she was settled and he'd put the bath items away, he sat down next to the bed. "How can you tell if someone's a threat, Jenny?"

His voice was as sharp as his knife.

"Watch the hands, always the hands. Tell me what you've seen my hands do, in hospital and here."

She thought back. "You undid my hospital gown, right after I met you."

"No, Dr. Adams did that. I covered you."

"You gave me a shot I didn't want."

He nodded. "It was necessary."

She remembered the first morning she'd wakened in this bed. It already seemed a long time ago. "You helped me sit up. You gave me my medicine. You held my waist so I could walk." Her voice shook a little at the memory. "You washed me. You cut my nightshirt. You wiped my tears." She stopped. Unshed tears were now constricting her throat.

"That'll do," he said. "Now repeat after me: A man proves himself through his actions."

She managed to force the words out.

He administered her bedtime medicine, removed the extra pillows from behind her so she could lie down, and adjusted the pillows she still needed under her left limbs.

She watched his hands.

CHAPTER 8

Every morning's activities were the same: medicine, breakfast, and exercises. Breathing hard still made her ribs hurt, but by Friday Jenny was beginning to feel more confident about her ability to stay on her feet. Her left leg did support her, as Sergeant Casey had said it would.

Saturday brought monotony, magnified by Danny's absence. He had been given a little time off. After lunch Brian found some sport on TV, but she stayed in her room to write letters. Laura, Alison, Mandy, Diane—Emily first. *Something bad happened to me in London, and I can't come home for a while.* She stopped. The things that weighed most heavily on her mind, she didn't want to write down. What could she say? That her physical therapist was an ex-Marine? No, she wasn't supposed to write about the men.

She could describe British TV. It would be a long letter if she related everything that they were allowed to broadcast—obscene language, sexual references, nudity—or a short letter if she mentioned the weather, which she didn't experience since she couldn't go out and didn't understand because the temperatures weren't given in Fahrenheit.

In the end, she wrote only a few lines. She was too tired to focus.

It was the distinctive aroma of Chinese spices that greeted her when she woke. Danny had returned with what he called takeaway food: appetizers—what the men called starters—chicken, beef, and pork entrees, and both steamed and fried rice. Their biggest consumer, Brian, had been given a day off. The meal was accompanied by English tea, of which she was becoming increasingly fond. Her fortune was enigmatic: *Interesting adventures await you,* it read. "If you define 'adventures' loosely, that might even be true," she said.

After dinner Sinclair and Sergeant Andrews stopped by. "Good news. We've arrested Scott's accomplices," Andrews said. He and Mr. Sinclair took another statement from her. "I'll make it as easy for you as I can," Sinclair said. "I'd simply like you to confirm exactly what events took place when you were in the little room. Every vile act Scott committed needs to be on record." He saw her bite her lip. "Jenny, I'll not ask you to describe anything, and I'll use yes-or-no questions."

Sergeant Andrews started the tape recorder. She had no trouble at first, but her dread grew as the interview progressed. She couldn't look at them during the final questions, and Mr. Sinclair had to ask her to speak louder so her monosyllabic replies would be recorded. Finally he thanked her, and she heard Sergeant Andrews conclude and stop the machine.

"As you know, Scott murdered other women," Sinclair said. "The detectives in charge of those cases have been working under horrific pressure for a long time. Finding you alive was a breakthrough, and we all want the case against Scott to be airtight. It's a very good day when we get someone like Scott off the streets. Without your help, we couldn't have done."

"How many were there? Other women, I mean."

"Six. We believe he killed six."

She was quiet, wondering why she had lived.

"Jenny, this inquiry has affected all of us. During your hospital stay, I was frequently asked to give updates on your condition." Concern had been expressed at every briefing in the incident room. The release of her statement—containing the facts of her abuse—had increased it.

"What did you tell them?"

That she was fearful, fragile, and easily upset. That it had been difficult to establish sufficient trust for the interviews to proceed. That her physical recovery was painful and slow. "That you're a lovely young woman who will make a very sympathetic witness," he said aloud. "That you have amazing resilience."

"Then why do I feel like a paratrooper whose chute didn't open?"

"Because you experienced evil. Evil is powerful and destructive, but you aren't facing it alone now. You have a very dedicated and powerful police service standing with you."

In the silence that followed, Sergeant Andrews thanked her and left, but Mr. Sinclair stayed, giving her a parcel with a Texas postmark. It contained family photos, a book by Anne Perry, one of her favorite mystery writers, and a letter from her parents. "I understand it's difficult for you to speak about traumatic things." He handed her a nicely bound journal. "It might be easier to write about them."

"Will it be subpoenaed?"

"It's for your eyes only," he assured her. "No one else need ever see it."

She gave him her letters to mail, wishing she'd had the nerve to seal the envelopes.

After he left, she sat quietly by herself in the living room. His questions had unsettled her. She wanted to forget the attack, not remember or record it. Hundreds of times each day something reminded her—pain when she breathed and moved, waking in her unfamiliar room. Even the faces of her protectors made her conscious of her need to be protected. She had not become accustomed to any of it. Write in the journal every day? It would be the diary from hell.

She was still upset when Casey helped her into the bedroom for her bath. She watched him and thought about the oceans of experience that separated them. "Why are you here? Instead of charging into barricaded buildings or something."

"My skills were needed," he answered in his concise way.

"Wouldn't you rather be out catching bad guys?"

He smiled. "There'll be some left for me."

Even after taking her medicine, she couldn't relax. Her mystery book was on the nightstand, but she didn't have the concentration to read it the way she usually did, trying to retain all the details that would figure in the denouement. The journal was there, too, and its pages were still blank. And Mr. Sinclair's Bible. She was 0-for-3. She remembered her daddy pitching to her; she had swung at every ball with all her might. He'd had to say, "You've struck out, Punkin. Let's try again." The lines from the baseball poem came to mind: "Mighty Casey has struck out." No one would ever say that about the sergeant.

CHAPTER 9

Sinclair left the protection flat and returned to the Yard with two jobs still to do. First he scanned Jenny's letters. What he read disturbed him, not because she had broken the rules—she hadn't—but because her notes bore a greater resemblance to newspaper reporting than personal correspondence. Each was a dry recitation of mundane facts followed by a request for news.

She wasn't as cold as these lines suggested. He had seen instances of warmth and humour, and in communicating with friends he would have expected these characteristics to be even more apparent. At the bottom of each letter, she had written, *My address is…* followed by a blank space and a direct request: *Mr. Sinclair, would you please fill this in?* He sighed. She was still cross with him. He provided the NSY address and readied the letters for the post. It wasn't her pique that concerned him as much as her use of "Mr. Sinclair." He had been unsuccessful in getting her to trust him. They could very well lose her when she was healed enough to go.

Next, a difficult phone call was in order—to her parents. He should have rung them already on the issue of visitation, and Graves had been puzzled by his dilatory behaviour. "Get it sorted, else they'll be here," he'd said, and he was right. They could have their passports soon.

He dialled the Houston number, wondering how you persuade a victim's family that their loved one will be safe in the city where she was attacked. "Mr. and Mrs. Jeffries, I want you to know that Jenny's progress is good. She has begun her physiotherapy exercises, and she's already stronger."

"Yes, she told us," Mrs. Jeffries responded, "that her trainer—or whatever you call him—was tough but capable. She's in a hurry to get back on her feet."

"She's adjusting well, but I need to discuss with you both what comes next."

"We'll be taking her home with us," Mrs. Jeffries said.

"I'd like you to reconsider those plans. Any attempt to see her at this time could jeopardise her safety. As loving parents, I'm certain you don't want that."

"Chief Inspector, what are you saying?" Mr. Jeffries said sharply.

"Sir, we have sound reasons for everything we have done in Jenny's case."

"Spit it out!"

"The man Jenny identified is an ambassador's son. He is ruthless and resourceful. She is willing to testify against him, and we are committed to protecting her so that she can."

"Does that mean she's still in danger?" Mrs. Jeffries asked in alarm.

"I haven't liked to frighten her. She is secure at the moment, and she is mending."

"You want us to stay away? We won't! Our daughter needs us, and we intend to be with her as soon as we can."

"Sir, we have an entire unit of police dedicated to the care and protection of witnesses. We will spare no expense in Jenny's case. I respectfully request that you not make travel plans without consulting me first."

"You can't expect us to leave her in the company of strangers after what she's been through," Mrs. Jeffries cried. "She has no one to support her."

"Mrs. Jeffries, your communication with her will not be restricted in any way. If you visit, however, attention will be drawn to the site. Inspector Rawson from our Witness Protection Unit will be contacting you. He will want to involve you in her relocation."

"Relocation? For how long?" Mr. Jeffries asked.

"Her case is a priority, sir. We have quite a large organisation assigned to the investigation, and we will press for the most expeditious prosecution possible. I can tell you that relocation will occur when Jenny's injuries have healed and she no longer requires medical oversight. Let me also assure you that nothing will be done without her consent."

"I don't know how we'll tell her," Mrs. Jeffries said.

"Allow me to handle that," Sinclair said quickly.

They were packed and ready to depart the minute their passports arrived, but Bill Jeffries didn't intend to tell the chief inspector. He didn't want any alteration in his daughter's care. "You have a charge to keep, Chief Inspector."

"Sir, I'm aware of that," Sinclair assured him. "I'll speak with you again soon. Goodnight."

He put the phone down, wondering why he didn't feel relieved. Jenny's parents had given him the answer he had wanted.

CHAPTER 10

At the protection flat, Brian was still gone, so Danny took charge of Sunday lunch. "The sandwich," he declared, "is a British tradition. Today: egg salad sandwiches!"

It was the strangest egg salad she had eaten. At home her mother had boiled the eggs, chopped them, and then mixed them with mayonnaise, a little mustard, salt, and vinegar. Danny's egg salad sandwiches consisted of slices of cooked egg, cucumber, tomato, and seasoning. Different, but tasty.

The chief inspector came by in the afternoon, interrupting Sullivan's explanation of English football rules. She asked Mr. Sinclair what sport he had played.

"I rowed. Eight-man shells."

"Casey's sport was target practice," Danny teased.

"Actually, I participated in water sport," the sergeant replied. "Swimming. Boating."

"I need a word with you," Sinclair told her. "Let's go in the sitting room."

When she turned to ask Sergeant Casey for help, he had disappeared. Danny had, too, so she leaned on Mr. Sinclair as she limped from one room to the other.

"I've spoken with your parents," he began. "They are willing to entrust you to our care."

"What does that mean?"

"They have agreed to postpone their visit."

"Postpone? For how long?" Had the sofa shifted? She felt queasy all of a sudden.

"For the immediate future."

It was a blow, almost as physical as when the monster had hit her in the stomach. "They're going to leave me here? Why would they do that?"

"Because they love you and care about your safety."

"What aren't you telling me?" she asked.

"Jenny, the man who attacked you is still dangerous to you. He has means. That's why we've taken the measures we have."

"If they 'agreed,' then you asked them not to come, is that right?"

"Jenny, if they visit you here, you will no longer be secure."

She remembered waking in the hospital, seeing his eyes, and thinking that he wouldn't hurt her. How wrong she had been. "I need Sergeant Casey."

Sinclair stood and summoned him.

"I want to lie down," she told the sergeant.

They woke her for dinner, Casey and Danny. It was leftover Chinese, but she spent most of the time just pushing the food around her plate.

"Would you like to ring your family?" Casey asked at bath time. Sinclair had briefed him—he knew they would not be coming soon.

She shook her head. "They've abandoned me."

"Will this help?" He held out his hand. "I know you're missing them."

"Don't you have a pill for that?"

"This is it."

"Then I'd better take it," she said.

CHAPTER 11

Jenny's second week at the flat brought change. Monday morning she was able to take her first solo steps. Monday afternoon men arrived to fit the flat with an alarm system. Casey moved her to his room while they worked. "Keep the door shut. Don't come out."

"Isn't it safe?"

"This security firm employs retired coppers, but I'd rather they not see you. They'll place sensors on the lower stairs, the windows in your room and the sitting room, and on the front door. That takes quite a bit of wiring, so they'll be here several hours, at least. It will all connect to the alarm unit on the wall between my room and the lads' room."

"I'll sit in your chair and read." In spite of her interest in her book, the time seemed to pass slowly. She didn't have a watch, and there was no clock in the sergeant's room, so she had no way of knowing if the work were nearing completion or not. When she became drowsy, she limped over to Casey's bed.

When the work ended and the security men had left, Casey, Sullivan, and Davies found her asleep. "I'll bet all the girls in Casey's bed fall asleep," Sullivan teased in a whisper.

"No, I usually find a way to keep them awake," Casey answered.

- -

When Sinclair came by after dinner with a job for her, she didn't want to see him. He was the ringleader in what she privately considered a conspiracy of cruelty. Why did she have to cooperate all the time? Something was rotten in the state of Denmark when someone like Sergeant Casey treated her better than her own family. She sat on her bed and opened her journal. She'd begun to use it to make lists. First she just recorded the things she'd seen Sergeant Casey do with his hands. Then she added general things that she hadn't seen him do, but knew that he had, like loading his gun. She entered a new heading: *Things I Know To Be True.* There weren't many items, and most weren't positive. Thinking of Mr. Sinclair waiting for her in the other room, she wrote, *People betray you.*

Sergeant Casey came to escort her to the dining room. “The boss is waiting for you, Jenny,” he said. “Front and centre.” With his arm around her waist, she had no choice but to go.

Sinclair took twelve colour photos out of the large brown envelope he carried and spread them on the table. All were pictures of women’s jewellery. “Have you ever seen any of these?”

She turned one photo face down. “That was mine. I don’t ever want to see it again.”

“You don’t want it returned to you when the case is over?”

“No. Give it to charity. Throw it away. I don’t care.” Then she set aside three more pictures: an oval watch with a silver band, a charm bracelet, and another necklace, a gold chain with a rose pendant. “I saw these in the little room. The others I don’t recognize. Did you find my ring? Or my watch?”

“Not yet, no.”

“Do you need anything else?”

“Not from you. These pictures will now be shown to the families of the other women.”

“Oh, those poor people,” she said. “Do they know about me? That I lived? That must make them feel awful.”

“No, they’re glad. They don’t want another family to experience their grief, and they know justice is possible for their loved ones now.”

As soon as he left, she regretted her lack of courtesy. His departure meant she could not postpone the dreaded bath. Cleanliness was overrated. “It’s as if the bath were the last straw. It’s not you,” she told the sergeant. “It’s Monday, and it’s been three weeks, and it’s thinking about the other women.”

“That’s not all,” he said. “It’s the trouble you’re having with your family.” Her mobile rang, three short rings, startling them both. He removed it from his pocket.

“Don’t answer,” she said.

“That won’t wash. Best all round to face things.” He pushed the talk button. “Sergeant Casey speaking. Yes, Mrs. Jeffries, she’s here. Talk to your mother, Jenny.” He handed her the phone and left the room.

At first he couldn’t hear her at all. Perhaps her mum was doing all the talking. Then he heard her begin to cry. It was a small flat, and before long the other men were drawn in. “What’s happening?” Sullivan asked.

“She’s on the phone with her mum,” Casey answered.

“It’s not going well,” Davies observed. And it wasn’t—Jenny’s distress was growing, not lessening.

“I can’t be brave anymore! I need you! How could you agree to leave me here? I was in the hospital, and I needed you! I’m still hurting, and I need you!”

Sullivan couldn’t listen to her tormented cries. He went to his room and closed the door. The older men stayed, knowing that when the call ended, someone would have to pick up the pieces.

"Mother, I can hardly walk! I'm all cut up, and I need you!"

Casey began to wonder if he'd done the right thing. He went to his room and retrieved his kit.

"Mother, he cut my face! And my body! I'm disfigured," she sobbed. "There are scars everywhere!"

Disfigured—Davies hadn't known she felt that way. She looked fine to him. He stood and began to pace back and forth between the sitting room and the dining room, his heavy tread the bass accompaniment to Jenny's shrill treble.

"I need you," she wept. "I need you. Now."

She couldn't sustain this much longer, Casey knew; either pain or exhaustion—or both—would end it.

"It's hard being here. My whole life has been taken away."

There were some spaces now between her phrases. "I'm sorry," they heard her say. Casey felt a stab of anger: What did she have to be sorry for?

"I don't know if I can do that, Mother." There was a pause. "But I'm not the same! I'm afraid all the time." Another pause, longer. "I love you, too, Mother."

Casey nodded at Davies to let him know he'd go in. He set his kit on the bedside table and sat down on the bed. "Can I help?"

"She said I have to trust Chief Inspector Sinclair. She said I don't have any choice."

"He knows what to do," Casey agreed. "He's an experienced officer."

"He has an agenda."

"So do you."

"My agenda right now is to sleep for a long time. Can you help me do that?"

"Do you want a jab or a tab?"

"No shots."

Casey opened his kit and called for Davies to bring a glass of milk. Then he waited with her for the medication to take effect.

Later that evening, he was reminded of her. When he went to bed, he could detect a hint of her perfume on his pillow, a light sweetness, but he knew her spirit wasn't light. Her physical condition was improving, but not her emotional state.

He dropped to the floor. Pressups first, then situps, one set for Scott and one for his low-life associates. One set for her family for deserting her, however briefly. One set for Sinclair, who had engineered it.

He was still angry. More reps would be required tonight for the pressure in his skull to ease. If looking after the Yank affected him this way every day, he would be in good shape when the assignment ended. Very good shape indeed.

CHAPTER 12

"I'm from the Met's Witness Protection Unit," Inspector Rawson began. "Chief Inspector Sinclair tells me you're doing well, and that you'll be healed sufficiently for a new placement in a few weeks."

It was late Tuesday afternoon, and Sinclair had brought Rawson to meet with Jenny at the flat. He was Sinclair's height, but his slim frame made him look taller. There was more gray in his hair than the lines on his face would account for.

"We'd like to relocate you," Rawson continued, "somewhere so safe that no one will be able to find you. You won't have to be guarded round the clock. You can go shopping, eat in restaurants, whatever you choose. You can have a normal lifestyle."

He was so soft spoken that she had to strain to hear him. Were all his conversations so secret that he had lost the habit of speaking out loud? Did he yell at sporting events? She resisted the urge to whisper herself. "Why are we talking about this? My parents aren't coming to me, so I'm going to them—when I'm better."

"Jenny, the man who hurt you is guilty of a massively serious offence. We want to continue to protect you. Inspector Rawson's recommendations are the result of our assessment of your risk."

"We have several locations in mind, places where a young American like you won't stand out."

"I won't stand out in Texas."

"We'll find you a flat, even provide you with an allowance until you have a job."

"In Texas?"

"No, Miss Jeffries. I'm afraid that's not part of the equation."

"Are you offering to protect me until my testimony is over?"

Rawson's voice oozed on. "In a manner of speaking, yes. I'm offering you a new life. We'll bring you back to London for your court appearances, of course. Afterward, you'll return to your new life. I am familiar with the facts in your case. I am recommending a permanent relocation."

"Permanent?"

"You'll have a new name, a new personal history. Jennifer Jeffries will be untraceable; she will no longer exist."

She shivered. He was talking about her in the third person.

"But the monster is in jail," she said, turning to Sinclair. "When I'm well enough to travel, why can't I go home? I'm not under arrest, am I?"

"Jenny, when you were attacked in hospital, Scott didn't come himself. He sent someone else. If these measures seem extreme, it's because we are taking your safety very seriously."

"Miss Jeffries," Rawson added, "I assure you, we are the best in the world at what we do. We can guarantee your safety. All we need is your cooperation."

First Mr. Sinclair convinced her parents not to come. Now Inspector Rawson wanted her to go. They had reasonable expressions on their faces, and she wanted to scream.

"We are offering you sanctuary," Rawson said softly. "We'll need two weeks, possibly more, to make the arrangements. And then you will disappear." He saw the colour leave her face. Most of the witnesses he placed were criminals who had agreed to testify against other criminals. They were eager for a new identity and change of scene. "It's a shock, I know," he said gently, "hearing this for the first time. Take a day or two to get used to the idea, and we'll talk again."

She did not speak. She watched the two men rise, managed to nod at Mr. Sinclair's good-bye, and heard him call for Casey and Davies to lock up.

She limped haltingly into her room. She couldn't think of a logical way to evaluate Rawson's proposal. He was offering her a safe future. Why did she feel like he was hammering nails into her coffin? Disappear: What a concept. A new name, Rawson had said. He can do what the monster couldn't, she thought: Erase her.

"Dinner's ready." Sergeant Casey was at the door.

"My name is Jennifer Jeffries. Jennifer Catherine Jeffries."

He frowned, not sure how to respond.

"I'm not hungry. You guys go ahead without me."

She went into the bathroom and looked in the mirror. No matter where she went, the scar on her face was going with her. The problem was, she didn't want the new life Rawson talked about. She wanted her old life—but that wasn't one of the choices. And they didn't want to keep her here.

She hobbled back into the bedroom and sat down in the big armchair next to the bed. She wanted out, out of everything. Out of her commitment to testify. Out of living with police. Out with cooperating. Out with letting other people make decisions for her. Out, out, out, echoed in her brain.

She pulled her suitcase from the closet and opened it. She had no purse, but she had her passport. The money she'd kept in her suitcase as backup was still there. Well, it should be: A policeman had unpacked it. She didn't have many clothes to pack. The slacks she chose rubbed against her tender bruises, but she'd have to tough it out. She willed her tears to stop—she didn't want to make any noise. She took several deep breaths—ouch—and added the toiletries from the bathroom. And her teddy bear—she couldn't leave him behind. She zipped up the suitcase. Heavy, but it had wheels. She'd have to pull it with her right hand; she still had the cast on her left arm, and she was limping on her left leg. She couldn't go fast, but she could go. All she had to do tonight was find a place to stay. After that—*que será, será.* Whatever happened, she was going to be in charge of her own life.

She should eat something first, though. She put her rolling bag back in the closet and closed the door. There was no one in the kitchen, but Brian came in to show her the meal they'd set aside for her. She thanked him, then ate slowly and silently. Brian was quiet, too, just offering to wash up for her when she finished.

She shuffled back to her room. Now was as good a time as any. She should start before she was too tired. She took her suitcase from the closet and peeked out her bedroom door. No one was in the living or dining room. Good. She headed slowly for the front door. She'd watched the men unlock it often enough to know that no key was required. She opened it, hopped into the hall, and closed the door quietly behind her. Stairs. There wasn't an elevator. Well, that didn't change anything; everything in life was accomplished one step at a time. She started down slowly, the suitcase thudding along beside her.

She heard a door open and a familiar voice say, "Cover me," but felt Casey's arms around her even before the sound of his feet had registered in her mind. She struggled, but she was locked in a vise, her arms pinned to her sides. Her ribs hurt, and she bit her lip but still couldn't keep from crying out. "Bloody hell!" he swore in her ear. "What's this about?" She looked up. Brian was at the top of the stairs, his pistol aimed high, Danny behind him. God, Brian looked gigantic! If he and Casey were both angry with her, she was done for.

"My name is Jennifer Jeffries," she insisted. "I was born in Houston, Texas, in 1975. I have a driver's license, and a social security number, and a passport, and they all say, 'Jennifer Jeffries.'"

The Vise had picked her up. When he reached the top of the stairs, Sullivan retrieved her suitcase. "Man the door," Casey told him when they were inside. "Davies, ring the boss." He sat her down on the sofa. "Do I have to cuff you?" he asked.

She raised her chin defiantly. "Yes," she said through her tears.

Damn! It had been a bluff. He didn't have any cuffs with him; none of them did. "Sullivan, your belt," he said.

"No, not the belt!" She struck out at him with her right arm, an impotent gesture, but one that caused the muscles around her rib cage to stretch and hurt.

He caught her wrist easily, as if she had merely extended it for him to restrain, wrapped the belt snugly around it, and then tied it to the one immobilised by her cast. "You little Yank fool," he said under his breath, "but I'm a bigger one for not keeping an eye on you."

Danny must have been listening for Mr. Sinclair, because she never heard the doorbell. He came in with no coat or tie, and his shirt was unbuttoned at the neck. "Jenny, what's this?" he began, stopping when he saw her hands bound on her chest and her tear-streaked face. "Casey?"

"I'd put her over my knee if I didn't think it would be counterproductive. Sir."

Sinclair drew a chair close to her and unwound the belt. "Jenny, talk to me."

"My name is Jennifer Catherine Jeffries, and I want out," she answered, her chin still high.

"I see that," he said. "Why?"

"I won't give up my name. I won't! It's all I have left—the monster took everything else." Her chin started to tremble. "I don't look the same. I don't feel the same. Only my name is the same." She whispered it. "I won't give it up." Her voice was trembling now. She clenched her teeth, hoping that would restore her firm tone.

Sullivan stood by the door, dumbfounded. Casey's face was hard, and Davies' was taut with tension. She started to get up, but Sinclair restrained her. "Let me go," she cried, frustrated because the tears were coming again. She did not want them to soften her resolve. "You said I couldn't stay here. I have to take care of myself. There's nothing else left."

"Jenny," Sinclair said calmly, "you don't have to run away from me. We'll sort this out together."

"We can't. I have to get away. You're not on my side."

"I want to work with you, Jenny. We all do. Don't you know you're not alone?"

Mr. Sinclair's voice was soft. It fed the lump in her throat, and she began to sob.

"Jenny, you are very important to us. You must know that. Your testimony against Scott is critical. We are asking you to do something none of us has had to do—face the enemy—with the exception of Sergeant Casey, and he was trained and armed. I can't tell you that I know how you feel, because I don't. I can tell you that we will spare no resource, no expense, to ensure your safety. What sort of coppers would we be if we took any chances with you?"

He was being gentle with her. Davies didn't think he'd be gentle with them.

"I can't do what Inspector Rawson wants me to," she said, the tears streaming down her cheeks.

"I understand that much," Sinclair answered with a wry smile. He handed her his handkerchief. "Davies, Jenny could do with some tea."

Brian brought cups for both of them. She sipped the warm liquid, sweetened just the way she liked it. It soothed the tightness in her chest. She looked at Sinclair. There was no anger in his blue eyes.

"Jenny, I think the best decisions are informed decisions, don't you? That means information has to come first, so I'd like to tell you why we've taken the actions we have." He stretched out his legs as if he had all the time in the world. "The protection we provided you in hospital was truly a precaution. We felt that an attempt on your life was a possibility but not a likelihood. Placing you in this flat was an emergency response to a critical situation. The Witness Protection Unit was not involved. I am not trained in witness protection. I am a detective. I direct and participate in criminal investigations."

Casey recognised the facts-of-life speech.

"This flat is suitable on a temporary basis because it was available when we needed it and because it allows me to have access to you. Although your formal interviews were completed in hospital, I knew there would be follow-on questions from time to time.

"The officers in the Witness Protection Unit plan very carefully. They do not advertise their methods. They have placed witnesses in countries all over the world, people who have used their fresh start to put down new roots. Their success rate is second to none.

"The WPU would consider this flat unsuitable—unsafe—for several reasons. First, it is in London. That is simply too close to Scott and his area of influence. If he has further actions planned against you, and we believe he does, he will look in London first. Indeed, he is already looking. Hospital security at one location evicted a man they considered an intruder. He had no weapon, but he could not provide a reasonable explanation for his continued presence in the corridors. Other hospitals have reported an excessive number of telephone enquiries about young adult female patients." He noted her tense, pale face. "Would you like another cup of tea? I would."

"I think I'm going to need something stronger," she answered.

Sinclair smiled. This time Davies brought biscuits as well as tea. The other men had settled in the dining room, well within hearing but removed from the immediate circle. Sullivan was mesmerised by the calm, logical way this senior officer was handling the crisis.

"Shall I go on?" Sinclair asked. "If you're tired or in pain, I can continue at another time."

"I am, but I need to know these things."

"I agree. Let's see—ah, the reasons the WPU wouldn't like this location. It's in a quiet neighbourhood. That's why you have a small team. Regular shift changes involving more officers could be noticed, so Casey, Davies, and Sullivan have to be on duty all the time. That's asking more of our men than we like to do, even on a short assignment. Also, for your own safety, you are confined. That means you are limited to the medical care Sergeant Casey can give, unless an emergency arises. Psychotherapy is recommended for all victims of violent crime, but that cannot be provided for you here. None of this is beneficial to you on a long-term basis.

"If you were living in another city—perhaps in another country—you would have freedom of movement. A policeman, called a handler, would be assigned to you. He or she would be responsible for dealing with any problems you might encounter as well as being the intermediary when your presence was required in court. You would then be returned to London and housed in a hotel, with several teams of policemen to protect you, monitor hotel entrances and exits, plan and execute safe transportation to and from the courthouse, and so forth. But I digress." He finished his tea. "Do you have any questions?"

"What is going to happen to me?"

"We're not going to decide that tonight," he answered. "In the meantime, I have some questions, if you're up to them." He leant forward in his chair. "What were you planning to do after you left the flat?"

"Find a place to stay for the night," she said. "Think about the next step in the morning."

"Would you turn left or right when you exited the building?"

She was silent.

"How far is it from here to a hotel?"

She shrugged.

"Assuming you found one, how would you pay for your room?"

"I have some cash in my suitcase."

"Were you going to register in your own name?"

"I guess so, because my passport is my only identification."

"And when you needed more money?"

"I'd call my parents collect and ask them to wire me some."

"That would leave a lovely paper trail for someone to follow. Were you planning to return to Texas?"

"No, not at first."

"Jenny, we have never found your handbag. We must assume that Scott had it, at least for a time, and that he knows your name, your family's address, and other pertinent information about you. It would not be difficult for him to have you tracked down, even in the States."

"Oh, God," she said, her shoulders slumping.

"Jenny, if no one is protecting you, you'll be a soft target wherever you are."

Hearing his words hurt.

"The man who attacked you in hospital did not use a firearm. In another venue, however, a firearm could be the weapon of choice. If so, it's unlikely that it would be a sniper's weapon. To ensure success, an assassin would probably prefer a spray of bullets. Others could be caught in the line of fire."

Her chin drooped.

"Fortunately, the alarm alerted Casey and the others that security had been breached." He paused. "I have another question. After hearing your description of Scott's attack, do you know what single impression stayed with me?"

She did not answer.

"His rage. He may be mentally unbalanced; I don't know. I do know that a very high level of protection is necessary for you. Jenny, I see what people go through, what violent crime does to them. It's one of the reasons I am so committed to what I do. 'The evil that men do lives after them…'"

"'The good is oft interred with their bones,'" she said, finishing the quotation. "Will the good I want to do die with me?"

"If you leave this flat unescorted, yes, because Scott's men will find you. And I don't think you could survive another assault. Refusing to testify is another course available to you. I hope you won't make that choice. 'All that is necessary for evil to succeed is that good men'—or women—'do nothing.' I believe that to be true."

"Me, too."

"Are you willing, then, to work with me to put that bastard away? In your heart you know he is guilty of serial murder."

She nodded.

"Will you agree to stay here for the time being? We won't plan to move you without your foreknowledge and consent, as well as Sergeant Casey's judgement that medical oversight is no longer needed."

"What about Inspector Rawson?"

Sinclair gave a sharp laugh. "I'll keep him away from you," he promised. "And I'll give a fair hearing to anything you want to do, as long as you'll allow me to present the safety considerations I think are important. Have we accomplished enough for now?"

"Yes," she said, relief flooding her face.

"Casey," Sinclair said, "it's Jenny's bedtime. Can you give her something to ensure a good night's sleep? Jenny, I don't want you worrying about anything tonight. We have several weeks to find a solution that is agreeable to both of us."

Sinclair watched them go. Jenny's gait was sluggish. He sighed, then stood slowly, his face sombre. "Stand by," he told Davies and Sullivan.

The younger men rose to their feet as well. They were apprehensive, Sullivan fidgeting slightly and Davies examining his boots. They heard a cry of refusal from her followed by Casey's even tone. Another negative, less emphatic, then an outburst: "Give it to Mr. Sinclair!" Finally Casey returned to the sitting room.

"She wouldn't accept the stronger sedative, sir," he reported. "I didn't think it wise to force her."

There was a tense silence, then Sinclair levelled his gaze at them. "It has not escaped my attention," he said grimly, "that if the alarm system hadn't been fitted yesterday, she might have got away. Then, possibly within a few days, I'd have to identify her body. I'd like to hear what additional security measures you plan to take."

"Sir," Casey answered, "I'd like to add a key lock on the inside of the door, as well as a camera on the stairs and at the front and back doors of the block."

"Her exit from the flat was hardly stealthy," Sinclair said between his teeth. "Anything else?"

"Yes, sir. From now on, the man on watch will monitor her whereabouts. We'll keep her door open, and the public rooms of the flat won't be unattended again."

"She's terrified of Scott, and she went anyway. Is there anything I need to know about what is going on here?"

Casey's jaw tightened in anger. Sullivan and Davies had the good grace to look offended. Casey answered for all three of them. "No, sir. Nothing."

"You'll be notified when the work will be done. Carry on." They locked the door behind him.

Sullivan bowed his head in relief. Davies caught Casey's eye and nodded his thanks. Jenny's attempted flight had occurred on *his* watch, but the sergeant had not offered him up to Sinclair. Casey returned to her room. He had treated her pain, but shock and despair were beyond the reach of the medications Dr. Adams had prescribed.

Sinclair entered his flat, poured himself a generous amount of cognac, and settled on the sofa in his dark sitting room. He was angry at the protection team for not being more vigilant, but if he'd rounded on them—which they deserved—Jenny would have heard, and she was already unhinged by Rawson's proposal.

Damned sods! They'd been caught unawares by her action. The security measures Casey had recommended would reinforce the flat, but that didn't mean they were home and dry. If she truly wanted to go, none of them could force her to stay. And that was the crux of the problem.

She had tried to run away. In spite of pain and fatigue. Her judgement had been appalling, but he could not bring himself to be exasperated with her. She had been desperate, and that was before he had given her the complete picture. Well, almost complete—he had not disclosed that her protection was conditional. They would not protect her unless she agreed to testify, but without protection, she would not survive to testify. He took another sip of cognac. The only way he could ensure her testimony—and her safety—was in keeping her on witness protection provided by the Met. Would he be able to persuade her to accept it? Would she be able to follow it through to trial? Her case called for a different approach. He'd have to have a word with Rawson in the morning.

CHAPTER 13

Casey was ready to be rid of this assignment. All day Jenny had lashed out at them without cause. Then she'd accused them of stalking her, which in a way was true. They were keeping a close watch. Outbursts: "All I did wrong was live!" "I didn't ask for any of this!" Sudden tears. None of them knew what to do with her.

She flatly refused to be bathed. He sent Sullivan to sit with her and left the flat. He needed a night run to clear his head and temper his frustration.

He took the quickest route to the Heath, counting on the cool night air in the park and the strenuous exercise to drain his anger. He was always conscious of his surroundings, alert for any unexpected sound or motion, but when he reached the path by the ponds, he found a rhythm in his stride that allowed him to reflect. He revisited his actions and decided he shouldn't have reacted to her lack of trust. Sullivan was the only one of them who had proved himself, saving her life in hospital. What had he, Casey, done? Bound her with a belt after she tried to go AWOL. At the time reestablishing his authority had been foremost in his mind, but the military model may have been inappropriate for someone not in service.

Damn it, the military approach was what he knew best. What had initially been learnt reflexes were second nature now. Were there any parallels between his experience and hers? She was young to be facing a death threat. He had been young, just twenty-three, when he was sent to the Persian Gulf prior to Desert Storm. Nervous as well. He'd had some second thoughts—no, uncertainty—although he'd not have admitted it to anyone.

They had expected the Republican Guard to be formidable opponents. His life had depended on his preparation, a sixth sense that warned of imminent danger, and his mates. She had no mates, only Davies, Sullivan, and himself. Would their support make a difference? Not likely—their assignment would end soon.

His military participation had been covert. Jenny's role, when it came, would be public, every word recorded and no doubt disputed by defence counsel. Her integrity, her character, would be questioned. How would she deal with that? She had questioned his, and that was one of the reasons he was running now.

Her identity was known. When his role in the Gulf conflict ended, no one had traced him back to England. Someone had already tried to assassinate her, and if Sinclair and Rawson could be believed, more attempts would be made. Fear can affect your reasoning. He'd seen injured, exhausted men lose courage. No wonder she had done. He should have been more patient. Indiscriminate attacks were a sign of desperation. If she lashed out at him, he shouldn't blame her.

He had covered enough ground. On the way back he recognised that his physical discipline had served its purpose, but Jenny's emotions needed to be defused. The bathing that she dreaded—she was strong enough to manage it herself now. A garbage bag tied around her cast would stop it getting soggy. And an exercise regimen could mitigate the stress she felt. He would have to get her moving again.

CHAPTER 14

In the morning Jenny suffered through her exercises. It seemed that Sergeant Casey pushed her even harder than he usually did. She was tired of him, of features so cold he could have been the fifth face on Mt. Rushmore. She was tired of Mr. Sinclair, who didn't look menacing but was. She was tired of hurting from injuries that had yet to heal. She was tired of being afraid. She felt like a ping pong ball, bounced from the London hotel to the little room to the hospital to the apartment. Next Mr. Sinclair—or Inspector Rawson—would smash her off the table into the unknown.

When the men coaxed her out of her room to play poker with them, her hands began to shake so badly that she couldn't hold the cards.

"You must have been dealt a terrible hand," Danny joked.

"No," she gasped. It was all she could do not to cry out. One minute stretched into two, then more. Her heart was pounding. She wasn't in the little room, but she felt as if she were.

"Jenny." Casey's tone was unyielding. "Take my hand."

When he used her name instead of the colloquial *love,* it was like hearing her mother call her Jennifer Catherine. She knew she had come up against an immovable object. She unfurled one fist, and Casey took it. Brian pushed his chair away from the table, startling her. "Time for tea," he said.

She returned to her room. "Truth doesn't change just because you look away from it," her father would say. She remembered his corollary: "The opposite of truth is not falsehood, but cowardice." She wished she were home in Houston filling out her travel diary, but clearly wishes weren't fulfilled in this new life. She opened her journal. In the past writing her feelings down had helped her to clarify them. She titled the page, *My Choices.* She could think of only four:

1. *Go home. Don't testify. Be in danger.*
2. *Go home. Come back to testify. Be in danger.*
3. *Don't go home until after testimony has been given. Be protected.*
4. *Don't ever go home. Be protected through loss of identity.*

Two things were immediately clear: there was no protection at home and no freedom in protection. The protection offered in options three and four came with strings.

Mr. Sinclair had made her realize just how powerless she was. She would be an easy target in Texas, and her presence there would place others at risk. She had done nothing to deserve the monster's anger or attack, but his actions had defined hers ever since. He was in custody, but he could pay others to pursue her. "Choose life," the chaplain at the hospital had said. That ruled out the first two choices, but none of the choices guaranteed life. In spite of herself, she began to cry.

Inspector Rawson had argued for anonymity. If she didn't give up her name, she could be found. Her four choices had been reduced to one: If she wanted to live as Jennifer Jeffries, item three was the only viable one. Her tears fell on the page, smearing the ink but not obscuring the path she had to take.

In practical terms staying away from home until she had appeared in court would be very difficult. It meant accepting a move to an as-yet-unknown site and adjusting to a new set of circumstances and faces. It meant—oh God—not seeing her family. What had Mr. Sinclair said? That if her parents visited, attention would be drawn to her location? If that were true now, wouldn't that same caution apply wherever they hid her?

She sobbed in despair. She *needed* her family. She had had the usual teenage skirmishes with them and had been glad for the freedom and independence that college offered, but she had always known that she was welcome at home. Now, when she most needed a refuge, the one place where she could be completely herself was denied her.

The Alamo had been a mission, a refuge of sorts, before Texas' war for independence from Mexico. Colonel Travis had drawn a line in the sand and invited all those who were willing to stay and fight to step across it. None had survived. Mr. Sinclair—*Colonel* Sinclair—had drawn a line in the sand for her. Would she die if she did the right thing? According to her father's words, there could be no compromise.

She threw the journal across the room. She'd been in London a month. Thirty days confined to a hospital room and then a small flat seemed like a long time, but legal preparations for the monster's trial would take months. Months before she saw her family, months before she could go home! The sergeant's voice startled her.

"Are you all right?" He took in her red eyes and pinched face. "Sounded like something fell."

She gestured with a nod. "My journal."

On the floor on the opposite side of the room. He retrieved it for her. She looked brittle, as if she'd been struck but the bruises had yet to appear.

She squeezed her eyes shut and waited for the sound of retreating footsteps. Who would tell her parents that she wasn't coming? She couldn't. It would break her mother's heart. Mr. Sinclair would have to do it. He was good at giving bad news. Mr. Sinclair—she shivered in spite of the blanket. He had been relaxed, detached even, when he spelled out the dangers she faced. She felt empty now. Like the dolls she used to play with when she was a little girl, her arms and legs moved, her eyes opened and closed, and she cried, but she had no stout heart inside to warm her. Her dolls had been very much alive in her make-believe world, with individual voices and likes and dislikes, and she had been too young to understand that they were not living beings. She had cut Annabelle's hair—butchered it, her mother had said in exasperation—with a pair of sewing scissors, not realizing that she could never outgrow the lopsided style. Annabelle didn't mind, she told her mother, pointing to the doll's fixed smile. And her mother's expression had softened, not wanting to dispel her daughter's innocence.

CHAPTER 15

"Dinner's on." Sergeant Casey was at her door again. Was the man omnipresent?

After dinner she continued to make additions to her book of lists. *Brian's Recipes.* Good, but he always put too much on her plate. *Danny's Jokes.* In her current mood, she couldn't recall a single one. Then she began *Things I've Missed or Will Be Missing.* The World Series would be starting soon. In Texas the fall would bring cooler temperatures, but the leaves on the trees wouldn't change color and drop until November. She would miss it all, as well as the family holidays that filled the autumn calendar. Family. No, she mustn't focus on what she could not have.

She would miss Emily Mitchell's wedding, she thought with a start. It was scheduled for late October, and she had been fitted for her bridesmaid's dress just before she left for England. Many of her college friends would be there. She wondered which one would take her place. She tried to think of something else, besides people laughing and Emily in her new husband's arms, welcoming his touch.

Things I've Missed. Her period. How long had it been since her last one? Five weeks? More? She'd been late before sometimes, though, when she was under stress.

At the week's end, Sinclair had a positive report for the investigative team. "It's a match! Scott's DNA. For all seven. We've got him bang to rights!"

"And his accomplices?" someone asked when the celebratory buzz had quieted.

"We've searched their flats but still can't implicate either of them in any of the assaults. Both have been bailed."

"How's our witness?" The question came from DI Haas, the spare, solemn man with dark circles under his eyes who had led the investigation into Barbara Bennett's death. She had been Scott's first victim, and he had felt very keenly his failure to apprehend her killer in time to prevent subsequent deaths from occurring.

"Rawson's recommendation for long-term protection upset her," Sinclair answered. "Security's been improved at her current location, but I have some fences to mend if she's to stay on board."

- -

On Sinclair's way home he resolved to rebuild Jenny's trust before initiating any discussion of future placement. When he arrived at the flat, he found her in her room. "There's good news on the case—forensic tests confirmed that it was Scott's DNA in all the victims, including you. We're standing on firm ground legally."

She was appalled. The monster hadn't worn a condom after all. "Will I get AIDS?"

"No, he's clear of all that."

But she wasn't clear of anything. This news made her late period more ominous.

He saw her tremble. "I've brought something for you." He handed her a parcel from Texas.

She thought idly about collecting the U.S. stamps; she'd taken them for granted before. Her mother had sent Jenny's Dallas Cowboys sweatshirt, several books, and a box of notepaper.

The next box was plain, the cardboard flaps folded closed. It was filled with chocolate treats. "From the officers at the Yard," he explained. "Andrews let it slip that you liked chocolate."

"I don't understand. Why would they do this?"

"Jenny, your case—it has an impact on everyone who works on it. This is the copper's version of Newton's Law: Counter each violent act with a decent one."

The last box was glossy, with a wide ribbon tied into a bow. She hesitated.

"Jenny, I'd like you to open it. There's no obligation involved."

"Mr. Sinclair, you shouldn't be bringing me gifts."

"I should, actually," he said, not understanding why she seemed distant still. "Your mother gave me *carte blanche* to spoil you."

She untied the bow. Inside the box she found a pastel blanket. The colors, aqua and pale blue, reminded her of summer days at home, when the sun was so strong and the heat so withering that it bleached the landscape. The tag said "silk fleece," but to Jenny it felt soft as cashmere and as warm. She wrapped it around her shoulders, feeling a wave of homesickness. "It has fringe," she said, her voice breaking. "That's so feminine." Why was he being so nice? Would there be a new set of policemen soon? In a new place? "Mr. Sinclair, is this my life?" she asked. "This room?"

"Only for a season, Jenny."

"It's autumn. Will things be over that quickly?"

"I was speaking metaphorically. It's your winter—but 'if winter comes, can spring be far behind?'"

"Shelley," she said, recognizing the quote. "But I think Shakespeare said it better: It's the 'winter of my discontent.'"

CHAPTER 16

Saturday passed quietly, the men occupied with cleaning chores. None of them seemed to mind, Brian acknowledging that there was housekeeping of some sort in every job. The sad thing was, she couldn't tell the difference between before and after—the flat looked just as bedraggled. Why did the British call their apartments flats? Was it because the people that lived in them had a deflated existence like she did? She'd have to start a new list: *Odd English Words.* She noticed, however, that no matter when she left her room, someone was in the living room, dining room, or kitchen, perpetual as the plague.

On Sunday Brian served the traditional British meal of roast beef with Yorkshire pudding. She loved the beef, but held her nose over the Brussels sprouts, accusing him of breaking his pledge to protect her.

Later in the day she watched Sergeant Casey unlock the door to the flat with a key to admit Sinclair. Brian was standing by. "Do I get a key?" she asked the sergeant.

"No key, no surprises."

"Am I in custody, Mr. Sinclair?"

"No, Jenny. I'll have a key made for you if you like." He had brought a four pack of some kind of beer for the men. He opened a bottle for himself and invited her to join him at the dining room table. "I've something to show you," he said, spreading out a series of postcards. "I'm going to take you armchair travelling. Every week we'll have a new destination."

She tried to listen between the lines. Destination?

"When you're able to visit some of these places, you'll be well informed. Tonight we're going to the British Museum, since your trip there was disrupted."

That was a kind way to put it.

"This is the façade. Typical classical design."

It looked like the Lincoln Memorial, because of all the columns, but it was not a three-dimensional tour. What was the Lincoln Memorial without the battle scars etched in Lincoln's face? And the sight of his massive marble hands powerless to heal his divided nation?

"Inside," he continued, "are ninety-four separate galleries. It's the oldest museum in the world, I think, and covers almost two million years of culture. There are thousands of items displayed, many more than you could see in a day's visit."

She broke her silence. "Well, no wonder! Your navy ruled the waves, and your empire dominated the world. I never could remember all the eighteenth- and nineteenth-century explorers that sailed from here."

"Captain Cook was one of them," he mentioned, relieved that she was finally participating.

"No, that's Brian," she corrected. "He's Captain Cook, and Sergeant Casey is Mr. Clean."

Sinclair smiled and pointed to cards showing the Rosetta Stone, a mummified cat from Egypt, and others. "Works of art, archaeological finds, coins, drawings, manuscripts, they're all there."

"Thank you for showing them to me."

"Jenny, they're yours to use as you please. However, there's one more thing I'd like to do with them." He leant two of the postcards together, then, separating the two slightly at the top, placed a third card across them. Two more cards were set on top of the flat card, and yet another across their top. The third level was not stable, and all the cards ended up in a pile. "Trust is like that, isn't it? It's easy to topple if you're not careful." He caught her eye. "I'd like you to accept, if possible, that there's a difference between a man and his job."

"I don't understand."

"Did your father ever have to give low marks to a student? Perhaps to a student he liked? It may have been necessary, but I don't imagine he enjoyed doing it." His voice was very soft. "I don't like having to tell a husband that he'll never again be able to embrace his beloved, because someone has murdered her; or a parent, that his child will never see adulthood. I don't like telling a father and mother that they shouldn't visit their frightened, injured daughter or telling the daughter that her loneliness and isolation will continue. At times like that, justice seems a very cold mistress indeed."

She felt a warm flush come over her cheeks. She couldn't look at him.

He continued in the same gentle tone. "The mistress of justice is often shown blindfolded, to demonstrate her impartiality, I suppose. However, the blindfold also keeps her from seeing the heartbreak that the pursuit of her ideal sometimes causes. Jenny, violent crime leaves no winners in its wake. That is one of the reasons I am so angered by it and so dedicated to its eradication."

"I've been blaming the messenger for the message," she confessed. "I should know better. I'm sorry."

"Look at me, Jenny. My name is Colin Thomas Dowding Sinclair."

Her eyes widened. "That's a lot of names."

"Only one more than Jennifer Catherine Jeffries," he pointed out. "And I'm only asking you to use one of them, if you will, and to be in composition with me, not opposition to me."

Then she chose: Sinclair. "Are you talking about my next placement?"

"Jenny, that's only one of the issues we'll have to face in the days ahead. I'm simply suggesting that there is no conflict of interest between us. We both value honesty, is that correct?"

She nodded.

"You want very much to be safe, and I want to keep you that way."

She was silent.

"I believe justice is precious. We don't see it in every case. And it's worth fighting for, in spite of the cost."

"Yes," she agreed, "but it's hard."

"It's easier when you're not alone."

"I will be. I could be."

"Jenny, I'm in charge of your case. You'll always be able to reach me."

Lincoln's hands rested on the arms of his chair. Mr. Sinclair's hand was open, outstretched—smaller than Lincoln's but perhaps more able to mend the rift between them. She placed her hand across his and watched his fingers close over hers. "I'm sorry—Colin," she forced herself to say.

He smiled. "Well done."

Later, when she thought about their conversation, she realized that he'd essentially called her a spoiled brat, but he had done it with gentleness and eloquence. She had been unfair to him, and he had responded by assuming that she had a better nature and appealing to it. She started a new list in her mind, *My Shortcomings,* and envisioned the first entry: *Rudeness to Mr. Sinclair.* No, *Colin.* He was asking her to act as a mature adult—not an unreasonable request—and he had done it with grace and not anger.

CHAPTER 17

Still concerned about Jenny's frame of mind, Sinclair decided to consult a psychiatrist. He had just arrived at the well-furnished reception room when a tall, slim man in his fifties opened an interior door and invited him in. "Mr. Sinclair? I'm Theodore Knowles."

Sinclair gave him the file he had brought. It contained a copy of Jenny's fact sheet, formal statement, and medical record, with her name blacked out everywhere it had appeared. "I'm a detective chief inspector with the Metropolitan Police. The file you're holding belongs to the key witness in the Crown's case against Cecil Scott. Dr. Gerald West at the Yard referred me to you."

"Gerry won't be seeing her?"

"He's contracted to treat the police community, not civilians."

"Then I trust she has not received any psychological counselling so far?"

"That's correct," Sinclair said.

"You'll give me a few minutes to familiarise myself with this material?"

Sinclair nodded.

Shock and sorrow crossed Knowles' face as he read. "He stripped her of her clothes, her defences, her sexual innocence—and in his final act, of her femininity, by raping her the second time the way a man rapes a man. He broke her, and then he discarded her." He sighed, leaning forward to return the file to Sinclair. "I've just made a few notes—medications prescribed, details of injuries that could have a psychological consequence, that sort of thing. May I know her name for the purpose of our discussion? I understand that security is a concern; I won't record it."

"Jennifer Jeffries. We call her Jenny. She is currently in our protection."

"Who is providing her medical care?"

"One of our officers received medical training from the Royal Marines."

"Let me see if I understand the situation so far," Knowles said. "A young woman, viciously attacked in a foreign country, isolated from her family, and with substantial physical and psychological injuries, is being guarded by police."

Knowles' summary made Jenny's distress seem reasonable.

"How may I help you?"

"She's having trouble," Sinclair admitted. "For security reasons, I had to ask her parents not to come to London for a time. That was a significant blow for her, and she is now suspicious of my motives. In addition, she had a meeting with an officer from our Witness Protection Unit. He meant to be reassuring, but his suggestion that she disappear—with a new name—was a source of upheaval as well. Indeed, later that evening she packed her bag and tried to leave."

"Could she have taken care of herself?"

"No. Either she didn't consider her physical condition or she overestimated her strength. It was a powerful demonstration, however, of her determination to maintain her identity."

Knowles nodded. "Her name—her 'self'—is all she has."

"That's what she said. And since then, the men have reported that she's having nightmares as well as spontaneous episodes of fear in the daytime."

"Panic attacks," Knowles confirmed. "Her trauma is beginning to manifest itself."

"That makes my job even more difficult, because we will need to move her soon."

"If you do, you'll be taking a terrible risk with her mental health and stability."

"Even if she's willing?"

"And you believe her? Clearly her judgement of what she can do is inaccurate."

"Damn," he muttered.

"How is she getting on with the officers protecting her now?"

"She's beginning to trust them."

"Let me summarise. Your witness was brutalised by a violent man. Since the attack, she has suffered several serious psychological blows. Your intention is to remove her from the only stable environment she has known since her arrival and require her to start all over again, adjusting to a new situation. Following this disruption, you expect her to focus on her role as a witness and testify clearly and effectively in a court of law."

"Even if she is determined to testify?"

"Her determination is not the issue," Knowles argued. "Her ability is the issue. You are expecting her to stay on her feet while you pull the rug out from under her. That's just not realistic. She is still emotionally vulnerable. You must understand—all her reference points are gone. Nothing is familiar to her, including herself. She needs a stable, predictable environment. You may be most comfortable with proven procedures, but in this case you must evaluate how your procedures will impact your witness. I'm suggesting you consider Jenny's surroundings, schedule, and relationships."

- -

Sinclair returned to the Yard with a distinct feeling of unease. Since his involvement in the case began, he had considered mainly how Jenny's actions would affect someone else, her statement in identifying her attacker and her eventual testimony in convicting him. Aside from recognising the painful nature of her recovery and the difficulty she would experience when she faced Scott in court, he had not stopped to consider the effect their procedures would have on her. Rawson had a record of success in keeping witnesses safe, but Knowles was advising that he depart from it. He required second-source confirmation, from someone who had at least met her. He rang Bridges.

"How's Jenny doing?" the SOIT officer asked.

"Her injuries are gradually healing, but she's having difficulty psychologically. The visit by our witness protection officer upset her. She didn't respond well to his proposal that she have a new identity."

"Sever all ties to her past?" Bridges echoed, making the brief silence that followed more obvious. "Permission to speak freely, sir?"

"Granted."

"That's too great an adjustment for her to contemplate. She was essentially anonymous when she arrived here, and Scott got hold of her. A new name won't mean a thing. From her point of view, it's the same situation. She'd be looking over her shoulder all the time."

"She'd have freedom of movement. She'd be able to work, make friends, have activities off the job."

"Sir, she's had a deeply troubling experience. Freedom—lack of police supervision—means vulnerability. At this stage safety is far more important to her than freedom. Has she adjusted well to her current location?"

"Quite well, actually."

"Traumatised persons don't adapt well to change."

This time the silence on the line was Sinclair's.

"Sir? I visited her in hospital several times following her statement. She knew the names of some of the men who were stationed outside her room. She was reassured by their presence. I think she'd like her protection to be visible."

CHAPTER 18

Sinclair's phone at the Yard rang. "Sir, there's a Mr. Jeffries here, insists on having a word with you," a constable from reception reported. Cursing under his breath, Sinclair grabbed his coat and headed down to Back Hall. He saw a lean, lanky man in his late forties or early fifties standing in front of the glass cases that memorialised police officers and civilian staff members killed since the formation of the force. An eternal flame accompanied the roll of honour book that recorded the circumstances in which each life had been lost.

Sinclair's visitor had specks of gray in his hair. He wore navy blue trousers, a khaki corduroy jacket, and a white shirt, open at the neck. His tan face looked tired. He met Sinclair's extended hand with a firm grip and said, "I'm Bill Jeffries. I've come to take my little girl home."

Sinclair recognised Jenny's dark eyes and the now familiar, slow drawl. The corridors weren't crowded, but police departments have eyes and ears, so he escorted him upstairs as quickly as he could. When Mr. Jeffries was seated in his office and Andrews had been sent to the canteen for tea, Sinclair brought his own chair from behind the desk and sat down next to him.

"Sir, I'd like very much to change your mind."

Mr. Jeffries had been quietly absorbing the untidy surroundings, files piled high on the desk and filing cabinets and charts of various kinds lining the walls. "That's not possible, son."

Sinclair tried anyway, outlining the safety procedures they had instituted for Jenny's protection and the qualifications of the men who were guarding her.

Mr. Jeffries listened patiently.

Next Sinclair explained the importance of the case and Jenny's role in it, stopping only when Andrews returned with the tea.

"Very impressive," Mr. Jeffries responded, but it didn't sound like a concession to Sinclair.

He knew that as an historian, Mr. Jeffries would have studied the influence men can have on events. He pointed out that very few people have the opportunity to impact lives the way Jenny would with her testimony. He mentioned the families of the other victims, who were now hoping that justice would be done for those they had lost.

Mr. Jeffries sipped his tea and regarded Sinclair with a slow smile. "Take me to my daughter, please."

"Sir, she's at very high risk. If she doesn't testify—if Scott isn't convicted—she will never be free of danger."

"As we say in cattle country, you've got something foul on your boots, son," Mr. Jeffries replied. "She'll be a far sight safer in Texas than she has been here. We know that someone came after her in the hospital."

"How do you know that, sir?"

"She told us," Mr. Jeffries answered with a steady gaze. "She was telling us why she liked Constable Sullivan."

"Sir, my men did their jobs. She wasn't harmed."

"Chief Inspector, do you have children?" He had only seen photographs of what appeared to be Sinclair's professional family in his office.

"No, sir. I'm sorry to say, I don't."

Mr. Jeffries did not break the silence that followed.

"How long have you been planning this trip?" Sinclair finally asked.

"I was always coming for her," Mr. Jeffries acknowledged. "I was just waiting for my passport to arrive and her health to improve. I was taught never to telegraph my punches."

Sinclair had met his match. "When are you scheduled to fly home?"

"Tomorrow afternoon. I have a hotel room reserved for tonight."

"Sir, I'd prefer it if your name weren't registered anywhere. I'll have my sergeant take you to collect your luggage. You'll stay with me, and I'll take you to see Jenny."

Mr. Jeffries nodded and rose to his feet. He was easily Sinclair's height. When he had left with Andrews, Sinclair called Casey. "We have a visitor. Command performance. Uniforms. Tell Davies to cook something special. We'll be arriving for a late dinner." He rang off.

While he waited for Andrews and Mr. Jeffries to return, he brooded over the roller-coaster nature of the case. For a long time they'd had nothing; then Jenny's identification had given them everything they needed to proceed against Scott and the others. Now, potentially, it could all be lost, and there wasn't a bloody thing he could do about it.

CHAPTER 19

Andrews was a good driver, but negotiating London traffic was difficult at best. However, it gave Sinclair time to brief Jenny's father about her appearance. "The bruises on her face have completely faded. There's a small scar on her right cheek, but we hardly notice it. She's still got a cast on her left arm. She'll be limping slightly, but—sir—she's made great progress."

Sinclair had expected to field all sorts of questions from Mr. Jeffries, but instead the American sat quietly, letting Sinclair shoulder the bulk of the conversation. He looked weary but alert, as if he'd found his second wind.

They finally reached Sinclair's block. There were trees and lots of leafy shrubs and hedges, but some of the brick exteriors were worn, and the houses were close to each other. Would his guest regard it as stately or crowded? He took Mr. Jeffries up to the flat.

Casey and Sullivan answered the door and were introduced to Jenny's father. Mr. Jeffries eyed the pistol on Casey's belt.

"Daddy! Daddy!" she cried.

Mr. Jeffries' long strides took him to her side in seconds. "Howdy, Punkin," he said, enveloping her in his embrace.

Davies came out of the kitchen and laid two places on one end of the dining room table.

"We ate already," she said, wiping her eyes. "Did you meet everybody?"

Davies stepped forward and extended his hand. "PC Davies, sir. Pleasure to meet you."

"You, too, son," Mr. Jeffries replied. "Jenny tells me you're quite the hand at the chuckwagon."

"I'll let you be the judge of that, sir," Davies answered. "We'll have your dinner warmed through soon."

Sinclair took the opportunity to show Mr. Jeffries about the flat, emphasising the security procedures and privacy afforded to her.

Davies had made what he called Quick Coq au Vin. He served it with rosemary potatoes and asparagus with olive oil, lemon, and parmesan cheese. As they ate, Sinclair could see the pain in Mr. Jeffries' eyes when he looked at his daughter. He didn't let it affect his words or actions, but Sinclair realised that what looked like improvement to him would be fathoms from normal for her father. Sinclair had first seen her in hospital, her body covered with bandages and invaded with tubes, but Mr. Jeffries would remember a flawless gem, with light in her eyes and colour in her face, not this pale, haunted expression that she couldn't conceal no matter how hard she tried.

After dinner, she took her father to her room, holding his arm and leaning on him a little as they went. Davies removed their plates, and Sinclair leant back in his chair, running his hands through his hair.

"Did you know he was coming, sir?" Casey asked quietly.

Sinclair shook his head. "I believe she did, however."

Casey agreed. She hadn't seemed surprised. "Why is he here?"

"He intends to take her home with him."

Her door was open, and they could hear her laughing at something her father had said. Sinclair had heard her laugh, but he hadn't realised until now how subdued she had been. This laughter was lighter, freer, sweeter, like the sound made when two pieces of fine crystal touch.

"Sir, can't you do something?" It was Sullivan.

"It's never done, but legally I could detain her—force her to testify. Her father would go to the American embassy and possibly the press. And we would have an uncooperative witness."

Davies spoke. "Perhaps she'll come back for the trial, sir."

"If she's not dead," Sinclair said. "There's big money out on her."

"And if she doesn't testify?" Casey asked.

"If Scott's defence team can get the DNA evidence suppressed, there will be no case. He will be released, and eventually other women will die."

"Can they do that, sir?" Sullivan asked.

"There's no accounting for the legal system," Sinclair replied.

When Jenny and her father returned, she didn't notice the men's solemn faces.

"Sir, she's needed here," Sullivan said. "And we'll protect her."

"I know you will, son," Mr. Jeffries responded, "but it's my job to do that now."

"Sir—with respect—we're better qualified," Davies argued. "Someone's always on watch here; Casey now, me overnight, and Sullivan in the morning."

"I appreciate that. I'll take it from there."

She put her arm around his neck and kissed him on the cheek. "I'll see you in the morning, Daddy."

"Davies, can you manage a proper English breakfast?" Sinclair asked.

"Yes, sir."

He and Mr. Jeffries left, and the door was locked behind them.

"Are you going?" Danny asked. "Are you leaving tomorrow?"

"Three guesses, and the first two don't count!"

"You've got to stay," Danny insisted. "I won't let anything happen to you. Haven't I proved that?"

"The boss will get the push if you go," Brian told her. "He'll be struck off."

Their concerted appeal surprised her. She turned to Sergeant Casey. "Aren't you going to put your two cents in?"

"What will you lose?" he asked.

"I beg your pardon?"

"If you go, what will *you* lose?"

She didn't know. She shrugged her shoulders and went to her room.

"I expected you'd talk to her about her mission," Davies told Casey.

"If she doesn't feel it, I can't make her," Casey replied.

Jenny floated through her bedtime ritual. Finally something good had happened to her: Her father had come! How could she not go home with him? It would solve the problem of her placement for Mr. Sinclair. He had been courteous, even gracious, to her father. Surely he wouldn't lose his job. Then she remembered Sergeant Casey's question, and he hadn't even used his "I-will-brook-no-opposition" voice. What made him think she would lose anything? How could she lose anything by going home? She held the soft pastel blanket against her chest throughout the long night.

CHAPTER 20

In the morning Davies outdid himself: pancakes, sausages, bacon, eggs, tomatoes, and fried bread. "Coffee, sir?" he asked Mr. Jeffries. "Black or white?"

Mr. Jeffries ate heartily. "Black, thank you."

Jenny sipped her tea. Conversation was sporadic. Casey gave her the egg-sized ball to squeeze so she could do a last set of arm exercises.

Mr. Jeffries thanked Davies for the Texas-sized meal and turned to his daughter. "Are you packed, Punkin?"

She didn't answer at first. "No, Daddy," she said finally.

"Do you need me to help you?"

"No, Daddy," she whispered.

Something in her tone made Sinclair's detective's ears prickle. Then he realised that she wasn't smiling.

"We have to be going before long," Mr. Jeffries reminded her patiently.

Her voice, when it came, was barely audible. "No, Daddy."

Davies wasn't certain he'd heard correctly. Sullivan's mouth dropped open, and he glanced quickly from Jenny to her father and back again. Dead-on, Casey thought. That was twice the Yank had surprised him. Sinclair wanted to cheer.

Mr. Jeffries looked at her with the question his lips couldn't form written all over his face.

She held the therapy ball in one hand and pressed the other against her chest. "I can't go. I want to so badly, but I can't."

"Why not, Punkin? This can all be over for you in a few hours. And your mother can hardly wait to see you."

She stumbled over the words. "Because you taught me the difference between right and wrong," she said. "I need her so badly, but if I go, it'll be wrong."

"Aren't you afraid, Punkin? Let me take you home, where you don't have to be afraid. You can fly back for the trial."

"I'm terribly afraid, Daddy, but I'll be afraid there, too. I have to do this. Here."

"Can't others do it?"

"No, Daddy. I'm the only one who lived."

Davies took a few steps back. The conversation between Jenny and her father was so intimate, he felt that he was eavesdropping. Sullivan was stunned into silence for a change. Casey was watching her very closely. She was holding the exercise ball in both hands now, and he wasn't certain it would survive the pressure it was under.

"Haven't I always known what was best for you, Punkin?"

"Daddy, I'm a target. If I come home, you will be, too. You all will. I won't do that to you."

"Did someone convince you to do this? One of these men?"

She shook her head. "They don't have that kind of power."

"What am I going to tell your mother?" he asked desperately.

"Tell her—oh, God—tell her I love her," she cried. She suddenly released the ball, and it rolled off her lap and onto the floor, its smooth motion a stark contrast to the tension that surrounded it. Her fingers were limp, as if her heart had quit trying to force blood through them.

"Isn't there any way I can change your mind?"

"No. If I go, I'll lose everything—myself, my integrity. If I endanger the people I love, I'll never be able to hold my head up as long as I live."

Casey was still watching Jenny, wondering if she would survive the pressure *she* was under. An umbilical cord had been cut, a lifeline severed.

Sinclair thought her action was the purest example of virtue he had ever seen. Milton had said something about virtue, he remembered: that "heaven itself would stoop to her." "We should be getting on soon, sir," he said quietly.

Mr. Jeffries stood and put his hands on her shoulders. "Jenny, I believe 'the ultimate measure of a man is not where he stands in moments of comfort or convenience, but where he stands at times of challenge and controversy.'"

"Dr. Martin Luther King," she murmured.

"I've never been more proud of you than I am at this moment." He embraced her, whispering a prayer in her ear.

"I love you, Daddy," she said, clinging to him.

"I love you, too, Punkin," Mr. Jeffries breathed. He released her and stepped back. "Gentlemen, you'll take care of my little girl?"

Casey moved behind her. "You can count on me, sir."

Davies and Sullivan closed and secured the door behind them.

She sank to her knees, unable to hold back the sobs.

Casey knelt down beside her. "Jenny, if you want me to go after them, I need to know now." He didn't know if she'd heard him over her cries. He raised his voice. "Yes or no, Jenny! *Now*!"

She shook her head.

"Davies, my kit," Casey said. "Sullivan, water." She took the tablet he offered, leaning heavily against him. Gradually her sobs subsided, and she went to bed.

"I was dead sure she'd take off," Sullivan said. "She'll have a rough go of it now, won't she? We have to do something to put it right."

"All we can bloody well do now is wait." He decided to keep watch in the armchair by her bed. Sedatives brought rest but not peace.

CHAPTER 21

Jenny was quiet for some time after she awakened. Casey didn't break the silence. "Have you ever been in a hurricane, Sergeant?" she asked finally. "In the worst storms, you could be lying on the ground and still be blown away."

"I'll not let that happen."

"What time is it?"

"Time for some of Davies' soup."

Sinclair arrived while he was preparing the tray. "You dodged a bullet, sir," Casey told him, "but I'm not sure she did."

"What do you mean?"

"She was in a sorry state. I sedated her. She didn't rouse until a few minutes ago."

"Was that necessary?"

"It was the merciful thing to do."

"Right. How is she now?"

"Subdued. Very."

"I'll take the tray," Sinclair said.

"Is he gone?" she asked when she saw him.

"I drove him to the airport and waited with him until he boarded the plane. He's very proud of you, and so am I."

She pushed herself up. "That soup smells like spaghetti." It had meatballs in it, with spaghetti noodles and Italian seasonings. When he brought her a second cup, the other men came in with him.

"I've rented a video," Danny said. "Won't you join us?"

"I don't want to. Maybe later."

"But it's Benny Hill," he piped up. "My parents always thought he was a riot."

"Thanks a lot, Sullivan," Sinclair grumbled. "I thought he was rather humourous myself."

Jenny smiled and trudged into the sitting room, curling up on the sofa with her pastel blanket. Danny hit the play button. She watched thoughtfully at first. "He reminds me of an American comedian my parents used to like: Johnny Carson. This man has the same reasonably attractive and remarkably expressive face." It was a highlights tape, and she found herself becoming distracted by the outrageous situations. “They also share the total inability to feel embarrassed by anything. Thanks, Danny.”

“It’s a winner, isn’t it, Sis?” he crowed.

“Sis?”

“Yes, we’re going to be your family now,” he declared.

“I like that, Danny,” she said when she could. “Brian, thanks for the soup. Mr. Sinclair, thank you for being so good to my dad.”

Casey checked on her at the start of the night watch.

“Don’t go,” she murmured. She wrapped her fingers around his arm.

He put her hand inside his instead and rubbed her palm with his thumb. “Today was tough. Nobody could have done it any better. I’m that proud of you.”

“Tears and all?”

“Tears and all. But you’ll be needing this more now.” He took her mobile phone out of his pocket and held it out to her. “It’s yours to keep.”

CHAPTER 22

Jenny was surprised when Mr. Sinclair came by on Saturday with a big package, and even more surprised by what was for him, informal dress: camel trousers, sports shirt, and burgundy sweater. "I've been shopping, and we're going to have a history lesson and do a bit of decorating." He handed her the parcel. "History lesson first. Open it."

It was the Union Jack, the flag of Great Britain. "Our flag is made up of three crosses: the Cross of St. George, the Cross of St. Andrew, and the Cross of St. Patrick. St. George is the patron saint of England, legendary for killing a dragon and saving the king's daughter. You're going to slay a dragon when you testify, and we're going to help get you there. The red cross in the middle—outlined in white—is St. George's Cross."

The other men were curious and had joined them.

"St. Andrew," he continued, "is the patron saint of Scotland. His cross is shaped like a white X on a blue background. See how the white extends to each corner of the flag? You have to use your imagination a bit, because the red cross in the middle appears to be in front of it." He traced the outline with his finger. "There's one more: the Cross of St. Patrick."

"Patron saint of Ireland?"

Sinclair nodded. "His cross is a red X on a white background, the same shape as St. Andrew's but slightly smaller. It also appears to be behind the Cross of St. George."

"So England's patron saint has prominence in your flag. That's appropriate, isn't it?"

"I think so," Sinclair agreed. "Now—what can you tell me about St. Patrick?"

"Isn't he the one who drove all the snakes into the sea?"

"That's the story, but did you know he was kidnapped when he was sixteen and forced into slavery in Ireland?"

"Kidnapped? He wasn't Irish? How did he get from slavery to sainthood?"

"He escaped—with God's help, he said. He returned to England, studied in monasteries abroad, and was sent, first to evangelise his native country, England, and then to be a missionary to Ireland. Catholic scholars consider his return to Ireland to be tangible illustration of the concept of forgiveness. That's probably where the sainthood comes in. He died at the ripe old age of seventy-four. You're doing a service for the Crown, and this flag acknowledges that. Where would you like us to hang it?"

She glanced quickly around the room. "There." She pointed to the wall opposite her bed. "It'll be the first thing I see when I wake up and the last thing before I go to sleep."

Sinclair tacked it into place.

"How'd you learn all that?" Danny asked. "I'm Catholic, and I don't remember hearing those details at Mass."

"It's called research, Sullivan," Sinclair answered dryly. "I didn't get it in church, either. Now for my last piece of trivia. We all know St. Patrick's Day is March 17, but when is St. George's Day?"

"Not a clue," she said.

"April 23," Sinclair reported.

"Gold star for you," she teased. "What about St. Andrew?"

"November 30."

"Good for Andrew," she said, and Casey noticed that Sinclair's presentation had brightened her face. In fact, the entire room was brighter, the colourful flag a powerful focal point.

- -

Davies sent Sullivan for pizza.

"That's the fifth food group," Jenny smiled, "at least for college students. Meat, milk, bread, fruit and vegetable—and pizza."

"You've got six!" Danny chimed in. "Chocolate!"

After dinner, she resolved to start one of the Manchester volumes on Churchill which Mr. Sinclair had loaned her. She read until bath time. When Casey came in, she looked at the flag and felt inexplicably stronger. "Are you on watch?"

"Until six a.m."

He heard a muffled cry during the midwatch and went in to her. Her eyes were wide, and her breathing was shallow and rapid: another of her spells.

"Don't you ever panic?" she gasped. In the daytime she could usually push her thoughts away. At night what was beneath the surface rose up.

"I was trained not to."

"That's no help," she said. "Talk to me. About anything." She wanted to be distracted from all her fears, the rational as well as the irrational. She still hadn't started her period. She cried too easily, but there were no other signs that anything was wrong.

He told her about long summer days and teaching his brother to bait his first hook, and gradually her fear receded, leaving her calm but spent. She slept, and he made a cup of tea for himself and wondered if her family knew about her precarious psychological state. He thought not. If her father had known, he wouldn't have left without her, no matter what her choice had been.

CHAPTER 23

Brian made lamb chops for Sunday dinner, with tiny little peas and salad. And potatoes—always potatoes! He watched her every time she took a bite of peas. "Peas are okay," she assured him. "It's just Brussels sprouts I don't like. Even fresh ones smell like they're not."

After the meal, Sergeant Casey told her he'd be taking some leave, and she was surprised to discover that she missed him. He was still formidable but not tough through and through, the way she had thought at first. Lately he had been gentle with her, and she found that almost more difficult to bear. The monster had taught her in a tangible way that men were capable of extreme violence. Tenderness struck a chord of longing that she must extinguish. She'd become accustomed to the sergeant's firm approach; she always knew where she stood with him. She wanted her relationships with men to be well defined.

Monday morning when she woke, Brian was gone. "Is he coming back?" she asked Casey. "Is this it? Am I moving?" Casey assured her it was only for twenty-four hours. When Davies returned, Sullivan would take off.

That night after dinner, Mr. Sinclair gave her another postcard tour. The last time he had brought postcards, he had asked her to address him by his first name. What was his agenda tonight? Would it be rude to ask?

He began at Parliament Square and Westminster Abbey. "All our monarchs were crowned there."

She had seen the Abbey and the Houses of Parliament. She remembered her awe when she'd looked up at the tower of Big Ben, taller than a football field is long. She had been a tourist, with as many expectations for good things as a child with a Christmas list. She looked at the three-by-five-inch souvenir postcard in her hand. She and Big Ben had both shrunk.

He had found individual postcards of the statues of Oliver Cromwell, Abraham Lincoln, and Winston Churchill and paused in his narration to give her a chance to respond.

"How ecumenical," she remarked. "One British hero, one American, and one half and half."

There were several postcards from the Tower of London, showing the royal palace, the fortress, and the prison. She remembered the movie, *A Man For All Seasons*, and knew that Sir Thomas More had been beheaded, as had some of the rulers. The Beefeater postcard reminded her of the *Yeomen of the Guard* operetta, and she was embarrassed that so much of her knowledge of British history had come from the world of entertainment. She oohed and aahed over the Crown Jewels and intoned, "Nevermore," when she saw the picture of the ravens.

"Legend has it," Sinclair explained, "that if the ravens leave, the commonwealth will come to an end, so their wings are clipped. They can hop but not fly."

"That's one way to preserve the status quo," she observed, "but it's sad to think they can't be free. I know what it's like to be stuck in a place. I wonder if, in their bird consciousness, they know how small their world has become." She thought about the vastness of some of the world's natural landmarks. What was the Grand Canyon without the perspective of space, or Niagara Falls without the roar of the water? "Will I be moving soon? Will it be sudden, or will I have some time to get used to the idea? Will you tell me where I'm going, or will it be a surprise, like this was?"

"Jenny, I don't know yet." Knowles is right. She's nervous about changing her living arrangements.

"I want to keep being Jenny," she stressed.

"We'll find a way to respect that," he assured her. "We're trying to take into account all your needs. We have no desire to make this difficult for you."

She smiled suddenly. "At least you'll be free. Think about all the spare time you'll have when you don't have to collect postcards."

"It's no bother," he answered. "It's a distraction for me also."

He left the postcards with her and returned to his flat, its décor reduced to shades of light and dark. On a regular basis he used only his bedroom and bathroom, rarely venturing into the kitchen. He never ate there, just keeping one cup ready for instant coffee if he were called out during the night. Every square inch of the witness protection flat was occupied and used, and it seemed cosy to him.

CHAPTER 24

Danny returned to the flat late Wednesday morning, his arms full of groceries and laughing about Jenny's additions to the list. She'd written *chocolate* every other line, and at the bottom, all in capital letters, *NO BRUSSELS SPROUTS.* "I didn't buy any," he grinned.

Brian was busy all afternoon on an Italian dinner, and the flat was filled with the scents of garlic and oregano. He made chicken breasts stuffed with mushrooms, mozzarella cheese, sun-dried tomatoes, and seasonings, with risotto and a salad on the side. Everything was delicious, but she couldn't resist teasing him about his salad, holding up a leafy green sprig, and asking, "Brian, what in the world is this? It looks like a weed."

"It's called rocket. It has more flavour than other salad greens."

"You are the captain of the kitchen!" she exclaimed. "Where did you learn to cook?"

"Scouting," he said with a smile. "There was a merit badge. I do my best work over an open fire."

"You didn't learn to make this in Boy Scouts."

"Actually, we had paying guests that we cooked for—people who wanted to see what a working farm was like."

"Did you make Eagle Scout?"

"We call it Queen's Scout. But then I got interested in girls, and that was the end of scouting for me."

"I didn't make it very far in scouting," she remembered. "Camping did me in. It was hot, and the bugs—ugh! Just about everything in Texas has a bite, or a sting, or a thorn. And I was afraid of snakes."

"Does Texas have poisonous snakes?" Danny asked.

"Yes, lots. Water moccasins, copperheads, rattlesnakes, and coral snakes. I've never seen the others, but I went to a rattlesnake rodeo once."

She had their full attention.

"A company that sold rattlesnake-skin cowboy boots sponsored it," she explained. "A man was in a fenced area with more rattlesnakes than I could shake a stick at. He climbed in a sleeping bag with some of them; things like that. They even served cooked rattlesnake meat."

"Did you eat any?" Brian asked.

"Yes," she smiled at the memory. "I took a very small bite. Actually all the bites were small, because there are so many bones in a rattlesnake. It didn't have a strong flavor."

After dinner the men seemed to be everywhere. She went to her room intending to read, but the noise from the television was distracting, so she set her book aside and just sat. Eventually the TV was turned off, and she heard the men move away. Her room didn't feel private, however. They made her keep her door open. The lighthearted exchange at dinner had amused her, but it wasn't bedtime yet.

Finally she sat down on the floor next to her bed but on the side that faced away from the door. When Danny knocked and called out to her, she didn't answer. She heard his voice asking, "Have you seen Jenny? Could she have got out?"

Other voices: "No. Door's secure." "The alarm would have sounded."

She could hear them moving around the flat. She knew she should call out, let them know she was okay, but she was mute, as if some powerful hand were gripping her throat. Their footsteps were coming closer. She wrapped her arms around her shins and pressed her head against her knees.

"What's this, love?"

All three of them were staring down at her, their startled faces meeting her sudden, silent tears.

"I'll deal here," Casey said. He sat down next to her, scanning her body quickly. "Want to tell me what you're on about?"

She couldn't even swallow, because of the invisible hand.

After a few minutes he began massaging her fingers.

"My friend, Emily, is getting married this weekend. She was one of the first girls I met in college. I wasn't sure of myself at first, so I was drawn to the more confident students, like Emily." She took a shaky breath. "She's a fiery redhead with a personality to match. She'll do anything, say anything. We all knew swear words, but she used them with more alacrity than anyone else. She kept all us 'earthlings' on edge, but it was exciting. She liked E words: When she met Morgan, her fiancé, she said she wasn't in love, she was 'enamored.'"

The tears were coming freely now, but she didn't move her hand away from his to wipe them. "She was spontaneous, outrageous, but she could plan. She and Morgan planned everything, every detail. An evening wedding, of course. They wanted to wait until he'd finished law school and she'd worked for a year, and it had to be past the worst of the summer heat but not too close to Thanksgiving. Rainbow dresses for the bridesmaids, so we could each wear a color we thought suited us."

Her voice broke. "She always took life by storm; she had no fear. I'd be afraid of her now. She'd have a word for me, some expletive."

Casey remembered an officer telling him that his actions on a particular mission had been "exemplary." A rare compliment: Exemplary behaviour was the expected norm.

"This police thing I'm involved in—it's taken on a life of its own. And my life is passing me by. It'll be too late to apply to graduate schools when I get out of here."

He hated the hopelessness. What had happened to the adventurous girl who had eaten the rattlesnake? But he knew—Scott had chewed her up and spit her out.

Finally she looked at him. "And you'll be moving on soon, you and Brian and Danny. Do you know when?"

He shook his head. "I don't choose my assignments."

CHAPTER 25

"Andrews said you wanted a word with me," Sinclair told Casey when he arrived at the flat.

"Yes, sir, a private word." He gestured toward his room, where he sat on the bed, leaving the chair for the boss. "Jenny's in a right state about her move. Some mornings she can't keep her breakfast down. She cries at night. It's not good for her."

"We're in a logjam at the moment, Sergeant. No decision has been taken."

"I may be able to help with that a bit, sir. She's been hard done by. I'd recommend strongly against any change of venue."

"This site is unacceptable to Witness Protection."

"Sir, I'm aware of the objections, but security improvements have been made. Do you really think Scott will expect coppers to put her up in Hampstead? As long as we stay low on the radar screen, we should be okay. Besides, any movement creates security risks."

"Sorry? 'We'?"

"If she's not ready to pack it in, then I suppose I'm not either, sir."

Sinclair glanced about the room. Smaller than Jenny's and even more bare. "Sergeant, this case may not come to trial for months, the construction of a new Crown Court notwithstanding."

"I've been on extended ops before. Besides, I promised her father I'd do it, or as good as."

Sinclair gave him a long look but did not remind him of his initial reluctance to serve.

"I have two recommendations," Casey continued. "The front door should be fortified with steel plates. And we'll need some regular short-term relief. Days only would do, sir."

"She'll be isolated; cut off from psychological help. She has to be able to testify."

"Sir, I've seen lads with combat stress. Most go back into action, but not until they've had a period to recover. I can't mend her inside, but keeping her moored should help."

"Will the others sign on?"

"I'll wager they will, but you'll have to ask them, sir."

"Sullivan?"

"He's good with her, sir."

"And Davies?"

"He's steady. Besides," he added with a smile, "he's a dab hand in the kitchen."

Sinclair was thinking aloud. "I'll have to run it by Graves; let him take the heat."

"There's one more thing, sir," Casey said. "A little opdec goes a long way."

"What are you suggesting, Sergeant?"

"If Scott and his scum are expecting a move, give them one, when the time is right."

Sinclair nodded slowly. He stood and held out his hand to Casey. "Thank you, Sergeant. Will you ask Sullivan to come in?"

Sullivan didn't hesitate to volunteer for the extended duty. "I'm learning a lot from Casey and Davies, sir. I'll stay on."

Davies considered the request. "I never fancied myself a protection officer," he admitted. "Thought the job was done when her father came. Sir, what's your best estimate of the length of the assignment?"

"Months, but not years—they're fast-tracking this case. However, no trial date has been set."

"We'll need some relief."

"It will be provided."

"If she can stick it, then I can as well. I'll not stand down until it's all over and done with."

"Tell Casey I'll get on to it then," Sinclair said, wondering if he could flatter his boss sufficiently to gain his amen.

CHAPTER 26

"Sergeant Casey!" Jenny called softly. He was on watch, but he didn't answer. She slipped out of bed and went to her door. "Sergeant Casey?"

"Something wrong?" He was coming out of the kitchen with a mug in his hand. With his lean, serious face, he looked like a Texas Ranger, minus the cowboy hat, string tie, and belt buckle.

"I can't sleep. I'm so worried about my move. It's bound to come soon. Do you know anything about it?"

He hadn't heard back from Sinclair since he'd told him of his intention to stay on. "Not a word." He set his mug down.

She peered in his cup. "You're drinking coffee," she exclaimed.

"Got used to it when I was in the service," he smiled. "Tea doesn't maintain its integrity in canteens."

"I didn't have any choice about coming here, remember?" she said. "You put me to sleep. What if they want you to do that again? What if I don't like the next place? I won't know where I am, and I don't have enough money to get home. And I don't know anybody, and—"

He put up his hands. "Full stop, Jenny." She'd put one of the sofa pillows in her lap and was kneading it with her fingers. Perhaps a good hot cuppa would slow her down. He went back into the kitchen.

She was waiting quietly when he returned. He'd never seen a woman in such a demure nightdress. Her trim little figure was lost in the long flannel. He set the steaming cup down in front of her and advised several slow sips.

"I'm afraid," she confessed after she'd tasted it. "Other people are making decisions for me. Mr. Sinclair said that I'd have a choice, but I don't know if I can believe him."

His coffee had cooled slightly, and he drained the cup in two long swallows. "He's working for you, not against you."

"Do you know that for a fact?" she pressed.

"Yes, love; but I can't tell you any more than that."

"Will it be soon?"

There was no response.

"Will I like it?"

He did not answer.

Tears were prickling her throat. "You wouldn't let them do anything bad to me, would you?"

"I'm on your side, Jenny," he said quietly but firmly.

It was no use interrogating that voice. She sipped her tea and tried to quell her nervousness and the myriad of questions she wanted to ask. She heard his mobile ring and saw him reach into his pocket.

"Casey."

It was Sinclair. "Is she about? I know it's late, but I'm just home."

"She's in the sitting room with me, sir."

"Two minutes."

Casey rose and went to the door, drawing his weapon in readiness. He admitted Sinclair and secured the door.

"I have news, Jenny. I wanted to tell you in person. Sergeant, you deserve to hear this." He looked down at her, and the delicate lace around the high collar on her nightdress seemed to emphasise her diminutive features. "I've received approval for your permanent placement. If it's acceptable to you, we'd like you to remain here."

She blinked rapidly at him but did not speak.

He sat down across from her. "There will be a few minor changes in security and personnel, but Casey, Davies, and Sullivan will remain as your primary protection officers. You should know that all three volunteered for the duration."

She looked at the tired man seated in front of her and felt a rush of regret that she had doubted him. "Oh," she breathed, "I'm so sorry—I'm so grateful—Colin, thank you. I can do this. Sergeant Casey, I don't know what to say—I can't tell you—Colin, did you say Brian and Danny, too?"

"Yes, Jenny.". He hadn't realised until this moment how very frightened she had been. And she'd called him Colin as if it were the most natural thing in the world.

"I won't let you down, Colin. I won't. Sergeant Casey, I'll do my best. I promise." She rose to her feet. Words didn't seem sufficient, but now that she was standing, she felt suddenly shy. Both men had risen, too, dwarfing her. She caught Colin's hand for a moment and felt its warmth. She turned to Casey and stood on her tiptoes to give a tentative kiss to his rough cheek.

They watched her go, her limp less pronounced, her bare feet quiet on the carpeted floor. "Well done, sir," Casey said. "Was there trouble at the top?"

"Not as much as I expected," Sinclair acknowledged. "The biggest snag was getting you. And there'll be periodic review. You'll let the others know?"

"If she doesn't first," Casey smiled.

CHAPTER 27

Jenny woke late, surprised by the slight queasy feeling in her stomach. She'd had fleeting nausea off and on for the last week, but now that she wasn't worried about having to move, it would probably pass.

She looked up at her battle flag. Had St. George been on foot or on horseback when he slew the dragon? He'd probably had a horse, but she'd have to do it on her own two feet. And he'd had a sword. Her words would be her only weapon.

Until the trial, this flat would be her only home. She'd have to find things to do or she'd go bananas. She needed some way to quell her fear, to stop "shaking in her shoes," as Gilbert and Sullivan put it. More music might help. Perhaps she should take up a hobby that would be time consuming, like calligraphy or sewing. She could design and produce an entire line of clothing with one sleeve larger than the other, for people to wear who had casts and didn't have an on-the-spot alterations expert like Sergeant Casey.

Brian was reading the newspaper in the sitting room when she came out. He surprised her, responding to her thanks with a lighthearted remark. "JJ, I'm not leaving until I teach you to like Brussels sprouts."

"Then you'll never get away," she laughed, warmed by the nickname.

Danny was next. She had expected a joke from him, but it wasn't forthcoming. "I wouldn't leave you, Sis."

She remembered that awful night in the hospital, after the man had tried to kill her. Danny hadn't left her then, either, and he hadn't even known her. There was a serious commitment beneath his banter. He hadn't joined the police for the fun and games.

Sergeant Casey was asleep, so she did her exercises after lunch. He seemed the same; in fact, all the men did. She was the only one who felt different. She watched while the three of them played poker. The terms weren't the same in England, and that and her poor concentration had put her at a disadvantage when she played with them. At first they had staked her with pence, but they had won their money back in no time. Then they had played for matchsticks and even small pieces of chocolate candy, which she had really hated losing. When they played without her, they played for serious money.

"Did you ever know any policemen before you met us?" Danny asked.

"No," she answered, "but when I was in Brownie Scouts—that's Girl Scouts for younger girls, Brian—we had a field trip to a police station. They locked us in a cell, and when the door clanged shut, we all screamed. That poor officer! It hurt my ears, and I was one of the ones screaming." She fingered some of the British coins while they talked. Sergeant Casey was winning, and he had a representative sample. All the coins had the Queen's profile on one side.

"We have sworn allegiance to her," Casey said.

Interesting. In the U.S., allegiance was sworn to the Constitution. "Why is the one-pound coin so much thicker than the others?"

"You can tell what it is without taking it out of your pocket," Brian answered.

"The two-pound coin is fancier," she observed. It was a two-tone coin with a series of capital letters around the edge: DEI GRA FID DEF REG. "I haven't had Latin since high school, but the first one means 'of God,' I think."

"No, that's the last part," Danny said. "REG—for Queen—comes first. Read them in reverse order, and you'll get it." He had folded his hand. It was between Brian and Sergeant Casey now.

"Queen—Defender—Faith or Faithful—Grace—of God," she guessed.

"Queen, the defender of the faith, by the grace of God," Danny said. "I had Latin, too."

"I call you," Brian said. Casey laid his cards down.

She watched Brian sweep up his winnings. It was amazing that those huge hands could mince onions.

CHAPTER 28

Everything about Jenny's trip to the hospital was cloudy in her mind. It was time for her cast to be removed, Sergeant Casey said, and he wanted to give her some medication to ease her nerves. She tried to tell him she didn't need it, but he spoke to her in his insistent voice so she swallowed the tablets as instructed. She had expected to be curious about seeing things outside, but it was long after dark when they left, and she was very sleepy. All three men were armed and dressed for cold weather; she wrapped a blanket around her shoulders and huddled in the back seat. The drive seemed to take forever, and she had no idea whether the flat was a long way from the hospital or the driver had followed a very indirect route.

Colin and Sergeant Andrews were waiting at the casualty entrance. They had a wheelchair for her, and she was glad. It had been a long walk down the flights of stairs from the flat to the street, and Casey had been impatient with her. Sergeant Andrews pushed her straight through the double doors and into an examining room, the other men on either side of her.

She sat under the bright lights on the treatment table, her shoulders sagging, and waited to be called for her x-ray. The room was small, so only Colin and Sergeant Casey waited with her. The others stood watch outside.

After the radiographer had finished, she lay down. Dr. Adams' entrance woke her. He was brisk, as usual, giving her an examination and questioning Casey about her condition at the same time. "You're healing beautifully," he told her, and she smiled sleepily at his stock phrase. "No need for you to tote this thing about any longer." The saw wasn't loud, and she found that if she closed her eyes, she didn't worry about it cutting into her skin.

"The itching under the cast drove me crazy," she told the doctor while he worked. She wanted to ask him if she could be pregnant, but she was never alone with him.

Then it was back to the wheelchair and into the van. She slumped against Brian. Finally they were back among the narrow streets and dark houses. "Stand by," Casey told Davies.

"Clear," Sullivan said.

"I can walk," she said wearily.

"Not fast enough," Casey said. His hand was on his gun, and his eyes scanned the street. "Take her now, Davies."

CHAPTER 29

Time passed slowly, and Jenny was often lonely, even in an apartment full of men. She felt more secure with them than she had at first, but her fear symptoms hadn't abated. If anything, they were worse, coming upon her suddenly and with an intensity she had expected to fade. Sometimes she woke from a nightmare not sure where she was. And not having a period had become a nagging worry. Was there an embryo inside her, growing like a cancer? How could she find out? What would happen if she put *pregnancy test* on the grocery list?

Desperate for distraction, she suggested that they celebrate Movie Week. She asked each of them to think of his favorite movie, explaining that they could rent the video, pop popcorn, and eat chocolate bars. Danny laughed at the way she always tried to bring chocolate into everything, but the movie idea didn't work very well. Casey said he had been away on extended missions, he wouldn't say where, and he couldn't remember any recent films except *Lawrence of Arabia*, which had been reissued the previous year. Brian liked the James Bond films but couldn't think of any specific titles. Danny couldn't think of a favourite, either, but said he'd look for *Men in Black* since he liked science fiction. Somehow an air of enthusiasm was lacking.

Movie Week was followed by War Week, Jenny regretting her movie idea. She was disturbed by all the scenes of men dying violent deaths. The blood on screen reminded her of her own wounds, and her dreams reflected her distress. The monster was standing over her, his hands on his belt, his face a dreadful mixture of anger and anticipation. He struck her, and she screamed. She woke suddenly. She was in her bed at the flat, and Sergeant Casey was there. She hugged Colin's blanket to her chest. "Sergeant Casey, did you ever think you were going to die?"

He didn't reply.

"People probably think that when you're dying, the fear blocks everything else. Or the pain. But it doesn't override everything."

He was still quiet.

"It ought to be a gift, a good thing, that you still have senses left when you're close to death. Maybe if you're dying in the arms of someone who loves you, it is a gift. Maybe seeing with such intensity that it will last forever—"

"Get to it, Jenny." It was The Voice, but throttled back.

"It's still so vivid. I had never really begged for anything in my life, the way I begged him to stop. But he didn't. All my senses went into overdrive. It was cold in that room, but my blood was warm. I felt his fingers digging into my thighs. He needed to trim his nails; they were sharp. The salt from my tears made the cut on my cheek sting. I remember his smell, not of his aftershave, but of his sweat."

"And in hospital?"

"It was the *same.* Another small room. Another violent man. I was in pain, and I couldn't get away. It happened very fast at first. I saw his eyes, cold and hard, darker than walnuts—I screamed—I saw the syringe—Danny hit him with his nightstick. Then—then—" She choked on her words.

"Steady on, Jenny."

"His hand was on my throat, and time slowed down. He had large pores on his face and a network of blood vessels under his skin. He was trying to squeeze the life out of me, and it was an eternity before Danny pulled him off." She brushed her fingers across her cheeks. A terrible fear gripped her chest. What did he think of her now? She shouldn't have said anything.

"It was bitterly cold," he said quietly. "Windy as hell. There were four of us. I was the team medic. We'd almost made it to the extraction point. We'd been moving fast, and we were well tired. My Bergen—my pack—was heavy, and my sides hurt from the exertion. One of my mates—behind me—was hit. I turned to grab him. Took a couple rounds in my thigh. Laid it open."

The scar he had shown her. The fear in her chest rose, and a single sob escaped her.

"I fell backward, onto the frame of my pack. There was steam rising from the wound in my leg, and the grains of sand that blew against my skin felt like needles. I had a cramp in my calf I couldn't relieve, because I couldn't straighten my leg or bend my ankle."

"Who took care of you?"

"I did, until I passed out. I slipped out of my pack and managed to get my kit. It was a nasty, dirty wound."

"What happened to the other man?" She held her breath.

Casey paused. "He should've been quicker."

"Oh, God." She felt her stomach turn over. "How did you—does it ever go away?"

"Not completely, no. It gets better, but there's no quick fix." He frowned at her expression. "Are you all right?"

"My stomach feels funny."

He'd drowned his sorrows in a pub sharing countless pints with a mate, but he couldn't offer that to her. "Time for tea."

This whole nation would suffer terminal withdrawal without tea. She took Colin's blanket with her into the kitchen and watched him heat the water. "How do you keep going?"

"Focus on the mission. And always keep training. Sometimes on long missions you have to work to keep the edge."

"Is that why you brought me those weights?"

"I'm changing the purpose of your exercises—from physical therapy to physical readiness."

"Promise? You're not just tormenting me?"

"Physical conditioning prepares you for mental challenges. You'll have to be alert in court. In order to be ready then, you need to start now."

He filled their cups. The warmth melted the shards of ice in her chest and soothed her stomach. "Did you learn all this in the Royal Marines?"

"Much of it. My medical training began there."

"Was it hard, what you had to do?"

"They kept us busy."

Typical Sergeant Casey understatement. "Were you ever afraid?"

"We called it apprehension," he smiled.

"Why did you leave?"

"After I was injured, I couldn't regain combat readiness. I wanted it, but I couldn't do it."

"So—an injury prevented you from going back to the way you were," she said slowly. "Sounds like me. My life has been changed forever by what I've experienced. I can't imagine going to graduate school now. Become absorbed in the study of fictional characters? I don't think so."

"Texas, then?"

"I don't know. My family lives in such an innocent world. It's hard to see myself fitting in there." She smiled. "I know—no quick fix."

They sat together finishing their tea in companionable silence.

"I'm sorry I was so afraid of you at first."

"Nothing to be sorry for. We expected it. Trust is earned, love."

"It certainly is," she agreed.

- -

In the morning she was putting on her exercise clothes when she heard an unfamiliar voice. The man it belonged to was too short to be Brian and too wide to be Danny. Besides, he had curly blond hair. When he turned around, she saw that his eyebrows were curly, too, and they gave his ruddy face a look of surprise. She hadn't been expecting anyone, and it startled her.

"PC Wilcox," the man said. "Joseph Wilcox. Didn't mean to scare you, Miss."

"I'm Jenny. Just Jenny."

"Nice to know you, Just Jenny."

"Tea?" Danny asked. "I'll be the mum."

"No, my stomach's upset. I'll have a Coke."

Danny poured cups for Wilcox and himself. "Davies took a short leave this morning," he said. "I'll take off when he gets back. Wilcox is going to fill in for both of us."

She tried to smile. "What dastardly thing did you do to receive this assignment?"

"Four days with a lovely lass? It's winning the lottery, isn't it?"

Wilcox's voice had a lilt to it. She didn't know enough about regional accents to place it, but it was relaxing to hear. Chivalry was not dead: He had called her lovely, and no one looked lovely in sweatpants. "Are you qualified to do this?" she asked him. "You need to be a poor poker player, a good listener, have an endless supply of handkerchiefs, and—"

"No one's as poor a poker player as you are, Sis," Danny teased. "Give the bloke a chance!"

Wilcox leant forward. He reached toward her cheek, the unmarked one, with a closed hand. She tensed, but he didn't touch her. "There's a little something already!" He held a fifty pence coin in his fingers.

"Magic," she breathed. "We could sure use some of that around here."

CHAPTER 30

Wilcox's four day shifts passed quickly. He entertained Jenny with his magic and his accent. Really, it was more than an accent—he was from Wales, and he spoke whole sentences which were unintelligible to her, all while remaining alert and armed.

Several days later it was Sergeant Casey's turn to be gone, and another new man arrived. She couldn't guess Sergeant Nick Howard's age. He had thick brows and dark hair receding slightly at the temples. There was no gray, but his lean face was weathered, with a myriad of fine lines around his eyes and the corners of his mouth. She was uncomfortable with his dark stare and couldn't get a conversation going with him. When she asked where he was from, he replied, "No place in particular. And I go where I'm sent."

"What do you tell people when you arrest them? 'I'm Nick, and you're nicked'?"

Howard did not laugh. Perhaps to compensate for his lack of humour, Danny declared it Comedy Week and rented funny movies. Like Gilbert and Sullivan, Monty Python made fun of established customs and rituals, and some of the characters had as much dialogue as a G&S patter song. However, many of the skits embarrassed her with their frankness about sex and bodily functions. She escaped to her room.

She could hear Danny and Brian laughing, but she had been infected with Sergeant Howard's sober demeanor. She could no longer ignore the fact that she might be pregnant. It was too much to bear—like having a second and then a third wave crash over you when you hadn't regained your footing from the first. The beating she'd received at the hands of the monster and his violations of her had crushed her. Now she might be carrying his child. What could she do? Was abortion legal in England? How could she arrange for one? Was it too late? Did she even want an abortion? No, she didn't think she could go through with it. She didn't want anyone touching her below the waist, not even a doctor.

What would happen to her? Would the police buy her maternity clothes? No, they wouldn't want her—how effective would she be in court if her belly crowded the witness stand? What if she went into labor during the trial?

She cried until she tired herself out.

- -

In the morning Howard was back, and so were her apprehensions. Did she look fatter already? How long could she hide her condition from the men? Casey would feel contempt for her. A good and decent man like Brian would never respect her. Danny wouldn't be able to find anything funny to say. And Colin: He was too elegant to listen to another sordid tale. She couldn't go home—Colin hadn't told her parents she'd been sexually assaulted, and neither had she. If a long-standing boyfriend had gotten her pregnant, they wouldn't be happy. If pregnancy had resulted from a casual encounter, that would be worse. But being impregnated by a criminal? Inconceivable.

When Sergeant Casey returned and learned she'd had only a Coke and a few biscuits to eat, he demanded to know why. Davies and Sullivan were clueless—they'd been watching comedies all day. "Howard's a bit formidable," Sullivan ventured.

Casey found her already in bed. "You have to eat."

"Are you going to make me?"

"If I have to."

She managed to get down part of a baked potato before turning off the lamp by her bed.

In the morning she felt a terrible weight on her chest, and the ghosts from the night haunted her. She'd dreamed she'd been watching *Rosemary's Baby* on late-night TV, but she had taken the place of Rosemary. *She'd* been the one who'd been raped by a monster. *She* was the one who'd become pregnant.

She couldn't keep down the breakfast Sergeant Casey brought, but she had no other kinds of discomfort to report to him. He pronounced her vital signs normal.

Rosemary's baby. What would happen to *her* baby? She couldn't keep it, but if she gave it up for adoption, some innocent family would be cursed with the devil's child. Better if it were never born. Better if it died. Better if she died.

- -

Sinclair was concerned by Casey's call. Not one to overact, Casey had described Jenny's situation as "worrying." She was withdrawn. Didn't dress. Wasn't eating. Wanted sedation. Cried until it took effect.

"She was functioning, sir, until the last day or two," Casey reported when Sinclair arrived.

"Could she have become upset by the change in personnel?"

"She adjusted to Wilcox. According to Sullivan, she kept out of Howard's way, but there was no conflict."

Sinclair was impatient to speak with her. "How long has she been in the shower?"

"Too long," Casey realised. He and Sinclair walked into her bedroom. The bathroom door was locked.

A catalogue of dire possibilities flashed across Sinclair's mind. "Let's have it down," he said. All it took was Casey's well-placed kick to break through. When he yanked the shower curtain aside, they saw her huddled at one end of the bath.

Sinclair put a towel over her shoulders and lifted her out of the water. It didn't cover her enough, so he took off his coat and wrapped it around her. "There's no blood."

"Let's get her in bed, and I'll have a look." Casey stepped close to the bed and opened Sinclair's coat briefly, revealing the pale skin and soft swell of her breasts. The left bore no scar, no evidence that she had been defiled so cruelly. Her face reflected the same before-and-after contrast, the pure, smooth, unmarred cheek on one side and Scott's signature on the other. "No new injuries," he said.

Sinclair sat down on the edge of the bed and took her hand, hoping to create a connection, a bridge, that she could cross. "Will you let me help?"

"You can't," she whispered.

"I want to try. What is it you want? Tell me, Jenny."

The silence lasted so long he wasn't sure an answer was coming.

"I want to sleep without dreams, dreams that are real."

"I can't grant that wish, Jenny," Sinclair said softly.

"I want to turn the clock back, before all this happened. Before the scars, before the shame. When my body belonged to me." She was lying on her side, her tears pooling on the bridge of her nose before spilling over.

Sinclair and Casey waited, neither sure what to do next. They could hear Davies and Sullivan talking in the kitchen, something being set on the counter, a cabinet being closed.

"Why did you take a shower?"

"To wash the monster away, but I can't. He's inside me. I can't get him out."

"Jenny, you're safe from him. You're alive. And I believe God preserved your life for a reason."

"For this? How could He? *How could He?* Damn Him! I don't even believe in Him!"

"Jenny, God is there whether we believe in Him or not. When we can't speak with anyone else, we can speak with Him. He's where we turn when we come to the end of the road."

"It's a dead end road."

"No, Jenny. I don't believe that. Choose life, the life God has for you."

As the mother of the monster's child? She shook her head very slowly. "Not this life."

"We need you, Jenny," Sinclair said.

"What about what I need? Sergeant, will you help me? I can't hold on any longer. Please..."

Casey retrieved his kit, ready to give her the tablets.

"That's not strong enough," she objected. "Or fast enough."

"You want a jab?" She'd never requested an injection before.

"I want you to knock me out."

He looked at Sinclair for permission. At Sinclair's nod, he filled a syringe.

The cold alcohol was a shock, but the sting was welcome, because she knew oblivion would follow. "To sleep, perchance to dream."

"No, Jenny!" Sinclair protested. "Not that sort of dream. Not Hamlet's."

"I'm sorry," she whispered.

When her eyes closed, Sinclair rose to his feet. "I have an unpleasant task to do, and I could use your help, Sergeant." He opened the door to her wardrobe. "A search of her personal spaces is in order."

"What are we looking for, sir?"

"Anything that could be dangerous to her. That line she quoted—when Hamlet said it, he was contemplating suicide."

Sinclair examined the contents of the closet, including the luggage. He checked every pocket in the neatly-folded clothes in her chest of drawers. Casey was equally thorough in her bathroom and bedside table. They found no loose razor blades but did confiscate her shaver and nail scissors.

"Any medicines here, even over-the-counter ones?" Sinclair asked.

"I keep everything," the sergeant replied.

"Brief Davies, if you will. I'll want him to be vigilant if she comes into the kitchen." He looked at her sleeping form. He knew he couldn't provide any comfort to her, but he was loath to leave. Strangely, he thought he might be comforted *by* her, by seeing her chest rise and fall, much the way watching his ill father breathing had given him solace. It had, however, not brought hope. Life was the first and most important step, the foundation for all the rest, but only the first step. A beating heart, a sustaining breath, these were only the beginning. What did the human spirit need to survive? Faith. Hope. Love. A reason for living. Whatever the cause of her upset, he must get to the bottom of it. He rang Dr. Knowles and arranged to bring him to the protection flat in the morning.

CHAPTER 31

When Sinclair and Knowles were admitted to the flat, Knowles took a moment to survey the surroundings. The flat was a bit dingy and dark with the curtains drawn; not a beneficial environment for a troubled young woman. PC Davies was rugby size. Sullivan was younger and quite a bit shorter, with a friendly face. Casey's was lean and stern—hardly the sort to confide in. Jenny's bedroom had a British flag on one wall. What looked like family photos were displayed on the chest of drawers.

"Jenny, I've brought someone to talk with you. This is Dr. Knowles," Sinclair said. She was wearing the nightshirt with the torn sleeve. His coat was nowhere to be seen.

"Sergeant, I'd like you to stand by," Knowles said. He sat down next to the bed. "I'm a psychiatrist, Jenny." He noted the shadows under her eyes.

Jenny saw a slender man with a placid expression, round nose, and graying hair. The lines in his face looked like laugh lines, and that made her feel terribly sad, because she couldn't remember anymore what it felt like to laugh.

"I realise there's a big difference between the absence of fear and the presence of trust, but perhaps together we can bridge that gap." He waited for a reaction.

Was she supposed to say something? She couldn't think.

"I know rather more about you than most patients I meet for the first time, and I'm sorry about that. I'd have preferred for us to start on an equal footing." He knew her history, and Sinclair had briefed him on her recent behaviour.

"Are you a medical doctor?"

"Yes, I completed medical school before choosing to specialise in psychiatry. I understand how severe your injuries were, both physical and psychological."

"I didn't know it was possible to hurt that much and still live."

"Are you in pain now?"

"I need Sergeant Casey. He puts me to sleep, like a vet putting down a dog, only I wake up."

"Listen to the doctor, Jenny." Casey's voice was firm.

"What's the point?"

"To ease the anguish you're feeling," Knowles answered.

"Are you going to put me in the hospital?"

"I'd rather treat you here, if you'll let me."

"It's no use."

Knowles wasn't discouraged. "What can you tell me about how you're feeling?"

How much could she tell him? Colin and Sergeant Casey were both there. Nothing she said would be confidential. "My stomach's been upset."

"That could be a result of anxiety. Are you afraid for yourself?" According to Colin, nothing had happened that would affect her safety, but her perception of it was what mattered.

She didn't answer.

"Are you missing your family? Colin told me that you didn't go home when your father came. Staying was a very courageous thing to do."

"Courage had nothing to do with it. I was afraid to go. I didn't want to put them in danger."

"Jenny, sometimes we take decisions we regret, or circumstances change and the decision we took is no longer right for us. Do you want to go home?"

"No. I'm different now. I'm tainted."

She doesn't want to be with her loved ones. A result of shame? "Jenny, shame is a normal consequence of sexual attack."

Shame wasn't the worst consequence. "Why didn't he kill me? Why did I live when other women didn't? Didn't he get better at killing? They should have lived, and I should have died."

Her most animated discourse thus far, and the subject was death. "Jenny, what you're feeling is survivor guilt. It's a symptom of your trauma, and it's unjustified. You are not responsible for the deaths of the others."

"There's no way out."

"Jenny, why do you feel hopeless? Are you feeling helpless?" He saw her face close. "Would you tell me why you're so sad?"

She slid down under the covers.

"Is there anything you'd like to tell me? To ask me?"

She turned her face away.

Somehow he'd lost her. He stood. "I'll see you soon, Jenny."

Davies and Sullivan were waiting in the sitting room. "How's Jenny?" Sullivan asked. "We've been off our heads about her."

"Still on crisis."

"Sir, how serious is this? Is she—" Davies didn't want to say the word.

"Suicidal? Why do you ask? Has she given away her possessions?"

"She's hardly got any possessions," Davies said.

Knowles nodded. "There are some indicators, but I'll be working to shift the balance a bit. In the meantime I'd recommend restricting her access to all medications."

Casey had followed him out of the bedroom. "I have everything," he said. "Even the paracetamol."

"And one of us is always with her," Sullivan added.

"Anything else we can do?" Casey asked.

"Yes. Continue to check her vital signs. Be alert for any change in coherence. Don't push her too hard to eat; liquids are more important. But I'd like you to withhold any sedatives. She wants to sleep, but I want her to feel whatever is causing this. Perhaps then she'll be more likely to disclose it."

CHAPTER 32

Sinclair and Knowles headed to Hampstead Station. "It's a rather dismal place," Knowles mused, "and I don't imagine your officers provide much emotional support. I didn't see fear or anger—mostly shame and despair. That concerns me. She may equate anger with loss of control, the loss of control her attacker demonstrated. Shame is safer but more difficult to treat. Have there been any changes in the case which could have upset her?"

"Stark and Michalopolous, Scott's accomplices, were bailed and released. The charges against them weren't sufficient for remand. But she wasn't told. The men censor the newspapers so she isn't aware of the media attention the Scott case is receiving."

"Then something else precipitated this. The best therapy occurs when good training and a strong relationship meet. I don't have the relationship yet, but it often takes more than one session for any sort of trust to develop."

"We found that to be true in the interview process," Sinclair commented. "We weren't successful in getting her to speak with us initially."

"Tomorrow afternoon then?" Knowles inquired. "I'm booked until three."

"I'll meet you here and escort you."

At the flat Jenny sipped a little Coke. Her stomach was still queasy from time to time, and the Coke seemed to settle it. She wished she could sleep, but the cold-hearted Sergeant Casey wouldn't give her anything. As time passed, the air grew thicker and heavier, almost like a fog, and the constant presence of the men ceased to register.

The pain started as a cramp low in her stomach, where she thought the baby was, an annoying dull ache that wouldn't go away. Danny was sitting with her, but she said nothing, trying instead to find a position that was more comfortable. Gradually the pain grew and found focus, becoming sharper and broader, insisting on being noticed. She asked Danny for a cup of hot tea, but it didn't help the throbbing. She broke out in a sweat and brought her knees up to her chest.

"She's restless," Sullivan reported to Casey.

She was doubled up when Casey went in. "What's this?" he asked.

"Hurts. Like knots being tightened in my belly," she gasped.

"Where exactly? Near your navel or below?" He lifted her nightshirt. No swelling. She didn't feel feverish. He felt through her knickers. No tenderness in the lower right quadrant. Not appendicitis then.

"Any pain when you piss?"

"No, it isn't any of that!"

"Then what the bloody hell is it?"

"I'm bleeding! I think I'm having a miscarriage! Do something!"

He wasted no time. "Davies! I need you now. Sullivan, take the watch." When Davies arrived, Casey took sterile gloves out of his kit. "Hold her still," he said.

Davies put the flat of one hand on her chest and restrained her hands with the other. He could not stop her screams.

Sullivan came running. "What's going on?"

"Give us a minute," Casey growled. His knife cut through her knickers like a scalpel.

Davies felt her whole body shudder when Casey examined her.

"I don't know much about women medically," Casey said, "but you're not aborting. Bleeding's not heavy enough. Must be your menstrual period. I'll treat you for the pain."

She was shaking and sobbing so hard Davies wasn't certain she'd be able to get the tablets down.

"How could you?" she cried. "How could you?"

Casey was stunned. "I did the right thing," he said with an edge to his voice.

"You call what you did *right?*"

"I placed your security first, yes."

"You were keeping me *secure?*"

"I was quick. I didn't hurt you."

"Didn't hurt me? You bastard! You raped me!"

"I never did!" he yelled, recoiling in shock and outrage. "Damn it, Jenny! You're bloody minded! Daft! You've got it all wrong—it was medical!"

"I couldn't stop you," she sobbed.

"Bloody hell!" he swore. "Jenny, look at me!"

Oh God, it was The Voice. If she didn't obey, there was no telling what he'd do.

"Don't—you—know—me?" he demanded.

She kept her eyes on his clenched fists. "I know you're really angry," she stammered.

He slammed his fist into his open palm, and she jumped. "Damn right! False accusation like that? If you were a man, I'd take you down!" He noted her white face and forced himself to speak more deliberately. "Jenny, I don't hurt women. Certainly not frightened little rabbits like you. If I'd wanted to grope you, I'd not have used gloves." He nodded at Davies. "Make Jenny a cuppa. Sweet."

Davies brought a cup for Casey also. "JJ, I know you're frightened, but there are some things you need to understand about Casey. He's treated men far from modern medical facilities. He was trained to be decisive, to do what had to be done as expeditiously as possible. There wasn't time for niceties."

"*Niceties?* He cut off my panties with his—his Bowie knife!"

"Jenny, listen to me. I used the quickest method. I did what I had to do. We're all here because you're doing what you have to do. You and

I—we're cut from the same cloth."

She hated it when he used her name; it was always bad news. "I don't scare people."

"You will," he said with a measured tone. "When you testify, the man who hurt you is going to be very afraid."

She looked back at him for the first time. His gaze didn't waver. "Stop using that voice!" she cried. "It's like a wall I can't break through, and I feel so alone!"

"You put the wall up, love. You have to take it down."

"Oh, you've turned the spigot on now," she said, tearing up at the word "love" and the gentle tone he used when he said it. She wept because she was in pain, because these men knew intimate things about her, and because she was exhausted. She wept because the fog of fear was still inside her, though dormant, like cool yeast.

"There's a difference between anger and violence, Jenny. It's time you learnt it."

"You were in the military," she countered.

"I have never fired a weapon solely in anger. My military service taught me to channel my aggression."

She didn't know what to say. His action had seemed aggressive to her.

"Anger's a feeling, Jenny. That's all it is."

"The monster's anger nearly killed me."

"No, his violence did that. Violence is an action, often uncontrolled, like the hurricanes you've talked about. Violence results in injury. Anger doesn't have to lead to violence. People get angry all the time, but they don't harm each other."

"Sergeant Casey—it's not an excuse, but—I was hurting so badly—and I was nearly naked—and Brian could see—and then it got worse, when you—" She stopped. "I was scared out of my mind."

"That's about right," he said. "Jenny, I had to rule out spontaneous abortion. That would have required immediate hospitalisation. Instead your body's working the way it's supposed to."

Sullivan had joined them. "Casey's action minimised your risk," he added. "When we took you to hospital to have your cast looked after, we planned well in advance. The time of day, the transport we used, having a treatment room available for you—every detail was prearranged. Taking you on short notice, in traffic, with medical personnel unknown to us, who hadn't been briefed—you can see how dodgy that would have been, can't you?"

"But Danny—"

"We've no transport, Sis. An ambulance would have taken you to the closest hospital. Bad for our security. And there's one more thing. If I'm ever hurt, I hope that Casey or someone like him will treat me fast. I don't give a toss what anybody sees."

Casey's medicine was beginning to bring her pain under control. She didn't need a sedative to sleep.

"She could charge you with indecent assault, mate," Davies told Casey later. "She didn't consent. And if Sinclair hears of this, he'll relieve the lot of us."

"Acceptable risks," Casey replied.

CHAPTER 33

When Dr. Knowles returned with Sinclair to the protection flat, he was surprised to see Jenny waiting in the sitting room, Sergeant Casey beside her. She was not completely dressed, however—covered only by a long robe of some sort—and there were lines of exhaustion in her face. A short session then. "Has something changed since yesterday?" he asked.

Casey wanted to control the flow of information. "Her monthly began last night."

"Why is that something I need to know?" Knowles asked.

"Because it had been so long—too long—weeks and weeks—"

"She thought she was pregnant," Casey interrupted.

"Jenny, weren't you told? You were given a drug at hospital to prevent pregnancy. It's standard operating procedure for rape victims," Sinclair said.

"Then all that worry—all that fear—it was for nothing?" She began to cry.

"I'm so sorry," Sinclair soothed. "There never was any possibility of pregnancy."

"I've never had a period hurt like that before. I didn't know what was happening!"

Emotions which had been blunted the day before were evident now, Knowles noted. A result of desperation? "Jenny, a woman's cycle can be disrupted by stress in any number of ways."

"Do we have to talk about this?"

"I'll leave you to it," Casey said and left.

"You didn't feel you could ask your protection officers? Or Colin?" Knowles persisted.

"Ask them what? 'What are the symptoms of pregnancy?' They're all guys!"

"Are you feeling isolated then?"

"I'm like Edvard Munch's screaming woman. Are you familiar with that painting? Her face is featureless except for her gaping mouth."

"And no one can hear her cries. Are you crying inside, Jenny, where no one can hear?"

"Inside and out," she sobbed, accepting Colin's handkerchief. "The monster's still here. Imprinted. He's in my pores."

"Monster?" Knowles turned to Sinclair.

"Scott," Sinclair answered.

"Jenny, Munch's woman is part of a landscape in upheaval. Do you feel insecure here?"

"Sort of," she answered, thinking of Casey's examination. "They're men, and I don't know what they'll do. The only thing I'm sure of is gravity—when I fall, I always go down." She twisted the handkerchief in her hands.

"It's my understanding that they volunteered for extended duty. That would seem to indicate a strong desire to help."

"But they can't! No one can."

"Why have you lost hope, Jenny?"

"Because I feel so lost! I can't change what happened. I've turned into a person I don't know, a despicable person. I belong in unconsecrated ground."

"Jenny, if I may—I think you're grieving. You've had a succession of serious losses. Innocence—independence—even identity."

"I'm not the person I was. He took it all away! And I can't get over it."

"There's no timetable on grief, Jenny. Sometimes grief is more intense, sometimes less so, but when you've had a significant loss, it never leaves you completely. Once you have grieved, it will always be a part of your experience."

She wiped her cheeks. "That doesn't sound like good news."

Knowles smiled gently. "Repeated shocks have worn you down, but you're going to come through. I won't lie to you and tell you that someday you'll forget. It just won't always hurt so much to remember."

"Hemingway said, 'The world breaks everyone, and afterward some are stronger at the broken places.' But I'm not."

"It's early days yet. You're doing much better than you think you are, actually. Let me tell you what I see: a very brave young woman, isolated from her support system, who is struggling to cope."

Sinclair realised he hadn't been a very good liaison officer. He'd have to call round more often.

"But you're rational. You're not without resources; you only need to use them. You have confused reality and memory a bit—reality and memory are not the same. I know your memories are powerful and frightening, but they refer to events past." He stood. "We'll speak more about grief the next time we meet, but let me leave you with two thoughts. First, grief has a purpose, always, although it may not become apparent for some time. Second, grief changes you. I'd be willing to wager that you're more protective of others because you've suffered."

She looked at her hands. She hadn't protected Colin's handkerchief—she'd mangled it.

Before he left, Knowles had a word with the men, explaining that the feared pregnancy had compounded her shame and emphasising the importance of reassurance and acceptance. "A burden has been lifted, but desperation and some suicidal ideation are still present. Talk with her. Listen to her," he instructed. "And Colin—I need more time with her. She's too upset to appear at court anytime in the near future."

"I can't face it," she told Casey later that evening. "Dr. Knowles—Colin—all of you can walk away. I can't get out of my skin, even when I sleep."

"I can help with that." Knowles had given permission for him to administer sedatives as needed.

"If I weren't so weak, I wouldn't need it."

"It's not weakness, it's trauma that's the cause of this. Knowles doesn't want you to have nightmares tonight, and neither do I."

She knew the routine. She turned on her side and closed her eyes while he moved her nightwear out of the way to give the injection. "I feel like the beach after a storm—trash and rubble everywhere."

"Beaches have beautiful things on them as well," he said. "Storm waves wash up shells and driftwood. You didn't live far from the water. Did you go to the beach with your family when you were growing up?"

"My dad liked crabbing. I liked finding sand dollars. It was rare, but sometimes I'd find one that wasn't broken. And we all cooled off in the water. I liked to go way out, beyond the breakers."

"You'll have those fun times again, love."

She shook her head. "No, with my scars I'll never wear a swimsuit as long as I live. Someone would call the police—indecent exposure."

He had to smile. Caustic humour. A sign of resilience. He respected that.

CHAPTER 34

"I love my morning cuppa," she told Danny in the morning. "I'm so sorry we dumped your tea in Boston Harbor."

"When did you do that?" he asked.

"1773. Big moment in American history. What's on today's schedule?"

"Flower arranging. I bought these for you," he held up a bouquet, "but I don't know what to do with them."

"I'm a novice myself." She removed one of the delicate petals, rubbing her fingers across its softness. What the monster had done—would she ever get over it? No. She removed another petal. No. Would she learn to feel comfortable with these men? Yes. No. Yes. Would she be able to testify? No. Yes? The table was covered with petals; she had stripped every stem.

Her sessions with Dr. Knowles continued. He encouraged her to accept that being affected by the significant losses she had suffered was not a fault but the normal reaction of a caring and capable individual. Likewise, the ability to accept help was an important factor in healing, not a defect or deficiency. He agreed that she couldn't change her past, but he challenged her to focus on what she could change in her future and how the officers who protected her could assist. The most difficult issue she faced was the shame she felt. Over and over Dr. Knowles stressed that there was a difference between what had happened to her and letting it become a part of her. One led to anger and the other to shame.

During the long afternoons she began to read a book on grief that Dr. Knowles had given her. According to the author, grief was a process, meaning she couldn't stay the same and she couldn't go back. That was good, but the idea that grief couldn't be rushed bothered her because she wanted so badly to put her sad feelings behind her. The chapter on the emotions of grief described far more than sadness, however: fear, anxiety, bitterness, helplessness, and dread. Anger—rage—was an important step, the chapter concluded, but she was afraid to open that Pandora's box.

She put the book down. Somehow the monster had assassinated her self-concept, causing her to reexamine everything she had previously felt to be true about herself. In a very important sense she was starting over. Perhaps if she'd grieved as a child, she'd know how to do it as an adult, but when the family dog had died, her parents had simply replaced it, bypassing the time for tears. She suddenly recalled a line from Elizabeth Barrett Browning's famous poem: "I love thee with the passion put to use / In my old griefs…" Passion as intense as grief? "Throw me in that briar patch!" she said to her empty room.

After dinner Colin came by. No tie—so he wasn't working. Finally a chance for a conversation that didn't center on her problems! The author of the grief book recommended expressing sad feelings to others, but she didn't want to go on and on about hers, and besides, she discussed them with Dr. Knowles. So she asked Colin to tell her something about himself.

He was from Kent, about three hours southeast of London. His father had been in the diplomatic corps, but he wanted to live in England, not abroad, so he hadn't considered a career in the foreign service. He had attended university and then applied at the police academy, wanting a practical, useful profession. His job performance had been good, and he had progressed through the requisite courses and examinations to his current rank. He liked detective work because it allowed him to use his reasoning skills. "Unlike jigsaw puzzles, not all the pieces of information collected in an investigation fit. I look for the relationship between the pieces."

"Like word association questions on exams—deciding which word doesn't belong."

"Exactly. Forensic police are often called upon to conduct what we call 'fingertip searches' of a site. I like to think that my mental scrutiny is every bit as thorough and painstaking."

On the personal side, he was divorced, but he had a sister who was married with small children. His mother lived near Ashford. "It's beautiful there, but I don't get down very often. Demands of the Job and all that."

"I owe you an apology, Colin. I criticized you for caring more about my testimony than about me, but I've benefited from your concern, no matter what motivated it. Your agenda isn't hidden, and it isn't too different from mine."

"Jenny, you're being too hard on yourself. You've no reason for regret." He hoped this chat and the others to come would cement his rapport with her; she had a long road ahead. Emotional involvement with a victim or a victim's family was unwise, but a certain amount of caring—he preferred to call it commitment—provided welcome motivation when days of drudgery occurred. Every investigation had its own ebb and flow. Odd how the commission of a crime—usually an event not overlong in nature—could spawn such complex and interminable consequences for so many.

CHAPTER 35

Colin brought postcards of St. Paul's Cathedral, the Cabinet War Rooms, and the Imperial War Museum on his next visit. As usual, he was full of interesting facts about the sites, particularly St. Paul's, mentioning the memorial to American servicemen who were killed in World War II as well as the tombs of famous Britons, like the poet John Donne; the architect of the cathedral, Sir Christopher Wren; and Admiral Nelson. Nelson, who was killed at the Battle of Trafalgar, was preserved in brandy for the voyage home. "Shocking waste of brandy," Colin remarked.

His hair was a little ruffled, and Jenny found that she didn't care about the postcards, even the dramatic image of the dome of St. Paul's rising high above a besieged London. She put her hand on his arm. "Colin, please—I know you've taken time to prepare this, but could you tell me about what's happening now? Instead of talking about the past?"

"Current events are in the newspapers, Jenny."

"No, I want to know about outside. I don't get to feel the sun or the breeze. Was it dark when you went to work? Was it cold? Did you work indoors all day? Can you—"

"Sshh," he said. "I understand. It was humid, but it didn't rain. Today was the chilliest it's been all week—didn't get above eight or nine, I believe."

"Eight or nine what?"

"Degrees Celsius. That would be—between forty-five and fifty degrees Fahrenheit."

"Was it windy?"

"Yes, a bit. I spent most of the day in meetings or with paperwork." He smiled. "I sent Andrews out when necessary."

"Do you have a car?"

"Yes, but the traffic in the city is horrific. I take the tube to the Yard. Most are quiet on the train, but London is an international city. On the streets you can hear persons conversing in all sorts of languages. I have a bit of a walk from here to the closest station. It's shorter on the other end." He left the postcards with her and departed.

Alive and bustling. Not like her day. She hadn't done anything except read and drink tea. She retired late but couldn't settle. She slipped out of bed and knelt by her window, pulling the curtain back slightly. She couldn't see much, just the side of the brick building next door. Only a narrow driveway and a few small trees separated the two structures. The trees hadn't lost their leaves yet. Her room must be near the back of the building, because she could see only a sliver of the street. There were several parked cars in view and a street light that suffused them with an amber glow. Nothing was happening out there either.

"Doing a bit of recce, are we?"

She jumped. It was Sergeant Casey.

"Shouldn't you leave that to us?"

She waited for his outburst, but he surprised her.

"Let's have some ice cream." He held out a hand to help her up.

They went into the kitchen, and he dished up a generous amount for each of them.

"Sergeant, what's it like out there? Colin said it didn't rain. In Texas, you could smell the rain before it fell and sometimes even see it coming. I'd give anything just to take a walk after it's rained, when the world has been washed fresh and clean."

"You like the outdoors, do you?"

"I like the smell of pine trees. I like the way cold weather gives everyone pink cheeks. I like the way people laugh when they come out of a cold wind into a warm room."

Casey paused between bites. "When I ran this morning, it was still dark. Foggy. Most mornings there's mist. We don't usually have hard rains here; it's more likely to drizzle."

"You don't mind running when it's damp?"

"The air is crisp early in the morning. Before too long there will be frost on the ground. It turns the leaves underfoot silver."

"And then you trample all over them," she teased. "How poetic." She rinsed their bowls and utensils and put them in the dishwasher. "It's back to bed for me."

"Keep your bloody curtains closed, Jenny."

She shivered. It was The Voice, and he'd waited until her guard was down to use it.

CHAPTER 36

Days in the protection flat passed slowly for Jenny. Sergeant Casey resumed her exercises, but they occupied only a small portion of her time. There were so few TV channels compared to the U.S., where everyone she knew subscribed to cable, so sometimes she was stuck watching rugby with Brian. It seemed like a free-for-all sport to her. The men wore no pads, and some played with obvious injuries, which upset her. Brian assured her that there were rules and tried to explain them, but it was a morass of obscene-sounding terms: props, scrum, hooker, and ruck. She preferred practicing the Italian phrases Sergeant Casey had been trying to teach her.

Colin called by regularly, short visits that only interrupted her tedium, but she enjoyed seeing him. He was an educated man, and she discovered that they shared many of the same interests: theater, movies, music, and books. It was mid-November, and she saw the weather reflected in his attire. He wore his overcoat now, with scarf and gloves. There were no changes of climate in the flat, however, only the storms of fear and despair inside her that continued to rage and abate, rage and abate. Colin had suspended her sessions with Dr. Knowles once he was certain her crisis had passed. She understood the premium Colin was placing on her safety, but none of the issues she had addressed with the psychiatrist had been completely resolved.

Packages continued to arrive from Texas, bringing warmer clothes for her and other reading material, but they were only fleeting distractions in the long days. She had no place to wear the clothes other than the flat, and it wasn't fun reading when that was all you had to do. She made the grocery list and now helped with the dishes and the laundry, but these chores were not very time consuming.

Mealtimes were likewise less than exciting. The food was good, but things that had seemed quaint to her at first, like their way of eating, were now getting on her nerves. It was ridiculous for grown men to mash their food on their forks like that! She was sick of potatoes, too, some form of which was served at every meal. She thought about adding *Ways To Serve Potatoes* to her journal, but that list would fill an entire book by itself. And if she heard one more man belch, she thought she'd scream. Of course, she was probably getting on their nerves, too.

At night the tornadoes still came. The inner gales were powerful enough to wake her, capricious in their regularity but destructive in their severity. They were short lived, like most cyclones, but left her shaking. Invariably she'd turn on her lamp and then move around her room a little. To balance the discord inside, she kept her room neat, always making sure each item was in its appropriate place before she turned out the light. There was a serenity in sameness, a reassurance in predictability—the framed photographs of her family next to Colin's CD player on the chest of drawers arranged just so and her uniformed teddy bear guarding the stack of books on her nightstand.

Tonight, however, her search for peace eluded her. She sat down on the floor next to her window and peeked out. All was quiet in the world outside, a world she missed being a part of. There must have been rain earlier in the day, because every detail of the landscape was evident, like a painting made with a fine brush. But no one would have painted this scene: It was boring. She heard Brian's footsteps too late. She let the curtain fall back into place, but it was still swinging slightly when he looked in, and his eyes went to it immediately. "Brian, I'm so bored."

He had learnt long ago that his size alone was enough to frighten most people. He knew better than to add an angry, explosive voice, so he kept it quiet and controlled. "We all are, Jenny. Do you hear me? *We all are.* You've done this for the last time."

He hadn't used her nickname, JJ. A bad sign. She climbed into bed and pulled up the covers, a pitiful attempt at self-defense.

He walked over to her, making no attempt to disguise his bulk. "This is not a game. You should know that better than anyone." He spoke slowly, making every word clear. "If we're found, someone could get killed. How will you feel if someone dies because you were bored?"

"How—how do you know there were other times?" It was a whisper.

"We brief each other."

"Are you going to tell Sergeant Casey?"

"Jenny, understand me. This just won't do. Will you play by the rules? Show some integrity? I need to know."

"Yes, but—what are you going to do?"

"For now, I'll keep you company." He pulled one of the armchairs to the window and sat down. "For the rest—I'm not prepared to say."

His stature and his silence were sobering. Oh, he was such a *policeman,* going on about the rules, making her feel like a disobedient child. What would he do? He wouldn't hurt her. He couldn't take away her privileges; she didn't have any. He could withhold chocolate. He could make her eat Brussels sprouts. No, that's silly. Oh—he could leave. They all could. They could decide they'd had enough and turn her over to someone else. Colin had said they were here voluntarily. Of course they were bored—the endless poker games and the books and magazines strewn all over the flat were evidence of their attempts to occupy themselves. "Brian, I'm sorry." It came out as a whimper. "You won't leave me, will you? Please don't. I need you guys." She choked on her words. "I don't want any of you to get hurt. Honest, I don't."

His tone softened. "JJ, you need to join the team. Work with us, not against us."

"I will," she promised. "Just tell me what to do, and I'll do it."

"Tomorrow. Sleep now." He turned off the lamp, and the room was dark except for the nightlight. The nightlight he had provided. She watched him seat himself again, still facing her, but his presence was no longer portentous.

CHAPTER 37

In the morning there was no indication that Danny and Sergeant Casey knew about her recent disobedience. Jenny did her exercises under Casey's watchful eye, trying to do at least one or two more in each set than he requested. She helped Danny with the lunch, washing the dishes afterwards. Brian woke after lunch, and when he began dinner, she decided to assist. Perhaps if she got on his good side, her sentence wouldn't be as severe. He set her to work peeling potatoes and made no reference to the night before.

After dinner, however, he came to her door. "Sullivan's rented a video. I'd like you to watch it with us. *Das Boot.*"

"Another war movie?"

"JJ, it's important."

At first she couldn't figure out why he wanted her to see it. It began with scenes of German officers in a nightclub, some of them drunk and disorderly. Then the action shifted to a submarine, cramped and crowded with many men. Not much was happening on the screen, but Sergeant Casey surprised her by explaining in a matter-of-fact voice how submarines worked and the different duty stations on board.

It was a long movie, and as Casey outlined some of the tactics of submarine warfare, the similarities between their situation and hers began to dawn on her. The submarine sailors missed their families. They were confined. They were safe as long as their location was not discovered. There were long periods of waiting—endless monotony—broken by moments of intense terror. Pressure could kill them. It was, at times, a psychological war.

There were differences, too. The sailors never bathed. Their hair grew long, and their beards looked unkempt. Sergeant Casey's baths had been frightening, but he had made sure she was clean. The three men whose eyes were glued to the television were neat and clean shaven. The living room was much larger than anyone's space in the U-boat, even the captain's. The submariners' danger was greater. The enemy—the Allies, she thought wryly—could be anywhere in that vast ocean. The Germans would have very little warning of an attack. She knew she was in danger, but there were safeguards and alarms, and she didn't feel that an attack was imminent. There was way more than the thin skin of a submarine protecting her, and she didn't have to worry about depth charges or fires.

At the movie's end, the German sailors thought they were safe, but gunfire cut them down. Their crumpled bodies bled on the wharf. She hadn't wanted them to die, and they were just characters in a story. She really didn't want these policemen to die, these flesh-and-blood men who kept continual watch over her. They hadn't jumped ship when they'd had the chance. They were willing to endure the dull days.

Danny gave her a pat on the shoulder and went into the kitchen to make himself a cup of tea. "I'd like a word with her," Brian told Casey, who left without inquiring why.

She had underestimated him. *Das Boot—Das Brian.* Sergeant Casey would have yelled at her, and he would have been justified. Brian had found a gentle way to drive his point home. "I learned a lot tonight," she said. "Those men were responsible for each other. They depended on each other for their safety."

He didn't interrupt.

"When the monster got hold of me, I thought I was going to die. I should know better than to endanger anyone else, particularly people I care about."

He waited.

"I've been selfish and immature. I wasn't always like this, Brian—but there's a price on my head."

"JJ, you can come to me when you're afraid. To any of us."

How could she tell him that in spite of his best efforts, the fear never left her? The monster had plucked her from a public street and fractured her future. Dr. Knowles had said that memory and reality weren't the same, but they hurt the same, and it didn't stop. "It's still hard for me to do that," she admitted.

"Then we'll come to you." He took her hand.

"You can tell Sergeant Casey if you want to," she said shakily.

"There's no need." He already had, of course, but he did not say so.

That was one blessing, and another was that this incredible hulk was on *her* side.

CHAPTER 38

Sinclair found no evidence of a special meal when he visited the flat on Thanksgiving. "No celebration?" he asked Jenny. "Isn't this a holiday in the States?"

"The Pilgrims had fled religious persecution in England," she said. "They were starving, and the local Indians fed them, so we usually honor the event by being thankful we can overeat. I wasn't in the mood today."

"Did you speak with your family?"

"With my brothers. My mom's still cooking. BJ's a sophomore in college and worried about finals and completing research papers. Matt's younger—a junior in high school. His soccer team made it to the championship game before losing. They played in a downpour, but rain or no rain, if I were in Texas, I'd have been there."

Sinclair heard the wistful tone.

"They wanted to know what it was like living with three policemen. I didn't tell them how it felt to be under surveillance all the time. I described some of Brian's more exotic recipes, like bubble and squeak." She liked the fried combination of leftover meat, potatoes, and vegetables as long as Brian didn't put Brussels sprouts in it. "And Matt said that by tonight they'd all be replete. Isn't that a great word? My mother used to teach me one new vocabulary word each week, and now BJ and Matt are her victims."

"And your father taught you quotations."

"Yes, he'd often leave a clipping at my place at the breakfast table. That was his not-so-subtle way of telling me I should learn it." She smiled. "Colin, you're wearing yet another tie. I don't think I've ever seen the same one twice."

He was a bit flattered that she noticed.

"And your cufflinks match. I didn't know men cared about such things."

"All day I deal with vulgar crimes and the depraved people who commit them. I need a reminder sometimes that beautiful things exist."

"I do, too," she said. "I've been reading the book you lent me on Churchill, and I've made a terrible discovery: The only thing I have in common with that great man is depression! I should probably read poetry instead."

"T.S. Eliot, perhaps?"

"*The Wasteland?* No, that's depressing too. Maybe one of your pastoral poets. They paint pictures with words of landscapes I can't see."

"A field's worth of words," he quipped.

"Wordsworth," she laughed. "One of the British 'big six.' He was aptly named! I also studied the romantic poets in school—they wrote about landscapes of the heart—but that's hard to think about now. Let's create a new genre: medical poetry. I could use some healing words."

Prayer can heal, he thought. I'll bring her a book of prayers.

CHAPTER 39

Jenny was finally asleep. It had been a difficult evening for her, Casey reflected, beginning with the news report they'd seen just before dinner. Another bail application had been made on Scott's behalf by his defence team, and his picture had appeared on the TV screen as the announcer delivered the details. She had fainted, then awakened shaky and distraught with no appetite for Davies' meal. After dinner she'd been alternately tearful and withdrawn, expressing her fear of seeing Scott in court—"What if I faint then, too?"—and her worry that they'd all be angry if she couldn't do what was expected of her.

Sinclair's news had been disturbing as well, and it had contributed to her distress. It was the boss' procedure to censor what she heard, but she had come into the sitting room during his report. She knew now that someone was offering a thousand quid for information about unusual police presence in any London area hotel. "Scott's on the wrong track," Sinclair had told her, but she had not been reassured.

Casey thought about the team. The more specialised his military training had become, the smaller the unit with which he was associated. That was one of the things he liked about the current arrangement. He knew their strengths and weaknesses, and they knew his, enabling them to cover for each other and make the team stronger than any single individual. Davies was solid and well trained. Sullivan had less experience, but he was clever, creative, and confident.

He'd told Sinclair some time ago that Jenny was suffering from combat stress. Bridges had called it rape trauma, but many of the symptoms he'd been taught to identify in soldiers, he saw in her. She was tense, jumpy. She had difficulty sleeping and was often fatigued. She experienced depression, and there were times she withdrew. She was far too introspective. Anyone who examined himself too closely came up short, and she always had her yardstick out.

The incidence of combat fatigue had been lower in the special forces than in the regular military ranks. In less extreme cases a man often regained his calm because those around him were calm. What made the difference? Training, of course. He had gone into combat prepared for what he would encounter, knowing that return fire was a strong possibility if not a certainty. His rules of engagement had been clear: Assess the odds and do whatever is necessary to tip them in your favour. And do it quickly to reduce the risk to yourself and others.

The attack on Jenny had been unexpected. There had been no rules. Scott had intended to murder her after he tortured her sufficiently to satisfy himself. Her statement had given no indication of the duration, but a beating that severe—and the sexual assault that followed it—could have taken an extended period of time. The crime scene was isolated. There was no danger of detection. He had not had to hurry. Bloody bastard.

It was not his practice to discuss his military experiences, even the nonclassified ones. Consequently she didn't know that he had been about her age when he was deployed for the first time. He had been inexperienced and far from home, but he had performed effectively when called upon because he had been trained. And the training that had qualified him for specialised service had been even more valuable.

He thought about some of the men with whom he had served. They had been intelligent, able to achieve intense mental focus. They were physically fit, understanding that the body had to be capable of responding to demanding circumstances. They were willing to push themselves beyond pain and fear. Knowledge and self-control were factors: It took the combination of the two to apply training appropriately. Understanding how their mission fit into the larger picture had given them an edge. And a sense of humour had been essential. Sullivan wasn't as crude as many of his mates had been, at least not in front of Jenny, but his playful personality had helped.

She was the wrong size and sex for soldiering, but surprisingly she possessed most of the characteristics he had just brought to mind. She was clever, resourceful, and motivated. Her injuries had healed, and she participated willingly in the exercises he devised. Physically she would be ready. She knew how important her testimony was in convicting Scott of his crimes. Her sense of humour indicated an inner resilience. Her overall lack of confidence, her reaction to psychological triggers, and her lack of training were her biggest drawbacks.

Would her trust in them—her unit—give her more confidence as a whole? Was it too late to teach her how to face her enemy? Battleproofing—simulating battle conditions—could offset her emotional reactions, but since her battlefield would be a courtroom, the CPS would have to handle that. Many men found ways to relax themselves before conflict began. Physical and mental relaxation were both effective, since either one affected the other.

Her state of mind was troubling. Her sessions with the shrink had provided only passing relief. Now she'd had a visceral reaction to seeing Scott on TV. She was a man overboard without a life preserver. Sinclair had promised to consult the psychiatrist, Knowles, but not to send for him this time. Combat by remote didn't work in the military, and he didn't think treatment by remote would either.

CHAPTER 40

Like Casey, Davies believed in tackling problems head-on, but he was uncomfortable with Sinclair's orders. Following a conversation with the psychiatrist, Sinclair had instructed the men to encourage Jenny to talk about her attack. Discussing her fears could relieve her inner torment, apparently. The shrink talk, they called it, and they all felt that the psychiatrist should do it, but Sinclair had not conceded. Their late-night poker game had decided it; Davies had been the biggest loser and therefore had to go first. "JJ," he began, "you're not the only one here who's been afraid. Arresting thugs with weapons can be frightening. We're trained, but that's no guarantee that everything will go right."

"What are you trying to say?"

"You fainted the other day. It's worrying."

The whole conversation was worrying: his insistence that he wanted to help, the pauses while he waited for her to answer, sitting with a clean, wholesome man who wanted her to talk about her rape. She ended it as soon as she could, and he seemed glad to let it go.

Danny told her about his football injury. "I had the ball, and a larger boy ran into me and spun me round. The biggest problem I had afterward wasn't the pain or the swelling—it was my fear of the older boys on the pitch. Talking about it helped." He promised to listen if she wanted to talk about what scared her, but she didn't.

Casey completed the triumvirate. "It's not good to keep things bottled up."

"You don't talk about the things that happened to you."

"They occurred in the context of missions I can't discuss. And I've healed: Remembering my injuries doesn't keep me up at night."

"Is this POW interrogation day? If I had a rank and serial number, I'd give them to you."

"And nothing more."

"No."

He couldn't argue with her reasoning.

She was quiet during dinner, expecting a combined assault, but none came. When she left the table, Casey rang Sinclair to report that none of them had been successful in getting her to engage. "Keep at it," Sinclair instructed.

CHAPTER 41

"Fall in," Casey told Jenny after lunch. "I want a word with you." He led her into the sitting room where Brian and Danny waited. "We know you're troubled. Stress shared is stress halved. Talk to us."

Her face paled. "You're ganging up on me!"

"We're the safety net, love."

"It hurts too much! I just want it to go away."

"JJ, things like that—they don't go away by themselves."

"At night he comes at me. I just can't face it in the daytime, too. Please don't make me."

"We know you're upset, Sis, but at some point you're going to have to tell about it in a courtroom. Wouldn't it help if you'd already been through it with us?"

The room was closing in on her. The walls were the color of quicksand. "I don't want to face things. I'd rather drink too much or spend too much money shopping or—or—run until I drop!"

"Facing it's the only way to beat it," Casey said.

Her chest was tight, and she couldn't get a breath.

"Cup of tea wouldn't go amiss, Davies," he added.

Brian rose to his feet, and suddenly the image of the monster standing over her flashed through her mind. She began to tremble. Casey spoke to her in the voice that stopped her in her tracks, and her eyes widened, but she couldn't answer.

He told Sullivan to fetch an ice cube and folded it into her fist. "Squeeze," he said. "Focus on the cold."

The ice cube didn't last long enough to make a difference. "Stand up and stamp your feet. Hard. Trample on that bastard Scott! Crush him."

She froze. He put his hand over her nose. "Open your mouth and breathe," he commanded.

She gulped the air and felt lightheaded. He eased her down on the sofa, and she began to cry.

"We'll leave it for now," he said.

Brian was there with the tea.

- -

Sinclair didn't make it to the flat until after dinner. Jenny was awake but in bed, her form lost under the blankets. He thought about the first time he'd seen her: comatose, her body frighteningly still, her life at the mercy of the machines which maintained it. He'd wondered whether she'd be coherent when she regained consciousness, whether she'd be capable of identifying her attacker. Much had changed since then, yet much remained the same. Scott was in custody, and her physical wounds had healed, but the memory of his violations was attacking her from within. Rape was destructive. It desecrated one of the most personal, private, and potent forms of communication there was. "I hear you had a bad patch," he said. "Better now?"

She sat up. "I lost it, Colin. I'm so embarrassed. The guys have seen me at my worst."

"That's when we can do the most good. 'If you can keep your head when all about you are losing theirs…' That sort of thing."

"Kipling," she said. "But there's more to that poem. Doesn't it say something about 'bearing to hear the truth you've spoken'? I couldn't do that. Colin, Churchill called his depression, his Black Dog. I'm worse than that—I think my fear's a black bear. It charges at me. How will I ever face an antagonistic lawyer?"

That had been his concern exactly. She had to be able to perform when the time came. "Fortunately," he smiled, "that's not on the docket today." He paused. "Jenny, when I'm on rough ground, I open the book." He gestured toward the Bible.

"Whose was it, Colin?"

"My father's, and his father's before him."

"Why doesn't your father have it now?"

"He died, Jenny. Of cancer. He was only fifty-six."

"Colin, I'm so sorry. I shouldn't have asked."

"I'll sit with you until you fall asleep," he said. The soft blue fabric of her nightdress exposed nothing. Awake or asleep, she kept herself covered. He thought about the case. They'd hoped for a lead, and they'd got far more: a victim who had survived, an intelligent, believable, sympathetic woman who was willing to be a witness. Who was so fearful that she couldn't talk about her experience.

She whimpered, and he found it tragic that her memories allowed her no rest. She had turned on her side, and the cheek with the scar was hidden by the pillow. She looked lovely, even with her tousled hair. He was tempted to stroke her cheek, very lightly, to reassure her. He didn't, however—it hit him like a blast of arctic air that stroking her cheek wouldn't have been a comfort, it would have been a caress.

He returned to his flat, but he did not sleep. He was haunted by the lovely, young, vulnerable woman upstairs and how powerless he was to help her. He hadn't been able to protect her from Scott's attack, and he couldn't protect her from the tribulations—trials—that lay ahead. Knowles had advised that they reduce the pressure she felt by encouraging her to talk about what she had suffered. The men had done so, with dreadful results. He felt more for her than simple empathy, and he didn't want to follow the orders he had given them. Damn! There was too much at stake to allow a conflict of interest with a witness to affect him.

Witness—that was the key. His job was to ensure that she was effective in her testimony, whatever it cost her. Casey, Davies, Sullivan, himself—there were only four of them. There would be a multitude in the courtroom, the jury alone three times as large as the gathering in the protection flat. Teams of barristers and solicitors would be in attendance. The press would be a significant presence. The public gallery would be full. The individuals on her side would be outnumbered by those who were required to be objective. Scott's defence counsel would be overtly hostile.

He wanted to go easy on her, but he could not. He had to know if she could delineate Scott's actions in front of others. Anything that distracted him from this course was unprofessional and unpardonable. His feelings were irrelevant. He knew what he had to do, and he had the rest of the night to nerve himself up for it.

CHAPTER 42

Sinclair rang Casey in the morning. "I'm going to give it a go. After breakfast. I want everyone there."

Jenny was apprehensive when she saw all of them in the kitchen. Sergeant Casey had been on watch all night; why wasn't he sleeping? Why was Colin back? He was dressed for work, in a blue and gray herringbone tweed jacket with charcoal gray slacks and a blue shirt that emphasized the blue in his eyes. She felt shabby in her exercise clothes.

Colin was strangely gentle, taking her hand as he led her into the sitting room. The others followed, Brian straddling a chair from the dining room and making it look like kindling.

Colin didn't ask her to say anything at first. He explained that he believed in her, in her strength and her commitment. He assured her that fear grew only in darkness; it could not defeat her if she exposed it to the light. And then he asked her to tell him about the day she'd been attacked.

She had one objection after another, and Casey listened while Sinclair eased her past each one, his voice seductively calm. Perhaps he and Davies and Sullivan had been too quick to allow her to stop.

"I feel like I'm at the edge of a cliff, and you're going to push me over," she said.

"No, Jenny," Sinclair responded. "I'll not push you. I'll catch you."

He seemed strong enough to catch her, his coat open, his chest broad.

"Look at me," he said.

He had the beginnings of crow's feet at the corners of his eyes. His dark pupils were surrounded by blue, as blue as the sky had been that day. She told him about walking to Selfridge's and the chill in the air that had made her hurry. She told him again about waking naked and sick in the dark and the icicles of fear that had pierced her.

"I've been in that room," Sinclair said. "I felt the cold, and I know how black it was. And I remember the smell."

"Wet and earthy, like being buried alive."

"Yes. It was a cellar. But I'm not there now, and neither are you. Shall we go on?"

She mentioned the two men who turned on the light, their identities no less concealed than her future. "Death row, and my family would never know what happened to me!"

Sinclair kept her on course, having her describe the room and her discovery of women's jewellery. He had an agenda, Casey realised, and it wasn't limited to alleviating her psychological pressure. He wanted the full narrative.

"He knocked me off my feet. Then he kicked me. My legs, my stomach, my ribs. Did he aim for the places that would hurt the most?" She described the sound of Scott's fury and how it felt. "Pain is alive, did you know that? It has a pulse, it beats, it throbs."

Sullivan knew the basic facts, but hearing them spoken between sobs—was this what detectives did? If so, he didn't want to be one.

"He used his hands, too, his fists. When he backhanded me, his ring—that sharp ring—cut me open." She covered her face. "I'm so ashamed—I should have fought more. I realize that now. But there was so much blood, and I hurt so badly."

"Jenny, it wouldn't have changed anything."

The morning dragged on, Sinclair inexhaustibly patient when she cried, assuring her that no one could have effectively resisted the onslaught of cruelty that had been directed at her.

"He removed his belt. He let it swing in his hand."

"Tell me what he did next, Jenny," Sinclair said.

"He ripped off my necklace."

"After that, Jenny."

Casey leant forward, alert for symptoms of panic. He would have welcomed an injury he could splint or suture. Psychological pain could not be anaesthetised.

She used verbal shorthand to describe Scott forcing her legs apart, the pain she felt deep inside that did not stop because he did not stop. "It was my first time," she wept.

Sullivan felt ill. The room seemed darker to Davies. He had given her a nightlight, wanting her to adjust to the darkness. He should have given her a floodlight, but that was what the boss was doing.

"When he finally pulled away, I thought he'd kill me. I wanted him to! Why didn't he?"

"Finish it, Jenny," Sinclair said quietly.

Silence, then fragments, none of them sufficient to describe Scott's vile actions. "He—over—and—and—I can't—no!—no!—don't!—oh my God—"

Casey could fill in the blanks. He sprang to his feet, stepping past Sinclair to grab her shoulders. He saw her red eyes and wet cheeks and spat the words out. "It was never an even match, Jenny! He drugged you, and he chose small women—did you know that? All his victims were *small.* And he's a bloody coward, that's why he beat you first. When you set foot in that courtroom, he'll cringe, and I'll be bloody glad to see it."

His anger shocked her into silence. She shuddered and settled.

Sinclair stood and forced himself to move away. Job done.

"Do you want to hear the rest?" she asked. She told them about being shy and overprotected. About not meeting the right boy—Rob—until she was in college. About how much they loved and respected each other. The pregnancy scare in her dorm that had made them cautious. The car accident. He had been killed before she had gotten the birth control prescription from the doctor. Her solo trip to London. At long last she'd been with a man, she cried, and he had been a monster.

It was all Sinclair could do, not to go to her.

Casey was still angry after Sinclair took off. Bloody senior officer hadn't cut her any slack. He'd opened her wounds and left them to deal with the mess. Even after she'd calmed, she'd wanted to hold onto somebody. Sullivan had obliged.

"Do you want to be reassigned now?" she asked. "Now that you know what a coward I am?"

"Not to worry, Sis."

"Promise?"

They saw to her as best they could, and Casey wished he'd had a pint or two to help him forget. It had been difficult, hearing her voice thick with remembered pain. Scott had terrorised her psychologically as well as physically. He'd made certain she was incapacitated. He'd stripped Jenny but not himself—bloody bastard had kept his shoes on. He'd broken her arm, several of her ribs. The sound made when a bone broke was unmistakable. She shouldn't have to know such things.

While she bathed, he stretched, breathed, ran in place. Thought about her helplessness. Her fear. Her mission. Bloody briefs would strip her in court. He didn't know how to predict her psychological suitability for the witness-box, but she was stronger than she looked. She'd taken everything that bastard Sinclair had dished out and hadn't quit.

Sullivan wanted to break something. "Davies, if that happened to one of my sisters—I wouldn't give a toss for the law! Scott had no weapon, mate—he didn't intend to kill her quickly."

Davies agreed. Having read her statement hadn't made it easier to hear; he would have stopped it if he could. "That bit about the necklace—she had to know when Scott took it that he meant to kill her. No wonder she doesn't want it back."

Both men were quiet for a moment.

"Are your sisters virgins, Sullivan?"

"My oldest isn't. When her boyfriend broke it off, she thought her world had ended. He was her first."

Davies recalled his first time. It had been Beth's, too. He'd fumbled a lot, but he'd got it done. "You remember your first time, Sullivan?"

"Yeah. I was afraid she'd say no." He paused. "I wish Jenny'd had it off with her bloke in Texas."

"Wish he hadn't been killed."

"She'd never have come here then."

"Scott would still be killing."

"How's she going to face him?"

"Hard to say."

"Why'd the boss move away when she finished telling everything?"

"Thinking of the trial, most likely. Besides, his job was done—he got her through it."

"Cold-hearted bastard, isn't he?"

Sinclair's afternoon at the Yard was less than productive. His relief at Jenny's cooperation was tempered with concern. She had required so much prompting. Prosecuting counsel would not guide her as gently as he had done. Still, it was a step forward, one they could build on. She had cried, but she had not lost focus. He was proud of her.

Her recitation hadn't yielded any new material, however. At least, nothing germane to the case. He was surprised that she had disclosed personal information, but he knew now what had given her the strength to send her father home: She had lost someone she had loved. Her grief was deep, and she would not put her family in peril.

His office was quiet. It had been quiet at the protection flat, too, all the times when she had stopped and he had hoped that she would be able to continue. He remembered hearing her radio during those moments, the music punctuating the information she had found so difficult to give.

She had never been fully loved by a man. Saying she was a virgin was more antiseptic, but now she was neither. Even more poignant was the definition of sex her mother had given her: "beautiful if it's with the right man."

He had done what he set out to do—maintain his professional reserve in front of the protection team—but there was no satisfaction in it. It had been a harrowing morning for her. She had still been upset when he left. "Nothing's private," she had said. "The trial will come, and they will see everything, ask everything." The men had rallied round her, but he hadn't. Would she start calling him Mr. Sinclair again?

CHAPTER 43

When Sinclair arrived at the flat after dinner, Jenny was on the phone with her parents, so he took the opportunity to address the men privately. "How's she doing? Any chat about this morning?"

"Titbits, nothing more," Casey said. "Told me she wished I'd been there. If I had, she'd be home now—no need for a trial."

"Anything else?"

"Wanted to know if I'd ever begged for anything. I hadn't."

Sinclair frowned. It didn't sound as if her mood had improved any.

She gave him a cautious smile when she saw him. "My mother was just asking about you."

"I hope you didn't tell her what I put you through earlier today."

"That you made me give my statement again? No. Colin, you didn't have a tape recorder, and you didn't take notes, so it wasn't official. What was it for?"

"In the long run I believe it will help you."

"To remember? Colin, it just hurts."

"What did you remember, Jenny?"

Did he *ever* stop being a policeman? "He had a birthmark. The monster did. Below his navel. Red—splotchy—like someone had spilled wine on his stomach." She shivered. "Aren't you going to write it down?"

"No, Jenny. You identified him already through other means." He waited. "Anything you'd like to add?"

"It's hard—remembering Rob. After he died, I went into remission from life. When I stepped on the scales, the reading hadn't changed, but I felt heavy, as if I'd put on more weight than my bones could carry."

He'd felt clumsy, ungainly, after his father's death. Focussing on work had helped. "What did you do after that?"

"I stayed in school, but it was hard to concentrate. I had to drop a couple classes to keep my grades from falling. I graduated a year behind schedule."

"And then came to London."

"There was nothing to keep me in Texas. I was used to making my own decisions, being independent, and I wanted a fresh start. I was planning to visit universities in the U.S., too—in New England, northern

California. Different landscapes. Colder climates. I thought if I went to a new place, I could find a new me. Instead I died, sort of. What you see now is a mirage. I'm that distant spot on the highway that disappears when you get close."

In his flat downstairs he stood for a long time looking at the family photos on his chest of drawers. The faces in the frames smiled at him, but tonight the snaps didn't bring solace. His father was dead. His mother now filled her days with a host of community activities. His sister had a husband and children of her own. He had kept no pictures to remind him of his marriage to Violet. The grief and loneliness in Jenny's voice mirrored what he felt. He had given her a professional, measured response, but in his heart he knew she needed more.

CHAPTER 44

Jenny was puzzled. Colin had brought her a book of prayers, *For Those Who Are Hurting.*

"I got it from a friend," he explained. "A chaplain. I know you're still struggling, and I want to help. What's your expression? 'Covering all the bases'? There's a spiritual element to us."

She thumbed through the pages. Each prayer followed a line of Scripture. "You think I need God?"

"He's the best source of strength I know of."

"He's the reason I'm in this mess," she said bitterly. "He left me."

"I don't believe that. God didn't cause any of this. Things just happen. I don't know why."

"I used to believe in Him, but since the attack, I've questioned everything. I was always taught that God was faithful, but I haven't seen that."

"I beg to differ, Jenny. You didn't doubt His existence when you were angry with Him. Sometimes our anger—or grief or fear—keeps us from hearing Him. You've had your foundations shaken, but you're still standing. You may not be certain about your belief in God, but don't give up on Him. I think He believes in you."

She was stunned and a little embarrassed by the compliment. Instead of replying, she took his hand.

Colin was also silent for a few minutes. He was glad they were holding hands. It made the intimate nature of the conversation more comfortable. "My father was in a lot of pain before he died. My mother and sister were leaning on me. I needed something stronger than myself. God was it. I sat by my father's hospital bed and asked God to give him one more day. Many times He did."

"Are you still grieving for your father?"

He was surprised by the question and even more surprised that he didn't mind answering. He hadn't spoken much about his father to anyone outside his family. "My father had postings abroad, so there were long periods when I didn't see him. The times we did have together were important to me. I was with him on a more consistent basis when he was ill than I had been since childhood. It made his death all the more difficult when it came. I'd say I'm still grieving for him, yes. The longer I live, the more things I'd like to discuss with him." He remembered telling her long ago something about trust being a two-way street. It had been a copper's line, calculated to inspire confidence, but it just might be true. Her trust had certainly engendered his.

"It's hard to believe we're talking about all this."

He smiled. "We met under unusual circumstances. You had to tell me personal details from the beginning. It's not so one-sided now."

In the morning when Danny brought her tea, she asked if he believed in God.

"I'm Catholic, Sis. Of course I do."

"Do you think He loves us?"

He was smiling. "He laid down the law, didn't He? My parents always said it was love when they laid down the law."

"And now you enforce the law. That's not love exactly, but it is in people's best interest. Do you pray?"

This time he laughed. "No, I just feel guilty for not doing it."

She tackled Brian next, early one evening when she'd felt afraid and had gone into the living room to sit with him. There was a rhythm of nature he'd seen on the farm, in the seasons and the reproductive cycles of the animals and the crops, that made him feel that Someone was in charge. It wasn't an accident that things happened the way they did. As far as good and bad were concerned, he'd seen too much of the bad during his years with the police to believe that human beings were the source of love—another Being, far greater and wiser, had to be. He confessed that he didn't pray. "I just hope for things," he said. "I hope you'll be okay. I hope we're helping."

Later that night she asked Sergeant Casey if they could talk for a little while.

"What's on your mind?"

"Sergeant, I feel like I'm learning to walk again. Remember when we first came here? I couldn't do it by myself. I had to lean on you." Her voice faltered. "I don't know who I am or what I believe any more. You seem so sure of yourself. You always know what to do."

"Get onto it, Jenny."

"I've been wondering about—God. Do you think He's real?"

She's searching. Not surprising after what's happened to her. "I've seen some things that would make me doubt it."

"Have you seen anything that would make you believe it?"

"Some things, yes."

"Like what?"

"Missions when the odds were against us, and we seemed to have supernatural luck. Men who were injured so badly that I couldn't save them but who lived anyway."

"I don't know how I made it."

"Some things you can't explain, but they're no less real. I've spent a lot of time outdoors, often at night. The night skies fascinate me. They're vast, and the orbits of the planets aren't random. The more I've learned about astronomy, the more I've wondered myself. About God, that is."

"Do you pray?"

"Men in combat face danger and uncertainty. Many use meditation and deep breathing to relax and focus. Those who believe in God, pray. Everyone needs to believe in something."

She smiled. "Sergeant Casey, you are the most unlikely evangelist I ever knew."

CHAPTER 45

As Christmas drew closer, the longing Jenny felt for her family became a continual ache. At home she would have been helping her mother bake Christmas cookies to give to the neighbors. They would have delivered the fresh treats on foot, then headed home for bowls of steaming hot soup and homemade bread. Her father and brothers would have taken the Christmas decorations from the attic so her mother could transform the house into a visual feast. Nothing at the flat dissipated the hurt, not the store-bought cookies or canned soup they consumed, and the tree which had given her enjoyment at first now looked lonely in the corner, its decorations not sufficient to lift her spirits. A number of her friends had sent Christmas cards, with notes shorter than their usual correspondence. They knew her letters were censored—perhaps they were afraid their mail would be read, too.

She wanted very badly to go shopping, to select her family's gifts herself, but no amount of wheedling would convince Colin to let her, either in his company or with one of the men. He arranged for her to send her mother a British cookbook, her father a book on the American Civil War by Winston Churchill, and sport shirts to her brothers, a Manchester United football jersey for Matt and a Henley Royal Regatta jersey for BJ.

Brian and Danny had taken some candid snaps of her. The one she selected for her parents showed her laughing, with the left side of her face—the unmarked side—toward the camera. It had been taken just after Colin had brought the Christmas tree into the flat. He hadn't been certain decorating a tree would be a good idea, fearing it might cause her to miss her family more, but she had been glowing with anticipation, and Brian's photo had captured it.

Sergeant Casey worked out a complicated duty roster which granted all three of them leave while ensuring that at least one of the original protective team members was still at the flat. Colin went home to Kent, and she tried to look past her homesick feelings. The men kept her busy, Brian waking her early on Christmas Eve to help him prepare the turkey, roasted vegetables, gravy, and special sauces, and Danny quizzing her about Texas traditions. Everything was ready by early afternoon, and they popped the Christmas crackers Danny had put at each place and savoured the dishes their combined efforts had produced. All except the

Christmas pudding. Jenny took a very small bite and chewed slowly. It was a long time before she swallowed. Her brother, Matt, would have called it revolting, but she knew she couldn't say that. "Is it an acquired taste?" she finally asked. "Like fruitcake?"

After the meal, Jenny gathered them in the living room. Her parents had sent a Texas-sized belt and buckle for a Texas-sized man, Brian. Danny received a buckskin leather wallet and a book about Chick Bowdrie, a fictional Texas Ranger. Jenny's father had selected a number of his favorite fishing lures for Sergeant Casey as well as a nonfiction account of the Texas Rangers. Jenny's parents had another box for the team, with a card that read, *With heartfelt thanks for taking such good care of our daughter.* It was filled with Texas pralines, UNO cards, Labyrinth, and a large jigsaw puzzle with Texas scenes. "Texas generosity," Jenny explained.

Then Danny spoke up. "It's your turn, Sis." He put a small box wrapped in gold paper in her lap.

"You didn't have to get me anything," she said.

"It's from all of us. Just open it!"

She did. A pearl cross lay on dark blue velvet. Rob had been the only person who had given her any pearl jewelry, and a lump rose in her throat. She closed the box quickly.

"Sis? You like it, don't you?" Danny's normally buoyant voice was quavering slightly.

She opened the box again. In her previous life her skin had been as smooth and pure as these precious stones. The pearls were creamy white, round as teardrops, and suspended on a gold chain. A single diamond marked the place where the two arms of the cross met.

"Did we do the right thing, Sis? You're happy with it, aren't you?"

His voice brought her back to the present. She smiled through her tears at the three worried faces. "Yes. Oh, yes. It's beautiful."

"Tea?" Brian asked.

"No. Hugs." She stood and put her arms around him. Then he undid the clasp and gently fastened it around her neck.

Casey watched her embrace Sullivan, remembering that he had been the one to suggest giving her jewellery. Brian had insisted on a necklace. Then she turned to him, and he realised that it was the first time she had reached out to any of them with affection, not desperation or fear. Excellent. Should he tell her he had decided on pearls? He had liked the idea that a speck, an intruder, had caused something lovely to grow inside a shell. No, the result was what mattered. "Happy Christmas," he said.

When Colin arrived on Christmas afternoon, Jenny was in her room listening to her new Kenny G album. She didn't know why her brothers had sent it—he wasn't that popular with her age group—but Danny was packing and the silent sergeant was on watch, so she needed a way to pass the time. The music touched her more than she expected, and she didn't hear Colin's first knock. She reached up to take his hand as he asked whether her tears were happy or sad ones. "Both," she said. "Happy because the music is so beautiful, and sad because I'll never have the love his music is about."

The saxophone was exquisite and the tune haunting. A lovely young woman was holding his hand. Certainly good manners dictated that he ask her to dance. He held her loosely at first, but as the music progressed, he pressed gently on her back, and she moved closer. They danced to "Forever in Love," "Sentimental," and then "The Moment." Casey heard the music and looked in. What he saw suggested to him that the boss fancied her. He wondered if she fancied him.

Several of the pieces didn't lend themselves to dancing, so she showed him the gift the men had given her and described the ones from her family. "It's so important to belong somewhere," she said. "I'm fortunate to have a wonderful family, even if I can't be with them." The strains of "Dying Young" began, and she lifted her arms to him again, feeling the ache in her chest ease.

"What's this one called?" The music was enticingly slow, and he held her near, so they'd stay in step, of course.

"Innocence," she whispered, and Colin felt how appropriate it was. The saxophone had a pure tone, and the melody was tender. She looked like a precious lily, with the collar of her white silk blouse high on her neck and the ruffles like petals at her wrists. The music ended all too soon.

"That was wonderful, Colin." She was eager to see his reaction to his present, so she led him into the sitting room and watched while he opened the two nicely-bound volumes of American poetry.

"I'll be able to identify your quotes now," he smiled. Then he took a small rectangular box from his pocket. When she opened it, she saw a gold wristwatch with an amethyst band, each gem carved into the shape of a heart. "Purple hearts," she breathed.

"The medal given to American soldiers injured in combat. You've earned it, Jenny."

"Not yet, but I will." She stood to hug him, and if it seemed that he held her a little longer than was necessary, it must have been her imagination.

While Colin and Casey tucked into Christmas leftovers, she called her family to thank them for her gifts. It was still morning in Texas, but they had opened theirs already, knowing they would hear from her. Her parents were very touched that the English police, as they called them, had been so thoughtful.

"I'm in very good hands," Jenny said. "These men are special. I wish you could meet them."

The Queen's Christmas message—which Jenny watched alone—also focused on families and the wisdom and trust that they could provide for each other. Jenny ran her fingers over the pearl cross. The gift from the men had already strengthened her, something else that families did. But the watch from Colin—was it a vote of confidence or a sign that he expected her to do her duty when the time came?

CHAPTER 46

Sergeant Andrews came by the flat on the 26th and explained Boxing Day to Jenny while they played cards. He was armed, which seemed unusual to her. "I'm an AFO," he said. "Like Sullivan."

"AFO?"

Andrews laughed. "Sorry! Alphabet soup, isn't it? Stands for authorised firearms officer. I completed a basic firearms course, but I don't carry in my usual duties. Regular training is still required, however."

Jenny examined her cards and couldn't see the beginnings of a good hand. She drew a card, then took a wild guess when she discarded one.

Andrews wasn't interested in her seven of clubs. He drew from the pack, at the same time sharing background information on the members of the protective team. "Sullivan's here because he saved your life in hospital," he said. "Showed judgement and initiative. He might not have made the cut otherwise."

"Is Brian an AFO?"

"No, he's an SFO, a specialist firearms officer. He patrols in an ARV—armed response vehicle. They're the first armed officers on a scene, so one of their jobs is control and containment. They also chase and apprehend stolen vehicles, conduct armed searches, deal with armed robberies, that sort of thing."

She had lost sight of her strategy in the card game and couldn't think which card would be least useful. "What about Sergeant Casey? Colin said he was in the special forces. He's probably pretty good with guns, too."

"That's an understatement! He's a member of an armed team and a marksman on all weapons. Specialist missions may be undertaken on short notice, but they're more likely to be planned. They give support to the ARVs, handle hostage rescues, terrorist threats, heavily-armed criminals. With his background and experience, he'll be a team leader one day." Andrews smiled and discarded.

"Having been a Royal Marine helped him, I guess."

Andrews chuckled. "Is that what he told you? He only started out in the Marines. From there he joined the toughest, most elite group of fighting men in the world. Have you ever heard of the Special Boat Service?"

She hadn't.

"Just trying to qualify can kill you, the process of selection is that difficult."

"He never talks about it." Deuce of diamonds. She didn't think she needed that card.

"They keep a low profile, but they're the ones who teach everyone else what it's about. Give them the worst odds and the most appalling physical conditions, and they'll still get the job done."

"I'm glad I didn't know that when he was giving me baths," she said, a little awed.

"They have a killer sense of humour also. Gin!" He laid his cards down.

"Oh, you are devious," she laughed, "distracting me before the final blow! You win." She decided that it was a good thing Danny and Sergeant Andrews weren't at the flat at the same time: They would be like two magpies.

PC Arthur Hobbes had accompanied Andrews, but she was unable to convince him to join them in the next hand. Food usually broke the ice, particularly with someone who obviously enjoyed it, so she offered him a sandwich. "Turkey or ham? I'm making one for Sergeant Andrews."

"Turkey, if it's not too much trouble, Miss." He didn't know how to look at her, not wanting to stare at her scar and not sure where he should look if he didn't look at her face.

She went into the kitchen to make the sandwiches. It was time to take the bull by the horns. "Constable Hobbes, have you read my file?" She handed him his plate and glass and set Andrews' down in front of him.

Hobbes ran his hand over his moustache and looked down at his lunch.

She tried again. "What happened to me isn't a closed subject here. And I'm much better now." Andrews was watching her with interest. Hobbes still had not replied. His discomfort was making her self-conscious. "I'm not a victim. I survived."

Hobbes' blush was easy to see with his buzz haircut. He choked on his sandwich, thinking about what she survived. "Yes, Miss," he said after he'd cleared his throat.

She sighed. He must be good for something. "Christmas pudding?" she asked with her sweetest smile.

He nodded eagerly. "Thank you, Miss."

She brought him a large portion. They were going to get along after all.

Hobbes came for only two days, but that was long enough to finish the dessert Jenny didn't like. When he left, Danny returned, along with PC

Linda Hewes and the sinister Sergeant Howard. With Brian gone, their meals were less lavish, to say the least. Linda helped Jenny prepare some lighter fare, mostly sandwiches from the Boxing Day ham and soup from the leftover turkey. Sergeant Howard never set foot in the kitchen.

Fortunately Howard's tour of duty was short. He was replaced by PC Derek Nicholson, a tall man with large eyes and slanted brows which gave him a look of perpetual sadness. His smile failed to dispel the grief-stricken countenance he wore and caused her to wonder whether everyone could see past her smiles. Nicholson had a deep bass voice and a gentle manner, and in spite of his downcast features, she found that she liked him.

Andrews spent another day with her, and Colin came by periodically, but she missed the regular team. Sergeant Casey returned late in the day on the 31st, his eyes bloodshot. His brother had been ashore, and the two of them had hit the clubs regularly, he confessed. When Colin uncorked the champagne, she noticed that Casey contributed to the toasts for a better year but never drained his glass. Of course, he'd probably had more than his share of alcohol on leave, but she still found it sad that his vigilance couldn't take a holiday. It was his night on watch, and she made a point of telling him how much his continued care meant to her. "I missed you this week. You're my rock. It felt like someone had chipped away part of my foundation."

He looked at her. She was wearing a black velvet trouser suit with silver beads and sequins around the neckline. Beaded earrings dangled from her ears. "What are you playing at?" he snapped.

"Why are you mad at me?" she asked.

Too late, he realised that he'd misread her, and he was angry with himself. He played hard when he wasn't on a mission. The women in the clubs had come on to him, and he'd welcomed them. This one hadn't done. "Sorry, love. Don't take offence." He wanted to tell her to be careful. If she said something like that to a bloke on the outside, he'd shove his tongue down her throat and scare the bloody hell out of her.

She slept late on New Year's morning. When she woke, she missed her mother's cinnamon rolls, which had long been a family tradition at home.

Later that day Colin called by. As she told him how much in his debt she felt, she took his hand. "From the very beginning, you've gone above and beyond the call of duty. You've kept in close touch with my parents. I know it hasn't been easy, giving them bad news, but I'm sure they appreciate your attentiveness, and I do, too."

Colin didn't answer right away but the silence between them held no tension. "In the beginning I wanted to make certain the protective team behaved appropriately. I made a promise to your parents, and I still feel bound by it. More important, I made a promise to you. Having you upstairs made it easier for me to evaluate how things were going." She was still holding his hand, and he had to make a conscious effort to keep his tone light. "I've come to enjoy being here. There's food in the fridge, and something's always on."

"If you think this flat is interesting, you must really have a dull life," she teased.

He smiled. "Nonetheless, when you've made all your court appearances, I hope you'll consider staying on for a bit. You'll be free to go, of course, but I'd like to take you on some tours without postcards."

She looked down and realized how natural it felt, holding his hand. "I haven't thanked you enough for the watch." She held out her arm, admiring it, but it was the delicacy of her wrist that attracted his gaze. "I don't know what I'll want to do. Such frightening things lie ahead of me."

"I have a quote for you then. King George VI said it on Christmas Day in 1939: 'I said to the man who stood at the gate of the year / "Give me a light that I may tread safely into the unknown." / And he replied, "Go into the darkness and put your hand into the hand of God / That shall be to you better than light and safer than a known way."' It bears thinking about—every year, Jen."

He had called her Jen. This elegant, formal man had spoken to her in an affectionate way. She felt a sense of peace and contentment steal over her. She leaned up against him, and he put his arm around her, the soft weave of her sweater warm against his skin. They sat that way for a long time, neither saying anything.

CHAPTER 47

The Happy New Year wishes had barely faded when everything about Jenny's world changed. After months of having the men censor the media for her, Colin brought her the Evening Standard, untouched, and opened it to one of the news sections. The headline read, "Scott Defence Team Confident." There was a picture of Scott, smiling. "Oh," she said with horror, "it feels like it just happened yesterday, and there he is, looking—benign. I'm all right," she said, as much to reassure herself as Colin. "I'm all right."

After that he brought her the paper every night and told Sullivan not to clip the columns about Scott from the morning editions. The press coverage increased exponentially, with long articles about Scott's background, childhood, education, and early adulthood. His world-wide travels and participation in charitable events were detailed. The stories left her shaken. Clearly he was a press favorite. "Will they be writing about me?" There had been references to a witness "the police were keeping under wraps," but nothing more.

"No," Colin answered. "They are not allowed to print anything that could lead to your identification."

There were photographs of the six murdered women, however. All had lived or worked in London. Two were close to Jenny's age or younger. Only Marilyn had been married. Several had had boyfriends, and all were mourned by their families. Their facial features weren't anything alike, ranging from Patsy's round cheeks and mischievous smile to Clarissa's lean, elegant face, but each one was attractive, and most had dark hair.

Still, it wasn't until she read the descriptions of their deaths that they became real to her, that their one-dimensional portraits donned flesh and blood. All had had massive internal injuries, but Barbara had been the first to die. Had Sally been stripped, too, with no clothing other than her soft curls? What had Emma thought when she awakened in that little room? Jenny felt a kinship with them, and she put their pictures next to the framed family photos in her bedroom.

She asked Sergeant Casey about the men he'd served with, who had been killed.

"It won't help you to know that," he said.

"Do you remember what they looked like? Did their deaths strengthen your resolve?"

"Your resolve is what matters now."

- -

Sergeant Casey wanted her to feel more confident physically, so the new year also saw the beginning of her lessons on self-defence. "There are ways a woman can disable a man. Even a very small woman. It's a matter of knowing what to do and acting quickly and decisively." The first exercises were mental, Casey insisting that her mindset had to be right before they moved to any physical manoeuvres. "People either hesitate or are tentative in their responses," he said. "They want to believe that if they cooperate, they won't be hurt, but that's a lie."

She learned that she had two fears to conquer: the fear of offending the other person, perhaps from misreading the situation, and the fear of being injured.

"It's better for you to anger or annoy someone than to be hurt, and it's far better for you to be injured than killed," he said.

"Terrible choices," she commented.

Casey created endless scenarios, all designed to teach her which actions she should be aware of and what her reaction should be. "If you're ever threatened, there's no time to think, but you shouldn't have to. It'll be second nature, I hope."

If she had considered the mental exercises challenging, she found the physical drills even more daunting. She did not want to square off against Sergeant Casey. "Are you going to come at me?"

"That's the idea."

They discovered together, however, that she couldn't do it. His sudden moves unnerved her. Finally he adapted his instruction, slowing his offensive and guiding her responses. "Every man has vulnerable points: his eyes, his bollocks, and his knees. Strike hard and fast in any of those places, and you'll be a free woman."

She didn't recognize the B word, but his gesture made the meaning clear. "Sergeant, what should I have done?" she asked. "With the monster, I mean. Could I have gotten away?"

He had known the question was coming. "You couldn't have anticipated being drugged at the bus shelter. It was broad daylight, and they had only to bump into you, which most people wouldn't consider a suspicious or aggressive move. When he entered the cellar, you were still under the influence of the drug. If you hadn't been, you could have been waiting for the door to open, ready to rush him. You wouldn't have been successful, but you had nothing to lose."

- -

Meetings with the instructing solicitor, Edmund Halladay, began. He worked for the Crown Prosecution Service, and it was his job to prepare Jenny for the trial. Sergeant Casey told her the session would take place in a London hotel. "Look about all you like, but don't ask any questions during transport. No chit-chat. It's not a social outing."

Brian rode in the front seat with the driver, and Sergeant Casey and Danny flanked her in the back, so it was difficult for her to see much. And it was a gray day, which she thought was grossly unfair. She hadn't seen London in the daytime since before the attack, and she didn't want it to look drab. When they stopped, she wasn't sure they'd arrived anywhere, but the men guided her through a back entrance and up several floors to a suite at the end of a corridor. There were two sofas, both with a scrolling leaf pattern on a champagne and cream background, separated by a walnut coffee table with a glass top. The

Persian rug beneath them had all the color—it was chocolate brown with shades of yellow from saffron to ripe corn: food hues.

She'd dressed for the cold weather, with dark corduroy slacks and a long-sleeved blouse and sweater, but she felt colder indoors than she had during the drive, and that scared her. She didn't know what the prosecution lawyer would be like, but she wanted him to have confidence in her.

Mr. Halladay set his briefcase on the dining room table and nodded curtly at her when they were introduced. Colin took off his overcoat, but Mr. Halladay also wore a hat, scarf, and gloves, which he removed and then carefully folded. He was a middle-aged man with small features and short greying hair, neatly combed. His moustache was also meticulously trimmed, and his nails were buffed.

He seemed a little uncomfortable at first with the presence of the protection team. He eyed the firearm each man wore and positioned himself on the opposite side of the table from them. Danny had volunteered to take the first watch outside, and Brian was thumbing through the magazines on the coffee table. Sergeant Casey hadn't seated himself yet. "Is it entirely necessary that these men be present?"

"I don't feel safe without them," she answered. She remembered her misgivings when she'd first met Sergeant Casey and Brian. She'd been intimidated by the sergeant's fierce expression and Brian's size. Now she saw strength and gentleness. Besides, they were all in street clothes today, not the black uniforms that had added to her fright.

"Yes. Well." He cleared his throat. "Most judges don't allow armed police in court."

Casey frowned. The defence would know that as well.

Halladay addressed Jenny. "I gather your current arrangement won't allow you to meet with anyone from the witness service."

"It's not possible," Colin answered for her.

"A case of this magnitude," Halladay said, "is always heard in one of the Crown Courts. There's a backlog at the Old Bailey, as usual. Your particular case has been assigned to Judge Thomas, who presides in one of the newer Crown Courts, St. George Crown Court. On the wall above his bench you will see the Sword of Justice, and above that, the coat of arms. The dais is raised so he will have a clear view of the entire courtroom, including the gallery."

He put on his glasses and took a legal pad from his briefcase. "I'll draw you a diagram," he said, turning the picture in her direction. "In Thomas's courtroom, the court recorder and usher sit here, in front of the bench. The witness-box is to the judge's right and faces the jury." He continued to fill in the drawing. "From where I sit, prosecuting counsel occupy centre right and defence counsel, centre left."

"Where will the monster be?"

"I beg your pardon?"

"Scott," said Sinclair.

"Ah. Yes. The accused will be seated here," he made a mark on the diagram, "at the back of the courtroom under the gallery. He will be escorted by two police officers who will remain with him during the entire proceedings."

"He doesn't sit with his attorney?"

"We say, 'lawyer,' or 'counsel,'" corrected Halladay. "No, he's in the dock."

"What's that?"

"A wooden enclosure. There's a railing round the top."

She found Halladay's precise speech mildly annoying, but his illustration and attention to detail gave her a clear picture of the courtroom.

"The prosecuting and defence counsel still wear the traditional wigs and robes, but they function in a contemporary environment, as exemplified by the polished wood panelling and clean lines of the furnishings."

"May I keep this?" she asked.

"By all means." Her question had disrupted his dialogue, and he frowned. "After you enter the witness-box, you will be asked what religious denomination you ascribe to and if you prefer to swear an oath on a holy book or to affirm."

"Will they have a Bible?"

"Yes. You will take it in your right hand and hold the card with the oath in your left as you read it."

Halladay then removed a stack of papers from his briefcase, and she saw the heading "Formal Statement" on one of them. She bit her lip. In spite of her continual exposure to the press coverage, she was not desensitized to her own experience. His questions were probing and specific, and he waited resignedly when she broke down.

They heard a knock. "Lunch," Andrews announced. Colin and Mr. Halladay ate their sandwiches at the dining table, but the other men had to make do with their laps, a real problem for Brian since his legs were so long that his lap wasn't horizontal. She took hers into the bedroom, where Sergeant Casey couldn't see how little she ate.

Then it was time to begin again. In the hospital, she had thought that Colin and Barry would never finish interviewing her, but Mr. Halladay's exacting methods took longer, and he recorded everything by hand, repeating her responses under his breath as he wrote. When he reached the end of her statement, he took off his glasses and looked at her severely. "Miss Jeffries, we have physical evidence that two of the other victims fought strongly against the accused. You did not. Why is that?"

"The attack was so sudden. Later I hurt so badly—there wasn't much I could do."

"Highly unsatisfactory," scowled Halladay.

She heard a rustle from the sitting room and turned to see Brian's hand on Sergeant Casey's shoulder. It wasn't a gentle gesture; Brian's fingers were digging into the sergeant's shirt.

"May I ask you some questions?" she asked Halladay.

He raised his eyebrows.

"Will I be asked about that in court?"

"I'm afraid so, yes."

"Will there be reporters in the courtroom?"

"Members of the press are allowed to attend, but no cameras are permitted." He replaced all the papers in his case and stood. "I won't trouble you any further today."

"Stand by," Sinclair told Halladay. "They'll depart first."

Casey flipped open his mobile, and she heard him give instructions to the driver. She rose, gathered her coat, and met them at the door. When they were well away, Casey rang Sinclair, and only then did he and the "weaselly bastard," as Casey called Halladay, exit the hotel.

CHAPTER 48

Several days passed before Jenny's next meeting with Mr. Halladay. To prepare her for what lay ahead, Danny rented DVDs of *Kavanagh, Q.C.,* which followed the cases of an eminent fictional barrister. Queen's Counsel was a designation conferred by the government, and barristers with that status wore silk gowns in court. Many of the scenes occurred in courtrooms, and they helped her visualize the elements of the court which Halladay had described.

Once again Mr. Halladay's pedantic approach made the time pass very slowly. It was difficult for the men also. They had no way to distract themselves, and the man who had been on watch the night before had to stay just as alert as the others. Their first session had been difficult but informative. The second was simply boring. She was surprised when a third session was scheduled.

As usual, she and the men arrived first. She hadn't slept well the night before, and the bed in the hotel room tempted her. The heavy curtains made the room dark, and the maid must have turned down the *matelassé* coverlet the night before and not replaced it. She suddenly remembered with a pang coming home from college and finding that her mother had turned her bed down in anticipation of her visit. She had taken her mother's love for granted then.

Mr. Halladay began by giving her some general instructions about effective testimony. "Mr. Benjamin, the barrister, will want you to be honest but concise. He will endeavor to keep his questions clear, and where possible, not require long answers from you. He's a Q.C.—quite capable, as we say. Little joke of ours."

A very little one. "Why are you telling me about him? Won't I be meeting him?"

"Absolutely not! There must be no personal contact whatever. Otherwise, charges of bias could be made."

"That's the strangest thing I've ever heard! Isn't he supposed to be on my side? How will I even know who's who?"

"The judge will address him by name," Halladay said. "May I continue?"

"Isn't he my ally?"

"Not exactly. You are a prosecution witness. It is his job to present the case for the prosecution in an objective manner. I assure you, Mr. Benjamin's preparation has been more than thorough. He has met with Detective Chief Inspector Sinclair on a number of occasions, as well as with the other investigating officers on the case."

Halladay was oblivious to her dismay.

"Listen carefully. You are required to respond only to questions, not to statements. If you don't understand a question, you may request that it be repeated. Take as much time as you need to answer clearly. We do not want you to be unduly stressed by the legal process."

"How can I not be? It's intrusive, it reminds me of a terrible time in my life, and the man who caused it all will be only a few yards from me."

"I realise it was a harrowing experience," Halladay said in a matter-of-fact voice, "but you don't have to look at the accused. Concentrate on Mr. Benjamin's questions."

"How long will it take? His questioning of me, I mean."

"Mr. Benjamin's examination will take at least a day. Defence counsel will likely use more than that. Mr. Benjamin may then reexamine you, if he deems it necessary." He removed his glasses and rubbed his eyes. "Alistair Alford, Q.C., will be leading for the defence."

"Leading?"

"The defendant has retained a team of barristers to represent him. Alford will lead the team because he is the most experienced."

"What will he—they—do to me?"

"We do not believe that he can dispute the evidence effectively. Therefore, he will try to discredit you."

It then seemed to her that Mr. Halladay tried to do the same thing. He queried her endlessly about her activities, particularly those during her college years, when she had been away from her parents' influence. Lunch came and went. The men had learned to eat slowly to pass the time, but she didn't have much appetite and wasn't revived by the meal. She assured Halladay that she had never been arrested by the local police, never reported for dangerous driving, never disciplined by the dean of students, and never cited for any infraction of dormitory rules. She had never cheated on written tests nor submitted any work that was not entirely her own.

She'd expected the meetings with the solicitor to make her feel more confident about her courtroom experience, but instead Mr. Halladay's colorless inquisition and the impersonal nature of the legal system conspired to shrink her courage. The law was like an amorphous structure of wheels and gears, each connected to the next, like a human skeleton without the heart and the features that gave it an individual personality. And she was the smallest cog on the smallest wheel. "If the monster—the accused—is convicted, will he get the death penalty?"

"We don't have the death penalty in England."

"He gave those other women the death penalty," she pointed out. "What if he had killed a policeman?"

“Not even then.” Halladay paused. “There’s one other item I should mention. My work with you is complete, but a meeting with the instructing solicitor for the defence will be scheduled soon.”

“What?” She looked at Colin. “Do I have to?”

It was Halladay who replied. “There is a rule in law,” he said, “which provides that there is ‘no property in a witness.’ It means that we have no sole proprietary claim to you. It is unusual, but the defence are well within their rights to request a meeting.”

She was stunned.

“Try not to worry. Your testimony is compelling, to say the least, and we have every confidence in you.” He collected his papers and picked up his briefcase.

“Not so fast,” Casey said in The Voice. “Ladies first.” He nodded at Sullivan, who retrieved her coat from the bedroom. “Now,” he told his mobile. Davies opened the door, checked the corridor, and they were away.

CHAPTER 49

The meeting with the instructing solicitor for the defence took place in yet another hotel. Brian was more heavily armed, and Jenny was nervous. The men exited the van first, shielding her from view when she stepped out and then surrounding her as they guided her inside.

The suite was large. A lustrous maple table dominated the dining room. The sofas were decorated in a tropical pattern, palm trees with mocha trunks on a sand background and an area rug the color of summer sunlight. It reminded her of a Caribbean island, and she tried to imagine how warm it would be on the white beaches. It was another cold day in London. The wind had gone right through her slacks, and the sweater she'd worn under her coat was acrylic, not wool.

Colin arrived shortly after they did, explaining that Humphrey Cooke had been sent to another location as a ruse and would be brought along shortly by Sergeant Andrews. It was barely ten a.m., and he expected their session to last most of the day. Sullivan set several glasses on the table with a pitcher of water and began to brew tea in the little kitchen. She had just wrapped her hands around the hot cup when Andrews and Cooke were admitted. Cooke was breathing hard, and he set his briefcase down and shed his overcoat and brown tweed jacket immediately.

"Sir, I'll have to search you," Davies announced.

"I've already been scanned by this officer," Cooke said, referring to Andrews. "Won't that do?"

"No, sir. Extend your arms, please." Davies patted him down. "Your briefcase, sir."

With a disgruntled snort, Cooke snapped it open for his inspection. Davies removed Cooke's phone. "Your mobile will be returned to you at the end of the session, sir." He handed it to Sergeant Andrews, who pocketed it and left.

Sinclair introduced Cooke to Jenny and took a chair at the end of the table. Cooke hefted his briefcase onto the table without the semblance of a smile and took a chair perpendicular to her, so close that his knees bumped hers.

She wasn't ready to face this well-fed bear of a man, with his black eyes and unblinking stare. She walked over to Brian and whispered, “I'm stalling. Think of something.”

“I'll get some for you, Miss,” he said. “Just one moment.” He collected some tissues from the bathroom at the back of the suite and brought them to her. She returned to the table but to a seat farther from the solicitor.

No reaction showed in Cooke's fleshy face. His voice was smooth and even as he began questioning her. Initially everything he asked was nonthreatening, clarifying her reasons for visiting London and detailing her early days there.

The men were quiet. She heard them change duty positions occasionally, but they didn't disturb the process in any way. She thought about how interminable these sessions must be for them, but it became rapidly clear that Cooke wasn't as bookish as Halladay had been.

As the questioning continued, he focussed on the events she had described in her statement. His voice never altered, but his eyes seemed to bore in on her, and his mouth never closed. Over and over he said, “You have stated that…” and then asked if she would care to rephrase her statement in any way, giving her an example. She noticed that the vocabulary he used was only slightly different in meaning from hers, and at first the differences didn't seem significant to her. If she accepted his terminology, however, his next sentence contained words that modified her meaning even more. Instead of being helpful by saying things for her, he was trying to get her to change them. It was confusing and mentally exhausting. She was glad she'd studied literature—she'd never have been as sensitive to the nuances of his words otherwise.

Eventually the lunch hour drew near, and Sergeant Andrews returned, offering to allow Cooke to make his sandwich selection first from the variety he'd brought.

“May I have my mobile, Sergeant?” Cooke snapped.

He was met with a bland smile and a negative response. She felt an undercurrent of support from Sergeant Andrews. She'd seen the duty smile he directed at Cooke but hadn't heard one in his voice.

“Then let's go on, shall we?” Cooke urged. “I never eat at midday.”

Sinclair stood. “Miss Jeffries does,” he responded.

That was her cue. She pushed her chair away from the table. When she rose, all the pieces of Kleenex she had shredded with her hands slipped off her lap, a tangible testament to her anxiety. She went into the bedroom, shutting the door. Almost immediately there was a soft knock. She tensed, but it was Danny, bringing her a Coke and a chicken salad sandwich on a croissant. There were rocket leaves instead of lettuce inside, definitely a step up from their other hotel lunches. “Save a little room,” he grinned, pulling a Penguin bar from his pocket. Chocolate! She could have kissed him.

The Coke settled her stomach a little, and she remembered as she ate that Colin had suggested once, when she was upset, to focus on something neutral. She studied the pale green silk curtains and matching bedspread. The fabric was dotted with embroidered lavender and blue hydrangeas, much larger than the ones her mother had grown at home. How far away home seemed now—farther even in experience than in miles. She had come to depend on the policemen in the other room. What would it feel like to go home to Texas and leave them behind? Would she find her family changed also? Was trauma contagious? It must not be, or Colin and Sergeant Casey would have caught it long ago.

This time it was Colin's knock that interrupted her. He came in with a concerned look and an extended handkerchief. She laughed through her tears, thinking of the headline, "Jennifer Jeffries in London—Handkerchief Sales Soar." She brought the handkerchief with her when she returned to the dining room.

The afternoon session began. Cooke had unbuttoned his waistcoat, and his white shirt glistened like a viper's new skin. She recalled the advice Mr. Halladay had given her about testifying in court: Take your time, and be concise. She decided to apply that wisdom here, so she answered all Cooke's statements which began, "You have stated that..." with one word: "Yes." When he asked if she wished to rephrase her statement, she simply said, "No."

Eventually it was the material laden with frightening memories that had to be covered. She did not want to cry in front of this man, but it still hurt to remember, and taking a deep breath or a sip of water didn't shield her from her feelings.

Cooke varied his approach. When she became upset, he softened his questions, trying to make it sound as if the things that had happened hadn't been so bad. He never used the word rape, referring instead to what he called energetic intercourse, and acknowledging in an understanding tone that such activity could be distressing for someone so inexperienced, however agreeable she may have been when it began.

Once again she took refuge in short, simple answers. When he mentioned unfortunate discomfort, she said, "Pain." When he referred to scratches, she insisted, "Gashes." She corrected Cooke, who suggested that perhaps she could agree that in the heat of the moment Scott had "just taken things a bit too far."

His deceptively soft vocabulary notwithstanding, he disputed everything. Parrying his repeated thrusts exhausted her. From time to time he made a note, his pen jabbing into the paper. Did she have to answer every question? There was no official recording being made of her replies.

Cooke leant toward her and raised his voice suddenly, startling her. "You don't want to admit to initiating this whole charade, do you?"

"It isn't a charade, it's all true," she insisted.

"Truth is relative, Miss Jeffries! A jury will decide whose truth will prevail."

She paled. Surely the jury would believe her!

"What did you think when you saw Mr. Scott's residence? Money?

You had a motive then, didn't you?"

She heard Brian rise to his feet. When a man of his bulk moved, it was impossible to disguise.

"Defending yourself wasn't an issue, was it, Miss Jeffries?"

His words cut into her. "Stop!" she gasped. "Go away!"

"Like a bitch in heat, you led him on!"

Colin's fist hit the table. "This interview is terminated! Casey, prepare to depart with Miss Jeffries."

Casey snapped his mobile closed. "We're off, sir," he told Sinclair, and then he was at her elbow. She wiped her cheeks and stuffed the handkerchief in her pocket for the trip back to the flat. This time she didn't feel the cold. The aggressive, accusatory attitude of the solicitor presaged worse to come. And the memory of her three protectors' wary, alert faces scanning the streets as they took her home haunted her.

CHAPTER 50

Over the next days Jenny tried to forget Cooke's insidious interrogation and the lurid nature of his vocal attack. Relaxing with a book and two new CDs proved impossible, so she chose instead to reread the correspondence from her parents. Her mother had sent short encouraging notes. Her dad relied on quotes, including Lincoln's: "Let us have faith that right makes might; and in that faith let us to the end, dare to do our duty as we understand it." He wanted to bolster her strength of will, and she needed it. The words that kept running through her mind were less positive: Hamlet's lament that "the time is out of joint—O cursed spite, / That ever I was born to set it right!"

Meanwhile the men worked. Colin brought a detailed map of the entire area between their block and the courthouse and described their destination. "St. George Crown Court was built to ease the case load at the other Crown Courts. The courtrooms are about the same size as Southwark or Middlesex, and judges hear a variety of cases there. The neighbourhood is primarily commercial." In response to Casey's questions, he reported that all the streets between the two sites were surface streets. There were no overpasses, tunnels, or railway crossings to negotiate. There were several one-way streets, including one behind the courthouse.

Brian began to highlight other important sites: the nearest police station, the closest hospital with a casualty department. Areas with potential traffic problems, such as factories, were designated. "Are there any bridges nearby?" he asked. "Wooded areas? How tall are the surrounding buildings?"

Sinclair answered what he could and made notes to determine the rest.

"We'll take it from here, sir," Casey said.

Sinclair left, and the team continued their heads-down. "We'll plot a primary and an alternate route. By the way," Casey continued, "I'll need both your medical records—blood groups, allergies, and so on. I have hers."

Davies then outlined the IIMAC model for Sullivan. "Information—that is, her needs—we know. Intention—keep her alive and well.

Method—we'll formulate that. Admin—getting vehicles, weapons, supplies—we'll leave that to the boss. Communications—radios, batteries, chargers, call signs—" He stopped. "What are we going to call JJ?"

"Phoenix," Casey answered. "It's a constellation."

"I thought a phoenix was a bird that came out of ashes," Sullivan said.

"That's doubly appropriate then," Davies decided.

The next time Sinclair called by, Casey had a list of requirements, which included a trained driver. He and Davies planned to do their own recce of the routes, driving them ahead of time to correlate distances and times. Any road construction not already indicated on the map would be identified. Their experience had taught them that there was no substitute for firsthand observation or repeated examination of their plans. Jenny didn't want to hear their concerns, but Casey's military voice carried, and she was sure she heard him tell Colin, "We're still vulnerable. At that spot. There's no way around it that I can see."

A jury was chosen, and the trial of William Cecil Crighton Scott began. The newspapers were full of information about the long line of witnesses, their expertise, their testimony, their possible impact upon the jury. Colin had told her that although she was a key witness, the evidence against Scott in the six murders would be presented first.

The tension level was rising for all of them. Her nightmares, which had abated, returned with a vengeance. The monster and his two men were there, but they were not alone. Cooke bit into her with his questions, and even the unsmiling Mr. Halladay played a supporting role.

Her days were filled with trepidation. The meetings with the solicitors had opened her eyes to the reality of what she faced. Even the questions asked by the prosecution would be invasive. If Cooke were any indication of what she would encounter from the defense, she would be in for a very rough time. How far would the judge allow the defense to go? Would he intervene at all? She snapped at the men for no reason, regretting her sharp tongue as soon as she exercised it. Sergeant Casey medicated her at night to help her sleep and probably wished he could do the same in the daytime.

One evening Colin came by early. "You're to be called first, tomorrow morning. I rang your mother this afternoon to tell her. She's waiting to hear from you."

"'My apprehensions come in crowds; / I dread the rustling of the grass; / The very shadows of the clouds / have power to shake me as I pass.' That's Wordsworth," she told him. "I don't have any words of my own."

Colin bent down and kissed her on the cheek. "You'll be fine. I'll see you in the morning."

After he left, she called home, wishing her father were there, even in the middle of the day. "I need a dress rehearsal," she told her mother. "It'll be unfamiliar as well as frightening." Then she said good-bye quickly, before her emotions overwhelmed her. She looked up at the Union Jack, still mounted on her wall, and let her eyes trace the long arms of the crosses of St. Andrew and St. Patrick and the dominating square cross of St. George which overlaid them. She wondered if she'd be the slayer, the slain, or—St. Patrick, her testimony driving the monster into a metaphoric sea.

Dinner was early, and it seemed to take forever. She felt numb inside her own skin and had to remind herself to use her fork, to chew, to swallow. It was the first meal that Brian had produced that had no flavor, although the men didn't seem to notice. Their focus appeared to be on fortifying themselves, because all three of them had second helpings.

"It's early to bed and early to rise for me," she told Sergeant Casey. He brought her a sleeping tablet, which she took gratefully. "Who's on watch tonight?"

"Sullivan."

He was still standing by the bed.

"Is there anything else?"

"Tomorrow—if there's any problem—do what I tell you to do. Don't think."

She smiled. He means, don't argue. "Piece of cake," she said. "Just use The Voice, and I'll fall right in line."

Later she thought about how fond she had become of these men, Brian and Danny like brothers, Casey like something more. Colin—she didn't know. He had kissed her, as encouragement. He had danced with her. Had that been encouragement, too? Her arms and legs began to feel heavy, as if she had been moving with the music for a long time. She slept.

CHAPTER 51

Sinclair arrived at the flat shortly after five a.m. Jenny dressed quickly, having set out her clothes the night before. Her mother had sent two wool suits and several silk blouses for her court appearances, but the royal blue with black and ivory strands in the pattern was her favorite. She wanted to wear her watch—the one Colin had given her, with the amethyst hearts—but didn't. It fit like a bracelet, showing below her cuff. The cross, on the other hand, was concealed beneath her blouse.

She ran a brush through her hair, curving it behind her ear on one side and letting it fall forward on the side where the scar was. She drank a cup of hot tea but couldn't get down more than half a slice of dry toast. The men were in uniform, and she could see the chevrons on the epaulettes that Sergeant Casey wore.

"You need to be kitted up, too, love," Casey said, adjusting her body armour on top of her suit. They donned theirs and added topcoats to disguise the fact that they were all carrying. Brian had a second weapon in his hands. It was very sobering.

They exited the block by the rear door. An unmarked car with a driver was waiting for them in the car park behind the building. They took the same positions as they had for the trips to meet the solicitors, with Brian riding shotgun and Jenny in the back between Danny and Sergeant Casey.

"I'll see you there," Sinclair said and stepped back. It was barely six. Jenny leaned forward to look through the front windshield. The weather was bleak—misty, overcast, and so cold that her breath was visible in the air. She had wished for a clear day, for a glimpse of sky so blue that she could imagine it stretching all the way to Texas, a vast firmament connecting her to her family. Instead it was metallic gray.

The circuitous route notwithstanding, they arrived at the courthouse very early. It was a large modern structure, looking more like an office building than a seat of justice. The driver slowed as he approached the back entrance. She could see police cars in a cluster and officers waving them into position. Sergeant Casey stepped out on the right side of the vehicle. Brian and Danny exited on the left, scanning the street before gesturing her to follow. The armor felt heavy, and it took her a moment to get her feet under her. She had barely risen when she heard a high-pitched whine and turned toward the sound. It was a courier on a small motorcycle, coming very fast, his briefcase in front of him.

Danny collapsed in front of her, his head red with blood. Then something hit her chest like a baseball bat, slamming her backward against the car. Searing pain tore at her shoulder. She would have screamed, but she couldn't get a breath. Her knees buckled, and she fell, slowly, it seemed. Sergeant Casey's face was over her, his hand pressing on her carotid artery. "Phoenix is compromised!" he yelled. "Officer down!" His fingers opened her mouth and swept it briefly.

He turned away, but others were there, positioning her arms and legs and rolling her gently onto her side. "Hold on, Miss," an unfamiliar voice said. Someone pressed a heavy hand on her shoulder where the pain was.

She didn't see Brian raise his MP5 for maximum accuracy in the crowded plot. She didn't hear his double tap or the squeal of the Suzuki as it hit the pavement on its side.

The sky—where was the sky? Her visual world had shrunk to mere inches. She couldn't see beyond the large dark shoes, trouser cuffs, one man's knee on the rough, damp concrete, and the sleeve of the officer whose fingers monitored the pulse in her neck. She felt light headed and weak. She heard men's voices and their shouted commands, loud at first, then fading. The dark uniforms surrounding her grew dim. She didn't see how quickly Sergeant Casey worked as he applied pressure bandages to Sullivan's wounds. She felt very cold. She didn't see Colin's white strained face or hear him notify Casey that the ambulance was on its way. She didn't hear Casey's terse response: "No time. Load Sullivan now."

She didn't feel her armor being removed or see the sergeant's combat knife slicing through her suit to expose her wounds. "Phoenix is stable. I stopped the bleed. Catch us up at the hospital later." She didn't see the cordon of officers around them. They still had a witness to protect, although she didn't know that. She was unconscious when she and Sullivan were lifted into police cars and whisked away.

Sinclair forced himself to focus. First, ring Graves. He'd need to assign a temporary replacement for Davies and a permanent one for Sullivan. Davies would have to turn in his weapons and all unused rounds to a Scenes-of-Crime officer for forensic examination. The shooter had been prepared—his body armour, his speed, the way he was jinking the bike—Davies was lucky to have hit him at all.

The ambulance had arrived, and the motorcyclist had been taken, under police guard, to a different hospital than his victims. Andrews had secured the scene behind the courthouse and would keep all the uniforms in place until their statements had been taken.

Judge Thomas would have to be notified about the attack, as would counsel on both sides. Sinclair wanted Scott remanded in isolation until the police investigation of this incident was complete, and counsel for the prosecution would have to make that petition. With the current emphasis on defendants' rights, he hadn't a hope that it would be approved, but for Jenny's sake, they had to try.

Dear God, he'd have to give Jenny's parents a bell as well as Sullivan's. Sullivan's personnel file was in his office at the Yard, and he needed to make the call himself, not delegate it, however tempting that might be. It was far too early in Texas for him to ring the Jeffries; he'd wait until after she had come out of the operating theatre. Having the latest information on her condition could reassure them. Her shoulder and upper arm were lacerated and torn, but Sullivan had taken the worst of it.

He had a long list, with Jenny and Sullivan at the top. A well-planned operation, with competent, experienced officers executing it, but two people were seriously injured. No, Sullivan was critical—Casey, a man of few words in normal circumstances, hadn't wasted any describing his condition. Jenny was stable. Casey's focus had been on getting Sullivan advanced medical care as soon as possible.

This case was Sinclair's responsibility, and correspondingly, it was his job to get his witness to court safely. Ensuring the lives of the officers who protected her was secondary but still important. If she had been residing outside London, would it have made any difference? They would still have had to transport her from a hotel somewhere in the city to the courthouse. Their point of vulnerability would have been the same. What could they do differently the next time? Mustn't think about that now. For the moment what mattered was that Jenny and Sullivan were in more capable hands than his bloody ones.

CHAPTER 52

Jenny woke in a hospital room, alone and with images of the attack vivid in her mind. Danny—was he even alive? Was anyone else hurt? Where was everybody? When the nurse came in, she was accompanied by a policeman.

"Dr. Gallagher will be round in a bit," the nurse said, recording Jenny's vital signs.

"Officer?" Jenny said when he turned to leave with the nurse. "Would you stay with me? Will it be breaking the rules if you do that? Have you heard anything about Danny? Constable Sullivan, I mean—he was hurt, too."

"PC Billings, Miss. I just came on. I'm afraid I don't have any news."

The door opened, and Sergeant Casey entered. There was dried blood on his sleeves and a smudge on his cheek. "There's no easy way to say this, love. Sullivan's in a coma." He saw the shock on her face. "One of the rounds hit him in the head. He has other less serious wounds as well. But it's early days yet. There's hope."

"Are you okay? What about Brian? Where's Colin?"

"I'm in one piece. Davies is fine. He did good work today. The last time I saw the boss, he was with Sullivan's family. He's probably in a slanging match with your doctor now."

"What happened out there?"

"The man on the cycle had an Uzi in his briefcase. Davies slotted him. He's in custody. A few of the plods picked up minor injuries. Some of the rounds ricocheted."

"Sergeant, I can't stand this—Danny—in a coma—"

Casey prised her fingers off his hand and checked her pulse. It was racing. "First things first, love. Deep breath."

She couldn't. "It hurts, Sergeant."

"Blow all your air out, slowly."

That hurt, too.

"Now take it back in, plus some."

She tried.

"Again. All out—back, plus some. Think on your breathing. No more talk until you've settled a bit."

Her pulse rate was better. He sat down on the edge of the bed. "Listen to me, love. Sometimes the body has to shut off a few systems to focus on a particular area. There are different levels of comas. It could be worse." He began to rub her palm and her fingers, being careful not to bump the drip needle.

She gripped his hand. "Do my parents know?"

"The boss took care of that." He stood. "The next few days are not going to be easy. I want you to have a rest. I'll be back."

She couldn't settle enough to sleep. The attack had been sudden and shocking. She knew it hadn't been the monster on the motorcycle, but it might as well have been. She could almost hear his snarl and see the cruel set of his mouth. In her mind's eye she watched his hand fall, sending the cyclist on his way in a desperate attempt to silence her. She tried to breathe out, but it was hard to force the air past the lump in her throat. She tried to breathe in, but it was a sob. Her chest and shoulder ached. The sling didn't help.

She heard voices outside her room: Colin's, full and assertive, and someone else's, raised in frustration. "Oh, Jen," Colin said when he saw her glistening cheeks. The other man consulted a chart before approaching her.

"I'm Dr. Gallagher." He reached for her wrist and frowned. Sergeant Casey joined them. They were like stair steps, with Gallagher the first step, Casey the next, and Colin at the top. Gallagher was showing the most dissatisfaction, however, his young face dark with distrust. "Chief Inspector, this won't do. Her blood pressure and pulse rate are still up. I'm concerned about bleeding. I want to keep her twenty-four hours." He turned to her. "Miss Jeffries, I am acting in your best interest. I can see you're upset. Shoulder bothering you? By this time tomorrow you'll feel much better."

"The longer we wait, the more danger there will be," Sinclair insisted. "I am moving her for her own safety. Casey can handle any medical situation that may arise."

"Miss Jeffries, significant risk exists for you—bleeding and infection are only two of the possible consequences. Post-op recovery time is critical. You are of age. The police cannot act against your wishes."

Did she have to choose between health and safety? She looked at Colin. His face was grim and worn. "Trust me," he said.

She blinked hard. "Sergeant Casey?"

"Best all round if you come with us."

"Miss Jeffries," Dr. Gallagher began. She closed her eyes, but she couldn't shut out his aggressive tone. "There's your answer, Chief Inspector—she's not well enough to make an informed decision."

"No—wait—" She looked at the doctor and almost felt sorry for him, having pitted himself against Colin and Sergeant Casey. "Someone tried to kill me today. The man who sent him isn't going to stop. I want to be safe. I'll take my chances with bleeding and infection."

Dr. Gallagher shook his head in regret. "How soon?" he asked

Sinclair.

"Within the hour."

Gallagher acquiesced. "Come with me, Sergeant." They left the room.

Sinclair stepped beside the bed. "I'm sorry for all this, Jen. Will you be all right for a few minutes?"

"Are the policemen still outside? Could one of them come in until you get back? I'm—"

"I know. Billings!" he called. "Look after Miss Jeffries." He was gone.

Billings stepped just inside the door. He reminded Jenny of Danny—older and taller, but with the same earnest face. "How can I help, Miss?"

"Just look fierce and be ready to fire," she answered. "Really. I'm not joking."

He looked as if he wanted to smile but wasn't sure if he should.

"Do you have sisters?" She was still thinking about Danny.

"A sister and a brother. I'm the oldest."

"Me, too. Sometimes I wish I weren't—fine example I'm setting."

"You are, Miss. Very fine."

Her shoulder was throbbing badly when Colin returned with Sergeant Casey and Dr. Gallagher. The only one who looked alert and capable was the doctor. Leaving him probably wasn't one of her better moves.

Gallagher spoke first. "Miss Jeffries, I have two jabs for you—one for pain and one to help you relax."

"I only want the one for pain. No sedative."

"Sorry?"

"Don't you need my permission to medicate me? Well, I'm not giving it."

"Jenny, you'll need it. It's not a short ride," Sinclair argued.

"I don't want it! Doesn't what I want count for anything?"

"Please. I don't want you to be in pain."

"He's going to give me something for pain," she said, her voice rising.

"You're already exhausted," Gallagher said, still holding the tray with the two syringes. "Further fatigue could delay healing."

"No, no, no, no, no!" she cried. "I don't want a sedative! Put it away! Don't you understand? I have to stay awake. If someone comes after me, I want to know. If I go to sleep—and a killer comes—I won't get to wake up!"

"Jenny."

Oh, God, it was The Voice.

"You're agitated. We can't transport you like this." The quiet firm voice continued. "Listen to me, Jenny. We've sent a decoy to UCH with a police escort. The transfer was reported on the news. We'll use unmarked vehicles. No one is going to know who you are or where you are. There will be no killing tonight."

"Promise?"

"On my badge."

She turned to Colin. "Are you going with me?"

He looked as if he had aged ten years. "For security reasons, it's best if I don't."

Gallagher handed the tray to Casey.

"If I don't wake up, I'll kill you," she sobbed.

"There's my girl," Casey said. He administered the injections.

She heard Gallagher's voice. "We'll keep the vein open," he said, leaving the needle in her hand and plugging the outer end. He inspected the drains in her shoulder and gave Casey instructions for their care and removal.

She felt sleepy. Whatever Casey had given her, it was already working. "Is Danny's family with him?" she asked Colin.

"Yes, they're all there."

"Colin, I don't want him to die."

"He's in good hands, Jen."

He had to lean over to hear her. "I don't want to die," she whispered.

Sinclair found that he could not reply.

CHAPTER 53

When Jenny woke in the flat, Sergeant Casey was with her. He used the drip to administer her pain medication as well as the light sedative Gallagher had prescribed for the first twenty-four hours. The doctor wanted to restrict her activity level; Casey wanted to postpone the emotional consequences. He'd seen hardened men suffer anxiety after being shot, and it was inevitable for her.

She stirred slightly when she heard PC Hawkins' cough, but she didn't waken. Casey took the offered tray and ate quickly. He returned it to the kitchen and made himself a cup of strong tea. Kirvin was asleep. The young PC had been on the transport team and had had the night watch. He would have to take it tonight as well. Hawkins, a wiry man with the odd patch of grey in his hair and a slight cleft in his chin, was on watch with PC Nicholson.

Casey watched Jenny sleep, managing to change the dressing on her shoulder without waking her. Her wounds were clean and draining well, but infection, if present, would not manifest itself this soon. He slept only for short periods, resting as best he could in the armchair he'd stationed next to her bed.

The second day Casey removed the drip and discontinued the sedative, giving her oral medication instead. Sinclair and Andrews called by late in the morning to take her statement about the shooting. Neither looked like he'd slept. They reported no change in Sullivan's condition.

The interview didn't take long, and Sergeant Andrews recorded everything in his notebook.

"Why isn't Brian here?"

"He shot a man, Jenny. That means temporary suspension. Every shooting is investigated."

"But that man shot Danny—and me! Brian did the right thing!"

"Yes, and fortunately for Davies, all the witnesses were coppers."

"Where are my clothes?" she asked.

"They were collected at hospital as evidence."

"Was there a photographer? Did you have to photograph me?"

"We did, yes," Colin answered.

"My shoulder?"

There was a long silence. "And your chest."

She frowned. Sergeant Casey had folded back the sleeve of her hospital gown to change the dressing on her shoulder. She hadn't seen her chest. The gown was tied closed in front, and she undid the bow and let it fall open. There was a laceration covered with a steristrip and several cylindrical bruises, wide and red with deep, dark centers, where the bullets had struck her body armor. She held her hand over her chest and began to sob. The gown was still open, and Colin didn't know what disturbed him more—seeing her lovely breasts exposed to others or the dark tattoos of attempted murder between and above them.

"I'm running out of lives," she cried. "He'll get me next time! Oh God—the next time it'll be my dead body you take pictures of!"

"No, Jen, I won't let that happen."

"It's all wrong—when I didn't care about dying, I lived, and now that I want to live, I'm going to die!"

Hawkins was in the sitting room. Casey heard his muffled cough.

"Look at me, Jen. We'll do better next time."

"How? I have to go back to the same place, don't I?"

He stood, his recrimination surfacing. "It was my operation and my responsibility. Do you understand? What happened to Sullivan and what happened to you—it's mine." He turned to Andrews. "Time to go."

"I don't care about justice anymore!" she cried after he left.

"Of course you don't!" Casey answered. "No one does, when they're in the thick of it."

"Those marks on my chest—I should be dead!"

He lifted her chin, wishing her defiance hadn't been replaced with despair. "Focus, Jenny. Battles are fought one day at a time. Today's battle—accepting that you're safe." Her tears were still coming, and they made her lashes glisten. He'd never been under fire with a woman, much less a civilian. He'd assessed her condition quickly and had reacted appropriately by treating Sullivan first, but now he found himself wanting to protect her from more than gunfire.

When she woke, she covered her face with her hand, not wanting Casey to see her upset again. "It's okay to cry, love," he said. "Being hit—seeing a mate go down—it's difficult. We've all been affected by it."

"I'm so scared I feel sick. He's determined to kill me!"

"Actually, he's desperate. That's why the nature of his attacks has escalated. But I know how to assess an enemy. I'll make sure you're all right."

He helped her don a dressing gown. When they went into the dining room, Brian was there. His eyes went to her shoulder. "Oh, JJ," he said, the smile sliding off his face as he came toward her. "I wish I'd been in front of you at the courthouse."

"I'll have none of that, Davies."

"I should have been," Brian insisted. "I'm a bigger target. She'd not have been hit. Nor Sullivan."

"Now's not the time, Davies!" Casey said sharply.

She eased into one of the dining room chairs, disturbed by the conflict between Brian and Casey. She needed Danny and his impish grin more than ever, but Brian put his arm around her, and being in the lee of the mountain made the trembling stop.

After dinner she called her family. They wanted her to come home, and she was more tempted to go than she had ever been. "None of you would be in danger anymore," she told Sergeant Casey.

"That's back to front," he answered. "It's not your job to protect us." By now he could spot all the signs that she was hurting, no matter how hard she tried to hide them: the tightness in her face, the halting way she spoke, her hunched shoulder, her careful breathing. He went into the kitchen and brought her a glass of milk and an analgesic. She took them without argument, another sign.

"God, I'm tired of all this." She shifted her left arm and winced. "I feel like the boxer who lost the bout. All that's missing are the gloves and the sweat. When can I shower?"

"Domani. Tomorrow. If you keep your shoulder dry."

She nodded. "I don't have the strength tonight. There's something I need to do, though." She punched Colin's mobile number and hardly recognized the weary voice that answered. "Colin, it's not your fault. None of this is your fault. The monster's to blame."

"Do you want me to call by? I'm still at the Yard, but if you need me, I'll come straight round."

"No. I just want you to know—you're a good man. You have good men here. We have right on our side. We'll try again."

"Jen—thank you. More than you know."

She climbed in bed, fatigued in spite of her nap but with a little less unrest in her spirit. When Sergeant Casey came in and changed the dressing on her shoulder, she encouraged him to rest, too. "I'll be all right. Please. I worry about you."

There was a quickening in his eyes, but his voice was even. "Jenny." It was the tone he used when there was going to be no more discussion. "I'll be right here."

CHAPTER 54

Brian was finishing a late lunch, and Casey and Jenny were still at the table. Her hand shook a little as she reached for her Coke, and Casey watched her press her palm against the table instead of drinking. Good thing he hadn't reported the news—according to Andrews, Sinclair was in for it. He'd been carpeted, and he and Graves were under review for the shootings. The timing couldn't have been worse, either for the Met, which desperately needed some positive publicity, or for Jenny, who didn't need a stranger in charge of her case. Andrews hadn't known if Sinclair would continue as their operational contact.

"It'll be the boss," Brian said when he heard the knock.

Sinclair was accompanied by a stocky, muscular man with thick hands and short, dark curly hair who threw his rucksack against the wall. He was more careful with his gun case.

"Hunt, I'd like you to meet Jennifer Jeffries," Sinclair said. "Jenny, this is PC Hunt. The super's assigned him to the protection team."

"Alan Hunt." He pulled out a chair and sat down next to her.

"You're putting someone else in harm's way?" she asked Colin. "How's Danny?"

"Jenny, there's been no change."

She could feel the new officer looking at her.

"You're the talk of the town," he said.

"I hope not."

"A girl who doesn't want to be the centre of attention? Not in a million!" His eyes were examining her face. "Why aren't you proud of it?"

"Proud? When every day it's a reminder of what he did?"

"Because he had three tries and didn't score. It's Yank three, Scott nil."

The flat seemed smaller. She had put on a tank top to allow Sergeant Casey easier access to her shoulder, but now she wished she weren't so exposed. She wished the surgical dressing were larger.

"Fancy watch," he said.

"Danny deserves the purple hearts more than I do," she responded.

Sinclair decided to put a stop to Hunt's examination. "Casey's in charge here."

Hunt nodded at Casey. He stood and punched Davies on the shoulder. "Haven't seen you around Old Street lately. Wondered where you'd got off to! How long have you been here?"

"Since late September."

"Hardly a peach job—and you haven't gone completely potty? I'd be climbing the walls!" He turned back to Jenny. He was curious about the little girl with the big file he'd had to plow through at his briefing. "Texas! I thought you'd be bigger."

Casey saw her raise her chin. "Size isn't everything," she said.

"Yes, it is!" Hunt whooped. "By the way—your president still mucking about with the ladies? He ought to keep his trousers zipped!"

Her face paled. There had been numerous headlines in the newspapers about President Clinton's infidelity. "Stop! Just stop!"

He threw up his hands in a gesture of defeat. "Sorry! Bull in a china shop."

She stood and left the kitchen. Hunt eyed her up as she went.

"See that you don't alarm her," Sinclair warned. He headed back to the Yard.

While Jenny rested, Casey and Davies outlined the ground rules for Hunt. Casey was a bit exasperated with him already. "Weren't you briefed? Don't get too close to her. She's scared enough."

"Throttle back, mate," Davies added. "She's fragile."

"She looks okay. Why the long faces?"

"She's been to hell and back," Casey answered. "Sullivan was shot right in front of her. She's not fully recovered either. She has nightmares. We wake her."

"You want me in her bedroom?" Hunt asked.

"Sod it, Hunt, I want you to be a copper first and a man second!"

"What's the physical layout?"

"Only one entrance to this flat," answered Davies. "The door's reinforced, with multiple locks and an alarm. Three remote cameras. The only windows are in Jenny's room and the sitting room. There's a radio on all the time in her room, and we have the telly in the sitting room."

"Why'd she get the windows?"

"It was a privacy issue," Casey said, "and her room's farthest from the front door."

When Jenny woke from her nap, Sergeant Casey removed the drains from her shoulder and replaced the dressing. Hunt took a quick look round her room before settling in the sitting room with the other two men. She put one of her caftans on and forced herself to join them. "I'm at a disadvantage, Constable Hunt. You know all about me, and I don't know anything about you."

"Don't hesitate."

"Can you cook?"

Hunt threw back his head and laughed. "Not as well as I can eat, but we'll muddle through."

He was built like a bulldog, thick and solid. "Do you play rugby?"

"Great game! Love contact!"

"What else do you like?"

"Winning."

"And your family?"

"Full of coppers—my dad, my brother—my sister even married one. They all live in Manchester, where I'm from. But I'm the first to be a bloody bodyguard."

She lifted her chin. "You don't have to be one. Take off!"

"You're not the boss of me," Hunt retorted.

"No, but Colin is."

"First-name basis with the guv—how'd you rate that?"

"Got attacked."

"What would you like to call me?"

"History!"

Hunt was impervious. "Alan's okay. Anything's okay. I'll call you Tex."

"You will not!"

He was undeterred. "Why'd you change clothes?"

"You don't converse, you interrogate," she said.

"Never learnt to walk on eggshells. Saves time to speak my mind." He gave her an appraising look. "Three of us to protect one of you. The odds are in your favour. What are you afraid of?"

She was dismayed. "Have you ever been shot, Constable Hunt?"

"Not yet."

"Has someone ever tried to strangle you to death? Or beat you to death?" She saw his surprised expression and didn't wait for him to answer. "Have you ever been in so much pain you were afraid you *wouldn't* die? Have you ever been so afraid you—couldn't—breathe?"

"Christ," he swore. "What'd I do?"

"Dismissed!" Casey said so sharply that she jumped.

Davies left with Hunt. "He was SBS. Don't cross him," he said in a tense whisper. The door to the bedroom closed behind them.

"He's a bit rough about the edges," Casey said grimly. "I'll have a word with him. I'd like you to wait in your room while I do."

That was the pot calling the kettle black. The men's voices resounded in the small flat, Casey's colder and harder than she had ever heard it. It was laced with profanities, one of which appeared and reappeared with frightening frequency. She knew Casey was acting on her behalf, but he sounded out of control. She had never heard any of the men swear like that.

- -

Dinner was a quiet affair. Hunt was sullen; he knew she had heard his dressing-down. When she told him that she hadn't been herself and was sorry, he scowled, swore under his breath, and left the table. Casey went after him.

She held her breath, but she didn't hear anything. "What's he doing?" she asked Brian.

"Showing Hunt his low and menacing side. And explaining that the wrong person apologised."

Sinclair made a brief visit after dinner and was told by Casey that Jenny didn't like Hunt. "We need him," Sinclair said. "He's rested. He has to take the watch."

"I don't like it, sir. He may be weapons qualified, but he's a loose cannon. Davies and I had to calibrate him this afternoon. I'd issue an RTU order."

"Return to unit? Not yet. We have to use him, at least for the time being."

CHAPTER 55

When Sinclair came by late the next day, Hunt was sleeping in preparation for another night on watch. Sinclair took the opportunity to ask Jenny about him.

"He doesn't want to babysit me. But if he keeps taking the night shift, I won't have to see him too much."

"Anything else you need to tell me?"

She hated to give him more worries. He looked tense as well as tired, and there was a shadow behind his eyes.

"Jen?"

She looked down, and her chin trembled slightly. "I dream about Danny now. I see him fall, and there's so much blood! I'm afraid for him, and for you, and for all the men, even Hunt. He doesn't know he could be dead in a few weeks." They were sitting together on the sofa, and she took his hands and pleaded with him. "I don't want anyone else hurt. I want you to send them away."

"That's just not on, Jen—it's irrational."

"I don't care. I want to go it alone."

"Jen, you can't make it through the night without help."

"I'll get better. I'll take a cab to court. It'll work. It'll be so unexpected I'll get away with it."

He just shook his head at her.

"I'll fire everybody," was her next approach.

"You can't—they don't work for you. They don't even work for me. They were assigned by a more senior officer."

"I don't want them in danger! I can't stand this! I nearly got Danny killed!"

He tried for a gentle tone. "Jenny, we're not going anywhere. Everyone who accepted this assignment accepted the risk. Besides, you still need care."

"'Risk'—I hate your politically-correct police words! You should have said, 'death sentence.' It isn't safe for them to be here!"

She was insistent, and he became exasperated. He and Graves were still under investigation for the incident at the courthouse, and he didn't know whether his role in her case would be reduced. In addition, portions of the McPherson Report had been leaked to the Sunday Telegraph and printed in the morning edition. The Met had been cited for institutional racism and poor investigative procedures in the Stephen Lawrence murder case. He felt personally slandered—every decent copper did. She knew nothing of this, however, and she was still his responsibility until notified otherwise. He took a deep breath and kept his tone even. "Jenny, their presence is needed more now than ever. Can't you see that?" Finally he remembered a Texas expression that would make his point clear: "That dog won't hunt!"

The Texas comment sounded incongruous with his English accent, but it didn't calm her. The danger was tangible—she had seen it, and she still felt it. Her emotions were heightened, and she began to cry in frustration and fear. It was then that he crossed the line for the first time. He put his arms around her and pressed his lips against her hair, then the tears on her cheeks. When he lifted her face to his, she could taste the salt from her tears on his lips. His kisses were tender and gentle. She didn't pull away. Against all odds, she felt herself responding. She opened her mouth, and when she felt his tongue enter it, she kissed him back. When they broke apart a few moments later, her heart was pounding.

He rose to his feet and ran his hand through his hair. "Jen—my God—I shouldn't have done that. You have every right to be upset with me."

Her heart was still beating rapidly. He had shocked it back into life, and she felt something akin to wonder: A cherished possession believed to be lost forever had been returned.

He saw her blush and was emboldened. "Jen, you're very important to me. When you were shot, I thought I'd lost you, and all I could think was—I'd never have the chance to tell you how much you mean to me."

She looked up at him, this gentle, decent, refined man with regret and longing written all over his face, and knew she didn't want to hurt him. She reached out and touched his hand. "It's okay, Colin."

He pulled her to her feet. "I don't want you to be afraid of me." He took her face in his hands and let his thumbs caress her cheeks. Then he tensed, and his hands fell. "I should go," he said. He had headed for the door and called for Casey to lock up before she had a chance to reply.

Later, Sinclair berated himself for his actions. He should never have kissed her! She had not pushed him away, but he should not have done it. It could compromise the case and complicate her recovery. He had never before been tempted to behave inappropriately with a witness. But—she had responded.

CHAPTER 56

Several days passed. Sergeant Casey changed the dressing on Jenny's shoulder for the last time. Even the steristrips on her chest would be gone soon. Since Hunt continued to take the night watch and then slept all morning, she found some relief from his cocky, irreverent behavior. She did have to admit that he was lively, although in a far less predictable manner than Danny had been. His card playing, for example—he was noisy in victory and likely to come to blows with the winner if he lost.

She had slept late, but she was still tired. She felt warm and sluggish and didn't want to get out of bed. It felt even warmer in the kitchen when she went in. "Who turned up the heat?" she asked Casey. "I think I'll have a cold drink this morning instead of a hot one."

He frowned. She looked a bit peaky, and she was never warm in the flat. She hadn't had much appetite at dinner the night before and then had gone to bed early, causing Hunt to grouse about having to keep the sound on the telly low. He'd reported that she'd had a restless night, repeatedly throwing off the comforter. "Don't drink anything yet."

His tone startled her. What had she done to deserve The Voice?

He came back with a thermometer. She held it obediently under her tongue until he removed it. "It's back to bed with you, love. You have a fever. I'll bring you something to drink in a few minutes." He looked at his watch. It was almost ten. Damn! She could have been ill for over twelve hours, and none of them had twigged it.

He brought two tablets and a tall glass of cold juice for her. She shivered a little from the juice and slid down in bed to warm up. When he returned an hour later, she had pushed the covers aside. He took her temperature again and offered her another drink.

"Is my fever high?"

"Reading's in Celsius. Won't mean much to you. Rest now."

He went into his room and rang Dr. Gallagher. "Fever's up."

Gallagher knew Jenny's history. She had no spleen. Consequently any fever was cause for concern. "Any sign of infection in the wounds?"

"No, sir."

"Check her for swelling, tenderness, or any other indication of a fever source. In the meantime, I want a blood sample. I'm prescribing a broad spectrum antibiotic which I'd like you to administer through a drip." He rang off.

Casey phoned Sinclair and reported Gallagher's orders.

"I'll send Andrews straightaway."

Casey returned to her room. "I need to have a look at you, love." She had the covers piled high, but she let him remove them. "Tell me if anything feels tender." Nothing did.

When he came back to take her temperature again, her fever was still rising, and she was restive, wiping the sweat from her face and trying to fan herself with her hand.

He paced the sitting room, willing Andrews to arrive. He took her another glass of juice. "Even my eyes feel hot," she said. He moistened a face cloth in the bathroom and placed it on her forehead. She squeezed the excess water over her chest, and he watched it bead on her skin. She closed her eyes.

Where the bloody hell was Andrews? He heard her swallow. He ran his fingers down the sides of her neck. No swelling. "Throat sore?"

She nodded. She was cold now.

Damn! He rang Gallagher to report. Andrews hadn't arrived at the hospital yet. "I'll need a throat culture," the doctor said. "I'll include instructions and supplies in the packet I give Sergeant Andrews."

"Her fever's higher now. Shall I bring her in?"

"We'll wait for the test results."

Casey was coming out of the bathroom with another face cloth when Andrews arrived. He unpacked everything Gallagher had sent. He took the blood sample from her arm first, having to explain that Gallagher needed it to isolate the reason for her illness. Then he set up the stand. Gallagher had sent two drips, one with glucose and one with saline. She was restless and apprehensive, and when he tried to insert the needle in her limp hand, she jerked her hand away, and blood welled up in a thin line. "Andrews, I could use some help here," he said without turning.

"I'll send Davies," he heard Andrews say. His lighter tread was replaced by Davies' heavier stride.

"Why are you doing all this?" she asked.

He'd not told her that her immune system was compromised. "Gallagher's orders. Your resistance is down because of your recent wounds."

"But IVs are for the hospital. You're scaring me! Why do I need it?"

"Gallagher believes in aggressive treatment," he told her. "Davies, hold her arm and hand still."

"If you don't get it the first time, you'll have to ask Hunt," Davies said, one hand over her fingers and the other squeezing her elbow.

Casey gave him a sharp look and got it the first time.

"The needle hurts," she said. "Do you always have to be in such a hurry? Is my next court date already set and you have to get me well by a certain time?"

"Nothing of the sort." He connected the tubing and set the bags on the stand, adjusting the rate of flow. Gallagher's instructions said to administer the antibiotic next. Then he sat down on the edge of the bed and patted her cheek. “Open wide, love.”

“What’s the Q-tip for?”

“Throat culture.” He wasn’t sure how far down her throat to poke it. “Davies, bring a torch.”

The light helped. He aimed for the redness. She gagged, but he was done. He sent Andrews on his way with everything that needed to be returned to the hospital. Gallagher had included a stronger antipyretic with instructions on how often he could give it. It would be time soon. The over-the-counter medicine he’d used in the morning hadn’t been effective. He waited. It hurt her to swallow, but she got it down.

The time passed very slowly. Periodically he brought her a cooler face cloth or something to drink. The cycle of heat and chills had not ceased. “I feel like a slice of Brian’s fried bread,” she told him. “Sizzling.”

He didn’t expect to hear from Gallagher today. He might get a reading on the throat culture quickly, but the blood sample would take longer to test. He realised he’d missed lunch. He went into the kitchen and made himself a sandwich and a cup of coffee.

“I hear Little Bit’s tits up,” Hunt said. He’d begun to tease her, calling her a Little Bit of Texas.

“Yes. She doesn’t have a normal immune system.”

“If you need a break, I’ll sit with her. I’m not as squeamish as Davies.”

Casey nodded and finished his impromptu meal. He went back to her room and took her temperature. The new medication hadn’t had any impact yet on her fever.

Davies brought him dinner and asked what else he could provide.

“More strong coffee.”

Hunt came in and coaxed her. “Time to eat, Little Bit.”

She was listless, but she did eat a few biscuits and some gelatin, to Casey’s surprise. He wouldn’t have thought Hunt the sort to have a decent bedside manner.

Sinclair rang, wanting to know if he should notify her parents before he left the Yard. Casey advised waiting for lab results and giving Gallagher’s medicine time to work. He promised to ring Sinclair in the morning, even if there were no change.

Sinclair didn’t wait for morning. He stopped in on his way home. Casey saw him sit down on her bed and stroke her cheek.

“I’ll be okay, Colin. Don’t worry about me.”

She protects him, Casey noted. Interesting. Something has changed between them.

CHAPTER 57

Twenty-four hours passed, but to Jenny it seemed much longer. There was nothing to do. She was too sick to read. Sergeant Casey turned up the volume on the radio, but it wasn't soothing. The slower and softer the music was, the sadder it made her feel. The tunes that moved, that had a beat, made her head pound.

Brian's sandwiches were dry and tasteless as sawdust. The only foods that appealed were Cokes—which were rapidly becoming cloying—and potatoes, which Brian boiled until they were so soft that she hardly had to chew. If she were home, her mother would have breezed in and out, checking on her, cajoling her. Sergeant Casey was always nearby, but he was not smiling.

It was so unfair! She should have testified already. Danny should be in the flat, calling Brian "Spuds" and making jokes to help her settle down after the courtroom experience. Spuds and Suds. Sergeant Casey was Suds because of the baths he'd given her, but Danny had never called him that to his face. Danny had been sly—involving her in his plans to play practical jokes on the others so she wouldn't suspect she was his first target. When she'd found bubblegum on her toothbrush, she knew she'd been duped twice. "You chewed it first, Danny," she said when she confronted him. "That's gross!"

"It is, isn't it?" he'd laughed. "Want a new toothbrush?" He'd set his sights on Brian and Sergeant Casey next, confessing that Casey was the hardest to get. "I want to replace his combat knife with a rubber one, but he's too vigilant." He'd had to settle for repeatedly moving his bookmark, but he'd promised her he wouldn't give up. Now he was in a hospital bed, and she might as well be. Her every movement was monitored.

She picked up her cell phone and called home. "Mother, it's Jenny. I'm sick, and I miss you."

Casey stepped outside her room, not wanting to be available to discuss her condition.

"Fever and sore throat. Sergeant Casey's taking good care of me, but I wish you were here."

There was a pause.

"I don't know, but he's talked to the doctor and everything."

Silence.

"Yes, I will. I just missed you, that's all. I'll call again soon." She saw Casey enter the room. Not the thermometer again! Every time he took her temperature, he looked more somber. Then he'd bring crackers, jello, juice, ice cream—and she didn't want any of it. "I've never been this sick. Am I contagious? Is that why Brian and Hunt don't come in anymore?"

"They've got their hands full, love. They've split the watch, and there won't be any day police for a while."

"You're here all the time. Are you going to catch it?"

"Not likely."

She jumped. "What was *that*?"

"Hunt's crushing ice for you. He must have used the frying pan."

The ice was delivered, but she was too dizzy when she sat up to consume any. The sheet felt heavy and hot. She pushed it away and rubbed one of the larger chunks of ice over her face and down her arms. The relief it brought was fleeting.

Colin came by and sat with her for a few minutes. "Your mother rang me. I reassured her," he said, but he didn't look reassured.

"Wash your hands before you leave," she told him. "I don't want you to get sick."

He was gone when she woke. There was only Sergeant Casey, who looked as solemn as an undertaker. She shivered and reached for the blankets at the foot of the bed. "Sergeant Casey, did your mother take care of you when you were sick? When you were little?"

"When she could."

"I wish my mother were here now."

He was silent.

"Should I have stayed at the hospital? None of this is helping."

His eyes were unreadable.

She realized how ungrateful she must sound. "I'm sorry," she whispered.

"You're a good soldier, Jenny."

"I don't want to be a soldier."

She waited for anger or his combat voice, but neither came. He touched her hand very lightly, as if he knew how tender her skin was.

CHAPTER 58

It was a long night for Jenny. Her skin was dry and tight, and it hurt to move. She felt imprisoned in the no-man's-land that exists between consciousness and restful sleep. The world outside her room did not exist, and within it, nothing changed. There was just her bed, the lamp nearby, and Sergeant Casey in the armchair just a few feet away.

The first throat culture had been negative. Gallagher had requested a second, and he rang late in the morning to report that it had been negative also. He recommended increasing the rate of flow of the drips and continuing the current level of both medications until the results of the blood test were received.

Davies and Hunt kept Casey supplied with tea and coffee and brought a succession of light snacks for him to consume. After lunch he found her fever again on the rise. With it came a dispirited attitude that concerned him even more than the physical symptoms.

"Is this how my world is going to end?" she asked. "Not with a bang, but with a whimper?" Then she called home on her cell phone. "I'm tired today, Mother. Tell Daddy—when he came here, that was awesome. I'll never forget it. Tell Matt and BJ—they're the best. I love you, Mother."

Casey realised she was saying good-bye, and he rang Sinclair. "Damn it, sir, she's given up. Thinks she's not going to make it. Tidying up loose ends."

"I'm on my way. Thirty minutes. Tell her I'm coming."

When Sinclair arrived, there was someone with him, but he went straight to Jenny's room, not even stopping to introduce his companion to Davies and Hunt. "Any change?" he asked Casey.

"Wanted me to remove the drip." He stepped aside. He had put so much tape around the drip needle that her hand looked gloved.

"Jenny, listen to me. Don't give up! 'Do not go gentle into that good night…Rage, rage against the dying of the light.' Tell me who said that. I know you know."

Her voice was muffled. "Colin—I'm sorry. But it is a good night. I'm not afraid."

Casey noted the clerical collar worn by the man who accompanied Sinclair and was immediately suspicious of his purpose. If Sinclair had brought the bloody God Squad to administer last rites, he'd give them both theirs.

The stranger took the chair Sinclair offered and grasped her hot little hand in his rough one. "I'm Neil Goodwyn, Jenny. Padre Neil. I'm a police chaplain. I'd like to help you."

Padre? Casey knew some Army chaplains called themselves that.

Her fever had made her vision a little blurry, but through the haze she could see a weathered face with warm brown eyes and an untroubled expression. His voice was soft. "I understand you have a job to do, little one."

She felt like a little girl again, when a missionary had visited their church and entertained them with his puppets, and he had been so full of love that none of them had wanted him to leave. "I did, but I'm not strong enough now."

"God's strength is sufficient when we're weak. He loves you, Jenny. He loves you so much He trusts you to do something that is very important to Him."

God would be disappointed in her then.

"He will cradle you in His arms, Jenny."

God hadn't held her in His arms, but Colin had.

"He carries you close to His heart, the way a shepherd carries a lamb."

No, Brian had carried her. And Sergeant Casey. She would miss them.

"His love never fails, Jenny. And when we're about His work, we can't fail, either." He leant closer to her, hoping he would hear her response if she made one.

It was almost inaudible. "I did my best."

"That's why He chose you—He knew you'd do your best. You can trust Him now. He'll do the rest."

His gentle voice drew her like a magnet, but she was too tired to follow him, even with her mind. She closed her eyes. His fingertips felt cool as they moved across and down her forehead. Someone's fingers were resting on her hair, and someone was holding her other hand. She heard Goodwyn ask God to heal and restore her, to fill her future with hope, and to lavish her with love. "She's in God's hands, Colin. She always has been."

Casey wasn't reassured.

"Davies and Hunt will need to see you out," Sinclair said.

"I'll have a word with them," Goodwyn replied. He extended a hand to Casey. "You're doing good work, Sergeant."

"Not good enough, sir."

"Neil." He clapped Casey on the shoulder and left.

Casey sat down next to the bed. Jenny smelled like roses—it must have been the oil Goodwyn had used. It still glistened on her forehead. A sign of God's presence, the padre had said. Casey would have preferred some tangible sign that her condition was improving.

Sinclair stayed, resting his chin in his hand, occasionally rubbing his face, his eyes never leaving her.

The room was still. After a very long time she heard Sergeant Casey's voice, his nice voice. He put the thermometer in her mouth. She didn't know when he removed it, because she was at the beach with her family, lying in the Texas sun. She had wanted to get a suntan, but she must have been in the sun too long and gotten a sunburn instead, because she was hot all over, even under her hair and on the soles of her feet. Her mother would be so annoyed with her. "Jennifer Catherine, you try my patience," she would say. She hated letting her mother down. She was supposed to have good judgment about things. It was hard being the oldest.

Casey and Sinclair heard her whimper.

"Damn! She's delirious. I'll run the water in the bath. We have to bring the fever down."

Sinclair waited with Jenny.

Casey returned and pulled the sheet aside. He leant over briefly, retrieved his knife, and slit both straps and the front of her nightdress. "Sir, hold the drip bags." He knelt by the bath and laid her in the tepid water, his arm under her shoulders to support her.

Sinclair could see her flat stomach and the curve of her hip under the water. Strange how someone completely naked could look so demure, but her knees were touching, and her legs were angled away from him. After the courthouse attack, Casey had cut off her clothes so he could treat her. Had that been necessary tonight? Sinclair supposed so—her nightdress would have become cumbersome when wet. Still, she was nude in Casey's arms, and Sinclair had to remind himself that the man was her nurse. He would insist that Casey clothe her as soon as this crisis had passed. He suddenly realised the room was quiet.

"She's asleep, sir," Casey said quietly. "We'll put her back in bed before she gets cold." He put his other arm beneath her knees and lifted her out of the water. It frightened Sinclair, seeing her limp form.

"Is she better?"

"For the moment."

"Sergeant, are we going to lose her?"

"Not on my watch, sir."

Sinclair nodded slowly. "Tea?"

"I wouldn't mind, sir."

- -

Sinclair and Casey sat in Jenny's room sipping their tea. She was still quiet, motionless under the sheet.

"Sir, are we in for a change of command here?"

Sinclair glanced toward the bed.

"She can't hear us, sir."

Sinclair didn't want to comment on his professional upheaval at the

Yard to the sergeant, but it appeared that Andrews already had done. He sighed. "Graves and I are under review for our handling of Jenny's protection. The Detective Chief Super has been uncomfortable with the unorthodox nature of this arrangement from the beginning. We've had monthly reviews, but the shooting has given him the perfect excuse to revisit each decision we've taken."

"It's a bit close to the trial for a move to be made."

Sinclair gave a harsh laugh. "The verdict may be more political than just, Sergeant. Supporting us—a vote of confidence—makes it appear that he's done nothing. The appearance of action is very important to Woulson." He set his tea cup on the floor by his chair. "The first change he'd make is venue."

"Bloody politicians. They should keep clear of operations."

"Some days I wish she'd gone with her father, actually."

"In spite of the danger to her?"

"I've not done very well on that score here, have I?"

"Sir, it's too soon for an assessment. Let's get her mended first."

The hours passed, Casey pulling a nightshirt on her, checking her vital signs, forcing liquids and medication down her, trying to make her comfortable as she alternately shivered and perspired. Hunt collected their cups and refilled them. Sinclair's eyes felt less heavy than his spirit. He thought about Goodwyn's visit. Sinclair had met him after his father's death and had seen him work with others as well. He respected the way Goodwyn's approach varied from situation to situation. He seemed to know what each person's inner need was. He knew Jenny was far from home and the love of her family. He had wanted her to feel God's love. He'd wanted to give her something to live for. Sinclair didn't know if he'd succeeded. What do people her age live for? "Sergeant, is there anything more we can do for her?"

"No, sir. It's a waiting game—lab results should be back later today. When they isolate the bacteria that's causing this, Gallagher can prescribe a more specialised antibiotic."

"Should we have taken her to hospital?"

"Sir, she's my only patient. Shorter response time."

Sinclair stood, stretched, and sat down again. Casey sat with his elbows on his knees and his chin in his hands. They heard Hunt's voice at the door. "Sir, Davies is coming on now. Any change?"

A thin thread answered. "Yes. I feel better."

All eyes turned toward the bed. Jenny saw Colin's unshaven face and Sergeant Casey's widening smile. Casey reached her first, his hand on her wet forehead. "Fever's broken, sir!" He turned to Sinclair, and without thinking, high-fived the senior officer. "Hunt, tell Davies we'll need his services."

There was a sudden flurry of activity, Casey reaching for the thermometer for confirmation and Davies wanting to know what she'd like for breakfast.

"No Brussels sprouts."

Davies laughed aloud, and Sinclair saw her weak smile and knew his presence was no longer required. He had a phone call to make—to Texas. "Well done," he said to Casey. "Will you let Davies take it for the time being?"

"Yes, sir. He'll give me a shake if need be. Good luck, sir."

CHAPTER 59

At the flat, the men were returning to a normal duty roster, but Jenny's recuperation was slow. She dragged herself into the kitchen to eat and crawled back into bed afterwards. After twenty-four hours, Casey removed the drip and encouraged her to dress and move about the flat a bit more. She did so halfheartedly. Later he found her asleep in her clothes. One night she slept on the sofa in the sitting room, wanting to be close to the man on watch. It was worrying. Casey reported to Sinclair that this last assault on her system had taken something out of her. Gallagher had prescribed regular injections of Vitamin B-12, but no improvement in her energy level had resulted so far.

With Graves' permission Sinclair requested a meeting with Commander Keating. The progress of the Special Homicide Squad had been reviewed periodically since its inception, and Keating was the senior officer in charge of the detectives who performed this function. Sinclair wanted to make an appeal on Jenny's behalf. He was aware that her medical condition and time in witness protection had already been documented, so he limited himself to more recent matters, the shooting at the rear entrance of the courthouse and her subsequent illness. He began by describing Sergeant Casey's level of medical expertise, which had allowed them to remove Jenny from hospital quickly after her surgery. He reported the severity of her illness and Casey's immediate and constant response. "We will benefit from her testimony in a number of cases," Sinclair pointed out. "It is in our best interest as well as hers to be wary of any unnecessary changes that may distress her. In addition, as late events have proved, it is impossible to guarantee that she will not require medical intervention in the future."

Keating regarded him with a steady gaze and thanked him for coming in.

Twenty-four hours after Sinclair's meeting with Keating, the determination came down. No fault was found either in Jenny's protection, which Keating called "irregular but effective," or in the planning for her transport to court.

"Sir," Andrews commented to his boss, "he must have remembered his operational days and recognised that no amount of preparation can anticipate everything." He made note of the sentence he wanted to relay to Sergeant Casey: "The standards of integrity that are essential to effective police work were maintained." It was a pity that so few coppers would see this report—they all needed to hear that they had handled at least one case well.

Sinclair did not speak of the ruling. Now that it was clear that he would still be involved in the case, he called an evening meeting to discuss new plans for escorting her to court. He brought a set of blueprints for the Crown Court building, leaving them on the dining room table before speaking to her briefly. She was in the sitting room, but her book was face down on her lap. He glanced at the title.

"Good book?"

She looked up at him. "I don't know. I've read the same page five times."

"Jenny, I need to have a word with the men."

"I'll go in my room. I don't want to know." But she did. What did they think the monster would try this time? When? How would they prevent his attack? Could they?

Troubled, he joined the men in the dining room. "The venue hasn't changed—it's the same court. What can we do differently?"

"Our tactics will have to change, sir," Davies said.

Casey glanced at him. "Make it more like a special op. Use the element of surprise."

"Sergeant, when I tell Judge Thomas that Jenny has recovered sufficiently to appear, he will reconvene. The day and time will be known."

Casey reached for the blueprints and unrolled them. "Which court will she be in?"

Sinclair consulted the plans and pointed.

"What are these other spaces?"

"Other courts and judges' chambers."

"Sir, I want to enter the building only once, and use someone's chambers or conference room as our bunker."

Davies picked up Casey's train of thought. "And wait until we're safely inside before letting anyone know we're there."

"Right. Give no one advance notice. Even our route should be a last-minute decision."

"How long will she be testifying?" asked Hunt.

"Hard to say. Depends on the defence strategy. Plan for at least three days," Sinclair answered.

"When she testifies, I want to be in the courtroom," Casey said. "I don't want her going in without us."

"I rather think Judge Thomas will see the necessity this time. Anything else?"

Davies nodded. "We'll need shifts of coppers outside the chambers and at all entry points."

"We should stow our gear on a weekend," Casey continued. "Easier to be covert. Take her in on a Sunday night, under cover of darkness. Have only a small contingent of plain-clothes officers on site when we arrive."

"What about the press?" asked Hunt.

"We shouldn't have any problem going in," Sinclair said. "Coming out is another matter."

"We'll need a decoy to leave in an official vehicle, probably with you, sir." Casey leant back in his chair. "We'll depart later with her."

"Agreed." Sinclair looked at the three men. "Weapons?"

"We'll be covered," Davies said.

Casey's voice was grim. "I want her to have body armour again. And Hunt will need some."

Sinclair nodded. "Medical supplies?"

"I'll be ready, sir." There was a moment's silence. "Sir, our best is going to be good enough this time."

"Sergeant, Judge Thomas will want to know when she can appear. What can I tell him?"

"Sir, just give him a window. We're going to need his cooperation in advance of our providing any specifics. At the moment I can't hazard a guess. She's not focussed. Her physical recovery's not what it should be. And we have to guard against a relapse if we can. Testifying and enduring cross-examination would tire most anyone, and she'll be weaker than most witnesses when she begins."

"I'll have a word with Judge Thomas in the morning." He collected the blueprints and went to Jenny's room. She had set her book aside and stretched out on the bed, one arm clutching her teddy bear. He sat down next to her. "Casey said you weren't yourself."

"I'm no good to anybody, Colin. I wasn't afraid when I was sick, but I am now. I'm afraid all the time. I wish I had a gun."

He smiled at her. "I can't grant that wish, Jenny. Private possession of handguns is against the law here."

She did not smile back. "Is Danny any better?"

"Not yet." Casey had briefed him on the psychological symptoms of gunshot trauma, but he was concerned because she was still experiencing them. Her illness had indeed set her back. "Jenny, what you're feeling is normal."

"Wanting to hold onto somebody all the time? It's not normal for me."

"Would you like me to bring Dr. Knowles by? Or Neil Goodwyn?"

"I liked Dr. Knowles," she said slowly, "but I felt so peaceful when Chaplain Goodwyn was here."

"I'll arrange it." His eyes lingered on her lips, but he limited himself to the thought.

"It's late. I know you need to go. I'm going to sit in the living room next to whoever's armed. Even if it's Hunt."

CHAPTER 60

Jenny woke with a start. It was pitch black and deathly silent. The radio by her window wasn't working. She felt the stirrings of panic. In the stillness she could hear Sergeant Casey's terse whispers: "All hands on watch. Hunt, cover the sitting room windows. Davies, put Jenny in the safe room. Cover her windows and door."

She could hear Brian's steps, then Casey's voice again. "Sir, we're on full alert. The power's off. Yours also? The lights across the street are on. Bring an SFO team to the pre-arranged lying up point and tell them to stand by. Put an ARV on patrol. We're closeted—need some eyes about."

Her flannel pyjamas were illuminated by the glow of Brian's torch. "Are you awake, JJ? Take your pillow and climb into the bath until I call you." His words were quiet—*sotto voce,* Casey would have said.

She took his arm and didn't want to let go. "It's dark. Brian, it's so dark."

"I know. You'll be all right. I'll not be far. Hush now."

She saw a gun in his holster and another in a sling across his shoulder. She heard him close the bathroom door. There was a sudden scraping noise, then the sound of something being dragged across the carpet. Was he moving her furniture? Why?

It was cold in the tub, but she shivered more from fear than lack of warmth. Had the monster sent someone to get her? How would he—or they—get through the front door? Would Colin hear them coming up the stairs? She had never seen him with a gun. Would he have any way of stopping them? Maybe they'd come through a window instead. Did they know which one was hers? With the electricity out, the alarm would not sound. Were there quiet ways to break glass? Would Brian have any warning? Dear God, please don't let anything happen to Brian! She closed her fingers around the pearl cross. She thought about Danny and how afraid she was for him still. There was a hard knot of dread in her stomach.

Time passed—she had no way of knowing how much. She grew stiff in her cramped position but was afraid that any movement would make noise. The stillness was scary. She missed all the everyday noises she'd become accustomed to, her radio, the TV, men's footsteps, cabinets being opened and closed in the kitchen, even the furnace. The furnace—with no power, it would have turned off. No wonder she was cold. And it was so dark.

Suddenly she heard footsteps approaching. The bathroom door sprang open, and she cried out involuntarily, pressing her face into the pillow at the same time. Then she heard a beloved voice say, "It's all right, JJ. All clear." The lights were on! She couldn't hold back any longer, and her racking sobs drew the other men. "Let me help you," Brian said, putting his arm under her shoulders. "Hush," he said. "It's all off now." He set her on the bed, and she rubbed her legs to restore the circulation.

She heard Sergeant Casey's voice before he entered the room. "Yes, sir, tell them to stand down. False alarm." Hunt followed Casey, Hunt's face showing more color than she'd seen since he arrived at the flat. "Unprofessional to show excitement over a possible engagement," Casey hissed at him. "You're a bit too keen. And get a bloody shirt on."

Naked to the waist, an elaborate tattoo on his shoulder, and holding a submachine gun in his hands, Hunt did look dangerous. "Would a fry-up help? I'll get it started."

"Are you okay, love?" He watched her stand.

When she got to the kitchen, Hunt had some of the breakfast ingredients on the counter and was heating milk in a saucepan, but he still looked coiled and ready to spring. "No tea for you, Little Bit," he said a little too loudly. "My mum said hot cocoa was just the ticket when something soothing was called for."

She watched while the men busied themselves. After the crushing quiet, everything they did seemed unnaturally noisy, but their voices were reassuring to her. She sipped her cocoa, so hot it almost burned her mouth but very relaxing when it reached her stomach. She felt her dread melt away, and her eyelids were heavy when she finished her meal. "Thank you, Constable Hunt."

"Alan," he said in a firm voice. "Alan."

She paled. She just couldn't do it. For better or worse, he was "Even" Hunt. Her chin drooped, her limbs felt like putty, and once again Brian was there to help.

"You spoil her," Hunt said.

"You bet we do," Brian agreed.

CHAPTER 61

Sinclair was concerned. The power-cut had been another frightening experience for Jenny, and its coming on the heels of other difficulties could undermine her fragile progress toward recovery. A thunderstorm to the north had left areas without power, but the cause had not been apparent at the time, and the lack of electricity had made the protection flat vulnerable. The response of the team had been appropriate. Any sort of alert required them to execute their procedures.

On the positive side, he had engaged the cooperation of Judge Thomas. Judge Lloyd's chambers would be unoccupied for a two-week period soon, and Judge Thomas had not pressed him about his timing for their use. He planned to leave the blueprints of the courthouse with the protection team this evening, with Judge Lloyd's chambers marked, so their final planning could proceed. While they worked, he and Neil Goodwyn would have a chat with Jenny.

- -

She was reading in her bedroom when they arrived, and Colin brought a third chair from the sitting room so that he and Goodwyn could speak with her privately. The men were working at the dining room table, and with her current state of mind, Colin wanted to prevent her from overhearing their plans and concerns.

"Jenny, how may I help you?" Goodwyn began.

"Why did you come to see me when I was sick?"

"Because Colin thought you needed my sort of medicine." He smiled. "And you do seem to be much better."

She looked at Colin. He had such a patient expression on his face. It would hurt him to hear what she had to say, and for a moment she wished she hadn't spoken to him about her malaise.

"Jenny, I've known Neil for some time. He's helped people who were afraid."

"I was an Army chaplain for almost ten years before assisting the police," Goodwyn clarified.

"Are you going to talk to me the way Sergeant Casey does?"

Goodwyn chuckled. "No, that's not helpful in my mission."

"You don't sound tough enough for the Army."

"There was more than enough toughness to go round. I didn't need to add to it."

"Were you ever afraid?"

"Yes, but not of death. At times I've been afraid of the process of dying, of what could come before death."

"There are worse things than death," she said.

"I agree," Goodwyn said very quietly.

"What has Colin told you about me?"

She was not giving anything away, Goodwyn noted. No matter. He was used to that. Usually it was his hand that was extended first to those who needed his counsel. "He said that your spirit was wounded, Jenny."

Even his words hurt, her spirit was so raw. "You said—when you were here before—that God loved me, but I don't believe you. The police are briefed about everything I do. Terrible things have happened to me, and everyone knows. I have scars from head to toe, and strangers have seen them. Do I look like someone God loves?"

Often people who were disappointed by God challenged Him. Goodwyn was glad that Jenny still had the pluck to do it, no matter how frail she seemed. "Jenny, nothing can separate you from the love of God. Not the height of fear or the depth of despair. Not your anger or resistance. Not gunshots." He paused before adding very gently, "Not even rape."

She flinched, and Colin felt it even as he saw it.

Goodwyn leant forward. "Jenny, I don't seek to embarrass or upset you. I'd like to reassure you with my conviction. In the Army there was no time for lies or dissembling. If I'd given pat answers, I'd not have lasted long. In spite of their arms and fortifications, soldiers are vulnerable, and they know it. It's necessary to tell the truth."

"I'm vulnerable, too," she whispered. "I'm afraid all the time. I saw what happened to Danny, and he's still not better. I saw what almost happened to me."

She was desperate to feel safe, and Colin knew he could not guarantee it.

"Why do you think there are so many verses in the Bible about fear, Jenny? Left to our own devices, we are a fearful lot, but that is not God's will for us. He has not given us a 'spirit of fear, but of power, and of love, and of a sound mind.'"

Those same verses were in the book of prayers Colin had given her. "What can I do when fear strikes?"

"The Word of God is powerful ammunition. In this case the Twenty-third Psalm is the antidote I would use. Learn it by heart. It tells us, among other things, that even in the valley of the shadow of death, we are not meant to be afraid. The presence of a shadow means that light is close by."

She had been in that valley more than once, and lately she'd felt threatened even in the flat. There was no safe place to hide. "Danny's there. Is he afraid?"

"No, little one. I've been to see him. There's no fear where he is."

"There's no fear when you're in a coma?"

"He's having a little rest in God's arms. I believe that he will awaken, in God's time."

"Why did you visit him? What's the point, when he can't hear you?"

"Jenny, it's his body that's in a coma, not his spirit."

She was the reverse: her body awake, her spirit in a coma. Strange—Colin had kissed her and wakened her, but now her fear had anesthesized her again. "I need God to help me, and He hasn't. Sergeant Casey has, and Colin, and Dr. Knowles, and the other men, but not God."

"Don't you know He uses people to accomplish His will? He did in the Bible, and He still does. I also believe that God has magnificent blessings in store for you."

She shook her head slowly. "I haven't seen any evidence of that."

"On the contrary. You are alive. Colin tells me that you had dreadful injuries, and clearly you have recovered from them. You have been well looked after by the police. I hear you have come to trust them. Life, health, loving care—those are all gifts of God."

"Wait until I tell Sergeant Casey he's a gift from God!"

Colin smiled. Her sense of humour revealed itself at the most unexpected times.

"There's a very simple reason that I'm convinced blessings are in store for you," Goodwyn continued. "Do you want to know what it is?"

She inclined her head.

"By agreeing to testify against your abusers, you have aligned yourself with God's will. Haven't you realised that every time your commitment has been threatened, something—or Someone—has strengthened your resolve?"

"You make it sound so personal," she said. "I was always taught that God loved us, but from a distance."

"It *is* personal. God knows your name. He knows how many hairs you have on your head. He knows how many tears you have cried. He knows your needs, He has provided for them, and He will continue to do so."

That was the message of *The Mysterious Island*, she remembered: What you need will be supplied. Danny had been reading a paperback copy before Christmas. At the time it was the concept of being an island that had occupied her. Britain was an island; that had been the most significant element in its history and literature. She had felt like an island, surrounded by savage waters and an ocean away from her family. Now Danny was the island, surrounded by his family but unaware of their presence.

"The most prominent symbol in this room is a cross."

"My flag? Those crosses belong to St. George, St. Andrew, and St.

Patrick."

"All saints of God," Goodwyn said calmly. "Don't you find its placement interesting? The Bible says that God watches over us while we sleep."

She had wanted the flag mounted where she could see it. It hadn't occurred to her that it was a symbol of the fact that God could see her.

"You were chosen to be a witness. We are all witnesses, either to our belief or our unbelief."

"So far I haven't been a witness to anything. Colin's a better witness than I am. He never gives up, and I do."

"I disagree. You're a witness to integrity, decency, and the rule of law."

"Then why—why—does it have to be so *hard*?" she asked, her voice breaking.

"To increase the impact your life has on others," Goodwyn replied without hesitation. "And I can tell you without qualification that your struggle has affected the men in this flat. They respect you."

"Why, when I put Danny in a coma?"

"That wasn't your doing, Jenny, but the light of God is with him, even there."

"You see God in everything."

"I certainly do," Goodwyn agreed. "You've heard people recommend that we stop to smell the roses? I like to go one step further—remember Who made the roses and gave them their scent. There are signs of God's presence all over our world, if we will only look for them."

Jenny finally smiled. "You're in the right profession. I just think you give God entirely too much credit."

"It's not possible to do that. God is here, Jenny. All you have to do is acknowledge Him."

CHAPTER 62

Sinclair had a smile on his face as he headed home on the Friday afternoon. Sergeant Casey had rung him earlier in the day to report that Jenny was restless, and they were seeking a way to distract her. As a further complication, her trip to the courthouse was scheduled for the Sunday, and the men needed time to move their gear into position. Casey was concerned that she would be upset further if she saw them preparing and realised that her exposure to danger was imminent. Sinclair had suggested that they bring her to his flat for the evening. He'd provide dinner and a bit of entertainment while the men recced the routes to the courthouse. Casey felt that a four-hour window should be sufficient, so he agreed to escort her downstairs at seven p.m. and pick her up at eleven.

Sinclair stopped by the video store on Finchley Road to rent a film and bought a pepperoni pizza at Domino's on his way up the hill. Simple fare, but it would do. He had a bottle of red wine at the flat, which Casey had assured him was not contraindicated with the antibiotic medication she was still taking.

He had just popped the pizza in the oven to keep warm when he heard the knock on the door. He was still wearing his work clothes, but he'd taken off his coat and tie and unbuttoned his waistcoat. "Dinner's warming. Glass of wine?"

She nodded, curious about his flat. It had high ceilings, and his sitting room was larger than the one upstairs, with a fireplace in it. He also had a bay window, which she supposed she shouldn't approach, and one wall was lined with bookshelves. Instead of wall-to-wall carpet, there were hardwood floors with an area rug between the leather sofa and the fireplace and another beneath the dining room table.

"To easier times," he said. They sat down on the sofa, and he cued up the video.

"*American President*, with Michael Douglas and Michael J. Fox," she exclaimed. "I love this movie." It opened with scenes of previous presidents, and she felt a little homesick. Colin served the pizza when the characters in the movie were enjoying a lavish state dinner at the White House, and both of them looked down at their sliced meal and laughed at the contrast.

"It's different, seeing this movie from another country. It might be easy to leave America behind for a vacation, but to be away from it like this—" She stopped. "It's so good to hear American voices!"

Colin hadn't seen the film before, but the character of the environmental lobbyist reminded him of Jenny. They both had pluck. When the American president kissed his leading lady, Jenny blushed. Colin found it charming and tried to remember the last time he'd seen a woman blush. It had been Jenny, after he'd kissed her when she was so upset about Sullivan.

As the film progressed, he spent more time watching her than the video. Even her t-shirts were feminine, with lace, ruffles, or embroidery. Tonight she had worn one embellished with lavender flowers which complemented her watch and curved gracefully across her chest. Knowles had said that the assault had destroyed her femininity; was that why she dressed the way she did? Was she attempting to recreate it? He couldn't ask, but he could compliment her. "You're lovely tonight," he said, and was rewarded with a quick smile.

"Will the press hound me like that?" she asked, watching the American reporters harass the President's girlfriend.

"If they could, they would—if they knew who you were and where you were."

When the video ended, he made coffee. She was in a pensive mood. "Don't you wish politicians really sounded like that? He was so inspiring."

"The lines aren't scripted for the real ones," he reminded her.

"And they won't be for me, in court. When will it be, Colin? Sergeant Casey won't say."

"The date hasn't been determined."

"I know it can't be long—I'm pretty much recovered."

"You gave me a fright, Jen."

"I've never been that sick, but after a while I wasn't afraid." She set her coffee cup down. "I dreamed that I was being buried at sea. You were there, and you wrapped me in the flag. The colors were bleeding onto my skin, but I didn't care because the water was so cool. Dying was like going to sleep."

He hoped desperately that she wouldn't cry. Her tears after she was shot had moved him to comfort her, and in a heartbeat it had changed everything. He had been unprofessional. He'd heard of other officers taking witnesses, even suspects on occasion, into their beds. That was not possible with this woman, not now, when her full concentration needed to be on her testimony, and possibly not ever. He was a weary thirty-seven years old, she a fragile twenty-three.

The musical soundtrack was still playing, and its romantic music made it difficult for him to show restraint. He reached for the remote and stopped the recording. She looked calm and relaxed. Yes, he was more in control this time. "Sergeant Casey will be along soon," he said.

"We'd better clean up then." They were in the kitchen when the knock on the door came.

"Thank you for this evening." She stood on her tiptoes, and he felt her lips, soft on his cheek. Very quickly he cupped her face in his hands and bent down to kiss her. Why hadn't he done it before, when he wouldn't have had to hurry? He straightened and saw her smile. That would have to satisfy him for now. She would be in court in three days.

After she left, he thought about her. It had been a long time since he'd valued a woman's kiss. Since his divorce, he hadn't looked for love. Sexual attraction had been sufficient, and he'd expected far more than kisses from the other women who had been in this flat. He was a confident man, and he'd never before considered it remarkable when a woman he fancied responded to him. Strange—instead of comparing Jenny to other women, he was comparing other women to her.

CHAPTER 63

In spite of the men's efforts to keep a low profile, Jenny knew that her time to testify was approaching, and their reluctance to discuss their plans made her even more nervous. It was a relief when Sergeant Casey sat down with her Sunday afternoon and explained the schedule and the measures they would take to keep her safe during the big event.

"Have I lost my readiness? I haven't exercised. And I need new spark plugs. I don't have any get-up-and-go."

"You have residual readiness, love. And the B-12 jabs should help. Roll up your sleeve."

Per his instructions, she packed an overnight bag with her clothes for court, toiletries, and linens. Fortunately there was room for her London policeman teddy bear, so she could have a stuffed bodyguard as well as stuffy bodyguards. She'd have to spot bathe in the judge's bathroom. The men would use Davies' flat, since it was closest to the court, and Davies and Hunt would sleep there. She wore her workout clothes and planned to sleep in them. The men were already wearing their body armour. Sergeant Casey adjusted hers carefully.

"I love this stuff," she said, trying to control the trembling in her voice. "I think I'll get some in every color."

They departed after dinner. It was raining fast, and the men were pleased. The bad weather would limit the number of persons on the street and reduce the visibility of any souls brave enough to venture into the downpour. In Texas they'd call it a frog-choker, but she knew better than to say anything aloud.

They didn't want to attract any attention, so there was no shadow car. Jenny rode with Casey, Davies, and Hunt in a nondescript vehicle, Andrews behind the wheel. She'd observed the other men at work: Sergeant Andrews was the revelation. She had seen Andrews the interrogator, logical, thorough, and direct. She had enjoyed the Andrews who gossiped and played Christmas games. She remembered a bland, affable Andrews unintimidated by the defence solicitor. Now she saw an Andrews as mute and focused as Sergeant Casey.

They saw no one near the courthouse as they approached. Andrews drove within a few feet of the rear entrance. The courthouse employed its own security men, Casey had told her, but plain-clothes officers would be expecting them. They waited inside the car while Hunt knocked on the door. Sergeant Andrews kept the motor running, and Brian and Sergeant Casey watched the street. When the courthouse door opened, Brian exited the right rear door of the vehicle. He opened Casey's door, his eyes sweeping the area while Casey reached for her hand. It felt safe in the car. Outside it was too dark to see a threat coming. "Now, Jenny," The Voice said when she didn't move. He and Brian kept her between them, and Sergeant Andrews didn't pull away until the courthouse door had closed behind them.

There was a lift just inside the door, but Sergeant Casey directed her past it. "We'll take the stairs," he said. "Try to keep up." She couldn't, not with Brian's long, rapid strides. "Move it, Jenny," Casey commanded, pushing against her back. Frightened by his urgency, she broke into a run, clasping her overnight bag to her chest. She could hear Hunt behind her, barely managing to keep his excitement in check. When they were inside the judge's chambers, Casey rang Sinclair. "Phoenix has landed," he said. "Call the backup units into position."

A short while later Sinclair rang back. "I reached Judge Thomas. Court will convene at half ten tomorrow morning. I'll see you before then. Good luck."

It was a long night. Armed police identified themselves when they arrived and were positioned outside the door to the judge's chambers. Occasionally Jenny was reassured by the sound of their voices or the sight of the shadows of their shoes under the door. She had never been in a judge's chambers, and she was surprised to find that the space was crowded with a desk, sofa, and two chairs. She found medical supplies in the small bathroom; Sergeant Casey was prepared for the worst. "Am I safe here?" she asked him.

"This place is crawling with coppers, not just outside our door. Some uniformed, some not. You'll be okay."

"Will they shoot?"

"They've been fully briefed."

"Will—they—shoot?"

"If necessary, yes."

He brought her a sleeping pill, and she lay down on the sofa with her bear and her blanket, but she was afraid, and sleep would not come. She missed Danny terribly, knowing that even in this situation he would have pierced the dread with his lightheartedness. She had learned the Twenty-third Psalm, as Padre Goodwyn had suggested, but she could not concentrate sufficiently for the words to register, so she prayed for Danny instead—to wake up, to laugh, to be himself. She prayed the trial would be worth what it had cost.

She left the light on in the bathroom, but there was no radio, and it was terribly quiet. The men had pushed the desk against one wall to make room for Sergeant Casey's sleeping bag, and she asked if she could sit next to him. "No, love, I'll sit with you," he said, so she made room for him on the sofa and held his arm.

"After all this time, I can't believe I'm finally here. Sergeant Casey, how am I going to get through it tomorrow?"

"The way all warriors do: by relying on your training."

"What am I trained to do?"

"Communications and demolitions. Just tell what that bastard did to you, and you'll destroy him."

"Promise?"

"Yes. Jenny, you'll be on point, but I'll be there to cover you."

"Promise?"

"Jenny, *yes.*"

The Voice reassured her, and she felt sleepy.

When morning came, Andrews arrived with breakfast beverages and rolls. She sipped a little tea and wished that she had a Coke to settle her stomach. She changed into her hunter green wool suit in the adjoining bathroom. Davies and Hunt arrived. They waited.

Sinclair was admitted just before ten. "It won't be long now." He squeezed her cold hand and bent down to give her a light kiss on the cheek. "I'll be sitting in the back," he said and was gone.

Sergeant Andrews knocked. "It's time."

Casey came up behind her and took her arm. "*Coraggio.*"

"I love you guys," she said, her voice breaking. "Even Hunt."

They followed Andrews and the black-robed court usher down the corridor.

PART THREE

Success cannot be guaranteed.
There are no safe battles.

— Winston Churchill

CHAPTER 1

"All rise!" cut through the buzz of excitement in the crowded courtroom. Judge Wilfred Thomas entered and seated himself, waiting for the rustle to subside. "Call your next witness, Mr. Benjamin."

"The Crown calls Miss Jennifer Catherine Jeffries."

There was a slight pause, and Jenny entered through the usher's door, her protection officers behind her. To her left and just a few feet away was the dock with Scott inside. She cast her eyes around the room, looking for the witness-box, and realized she'd have to walk past him to get there. Why was everyone so calm? Didn't they know what he was capable of? She stopped, wanting a moment to quell the rising tide of panic. Almost immediately Sergeant Casey moved beside her, placing himself between her and the monster and using his hand to apply firm pressure to the small of her back. Her legs began to work again, and he escorted her to the witness-box as if that had been his prescribed role all along. He positioned himself on the wall to her right.

She was alone in the witness-box. Halladay had said that the monster would be seated in the dock, and he was, but she felt as if the balance of power had shifted and he were standing, not she. No one had told her how small she would feel and how vulnerable. There was a cramp in the pit of her stomach, and she leaned forward slightly and put a hand on the side of the box. She heard Sergeant Casey take a deep breath and let it out slowly, and she followed his example.

She had a good view of the entire courtroom. Moving her eyes to the left, she saw the judge, the jury, all staring at her, and Hunt by the door they'd just used. Her eyes ran across the public gallery above the dock and down again, finding Brian by the door at the back of the room, a clock on the blue-gray wall next to him. A group of individuals, some bespectacled, with pens poised, peered at her—the press. She spotted Colin, Sergeant Andrews, several other men in suits, and in front of them, the legal counsel. She felt unsteady on her feet and took another deep breath. Why did she have to stand? In the States, where they called it the witness stand, participants were seated during their testimony.

The clerk, looking bored already, approached her with the Bible, and she remembered suddenly a line of Carl Sandburg's: "like I was one more witness it was work for him to give the oath to." Her mouth dry, she swore that the evidence she was about to give was the truth, the whole truth, and nothing but the truth.

One of the bewigged creatures stood, and she observed that none of the wigs were long enough to cover the sides of the head, nor were they really white, more the color of sheep's wool. Some of them would be wolves in sheep's clothing.

After bowing to the judge and the jury, the barrister, Peter Benjamin, introduced himself to her. He had deep lines on his thin face, as if he'd lost weight but not worries. He sounded friendly, almost conversational, as he confirmed her vital statistics and inquired about her life in Texas, and she realized that he was trying to put her at ease.

More questions about her background followed, covering her brothers' activities growing up as well as her own, and their parents' guidance and involvement in their lives. He was painting a picture of her, and he used a fine brush to portray a close-knit family that found time to take regular holidays and engage in other types of shared recreation. He rarely referred to notes, and no one interrupted him. He complimented her on her university performance and confirmed the date of her graduation. The morning had come to a close when he finally inquired about her purpose in coming to England.

After answering a series of questions about her activities between September 9 and 13, Jenny heard the judge's voice.

"Mr. Benjamin, we are nearing the lunch interval," he said. "I'd like to adjourn."

"As your honour wishes."

"We'll reassemble at half one."

She didn't hear a gavel, just the usher's voice intoning, "Will you all please be upstanding."

When she turned to step out of the witness-box, Sergeant Casey was there to shield her, but the defendant had already left the dock when they passed it. They returned to Judge Lloyd's chambers, where Sergeant Andrews was waiting with tea and sandwiches from the courthouse cafeteria.

"The hot courses weren't ready yet, and the Coke machine is on the blink," he reported.

She didn't take more than two bites of the sandwich. It tasted like last week's, and she felt more tired than hungry, so she slipped her shoes off and rested on the sofa with her feet elevated.

Hunt tossed his sandwich in the dustbin. "Come on, Davies. We can do better than this."

Andrews must have thought so, too, because he hadn't brought a sandwich for himself.

It was quiet. She was alone with Sergeant Casey, and it seemed seconds later when he shook her shoulder gently. "It's gone one, love. Lads will be back soon."

She sat up and rubbed her face. When she returned from the bathroom, she discovered that her shoes didn't want to testify any more than she did. They wanted the afternoon off.

Shortly after Davies and Hunt returned, the call from the usher came.

CHAPTER 2

When they entered the courtroom, all eyes were on Jenny. Once again Sergeant Casey pushed her past the defendant. He helped her step up into the witness-box, where she was reminded of her oath.

"Mr. Benjamin, you may begin," the judge said.

The prosecutor stood. "Miss Jeffries, what is your status in this country?"

She was tempted to reply that she was there to shop for more comfortable shoes, but she didn't want to appear flippant. "I am a visitor."

"You are here—and in this court—of your own free will?"

"Yes, sir."

"Has anyone pressurised you to testify in this case?"

"No, sir."

"Have you been in contact with the press or any members of the media?"

"No, sir."

"Have you been offered any sort of compensation by anyone for your story?"

"No, sir."

"Miss Jeffries, I'd like to focus on the events of September 14, 1998. Let's take it in stages, shall we?"

The prosecutor phrased his questions so that her answers could be short and clear, but she was still nervous. She described what she was wearing, her loss of consciousness at the bus stop, and waking up naked and sick in the dark. She told about the two men she saw when the light was turned on, her search for her clothes, and her discovery of women's jewelry instead. Mr. Benjamin had her identify the specific pieces of jewelry before enquiring about the defendant's entry into the little room, which he referred to as the "cellar in the ambassadorial residence."

Sinclair respected Benjamin but wished for Jenny's sake that Graves' request for a woman to present the prosecution's case had not been denied.

"The man who attacked you in the cellar—do you see him in the courtroom today?"

She looked away from Mr. Benjamin. The monster was staring at her, and when their eyes met, she could feel his malevolence. Instinctively she backed away as far as she could, trying to flatten herself against the back wall of the witness-box.

"You must give an audible reply," the judge told her. "There's nothing to be afraid of."

It didn't help. Even guarded, the monster was still too close.

"Miss Jeffries!" Mr. Benjamin said sharply. "Look at me! Is the man who attacked you in the courtroom?"

"Yes, he's sitting in the dock with the two policemen," she managed to say.

"Miss Jeffries, please speak into the microphone," said Judge Thomas.

She took a few steps forward and repeated her answer.

"Let the record show that the witness identified William Cecil Crighton Scott, seated in the dock," said Mr. Benjamin. He frowned at her pale and tense face. "Miss Jeffries, are you all right?"

"Sir—I need to sit down, please." She looked at the judge.

"Of course," he answered. "A chair will be provided."

She noticed for the first time that Judge Thomas was clothed in more than a black robe and white neckpiece: He had a purple stole, purple cuffs, and a red sash. The light gray hair on the sides of his head matched his wig. They all waited while a chair was brought from the court down the corridor and the height of the microphone adjusted.

"Proceed, Mr. Benjamin."

"Miss Jeffries, were you acquainted with the accused?"

"No, sir, I was not," she said.

"Did you recognise him when you saw him in the cellar? Did you know his name?"

"No, sir."

"Did he speak to you?"

"No, sir."

"Did he approach you?"

"Yes, he grabbed my arm and pulled me to the center of the room."

"What did he do then?"

She was feeling shaky, and her voice quivered. "He nearly beat me to death."

"Nearly beat you to death," Benjamin repeated, his enunciation unusually clear. "Could you be a bit more specific, please? What sorts of blows did the defendant use?"

"He hit me in the stomach and knocked me down. He kicked me all over, and he hit me with his fists."

"The scar on your face—was that a result of the defendant's actions?"

"Yes, sir, it was. He wore a sharp ring that made gashes in my skin."

"A ring that cut like a knife?"

"Your Honour, my learned friend is leading the witness." The voice came from someone across the aisle from Mr. Benjamin.

"Indeed he is."

Mr. Benjamin bowed slightly in acquiescence. "Miss Jeffries, for the benefit of the jury, would you push your hair aside and turn your right cheek toward them?"

Both cheeks burning, she did as requested. She didn't see the sympathetic faces of those who leant toward her—she closed her eyes, and Mr. Benjamin's next question seemed a long time in coming.

"Thank you, Miss Jeffries. Can you tell us, please—did the defendant exhibit any unusual behaviour while this physical abuse was taking place?"

"Yes, he made a noise in his throat, like a growl. It made him sound like an animal. A monster."

"Your Honour," said the defence counsel, rising.

"The witness has a right to her opinion of the sound," said Judge Thomas.

"The defendant's attack was brutal, was it not?" asked Mr. Benjamin.

She swallowed. The questions were becoming harder for her to answer calmly. "I was bruised and bleeding. I had broken bones. I was in such terrible pain that I couldn't move."

"Bruised and bleeding," Benjamin echoed. "Broken bones. Immobilised. What happened next, Miss Jeffries?"

"He tore off my necklace." At Benjamin's direction, she described it. "That's when I knew he had done this to other women. As we say in Texas, it wasn't his first rodeo."

"Because of the jewellery you found?"

"Yes, sir."

"Your Honour, the witness is drawing a conclusion," said defence counsel.

"Miss Jeffries," said the judge, "you must confine yourself to what you know."

"What did the defendant do next, Miss Jeffries?"

The courtroom was still as a tomb. She looked away from Mr. Benjamin and saw the jury looking back at her. There were both men and women, some who looked about her age and others who appeared significantly older. Most were dressed informally, with sweaters or sweatshirts instead of suits. Some had pencils in hand, and she noticed that the ledge in front of them held pitchers of water and glasses as well as red folders. She didn't want to speak in front of them, and she began to cry.

"Miss Jeffries?" It was the prosecutor.

"He—he raped me."

The word "rape" pierced Sinclair's heart. It was the first time he'd heard her say it, in all the months since it had happened. Again he wished prosecuting counsel were female.

"Miss Jeffries," Mr. Benjamin said in a sympathetic voice, "I regret the necessity of such personal questions. However, for the record, we need to know. Had you ever had sexual intercourse with anyone prior to this dastardly attack?"

She felt naked, her private life laid bare. "No," she wept.

The prosecutor waited a minute or two before continuing, whether to give her a chance to collect herself or to milk the dramatic moment, she didn't know. "A virgin at the time," he said gravely. "Miss Jeffries, did the defendant abuse you in any other way?"

She was crying harder now. "He pushed me onto my stomach, but I can't—oh, God—"

Sinclair leant forward, hoping the prosecutor could guide her through her distress.

"It was a despicable offence, was it not?"

"My statement—can't you just—"

"Do you need a few minutes, Miss Jeffries?" asked the judge.

"No, sir," she sobbed. "It won't help. I'll never be able to say the words, not ever."

"Mr. Benjamin, would you care to rephrase the question?"

"Yes, Your Honour. Miss Jeffries, the accused has been charged in your case with two separate counts of rape, rape per vaginum and rape per anum. Do you understand these terms?"

Colin had told her that the separate counts of rape mattered. The more charges they could lay against the monster, the stronger their case, but she still felt humiliated by it.

"Miss Jeffries, we need a verbal answer," instructed the judge.

"Yes," she gasped into the microphone.

"Can you confirm for this court that both counts of rape took place?" Mr. Benjamin continued.

"They—they did." Her soft words seemed jarring in the silent room.

Again Mr. Benjamin paused. "What did the defendant do next?"

"He kicked me on the head, and I lost consciousness."

"Where were you when you regained consciousness?"

"In the intensive care unit at University College Hospital."

"Intensive care—of course. How long were you in hospital, Miss Jeffries?"

"Almost two weeks, I think."

"Were you completely recovered from your injuries when you left hospital?"

"Oh, no," she answered. "I couldn't walk. I had a cast on one arm. I was very weak. I was still in pain."

"Still in pain," he nodded. "Why, then, did you leave hospital?"

"Because I was attacked there," she said. "Someone tried to kill me."

"Where did you go when you left hospital?"

"I was taken into witness protection by the police."

"Miss Jeffries, were you scheduled to appear in this court before today?"

"Yes, sir."

"Why was your testimony delayed?"

"I was shot on my way to court the first time. One of the policemen protecting me was nearly killed."

"Yet you still had the courage to come here today," said Mr. Benjamin. "Why was that, Miss Jeffries?"

"Because I have to keep him from doing this to anybody else. And I have to speak for those who can't. What happened to me was monstrous, but what happened to them was worse."

"Your Honour," began defence counsel.

"Indeed," said the judge. "Miss Jeffries, you are permitted to speak only of your experience."

"Your Honour, the Crown has no further questions for Miss Jeffries at this time."

"Thank you, Mr. Benjamin," said Judge Thomas. "Court is recessed until half ten tomorrow morning."

"Court will now stand," said the usher, sounding just as bored as the clerk had in the morning.

CHAPTER 3

It was just past four p.m. when Jenny and the men returned to Judge Lloyd's chambers. Brian and Hunt left almost immediately, having complimented her on a productive day of testimony. When Colin came by with dinner and Sergeant Casey departed, she realized that all their movements had been preplanned.

Colin brought vegetable soup and beef baguettes, and she celebrated a meal without potatoes. Well, almost—there were diced spuds among the other vegetables. The meal revived her only slightly. It had been difficult describing the monster's crimes in front of such a large audience, but even more difficult doing it while he watched and listened. Every response she had given was an accusation. He had been angry at her before; she couldn't comprehend the depth of rage he must feel now.

When Sergeant Casey returned, Colin left. She made a quick call home. "Please, no questions, Mother," Casey heard her say. "All I've done today is answer questions for the prosecution. It was tiring—I had to stand most of the time. Talk to you tomorrow."

She changed from her court clothes into sweatpants and a t-shirt. Was it her imagination, or were her scars more prominent? The monster's shadow was still with her, growing larger as the night progressed. She didn't think he'd paid much attention to her face before, but after watching her all day in court, she knew without a doubt that he could spot her in a crowd now. The public gallery had been full; had he arranged for criminal associates to attend and memorize her looks? Did he know where she was hiding? She knew there were armed men outside, but she wanted all the ones she knew and trusted to be there, layer upon layer of human insulation.

Her hands shook when she bathed herself in the judge's bathroom, but she didn't hurry, hoping that the cleansing and rinsing strokes of the washcloth would be soothing if she forced herself to do them slowly enough. They weren't; every touch reminded her that she had been at the monster's mercy and in many ways still was. He seemed omnipresent. Was he in custody in the cells below the court? Were they both confined in the same building?

When she finished, she left the light on and pulled the door almost closed. Sergeant Casey had stretched out on his sleeping bag, and she sat down next to him and leaned against the wall. "It'll be worse tomorrow," she said. "He'll have an army of attorneys. And they'll be harder on me than that solicitor was."

He shifted her to the sofa. "You're capable of bringing it off. And you'll not be alone in there."

CHAPTER 4

Judge Thomas was already on the bench when Jenny followed the usher to the witness-box. The chair was gone.

"You may begin your cross-examination, Mr. Alford," the judge said.

A man with a wig and a patrician face stood. Was he taller than Mr. Benjamin, or did he just seem so because he was directly in front of her? She could see his long thin nose and smooth pale skin clearly. He gave a slight bow to the judge and jury, as Mr. Benjamin had done. "Your Honour, I am expecting some information to be delivered momentarily from my enquiry agent in the United States. Might you indulge me with a brief delay?"

She was thrown off balance. What could they be doing in the States? Already she was glad she'd had an unusually light breakfast, even for her—only the Coke that Brian had brought.

"No, Mr. Alford. We have had enough delays in this case already."

"As Your Honour pleases," the defence counsel replied smoothly. He faced Jenny. "Miss Jeffries," he said in a silky voice, "we're very sorry for your injuries and glad to see that you've recovered so well from them."

She sat quietly, listening for the question as Mr. Halladay had advised and trying to ignore the slightly sanctimonious tone he used. If he's a real patrician, then he considered her a colonial. His friendliness was false.

"As a matter of fact, you look lovely today. Did prosecuting counsel help you choose the clothes you're wearing?"

"No, sir."

"Oh—so you figured out all by yourself that a demure look would be best. Good for you."

She wanted to counter his sarcasm but didn't know how, and he didn't give her time to explain that her mother had sent her clothes from Texas.

"Miss Jeffries, what is your father's occupation?"

"He's a college professor."

"And your mother?"

"A homemaker."

"Your Honour, these facts are already on record," Mr. Benjamin pointed out.

"I'm well aware that Miss Jeffries' fairy-tale family life has been documented," Mr. Alford responded, not waiting for the judge to rule. "I intend to show this court that my learned colleague has built a house of cards."

She thought about the demonstration Colin had used, to show her how fragile trust was. Was the prosecution's case solid?

"Miss Jeffries, your father is a strict disciplinarian, is he not?"

"He set rules for our behavior and expected us to obey them."

"But the rules weren't as strict for your brothers, were they? In fact, your brothers enjoyed many privileges that you didn't, isn't that true?"

"Your Honour, I don't see the relevance," objected Mr. Benjamin.

"Goes to character, Your Honour," responded Mr. Alford.

"You may answer, Miss Jeffries," directed the judge.

"Parents are usually more strict with their firstborn, I believe."

"My, what a mature point of view! However, in your younger years, you resented his rules and raged against him, didn't you?"

"I felt I was responsible enough to deserve more freedom," she answered cautiously.

"Miss Jeffries, you are misleading this court! Your father's rules were necessary to keep you in line, weren't they? And you rebelled against him on more than one occasion, did you not?"

"All teenagers rebel."

"Miss Jeffries! We are not speaking theoretically, we are not speaking generally, we are talking about *you*. You resented your father's rules and rebelled against him, *didn't you*?"

"No—yes," she admitted.

"You wanted liberties."

"No, I wanted choices."

"You wanted to be free from parental supervision."

"I was the oldest—I wanted to be treated as an adult."

"Your mutinies resulted in tighter controls and more severe consequences, did they not?"

She didn't know how to answer. If she said yes, it sounded as if she accepted the term "mutinies." If she said no, it would be a lie. Her father had not eased his restrictions. He had intended for her experiences to serve as examples to her brothers.

Alford raised his eyebrows and waited.

"Miss Jeffries, you must answer," the judge said.

"Yes. Sir."

"Your father taught you to resent men, didn't he?"

"No, your client did that."

That's one for the Yank, thought Hunt.

Mr. Alford put on his glasses and shifted his papers. "You testified that you attended Prescott University. Why did you choose a university so far from home?"

"They had a good English department."

"I am not satisfied with that answer, Miss Jeffries. There were other reasons you chose Prescott, were there not?"

"They gave me a scholarship."

"Miss Jeffries, once again you are not telling this court the whole truth. You wanted to be rid of your father's restrictions, isn't that the truth?"

She paused. How did he know?

"Yes or no—you wanted to be free from your father's constraints!"

"Yes."

"Thank you very much, Miss Jeffries," Alford replied with false sincerity. "To continue—what was your primary subject at Prescott?"

"English. I majored in English literature."

"How appropriate!" exclaimed Alford. "This court has already seen repeated evidence of your ability to create fiction!"

Sinclair had heard her use the poetic phrases she'd learnt to give meaning and clarity to life—to express her feelings and desires when circumstances stressed her and she could find no words of her own. Now defence counsel was using the English language to throw mud at her.

"Your Honour," said Mr. Benjamin, "my learned colleague is testifying."

"Agreed," said Judge Thomas.

"Miss Jeffries," Alford continued smoothly, "you have been portrayed by the Crown as a devout young woman. How often did you attend religious services while you were at university?"

"Not often."

"We'd like you to be a bit more exact in your answer. Can you be a *bit more* exact, please? Did you *ever* attend church services whilst you were attending university?"

"Yes," she said stubbornly.

"Where?" demanded defence counsel.

"At home," she answered, feeling cornered.

"Ah, the truth at last. Thank you, Miss Jeffries." Mr. Alford bowed slightly in her direction and removed his glasses.

Mr. Benjamin rose quickly. "Your Honour, has my esteemed colleague completed his examination of this witness?"

Alford smiled. "Not at all." He continued in a conversational tone. "I imagine you enjoyed your time at Prescott, made good friends, and learnt a good deal from your professors."

She was quiet. It seemed such an innocuous statement that she was tempted to reply, but she hadn't heard a question.

"In point of fact, you had such a good time that it took you five years to graduate instead of the customary four, isn't that correct?"

"I did graduate in five years," she confirmed.

"Some years you didn't even carry a full load of courses. Too busy partying, weren't you?"

"No, sir. A good friend was killed, and I needed time to grieve."

Sinclair had a very uneasy feeling in his stomach, but Alford appeared to ignore her answer.

"Miss Jeffries, did you find employment after your graduation from university?"

"No, sir."

"Did you even *seek* employment after your graduation?"

"No," she admitted.

"You wanted a free ride, did you?"

"No, sir."

"You let your parents support you, did you not?"

"Yes, but—"

"You didn't want to work," concluded Mr. Alford, interrupting before she could point out that her scheduled trip to England precluded long-term employment.

"Mr. Alford, where are you in your examination of this witness?" Judge Thomas asked.

"I have more questions for her, Your Honour."

"Then now is an appropriate time to break for lunch," Judge Thomas said. "Do you agree?" He stood, and everyone rose with him. "See you all at a quarter to two. Court is recessed."

Apparently the judge was the only one who could ask rhetorical questions. The courtroom was in motion, but she seemed rooted to the spot.

"Miss Jeffries?"

She stepped out of the witness-box and followed Casey back to Judge Lloyd's chambers. Sergeant Andrews was already there, unpacking a large bag. "My wife did the catering today," he said. "Turkey or roast beef sandwiches, crisps, and brownies. Tea and sodas."

"Yum," she said, kicking off her shoes and reaching for a brownie. She opened a Coke and selected a sandwich.

Casey smiled at Jenny's priorities and Susie Andrews' lunch. Even Hunt's culinary critique was positive. Everything Andrews had brought was summarily consumed.

She freshened up in the bathroom. When she returned, Hunt was giving irreverent characterisations of the various players in court. "Upper-class twits, every one of them," he jibed.

Casey heard her short, frenzied laugh, but the usher's knock wiped even her feigned merriment away. "Oh, God," she said, hiding behind Brian. "Is it too late to change my mind about this?"

"Don't get your knickers in a twist," Hunt advised.

Brian frowned at him. "Come on, JJ. I'll walk with you to the usher's door."

CHAPTER 5

"Mr. Alford, are you ready to resume your cross-examination?"

"Your Honour, my trusted colleague, Miss Caroline Hayden-Welles, will now question the witness," Alford replied.

Jenny watched another black-robed figure rise. She must have swept her hair under her wig, the way PC Hewes had done with her police hat, but she could not disguise her creamy complexion or dark graceful brows. There was a slight flush to her cheeks. Either she was very careful with her makeup or the adversarial nature of her role energized her.

"Miss Jeffries," Hayden-Welles said in impeccable diction, "did you enjoy the night life after you arrived in London?"

"I didn't go out at night by myself."

"We know you weren't by yourself," Hayden-Welles nodded. "I'll come back to that in a moment. However, at present, I'd just like to confirm that you were travelling by yourself. Is that correct?"

"Yes, it is."

"Let's deal with the events leading up to your alleged attack by my client," the polished voice continued. "Can we just establish that you made your own decisions about the type of entertainment you chose to experience in London?"

"I didn't go out after dark."

Hayden-Welles frowned. "Miss Jeffries, I beg your pardon, but that was not my question. Did you plan your activities here?"

"Yes, I visited tourist spots in the daytime and ate dinner in some of the restaurants near the hotel."

"Your Honour," Hayden-Welles said coolly.

"Miss Jeffries, the court requests that you answer only the question that is put to you," Judge Thomas said.

"London has many wonderful night clubs, Miss Jeffries. Which of them did you visit after your arrival?"

"None of them."

"Perhaps the names have escaped you for the moment. I suggest that you frequented either Camden Palace, the Ministry of Sound, or both. These clubs are very popular with our American friends."

"I wouldn't know."

Hayden-Welles arched her eyebrows. "Miss Jeffries, I can't help feeling that you are not being entirely truthful. Like most young, attractive women, you enjoy being in the company of members of the opposite sex, do you not?"

Neither yes nor no seemed an appropriate response. "I used to, until your client got through with me," she finally said.

"Ah, yes. Thank you for acknowledging that you have met my client," Hayden-Welles said with exaggerated politeness. "But that's the problem, isn't it? It's the dangerous ones that attract us, don't you agree?"

Jenny shook her head. "No."

"There's an excitement in the unknown, isn't there, Miss Jeffries?"

"No."

She was met with a look of disbelief. "Miss Jeffries, it is agreed evidence—by your presence and your testimony—that you came to London alone. Do you intend for this court to believe that you felt no excitement about visiting unknown shores?"

"No, of course not."

"Miss Jeffries, would you agree that alcohol can affect our judgement?"

"Yes."

"What I really want to know is, did you flirt with my client before or after he bought you a drink?"

"Neither."

"Of course," Hayden-Welles said with mock regret. "I did not phrase my question properly. You flirted with him both *before and after* he provided you with alcohol, didn't you?"

"No."

"Miss Jeffries, we have no way of knowing that, do we? I can, however, tell you that you were not the first woman to find my client attractive. He's tall, blond, lean, with a healthy athletic face—in total, a very alluring individual." Hayden-Welles turned away from her podium to regard the defendant.

Jenny looked at the floor of the witness-box.

"Your Honour, would you be so kind as to instruct the witness to look at the accused?"

Bloody bitch. Casey hoped Jenny didn't have to comply.

Jenny was still looking at the floor. She spoke into the microphone. "I can't do that. I'll answer every question, but I will not look again at the man who abused me."

"Miss Jeffries—" the judge began.

"Hold me in contempt," she said. "Put me in jail. I won't do it." She started to cry. "I don't ever want to see his face again, as long as I live."

Sinclair stole a look at the jury. Their faces all had one thing in common: an expression of sympathy fixed on Jenny. Hayden-Welles' strategy had backfired.

"You do not have to look at the defendant," the judge said gently. "No one will force you to do that. Miss Hayden-Welles, I'll thank you to leave your theatrics out of my courtroom in the future."

"Yes, Your Honour," the cool voice replied. "My apologies, Your Honour." There was a pause. "Miss Jeffries, I believe we can agree that my client was a bit more of a man than you bargained for."

It wasn't a question. Jenny wiped her cheeks and waited.

And so the afternoon progressed, the cool, clipped voice asking one Catch-22 question after another. According to the defence, Jenny had met Scott in a club. She had come on to him. She had left with him voluntarily. She had been eager but not completely prepared for Scott's enthusiastic physical overtures when they were alone.

"We women tend to be overly emotional, don't we?" Hayden-Welles enquired, her arms crossed.

Yes? That answer meant that her tears over the monster were to be disregarded. A negative answer was impossible—she had already cried in the witness-box more than once. "We are not alike," she said slowly.

"Miss Jeffries," Hayden-Welles sighed, "I find I must agree with you. My time in this courtroom and others has been engaged in a search for the truth. And this story about my client's cruel attack—it's a fabrication, isn't it? A lie. I realise it's a bit embarrassing—well, more than a bit, actually—to admit that you were mistaken—we all understand that, I'm certain—but isn't that far better to do here and now, when the injustice can be rectified, than to wait? The longer you wait, the more intense your remorse will be."

Jenny had lost the question and had to ask for it to be repeated. "No."

"Miss Jeffries, this can all be over for you," Hayden-Welles soothed.

She remembered the last person who had spoken those words to her: It had been her father, wanting her to come home. She loved him, she missed her family terribly, and she had wanted desperately to go, but it would have been the wrong thing to do. And giving in to this Chinese water torture, no matter how tired she was, would be wrong, too. "I have not lied."

"Miss Hayden-Welles," Judge Thomas said, "do you have further questions for this witness?"

"Not today, Your Honour. The defence is willing to postpone its examination until the morning."

"We're off, then. Mr. Benjamin—Mr. Alford—will ten tomorrow be agreeable to you? Court is adjourned."

CHAPTER 6

The fireworks began as soon as the door to Judge Lloyd's chambers closed. "So much for posh!" Hunt yelled. "No disrespect intended, sir," he said quickly as Sinclair came in.

"None taken," Sinclair assured him. He sat down next to Jenny on the sofa.

"It's not fair," she said. "I feel like I'm on trial, too. It's a 'trial by existence.' That's what Robert Frost called it. And trials by jury end, but trials by existence don't. It will be over for the monster but not for me." Exhaustion covered her like a blanket, and she heard nothing until Hunt's voice penetrated. "Smelled so good, Davies and I had some ourselves," he said.

She sat up and rubbed her eyes. "Roast chicken. And mashed potatoes!" It struck her as funny that Brian, who always cooked potatoes, had brought her potatoes.

"Same schedule in the morning," Casey told Davies and Hunt. "Sir, I'll be back in a couple, if that's acceptable."

At a nod from Sinclair, the three men departed.

"Jenny, they cannot win. I'm sorry this is so difficult, but you must know that your cause is just. Your very presence in court means victory."

"Every question was a trap. It was worse than I expected. Well, to be honest, I didn't know what to expect."

"Their approach is to place the focus—and the blame—on the victim. It's not going to work."

She pushed her plate away. "I know now what it feels like to be raped by a woman," she said with a bitter smile. "She spent all afternoon raping my reputation, and there wasn't a thing I could do about it. Except stand there knowing I have to report tomorrow for more of the same."

"Once more into the breach."

"*Henry V*," she replied. "He was trying to encourage his men to attack again."

"Jenny, is there anything I can do for you?"

"Will tomorrow be my last day?"

"There's no way to know."

"Then I'll need more clothes. I only have this one suit—and one more clean blouse." She cleared the desk. "Were the families of the other women in the gallery today?"

"They've been there every day, Jenny."

"If you see them, will you tell them I'm doing my best? And will you tell Danny's family the same? I think about him all the time. I wish he were here."

Colin smiled. "I can't grant that wish, Jenny. All I can do is wish it with you. And I do."

Casey gave her a sleeping pill as soon as he returned, hoping she'd have an undisturbed eight hours.

"Sergeant Casey—do you think I did okay today?"

He chose his tone carefully. "Jenny—yes."

"Promise?"

"Yes. And Sullivan would think so as well. Rest now." As he waited for her to fall asleep, he wondered what he could do tomorrow to ease the weight on her shoulders. He had known her court experience would be difficult, and he feared that the defence's posturing was simply the prelude to a full-scale assault.

CHAPTER 7

The door to Judge Lloyd's chambers opened. It was Colin, bringing Jenny his Bible. There was an envelope on top with her name on it. "I can't stay," he said. "Super's outside. Good luck."

She sat down on the sofa and opened the envelope. *Read the end of Ephesians 6:13*, his bold handwriting instructed. *It's what you did yesterday. You can do it today.* He had signed his name.

She flipped through the pages and found the verse. He had underlined it: "that ye may be able to withstand in the evil day, and having done all, to stand." She read the rest of the verse and several that followed. They spoke of putting on the armor of God, wearing truth, walking in peace, and being shielded by faith. She needed all those things. The armor could keep the barbs of the defence counsel from getting through, and it could cover her poor rumpled suit, too.

Colin's note was still in her hand. She wished she could take it into court with her, and in her mind she heard him answer, "I can grant that wish, Jenny." She folded it carefully, unbuttoned her blouse, and slipped it inside her bra.

- -

She took a deep breath as she stepped into the witness-box and felt the edges of Colin's note against her skin. Unwittingly, he had called it: She would have to stand. There was no chair.

"Proceed, Mr. Alford," Judge Thomas said.

"Your Honour, the cross-examination will be led by my excellent colleague, Mr. Kevin Rhoads."

Another barrister rose to his feet. He was younger and broader than Mr. Alford, and everything about his features was exaggerated slightly, his high forehead, overlarge eyes, full lips, and jutting chin. His black eyebrows looked out of place with the white wig he wore. She would have known he was a predator even without the aquiline nose. He completed a series of questions Mr. Alford had started, about her employment history, or, as Rhoads emphasised, her lack of it.

Next he turned to her recreational activities, and she fielded one query after another about her participation in sports and entertainment. He made her sound as if she had been active only outside the classroom. He did not refer to her university transcript, which would have proved that she had spent some productive time in study. He paused. "If Your Honour could give me a moment," he said to the judge, looking through a stack of papers.

"Don't try my patience," Judge Thomas warned.

"Your Honour, I wouldn't think of it," Rhoads responded. "Ah, here it is." He opened a large brown envelope. "Could the witness be shown Defence Exhibit H, please?" He handed something to the clerk, who took it to the judge.

Judge Thomas frowned. He passed the exhibit to the clerk, who gave it to Jenny. She gasped, the color drained from her face, and she collapsed.

Sergeant Casey went to her without waiting for the judge's permission. He knelt down beside her and lifted her head slightly. Judge Thomas stood, as did the members of the press and a number of other observers. Both Davies and Hunt took several steps closer to the box, Hunt unable to keep anger from flooding his features. Rhoads turned away, hiding his satisfied smile from the jury but not from Sinclair. Benjamin was on his feet, an expression of horror on his face. "Your Honour—"

"Give us a moment," the judge replied.

Casey patted her cheeks. "Miss Jeffries, Miss Jeffries, are you all right?"

She could hear the sergeant's voice—but why was he calling her "Miss Jeffries"? She opened her eyes, and it all came back to her: the courtroom, the questions, and the picture of poor, dead, naked Rob. She doubled up and began to sob.

"Does she need a doctor?" asked the judge. "Should we recess?"

"Wait one, sir," Casey replied. He ran his hands over her quickly. "There's no evidence of fracture, sir," he reported. "Could she have a glass of water?"

The water was brought, and the sergeant helped her to sit up. He saw then what she had seen: a morgue photograph of the completely nude body of a young man—a young man who might have been attractive before physical trauma had crushed his chest and bloodied and distorted his other features.

"Bloody hell," Casey swore softly. He wasn't surprised to see Sinclair nearby. He handed him the photo and saw a dangerous expression cross his face. After a minute Sinclair gave it to the clerk, who passed it back to the judge. A member of the defence, managing to maintain a blank look, provided a copy for the prosecution.

"Sir, she needs a chair."

It took a few minutes to locate one, and the judge remained on his feet until it was provided. Casey helped her into it and gently pressed her head between her knees.

"Take your time, Miss Jeffries," the judge counselled.

Slowly she straightened.

"Any dizziness?" Casey asked.

She shook her head.

There was a rustle of concern in the court, and Sinclair could see why. Her face was stark white. Why had that bloody defence counsel done this?

"Take another sip of water," Casey suggested, wanting to buy her some time. It wasn't his no-nonsense voice; he sounded much kinder, but she obeyed anyway. He set the glass on the edge of the witness-box and took her elbow. With a little pressure he closed her arm so that her fingers rested on her neck where the cross was.

She thought suddenly of the flag in her room with the crosses on it, and Padre Goodwyn's belief that God used people to carry out His will. "Thank you, Sergeant," she whispered.

Casey nodded at the judge. "She'll do, sir." His heart heavy, he left the witness-box. He had done all he could. The rest was up to her, as it always had been, but she looked weak and small as she sat there alone.

Her microphone was adjusted. Sinclair returned to his seat.

"You may proceed, Mr. Rhoads," said Judge Thomas in a thin voice. He nodded for the clerk to pass the photograph to the jury.

"Miss Jeffries, do you need to see the exhibit again?" Rhoads' stout voice rang in the still room.

Tears ran down her cheeks. "No, please, no."

"Then please identify for the court the young man in the photograph."

"His name is Rob Morris."

Sinclair was shaking with anger. She was bleeding. Her tears were the external symptom that inside she was broken.

"Who is Robert Alan Morris, Miss Jeffries?"

She hated hearing Rob's name on Rhoads' lips. Rob had been everything this man was not: gentle, compassionate, loving, and funny. "A friend from college."

"Miss Jeffries, this court is tired of your half-truths. You supposedly swore to tell the whole truth. Isn't it true that you were more than friends with this Robert Morris?"

"Your Honour, I don't see the relevance," said Mr. Benjamin.

"Your Honour, that will become clear," Rhoads said quickly.

"See that it does," said the judge.

"Miss Jeffries, what exactly was your relationship with this young man?"

"I was in love with him." She saw the jury out of the corner of her eye. Their faces were shocked, and several of the women had wet cheeks. They had also seen the picture.

"Do you drink, Miss Jeffries?" Rhoads demanded.

"I beg your pardon?" She was confused by his sudden change in tactics.

"Don't be obtuse, Miss Jeffries! Do you consume alcoholic beverages?"

"Occasionally," she said. "I am of legal age."

"On the evening that Mr. Morris was killed—in a horrific automobile accident, I might add—were you drinking, Miss Jeffries?"

She bit her lip. "Yes."

"I didn't catch that, Miss Jeffries."

She had spoken too softly. She repeated her answer.

"And were you *of legal age* then, Miss Jeffries?"

"No."

"You and Mr. Morris were drinking together, were you not?"

"Yes."

"You knew he had a long drive ahead of him later that evening, didn't you?"

It was a question; she had to answer. "Yes."

"And yet you still enjoyed that bottle of wine and encouraged him to do the same—didn't you, Miss Jeffries?"

"Yes," she gasped.

"Miss Jeffries, please try to calm yourself," Judge Thomas said.

"I can't," she wept. She spoke into the microphone, but she hadn't looked in Rhoads' direction since seeing the photograph.

"You sabotaged him, didn't you, Miss Jeffries?"

"No! It was an accident."

"You sent him to his death, didn't you?"

"No, no, no! We didn't drink that much. I loved him!"

"Your irresponsible behaviour caused his death, didn't it?"

Davies wanted to throttle Rhoads' thick throat. Casey wanted to get Jenny out of the line of fire, then take him down.

"Your Honour, you must require the witness to answer," Rhoads declared.

"Mr. Rhoads, you have gone quite far enough," Judge Thomas responded. "You are not empowered to require me to do anything I do not wish to do. And in view of the time—and the obvious emotional distress of the witness—my wish is to recess until two."

"Your Honour, I have more questions for this witness," Rhoads protested.

Judge Thomas threw his pencil on the desk. "They'll have to wait," he snapped. "You cannot proceed without me, and I am leaving."

"Rise! All rise!" the usher exclaimed, caught off guard.

"Can you stand?" Casey asked her. The word reminded her of Colin's Bible quote. Oh, God—she had not even been able to stand. Casey put an arm around her waist and wrapped one of hers around his neck. "Davies!" he called. "Bring the chair."

When they reached Judge Lloyd's chambers, Casey set her down on the sofa and examined her properly. She had fallen onto a hard floor, and he found numerous places that were tender.

"What the bloody hell was that about?" Hunt yelled.

"It was a morgue shot," Casey said, "of her fiancé in Texas."

"We were celebrating our commitment," she cried. "We weren't drinking on an empty stomach—we'd had dinner. It wasn't late. We didn't even finish the wine. Alcohol wasn't a factor, it wasn't."

Sinclair came in. "Jenny, can you continue?"

"If I quit, he wins," she sobbed. "I don't have a choice."

Sinclair sat down next to her. "Yes, you do have. At two o'clock I can tell the judge he'll have to adjourn." He handed her his handkerchief. "You can't testify in this condition."

"I wish I were made of sterner stuff."

The boxed lunches Andrews had delivered were on the desk. Casey looked through them. The sandwiches looked decent, but he didn't think the beverages were sufficient. "Davies, Hunt—Jenny needs hot tea, as strong and sweet as you can make it. We'll give her some caffeine courage. Fetch some biscuits, the milder the better." He pulled the chair Davies had taken from the witness-box in front of her. "Sit here, Jenny," he commanded.

Sinclair took her arm and helped her change places.

"I'm going to start counting," the steely voice continued. "Count after me. One."

"One," she sobbed.

"No, you say the next," he ordered.

"Two," she repeated.

"Three."

"Four."

They had passed twenty before the sobs were completely gone and fifty before the shakiness had left her voice. Casey sent her to the bathroom to wash her face. "Sir, we got her mended and well for this? Frankly, sometimes I think our system sucks."

"My sentiments exactly, Sergeant."

They were both quiet when she returned. Davies and Hunt came in with their purchases and tucked into the sandwiches while Casey started her on the tea. After several sips, he opened a package of biscuits. He couldn't treat the soreness he knew was coming unless she ate something, and she'd have to have sustenance to carry her through the afternoon. "Take one bite." It was the voice no one said no to. "Another. Another."

Sinclair handed him a sandwich, and Casey gave her half. "Drink some tea, then eat a bit." He devoured his portion and nodded for more. She stopped eating. "One more bite, Jenny."

She started again, slowly. He finished the rest of his. "One more," he said over and over. Finally it was enough. He retrieved his kit and shook out two analgesic tablets. She washed them down with the tea.

Sinclair had watched the slow progression of Casey's recovery plan. It was nearly two. "Jenny, what shall I tell the judge?" he asked.

Her voice was weak but steady. "He killed those women, Colin. I'm not quitting."

When the knock on the door came and with it the usher's voice—tentative, this time—Casey helped her to her feet. "Every time I say a number, you take a step. Davies, bring the chair. Let's go."

Fortunately he didn't count too quickly, and the higher the number, the more time she had to respond. By the time they passed the monster, she wasn't waiting for his vocal commands. The glue was holding.

CHAPTER 8

Jenny felt a rush of relief when Mr. Alford rose to question her instead of his colleagues. It was short lived, however, because his interrogation continued the attack the defence had adopted from the beginning. He referred repeatedly to the statements she had made to the police and to the prosecutor's solicitor in examining her activities prior to what he called "her meeting with the accused."

She was tired when he began, and his ceaseless shuffling of papers exhausted her further. He asked one trifling question after the other, pausing briefly after she responded. Then he shifted gears. He explored the common belief that provocative clothing contributes to the incidence of rape and that most women who claimed to have been raped had invited it. He analysed the role of alcohol in irresponsible behaviour. He wondered aloud how many other men had been damaged by her callous, unthinking actions. He implied that she had been purposefully playing with fire when she aroused his client's interest, pointing out in a matter-of-fact tone that all adult males needed to experience sexual release following arousal. The frequent objections by the prosecution only prolonged the process.

When she was almost completely worn down, he increased his tempo, firing questions at her so rapidly that she had barely finished answering one when the next erupted. He added detail to the defence portrait of her as wild, immature, untruthful, and resentful of men.

She was apprehensive, expecting him to broadside her with some approach she could not anticipate. The courtroom was stuffy. No air was circulating. She felt a little dizzy, and she began to perspire. She missed a question and then stumbled in her answer. She gripped the sides of the chair to still her trembling.

"Pay attention if you please, Miss Jeffries," Mr. Alford scolded. He paused, sucking in his breath like a lion preparing to pounce.

As she waited for the panic to pass, she thought about the contrasts that existed in the court setting, the battle between the prosecution and the defence being only the most obvious. Truth was supposed to be the victor, but there were so many ways of shading the truth and coloring falsehood that it was sometimes difficult to tell where one ended and the other began. What would have been considered vocal abuse in a family was acceptable behavior here. This was not an old historic court, but the processes that took place were. People came and went—were they affected by what happened? Were the officers of the court changed, were the counsel, or were those who appeared in the witness-box the only ones altered? The impartial body of law that supported the whole process was an unfeeling observer, as Colin had said, devoid of mercy, while she felt just as exposed and bloodied as she had on the monster's rug. His symphony had had three movements: destroy all resistance, rape, and kill. Somehow in the final movement he had dropped his baton.

Mr. Alford said something about her emotional performance having an adverse effect on the fairness of the trial but did not concede that they bore any responsibility for her distress.

"Thank you, Mr. Alford, for explaining that," the judge sighed. "Need I remind you of the hour?"

"Your Honour, I would like to question this witness further."

"Then I suggest that you resume your examination in the morning. Half ten? Is that acceptable to you as well, Mr. Benjamin?" He did not wait for their verbal responses. "Court is adjourned."

Another day in the witness-box. She felt like the Greek figure Sisyphus, doomed forever to roll a huge stone up the mountainside. Sergeant Casey helped her rise, Brian collected her chair, and her little entourage escorted her back to her temporary haven.

She went into the bathroom to change out of her court clothes. When she came out, Davies and Hunt had already left. She had wanted to explain to Hunt why she couldn't call him Alan—because it had been part of Rob's name—but he had gone. She curled up on the sofa, but when she closed her eyes to rest, Rob's face was what she saw. She covered her head with her arms and sobbed, grieving again, not only for his loss but also for the manner in which he had died, because she knew how it felt to be broken.

The door opened and closed behind her, and she heard whispered voices. Someone left, and there was just one voice. "I've brought dinner, Jen. Would you eat with me?"

She sat up gingerly. In spite of the medication Sergeant Casey had given her during the lunch recess, she ached all over from her fall. Colin had brought soup with noodles, chunks of chicken, peas, and tiny slices of green onion. Brian would have watched to see if she ate the peas. There was French bread and hot tea. "Colin, I didn't help anybody in there today. I couldn't even stand."

"Jen, you never gave up. You never gave in. That's the same thing, in my book."

She shook her head.

"Would it help if I read you the Twenty-third Psalm?"

"I learned it, but I'm stuck on one of the middle lines: 'Yea, though I walk through the valley of the shadow of death, I will fear no evil.'

No matter what I do, I'm afraid. Not just of the monster, but of all the people who work for him, legally and otherwise."

Colin looked up the verse. "I'm no scholar," he said, "but it does say 'walk through.' You're not meant to stay in that accursed valley. And it also says you're not alone."

He reached across the corner of the judge's desk and took her hand. "Jenny, I talk to your family every night. They're very proud of you, and so am I."

"Proud of what?" She began to cry. "I was terrible out there!"

Colin moved his chair next to hers. "Proud of everything—your commitment, your tenacity, your inner strength." She accepted his handkerchief. The gentle voice continued. "They tried to destroy you, and they failed. Jenny, you are testifying in St. George Court. That's appropriate, don't you think? Dragons are slain here." He put his hand on her shoulder, and she leaned her wet cheek against it.

When Casey returned, he saw Jenny gripping Sinclair's handkerchief and trying to absorb his encouraging words.

Sergeant Andrews knocked and entered. "Give her my best," he said, handing Casey a carrier-bag. "Susie picked these up today. I hope they fit." He and Sinclair left together.

Casey gave Jenny medication to ease her aches and pains and something to help her sleep. He settled her on the sofa and climbed into his sleeping bag. He hadn't been there long when he heard her voice.

"Sergeant Casey—please—let me hold onto you. All I see when I close my eyes is that awful picture of Rob."

He let her crawl into the sleeping bag, and he sat next to her on the floor.

"Thank you for today, Sergeant Casey. The way you helped me after I fainted. I'll never forget it."

He wouldn't either, for other reasons. He'd understood with unwelcome clarity how Sinclair had felt when he'd seen her body bleeding behind the court block. It was a complication he did not want. When she finally fell asleep, he tucked her hand inside the sleeping bag and took her place on the sofa. He searched his mind for some way to help her in the morning, and he would have vehemently denied that it was a prayer.

CHAPTER 9

Jenny didn't sleep at all well, crying repeatedly during the night. Once Casey saw her trying frantically to brush nonexistent spider webs from her face, chest, and arms. "There's a spider in Texas whose poison makes your flesh rot," she explained. "I dreamed it was here."

He woke early and rang Davies, telling him to parade thirty minutes sooner than the previous mornings and to have Hunt with him. He phoned Sinclair, explaining that since she'd had a rough night, it would take some extra time to get her ready for the day and would he schedule his pre-court visit well ahead of time? Last, he gave Andrews a bell, explaining that he would have to medicate Jenny before her court appearance and they needed breakfast as soon as he could provide it.

When she woke, he handed her the carrier-bag with the new clothes and sent her into the bathroom to dress. When she came out, breakfast had been delivered. She saw the container of pain pills in his hand and gave him a weak smile. "That's the carrot in front of the horse."

"Right. You have to eat first."

Susie Andrews had found a two-piece sweater set, soft yellow with a hint of pink, to go with Jenny's dark green wool suit. Jenny tucked a napkin in the crew-neck sweater and ate what was necessary. The color of the sweater made her look like a ripe peach, tender and easily bruised.

Casey watched her receive Sinclair's words of encouragement with a brave smile, only to break down the moment the door closed behind him. When Davies and Hunt arrived, he took the opportunity to brief the officers stationed outside. "I'm going to give the witness a pep talk. No matter what you hear, stay out and keep everyone else out."

"Back me up," he told Davies and Hunt. "Jenny, pay attention."

She had no choice: It was The Voice.

"Long ago, before we met you, we were briefed—Davies, Sullivan, and I. Graves and Sinclair described this assignment, and I didn't want any part of it. I wanted to get armed criminals off the streets. I wanted to join other armed officers in fighting the war against drugs. I did not want to be shut up in a bloody flat day after day minding some Yank—a friggin' *female* at that—who was overimpressed with her own importance."

He had made her cry. He had expected that. He raised his voice slightly and kept the same firm tone. "Do you want to know what changed my mind? Do you? I saw pictures of what Scott did to you, photos taken at hospital, and I got angry. Not yell-at-persons angry—not throw-things angry—but determined angry, deep-in-the-gut angry. Remember where your pain was that time I examined you?" He reached out and touched the fabric of her skirt just a few inches above her pubis. "There, Jenny. I want you to fill that place with anger."

He raised the volume another notch and his intensity with it. "I don't give a toss what your reason is—God knows, you've got enough to choose from. Get angry for the other women! Get angry for your scars! Get angry for the months of your life that scumbag has taken! Get angry for Sullivan, Jenny!" He grabbed her arm and jerked her to her feet. "Give me a bloody pillow, Hunt!"

He faced her. "All these months we've watched you struggle—heard you cry—because of what that bloody bastard did! Haven't you been a punch bag long enough? Now hit it! Take a swing, and hit it like you mean it!"

She saw his fists clenching the sides of the pillow. She remembered the monster's fists coming at her. She was sobbing out loud now.

"Hit it like it's his bloody face!"

She struck out blindly, unable to see because of her tears.

"Damn it, hit harder, Jenny! Does he still have power over you, or are you going to take your power back?"

She slammed the pillow. She pounded it. She pummeled it.

"Texas, go, go, go!" yelled Hunt.

"Take him down, JJ!"

"I hate you!" she screamed, punching harder and faster, the tears streaming down her face. "I hate you!"

He dropped the pillow to grip her shoulders, stopping her next swing. "Well done!"

He saw her shake her head, trying to refocus.

"Healthy anger can make you stronger. Hold onto that power! Take it into the courtroom with you."

When they heard the usher's voice, she turned toward it, her shoulders straight. There was strength in her step for the first time. When she seated herself on the chair Davies had supplied, they saw her gather her feet beneath her, rest her fists loosely in her lap, and raise her chin.

Mr. Alford rose slightly. "Your Honour, my worthy colleague, Mr. Rhoads, will continue the cross-examination of this witness."

It was the pit bull. Hunt had other names for him, more colorful ones. She was ready for him.

"Did you have a good rest last night, Miss Jeffries?"

"I slept like a baby," she answered with a fixed smile.

Casey had told Sinclair that she'd cried half the night. Oh—just like a baby!

"How old are you, Miss Jeffries?"

"Your Honour," said Mr. Benjamin, "her age is a matter of record."

"So it is," said the judge. "Move on, Mr. Rhoads."

"Miss Jeffries, do you actually expect us to believe that you were still a virgin at the mature age of twenty-three?"

"Your Honour," said the prosecutor, "the Crown will present objective evidence of that."

"Quite. Be very careful, Mr. Rhoads."

"Bleeding," continued defence counsel undeterred, "can occur for all kinds of reasons. Were you in your menstrual cycle at the time of the alleged attack?"

"Your Honour," objected Mr. Benjamin, "Miss Jeffries has testified to the cause of her vaginal bleeding. The medical report, a copy of which was provided for the defence, confirms it. Her hymen was ruptured by the defendant!"

"I will not warn you again, Mr. Rhoads," the judge said.

"Miss Jeffries, the description you gave of your attacker was quite particular. More of your fiction?" Rhoads asked.

"No."

"Then how do you account for the details you provided?"

"The light was on in the room, and it was happening to me."

"Miss Jeffries, the record shows that you identified my client from an artist's sketch. Is that correct?"

"Yes."

She had dropped the respectful form of address, Sinclair noticed.

"But you were in hospital at the time, were you not?"

"Yes, I was."

"Did you subsequently identify my client from a photo array prepared by the police?"

"I did."

"While you were still in hospital?"

"Yes."

"You never identified him in person?" Rhoads asked in mock outrage.

"No. As you pointed out, I was in the hospital."

"The medical record shows that you had a concussion. Is it possible that your memory was affected by the concussion, causing you to identify the wrong man?"

"No. I don't have trouble remembering your client. I have trouble forgetting him." She heard Casey chuckle under his breath.

"Your Honour, the witness has identified the accused in this court," prosecuting counsel said.

"Indeed she has," agreed the judge.

"Miss Jeffries, how old would you say that I am?"

"Your Honour."

"I'll allow it, Mr. Benjamin."

She pressed one of her fists against her belly. "In your thirties."

"Would you please be more specific?"

"Mid to late thirties," she guessed.

"Miss Jeffries, I am forty-two. Appearance of age can vary widely, can it not?"

Damn. He had spent too much time in the law library. She had to answer yes.

"The judgement of a witness can be far from accurate, isn't that so, Miss Jeffries?"

Again she had to answer in the affirmative.

"Would you describe for the court what you were wearing on the day you claim you were attacked?"

"Dark blue slacks with a white blouse."

"That's all? No knickers?" he sneered. "Perhaps I did not make myself clear. I am asking you to describe *all* your clothing."

She turned to the judge. "Do I have to do that, sir? Describe my *underwear*?"

"Miss Jeffries, you don't have to answer the question if you don't understand the relevance. You may ask counsel politely what the relevance is," Judge Thomas answered.

"You want to know about my underwear?" she asked Rhoads.

He gave her a mock bow, arms extended and palms up.

She lifted her chin. "It was clean."

Laughter rippled through the court.

Rhoads waited a minute before continuing. "Your blouse and your trousers are not listed amongst the evidence recovered by the police. Where are they?"

"I don't know."

"Then I'm afraid—since we have only your word—that we cannot accept your version of what you were wearing. You are an attractive young woman. Are you certain you weren't dressed more provocatively?"

"I wasn't, and I'm sure."

"Miss Jeffries, are you expecting this court to believe that you don't choose your clothes to attract men?"

"Mr. Toads, you're wearing an expensive watch. Do you want to attract thieves?"

There was a restrained chortle from the prosecution barrister and others. Sinclair wasn't sure he'd heard correctly, but he hoped he had: It was a sign of pluck on her part.

"Your Honour." Rhoads appealed to the judge.

"You introduced this line of questioning," Thomas pointed out, choosing to ignore Jenny's incorrect appellation.

"Miss Jeffries," Rhoads resumed in a firm tone, "my client has wealth, position, and is very attractive to women. When did you decide to pursue him?"

"I didn't," she said. "I'd never heard of him."

Rhoads feigned surprise. "How can that be? Son of such a well-known British family? He is often pictured in the newspaper for his participation in various charity events."

"I'd been in England only a short time when I was attacked by him."

"But you have a degree—in English, no less—from a well-respected university. You testified to that yourself. Surely you are capable of reading a newspaper?"

"Mr. Rhoads," she used his correct name to ensure his attention, "can you tell me the name of the son of the current governor of Texas?"

"Your Honour," objected Rhoads.

"I rest my case," Jenny said quickly.

This time the laughter was more pronounced.

"I request that these irrelevant comments be stricken from the record!"

"Mr. Rhoads, I'm not going to do that," Thomas said. "I'm curious. Miss Jeffries, what is the name of the son of the current governor of Texas?"

She smiled up at him. "Sir, the current governor of Texas doesn't have a son. He has two daughters."

Even the judge laughed aloud.

Defence counsel began again. "Miss Jeffries, you are making light of very serious proceedings. This is not a time for levity. If I may continue—on the day in question, you went to my client's family's residence, didn't you?"

"I didn't go willingly to that little room, wherever it was."

"But you do admit to being in that room?"

"Yes." She squeezed her fists.

"You admit to being in a private room, fully naked, with my client?"

"He took my clothes!"

"Did he, Miss Jeffries? Can you testify under oath that he—and no one else—removed your clothing?"

Her fingernails dug into her palms. "No."

"You were hoping to seduce my client into doing something you could blackmail him for, weren't you?"

"No."

"You hate my client, don't you?" Rhoads pressed. "You'd say anything to convict him."

"Only the truth can do that."

"And humiliating him—putting him through this distasteful process—isn't enough, is it? You want revenge on him as well, don't you?"

Rhoads had raised his voice, but she didn't think he could hold a candle to Sergeant Casey when it came to using an intimidating tone. "I don't want revenge," she declared. "Revenge means my doing to him what he did to me plus some, and that's not possible. Justice is submitting the facts to an objective body and abiding by their decision. I am here for justice."

"Your Honour, I object. Miss Jeffries is not a legal professional, and these lines of testimony should be removed."

"Mr. Rhoads, legal definitions do not harm your case. Besides, it's as good a description of the two as I've heard in a while, so I'm going to let it stand."

Rhoads paused for a moment before continuing. "Then the truth is, you couldn't wait to spread your legs for my client, could you? Handsome man that he is!"

She recoiled, feeling shamed by the crudeness of the question. "No!"

"No? Then you desired rough treatment to excite you before intercourse?"

She gasped in shock and did not reply.

"Your Honour, have we disregarded the standards of decency entirely?" asked Mr. Benjamin. "When decency leaves, truth is not far behind."

"Mr. Rhoads," remonstrated the judge.

Rhoads either wasn't aware or didn't care that she hadn't answered his last question. "And you wanted more, didn't you? Tell me—after sexual intercourse, how did you get a clean-cut well-bred young man like my client to participate in deviant sex?" He turned toward the jury with a disgusted expression on his face.

"Mr. Rhoads, I'll thank you to direct your opinions to the bench," Judge Thomas said severely.

Her body was beginning to ache again. Even her fists felt sore when she squeezed them. "Mr. Rhoads—I never had sex with your client. Sex is—"

Rhoads started to interrupt, but his objection was waved aside by the judge.

"—what happens between two consenting adults. I never gave my consent. What happened to me was a crime, and that's why it's called by other names."

Sinclair wanted to cheer.

"Miss Jeffries," scolded Rhoads, "first you ask us to believe that you were a virgin, and now you lecture us about the nature of sex. I find it very difficult to believe that you are as much a victim as you pretend to be."

"Your Honour, my learned friend is testifying," objected the prosecutor.

"Indeed," said the judge.

Her shoulders slumped. All of Sergeant Casey's medicine was wearing off.

Mr. Benjamin had remained on his feet. "Your Honour, might I suggest that we recess for lunch? It is past the hour."

"We'll resume at a quarter to two." Thomas nodded at the usher.

"All rise!"

They did, some of them even more slowly than Jenny.

CHAPTER 10

No one spoke until the door to Judge Lloyd's chambers closed behind them. Hunt was seething. "How much more of this legal claptrap does she have to endure?"

Sinclair and Andrews joined them, the younger man with their lunches. Sinclair saw the lines of exhaustion on her face.

"They're wearing me down," she said. "I just want it to be over—the questions, the rudeness, the attempts to humiliate me—I'm tired of the whole sordid mess." She turned away, not wanting to face Hunt's anger, Colin's expectations, and Sergeant Casey's intensity.

Colin's voice followed her. "I know it's difficult, but you're the best witness we've got. We'd be nowhere without you."

"Eat a bit," Casey advised. "Then stay quiet. Save your strength."

She accepted the sandwich he offered and moved to the end of the sofa. Sinclair watched her take small, slow bites. The men ate noisily, Hunt punctuating the silence occasionally with a comment about the food.

"It's nearing the time," Casey told her. "Ready yourself. Splash some water on your face." He was waiting for her when she returned from the bathroom. "Tell me their names, Jenny. The ones you're speaking for."

"Barbara. Clarissa. Emma." She took a breath. "Marilyn. Patsy. Sally."

"One more," The Voice said.

Hers shook. "Jenny."

He took her arm and nodded at Davies to bring the chair.

They returned to the courtroom, Sinclair and Andrews to their chairs behind the prosecution, Casey, Davies, and Hunt to their appointed positions of observation, and Jenny back to the witness-box.

"Mr. Alford, who will be continuing the cross-examination?" Judge Thomas asked.

"I will, Your Honour." He faced Jenny once again. "Miss Jeffries, this business about taking the bus—it's a fabrication, isn't it? You never took the bus at all."

"Someone drugged me before I could buy the ticket."

"Who, Miss Jeffries?"

"I don't know."

"Allow me to read from the statement you gave to the police. 'It was a man's hand. A man's arm.' You can't do any better than that?"

"No, sir."

"I submit that you cannot remember—or give a better description—because it never occurred, Miss Jeffries. Now let's look at the alleged rape."

Alleged—her heart sank.

"Did my client threaten you with a gun?"

"No, sir. He didn't have to, he used—"

"A knife?" interrupted Mr. Alford.

"No, sir. He hit me! He kicked me!"

Alford appeared to consider this. "Then we understand correctly that there was no weapon."

"His ring was a weapon."

"Are you trying to tell this court that my client aimed his *ring* at you?" Alford asked in a scathing tone. "And you submitted because he had a *ring*?"

I will not answer yes. *I will not.* "I did not submit."

Alford paused. "Miss Jeffries, did you resist my client's advances?"

"Yes, sir."

"I challenge that, Miss Jeffries! According to your statement, and I quote, 'I didn't defend myself. I won't be a good witness.' Are these your words, Miss Jeffries?"

"Yes, but you're taking them out of context."

"I think not! The sex you had with my client was consensual, was it not?"

"No. I was a virgin."

"Miss Jeffries, it is not rape just because you lost your virginity. If that were the case, many a young man would be arrested and charged before his wedding night."

There were several chuckles in the courtroom.

"Let's continue. Miss Jeffries, if you didn't struggle, it wasn't rape."

"He had to pry my legs apart. What does that tell you?"

"That you were a tease, Miss Jeffries—that you wanted to be overpowered."

"I squeezed my knees together. It was all I could do," she insisted. "He had broken my arm."

"Both arms?"

Casey wanted to break Alford's.

"My left arm."

"So you had the use of your right arm?"

"No, it was bruised. And the drug made me sluggish."

"Then—and I must stress that we do not concede that my client caused any injury whatsoever to your left arm—why didn't you push him away with your right arm? Being bruised doesn't render one incapable."

"Because my face was bleeding. He had struck me across the cheek and cut me badly."

Alford's patient tone made him sound as if he were genuinely trying to understand. "You could have reached him with your right arm, but he had struck you across the cheek." He shook his head. "I don't see the connection—a cheek injury wouldn't affect your arm, would it?"

"No, sir, I—"

"I have it!" Alford exclaimed. "That blow—the one on your cheek—was of more concern to you than allegedly being forced to engage in sexual intercourse!"

"No, of course it wasn't, I just—"

"You were more concerned about your appearance! Miss Jeffries, that is your testimony, is it not? In the whole of your statement to the police, and indeed, in all your testimony to this court, you cite only one act of restraint, and it was short-lived, because, in your own words, 'I was concerned about my face.'"

"You don't understand, I couldn't—"

"Miss Jeffries, I understand very well, but perhaps you would like to explain it for the court—why you chose to shield your cheek instead of your vagina."

She shuddered. She hated hearing him say "vagina" out loud. His intonation made it sound obscene. "No—"

"What does that tell us about you, Miss Jeffries?"

"I was hurt so badly—I couldn't think clearly—"

"No, Miss Jeffries. I believe it tells us that you, like many women, may have thought no, but you meant, yes. You were not forced. My client did not rape you."

"Your Honour," Mr. Benjamin began.

"Save it for your concluding statement, Mr. Alford," directed the judge.

"Yes, Your Honour." Alford thumbed through a stack of documents. "One moment, please, Your Honour."

She needed a break. It was all catching up with her, the nights of poor sleep in the judge's chambers, the days of mental exhaustion, parrying the endless questions of counsel. She looked around the courtroom. There was Brian, her gentle giant, who had nursed her back to health with food too tasty to resist, held her accountable for her actions, and guided her into behaving responsibly. She saw Hunt, confrontational Hunt, who would never give an inch to anybody. She thought about Danny—his laughter stilled, fighting a silent battle. Behind her was Sergeant Casey, who understood what it felt like to face death, who was clear in his purpose and had helped her to be clear in hers. Her eyes rested on Colin. He had made her forget, however briefly, that she was scarred and would never be loved.

So many times she had been discouraged. When she wanted to go home, Colin had brought her a book about Churchill, who had never given in. She had asked Sergeant Casey how to fight something invisible, and he had advised her to focus on what she could see and to keep her body ready for the conflict. She had told Padre Goodwyn that she had done her best, and he had told her that God was with her.

Alford's voice interrupted her reverie. "Miss Jeffries, you have caused serious charges to be laid against my client. Would you like to hear the list of counter-charges my client intends to lay against you?"

She raised her chin. "Yes, sir, I would."

He raised his eyebrows slightly. "Perjury, Miss Jeffries. Giving false evidence. Slander, the most malicious I have encountered. These are only a few of the offences. I will place *you* in the dock next time."

The dock—the monster was sitting there, looking elegant in his expensive suit, an attentive expression on his face. If he went free, other young women, currently going about their daily lives with no warning that a monster was coming, would be in mortal danger. He had caused incalculable fear, pain, and sorrow. Colin had never condemned her. He had held her when she cried. He had always believed in her. Sergeant Casey—formidable in his anger, frightening in his focus—had gripped the pillow for her to hit. She thought about her family, her long distance lifeline, so deeply missed for so many months. Her daddy would say that it was time for her to step up to the plate. She pushed herself to her feet, lifting her chin defiantly and raising her voice so the microphone wouldn't be necessary. "Then bring it on, Mr. Alford!" she shot back. "I'm a Texan, and I won't quit. I'll fight for my integrity. As God is my witness, I did not lie. I remember—"

Judge Thomas interrupted Alford's objection. "You invited this, Mr. Alford."

"—everything your client did to me, from the first blow until I lost consciousness. I haven't forgotten the fear, and I haven't forgotten the pain, and I'll never forget—" she turned toward Scott and pointed her finger at him—"his face! Do you have a daughter, Mr. Alford? God help her, if you let her anywhere near your client!"

"I'll see you in court," Alford said coldly. "Your Honour, I have no further questions for this witness."

"Mr. Benjamin, would you care to re-examine?" Judge Thomas asked.

"Yes, Your Honour," answered Mr. Benjamin, bowing as tradition dictated. "Do you need a moment, Miss Jeffries?"

"No, sir, you'd better do it now."

"Miss Jeffries, when you first appeared in this court, you took an oath to tell the truth, the whole truth, and nothing but the truth. Have you upheld that oath?"

"Yes, sir, I have."

"In all your testimony, have you uttered any fabrication or falsehood?"

"No, sir, not one."

"Were you forced to testify in this case?"

"No, sir, I was not."

"Have you told this Court everything you can recall about the events that took place on September 14, 1998?"

"Yes, sir."

"Miss Jeffries, did William Cecil Crighton Scott hit you?—Kick you?—Cut you?"

She answered yes to each question.

"Did he in fact beat you so brutally that you had multiple broken bones?—Did he cause massive bruising?—Internal injuries so severe that your spleen was removed and repair to other internal organs was required?"

Again she responded affirmatively in each case.

"Were you in excruciating pain?"

"Yes, sir. At the end, it hurt so much to breathe that I stopped screaming."

"Were your injuries so extensive that they necessitated intensive care in hospital?"

"Yes, sir."

"Did William Cecil Crighton Scott rape you, Miss Jeffries?"

"Yes, he did."

"Did he kick you in the head, causing you to lose consciousness?"

"Yes, sir."

"Are you absolutely and completely certain—no doubt whatsoever—that William Cecil Crighton Scott was the man who committed these heinous offences against you?"

"Yes, sir. When I sleep, his face is in my dreams. Every time I look in the mirror, my scars look back at me. He was a monster. I'll never forget, not ever."

"That concludes our examination of this witness, Your Honour," said Mr. Benjamin, bowing to the judge and sitting down.

Judge Thomas glanced at defence counsel, who shook his head. The judge then turned to Jenny. "Miss Jeffries, thank you for your assistance. You are excused. You may stand down. Court is adjourned until half ten tomorrow morning. Off we go." He left the bench.

Was it finally over? She had heard the judge's words, but they hadn't registered. She was so exhausted she could not have testified to the hour or even to the day. She saw the sergeant holding out his hand to her, and she couldn't think what she was supposed to do.

"Time to go, Miss Jeffries."

His voice was firm, and automatically she obeyed. She found herself on Judge Lloyd's sofa, and she curled up and closed her eyes.

"Don't wake her," Sinclair said when he arrived. "Just tell her she did brilliantly. I'll phone her family later. I'll be off with the decoy straightaway." He smiled. "It's a bit like being the Pied Piper, at least for the press. Ring me when you've landed."

The protection team wouldn't leave until after the entire courthouse had cleared, so Andrews brought pizza, and Casey woke her to take a few bites. The men changed out of their uniforms, and Casey decided that a raincoat and hat were sufficient to conceal her identity. At the appointed time, the armed police outside the judge's door accompanied them to the waiting vehicle.

- -

When they returned to the flat, Casey rang Sinclair. Hunt volunteered to take the night watch. "So our chef will be rested and ready for kitchen duty tomorrow," he joked. Casey didn't wait to hear Davies' response.

The flat was quiet. Hunt made himself the first of many cups of tea and went into the sitting room. He recalled his early days with the team, how Davies had threatened to throttle him—more than once—when he'd whinged about being stuck there. Shut it until you hear her tell it, he'd said. Then you'll know what you're here for. Well, he'd heard it now, heard Little Bit describe everything and heard those bloody briefs at court maul her.

Coppers saw things other persons didn't—beastly things—but those who lasted on the Job learnt to insulate themselves. They had to pay attention on the outside but stay detached on the inside so they could process what they saw and take the appropriate response. It was a struggle; some nights his PC father hadn't gone down the pub. Sat by himself instead in the front room. In the dark. "Leave me. It'll not help to bring the heartache home," was all he had said.

Now he was living in a flat with someone who'd been through bloody hell. What should he do? What Casey had done in court when she'd fainted: Get her back on her feet. Help her get on with it. So the rest of them could also. Easier said than.

CHAPTER 11

Jenny nearly slept the clock round. Finally Sergeant Casey woke her with a cup of tea. Another list for her journal: *Uses for British Tea.* It put you to sleep, woke you up, soothed frazzled nerves, calmed upset feelings, welcomed visitors, and warmed cold hands. Did it reduce swelling? Assist in the quest for world peace? She felt like she had jet lag, and it probably cured that, too. "Have you had breakfast?"

"We've had lunch."

She put on a dressing gown, sipped some hot soup, and snacked on some biscuits. After a long nap, she showered and dressed.

When Colin came by after dinner, she was wearing a bright turquoise t-shirt with blue jeans but there was no colour in her face. She greeted him briefly and then went back to bed, not bothering to change into her pyjamas.

"Must have been something in the food," Hunt joked. Their mission—getting her to and from court safely—had been a success, and he was still in good spirits.

"Did you medicate her?" Sinclair asked Casey.

"No, sir, there's a natural letdown after a mission," he explained. "Combine that with physical exhaustion, and you have the thousand-metre stare. Men who've been in combat for a long time sometimes get it. She gave it all she had, sir."

"I'm still furious that so much was required," Sinclair said.

"She has the ability to stand in the door," Casey added. "I respect that."

"That another of your military expressions?" Hunt asked.

Casey smiled. He enjoyed baiting Hunt; he always bit, hook, line, and sinker. "Airborne troops coined it. When you're ready to jump, you stand in the door. You're committed 100%."

The second day passed much as the first. The third day her numbness was gone. She thought about her testimony, and the memories hurt. "It was a feeding frenzy, like letting a pack of ravenous dogs loose with the

Easter bunny! Alford—Rhoads—they beat me up in front of everybody."

"I'd like to beat them up in front of everybody," Hunt said.

"I'd rather do it in private," Casey said.

"They hit below the belt," Brian agreed, "but you played hurt, like the rugby blokes I see on TV. I was proud of you."

"But they sent people to Texas—they dug up all that dirt about me!"

"What dirt? Sounded normal," was Hunt's opinion. "I do have a question, though. If you loved that bloke, why didn't you have it off with him?"

Casey frowned.

"What! Did I go too far?"

"No, it's okay," she said quietly. "The truth is, I was planning to. If he'd lived just another week, I would have. I wish I had. I wish he'd been my first and not the monster." Her voice shook. "That photo—he was all bloody. His chest had caved in." She turned to Casey. "Sergeant—that last morning—did you really mean all those things you said? You didn't want to take care of me?"

"I wanted you angry."

"But—all those times you were good to me—were you lying?"

"Leave it, Jenny." His voice hardened. "Don't start messing me about. It's been a long time since I felt that way."

Why was he so gruff? She knew he rarely talked about his feelings, but she needed to know. "Is it just a job to you?"

"It's a job I like. I can't say any fairer than that."

Hunt left, returning a few minutes later with hot cocoa for her. "My prescription—administer chocolate. Dosage—one cup."

When Sinclair arrived after dinner, Casey told him Jenny was in phase two: feeling again. "Don't be surprised if she cries, sir."

"I'd prefer that actually," Sinclair said, "to stupor."

And cry she did: "Did I let you down, with my testimony? Was it good enough? Colin, will he get off?"

"Benjamin is confident he'll go down."

"But the monster is famous—and nobody's ever heard of me! Why should they believe me?"

"Because you were a wonderful witness, Jen. You kept fighting back, no matter what the defence threw at you. Your character was evident, and a number of persons testified as to the good characters of the women who were killed. You know their stories—none of them were promiscuous, but all had had intercourse shortly before they died. Your testimony established the link—not just Scott's DNA but his treatment of them. I don't think there's a member of that jury who won't consider the injuries that led to their deaths and not hold Scott responsible. And Benjamin doesn't think that Alford will dare to put Scott in the witness-box. His arrogance alone could put him away."

"Colin, he threatened to charge me with all sorts of crimes! Can he do that? Will I go through all this and then have to go on trial, too?"

"Jenny, when Scott is convicted, none of that will be an issue."

"Did you see Rob's photo? Have you seen others like that?"

Yes, and more—bodies on the scene, bodies at the mortuary, photographs in the files. And the faces of persons who loved the deceased. "Jenny, I'd like to tell you that over time that image will fade, but I can't. Some do, and some don't." He remembered his first. He remembered the worst. And over the years his mind had been imprinted by others whose circumstances had been particularly tragic. After his father's death, seeing any body without the spirit of life had been difficult. "Bodies die, Jen, but spirits don't. Scott might have been able to kill your body, but he could never eradicate that indefinable thing that makes you, you."

The photos the police had taken of her at the hospital probably hadn't looked much better than Rob's, but somehow she had survived. Her body had recovered. "I think he did, Colin. There's nothing left inside. I can't seem to find—*me*."

"You're like an athlete after a particularly grueling race, Jen. You need time to recharge."

"I feel more like a politician after the polls have closed: helpless. I'm waiting for the vote to come in to tell me whether my words were believed."

CHAPTER 12

Scott's trial continued, and Jenny's internal battles did also. Her skin had knit itself back together since his attack, but there were tears inside that her court experience had reopened. They had talked about her vagina in open court! It had been humiliating. And she had endured four days with the monster who had seen and abused her naked body. Four days with strangers watching her. Four days of endless questions. Four days with all her weaknesses exposed. Her testimony had been so *public*—all who were present had heard her delineate—describe—defend. How many had viewed her nakedness? Counsel on both sides—the judge—the jury—who else? Had the men in the flat been shown photographs of her shame? She knew the water couldn't wash it away, of course, but at least in the shower the men couldn't hear her crying.

After the shower she curled up in one of the armchairs in her bedroom, clothed in her roomy blue caftan, her journal on her lap. What kind of list could she make that would distract her? All she could think of were the things she used to be: healthy, productive, active. And do: play tennis, work on the college newspaper, eat out. She remembered going where she wanted, when she wanted—to the mall, movies, museums, plays, lectures, concerts, sporting events, bookstores. Texas had more warm months than cold ones; she'd gone to the beach, lounged by the pool, never worrying what her body looked like, never choosing her clothing to cover her scars. In court she'd had to display the scar on her face. She had a scar on her breast, too. A photo of that injury would have revealed her whole breast to whoever viewed it. Or did the photo show her entire chest? A record of physical evidence, the police would consider it. Mortifying, she called it. Surgeons had left scars on her midriff. The man on the motorcycle had made his marks on her shoulder—evidence for another jury to examine. She had not made one useful entry in her journal. It was time for another shower.

- -

New day. Same faces in the flat, but one more in her dreams: Rob. She woke up remembering what it felt like to be loved and how it felt to have love torn away. She'd first started saying "piece of cake" when she was loved, because she was enveloped in a soft cloud that filtered out the sharp edges of life. Mid-term exams? Major paper due? There were no negatives. Piece of cake.

She hadn't known Rob was dead until she'd seen the headline: "University Student Killed in One Car Collision." His parents hadn't notified her because they didn't know how serious his relationship with her had been; he'd been on his way home to tell them. He'd left on a Friday evening, and she remembered wondering why he hadn't called when he arrived, or sometime the next day. But she hadn't been worried—there were so many reasonable explanations, and she loved and trusted him. The black-and-white newsprint had taken all the color out of her life.

He had given her a ring, not an engagement ring but a promise ring, gold with several small pearls. "I, Robert Alan, take thee, Jennifer Catherine," he had said with a smile. She had been wearing it the morning she had left the hotel for the British Museum. It had never been recovered.

London. She would never have come if he had lived. She would not have flown across the Atlantic with her black and white perspective. But she had come to London, and the monster had colored her red. She had awakened in the hospital, and in that world of sterile white, Colin's blue eyes had been striking. Then the courthouse. A gray day with Danny's blood bold against his pale skin and dark hair. Would he die, too? Would Colin tell her, or would the heartless prose of the newspaper announce it?

CHAPTER 13

"Jenny, wake up."

"What's wrong?"

"You were crying in your sleep, love."

She touched her cheeks. Yes, she had been. "Rob and Danny—sometimes their faces are so bloody I'm not sure who's who."

She'd been alone in the witness-box, separated from the team. Then kept to herself in the flat. Had too many long showers. It was time for the team to reconnect. "Want to go running with us?"

"In the middle of the night?"

"We can't take you in the daytime. Put on your sweatpants and a shirt if you want to go."

When she met him in the sitting room, he'd brought his hooded sweatshirt for her to use also. He didn't trust the darkness alone to guard her features.

"Quiet past the boss's door," Brian whispered.

Hunt led the way down the stairs and out the front door. There was no smog or smoke, just the mist from her mouth when she breathed. The air was crisp, clean, fresh. Too cold, and all aroma is paralyzed at birth. Too hot, and even the subtlest scents are suffocating. It was chilly, but she caught a whiff of a faint flowery perfume—even in this winter month, something was in bloom. Trees lined the streets like sentinels. Some of them were bare, but many still bore their foliage. The streetlamps were on, giving an ethereal glow to their excursion. Nothing was moving, except the four of them: Hunt, jogging ahead; Davies, loping effortlessly behind; and Sergeant Casey, his steps synchronized with hers across the uneven sidewalk.

The street was narrow, with funny little cars parked on both sides of it. It had a slight incline, and she realized that she'd never walked outside the flat, except to cars waiting either in front of or behind the building. Indoors Sergeant Casey had made her run in place between exercises, but it had been—flat. They reached an intersection where the road levelled, and she saw Casey signal left and Hunt's acknowledgement.

They passed one house after another, all of them at least three storeys, silent in sleep. The gabled roofs had chimneys, and there were bay windows on the lower floors. Brick walls lined the small front yards. She could hear her feet lapping against the ground and her breath, barely audible at first, then discernible, and soon, readily apparent. She stopped and bent over, her hands on her knees, and heard Sergeant Casey's soft whistle to alert the others. She was panting, he was breathing normally, and it was all very infuriating.

She straightened, and Casey again gestured to Hunt. They turned and ran on, past houses with windows blindfolded against the rising sun and trees cradling the railed porches that designated each doorway. The street dipped, then rose, then dipped again.

She was breathing through her mouth, faster now, and she missed Casey's direction, trotting a few steps away from him until he caught her elbow and pointed. She had no idea where she was—she'd been so enthralled by the surroundings that she'd looked ahead, not back, not paying any attention to the appearance of the block of flats they had left. It was shrouded in shadow now.

Hunt had stopped, allowing them to draw even with him, so they must be home. Sergeant Casey nodded to her and waved to the others. He hadn't even begun his run; her circuit had been a preliminary lap for him.

Brian and Hunt waited outside with her until her breathing had quieted. It was still dark. Then the three of them crept up the stairs and back into the flat. Hunt made her a cup of hot chocolate, but even after entering the flat, none of them spoke. This mission hadn't been on the books.

CHAPTER 14

The prosecution rested their case Friday afternoon, marking the end of a very long week for Sinclair. His days in court had been followed by evenings at the Yard, and there had repeatedly been times when the undemanding anonymity of his flat was welcome. Tonight, however, he stopped in at his flat to don a fresh shirt and then went upstairs. It was late, but he never worried about the hour. According to Casey, Jenny still had nightmares and consequently was never eager for the day to end. Knowles had warned him that new traumas revived old ones, and her court experience had been devastating. "I hear you had a difficult week."

"I feel so useless. I can't do anything else to convict him. And he'll have scores of witnesses to say what a great guy he is."

She had every right to be upset. What losses had he suffered by age twenty-three? Not coming in first in a boat race? "Jenny, that's window dressing, nothing more. He'll not be acquitted." He watched her unfasten the clasp on the amethyst watch he had given her. She held it out to him.

"Colin, I can't keep this. I didn't earn it."

"Jenny, it wasn't a conditional gift."

"But I wanted to make a stronger showing—be so persuasive that no one would have any doubt about his guilt."

He closed her fingers over the watch. "I believe you did. Your testimony was the most powerful thing I ever saw."

"It was desperation, not courage, with some of Sergeant Casey's anger mixed in."

"Courage doesn't guarantee the result, but I'm confident in this case, and you should be also. He had means and opportunity. No credible alibis for the dates in question. DNA ties him to all of you. And the CPS doesn't prosecute a case unless they think they can win."

"Those lawyers crushed me. I've been reduced to the lowest common denominator."

"When we're under the greatest pressure, we find out who we are. In nature pressure produces precious jewels. I think your lowest common denominator, as you call it, is lovely. Essence of Jenny—a new fragrance."

"My essence is—tears. I'm a fountain that always overflows."

Her tears had spilled over. He wanted to embrace her, but there were three men patrolling in the next room. "Jenny, you cry because you're all heart—heart of courage in the courtroom, heart of caring for Sullivan, heart of concern for the protection team. I hope there's some room left in your heart for me."

He refastened the watch around her wrist and then offered her his hand and his handkerchief. She took both and watched him kiss her fingers.

"These last few weeks have been rather intense. How about a night out? Come to my flat Sunday evening, and we'll listen to some music and keep all legal topics off the table."

She smiled suddenly. "Is that a prescription or a subpoena?"

Before he left, he spoke to Casey.

"A run ashore will do her good, sir. With your permission, I'll let Davies and Hunt take off during the time she's with you."

"Sergeant, I suggest you take twenty-four hours yourself. No, make it thirty-six. You were on duty round the clock during Jenny's court appearances. Davies and Hunt had regular shifts. Let them handle it for a while."

Hunt had been unable to get a rise out of her all week. He couldn't resist teasing her now about her date. "You don't have to get away from here to have fun," he grinned. "You should have come to me. I'm a helpful bloke."

"What do you have in mind?" she asked, refusing to be drawn.

"Instead of poker, how about strip poker? I'll even let you deal the first hand."

To her surprise, she found she could appreciate his outrageous humor. She knew he didn't mean anything by it. "It wouldn't be much fun if you guys were the only ones stripping," she laughed.

"You wouldn't play?"

"Not a chance! I'm terrible at it—I lose too often."

Hunt smiled and snapped his fingers in regret.

CHAPTER 15

"A twenty-three-year-old with armed chaperones," Jenny smiled when the men brought her to Colin's flat.

"Beef cannelloni's cooking. I picked it up from Sainsbury's. They have a good bakery, so I bought some rolls. And there's fresh parmesan in the fridge." He rolled up his sleeves and began to toss a salad with Italian dressing.

"I'll do that," she said. She'd become accustomed to working with men in the kitchen.

When the cannelloni was hot, Colin lit the candles and uncorked a bottle of cabernet sauvignon. "To easier times."

"Do easier times lie ahead, Colin?"

"You should have a nice respite. The CPS will see the Scott trial concluded before prosecuting the others."

"How much longer will I have to stay upstairs?"

"Until Scott's case and all related cases have been adjudicated," he answered, wishing his toast hadn't reminded her of her legal commitments. "Has Casey resumed your Italian lessons?"

"Si," she laughed. "We've covered money, weather, and travel topics, just to name a few. We all excelled on the food chapter, and he even knows a lot of medical terms. Not much on sports or the arts. Hunt's a little behind, though, so we've been reviewing." She smiled. "It's not graduate school, but I'll also be a better cook when this experience is over, thanks to Brian. And I've learned the importance of family. I took them for granted before."

"I didn't appreciate my family until I was separated from them, either. My father was in the foreign service, as you know, and when I was twelve, I was sent back to England to boarding school so I'd have the requisite preparation for university examinations. Once or twice a year I'd fly to see them wherever my father was posted. I had fun exploring new places, but none of their residences abroad ever seemed like home."

There was a bit of wine left. He refilled her glass.

"Boarding school—university—then marriage. Did your wife live here?"

"Too modest for her taste. Now I'm glad—no memories to overcome. Ready for pudding?"

"No room left."

They put their dishes in the sink, ran water over them, and sat down together in the living room. Colin's sofa was the color of espresso. "Let's make coffee," she said, wanting a distraction.

She stood with him, but he stepped toward her, not the kitchen, and put his arms around her. She thought of the other times he had held her and how safe and comfortable she had been. She felt safe this time, too, but there was a tinge of excitement in her stomach that was completely new. She shivered.

"Are you cold?"

No, the air seemed warm and very close.

He bent his head down and kissed her. There was just a hint of perfume. He couldn't place the scent, but he liked it. He kissed the gold chain that held her cross and then the skin below the cross. He heard a quick gasp.

"Colin, stop. I'm not on *terra firma* here."

He took her hand, not wanting to lose the connection he'd felt with her.

"Why am I in your flat? Does Sergeant Casey have an agenda, or do you?"

"I gave the men some leave, yes, but there's no agenda, Jenny."

"Colin, I'm in an impossible situation. I can't pretend I'm not available, and if you make a pass at me just because I'm available—that's creepy."

"It's not like that, Jenny. I have no intention of taking advantage of you." He had not released her hand.

"Where men are concerned, I have to look out for myself."

"Are you worried about your safety upstairs?"

"No. They're good guys. Besides, if one of them stepped out of line, I could call out to the others."

No competition then. "If you were in Texas, would you be asking these questions?"

"No, but I wouldn't be in a man's apartment on the first date. If this is a date. I'd be in a restaurant or at the movies or a ball game. Somewhere public."

"If circumstances were different, I'd take you those places, Jen. I invited you here because I enjoy spending time with you, and I hoped you'd be more relaxed without the men hovering."

"And so would you."

"Yes, of course."

She looked down at their clasped hands. Despite the nature of the conversation, he hadn't pulled away. "Colin, I'm sorry. I didn't mean to insult you."

"Needing a bit of reassurance is normal, Jenny."

She looked up and smiled suddenly. "When you kiss me, I feel normal."

"Jen, so many things are right between us. One step at a time is all I ask. Will you do that?"

She began to blush. "Can we repeat some of the steps?"

Her warmth and humour had returned. He leant forward and kissed her again, lightly at first and gradually more intensely. "The men will be here soon," he smiled. "I should give you time to stop blushing before they arrive."

"Please do," she laughed.

She was glowing, and he was very pleased with himself. "Coffee?"

She laughed again. "What would Sergeant Casey call that? Opdec? Yes, please. It's a good thing they're not detectives."

- -

After she left, he remembered her frankness. He had not been put off by it; rather, he respected her ability to face things. He spent his days investigating crimes, often dealing with persons who either didn't know the truth or were unwilling to share what they knew. Jenny's direct manner was refreshing.

And her laughter—a sign of her resilience. So unlike Vi's forced gaiety, her terrible compulsion to experience everything straightaway. Vi's mother had died when Vi was a child, and he hadn't begrudged her the happy times she sought. At least, not at first. His parents had been active socially, entertaining and attending others' parties. It seemed a natural thing for him to do as well. Vi was a stunning woman, always on the go. In her company the bright lights of London's night life had appealed to him. He had wanted to forget the things he saw in dark alleys, the intense nature of some cases.

As he matured, however, helping someone gave him more lasting satisfaction than what was in vogue on the entertainment scene. If he arrived home late, he would find the flat empty. Married colleagues began to have children, and their lives seemed more balanced, more fulfilled than his. Having a family demonstrated a faith in the future. Vi's only faith had been in the pleasure of the moment, but she had known how to give and receive pleasure. The nights he'd waited up for her had been worthwhile.

Then his father had become ill. He had expected Vi to understand: She had lost a parent. But she had not been able to deal with the dark side of life. She wouldn't even accompany him to the hospital, and he had been deeply hurt. Their late-night couplings ceased. She wanted to receive passion and excitement, not give comfort to a man who had joined the ranks of the bereaved.

He had been on his own a long while now, and he hadn't had to look beyond his own needs. Although Vi had accused him of it, he didn't consider himself selfish. His role models were in professions of service.

And now there was Jenny, who expected so little from him: safety, which he could not guarantee, and honesty, which he thought he could. Jenny, who had proved she could survive the hard times. Jenny, whose courage impressed him and whose enthusiasm infected him. Jenny, who could make the bright lights fun again.

CHAPTER 16

Jenny didn't know what to think. Sergeant Casey was inscrutable, telling her only that they were going out and not to wear anything colourful. The other men were alert but not somber. She was alternately irritated because they knew something she didn't, apprehensive because Casey had brought his kit and his backpack, and afraid that some legal problem had arisen suddenly.

Sergeant Andrews was behind the wheel. When they pulled into a hospital emergency entrance, Casey opened his kit and covered part of her forehead and right cheek with gauze. "I'm not hurt," she wanted to say, but he had warned her in The Voice to be silent. He wrapped her hospital gown around her before they exited the car.

Colin had a wheelchair waiting for her. She sat down and tried not to react at the sight of Casey donning his white doctor's coat. Colin led the way, his face giving nothing away. Casey pushed the wheelchair, and Brian and Hunt brought up the rear, their eyes constantly scanning the corridors and preventing other passengers from taking the lift with them.

"Left," Colin said.

There was a policeman outside someone's door. Colin stood to one side, and Brian pushed the door open in front of her, his smile as bright as the rising sun. She saw Danny sitting up in bed, Danny pale but grinning, Danny disappearing behind her flood of tears.

"Sis, you're bandaged! Are you okay?"

She'd forgotten her disguise, and she laughed and cried at her silly memory as she tore it away, laughed and cried at the whole charade, laughed and cried at the expression on Colin's face, laughed and cried when Danny teased, "Some things never change!"

She stood next to the bed and held his hand. He looked so thin! "Danny, I was so afraid for you!"

"I hear you did well, Sis."

"That's not important now. You're all right. I'm so glad!"

"Have you heard my new nickname? Rip Van Winkle. You're the only one of my sisters who didn't age while I was asleep!"

There were cards everywhere, and flowers, too—in the hospital, even men got flowers! “Did you get my card?”

“Trying to see if I can count? You sent more than one, Sis.”

Danny’s bandages were small, but he looked so weak. “Will it hurt you if I hug you?”

“Don’t give a toss if it does!”

She sat beside him on the bed and put her arms around him. His heart sounded strong, oh, thank you, God. Thank you, God.

“Sir, my mum said you’ve been by almost every day. It meant a lot to her. Thank you.”

“None required.”

She gave Danny a quick kiss on the cheek and climbed back in the wheelchair. Sergeant Casey shook hands with Danny. “Good job, Sullivan.” He looked at Jenny. “Sir, we’ll never muzzle that smile.”

“I’ll look down.”

Sinclair wished she didn’t have to conceal it. He had never seen her look so lovely. He pushed the door open slightly. “Clear?” he asked Hunt.

“I miss you, Danny!”

“You’re good medicine, Sis. Good luck.”

Following their visit to see Sullivan in hospital, Sinclair felt a celebration was in order. He splurged and took a bottle of Pol Roget and a corkscrew to the flat. Eager for the drink, Hunt gulped his and challenged Jenny to do the same, but she declined, punching him playfully on the shoulder and teasing him about wanting her lightheaded as well as lighthearted. “Colin, I feel like the sun is shining all the time, because of Danny,” she said. “Thank you, thank you, thank you for taking me to see him.”

Then she clasped his hand and begged him to stay for a few minutes, even though the champagne had been quickly consumed by the five of them. He joined her in the sitting room, unable to resist her effervescence. She was still dressed in the dark and plain clothes she’d worn to the hospital, but her resplendent face would have outshone any attire, no matter how fine. She had a toast of her own for Sullivan: “*Salud y pesetas y el tiempo para gustarlos.*”

“Health, wealth, and the time to enjoy them,” she explained. “The toast used to be for health, wealth, and love, but someone decided that if you had health and wealth, love would find you, so they changed it.”

Her bubbly demeanor made him expansive, and he recounted the early history of champagne. She hadn’t known that it wasn’t originally intended to have bubbles but agreed that they’d be so much poorer without them. She was cheery and relaxed, and more physically affectionate as well, if her spontaneous kiss were any indication. She touched her lips to his mouth, not his cheek, and he made the most of it, receiving one last taste of the Pol Roget.

He wanted a relationship with this girl. His glimpses of Jenny’s body had only whetted his appetite for her, but he understood that intimate physical contact could be a long time in coming. In the meantime, what could he do? Most women seemed to measure a man's seriousness by the amount of time he was willing to devote to them. Time—but how to occupy it? The postcard excursions were not sufficient now. He wanted to engender more personal topics, the discussion of which would draw them closer.

Thoughtfulness—women wanted to know you'd thought about them when you weren't with them. Talk—they wanted you to listen. That would be easy—he still found her Texas accent so charming that he even wanted to smile from time to time when she was describing sad events. In her case, one more element would be crucial: tenderness. She had been so abused.

CHAPTER 17

The next week saw the continuation of the defence case and the influx of day police, some old faces, some new, to relieve Jenny's favorites. Sergeant Casey left first, followed by Brian on Casey's return. She was in charge of the kitchen in Brian's absence, which gave her something to do. He'd taught her to make pot roast with vegetables—she wondered if she could omit the potatoes without his hearing about it—and Cornish game hens with seasoned rice.

The newspapers were full of quotes from the various witnesses the defence had called, and she identified each page with Scott's name and meticulously tore it into tiny shreds, not caring if she defaced the broadsheet before others had read it. Danny's recovery notwithstanding, she still felt residual anger toward the monster, and she wanted to feed the flame so it would not go out. Other trials and testimony lay ahead of her, and she now saw anger as a resource she could draw upon in time of need.

The redoubtable Sergeant Howard was one of the substitutes, but his dark stillness didn't faze her this time. She teased him about not paying close enough attention to the security cameras, although his focus was exemplary. She found the most idiotic game shows on TV and the deadliest farm report, but he didn't react to sound or silence. He was the oyster without the pearl. She knew he didn't like the assignment, but she didn't hold it against him. Something had made him the way he was. She didn't have to know what it was to accept his guarded nature. Somewhere in the recesses of his mind he had decided to align himself with the law, and that was enough. She brought him his lunch and refilled his tea unasked.

She didn't see much of Colin, but one morning he called by while she was still asleep, leaving a book for her. It was a paperbound volume of poems by Louis MacNeice with a note for her to enjoy them at her leisure. She found that funny—how else would she enjoy them? In the hectic rat race that was life in the flat? Please!

She'd heard of MacNeice. There had been selections from his *Autumn Journal* in one of Rosamund Pilcher's books. "London Rain"—she'd love to feel it on her cheeks, but the poet was writing about an internal climate of conscience and concluding that without God, there was no moral law at all. She wondered if that were true: Did all moral law come from God? If you did not know God, could you still be a moral being? Could God supply you with His law unawares? What would Colin think? He had certainly seen a lot of lawlessness.

Other verses were equally provocative: "... this land / Is always more than matter—as a ballet / Dancer is more than body." His poetry posed more questions than it answered, drawing her thoughts beyond the outward appearances he described and outlining choices but not doing the discerning for her. She thought about Colin's face. What lay behind his smile?

It was Friday evening before she saw him. He had a bottle of wine with him. The men were playing cards in the dining room, and she could hear Hunt's exclamations, good and bad, as the games progressed. Sergeant Casey was always quiet as he contemplated and strategised, and Brian spoke only when announcing the type of poker or requesting the number of substitute cards he required.

"I want you to start a new list," Colin said. "Call it *Wines I Have Enjoyed with Colin.* The first is sauvignon blanc."

The first? What was he doing?

He had chilled the wine, and he poured some for her and watched her lips through the glass when she drank.

She thanked him for the book of poetry, and the issues raised by the verses were a springboard that launched them into far-ranging discussions. One's values might be forged in crisis, he believed, but if one were lucky, their seeds had been planted and nurtured long before. In his experience, those without strong values collapsed when trials came.

"No kidding," she said.

"Faith doesn't make rough times easy, it makes them bearable," he countered. "You didn't collapse. You reacted, then rallied."

"And all because of words and pictures—well, one particular picture." She was thinking of Rob's. "Regardless of other media, won't we always need words to communicate with each other? Think how many of our institutions revolve around what people say: politics, the legal system, the church, even much of our entertainment."

Colin would have preferred to communicate with her by touch, but circumstances weren't going to allow it.

"Studies show that people are reading less, but that doesn't mean they're thinking less, does it?" she asked. "Anyway, I loved the poetry. Poets need to have a better vocabulary than the rest of us because they rely on an economy of words."

The poker games ended. Hunt liked to stop when he was on top, and the others knew there would be games on other nights, so they put the cards away and left Colin and Jenny alone. She began to wish that he were seated next to her on the sofa. Too soon, he rose to his feet.

"I'll be in Kent for Easter," he said. He called for the men to lock up behind him.

CHAPTER 18

The days following Easter brought more day police—"fresh meat," Hunt called them, because Jenny's boredom led her to question them so extensively—and less Colin. She stopped reading the newspaper accounts of the continuing efforts of the defence in the Scott trial and turned to the notices of spring events in the London area. There were flower shows, music festivals, walking festivals, and celebrations scheduled for Shakespeare's birthday later in the month.

Houston in April would be beautiful, too. Baseball season would be beginning, and all over America people would see the green baseball diamonds and hear the crack of the bat. Wild blackberries would be ripe and sweet. It was too early for Indian paintbrush to bloom—she'd always thought Indian sunset would have been a more apt name because of their fiery orange color—but there would be masses of white, pink, and red azaleas, and the most unusual floral color, blue, would be finding dramatic expression in the bluebonnets along the Texas highways.

None of the day police had ever attended any of the festivals. They'd all walked a beat and didn't consider walking a festival. Their mums liked the flowers, they said, but their own disinterest was so marked that Jenny felt they wouldn't have noticed the tulips or daffodils unless someone had dropped dead in them.

She made a list of scenic places she had been and asked Sergeant Howard if he would tell her what his favorite place was.

He thought for a few minutes. Old Street, after a successful mission. The crack between a woman's thighs. He could not speak of those. "No, sorry," he said.

She gave up on Howard, choosing instead to corner Hunt with the World Series videos, which Colin had had converted to the British VCR. "Want to learn a little about baseball?"

"Cue it up!"

As the first game unfolded, she explained. "Baseball's a game of statistics. They record everything you do, good and bad. Good things are getting a hit, batting someone in, stealing a base, catching a fly ball. Errors are when you mess up."

Hunt thought the pace of play was a bit slow. "Why'd that bloke get on first? He didn't do anything."

"Poor pitching. It's like life—in some cases you benefit from someone else's mistakes."

The game progressed.

"What sort of pitch was that?"

"Curve ball," she said. "They're really hard to hit."

"What else do I need to know?"

"Individual stats are important, but sometimes a player will sacrifice himself for the good of the team. Like that guy—he didn't get on base, but his play allowed the man on first to advance to second."

It was not a concept that appealed to Hunt. In a rare philosophical moment, he asked, "Do you ever wonder why so many games are about balls?"

He was lively—occasionally shocking—but not malicious. "Because they were all invented by guys," she answered. "Think about the terminology. In football, you make a pass; in baseball, you want to get to first base; and all games are about scoring."

Hunt's interest level rose. The ball, the bat, the squeeze play, first base. A home run was "going deep." He had certainly struck out more than once himself. Baseball began to make sense. It was like life, too right.

Friday evening Colin came by bearing gifts and good news. Cambridge had beaten Oxford in the annual boat race the weekend before—"Light defeats Dark again," he said—and the defence in the Scott case had rested that very afternoon. Closing arguments were scheduled for the Monday, and following the judge's instructions to the jury, deliberations would begin.

As he uncorked the bottle of wine—a pinot grigio—she looked through the sheaf of pages he had brought. They were all poems by Siegfried Sassoon, who had written during and after World War I. She tried to remember her world history. England and France had been in a stalemate against Germany, all three countries paralyzed in trench warfare across no-man's-land. Sassoon's work was dark, expressing his anger at the senior officers who continued to send young men into battle when nothing was accomplished by their deaths, cynicism for the futility of war in general, and grief for untold friends who had died. "He thought Death was a person," she said.

"I imagine most soldiers do. And for those who were wounded, Life could be a person as well, in the form of the medic, for example."

Like Sergeant Casey. "Evil is a person—I encountered him. Do you suppose Good is a person?"

"I know He is."

She read further. "Frail Travellers," Sassoon had called butterflies. "A man wrote these lines—how fragile we all are, and how fleeting life is!"

"Men can have tender feelings, Jenny, although we generally don't advertise them."

She looked up from the printed page. He didn't look fragile. Where did his vulnerability lie?

"We'd best make the most of today, wouldn't you agree?"

"How can I do that, locked in this flat?"

"Your thoughts and feelings aren't locked in, are they?"

"Is that the nature of freedom? Being able to look past the limitations of your body to see a vista of what is possible?"

"That's the challenge of every age, isn't it? From the child to the elderly adult? And of every circumstance—none of us are what we wish to be."

"But you're healthy and capable—you have an important job—you can choose where you go and what you do."

"Policing requires an inordinate amount of time. I live an unbalanced life. When I was your age, I thought I'd have my own family by now."

She was aware of the men coming into the kitchen occasionally, but none of them interrupted the conversation taking place in the sitting room. Colin insisted that marriage was no less holy an institution because his had not survived. "Love lasts. My parents weren't unhappy with their lifetime commitment. My mother followed my father all over the world, and she still loves him, even though he's been gone over six years. I was wrong in my priorities, that's all."

They were not touching. Colin was sitting at the opposite end of the sofa, and her outstretched legs did not reach him. "Your mother's love made her more susceptible to grief."

"And gave her greater remembered joy." His face was gentle.

The wine had warmed her face and chest. "I missed you this week," she said.

The flat was quiet, except for the radio in her room and the soft whoosh of the heater when it came on. He stood and held out his hand. "Come here to me, Jenny," he whispered.

His eyes were intensely blue, and he looked particularly strong standing. She remembered his embrace—feeling safe in it, feeling alive. Her stomach turned over, and his kiss did nothing to settle it. Afterward he held her close, his lips against her hair, and she tried to catch her breath. Then he stepped back and called for the men to see him out.

CHAPTER 19

Monday: Colin had said that the case would go to the jury on Monday. All afternoon Jenny pestered the men to go for the evening newspapers. The late editions would precede the nightly newscasts on TV, and she wanted to know how the testimonial phase of the trial had concluded. She didn't retreat until Hunt threw up his hands and threatened to charge her with harassment.

In the end the reports did nothing to settle her. Prosecuting counsel, Mr. Benjamin, titled his summation "Beauty versus the Beast" and began with a broad overview of good versus evil. He referred to the defendant as a "sadistic and depraved individual" whose "total disregard for suffering and human life" had finally been discovered, following a valiant act of identification by a surviving witness. Then he reiterated each piece of specific evidence that tied the cases of the seven victims together. "I am often asked," he said, "what justice looks like. It is a wall, built brick by brick in a court of law, constructed of courage, held together by truth, and reinforced with scientific and medical data. It is a wall tall enough and strong enough to contain a monster. Your verdict, guilty on all the counts that have been presented to you, will make it a lasting wall."

Mr. Alford had spoken for the defence, disputing the evidence and citing the "character (reprehensible), calumny, and consent" of the primary prosecution witness. He had spoken of her with contempt, condemning her irresponsible conduct. "My client never claimed to be celibate," he argued, "but no man with his heritage, resources, and attractiveness has to force his attentions on members of the opposite sex. With no shortage of opportunities for mutual sexual enjoyment, what possible motive could he have for doing so?" Alford had then returned to the issue of consent, and Jenny finally understood why, after her tearful statement to Colin and Barry in the hospital, Colin had asked if she'd given her consent. "A wall?" Alford had scoffed. "Rubbish. Rubble."

Judge Thomas's instructions to the jury were not recorded in the newspapers, but they had evidently been lengthy, because several reporters had filed their stories before he had completed them. The waiting game began, and she was not very good at it.

Tuesday came and went, with Jenny preoccupied. What could the jury be thinking? Why wasn't it a slam dunk? Hadn't they believed her?

What about all the other evidence that had been given? He is *guilty*. All they had to do was say it. Why didn't they?

Hunt was the first beneficiary of her short fuse. On Wednesday he needled her about the university logo on her sweatshirt: Prescott Pumas. "What the hell's a puma?"

"A wildcat."

"Your mascot was a pussy?" Hunt elbowed Casey, whose mouth twitched suspiciously.

"No, they're *big* cats," she said, blushing. "Aggressive. Fierce. They pounce on their prey from great heights."

Hunt slapped his knee and roared with laughter. "Every bloke's dream—being attacked by a wild pussy!"

Casey made a choking sound in his throat and turned away.

"Damn it, Hunt, do you have to be so crude?" she yelled.

"You've got to learn to take it, Little Bit," Hunt said, still chuckling. "The Prescott Pussies—wait 'til I tell Davies."

Later during her exercises she erupted at Sergeant Casey. "What am I doing this for? So I can sit down the rest of the day? Who cares if I stay in shape?"

When he counselled using her anger to complete an additional set, she became even more irate. He held out the pillow, but she batted it away. "I don't want to hit that, I want to hit you!"

Casey laughed softly. He held out his hands and beckoned to her with his fingers. "Come on then."

She went for him, but he took one diagonal step back, easily deflecting her frontal attack, and she had forgotten to watch his hands. Damn his efficiency! One minute she was on her feet attacking, and the next, he was behind her. Her knees buckled, and she fell against his thigh. Her position on the floor was discouraging, but maybe she could use it to her advantage. She went limp. When she felt his grip relax, she aimed again, but she was no more successful.

"Don't give up, Little Bit!"

Sergeant Casey's face was close to hers. Was he restraining a smile? Damn him! She lurched at him with her chin but succeeded only in grazing his cheek with her lips. She couldn't think of anything else to try. "I'm through," she said. "No lie."

He helped her sit up. Her head bowed, she hugged her knees and waited for The Voice. Instead she felt his hands massaging her shoulders. She was so tense that even his gentle pressure hurt. "I've been in this flat over six months. Except for my Paul Revere midnight run, I've never gone anywhere that didn't have some medical or legal purpose. Tomorrow I'm going out. Would you like to pick the place?"

Casey didn't answer, but the massage stopped.

"Can't I go somewhere that's so crowded that nobody would notice me? Or so deserted that no one would see me?" She scooted over to the sofa and leaned against it. "Don't you understand? I want to see the light. The little room was dark. The courtroom had artificial light—no windows. There are windows here, but they're shrouded, and I'm not allowed to look through them." Brian was still sleeping from the night watch, so she turned to her only ally. “Hunt, help me here. I know I'm locked in, but I can call Colin and raise a ruckus. Or call the police—regular police—and scream when they come to the door until you let them in.”

Casey smiled at her determination. “What address will you give when you ring?”

“I'll tell them I'm being held against my will in Detective Chief Inspector Sinclair's building.”

Hunt laughed aloud.

There's my girl. “We'll get it sorted, love. Best not to call in fire on your own position.”

In the morning Brian fed her marmalade and toast for elevenses, and they all trooped downstairs to wait for the car Sergeant Casey had summoned. The men wore coats to conceal their firearms, and she wore a sweater under her raincoat. It was brisk and cool, and the sky was strewn with heavy clouds.

“Hyde Park Corner,” Casey told the driver, and her adventure began.

They hadn't been in the park long when men on horseback rode by, colourful tunics across their chests and plumes on their helmets. “From the Changing of the Guard at Buckingham Palace,” Brian said. “Their barracks are nearby.” Casey had explained that they wouldn't stop anywhere for long, so she kept walking, although she couldn't resist a backward glance.

Ahead of her lay vast open grassy fields with groves of trees in the distance and to her left, Serpentine Lake. They strolled alongside it and crossed the bridge into Kensington Gardens. The flowers here had been expertly planted, with an eye toward variety in color, height, and type of blossom. Everything looked a little bedraggled, but the colors were no less bright for the drops of rain that clung to the petals. She saw tulips in every shade of the artist's palette, daffodils, iris, and many florals she didn't recognize. Delicate yellows, the palest peach, lavender, hot pink, and royal purple. Why, she wondered, was the word “royal” used to describe the most intense hue? She would have called all these colors royal—the pastels were no less glorious than the others. Her enjoyment progressed from muted to vibrant, and she had to bite her lip to keep from laughing out loud.

They did not enter any of the structures they passed, even the visitor centre near the Albert Memorial. Sometimes Sergeant Casey walked beside her and sometimes Hunt, but evidently they felt the difference between her height and Brian's would attract attention, so he was usually at least a few feet away.

She liked the gentle little primroses the best, aptly named since the true roses would not be at their peak until warmer and drier weather arrived. Many had star-shaped yellow centers, but the colors that surrounded them ran the full spectrum: There were lovely lavender blossoms, shades of rouge from the softest pink to the deepest red, and petals of pristine white. She could smell the moisture in the light breeze. They were far from being the only visitors, but the natural show was such a feast for the eyes that she didn't think anyone in the park was paying attention to anything else. The flat was subdued, and many times her feelings had matched it. She did not want to go back, either to the site or the frame of mind. "How much time do we have?" she asked Sergeant Casey.

"The car won't collect us until I ring."

So she walked on, wanting to skip but knowing she shouldn't. She knew she was deceiving herself, but the air smelled like freedom, fresh and clean. Sergeant Casey kept a discreet distance between the two of them and other groups, but his caution didn't diminish her pleasure. When she began to feel hungry, she didn't say so. She didn't want to do anything to spoil the sensation, not of being tired—she wasn't exerting herself—but of being relaxed. For the first time in months, her movements were unrestricted, not choreographed by someone else. What a joy, not to be on her way somewhere but just to be going, strolling, having no purpose except enjoying the moment! She put her arm around Sergeant Casey's. "Thank you," she whispered.

His eyes left the path ahead of them for a minute, and she saw him smile.

Her stomach felt empty now, and she was sure the men were ready to eat, but none of them had hurried her. She took a deep breath and held it, wanting to keep some part of the experience with her as long as she could, because it was time to go. "I'm ready," she told Sergeant Casey, trying to keep her voice from breaking. She heard him speak quietly into his phone.

CHAPTER 20

Jenny slept through the night, with no dreams to disturb her. She did her exercises dutifully and then settled in for what promised to be another slow day. The air in the flat seemed stale after the freshness of the outdoors. She wished they could open a window.

After lunch Casey startled her out of her reverie. "Boss rang. He's on his way."

"Is there a verdict? Did he say?"

"He wants to tell you himself."

"Why? If it's good news, wouldn't he have told you?"

Casey didn't reply.

"Wouldn't he?"

"If he hasn't given it up yet, he's not going to," Hunt said.

That was true. Sergeant Casey had two modes: direct and silent. His infernal military training.

"How far away is he?" she asked. "Sergeant Casey, shouldn't you have your key ready?"

"Not yet, Jenny."

She slipped on her shoes and went into the sitting room. "Did you hear footsteps?" she asked Brian. "Was that his knock?"

"Take it easy, JJ."

"How? I've waited so long for this! What if it isn't the right verdict? If the monster gets out, he'll come after me—he heard me say all that stuff in court!" She sank down on the sofa. "Why isn't Colin here yet? Where is he?" she wailed.

"Deep breaths, Jenny."

When Sinclair's knock came, she jumped up, wanting to see his face. Surely she'd know when she saw his face—he wouldn't even have to say anything!

He was beaming. "Guilty! Of serial murder—serial rape—and a host of other charges."

She burst into tears and threw her arms around his neck. He returned the embrace. "Sshh. It's over now. Well done. Benjamin sends his congratulations."

Hunt punched Davies on the shoulder.

In a moment she released him, her face flushed with relief. "Colin, I thought the verdict would never come! I know they had to get through the rest of the dog and pony show, but it made me wonder if I'd made a difference, if what I'd been through counted for anything."

"It's an important victory. You've served the cause of justice."

"What was his sentence?"

"Sentencing will take place after counsel on both sides have prepared their briefs."

"That's okay. I'm still happy. I want to give my parents the news."

Casey had spoken to Sinclair on the phone. He withheld his question until Jenny had left the room. "Guilty of everything?"

"Guilty of the rape and murder of the six other women. In Jenny's case he was convicted of two counts of rape, false imprisonment, and attempt to cause grievous bodily harm with intent."

"Not attempted murder?" Hunt asked.

"That's a difficult offence to prove. Intent to kill has to be demonstrated. Evidence of careful and calculated planning. For example, that a deadly weapon was chosen and used. Threats—uttered aloud and taken seriously—are considered evidence also of intent. It helps if the length of the attack can be established, and if the accused acknowledges some pertinent information, however slight."

Bloody bastard, Casey thought. There'd been no weapon. According to Jenny's statement, Scott hadn't spoken. She hadn't been able to give investigators any clues about how long the attack had lasted. "Sir, is there more?"

Sinclair nodded and lowered his voice. "Scott threatened her. When the judge said, 'Take him down!' Scott turned to the prosecutor and screamed, 'This is war! Tell that Yank bitch I'll get her yet! I'll find her—she'll never be safe!' I don't mind telling you, it made my blood run cold. His rough, guttural tone—it must have been a sample of what she heard. I'm inclined to take him seriously."

"What can we do, sir?" Davies was concerned.

"Keep the TV off, and censor the newspapers for the next day or so. Distract her, if you can."

"You're not telling her?" Hunt asked.

"Let's not spoil her mood," Sinclair said. "She's safe. Let her enjoy her success."

Colin came by briefly on the Sunday evening. The visits scheduled for the upcoming week by day police had been cancelled due to a bombing in Brixton, south London. No casualties, but scores had been wounded.

"Do I have to go anywhere soon?" Jenny asked.

"You'll have a bit of a breather. The other trials won't begin until after Scott is sentenced."

She couldn't convince him to take the time to sit.

"We need to track down the bomber before he plants another."

Another bomb—a terrifying thought. She had felt like a human pincushion in the hospital, but each prick of the needle had been part of her medical program, intended for healing, not hurt. The nails in the bomb had become projectiles when it exploded. So many people had been injured! She respected what policemen had to do, but she missed Colin the man, who brought wine and wore casual clothes and a smile.

CHAPTER 21

When Jenny saw Colin late Tuesday, he was still dressed for work, but he did sit down with her in the living room. "Jenny, the families of the women whom Scott murdered want to meet with you. They've been ringing the officers who were their contacts on the case. I've had coppers in and out of my office all day yesterday and today wanting to know if it would be possible. If you could be made available. If you'd be willing."

"What do they want with me?"

"To thank you, I believe. They were present during the trial, and they know how difficult it was for you."

"Would I have to say anything?"

He smiled. "No speeches, no."

"What do you want me to do?"

"It's down to you, Jen. They know you're being protected. If you don't want to go, I'll tell them you're not accessible."

"They'll know that's not true. I was accessible for court."

He waited.

"How many handkerchiefs do you have?"

His face relaxed. "I'll let you know when it's scheduled."

The day, when it came, was an object lesson in the difference between restraint and excess. Cautious as always, Sinclair sent Andrews with an unmarked car to the flat, but instead of proceeding directly to their destination, Andrews exchanged the nondescript vehicle for a police van at the station in Islington before heading out again. Jenny didn't know where they were going, and she would not have recognized the headquarters of the Metropolitan Police if she hadn't seen the revolving sign in front and the uniformed guards at the gate around the corner.

She was curious about the glass cases in the lobby, but Colin did not allow her to linger, escorting her to a waiting elevator and then along an empty corridor. The carpet absorbed the sound even of Brian's feet, and neither Sergeant Casey nor Hunt spoke. They passed closed doors, and she imagined officers behind them, fighting crime quietly.

"Here we are," Colin said, opening a door into a large conference room. The table and chairs had been pushed against one wall, and all heads turned toward her. She felt suddenly shy. Who were all these people? There were so many men in suits. She had agonized over what to wear, finally rejecting the clothes she'd worn in court in favor of a pair of dark wool slacks and a pale sweater. "Better to be underdressed than overdressed, Jennifer," her mother always said, but she felt drab and plain.

Colin took her elbow and guided her forward a few steps so the men behind her could enter and close the door. A tall man with graying hair and the slack skin that would eventually become jowls approached her. Did all policemen have that watchful look?

"Miss Jeffries, I presume," he said. "I'm Detective Chief Superintendent Douglas Woulson. Thank you for coming. Would you care for a refreshment?"

"Yes—no—no, thank you."

"This is an informal gathering, Miss Jeffries. I hope you'll alert us if you change your mind."

She felt a little unsteady on her feet and leaned slightly toward Colin, hoping he wouldn't release her arm.

"Gentlemen," Woulson nodded. "I'll leave it with you."

Colin introduced her to Detective Superintendent Graves, the man with the thinning hair who had sat next to him in court, and the procession began. She could tell who belonged and who didn't—those who belonged didn't have a visitor's badge.

The detective in charge of Clarissa Hundley's case introduced himself and Clarissa's parents. They had brought a picture of their daughter, and they thanked Jenny for coming forward. "You gave us such hope."

A bald, sombre man introduced Jenny to the Bennetts, Barbara's mother and father. They praised her testimony.

"I wish you hadn't had to hear all that," Jenny said.

"We cried with you," Mrs. Bennett said.

The next couple was older. "We're the Saunders," the man said, not waiting for the officer standing with him to do the honours. "Emma was our only child. We adopted her."

Jenny felt her heart breaking. They had lost their only child.

"She liked stuffed animals, she did," Emma's mother said. "Even after she grew up, she collected them. Wild ones, like the ones she saw when we took her to the zoo." She held out a small gray elephant to Jenny. It reminded Jenny of the Babar stories she had read to her brothers.

There were three people in the next group, not counting the detective, and the younger man had a different surname. Marilyn Albritton had been married. Her husband must be the one who could not smile. Marilyn's father rested his hand on his son-in-law's shoulder. Marilyn's mother squeezed Jenny's hand.

Sally Coale must have inherited her curly hair from her mother, because her father had very little hair left, just a few straight strands carefully combed from one side of his head to the other. "Banana loaf," Mrs. Coale said, handing Jenny a foil-wrapped parcel. "For you to have with your tea. It's got raisins and nuts and bits of chocolate in it. Just the way Sally liked it." She smiled at the officer next to her. "I brought him a treat as well. All his hard work."

The tears had started, and Jenny could not speak. She took the little package and tried to hold it gently.

Patsy Hayes' family was the last. Detective Chief Something-or-other gave Jenny their names and then stood aside. Patsy's mother held out a small handkerchief, embroidered in bold colours. "Her gran tried to teach her, but she didn't like to sit still." The stitches were uneven and gave the flowery shapes an air of surprise. "Wanted to kick the football with the lads."

Jenny could imagine Patsy's plump, childish fingers impatiently pushing the needle through the soft linen, certain that she was missing something much more fun outside. "I can't accept this."

"Patsy won't be needing it now," her mother said.

That broke the dam. Jenny cried for all these families, who had lost so much more than she had and still had the strength and compassion to reach out to her. She cried for the young women who had died and left these loved ones behind. She cried for the months of isolation from her own family. Her hands were full of the offerings she had been given, and she couldn't shield her face or wipe her tears away. And no one seemed to know what to do.

Then Emma's mother stepped forward. She took the things from Jenny's hands and gave them to Colin. She put her arms around Jenny and held her close. "How long has it been since you saw your family?" she asked. "You miss your mum, don't you?"

Jenny hugged her back desperately, all control gone.

"It's like knowing you, you see," Emma's mother continued. "Knowing what you went through, like our Emma. But don't you be crying for us now. Emma liked to look on the bright side—said we were the family she always wanted. She'd want us to do the same."

Jenny had cried at the flat and been held, sometimes by Sergeant Casey and sometimes by Colin. Their muscular embraces had reassured her, but a woman's hug—being pressed against soft flesh, smelling another woman's perfume—was the comfort of home, the maternal acceptance that knew no geographical boundary.

"We're at peace, we are." The voice was gentle, and Jenny relaxed a little, taking a quivery breath. "There, there. You'll have happy times ahead. We want you to. We do."

Emma's mother took a step back. "You're lovely, you know," she smiled, and Jenny realized that no one in this gathering had reacted to the scar on her face.

"Emma is my sister," Jenny whispered. She turned to the silent onlookers. "They all are. They strengthened me during the trial. They thought of you in their last moments. I don't know why I lived and they didn't. I'm so sorry."

"No dark thoughts now," Emma's mother said. "Life's too short. You find the light, like our Emma would." She patted Jenny's shoulder.

"Andrews! Punch for the lady," Graves ordered. He offered Jenny his handkerchief. It must be part of a detective's uniform. While she sipped the sweet beverage, Graves made what sounded like closing remarks to the group, thanking the officers for their dedication and the families for their cooperation. He then brought the event to an end, shaking her hand. "Thank you for coming, Miss Jeffries. It'll be best if you depart first."

She saw Brian toss back his tea and Hunt stuff one more cookie into his pocket. Sergeant Casey was standing by the door with Sergeant Andrews. Colin led them all downstairs. She sat in the van between Hunt and Sergeant Casey and marvelled at the unusual makeup of families. Her American unit was two parents and two brothers. Her British family comprised of six sets of parents, three flatmates, one recuperating constable, and Colin.

CHAPTER 22

Another nail bomb, this time in Brick Lane, Spitalfields, in London's East End. Leaves were again cancelled, and the men were just as tied to the flat as Jenny was. They all waited for developments in the bombing investigations.

In the fall Jenny's correspondence with friends had been more frequent. Letters of encouragement had arrived often, filled with news about jobs, recreation, and relationships. They kept her up to date on the latest and greatest restaurant, movie, fashion, you name it. They had lots to write about, and that was part of the problem—they were busy. Over time they chose to live their lives, not chronicle them for her.

If your friends were the people you spent the most time with, then the men in this flat were her friends now. They cooked together, ate together, watched TV together, played games together, talked together. She envied Brian's equilibrium. Hunt's mercurial nature kept her on her toes, and Sergeant Casey's remoteness occasionally blossomed into a humaneness that touched her deeply. Each in his own way had made her face the truth about herself at one time or another, which only a true friend would do.

Her relationship with Rob had begun as a friendship, with instant rapport, shared interests, and similar senses of humor. There'd been a liveliness to his face, as if he were always on the verge of jocularity. They'd told each other the best thing that had ever happened to them and then the worst and laughed because there hadn't been much difference between the two. They'd talked about what their lives had been like before they knew each other. It had been so simple—they had laughed, and then they had fallen in love. Trust was a byproduct, although untested. There had been no fear and no tears.

She had gone from class to class as if she were skipping across a flower-strewn sidewalk. Even their postponement of sex hadn't been a problem. They were committed to each other, and they both knew it was inevitable—not a rejection but only a delay until the birth control issue was solved. What difference would a few days make, except to enhance her eagerness?

What would Rob have done, if she'd met a monster in Texas? He would have held her and cried with her. He would have tried to respect and be sensitive to her feelings. He would have been patient about initiating physical contact. That was just what Colin had done, but he had been trained to do it. How much of his tender treatment of her was due to his role as a policeman, and how much to his personal regard for her? He had been gracious, patient, and thoughtful. Would he have behaved that way if he didn't really care about her?

She looked forward to his visits, but it was more than that—she looked forward to his touch. His kisses were amazing, sometimes so soft that her lips tingled and sometimes so passionate that even the memory left her breathless. Her trust had come in fits and starts, but it was now tested and proved. But trust wasn't the same as love, was it? Maybe she was imprinted, like the baby geese in the scientific experiment who had fixed on whatever they saw when they hatched. Colin's had been the first face she had seen when she woke in the hospital. Perhaps what she felt for him was simple dependence.

Colin's face: He had a studied seriousness. A laugh took him by surprise, but it was no less genuine when it came. He had made her laugh, made her forget for a moment how scarred she was. It was so unfair—all a man had to do to be attractive was roll up his sleeves and expose the dark hair on his forearms. She felt the need to wear something colorful and apply her makeup carefully. But he had kissed *both* her cheeks, even the one with the scar—kissed it, instead of pretending that it wasn't there. And he had brought her a slim volume of Shakespeare's timeless and elegant *Sonnets* and suggested that she read the twenty-third because she was twenty-three. The lines described a man who wanted his visage alone to speak the words of love his tongue could not express. She had been too filled with wonder to cry at the sweetness of it.

Rob had been killed before grief or major disappointment had touched him. Colin had experienced loss but had not been defeated by it. He was a mature man, educated, supportive, and stable. He worked hard and understood the importance of family. Rob had been willing to wait until she was ready for a sexual relationship. Colin hadn't been specific, just saying that he wasn't in a hurry.

Dear God, what was she doing? It was lunacy comparing them—she was the one with the fears and the flaws. She picked up her journal and turned to a blank page. *Reasons Colin Should Have Nothing To Do With Me*, she wrote. *I'm scarred for life, in lots of places.* She thought for a moment and felt the shame all over again, wishing he didn't know what had happened to her. *I'm not intriguing. I still have night terrors. I haven't had a haircut since September.* There was one more: *I'll be going home.*

CHAPTER 23

Colin came into the flat with a smile. "Seven life sentences!" he reported to the four expectant faces. "Scott will never spend a day outside the nick as long as he lives."

"Wow! The judge considered what was done to me to be equal to what was done to the others!"

"There's more. He adopted your terminology for Scott, Jen—said that the use of the word 'monster' was entirely appropriate. He called Scott 'merciless' and his actions, 'contemptible.' There were shorter terms given for the other related charges, but the number of life sentences imposed mean that Scott will never be a free man." He shook his head admiringly. "You did it, Jen. You put him away. How do you feel?"

"Ready to celebrate! Can we go out? It's after dark, Colin. No one would see me. I'll disguise myself—I'll fold my collar up. Let the guys take off for a few hours. If I went somewhere with all of you, it would attract attention for sure."

Her enthusiasm eroded his resolve. Davies would take a twenty-four-hour leave. Casey and Hunt would return to the flat by midnight. "Where will you take her, sir?" Casey asked.

"Somewhere crowded, noisy, and dark. There are several choices on the High Street."

"I'll ring you when I'm back, sir."

Her sweater was bright pink. She saw Colin and Sergeant Casey's expressions and was afraid Colin would change his mind about the evening. "All *right*! I'll wear a dull sweatshirt instead."

Downstairs Colin shed his tie and traded his coat and waistcoat for a pullover sweater and a windcheater. Then they walked down the narrow streets to a wide one that was bustling with people. Colin found a restaurant that fit his specifications, and he and Jenny were given a table in the back. He watched the wine and the buoyant atmosphere bring colour to her face. How could anyone in blue jeans be so alluring? Instead of her usual understated earrings, she was wearing a pair that dangled and moved when she turned her head. He was lost. "I missed you," he said.

"You seem tense."

"I don't mean to put a damper on your good mood, but I'm concerned about the public's safety. Bombs are an indiscriminate form of violence. Many innocent people have been hurt."

"Turn about's fair play, Colin. All I've done to you since September is burden you with my feelings."

As they left the café and climbed the steep streets to his block, he tried to explain. "Jenny, we've lived under the IRA threat for a long time. I've never got used to it. It's the helplessness that's the worst—not knowing anything, not knowing where or when or even if another act of terror will occur. Policemen don't like to feel helpless. We don't believe the IRA is behind the recent bombings, but we haven't found who is. You don't have this sort of violence where you come from."

"No, in Texas we just shoot each other."

When they entered his flat, he took her hand. "Jenny, the time we spend together is very important to me. *You're* very important to me." He watched a rosy tint creep over her cheeks. He moved closer to her on the sofa and kissed her forehead, her eyes, her nose, her mouth.

His lips were still close. She brushed his nose with hers then kissed him back. She wanted more than kisses, but she was afraid of what lay ahead. Fortunately Sergeant Casey would act as her curfew.

CHAPTER 24

Colin was sombre when he came by Sunday afternoon. "I have news, Jenny. Sergeant, I'd like you to stand by."

"It's going to take both of you? It must be serious."

He had waited until the last possible moment to tell her, partly because he didn't want to disturb her more settled demeanor but mostly because he didn't want to disrupt the closeness that was developing between them. When she sat down, he realised that she was barefooted. She'd put polish on her toenails, ten little blood-red half moons. He had to force himself to begin. "Leonard Stark has done a runner, Jenny. Fled our jurisdiction. But this week you're scheduled to meet with Halladay to review your testimony against Anthony Michalopolous."

"Why is that making you look so grim? He didn't do much to me."

"There's something you need to know about him. About both of them, actually. When you described the room in the cellar, you mentioned a mirror. It wasn't a mirror; it was a window. Reflective glass was on one side only. The other side opened into a small storeroom. Both Stark and Michalopolous's fingerprints were found there."

Her stomach tightened. "What does that mean? Colin, you're scaring me."

"We can't prove exactly when they were in that room, but we believe that it may have been during the time Scott was with you. You reported that they checked on you shortly before Scott entered, and we believe that they were the ones who removed you after he left. It is reasonable to assume that they were on the premises during the time he was attacking you."

"You think they watched. Watched and did nothing. Saw me bleed and did nothing. Heard my screams and did nothing." She stifled a sob.

"Not exactly. Stark's semen was also found in that room."

Her horror bleached the color from her face.

"As a result the CPS decided to prosecute both of them for rape, conspiracy to rape, and aiding and abetting rape, as well as for false imprisonment and other charges. We consider them equally as culpable as Scott."

Casey was watching her carefully, and he did not like what he saw.

She had begun to tremble, and she had crossed her hands in her lap, as if she were covering a nakedness they could not see.

"Jenny, I'm so sorry."

The ground beneath her feet seemed to be shaking. She wanted to run—somewhere, anywhere—but she was afraid that if she stood, she'd lose her balance. And her lunch. "How long have you known this?"

"The window was discovered the day we found the crime scene."

September. Months and months ago. "Colin, I thought this next trial would be easier." She shook her head bitterly. "That's a contradiction, isn't it? An easy 'trial.' How much time do I have to deal with this before the meeting with Mr. Personality?"

He smiled at her ironic term for Halladay. "Three days."

She asked Casey for a Coke. When he stepped into the kitchen, Colin reached out to touch her hand. "Jenny, I wish I could give you more reassurance, but I've got to be a policeman today. You understand, I hope." He called for Davies and Hunt to lock the door after him.

When Casey returned with the Coke, she barely sipped it. She felt rooted to the spot, as if the information had paralyzed her, preventing any forward movement. Her relief at not having to testify against Stark was overshadowed by Colin's revelations. Now she dreaded the Michalopolous trial. "That's it," she said. "I've had it. I've done enough. I quit."

"You can't do that, Little Bit," Hunt objected. "You have to come up to the plate again. Think of it as a sacrifice play, like you taught me in baseball. Not good for your stats but it helps someone else. Justice is a team sport."

"When I'm in the witness-box, I don't feel like I'm on a team."

"Not on a team?" he thundered. "Open your eyes! Who the bloody hell do you think we are? And we're just the team you can see. What about all the coppers who've investigated this case and the ones who've taken turns minding you?"

"No, I won't do it. I feel sick just thinking about it."

"Dinner soon, JJ," Brian announced. "Something mild for you? Bit of potato?"

Oh, that'll really do it. Potato. "Their behavior was so obscene! It makes me feel dirty."

"No, JJ. It was *their* action. You had nothing to do with it."

Hunt's face brightened, his anger defused. "Strip off, Little Bit! I'll help you wash."

Even Hunt trying to help. Outrageous, inappropriate Hunt.

Casey sat down next to her. Despite her outburst, he knew she'd not quit. "There's something it might help you to know," he said. "After the window was discovered—and forensic finished their tests—Sinclair broke it. He was so angered by its purpose that he put his fist through it. Andrews saw him, and I later treated the lacerations on his hand."

She looked up at him. "I remember—he had a bandage. The night I was moved from the first hospital to this flat." She sipped a little of the

Coke. "Those men were voyeurs, and the lawyers will be talking about it in court. How will I get through it?"

"I'll bandage your hand when the time comes," he said. "As a reminder to be angry."

CHAPTER 25

For the first time Sinclair was thankful for a workload so heavy that it required a Saturday appearance at the Yard. Several parcels were waiting for him in his office, all from Texas. Boxes for her arrived frequently, evidence of her conversations with her mother, but never had so many appeared at the same time. End-of-testimony felicitations? Congratulations on the sentences Judge Thomas had handed down? He didn't think so—the timing wasn't right for either of those events.

He slit the cardboard and lifted the flaps. Whatever the boxes contained had been wrapped with brightly-coloured paper—damn, with birthday paper! He pulled her file from the cabinet and checked her date of birth: May 8. Jenny was twenty-four years old today. If this date had slipped by, he might have lost his campaign for her affections even before he'd truly begun it.

It was too late for a carefully-selected gift. Too late for a traditional cake. He rang the flat and spoke to Davies. JJ wanted to learn how to cook fish, he reported, so Hunt had been sent out to buy salmon. Davies planned to teach her to season and serve it with a lemon butter sauce. They'd have asparagus and wild rice as well.

"Excellent," Sinclair said. "Set a place for me. It's her birthday. I'll provide everything else."

His paperwork postponed, he decided to call this birthday her international anniversary. He chose the most decorative cake he could find, rejecting the ones with glazed fruit on the top and ladyfingers and ribbons on the sides in favour of a three-layer chocolate cake. The rosette of chocolate icing on the top was so large that it covered the entire layer, and it had been dusted with confectioners sugar. After considerable shuffling from shop to shop, he arrived at the witness protection flat with his purchases.

"Don't sing," she begged.

"Don't worry," Hunt said.

They ate first, enjoying the meal she had helped prepare and the chocolate extravaganza he had provided, then watched as she opened the gifts from her family. All clothes—including a pristine white sweater and a black silk jacket splashed with lavender and ivory flowers and a pink lining as soft as Jenny's blush.

Sinclair gestured to the arrangement on the dining room table. "English flowers." He then presented her with French perfume, an Italian liqueur, and earrings with tiny German crystals suspended on gold threads. "All for an American, in Britain." He uncorked the limoncello liqueur and poured a bit for each of them. "Good for your digestion," he smiled.

"I need an extra dose for the next time Little Bit cooks," Hunt teased.

His comment didn't upset her. "I love everything," she said, opening the Chanel fragrance and dabbing a little behind each ear. "Something to taste, something to smell, something to see—Colin, you have covered the territory."

The other men finished their limoncello and drifted away, Hunt to help Davies wash up and Casey to make himself a strong cup of coffee before the night watch.

Sinclair had tested the perfume at Selfridge's, but he found himself wishing he could determine how it smelled on her skin. He watched her sip the liqueur.

"This is a new flavor for me," she confessed. "Crème de menthe on ice cream is the sum total of my experience with liqueurs until tonight. Thanks for making me feel so grown up."

Her mobile phone rang before he could respond, but she didn't hurry into the bedroom to answer it. "My family, I bet," she said. "I'll call them right back. Colin—I didn't feel very festive, with the other trial coming up so soon. This was just right. Thanks so much."

He accepted a demure kiss. "I hope I'll have a chance to do better next year."

"Next year? Alive at twenty-five will be good enough for me."

CHAPTER 26

Colin didn't expect Jenny's testimony against Anthony Michalopolous to be protracted, so her protection detail planned to take her to the courthouse in the morning and return her the same day. She was concealed in a borrowed foodservice van and waited in a small conference room until her turn to testify.

Colin was in the courtroom, but Judge Leyton would not allow her protection officers to be present. Stephen Eliott—not Q.C.—led the prosecution. Judge Leyton's manner was brisk, and he did not allow Mr. Eliott to "dawdle," as he put it, between her response and his next enquiry. The police had provided the most logical reconstruction of events they could, based on the evidence they had been able to collect, but she felt that every amorphous response she made diminished their efforts. When Mr. Eliott asked if she'd felt—at any time during Mr. Scott's physical attack and rape—that anyone was watching her, she deeply regretted having to say no.

After lunch the defence barrister rose. "Henry Whitaker, Your Honour," he said. He looked placid enough to her, with his thin, pale cheeks and lips, but as his strategy unfolded, she realized that he was still capable of a robust cross-examination and the session with Mr. Halladay had prepared her only for what the prosecution would do. Various legal people bowed and left the room and then bowed upon re-entry, making it difficult for her to concentrate on his questions. At one point Mr. Eliott, at the prosecution table, took off his wig, rubbed his bald head, and replaced his wig. In another context it might have been funny, but Mr. Whitaker was engaged in an effort to knock her off her feet, legally speaking.

He skipped over her identification of his client, evidently not intending to dispute the false imprisonment charge, and focused almost exclusively on the rape scenario described by the prosecution. She was frustrated by her inability to make a stronger statement and humiliated by the nature of the questions. From time to time she glanced down at the gauze Sergeant Casey had wrapped around her hand and felt a surge of resentment against a system that required witnesses, not defendants, to be subjected to examination and cross-examination.

Finally Mr. Whitaker stopped and addressed Judge Leyton, requesting that the rape charges be set aside. “Another individual has already been convicted of this crime.”

Mr. Eliott rose rapidly to object, but Judge Leyton ruled immediately. “Mr. Whitaker, your motion is premature. This case is closer to its inception than its conclusion.”

Defending counsel used the rest of his questions to try to suggest that the protection the police had provided for her had biased her judgement against his client and rendered her entire testimony suspect. Finally he said he had no further questions for her and sat down.

Colin turned her over to the protection team. Casey explained that they’d leave as soon as the decoy had exited the courthouse. Since someone could have been planted in the gallery to give the alert when she left the witness-box, they had planned a very visible departure—a small plainclothes policewoman with a large escort. They took Jenny out through the back door.

CHAPTER 27

The men were confident as they planned for her transport for the next trial, to be held at Middlesex Crown Court. She didn't see the need for the continued protection. "This case is small potatoes compared to the others," she said.

"We follow through," Casey answered. "Plan for the worst case. A different courthouse and different conditions mean a different risk, not no risk."

When guilty verdicts were given against Michalopolous, the Bates trial really seemed anticlimactic to her. Again the men took her to the courthouse early in the morning, grumbling over the delays on the crowded streets and vigilant when they pulled up to the rear entrance. She left her jacket in the conference room when she was called into court, stepping into the witness-box in a simple long-sleeved white blouse and dark slacks. Not every seat was filled in this court, either with legal personnel or curious onlookers. The barristers were younger than any of her previous questioners, and one had long sideburns that sharply illustrated the contrast between the traditional wig and contemporary hair styles.

The barrister for the prosecution, Eric Foxcroft, asked her to identify the defendant, Marcus Alvin Bates, as the man who had claimed to be a psychiatrist and attacked her in hospital. He consulted his notes and added the date of the attack. As his examination of her progressed, it became evident that he hadn't the attention to detail as the solicitor who had instructed her. Several times the judge, William Rye, asked him to rephrase, stating that if the question were unclear to him, he was certain that it was unclear for the witness. Since Foxcroft did not always have his next question prepared, the judge had to prompt him from time to time. Defending counsel were silent, making no objections of any kind.

She hadn't been in the witness-box very long when a security officer entered the courtroom and interrupted the proceedings with the announcement that a bomb threat had been made. He requested that all present leave the courthouse in a calm and orderly manner until the matter had been resolved.

Casey and the others were not in the courtroom, so Colin came forward to escort her. The nail bomber had been arrested, but they were taking the threat very seriously. In the corridor, however, Casey intercepted her and turned away from the entrance, leading Jenny and the team to the conference room they had occupied prior to her testimony. Sinclair followed him, frowning but not speaking until they were inside. "Casey, what the bloody hell! The order is to evacuate!"

"Sir, with respect, it's a ruse," Casey replied.

Brian had remained outside the door, but Hunt's full attention was on the altercation between Sinclair and Casey.

Casey ticked off the reasons. "One, the threat came after she entered the witness-box. Two, evacuation would make her an easy target for a sniper. Three, it's unlikely any explosive has been planted in the building. Have the bomb squad search Rye's court and the conference rooms first."

Sinclair took the stairs down instead of the lift, hoping to intercept the bomb squad upon their arrival. The uniformed officers on site had directed the occupants of the courthouse away from the building and into the grassy area in the centre of Parliament Square. They were restricting traffic around the building also, a daunting feat in this popular tourist site. He heard screams and saw persons scattering toward the trees. Sniper attack. A silenced weapon. There were not enough trees to shield all of them. He ran toward a PC kneeling next to a prone figure. A dark-haired woman in a white blouse had been hit. No one else was down. People were huddled together, all their festive, nonchalant attitudes gone. The officer was giving first aid.

"We've got it covered, sir," Sinclair was told. "Ambulance and backup on the way." He scanned the buildings around the square but could see no sign of a shooter or a weapon. He saw the bomb squad van disgorge its personnel, their dark blue uniforms appropriate, because if Casey were wrong, it would be a very dark day indeed.

It was quiet in the conference room. The corridors which had been crowded when Jenny had been called to testify were now deserted. She had never experienced a bomb threat, and she paced back and forth, wanting to run but not knowing where safety lay. When they heard a loud crash not too far away, Hunt shoved her roughly to the floor behind him. He drew his weapon and sighted on the conference room door. "Stay down," he hissed. She had already been on edge, and she was shocked by the suddenness of Hunt's move.

Casey's pistol was drawn also. "Under the table with you."

She scooted across the rug. The table cast a shadow over her, but she was sure her white blouse stood out against the dark carpet.

The door swung open, and Brian reported, “Stand down. The bomb squad made the racket.”

Casey replaced his weapon, and Hunt relaxed his stance. She crawled out from under the table but stayed on the floor. “What’s happening? Where’s Colin?”

“Probably playing detective,” Hunt snapped.

When Sinclair returned, he had two members of the bomb squad with him. They had brought their dog, and even Jenny’s fear didn’t keep her from noticing how cute he looked in his official yellow coat. They worked quickly and moved on.

Sinclair summoned Casey outside. “Sniper. Only one casualty—a young woman dressed like Jenny. No fatalities. The unoccupied building northeast of the square is the most likely site.”

“He’s not ex-service, then,” Casey concluded. “At that range, we’d not have missed.”

Sinclair opened his mouth to argue then reconsidered. Casey’s assessment was correct. The sniper had shot to kill. He had not been successful. The victim was on her way to St. Thomas’s. They went into the conference room. “You’re safe here, Jen. There are coppers all about.”

“What’s going on? Did they find something? Please tell me it’s all over!”

“Not yet. A shot was fired in the square. We’re looking for the shooter.”

She paled, thinking of Danny and the last time shots had been fired near a courthouse.

He brought sandwiches and sodas on his next visit. “The courthouse is clear. All the appropriate buildings are being searched.”

“Will the trial resume?” Casey asked Sinclair.

“Yes. At this point people are safer inside the courthouse than out of it. Judge Rye has located the principals, and the jury was kept together, so after everyone’s had a chance to eat, Jenny will have to return to the box.”

“No,” she begged. “I’m scared! I don’t want to go in there without Sergeant Casey and Brian. If you’re searching buildings, then the shooter’s still out there somewhere. I want some guns on my side.”

“Jenny, it’s more likely he’s gone. The Westminster tube station is close by.”

“Colin, please!”

He looked at her pale face and rumpled clothing. “Casey, you and Hunt stand on the back wall. We’ll station Davies outside. If the judge objects, I’ll tell him it’s standard operating procedure following a bomb threat.”

When she returned to the courtroom, Judge Rye thanked the officers for their presence. “We’re all a bit more reassured, aren’t we?”

The young barrister for the prosecution completed his examination.

Then the counsel for the defence, Clive Tillotson, began. He also received gentle guidance from the judge, and she was glad that the barrister's somewhat tentative style allowed her more time to respond. Sergeant Casey was wearing his fierce look, and even Hunt looked a little menacing, but she still felt unnerved. It was sobering to realize that lives were still affected and the decisions made in this court just as binding, regardless of the quality of legal representation and the events that had nearly derailed them.

When Tillotson finally bowed to the judge and sat down, the prosecutor stood. "Your Honour, may I request a short recess? I would like to reexamine this witness, but she is clearly still shaken by the events of the day."

The judge agreed to a thirty-minute recess, and Colin led her to the corridor outside. She was surprised when her protection detail headed for the rear of the building. They were in the van and pulling away before Casey told her that the prosecutor had no intention of recalling her. Their departure had been rescheduled to take advantage of the heavy police presence in the area and to give them a head start on anyone who wished to follow them and do her harm. As further opdec, Sinclair had returned to his seat in the courtroom as if expecting her to reappear. A decoy had been previously arranged, but when Jenny and the team arrived at the witness protection flat without incident, Casey rang Sinclair to tell him it was not necessary.

CHAPTER 28

The newspapers the next morning were full of reports about the bomb scare at the Crown Court building and the sniper attack in Parliament Square. Colin had mentioned a shot being fired but hadn't said that anyone had been hurt. Jenny looked closely at the picture of the woman being loaded into the ambulance. Her face was turned away from the camera, but Jenny could see the collar of her blouse, a light-colored blouse—possibly white?—and her medium-length dark hair. The caption read, "Camden woman, 28, sole victim of sniper fire."

"Sergeant Casey—does she look like me?"

His eyes ran over the snap. "Hard to say."

"But look at her hair, her clothes—"

"There's a superficial resemblance," he said cautiously.

She frowned. "Okay, Sergeant Secretive, it's time for the truth. You thought this would happen to *me*, didn't you?"

"Diversions are a military tactic. I thought the bomb threat was a diversion, yes."

"Tell me the monster's not behind this!"

"I can't do that, love. We won't know who's behind it until we catch him."

Later she thought about how angry the monster had been when he was in the little room with her. He'd had months in jail for that anger to fester and flame. He was in prison now somewhere. Would he ever stop being angry at her? After several days, the newspapers went on to other stories, but her mind could not get past the fact that once again Sergeant Casey had saved her life.

Colin continued to stop by the flat, during the morning on the weekend—she needled him for not coming in time to interfere with her exercises—and after dinner on the other days. Bates was convicted, and when Colin arrived in mid-afternoon the next week—with lager for the men!—she knew it was a harbinger of other good news.

"Your responsibility is over, Jen. Moraga—the motorcycle attacker—

isn't going to trial. An informal arrangement has been worked out between his solicitor and the CPS." He set the beer on the dining room table. "It's a wise decision. He had no defence, what with Davies' slugs in his thigh and a score of police witnesses."

Hunt wasted no time in opening a bottle.

"Tomorrow's your last day. Casey—" He nodded at the others. "Report for reassignment Monday. You'll have some leave coming. Well done, all of you."

"Colin, I didn't think I'd have so little notice. Will I be able to get a flight out tomorrow?"

"Andrews is checking availability, Jen. It may be a day or two before we can get a reservation for you. I'll know more in the morning." Actually, he had instructed Andrews not to schedule anything before Monday.

She pulled out a dining chair and sat down. "What if there's no flight? Will I have to stay here by myself? I don't have enough money for a hotel."

"We'll provide for you, Jen. Don't worry over it." He smiled. "I'm due back at the Yard. I'll ring you tonight."

There was still a lot of food in the fridge, so Brian declared dinner a hotchpotch meal, and they'd finish whatever remained at lunch the next day. "You can look out your window now, JJ," he told her.

"And turn off your radio," Casey added.

"And you can all sleep tonight—nobody on watch," she said.

Instead of calling, Colin came by the flat to have a private word with her. "You're scheduled to fly out on British Air Monday morning."

"Tomorrow's Friday."

"I'd like you to consider staying the weekend with me, Jen."

She felt a warm flush on her cheeks. She shook her head. "It's just not right."

"Trusting me *is* right," he insisted. "You have every right to be suspicious of a man's motives, but you're safe with me, I assure you."

"Colin, I don't know what your expectations are."

He took her hand and drew her to her feet. "Look at your flag, Jen. Its arms are open ended. Our relationship is the same—you can step forward or back. What would you like to do?"

She was flattered by his attention. He was respectful, even solicitous. She should start a new list: *Pairs of Similar Words with Dissimilar Meanings.* Solicitous and solicitor would be the first two.

Jenny was so quiet during the rest of the evening that Hunt remarked on it. "Hunt, there's a Texas expression you need to learn: 'Never miss a chance to shut up.'" She was smiling when she said it, but Hunt wouldn't have taken offense either way.

She said goodnight early. She turned off her radio, but when she climbed into bed, her room seemed unnaturally quiet. She turned it back on.

It was a strange feeling, knowing that all the men were asleep. She didn't really need anyone to protect her anymore, but it felt lonely, not having someone awake nearby. She was going home; she was finally going to have a life, so why did she feel so sad? She thought about Danny and how glad she was that he was doing well. She would not have to go home with anyone's death on her conscience, thank God. She thought about Hunt, how jarring he had seemed at first and how harmless now. She thought about Brian and all the times he'd helped her in his quiet way, seen a need and responded, carried her and comforted her. She'd miss them. Her departure from the flat seemed as sudden as her arrival.

She thought about Sergeant Casey and got a lump in her throat. He'd been everything to her—saved her life, nursed her wounds, always put her needs first, as Colin had said he would. She forgot it was the middle of the night. For months in this flat, someone had been up no matter what time it was. She slipped out of bed and walked through the empty sitting room and knocked softly on Casey's door. It was slightly ajar. "Sergeant?" she whispered. "Could I talk to you?"

He didn't sound sleepy when he answered. "Are you okay, love?"

"No."

"Steady on then. I'll grab a shirt, and we'll chat in the sitting room."

She didn't even wait for him to ask. "I should feel safe, and I don't. I should feel glad that I won't have to be here anymore, but I'm not. I should feel excited that I'm going home, but it hasn't sunk in."

"Are you going home tomorrow?"

"No, I'm going to Colin's. My flight isn't until Monday."

"Are you okay with that?"

"It's just for the weekend. And he didn't ask for anything."

"He will, Jenny. He's got an agenda, and you don't have to be a detective to figure out what it is." He watched her brow tighten and took the edge out of his voice. "Are you afraid of this?"

"No, I'll be okay. He's courteous." She smiled. "Besides, he's big on consent."

He moved on. "There are some things you need to know about homecomings," he said. "Don't expect too much. Your family will mean well, but it's odds on they'll not know what's right for you. You've changed. Make your own choices. If you don't, you'll trade one prison for another."

"It doesn't feel like a prison now, this flat. But Texas—I don't know what I want to do there or even what I can do."

He leant forward. "Listen to me, love. Testifying—it was your mission, not your family's. They'll not understand. I've completed military ops without injury and found it hard to adjust to less intensity, less focus. I fulfilled a mission with an injury, and that's even more difficult. Bodies heal faster than minds do."

"Will you have to adjust after this one is over?"

"Yes, but I've learnt to let go. We've got a saying: 'You can't land on the same beach twice.' Militarily, you can't, because the enemy would be ready for you. For the rest, it's because you're different. The beach is different. If we were to return to this flat six months from now, nothing would be the same."

"I'll miss you. Will I ever see you again?"

"If you come back to England, you will. I'll give you my mobile number, and you can ring me."

"You'll have another life."

"I'll have another assignment, but you can phone me, can't you?"

"What if you're working?"

"Then I'll tell you that I am, and I'll be with you as soon as I can," he answered.

"What if you're with a girl?"

He chuckled softly. "Then I'll tell you that I am, and I'll be with you as soon as I can. But our relationship will be different, so perhaps it's time you called me by my name—Simon."

She felt giddy. No wonder she'd always done what he had told her to do. "Simon Says." The child's game in an adult edition. "Simon Casey," she whispered. "I love that name: Simon. I know I'm leaving, but I don't want to tell you good-bye."

He could see her pulse beating in the little dip above her collarbone. "Listen to me, love. Looking after you has been a privilege. You could have been a tart, or a whinger, or worse. Instead you were a good soldier. You saw it through." What would his life be like without her, this Yank he hadn't wanted to know? There would be a letdown all right.

"Sergeant—Simon—I would have died without you. I'll never be able to thank you for all the things you've done for me, and you've never asked for anything in return."

"How about a midnight run?"

"With everybody?"

"No, just the two of us. Get your jog pants on, and I'll grab my trainers."

She laughed aloud, excited at the prospect. It felt so—*clandestine,* exiting the flat, seeing the keys in Casey's—Simon's—hand. They ran slowly through the dark streets. Several times he ran to the top of the intersection, looked both ways, and waited for her to catch up. When she became too tired to run any farther, he took her hand and walked with her. Her muscles were relaxed, and she felt no need of words. She could hear sirens in the distance occasionally, but their section of the city was quiet. They walked and walked. Finally he said, "We're back."

She was still holding his hand. "I'm sorry I woke you, but I feel better. And I'm not going to say good-bye. I'll tell the others good-bye, but not you."

"I'm not sorry you woke me," he said.

"Promise?"

He put his arms around her, and she hugged him back tightly. Simon—her rock.

It took every ounce of discipline he had, not to turn his face and accept her show of affection on his lips.

They went in.

PART FOUR

To everything there is a season,
and a time to every purpose under the heaven:
a time to be born, and a time to die;
a time to plant, and a time to pluck up that which is planted...

—Ecclesiastes 3:1-2

CHAPTER 1

The day Jenny had been anticipating for months—freedom from the confinement of the flat—arrived. She packed her suitcases, then laid her remaining clothes on the bed.

Colin was all smiles when he arrived after lunch. He removed her flag from the wall. She carried the blanket he had given her and the bobby bear from Bridges. The men hung her clothes in Colin's extra bedroom and set her suitcases in the corner. The walls were the color of peaches, and the rosewood chest and nightstand seemed to reflect the warm glow. She put her bear on top of the chest of drawers, next to the vase of fresh flowers.

Opdec, Casey thought. "We'll collect our gear from upstairs and be off. Sir."

They all moved toward the door. She wasn't sure she could get any words out but knew she had to try. "Hunt—are you going to talk about me?"

"Too right," he said bluntly. "I'm going to tell everyone you're ten feet tall."

That made her smile. "Thanks for being lively," she said. "For standing up for me. For adapting so quickly."

"No hug? You'll ruin my rep."

She laughed and obliged and then turned to Brian. "I was so afraid of you at first," she admitted. "Now I can't imagine why I ever felt that way. Thank you for all the little kindnesses."

"No problem, JJ," he said, holding out his arms. "Glad to do it."

She embraced him and stepped back. She couldn't look at Simon. He put his hand under her chin and lifted her face. "That's a switch," he commented. "You used to cry when you saw me coming." His voice softened. "Ring me if you need me. Have a safe landing."

Sinclair shook hands with each man. Hunt opened the door, and they were gone. "Think where man's glory most begins and ends, and say my glory was I had such friends," she said. "Yeats."

Colin put his arm around her. "Cup of tea?" he asked.

In spite of everything, she smiled. "Tea cures everything! It's better than penicillin."

He set the water to boil and took two cups from the cabinet. "I'm glad you have your trainers on," he said. "When we finish our tea, I'll change clothes, and we'll go for a walk on the Heath."

"What's a heath?"

"A natural park. This one's almost 800 acres."

"Texas size!" she exclaimed.

"Yes," he smiled, "but in Hampstead—north London."

They walked down the stairs and left the block. They passed little shops on their way to the park and a bicycle with a small dog in its basket waiting for its owner to make his purchases and return. He took her past the ponds—"People swim in those?" she asked—and up the path to Parliament Hill. They sat on the grass, and he pointed out the spire of St. Paul's Cathedral. She leaned against him, listening to his voice and feeling the wind on her hair. Most of the poets she had studied had written of the winter wind, likening it to the cold hearts of men and the bleak power we have to hurt each other. This wind felt as warm as Colin's hand on her arm, and it was sufficient to lift the Frisbees off course, causing the intended recipients to laugh and run after them. She wanted it to sweep her spirit clear of the cobwebs that had accumulated during her three seasons in the flat.

They took a different path out of the Heath, stopped in at a French bakery, and selected a variety of chocolate confections for dessert later. Then they entered Café Rouge, which she remembered from central London. She was glad to see that only his entrée was accompanied by French fries, miniature and very tasty but a potato product all the same. They enjoyed decaf coffee when their bottle of wine had been emptied. He did not hurry her back to the flat, stopping with her whenever she wanted to linger. They climbed the quaint streets slowly, hand in hand.

Inside the flat she felt the nervousness of a fourteen-year-old, not the calm and poise she thought she should have at age twenty-four. He sat beside her on the sofa and ran his fingers across her cheek, along her jaw line, and down her neck. When he kissed her, his pace was slow, and then he stopped altogether. "I think I've fallen in love with you, Jen," he whispered, "but I'm not asking for a commitment now. I just want you to listen. I expect you're a bit uneasy about men, but Jen—I believe we can wipe away whatever fear you have, one kiss at a time."

"I wish I had your faith. I love being with you, but I just don't know—"

He put a finger across her lips. "Sshh. I know it's an adjustment, but I'm convinced that love can develop from trust. I know you trust me. I want you to trust yourself." He leant toward her again. There was an assurance to everything he did which she wished she felt. Gradually her universe shrank to the sensations from his fingers on her lips, from his breath in her ear, and from his mouth on her mouth.

He stopped again to serve the dessert. Chocolate had never tasted so sweet, nor wine so smooth. She could see the twinkle in his blue eyes. She laughed aloud and curled her legs beneath her, responding in kind to his light conversation.

Finally he said, "I want you to feel safe with me. I'll not pressure you in any way." He gave her a quick kiss and took their dishes into the kitchen.

She showered and climbed into bed. A different bed. Different sheets. Everything about her life was going to be different now. No ghosts from the past. But it was too quiet. She missed the radio. It had been a security device, but over time it had signaled someone's presence, as if the team were telling her that she was not alone. Was Colin asleep already? She slipped out of bed and tiptoed through the sitting room to his door. "Colin?"

She heard a rustle. "Yes?"

"Could I turn on the radio? Would it keep you awake?"

"Not at all. I'll find a station with soft music. Just give me a moment." He pulled on some trousers and came into the sitting room. She looked irresistible in her pyjamas and bare feet, but he would gain nothing in the long run if he pushed her now. One more goodnight kiss would have to do.

When she walked back into her room, she realized that it wasn't completely dark. There was a nightlight plugged in by the bed. Thank you, Brian. She could hear the faint strains of the radio, and she pulled the flowered duvet over her and remembered Colin coming into the sitting room bare chested. After a long while, she slept.

CHAPTER 2

When Jenny woke, she was unsure for a moment where she was. Then her eyes fell on the chrysanthemums, the beautiful soft pink chrysanthemums Colin had left on her chest of drawers. She almost laughed aloud, wondering if he recognized the irony—mums when she no longer had to keep silent to be safe, mums when she could shout from the rooftops that she was free and going home. She pulled on jeans and a t-shirt and went to find him. He'd either been out while she was sleeping or had planned ahead: There was a chocolate croissant waiting for her. "You'll need sustenance," he told her. "We're going to do some travelling today—on foot." He poured her tea.

And travel they did—up one side of Hampstead High Street and Heath Street and down the other. They bought ham and cheese crepes and stood on the pavement eating them. He purchased strawberries from the market. At the bookstore he chose two Hampstead books for her, one composed of picture postcards and the other, a history of the area, detailing the struggle to preserve the Heath from commercial development. It was late afternoon before he guided her past the library and Keats House and back toward his flat.

After a brief respite and time to wash and change clothes, they walked to an Italian restaurant for dinner. It had a French-sounding name, but everything inside was Italian: the waiters, the menu, the wines. A romance language, a romantic meal, and a man across the table from her, romancing her, asking her questions about less turbulent times and teasing her when her cheeks warmed from the glass of vino rosso that he kept filled. Their waiter taught her an Italian proverb: "Buon vino fa buon sangue," or "Good wine makes good cheer." He was right.

"I wish we had more time," she said after they returned to his flat. The warmth she felt now had nothing to do with alcohol—his touch had kindled it.

"That's what I'm asking for. We've been under horrific pressure, artificial time constraints. It takes time for things to unfold as they're meant to. Postpone your trip."

"I'd like to see more of England than hospitals and courtrooms. But how can I not go home? I've missed them for so long."

"Jenny, I'm in love with your optimism, your vitality, your humour. I want more of them."

She wanted more kisses. Her chest rose and fell to his touch. His fingers explored the skin under her t-shirt. "I don't want you to stop, but my scars are there. I don't want you to see."

He reached across her and turned out the lamp on the end table. The only illumination came from the kitchen behind them. When he kissed her neck and eased his hand over the cup of her bra, she began to feel shivery. Did he feel that way when she kissed him? She felt his fingers inside the cup. Why hadn't she worn a blouse with buttons? With the t-shirt it was all or nothing—she was either covered or totally exposed. "I can't—I want—I don't know what to do."

That meant stop. Damn. She had been responding. "My love is real, Jen. It's not going to go away." He moved his hand away but continued to kiss her, lightly, gently. He wanted to prolong the experience, to tempt her to stay, to make her remember his touch after she'd gone.

CHAPTER 3

On Sunday they packed a picnic lunch, sandwiches, strawberries from the day before, and a bottle of wine. Eventually they found a relatively private spot to sit on the Heath and watched the motley world go by, laughing together at the snippets of conversation they heard and what they imagined a companion's response might be.

They walked back with the empty picnic basket. He watched her open her suitcase and survey the space she had left in it. "You won't be needing your winter things in Texas," he remarked. "Or the books you've finished reading. Why don't you leave them here? I'll post them to you. It's far more important that you take your flag."

She felt a terrible ache in her chest when he handed it to her, the flag he had given her as encouragement when she had sent her father home without her. The flag that had been an integral part of her life, waking and sleeping. "You've been such a gentleman, Colin—no pressure, no anger. I'm sorry. I know I've let you down."

He sat down beside her on the floor and took both her hands in his. "Jenny, physical love between a man and a woman is God's creation. It's too fantastical to have come about in any other way. I want you to experience it with me, but I want you to experience it because you love me and you want it as much as I do. You haven't let me down, and you aren't burning any bridges by visiting your family. Families are important. I respect your commitment to them."

He had pizza delivered. After dinner he held her. His kisses were gentle. He rubbed her back and massaged her shoulders to ease the tension he felt there. "I'd like you to take something of mine home with you." He went into his room and retrieved his Bible. "It's a book of love and hope, Jenny. Think of it as a bridge between us, as proof positive that nothing has ended here, because I'll want you to return it."

"How is that possible? I live half a world away."

"Love doesn't know any boundaries, Jen. My feelings for you aren't going to change. I'll be ringing you while you're in Texas."

Her hands were full. His were empty. She had nothing to give him, this handsome, cordial man. She had lost consciousness—died, in a sense—in a little room with a monster. She had awakened to pain and to this man's face and voice. Her injuries had healed, her pain had receded, but this man had not stepped aside. He had walked with her through the corridors of fear and the halls of justice. The thought of going home had been her guiding star for so long. Now she was going, and she thought her heart would break.

CHAPTER 4

In the morning Colin drove Jenny to Heathrow. His final professional responsibility was to get her on the plane safely. At the corner of the jet way she turned to see if he were still there. He was, but he did not wave, and neither did she. One hand was on the handle of her rolling bag and the other swiping at her tears. She had not expected to cry leaving London.

She cried at the Houston airport, too, glad to be in her parents' arms. Her brothers hung back until she teased them about being the only girl they were shy with—her mom had told her that BJ had a girlfriend and Matt spent all his money on weekend dates. She sat between them on the drive home, tired from the long flight and slow march through customs. She listened contentedly to the voices of her family and watched the landscape through the car windows, broader and brighter than she remembered it, and hoped it would be a metaphor for her future.

Seeing her room, however, was a shock. It was a little girl's room, and she realized with dismay that she didn't belong in it. She wasn't sweet and innocent anymore. With a wave of panic she missed the witness protection flat, so used and worn it never looked really clean, its furniture a little battered from previous occupants. She swept the pink pillows from the bed, reversed the spread, and wished she could tear down the frilly curtains. She called Colin to let him know that she'd arrived safely and felt hollow inside when she hung up the phone.

Her dad grilled steaks for dinner, and her mom served potato salad she'd made earlier in the day. Jenny found it difficult to explain why she laughed at the potato salad, having to assure her mother that yes, she still liked it, and that no, she wouldn't have preferred anything else. Angel food cake with fresh peaches was the dessert.

Before she went to bed, she opened her journal and started a new page with the heading, *Things That Are the Same. 1. Men are sleeping in the other rooms.* No, her brothers were boys, old enough to drive and date but not likely to be much help if a threat came. *2. I'm safe.* No, the house has no alarm system. Her father would have to defend her mother, too—bad odds. Did he lock all the doors at night? Would she have any warning if someone tried to break in? Maybe they should get a dog.

She looked at her list. Short, but it demonstrated how different everything was. Colin was not downstairs, a mere phone call away. He would not be calling by. She smiled at herself for adopting the British expression for coming over and began a new list: *Things I Wish For. 1. Colin's touch.* Amazing—after the monster's attack, she hadn't thought she'd want any man to touch her, ever. *2. A feeling of safety.* When bad things had happened, the guys had known what to do. Danny had saved her life at the hospital and Sergeant Casey at the courthouse, twice. Colin had, too, in a way, with his attentiveness and affection. *3. A sense of belonging.* She imagined Colin saying, "I can grant that wish, Jenny." Could he? *4. An identity separate from the events of the past months.* Was that possible? *5. A sense of purpose.* A new mission, Sergeant Casey—Simon—would say. Having a normal life would be good. "What does that mean, Jenny?" he would ask. He wouldn't be satisfied when she confessed she didn't know.

In the morning she discovered that there was no tea in the house, except the iced tea variety, so she asked her mother for a Coke.

"For breakfast?" her mother asked with surprise.

"To settle my stomach," she explained.

She had her hair trimmed and shaped, but there was no man to admire it except her dad. Her parents had been busy since hearing the news of her return, and by the end of her first week home, she had already been to the dentist, the family doctor, and her first appointment with a psychologist.

Sergeant Casey had given her a copy of her medical report, which detailed her injuries and treatment. Dr. Morgan, the family physician, took most of it in stride, although he could not entirely mask his pity. He patted her on the shoulder and assured her that he understood her nervousness. He must have—he did not make her disrobe completely for the examination.

She gave the psychologist, Dr. Abramson, a copy of her medical history also, hoping that having the record would spare her from having to relate everything. He seemed a little lost with all the medical data, preferring to focus on how she felt. Dislocated. Lost. Lonely. She mentioned Colin's love and then regretted exposing it to Abramson's psychological scrutiny. She looked repeatedly at her amethyst watch, deciding not to disclose who had given it to her.

On Saturday morning when her mother took her shopping, she bought a variety of postcards to send Colin and then went into the department store. She was trying on a blouse in one of the fitting rooms when she heard her mother gasp and then go suddenly silent. She had seen Jenny's shoulder and the flaws on her torso. Jenny sank down on the little stool in the dressing room, shaken by her mother's shock. "Mother, I was badly beaten, and I had surgery, you know that," she said, her enthusiasm for shopping completely deflated. "There are marks from everything."

Saturday evening she put on her baseball cap and went to a game with her dad. It was the most crowded place she had been since her return home, and although she enjoyed the play on the field, hearing so many American accents did not make her feel less like a foreigner. And she missed Colin's call from London.

Coming home should have been comfortable, like putting on a pair of old shoes, but Simon had been right: You can't go home again. These shoes chafed. That night she dreamed a gunman fired at her. She had her bulletproof vest on, but it didn't help, and the sergeant wasn't there to stop the bleeding.

Sunday she attended church with her family. The minister's text for the day centered on the love passages from the New Testament. He used Christ's death as the perfect illustration of love, adding that by following the guidance of Scripture, we could also demonstrate the depth of our love. Jenny's mind heard a new voice inside her, telling her that Colin was patient and kind. Colin was not rude or easily angered. He was a policeman—he certainly didn't delight in evil! Why had she been in such a hurry to leave him? She had his Bible but not his handkerchief. She had to settle for the stale Kleenex in the bottom of her purse.

After church her parents spoke to her about her plans. When she told them that graduate school was no longer a consideration, they encouraged her to think about what kind of work she would like to do. At her age they felt she should be self supporting, and the routine of employment, having office hours, would settle her. Practical shoes, she thought. She tried to imagine a work environment in which she'd feel comfortable—safe—but when she mentioned the police department as a possibility, her parents thought she was joking. When the conversation was over, she called Colin, preferring to think about romantic shoes.

She didn't tell him how difficult it was—how her parents' expectations, not unreasonable, seemed like a mountain too steep to climb and how adrift she felt in a room with too little wall space to mount her British flag. Hearing his voice was reassuring, even with the transatlantic echo, but it wasn't enough. Severing the phone connection gave her an emptiness that ached, like having a part of you surgically removed and still feeling the slice of the scalpel when it was gone.

During her second week home, Jenny went to see college friends who had settled in the Houston area. Mandy Edwards had married before either she or her husband had graduated from school, and they had a baby already, a baby girl. Mandy was excited and proud, and Jenny was happy for her but felt the chasm between them widen. Mandy didn't know what to say about Jenny's experience, and Jenny didn't want to tell her how dangerous the world was for girls.

Emily Richards was as ebullient as ever, laughing about how she'd spent her year in the company of children while Jenny had had adult conversation, at least if you could consider cops to be capable of adult conversation. Jenny tried to explain what the men meant to her, how wise and supportive they had been. They weren't the dreaded enforcers of speed limits on holiday weekends, but the difference between death and life, fear and safety, chaos and control. You were involved in an in-depth study of the British legal system, I'll grant you that, Emily had replied, but you don't have to get emotional.

Her second appointment with Dr. Abramson went less well than the first. She told him about Danny, Brian, and Simon, and how close she had become to them. She described Hunt's irreverence. Abramson agreed that they were good men but suggested that since their job was over, her dependence on them was unhealthy. He explained that disengaging was an important factor in moving forward. If she had been unable to say good-bye to Simon in person, writing him a letter would be a useful exercise, even if she didn't mail it. Say good-bye when he had finally told her his name? It was unthinkable. She had released too much already. What did Dr. Abramson know about loss? She'd write *him* a letter. "Buh-bye," as they said on the British chat shows.

When Jenny refused a third session with the psychiatrist, her parents took her to see their minister, Walter William Keith. She thought of him as the man with three first names, but the congregation affectionately called him Walter Will, because in the short time he'd been with them, they'd learned that no matter what needed to be done, Walter would pitch in.

"Your parents have told me how difficult this past year has been for you," he said. "How can I help?"

"Everyone wants me to forget it and move on," she told the trim man who had looked taller in the pulpit. His liturgical robe, which had hidden his slight frame, hung in the corner of his office. "And I can't, because it changed me. With my friends—their futures seem so bright, and I'm a real-life law and order victim, not an entertaining TV plot. I don't really want them to know how violence feels, but I'm not over it. I'm different, and it's lonely."

"They mean no harm, but trust comes so easily to them, doesn't it? Jennifer, sometimes we have to forgive others their innocence. More than that, not spoil it."

"How do you know?"

"I have alcohol-related violence in my family." He paused. "I was affected by it, but I'm not defined by it."

"Is that why you became a minister?"

"I sought peace, and Someone I could trust. Who do you trust?"

"My family, sort of, but they're not on the same page with me. The guys who protected me are, but Dr. Abramson said I should stop thinking about them."

"You must know them very well." He leaned back in his chair, wanting her to know he wouldn't rush her. "Tell me about them."

She described the ones she knew best, the commitment they had made to stay with her, the hard times they'd come through together. She told him about Danny and how much she wanted to hear his laugh; Brian, patient with her fear; how tough Simon had been but how they had come to respect each other. Even Hunt, who didn't change his behavior when he was around her, who treated her like she was normal. And Colin—faithful, considerate, loving, with enough hope for both of them.

"The connections God establishes aren't meant to be broken."

"God chose them?"

"Of course. God knew what you needed."

"How do you know God was a part of it?"

"Because when you talk about them, your face relaxes. And they made sacrifices for you, which is a godly thing to do."

"They were so good to me, and I didn't deserve any of it."

"God's grace is always unmerited, Jennifer. And His grace is often accompanied by peace, a sense of inner calm despite stormy circumstances."

"I felt that, sometimes, when I was with them."

"Jennifer, God works through His people. When people truly listen, it's a sign of God's presence. When they don't judge. When they accept your love without having to shape it to meet their own needs. When their actions make you want to give something back."

"It looks like you gave something back," she said, gesturing toward his swollen thumb.

"Habitat for Humanity," he smiled. "Our spiritual beliefs can lead us to actions of all sorts, and I have witnesses that my tools were effective, at least some of the time." He looked at her thoughtfully. "The Bible is a kind of hammer, you know—we can use it to drive our beliefs home."

Colin had given her his Bible. "I don't know where to start," she confessed.

"Start at the end, with Revelation 21:5: 'Behold, I make all things new.' Or if you prefer the Old Testament, Ezekiel 36:26: 'A new heart also will I give you, and a new spirit will I put within you…' God lives through His Word and through prayer, and we can also experience Him in our relationships with others."

"Will the nightmares stop? If I pray?"

"You still need healing, I think, although your protection officers began the process without realizing it. If you'd had female officers, your trust of men would have come much more slowly. Regarding the nightmares—time will tell."

No quick fix, as Simon would say.

"It'll help if you reach out to Him—to someone—when they occur."

- -

That night she dreamed that she was in a dark room, and the darkness had substance. She cried out for Colin, but he couldn't hear her. She woke in a panic, sweating and shaking. It was four o'clock in the morning. But it was mid-morning in London! She called him, and for the first time, she cried on the phone, telling him that she missed him, she needed him, and she wished she hadn't left so quickly. "Home isn't home, Colin. It's not the haven I thought it would be. Love and acceptance aren't the same."

"For me they are."

She slept late, and her family went to church without her. After Sunday dinner—served in the middle of the day, just the way Brian had always done it—her parents again spoke to her about her future, stressing their love but pointing out that the violence against her had happened in September the previous year. Perhaps it was time for her to stop talking so much about the English police and start focusing on the present. Nine months ago, Jenny thought: long enough for a baby to be born. What have I birthed?

That night when Colin called, she told him that she was having to appear in another trial after all, this time as the defendant, and there were way too many judges. "You never judged me," she said. "Not once, not matter how bad it got. And I hurt you, and I'm so, so sorry."

It was very late in London, and he sounded tired, but he spoke of understanding and comfort. "This has been a crisis for your family as well as for you. They almost lost you, more than once. That makes some persons hold on more tightly."

"You didn't."

"Jenny, sometimes love is letting someone go."

"Not for me."

"We'll sort this out together then. Jen? Together."

CHAPTER 5

Colin looked over at Jenny, asleep in the airline seat, her face relaxed, her cheeks still slightly flushed from the champagne, her hand in his. When the plane bound for London had lifted off the runway, he'd felt a surge of hope. Gravity had released them—perhaps she would be released from her misgivings as well. The plane was high above the clouds now, and the roar of the engines was softer, soothing even, a sign that he and Jenny were on their way together. The sky's the limit for us, he thought.

When he had arrived in Houston three days earlier, he hadn't been certain he could win her over. Then he came through customs and spied her, his heart skipped a beat, and he knew he must convince her that they could overcome any obstacles that lay ahead of them. Her hair was a bit shorter and more graceful, her shirt Royal Mail red, tied at the waist. He'd never seen her in shorts, and he approved heartily of her tan legs and red sandals. Her face was tan also, and although it put the narrow scar on her cheek in sharper relief, he felt unreasonably proud when he saw it. She had been laughing and crying and had hugged him as if she didn't ever want to let him go.

Houston was flat, and her home was correspondingly a single elevation ranch-style design, the southwestern influence apparent in the colours and the comfortable informality of the furnishings. Mrs. Jeffries was taller and rounder than Jenny, with curlier hair. Jenny was poised and happy, teasing her brothers good-naturedly. Over a meal of potato and leek soup, pecan-crusted salmon, and spinach salad with strawberries and black pepper, they quizzed him about his work. He described the concept of policing by consent that governed the actions of the Metropolitan Police. Then he fielded questions about their lack of firearms, explaining that they didn't consider themselves to be lacking, since their skills and training were sufficient for most situations and they could call upon specialist units when necessary.

"Like the ones that protected Jenny?" Matt asked.

"Exactly, yes," he responded.

On Friday Jenny took him to an upscale shopping mall, where they wandered about hand in hand, stopping for a late lunch at La Madeleine, a country French restaurant near the ice arena. Over a plate of Caesar salad, he asked her to go back with him, confessing that he had already reserved a seat for her on his return flight.

"I love you," he said. "I want you to come home with me."

"Colin, I'm not sure how I feel."

"On this journey only one of us needs to know the way. Trust me and accompany me."

"What if I can't be what you want me to be?"

"Jenny, I've investigated cases which involved bodily harm. I've investigated rape cases. As a result I think I have more understanding than most men about what it takes for a woman to regain her confidence. I'm offering you an old-fashioned courtship."

"While we're living in the same flat?"

"Why not? Life is full of contradictions." He smiled. "It's important to me, a physical relationship. I'll not deny that. But I want more than that. I want to spend time with you. I want you to meet my family. I want to show you my city, my country. And I promise you patience. Gentleness."

Her cheeks flushed, but she did not say yes.

Mrs. Jeffries did not cook Friday evening. Instead, Jenny's father took them all to The Taste of Texas, a restaurant with Texas fare and Texas-sized servings. The décor, including cowboy memorabilia, historic relics, and skins of wild animals, was not sufficient to distract him from Jenny's appearance—striking in black cotton trousers with a bright pink gauzy shirt—or the culinary delights. He tasted crab cakes and bits of quail meat wrapped in bacon and served on skewers with creamy dressing. There was an extensive salad bar complete with freshly baked bread and sweet summer fruit. He was a bit amused that Jenny's younger brother ordered the same beef entrée that he did, a fourteen-ounce prime rib, prepared medium, and aped his table manners as well. Mr. Jeffries gave him a summary of Texas history by referring to the six flags of sovereignty that were displayed at the restaurant's entrance, all to the accompaniment of Matt's rolling eyes.

"We've heard that spiel before," Jenny said. "We could all give you chapter and verse!"

During the night Friday, Jenny had a nightmare. He turned on his light, pulled on trousers and a shirt, and opened his door, wanting to be available if needed. In a few minutes Bill Jeffries told him that Jenny was asking for him. She was sitting up in bed, her pyjamas edged in lace and as pale as her face.

"The monster and his thugs came home with me," she said, "like excess baggage."

He pulled her desk chair next to the bed and took her hand. "Care to tell me about it?"

"I don't dream about all of them," she answered. "When I was in the hospital and Mr. Bates attacked me, I wasn't alone. Danny was there. And when Danny and I were shot, Sergeant Casey was there. In the dreams it's the being alone that's so frightening."

"Speaking of Sullivan, he received a citation. I meant to tell you. There was a do at the Yard with his family present. Woulson presented the certificate, which was signed by the commissioner."

"Colin, I'm such a mess. Are you sure you want me?"

"Oh, Jen. There's something special about you—a spark. When you left, the lights went out in my life. My flat has never seemed so stark and cold. So empty. I couldn't bring myself to post your winter clothes to you—I kept hoping you'd come home to them."

"But I can't make a complete commitment. Will you take me on—on consignment?"

With a soft laugh, he kissed her cheek and assured her that he would.

Bill Jeffries was waiting for him in the kitchen with two liqueur glasses and a bottle of Bailey's Irish Cream. "You've done this before, haven't you?"

"Comforted her? Yes, sir," he answered. "I didn't like to hear her cry."

"She won't tell us what the dreams are about."

"She's protecting you, sir."

"You've come to take her back, haven't you?"

"I've invited her, yes." He smiled at the older man. "I love her, sir. My intentions are the very best. I'm perfectly capable of providing for all her needs, whatever they may be."

"We'll talk more in the morning," Mr. Jeffries said.

And they had. Bill and Peggy Jeffries slept rather late, but they had all waited for Jenny. When she came into the kitchen, her mother poured her a glass of juice, and her father suggested that she bring it into his study, where they could have a private conversation.

"What's wrong?" Jenny asked.

"Your mother and I would like to talk with you and Colin about your plans."

Jenny drained her glass and took Colin's hand.

"Are you serious about this man?" Jenny's mother asked as soon as they sat down. "We like him very much, but do you think a relationship that began the way this one did, can last?"

"I know Colin and I met because of a crisis, but that's an advantage, I think. All the artifice was stripped away. I feel very close to him. I know I can trust him. I feel safe with him."

"Safety isn't love, Jennifer," her mother said.

"No, but I'll never love someone without it. Colin's a gentleman, Mother—more than anybody, he understands."

"What does he understand, dear?"

"That I need to prove some things to myself. That I need time. And that is the one thing I'm sure we can give each other."

"But do you love him, Jennifer? How can you consider this without love?"

Colin answered for her. "The legal process was very difficult for Jenny, Mrs. Jeffries—the preparation as well as the trials themselves. She hasn't had the time to examine her feelings fully." Jenny's grateful smile encouraged him. "I've seen what her commitment can accomplish," he said. "And her commitment is worth waiting for."

"Mother, if he leaves without me, I don't think I'll be able to stand it."

Peggy Jeffries looked at her husband.

"Punkin, we want to help you however we can, wherever you are. You will need some financial support. I know Colin is willing to provide for you, but that's still part of my job as a father. Another is to assure you that you can come home if this relationship doesn't work out. And I hope you'll seek psychological help in London. I know you didn't like Dr. Abramson, but I'd feel better if I knew you were taking some steps to accept responsibility for your recovery."

Colin leant back in his seat. The flight to London had been smooth so far. The rest of the weekend couldn't have been easy for the Jeffries, but they had responded with courtesy and humour, two qualities he often recognised in Jenny. Saturday evening over a meal of grilled chicken and cole slaw, he had responded as generously as he could to Bill Jeffries' questions. It was an interrogation of sorts, albeit more restrained than many he had conducted, and he understood that Jenny's father needed to know more about him.

Sunday morning they had all attended church together. He saw Peggy Jeffries take her husband's hand during the minister's homily, and he thought about love and sacrifice. He was taking their daughter away on Father's Day, but he hoped that they knew he was taking her to something. Jenny had come so far since he'd first met her, but he wanted much more for her, for both of them. She had been so excited over their seats on the plane—she had never flown first class before—and he promised himself that this trip would be only the beginning of her first class treatment.

CHAPTER 6

It seemed a long drive home from the airport. Several times Bill Jeffries checked the speedometer as he drove, certain that the car was not maintaining acceleration. It was the departure of his daughter, however, not the rate of rotation of his tires, that caused his sluggishness of spirit, and it continued throughout the evening.

"I wish this hadn't happened, Bill," Peggy said, "but I like Colin. Jenny seems happy with him. And she's an adult. We had no way of preventing her from going."

"She'll be dependent," he argued. "Her tourist visa won't allow her to work. She has no friends there. What kind of a life will that be? I don't think she has any idea what she is doing."

"Oh, Bill, I know what living with a man means, and I don't approve, but if we had opposed her, what would the impact have been?"

He sighed. "He says he loves her, Peg, but that doesn't mean that he'll stay with her—his marriage ended in divorce. Or that what he wants is best for her."

"No, but I don't want to do anything that will drive a wedge between us. Remember what the Harveys said last month? When their son told them he wanted to drop out of school to play in a band? 'To keep your children, keep your mouth shut.'"

"She'll be hurt, and we're too far away to help."

"Nothing can separate her from our love, can it? Now more than ever, we should make sure she knows that." She gave him a quick kiss. "Get some rest. I know it was a blow for her to leave on Father's Day, but she'll be all right, and you will, too."

Now as he watched his wife sleep, Bill Jeffries thought, not for the first time, what a fortunate man he was. He wasn't worthy of his wife's love, but he was thankful for it, and for her strength, too. When he had come back from London without Jenny, it had been Peggy who had sustained him, not the other way around. He had been proud of Jenny's determination to see justice done, but afraid for her and bereft from leaving her behind. Now he thought about what her scant three weeks at home had revealed. She'd seemed fine when she arrived on Memorial Day. They were confident that she'd received good medical care in England, but they wanted the reassurance of a good report from their family doctor. They were also cognizant of the fact that she needed counseling, and after all the months of not being able to help, they made the appointments for her, feeling profoundly relieved that they could take positive action on her behalf at last.

Her fear of going out alone had been the first indication that her condition was more serious than they had supposed. Then they began to notice other signs of distress. She was tense and easily upset. She had a short attention span. Her appetite was poor. And she had bad dreams—shattering their illusions as well as their sleep. They certainly didn't want to upset her further by referring to her experiences, so they encouraged her to look ahead, but she was confused about her future.

Peggy had taken her shopping, and the sight of their daughter's scars had shocked her. He looked over at his wife, her face relaxed in sleep, her skin still smooth, and wished that he could erase the last year of Jenny's life, the marks and the memory. They had spoken to her often during her time with the police, and the forced optimism they heard in her voice had concerned them. Chief Inspector Sinclair was more direct, never minimizing the seriousness of her case, but he had not disclosed the degree of violence she had suffered. Could they believe him now, when he said he would take care of her?

When she told them that he wanted to visit, he suspected the reason immediately. She had been on a first-name basis with him for some time, and he had kept in touch with her following her return to Houston. Then he had arrived, gracious, charming, attentive. Her emotions were less guarded in his company, her smiles were genuine, and her laughter spontaneous. There was something Old World about the two of them drinking together and bonding over the spirits in their glasses, but it had given him a chance to thank Sinclair for his commitment to her safety. Sinclair had responded by declaring his love for her.

In other ways Sinclair had acquitted himself well, too. He had stood whenever Peggy or Jenny entered the room. He had been willing to discuss his background and his work. He'd mentioned his father's example of service, his own schooling in England, and some of the more interesting places he'd lived, the exotic creatures, beautiful beaches, and lush landscapes. As a child he hadn't fully grasped the larger picture—the poverty, disease, and unrest. His mother had made each posting a new holiday.

As he grew, however, he'd realized that some families were frightened. The fathers of some of his playmates didn't come home. Some days they weren't allowed to play outside because there were soldiers on the streets. Later his father had described despotic regimes, egotistical rulers, and the effects evil men had on society, but for him it had always been personal. Lawlessness led to human misery. A society, to be productive, had to assure its citizens that order was possible, that justice was real, and that there were consequences for bad acts. He'd wanted to participate in that process, to redress the imbalance caused by violence and fear, and that was why he'd chosen a career in policing.

Yes, Sinclair had been eloquent, and Jenny had hung on every word. Even his sons had not excused themselves from the dinner table. Sinclair had come from a loving family, he'd been able to adapt to a wide variety of circumstances, and he had made good progress in his profession. None of that, however, could predict what his relationship with Jenny would be like. He was significantly older than she was, and he was used to directing others. Would he respect her wishes?

In the course of his investigation, Sinclair had uncovered everything that had happened to their daughter, and he had not judged. He must have seen her injuries—long before she had healed from them—and he had not judged. He had witnessed her tears, and he had not judged. They hadn't become accustomed to the scar on her face, but Sinclair had. His eyes never rested on it. Sometime in the last months love had become a factor for him.

Will they marry? he wondered. Would that give Jenny the security that she needed? He stretched his legs carefully, not wanting to disturb his wife. Love was the most powerful force there was, and Sinclair was offering it freely to their daughter. Love and more—hope, the element that Bill Jeffries now thought had been missing from their daughter's disposition since she had returned home. We are all drawn to the light of hope. If the light in her eyes that was now fleeting could become permanent—if Sinclair's love could push the darkness in her spirit away—it would be worth letting their daughter go.

CHAPTER 7

The flight from Houston had been long, and Colin had made only a quick stop at his flat before reporting to the Yard. He must have been tired; she was, and she had slept on the plane. She smiled as she remembered how close she'd felt to him when the British Airways attendants had turned the lights down. Most of the people around them had fallen asleep, and Colin's gentle whispers had lulled her, too. She'd been reassured by his presence. Now he was gone, and the flat was quiet. She hadn't paid much attention to it before; her focus had been on going home.

He had left the makings for tea on the counter in the kitchen—how thoughtful. He was generous, too. He had brought her parents a blue jasperware bicentennial plate depicting Paul Revere's ride. "The British are coming!" she had teased. He had given her something, too: a musical jewelry box with flower designs in the royal blue exterior and two velvet-lined compartments inside.

She took her tea with her and surveyed the living and dining rooms. Like the flat upstairs, all the rooms had wainscoting separating wallpapered and painted walls, but Colin's flat looked larger, perhaps because there were two bedrooms instead of three and the background color was ivory instead of beige. Watercolor paintings and several photographs which looked custom framed hugged his walls. Had Colin taken them? She put her empty tea cup in the sink.

She decided to peek in his bedroom. He'd told her to make herself at home, but his flat didn't feel familiar enough to be home. Could she and Colin make it a home? There were a number of photos on his chest of drawers, and she thought she could guess who most of the people were—Colin's parents with Colin and his sister when they were children; Colin's sister and her husband with their two youngsters. Colin looked like his dad—tall, with strong features and blue eyes. And there was a picture of her, with her good side to the camera. She looked happy. When had that been taken? Before Christmas, when she'd wanted a snapshot to send her family? Colin had had it all this time? He also had an old roll-top desk in one corner, a little battered but still handsome. Had it belonged to his father? He had a computer, but the screen was dark. There hadn't been a computer in the witness protection flat.

Having noted everything else in his room, she could no longer ignore the large bed. She sat down on the edge and fingered the blue spread. He loved her, he said. Would he make love to her in this bed? Did she want it to happen? She knew so little about him. Did he eat breakfast? What were his favorite foods? Did he shower in the morning or at night? Did he exercise? How did he spend his spare time, if he had any? Did policemen have hobbies? Would her body disappoint him? Did she belong here?

She went back into the living room. She remembered the leather sofa and armchairs. The weather was not cold enough to need the fireplace—too bad. The bookshelves contained lots of science fiction titles and some nonfiction ones, a smattering of history, art, and the classics. His CD collection revealed an eclectic taste in music.

She made herself a sandwich and ate in the dining room while thumbing through one of the art books. There were so many museums in London—some of the paintings she saw might be exhibited here. Would Colin have time for such things?

She washed her dishes and put them away. It was a strange feeling, being completely alone. She hadn't had a cup of tea by herself, much less a meal, in months. The witness protection arrangement had been unusual, but the initial awkwardness of living with three policemen had been replaced with a closeness she hadn't anticipated. She'd been nurtured by that group of men. Was Walter Will right? Had Danny, Brian, and Simon been chosen by God to teach her to trust men again? Even Hunt? If so, God had a sense of humor.

- -

She had just put the phone down when she heard Colin's key in the lock. She hurried to meet him, but if he hadn't smiled, she wouldn't have been able to hug him, he looked so official in his dark suit and tie. He changed clothes and took her out for Chinese food, to the same restaurant he'd used when buying takeaway food for the protection team.

"I called the guys today," she told him. "I wanted to congratulate Danny. He said that his injury—since it was followed by a citation—multiplied his chances with the girls, so it was all worth it! Brian's going to come by tomorrow to give me some recipes, and Simon wanted to know where I was. When I told him London, he invited me to lunch on Thursday. It was good to talk to them."

"Even Hunt?" Colin asked with a smile.

"Well—no. I didn't call him yet."

After a short walk back to the flat, she welcomed Colin's kisses but felt a little shy still. How do you date someone you're already living with? When does the date end? She leaned against him. "You have a photo of me."

"It's lovely, isn't it?"

"It was taken from the right angle."

He realised she was talking about more than the snapshot. "There are no wrong angles, Jen." He pushed her hair back. "I want to see your face, your whole face." He traced the scar with his fingers.

"When I close my eyes, I pretend that you can't see it," she whispered.

"Then keep your eyes closed." He kissed her mouth, then the smooth skin on her throat.

She watched his fingers play with the buttons on her blouse.

"Jenny, seeing you excites me." Her lacey bra did not hide the skin beneath. He touched the curve of her breast not covered by the bra. "Do you want me to stop?"

"No," she said. She could hardly breathe.

He reached behind her, unhooked her bra, and pushed it aside. "You're beautiful, Jen. I love you." He caressed her bare skin, first with his hands and then with his mouth.

She was tingling in places he was not even touching. She wanted—she wanted—but when he put his hand on the waistband of her slacks, she gasped.

"Jen?"

"I'm not ready," she said.

He had hoped she was.

CHAPTER 8

Jenny woke up relaxed, stretching her arms and legs and remembering Colin's loving restraint. She was glad she had slept as long as she had—less time to wait for him to come home. And Simon was taking her to lunch today. That would help the time to pass, too.

He arrived well before noon, but she was ready. They walked down to the Finchley Road tube station, and she told him how much she missed everybody.

"You're the first witness to want the coppers to come back," he commented.

"I know it's crazy," she laughed, "but I miss the camaraderie. At least in protection, when there was nothing to do, there was always someone to do nothing with."

They left the tube at the Baker Street Station and climbed up the steps to Marylebone Road. He guided her down Nottingham Place past the hotel where she'd stayed when she first came to London and over to the High Street. "Where are we going, Simon?" she asked, trying to quell the rising tide of dread in her stomach.

"Trust me, love."

Oh, God, they were heading toward Oxford Street. Her feet were heavy. "Why are you doing this to me?"

He put his arm around her. "Love, I'm doing this *for* you. Let's go."

Toddlers with short pudgy legs passed them by, their mothers not hurrying them. Finally they turned the corner, and Selfridge's was on her right, the bus stop just ahead on her left. She clung to him, too terrified to be embarrassed. Breathe, she told herself. Simon is here. I'm not alone.

"Look about, love. It's just a place. They're just people." His arm was firm around her waist. "Don't you remember? It's not the same beach."

"I really hate your beaches," she declared.

He had hated some of them, too. "Tell me what you see, Jenny."

Her name, but not The Voice. "Lots of people, in a hurry. Lots of cars. A bus pulling up. A policeman." He was young, like Danny, but with Hunt's jug ears.

"Everything all right, sir?"

She looked at the constable's concerned face and realized that everything was. It wasn't Monday, September 14, it was a warm day in June and she was standing on a busy sidewalk next to two policemen. She wasn't wearing fall clothes she'd never see again, she had on khaki slacks and a cotton blouse. "Afraid of Selfridge's," Simon answered.

"Afraid of the prices, more likely," the constable quipped.

She laughed and relaxed her grip on Simon. "My credit card's not afraid," she said.

"Good luck to you, sir," the constable smiled as he moved on.

"Ready to go in?" Simon asked.

Over lunch in Selfridge's, she told him about her Houston trip, how right he had been about the things you left not being the same when you returned. She told him about the doctors and about her mother's reaction to seeing her scarred skin. "I guess that's what most people would do—feel shock, then pity." She paused. "Simon, are they that bad? I've gotten so used to them, I forget that other people aren't." He was quiet for so long that she began to regret her question, and she swallowed hard. "Are they so bad you can't figure out how to tell me?"

His eyes rested on her face. "Just the opposite. I've never known you without them, so to me they're just part of who you are, like your brown eyes or the little bump below your left knee." He looked away briefly.

"Or the scar on your thigh," she said slowly. "I remember when I saw it, I respected you. It didn't put me off at all."

"When did you get that bump on your knee?" he asked in a lighter tone.

"I fell off my bicycle," she smiled, "when I was ten. I was going too fast on a turn and lost control. The bike flew out from under me."

They'd finished their meal. "Come on then," he said. They made their way to the Bond Street tube and finally back to Colin's flat in Hampstead. "I'm proud of you for today, love. Shall I ring you next week?"

"If you promise to take me somewhere dull."

Nowhere in her company was dull.

She locked the door behind him and went to change her blouse. She felt tired, but alive. With Simon's help, she had slain a dragon.

CHAPTER 9

Colin was wonderful. He'd promised her an old-fashioned courtship, and he had kept his word. He took her to a different restaurant every night and held her hand as they walked the Hampstead streets. Their physical relationship had escalated, but not completely, because he switched from passion to affection if he sensed any hesitation on her part. Her regard for him was deepening, as was her desire. Now they were on their way to Kent so she could meet his mother. He drove his black Audi fast, slowing only slightly when the roads became narrower and the vegetation hugged the winding lanes. There were rolling hills dissected by wooded areas with deer signs nearby and horses and sheep in the distance.

The interior of the car was dark, and as the light outside faded, Jenny felt as if she and Colin were encased in a little bubble. It was intimate, the two of them closed off from the rest of the world. She remembered how her parents had reacted when she came home and wondered what sort of a welcome she would receive from Colin's mother. "What does your mother know about me?" she asked.

"That you were the Scott witness," he replied. "That a team of coppers protected you. That we all came to love you, but I'm the luckiest of the lot."

"Did she like your wife?"

"My ex-wife."

"But did your mother like her?"

He glanced over at her. It hadn't occurred to him that she would be concerned about making a good impression. "Oh, Jen, we were young, too young to know we didn't want the same things in life. You'll be fine. It's not much farther now."

He slowed and turned down a long, wide drive. The house was large, three storeys, with ivy climbing the red brick walls, a softer creamier red than the houses in Hampstead. A stone walkway extended from the drive to the front entry. He turned off the motor.

The woman who approached them looked blonde in the halo of light from the front door. She gave her son a quick hug, then held out her hand to Jenny as Colin rounded the bonnet and opened the car door. Her hair was brushed back and gathered loosely in a barrette at the nape of her neck. Some strands had broken free, but she wasn't bothered by them. Her focus was on Jenny. "I am indebted to you," she said, putting her arm around Jenny's waist. "You've brought my son home! How ever did you accomplish that? Colin, I'm putting Jenny in the Rose Room. It's one of the few on the first floor with a private bath," she explained. "We'll let him fuss with the baggage, and you can practice calling me Joanne."

She led Jenny up a wide staircase and into a spacious room with a walnut desk, a dressing table with a vase of fresh flowers on the glass top, and a wardrobe, painted yellow to match the duvet with the embroidered roses. "Colin's room is just down the corridor on the left. When you've freshened up, won't you join us in the drawing room for a bit of cheese and fruit? It's on the ground floor. Down the stairs and to the right."

When Jenny closed the door, she spied a small silk bag hanging on the inside doorknob. Curious, she removed the ribbon that held it closed. There were small soaps, miniature lotions and creams, and tiny sachets, everything with a light floral fragrance. She opened her suitcase, hanging several things in the wardrobe, and then opened the roll-top desk. A small envelope with her name on it contained a note of welcome.

When Jenny woke in the morning, she reflected that if her first night in Kent had gone well, all the credit belonged to Colin's mother. Joanne had offered her a glass of wine to accompany the snack, explaining that she had learnt early in her husband's foreign service to serve alcohol with every official meal, to make any *faux pas* less noticeable. "I made all the mistakes in the book, culinary and conversational, but somehow Cameron was successful in spite of me."

Jenny had laughed and requested a second glass "for insurance," and the ice had been broken. The experienced hostess had made it easy.

She hadn't noticed the bay window in her bedroom the night before, but now the sun was shining through it, giving an amber cast to the floral shapes etched in it. "No alarm clocks here," Joanne had said. "Agnes, my cook, doesn't do breakfast. I do—so just follow the smell of burnt toast when you're ready and we'll be there."

Following their morning cups of tea, Joanne gave her a tour of the house. Jenny lost count of the number of rooms—sitting rooms with high ceilings and wide windows as well as a drawing room, a library with a marble fireplace, a kitchen with an adjoining breakfast room, a formal dining room, and a conservatory—and that was just the ground floor. Adult bedrooms and baths occupied the first floor, and children's spaces were above that. Grand in size, the house was, however, not grand in décor. The Sinclairs' years abroad yielded a blend of cultures, a tapestry here, an interesting rug there, or a piece of pottery too individual to have sprung from an English bone china designer. "Most countries had a speciality," Joanne said. "Some diplomatic wives could even decipher your postings from your furnishings. I'll let Colin show you the grounds."

Summer in Kent felt like early spring in Texas. Colin took her past the cultivated gardens near the house, through the greenhouse, and down to the stables, empty during his lifetime, because there were such long periods when the house was vacant. They made a long circuit through groves of trees. She could identify only the oaks and sycamores. Colin had to point out the rest: walnuts, hawthorns, chestnuts, and yews. Willows—very different from the weeping willows with which Jenny was familiar—and poplars. How far did the property extend? She saw no fences.

After a soup-and-salad lunch, they exited the house and walked in the other direction. "Now you know why I live where I do," he told her. "The Heath reminds me of home." They sat down beside the duck pond and watched the swimmers glide past. "Jenny, I want you to know—I have resources beyond my police salary. Whatever you want, whatever you need, I'll give it to you."

"Has this property been in your family a long time?"

"Generations."

"It will all be yours?"

"It's mine now. Upon my death it will belong to my children, if I have any. If not, to my sister's children."

"Do you want children?"

"Yes, very much."

"Colin, I'm a commoner. What in the world are you doing with me?"

"Jenny, I'm a policeman. What are you doing with me?"

"Looking for a new life."

His blue eyes spoke of cloudless days. "I can grant that wish, Jenny."

Dinner was served in the formal dining room, its serenity the closest to a true British ambience that Jenny could imagine. Ivory, pale gray, and almond had been blended throughout, so the only colors in the room came from the decorative plates on the shelves, the food, the wine, and Colin's eyes. He took her hand before asking the Anglican blessing: "Our heavenly Father, we thank Thee for all the blessings of this life, and ask Thee to make us ever mindful of and responsive to the needs of others." Joanne used her gold and white china, and Jenny thought that she—or Agnes—could teach Brian a thing or two: carrot soup with orange zest was followed by mixed salad and sorbet. The main course was roast pork, served with apples and sugar-snap peas.

Joanne entertained them throughout with stories of life abroad. Often you couldn't communicate with your foreign cook, she said, so you mastered a few basic recipes and demonstrated how to make them: one with chicken, one meatless casserole, and a plethora of rice recipes, because rice didn't spoil. "I'm never making another fruit mousse," she laughed. "We're having raspberry tarts instead. I've made mango mousse, apricot mousse, peach mousse, you name it—I learnt the art of substitution."

After-dinner coffee came in *demitasse* cups with a small square of fudge on the saucer.

"You *had* to have people in," Joanne continued, "no matter what foods you were lacking or how many place settings you had to borrow from the neighbours, because you wanted to make friends. When the children were with us, I made friends through them, but when they went back to England to boarding school, I joined the women's club. There were exercise classes, arts and crafts, even foreign languages, although for some reason the language of the host country was rarely offered."

"Was it hard to send your children away?" Jenny asked.

"Oh, yes, but they came for holidays, and of course we had annual leave. It was more difficult seeing the conditions the local children endured. We all participated in charitable projects, but you could not impact their poverty in any meaningful way."

"How long were your husband's postings?"

"On paper four years each, but in practice that varied widely. Some of the places where we lived were lovely, but we always shared our house with some sort of creature—in fact, many times I think the creatures shared their house with us! I enjoyed our time abroad, but I was always glad to come home." She smiled. "Colin's rolling his eyes at me. Time for me to stop my chatter."

Jenny and Colin helped with the washing up. "Sunday dinner's at midday," Joanne said. "I'll finish here."

Colin sent Jenny for her sweater, then took her hand and led her outside. The night was clear, and the stars so bright that she felt she could feel their warmth. No, it must have come from Colin's kisses.

"How did you do it?" Jenny wanted to know over the Sunday meal. "Move so many times, start over so many times?"

They had finished the watercress soup and were savoring roast lamb with mint sauce, fresh asparagus, and baked tomatoes. Joanne had explained the trinity that underlay most soups and sauces in England: carrots, onions, and potatoes.

"COP," Jenny laughed. She countered with the southwestern trio of bell pepper, onion, and garlic.

Colin leant back in his chair and watched the two women bond. It was what he had hoped for. His ex-wife had never been interested in his mother's stories. Violet—tall, slender, blonde, an only child who thought his choice of profession was exotic and assumed he'd settle down eventually into a more socially acceptable role. In point of fact, she was grooming him to work with her father, who had a very successful distillery and no sons to take it on when he retired. She had misjudged him. They had misjudged each other, actually.

"I took my faith with me, but sometimes I thought I would wear my sense of humour out," Joanne said. "There were negatives about every locale but compensations, too—things that helped you look past your immediate circumstances, like a beautiful countryside or adventures that kept your heart in your throat."

"I've had a few of those," Jenny admitted, and Colin was amazed that she had referred to her experience, however obliquely.

"Friendships formed in adversity, last," Joanne said. "Besides—I mastered Scrabble! One of the few games you could play by candlelight, when the power had failed."

"And your husband?"

"Cam loved what he was doing, and I loved him. I would have followed him anywhere." She paused, running her finger across the wedding band she still wore. "I did follow him, everywhere I could. This last time—I couldn't go where he went."

Jenny's throat was tight. "I'm sorry," she whispered. "I cry so easily now."

"Some things are worth crying about, aren't they?" Joanne answered gently. She glanced at her son, whose eyes were on Jenny. He wants to go to her, and I should make myself scarce and let him. "Pudding coming straightaway," she said and took a bit longer in the kitchen than was necessary. Jenny was the first girl Colin had spoken of—not to mention, brought home—since that minx Violet had left him. She had never loved Violet, but she wished Jenny had some of her self-assurance. Colin was clearly enthralled with her, and she was so tentative.

The final course was fresh strawberries with a vanilla cream sauce that Jenny found delicious. When Joanne confessed that it was an upscale brand of vanilla ice cream, melted, they laughed almost until they cried. Of course, the wine that had been consumed during the feast might have had something to do with it, as well as the loving acceptance that Joanne brought to every meal she served.

They lingered over their coffee, and Colin thought again about how different Jenny was from his ex-wife. Violet had always been in a hurry to leave his mother's table, remaining only as long as was necessary to fulfil her familial commitment. Her bag would have been packed long ago, and only her extraordinary self-discipline would have kept her from drumming her fingers in her lap. He saw Jenny smile and touch his mother's hand and knew he could forgive Vi now.

- -

Jenny was quiet on the drive back to Hampstead. She had a new list for her journal: *Things I Learned from Colin's Mother. Family matters most* was the first item, followed by, *Having friends helps.* So many more, though: *Be resourceful; Take the long view; Starting over is a part of life and not necessarily a bad thing;* and, *Happiness can be found anywhere if you love the man you're with.* She'd learned why Colin wasn't affected by the disorder around him—as a child, there had been chaos in nearly every third world country they'd lived in. Corruption was rife in countries with unstable political systems. No wonder he was so committed to the process of justice now!

Joanne kept a journal, too, filled with simple sketches of recreational activities she'd shared with her children. She'd given Jenny a drawing of a preadolescent Colin flying a kite, one of the last times he'd been unrestrained, she said, because after he'd started boarding school, he'd been so serious about modelling adult behaviour. She'd also presented her with a photograph of him in his constable's uniform, taken just after he'd completed the introductory course of instruction at the academy. With a hug and a promise to invite Colin's sister, Jillian, and her family the next time Jenny came, she had let them go.

CHAPTER 10

Jenny woke up thinking about Colin's caresses. She had wanted more. She dressed, wondering as she donned each item what it would feel like when he removed it. A whole new set of feelings welled up inside her: excitement, joy, anticipation. She was giddy, laughing out loud, wanting to celebrate because she was in love. Should she call him? No, this was too big a deal for that—and besides, she wanted to see his face when she told him. And if they were together, then physical love would follow. Wouldn't it? That was scary, but thrilling too. She decided to get a bottle of wine. She could find her way to the High Street; there was bound to be a place there that would have some. After dinner she'd ask him to open it and she'd tell him how she felt, if she could wait that long! She picked up the keys and left the flat.

It was the first time she had been out by herself. The High Street hadn't seemed far when she had been with Colin, but now each step led her farther from the safety of his flat. She didn't find a liquor store or grocery right away and had to ask at the bookstore where the closest supermarket was. Sainsbury's, she was told, on Finchley Road. She didn't know where that was, so she bought a map of Hampstead.

That almost defeated her. She'd have to retrace her steps to Colin's flat and then start out in another direction. She tried to recapture her happy feelings but succeeded only in feeling exposed. No one was paying any attention to her, she was sure, but nevertheless she hurried.

The store was crowded, and there were long shelves of wine. First she had daydreamed the time away, then she had gone the wrong way, and now she was rooted to the spot, not being able to choose from the many varieties. She remembered some of the names from her list of *Wines I Have Enjoyed With Colin,* but there were so many brands which bore those titles. She closed her eyes and purchased the one her outstretched fingers touched.

Now all she had to do was follow the map to Colin's and she'd be home free. Her first solo flight—she'd been scared, but she had done it! When she let herself into the flat, Colin was already there. She had wanted the wine to be a surprise, but he came toward her immediately.

"Where have you been?"

He didn't sound happy. She was startled and short of breath.

"You went out by yourself? For *wine*?" His voice was rising. "We shopped yesterday. How could you do such a thing? What were you thinking?"

Her mouth dropped open. He was angry!

"Answer me!" he yelled. "Why would you take such a risk?"

"What—what risk?" she stammered.

"What risk? Damn it, Jenny!" He shook his head in frustration.

"Colin, you're scaring me." She gripped the bottle of wine tightly. Her mind said, he won't hurt you. Her body said, run! No, she thought, I am not retreating.

He turned aside, took several deep breaths, and ran his fingers through his hair. "What have I done?" he said to himself. He turned back and held up his hands, the fingers spread in a gesture of concession. "Sorry. I just reacted." He let his hands fall to his sides. "Jenny, could we sit down and talk about this?"

She waited until he was seated before occupying the other armchair. She was still holding the bottle of wine. She rested it in her lap, one hand on the neck. The sofa separated them. Now that the shock of his anger had passed, she felt only a sense of sadness.

"Jenny, I was afraid for you. If anything happened to you, I'd never forgive myself. I'm terribly concerned for your safety."

She tried to clear her throat. "Why? It's over. Isn't it?"

He didn't answer right away, and her dread deepened. She had thought her fear was irrational. "I don't know," he said finally. "When Scott's verdict was read, he threatened you. I've heard other threats made in anger, but none had the intensity of this one. I didn't think I should take it lightly."

The fear in her chest had nothing to do with Colin now.

"Jenny—when you were in protection, things happened on the outside, things that would have frightened you. You had been through so much. We wanted to protect you in every way we could, so we didn't tell you everything. Please understand."

"That was then. Now we are supposed to be equals. How—if you love me—could you bring me back to danger?"

Her words cut him to the quick. "It was one of the most selfish things I have ever done."

"How bad is it?"

"Revenge is a powerful force. It's possible I overreacted, however. Protecting you has become a habit, but the more time that passes, the less likely any retaliation will be." He noticed suddenly the bottle in her lap. "Why did you buy the wine, Jenny?"

She looked at it as if it were a foreign thing. "It doesn't matter now." She put the bottle on the floor.

He stood slowly. "Will you let me hold you?"

She felt his arms around her and discovered that it was possible to feel alone in someone's embrace.

CHAPTER 11

The same question that haunted Jenny all evening returned with a vengeance in the morning. What should she do?

"Why do you need to do anything?" Colin had asked.

Because doing something—anything—meant that she was not powerless.

He had tried to explain about the double standard in detective work: Find out *everything* but release information only on a need-to-know basis to anyone outside the investigation. It was hard to shift gears, and married officers sometimes took that attitude home with them, almost always to their detriment. It wasn't just the long, sometimes unpredictable hours that made married life difficult for coppers. The contrast between the need for discretion on the Job and the need for openness at home contributed, a continual tug of war between what could be said and what could not.

She had called it the I-need-to-know-but-you-don't attitude, and she didn't like it.

Simon's call was a welcome distraction. After lunch he took her to St. Paul's Cathedral, and she was sure that her awe at what she saw concealed her unusual quietude. The Grand Canyon was vast, but that was God's creation. This magnificence was man's achievement, the vision Sir Christopher Wren's, and the execution, thousands of nameless artisans. This cathedral had been an inspiration since its construction, and it still conveyed a sense of holiness to those who entered. People trod softly on the marble floor, and their voices had a respectful hush.

She was touched by the memorial to the American servicemen who had died defending Britain in World War II. They passed the tombs of the Duke of Wellington, Lord Nelson, even Florence Nightingale. T. E. Lawrence's statue was labeled with his movie name, Lawrence of Arabia! And there was a bust of George Washington, who had surely been regarded as a renegade on these shores. Simon asked if she'd like to climb to the whispering gallery, but when she heard how many steps there were, she shook her head, not confident that she had the energy after tossing and turning all night.

They stopped for a cold drink at a sandwich shop nearby. She had given him a brief description of her trip to Kent on the tube ride to the city. Now he wanted to know more. "Talk to me. You're not yourself."

How could she? If he had to deal with a crisis every time they were together, he would not want to take her places any more.

He switched his voice to the tone she could not ignore.

"Colin lost it yesterday," she answered. "I've never seen him so angry. I'd gone out by myself. That was what brought it on. He'd never told me about the monster's threat."

"Your safety has been his primary consideration."

"You protected me, too," she commented. "Would you have lied to me?"

If lying meant not disclosing everything, yes. "Jenny, you have to sort things out with him. You're part of a couple now. That means you don't take decisions by yourself."

"He did."

"Water over the dam. Time for us to move out."

CHAPTER 12

Colin came toward the door as she opened it. "Jenny, I feared you'd gone. Or that something had happened to you."

"We need to talk, Colin."

"Indeed we do." He gestured toward the sofa. "What were you doing with Casey?"

"Touring St. Paul's," she answered with a frown. "Are you going to attack me for that?" Her chin went up. "I needed a friend today. He was your friend, too, if you must know. He defended you."

"Jenny, our dispute has been on my mind all day. I admit I withheld information from you, but I'll not carry the can by myself in this misunderstanding."

"What do you mean?"

"You accused me of bringing you back into danger. That doesn't tally."

"Are you telling me that there's no danger?"

"No. I'm suggesting that you may have suffered from selective memory. We all do, from time to time."

Colin had a Voice, too—a tone of professional detachment. She didn't like it any more than she liked Simon's voices.

"The sniper attack during Bates' trial came *after* Scott's verdict and sentencing. You suspected the source of the threat then. Nothing significant has altered since."

She remembered thinking that the sniper's victim had borne at least a slight resemblance to her and that Simon would neither confirm nor deny it. "Ouch," she said. "That's true." They were sitting only a few feet apart, but she felt as if there were still miles between them, and she didn't know how to bridge the distance. "Feeling safe is important to me. I'm so tired of being afraid. I shouldn't have criticized you for wanting to protect me."

"In my view the risk level is the same. Your whereabouts are still the issue."

Her frustration surfaced. "Oh, please stop sounding like a detective! I can't live here like a prisoner. Help me figure out what to do."

"Do you want to stay?"

"Yes, and I want a job, and I want—chocolate." She gave a shaky laugh, and he felt a weight rise from his shoulders. "I need something to do while you're at work, and I need to make friends. Besides Simon."

That would be a good idea.

"I know I don't have a work permit," she continued, "but couldn't I volunteer somewhere? Somewhere nearby?"

He raised his eyebrows, and she squirmed under his gaze. "Colin, I haven't been completely honest, either. I'm—I'm—afraid to go out by myself. I should have told you, but I didn't want you to know how crippled I was."

No matter—he had already known. "My independent daughter—gone," her father had lamented to him when he was in Houston. "One of us has to take her everywhere she goes."

"Close to home works for me," he assured her. "I'll make some calls for you tomorrow. In the meantime, where would you like to go for dinner? French, Indian, Italian?"

"That Italian restaurant on Heath Street."

While Colin ate his Dover Sole Amalfi, he promised to be proud, not angry, when she left the flat. She feasted on an herb-broiled chicken breast in basil cream sauce and agreed to leave him a note when she did and not to use her credit cards. They'd had a pasta course before their main meal, and the wine they drank was light and smooth. "Why are you willing to stay with me, Jenny?" he asked.

He saw the slow blush. "I can't answer that here," she said.

He put a generous assortment of pound notes on the table and left with her before the coffee and fudge cake had been served. She had trouble keeping up with his long strides. Inside the flat, he took her face in his hands and asked, "Why, Jenny?"

She was still panting from the dash home. "You have to kiss me first."

He was happy to comply.

Her heart was racing. She would never get her breath back! "Because I love you, Colin. Because I love you."

CHAPTER 13

Jenny's confession of love made Sinclair want to celebrate: They had a solid foundation to build on now. He had flown to Texas with no more than a wish and a prayer, fearing that it would take repeated visits to establish the connection he sought. Since she had come home with him, a second prayer had been answered: She loved him. A woman's love is precious, his father had told him. You must safeguard it. He would—he already felt more tenderly toward her than ever before. Yes, there was much to celebrate—the woman he loved, loved him. She—damn! He'd missed his tube stop. This morning he'd have a longer walk to the Yard.

As he took the lift to his floor, he thought about her quest for a meaningful way to spend her time. She would be occupied today watching some of the Wimbledon tennis matches on TV, but the finals would take place on the Sunday, and another week would then stretch in front of her with little to do. He was not unsympathetic with her desire to be productive, but he had come close to losing her on several occasions, and as a result, he had probably overstated the amount of risk she faced. "Downshift!" she'd said. "You're in overdrive!"

Nevertheless, her taking the tube to another part of the city was out of the question. That ruled out museums and universities as sites for her activity. The Hampstead library wasn't large, and he didn't imagine that reshelving books there would be very challenging.

He decided to ring his sister, Jillian. Her husband, Derek Horne, worked in finance in the city, and they were more socially active than he was. Jillian couldn't think of anything offhand that would suit but promised to discuss it with Derek when he came home.

- -

Jenny had had a rough night, and Colin was tired. He leant back in his chair and stretched his limbs to revive them. Years of being called to crime scenes at all hours had made him a light sleeper, so he'd heard her rustling about in the kitchen. She couldn't take pain meds on an empty stomach, she explained, and he'd embarrassed her by asking why she needed them.

Violet's menstrual cycles had always been a surprise to him. Later in their marriage he suspected she used them as a contrivance to keep him at arm's length, but he knew Jenny had no such purpose. She'd been more expressive that evening than ever before.

The jangling of his phone interrupted him. It was Jillian, with good news. "Would Jenny be interested in working in a bookshop? Antiquarian and secondhand books, that sort of thing. A friend of Derek's—an investments counsellor—retired at the end of last year and joined his wife in her venture. They're looking for help."

"Where?"

"It's not far from you, Colin—in Hampstead. Esther and Reginald Hollister are the proprietors, but it's been small beer for years, so you might not know of it. Esther knows books, but Reggie's a businessman. He has secured additional space and plans to use the internet for sales as well." She gave him a phone number. "Reggie's the one who wants to make it a going concern—probably retired from the city too soon, Derek says!"

He could hear children's voices in the background and Jillian remonstrating them. "Derek would have rung him for you, but we didn't know what you'd want him to know about Jenny. By the way, Mother loves her, and we want to meet her. Soon!" The youthful voices were more insistent. "Must run!"

- -

The answer phone had a woman's voice. "Hollister's Books, but we want to make them yours! We're off finding more treats for you to add to your collections. Buying trip to end on Sunday, selling spree to begin on Tuesday. The tea is free! Cheerio!"

CHAPTER 14

Wednesday morning Colin left early for the Yard, and Jenny reviewed the directions he had given her for finding Hollister's Books. It was about ten minutes' walk from the flat, in an area of Hampstead not too far from Royal Free Hospital. The gold script with the owner's name sparkled in the morning sun, and the broad windows beneath the marquee would let in as much of the natural light that the London climate could provide. When she entered, she felt as if she had stepped into someone's sitting room. The ratio of books to furniture was a little skewed, but care had been taken in the selection of love seats, chairs, small tables, and shaded lamps that would make the shop seem cozy on cloudy days. "Hello?" she called. No one was in sight.

"Yes, yes, here we are," a voice replied. "Look, Reggie, it's our volunteer! Our regular clientele are never here this soon after opening," she explained.

Jenny smiled as the superficially mismatched couple approached. Mrs. Hollister—"No, no, you must call me Esther,"—was a spare, big-boned woman with a baggy dress and flyaway gray hair. Her husband, who did not immediately encourage Jenny to address him by his first name, was short and nearly bald. His clothes were tailored but sufficient to cover his substantial girth.

He and his wife started to talk at the same time. "I haven't got used to Reggie being about all the time," Esther laughed. "I've had this little investment since the children started school, and that was years ago! Reggie has been involved just since the beginning of the year."

"Essie, Miss Jeffries isn't interested at all in your history."

"It's Jenny, and I am."

"Ladies first, then," he said graciously.

Esther Hollister gestured as she narrated. "Nonfiction downstairs, fiction upstairs, all arranged according to category, except for the first editions on the north wall, well away from the sun. I can't permit any damage to be done to my little lovelies!"

Jenny had always been more concerned with what was printed on the pages, but she couldn't deny that some of the Hollisters' books were beautiful. Esther opened one case and handed Jenny a leather-bound volume with gilt-edged pages and marbled end sheets.

"Some of these are purchased more for home decoration than for consumption," she said. "To make a room appear more masculine or complement its colour scheme. Isn't that sad? Books are lonely if they're not opened, I think." They squeezed past a ladder on wheels. "Reggie's idea," Esther continued. "I never had any difficulty reaching the top shelves, but he feels that if we're an antiquarian shop, we should look the part."

They arrived at the back of the store. "Here's the children's area. I wanted it at first so my little terrors would be occupied while I worked, but mothers seem to appreciate the fact that they are welcome with their children, and to be honest, they almost always buy a book for their little ones before they leave, so I sell twice as much. Although this section of the store stays a bit unruly, you can't see it from the street, so it's not a deterrent to those who don't have youngsters."

They had completed the tour of the ground floor, passing a small bathroom and an equally small workroom.

"My turn, dear?" Mr. Hollister asked. He turned to Jenny. "We have two target groups, the visibles and the invisibles. Essie prefers to deal with the visibles, those who come into the shop. You'll be helping her periodically to stock the shelves with our new acquisitions and to remove the ones that are past their prime."

"I've never met a book that was past its prime," Esther said.

"The rest of the time, you'll be working on the computer." He led the little group upstairs. A desktop computer rested on one end of a glossy wooden table. Matching wooden file cabinets stood underneath and to one side. Jenny smiled. These modern furnishings could not be seen from the street, any more than the cluttered children's area could. "I've had a website designed and installed. I'm now in the process of entering all the books in our inventory online."

"Your invisible buyers," Jenny commented.

"Exactly so," Mr. Hollister agreed. "Of course, whenever a book is sold, the inventory online must be updated. Periodic printouts can tell us when a book came in, when it sold, which categories are the best performers, and so forth. Are we pricing our books correctly? Internet searches can answer that question. Keeping a record of our expenses on each buying trip will show whether such excursions are profitable. I've already begun to scan online sources for reviews of books that may be interesting. Expanding our stock via online purchases could be more economical."

"Reggie, a book must be held," Esther said. "A book has its own personality. You won't be able to tell from your computer whether a book will belong here."

"At the very least," Mr. Hollister continued, "I'd like to be able to order books online for our visible customers, notify them by e-mail when a special order has come in—"

"Enough!" Esther exclaimed. "You'll discourage Jenny before she has even started."

Mr. Hollister cordially relented.

"We're just back from a trip," Esther said. "I priced our new selections yesterday, and if you'll help me put them on the shelves, you can familiarise yourself with our system and make friends with some of our long-standing residents."

"Miss Jeffries, how much time will you be willing to give us?"

"I can come in most afternoons during the week. No weekends."

They heard a bell tinkle. "Gracious, there's our first guest, and I don't even have the music on," Esther said. "Jenny, if you see a book you like, you may borrow it. In the meantime, could you turn on the radio in the little office downstairs? And there's a fridge there if you'd like to have a cold drink. And we always have the kettle on for tea."

Jenny couldn't wait to tell Colin about the Hollisters, how Esther wanted to hold the books and Mr. Hollister wanted to catalog them. How Esther loved to talk to her "guests" and didn't pressure them to buy, although her enthusiasm for her "little charges" usually had a positive result.

Mr. Hollister knew that technology was necessary to help a business grow. He didn't mind nudging the customer toward the cash register. "The furniture encourages indecisiveness," he'd said. "Let 'em stand, and they'll say aye or nay faster." He placed a high premium on accuracy, but that didn't bother her. Besides, with his emphasis on technical information, he would be less likely than his wife to ask personal questions. They were the first two people Jenny had met who didn't know how she'd spent her last year, and she wanted to keep it that way.

CHAPTER 15

Jenny had only worked at Hollister's several days, and already it was a big plus. She was happier, and Colin was the beneficiary. When he opened the door to his flat, she greeted him with a hug and a smile. And the way she kissed him: He would give "all his worldly worth for this; / To waste his whole heart in one kiss."

"You and Tennyson," she laughed.

The weekend weather was glorious, and during their Saturday walk on the Heath, she had asked about birth control, accepting his assurance that he would see to it. That night after they'd been involved for a few minutes, she surprised him by asking if he wanted to go into the bedroom. He did, very much. They'd already shed their shirts, and she lifted her arms so he could remove her bra. "Jen, you're beautiful," he said, kissing her. She stepped out of her jeans. He stretched out next to her and took her in his arms. "I want to make love to you," he whispered.

"Colin, yes," she gasped. He began to undo his belt. She went suddenly still. He heard a strangled sound and looked up.

"Stop—you have to stop!" she cried, rolling away from him. The tightness in her chest made it hard to breathe. "I can't, I can't!"

It took a moment for his shock to pass. "Jenny, did I do something wrong?"

"No—I don't know—all of a sudden—like someone flipped a switch—I was afraid—of being naked—of what you'd do—"

"Jen, I wouldn't hurt you."

"I know. I shouldn't have panicked."

"What now?"

She shivered. "I think I need to get dressed."

He collected her clothes. She pulled them on haphazardly, and he watched her go. In a few minutes he heard her shower running. He took his own shower then decided to check on her. "Jen, we should talk."

He looked so handsome standing there, the light from the sitting room behind him. His voice was gentle. How could she have pushed him away? Her failure gripped her chest like a vise. "Do you want to call it quits? Do you want to send me away?"

He went to her. "Jen, of course not—why would you think such a thing?"

"Because I can't satisfy you. I wanted to, and I couldn't."

"Jenny—Jen—I love you. I'm not going to desert you at the first sign of trouble."

"Colin, I wish—I wish—"

"Jenny, listen to me. I want to give you pleasure. If the pleasure stops, then I'm going to stop." A frightening thought occurred to him. "Jen, do you want out? Do you want to go?"

She shook her head.

"Then let's see this through. Every couple has problems—this is ours, that's all."

She leaned against his chest, and she felt safe in spite of everything. "Colin, I love you so much. You made me feel—wonderful. I wanted you very badly. I don't know where it went."

"Jenny, we'll try again, when you want to. But I want you to know—the further we go, the better it will be. For both of us." He reached out and caressed her face, running the tips of his fingers across her cheeks and lips. "The loving feelings between a man and a woman make sex beautiful, Jenny. It'll happen for us."

On Saturday evening, after a second disappointment, Colin held her close, wishing his kisses could comfort her.

"Why isn't love enough?" she sobbed.

"Because love and trust are both required."

"But I trust you with my life!"

"This is a different level of trust. When a woman opens herself to a man, she is at her most vulnerable. I'm not surprised you're having trouble—I know what you've been through. It's bound to affect you." She had calmed somewhat. "I owe you an apology, Jen. I promised you an old-fashioned courtship. Perhaps it would help if you knew what my intentions are: marriage and family."

Her mouth fell open. "Is that a proposal?"

He smiled. "An informal one."

"How can you ask me that when I've just failed you?"

"Because you haven't failed. Because I love you and believe in you. I know the sort of determination you have. I've fancied you for a long time, and I want us to have a life together, here and hereafter."

"You believe in that?"

"God is infinite, Jenny—infinite in power, infinite in love, infinite in second chances. Would He give us a limited life? I don't think so."

She rested her head against his chest, soothed by the sound of his heart and his voice.

"The Bible says that faith is hope made certain. I think commitment makes love certain. You don't have to give me an answer now, though. It takes time to heal."

"Colin, I love you so much."

"I'm going to enjoy buying you jewellery—an engagement ring to start, when you're ready."

She sat up suddenly, and a giggle escaped her. "So that's why you gave me an empty jewelry box!"

Just one of the parts of her life he wanted to fill. He kissed her.

CHAPTER 16

Mr. Hollister had been busy. Over the weekend, he had purchased a digital camera. He had spent the Monday asterisking the books on the online inventory list that he wanted a fuller description of. When Jenny came in on Tuesday, he explained that she needed to locate each starred title on the shelf, determine if the cover were sufficiently attractive to stimulate visual interest, and if so, insert the photo of it into the computer before adding the rest of the requisite information. He wanted a greater percentage of sales among the more expensive volumes and hoped this special treatment could bring that result. Clearly no grass was going to grow under Mr. Hollister's feet—this was only her fifth day at work, and he was already procuring equipment for her use. She wondered how many of the photographed selections would have to sell to pay for it.

"Jenny, there's a man here to see you," Esther called out.

She hurried down the stairs. It was Simon. She looked at her watch. He must be on his way to report in. She introduced him to Mrs. Hollister. "Could I take a short break?"

"By all means," Esther said, noting the policeman's stern expression and wondering if she should endeavor to keep them in the shop. "May I bring you both a cup of tea?"

"No, ma'am, thank you, but we'll be going for a walk." He took Jenny's arm.

Esther watched them go. Reggie had said a Chief Inspector Sinclair had recommended Jenny. This young officer was a sergeant. Had the chief inspector introduced Jenny to his colleagues?

Simon guided her up South End Road and into the Heath's South Hill Park. The path was lined on both sides with lofty plane trees in their summer fullness. A young man in faded blue jeans walked by, his dog more eager to reach the park than his master. She saw a toddler in pink overalls welded to her mother's hand.

"What's the news about your family?" she asked.

"My mum's a sister now. A senior nurse," he explained.

"You come by your medical talent honestly," she decided. "And your brother?"

"Martin's just received orders to *HMS York*. He's a sonar tech. That's his warfare specialty."

"When can I meet him?"

"He won't have leave for a while, but that's okay. He sounds like the sailor he is—salty language. Might upset you."

"Still protecting me?" she teased. "Have you been busy lately? At work?"

"No, my team's spare at the moment, but we still need to be ready for the off."

"Speak English, please," she said, wanting to keep him talking, to feel a connection. He must be relaxed or he wouldn't have lapsed into the vernacular, but her recent difficulties with physical communication made oral communication critical.

"Spare—extra, backup. But you have to have your equipment and your mind prepared. If a call comes, you may have to move fast. No time to think. You go on automatic." He paused. "It's strange. After hours of training—extended briefings—long waits—a deployment may be over in seconds." She wasn't looking at him. "You're tense. Has something happened?" They stepped off the path, and he put his arm loosely around her shoulders. "No one will pay us any mind, love."

She leaned into him. "Simon, I'm in trouble. Don't laugh—but I've been feeling so normal! I have a job, I go shopping, I cook dinner."

"Those are important steps."

"But not enough. Real couples do more than that."

He knew all about what real couples did.

"We were—close—and then I was afraid, and—and—"

He waited, knowing, not wanting to know.

"I—I couldn't do it. All I could think of was getting away."

He was glad Sinclair had been patient. Glad Sinclair had been denied. "Did he do anything you didn't want him to do?"

She shook her head.

"Was he angry, Jenny?"

It was The Voice, but it was a comfort, because that voice always knew what to do. "No, and I hurt him. I never thought anything could hurt so much. I need to find a way to get through it."

"No, Jenny. If a man fancies a woman, he wants her to fancy him as well, not endure him." He took a deep breath. She had changed her shampoo. Her hair smelled like peaches. "Physical love is very important to a man," he said quietly. "A man needs—"

"An outlet?"

Sometimes, yes, but he didn't want to think of her as someone's outlet. "More than that. A man needs to know that he is desired."

"I felt that, until—until—the last step," she whispered.

"Jenny, the last step is the most important one."

"If I could learn to take it, wouldn't that be enough?"

She spoke of it like a punishment. "Not if he loves you. It wouldn't be enough for me."

Her tears welled up, and she dug in her pocket for a tissue. Simon never had any handkerchiefs.

"Jenny, there's no easy answer here. You have more to overcome than most women."

"Then the monster wins," she said bleakly.

They walked a little farther into the park. "No, but you're going to need help. What about Knowles?"

"I wish I didn't need Dr. Knowles. I wish the monster were dead!"

If he ever had the chance, he'd rip his heart out.

They turned back toward the bookstore. "I promised my father I'd get help and I haven't. Things were going well. I thought I could handle it all by myself."

"Haven't I taught you anything? Don't go it alone. Better to combine forces."

Alone—that's what she was a lot of the time. Most days only strangers spoke to her, except for Colin and now the Hollisters. She remembered how Simon had rubbed her hand long ago, and she took his now, wanting to connect with someone. Combine forces. "Thank you, Simon. For telling me the truth. For not showing pity."

Esther Hollister watched them through the picture window. The young policeman did not kiss Jenny. She could not tell whether the hug he gave her was a romantic one. What was the relationship between these two?

CHAPTER 17

Colin and Jenny tried varying the setting and the approach to their lovemaking, to no avail. Less light, more light, glass of wine, no wine—none of it made a difference. Each time there came a point beyond which she could not go, and each time she felt worse, because she couldn't accept his proposal if this problem weren't solved. Marry a man you couldn't make love to? Their wedding night would be a disaster. She was desperate, alternately at war with and grieving over the actions of her body. "Colin, I want to see Dr. Knowles."

Relieved, he had rung the psychiatrist. "Jenny's back," he said. "We're serious about each other, but she's having trouble with the physical side of our relationship. She wants to follow through, but her passion turns to fear, and her physical responses shut down. She's willing to come in."

"Are you?"

"Sorry?"

"Colin, this problem concerns both of you. I trust you want to be part of the solution?"

"I do, yes. We'll need to come after hours, then."

Friday evening Colin and Jenny arrived at Dr. Knowles' office. He greeted them both in the reception area before asking Colin to stand by for a few minutes. "There are some questions I need to ask Jenny by herself," he explained.

She stepped into the consulting room and looked around. Good place to crash and burn—all the upholstered furniture would give her a soft landing.

Knowles closed the door and seated himself across from her. "Jenny, how did you come to be here?"

"I went home after the last trial, but it didn't work out. I missed Colin so much! When he offered me the chance to come back, I took it."

"Returning was entirely your choice?"

"Yes, and then I fell in love with him, but love isn't enough. I want to show him how I feel, and I can't."

"Jenny, he is committed to you, but he is also accustomed to being in charge. Did he push you to have a physical relationship before you were ready?"

"No. One minute I wanted him more than anything, and the next minute this wave of fear kicked in out of nowhere, and all the good feelings went away. Dr. Knowles, I've hurt him so badly. You have to help me."

"I'll ask him to come in then." He opened the door and beckoned to Colin, who stopped pacing and joined them.

Knowles collected a clipboard and pen. "Jenny, I hope you won't mind if I make a note or two while we're speaking. In our previous meetings, we made reference to your attack by William Scott, but we didn't examine it fully. That's where we need to start, I think."

"Why? The trial is over, and he was convicted."

"It's likely your attack is the primary source of the problem. Trauma doesn't disappear quickly. It is imprinted on the brain and reflected in the body. Untreated symptoms can last for years."

Her face fell. "But I want to leave that part of my life behind."

Victims of violence often avoided discussing the acts they had endured. "Jenny, I don't believe that's possible without counselling, but I'd like to reassure you. Saying the words aloud may be frightening, but they won't recreate the event. My purpose is to bring to light the feelings you have associated with it."

"Can't you just teach me to relax?"

"If you proceed physically when you're not ready emotionally, you will be further traumatised."

She shook her head in frustration. "Are you telling me I'll get worse?"

"I hope our work together will avert that, but the choice to participate in these sessions, as well as how you participate, is yours."

Colin took her hand. "I'm here to support you," he said softly. "Tell him."

She sighed. "I had been drugged. When I woke up, I was naked, nauseated, and cold. It was completely dark, and I couldn't tell where I was. I've never been so scared."

"Go on."

She took a deep breath. "When the monster came in, the first thing that struck me about him was how angry he was. He nearly beat me to death. I don't ever want to feel that powerless again. My pain didn't matter. My screams didn't matter. I didn't matter." She looked down at her hand, still locked in Colin's, and began to cry. "Colin, I'm so sorry. I wish we didn't have to go through all this."

"Jen, you didn't heal physically overnight. It's all right if we're a bit slow at the start."

"Seeing his hands on his belt—I should have known what he meant to do, but I didn't realize he was going to rape me until he unzipped his pants and dropped his boxers. How stupid is that? I was naked!"

"Not stupid at all," Knowles countered. "How could you possibly predict the actions of a madman?" He waited for her to regain control. "Why do you call your attacker the monster? Do you ever refer to him by name?"

She shook her head. "It would humanize him." Colin handed her his handkerchief, and she smiled in spite of herself. He had an unending supply! At least now she was laundering them.

"You've made a good start." He set his clipboard aside. "Now it's my turn to talk a bit. You had a terrifying experience not too long ago, and it made a big impact on your brain. You're intelligent, and your brain learnt very quickly that in certain circumstances you had to focus on survival. In the process some of your feelings found a home where they didn't belong. Our task is to rearrange them a little so that you're not afraid to love the man who loves you."

He reached for a dictionary on a shelf above his desk. "Let's define some terms. Beat: to strike someone repeatedly. Did you do this?"

"No, I couldn't hit him at all."

He thumbed through the pages. "Assault: a violent attack. Did you attack him?"

She shook her head.

"One more. Rape: forcible sex. Did you force Scott to have sex with you?"

"No, of course not."

"Who committed the crimes, Jenny?" Knowles asked.

"He did," she said.

"Yes. Everything he did to you was unlawful. I want to be very clear about who is at fault here." He set the book down. "Are you taking any medication? No? Good. I'll write you a script for a mild anti-anxiety medicine. We're going to relax that brain of yours a bit."

"Now I have a very important point to make. Hear me on this: *You* are in charge of *your* body. For a time your attacker was in charge of it. Then there were doctors and nurses who were in charge, but now *you* are in charge. Not Colin, even though he loves you. And not I, because although I hope you'll follow my recommendations, I can't and won't make you. Do you understand?"

"Yes."

"Next, I'm going to give you a homework assignment. I want your physical relationship to be completely nonthreatening, so I'd like you to restrict yourselves to touching each other above the waist only. Let me be very clear: No caresses of any kind below the waist. Absolutely no attempt at intercourse." He saw Jenny give Colin an apologetic look. "It's not as clinical as it sounds. I don't want to limit your love, just your expression of it."

She had not maintained eye contact.

"Accept that this may be a stressful time. Do special things together outside the bedroom." He picked up his calendar. "Will the same time next week be convenient for you?"

"No," Colin answered. "We need to vary the day. I'll ring you."

"One final question. Jenny, who is in charge of your body?"

She raised her chin. "It appears that you are, Dr. Knowles."

"No, Jenny. My role is to work with you, to ease the pressure you are putting on yourself."

Colin reached for her hand. "I'm okay with this, Jen."

Deep in thought, Knowles watched them go. She equates darkness with danger, sex with pain and brokenness, and nakedness with being vulnerable and afraid. Against this lineup stood his training and experience and their love and trust.

CHAPTER 18

On Saturday Colin decided to spend time with Jenny outside the flat. She had expressed an interest in the artists of the impressionist period, so the two of them spent a long afternoon at the Courtauld Institute in Somerset House.

Jenny was surprised at the vitality of the colors in the medieval paintings. The gold leaf still shone! There was an entire room full of works by Rubens, and every room was decorated by more than the artwork displayed. The ceilings were ornate, with carved roundels and chimneypieces as well as sepia-toned paintings.

She was fascinated by Van Gogh's Self-Portrait with Bandaged Ear. "I guess I'm fixated on people with injuries, but he looks like he's still hurting! I wonder why he painted himself. I wouldn't have wanted anyone to paint me when I was covered with gauze from head to toe."

They feasted on the genius of Monet, Gaugin, and Cezanne. Colin was a bit ahead of her when he heard her laugh softly. Curious, he went back.

"Colin, I've just done the silliest thing!" She gestured to the blues and greens in the landscape painting. "See the sunlight on the sides of those mountains? There, and there? It looks so real that I thought it must be coming through a window somewhere, but of course it isn't. The light's in the color of the paint and the strokes of the brush. Amazing!"

Colin had comments of his own to make about some of the works they saw, perceptive comments, and she realized that he must have a visual orientation to life. She supposed having visual acuity was necessary for a good detective, but it disturbed her. How could he accept her scars? On their way back to Hampstead, they stopped for tandoori food, and she asked him about them.

"Jenny, it's just a little white line here and there. I think you see them as worse than they are."

"But there's one on my breast," she whispered.

"Yes, and when I see it, I see what lies beyond it, and all I want is to caress you."

She blushed, and they ate quietly for a few minutes. "My shoulder's bad, though."

He put his fork down. "Jenny, it reminds me how close I came to losing you—how lucky I am to have you—and how much I'll do to protect you. Your scars demonstrate how far you've come. I wouldn't erase them if I could."

Their discussion helped, but she was still upset when they returned to the flat and began their homework assignment. She knew he wanted more physical contact than they were allowed. His approach, however, was to prolong what they could do. He kissed her slowly and deeply. He didn't remove her blouse until he had explored what lay beneath each button. He introduced her to the concept of sensual as opposed to sexual touches.

She learned from him to look, and she liked what she saw of his body. She tried to make each touch a goal in itself, not a means to an end. She resolved to start a new list: *Things Colin Has Taught Me*. She wished she could put *patience* at the top, but she was not patient with the problem that had come between them.

She was downstairs on Tuesday afternoon when Brian came by the bookstore. As a way of escaping the dreary computer work, Jenny had asked if she could make displays with some of the books, beginning with the children's section, since there were so many young visitors to the shop in the summer months.

"Please introduce me to your giant friend," Esther said.

"Brian, meet my boss, Esther Hollister. Esther, this is Brian Davies. PC Davies."

Another policeman. Esther watched the two young people walk up the street toward the coffee shop.

Fortunately there weren't many customers in the coffee shop, and Brian was able to stretch out his legs. "JJ, I want to tell you about Beth. She's a schoolteacher, grew up on a farm near Norwich, like me."

"You mean she knew you when you were small?"

He smiled. "Yes, but when I joined the police, she went to university, and we didn't see each other for a while. She's moved here, though—she found a job teaching juniors."

"Junior high? Young teenagers?"

"No, juniors are younger than that—between seven and eleven. She likes kids."

"She must like you, too," Jenny teased. "Those phone calls you used to get—were they all from her? It must have been difficult, not being able to see her."

"I think it helped, actually. Not being available all the time."

"Did she move to be closer to you?" Jenny had, to be close to Colin, only now they couldn't be close.

"She won't say."

"What does she look like?"

"She's short."

They both laughed. "Brian, you have to do better than that! Give me a policeman's description."

"Right," he smiled. "Twenty-five years old, 5' 4" tall, dark eyes, dark curly hair." He paused and smiled again. "Lovely all over."

"Brian, you're such a good man. I hope she'll love you, if that's what you want."

"That's what I want, JJ."

She had to look away. That was what Colin wanted, to be loved. No, it was what they both wanted, but something inside her had locked up, and she couldn't find the key.

They walked together back to the bookshop. Esther Hollister was still downstairs. Second policeman, second hug. My, this policeman had to bend down a long way to do it!

CHAPTER 19

When Colin and Jenny came for their next appointment with Dr. Knowles, she was not very forthcoming about their week.

"Perhaps this would be a good time to discuss how the issue of sex was handled in your families when you were growing up. What sort of relationship did your parents have with each other? What did they tell you about sex?"

Jenny didn't reply, so Colin began. He was uncomfortable, so his explanation of things was rather abbreviated. "My information came from my father. He explained about the various parts and what they did, just in case I'd got wrong ideas from other boys. He and my mother were very close—moving as many times as they did taught them to depend on each other, to turn to each other first when there was a problem."

Knowles turned to Jenny.

"I can't report the same sort of education. My parents were affectionate with each other, but they didn't talk to me about sex much. My mother told me what a miracle my body was, that it was a privilege and a joy to be a woman. I've never been able to tell her that the monster took it all away."

"What about your brothers?"

"What about them? I don't know what they were told. It doesn't matter now anyway."

The wrinkles around Dr. Knowles' eyes deepened. "Colin, did your father address the issue of consent?"

"He didn't call it that. He simply said that force had no place in any relationship between a man and a woman. A man's superior physical strength brings responsibility, not licence."

"And your first sexual experience?"

"She was older, and she was willing. I was grateful."

Knowles smiled and turned to Jenny. She wasn't smiling. "Jenny, you're here because you're afraid of intercourse. Would you allow me to give you some information about it?"

"What's the point?" she asked. "I was raped. What else do I need to know about what a man does?"

Knowles lifted an eyebrow. How does he do it, she wondered—look concerned but not worried? Do they teach that in shrink school? They probably have a whole course in it: "Facial Expressions Permitted in Psychotherapy." If so, Dr. Knowles had aced it. She wondered what her facial expression was revealing. Probably exasperation. She didn't need a biology lesson. She didn't need to be told why rape hurt. She needed to be told how to forget it. "I want—to get through it," she said.

"And I want you to give yourself some time. You may choose to allow Colin to touch you anywhere. I would, however, recommend strongly that he remain clothed, at least below the waist. I want you to feel safe enough to experience consistent sexual arousal."

"Colin, you deserve better than this."

"Jen, you are thirteen years younger than I am. Do you have any idea how good that is for my ego?"

"Colin," Knowles asked, "are you willing to participate in a sexual relationship that will be a bit one sided for a time?"

"I am, yes."

CHAPTER 20

Colin kept Jenny away from the flat most of the weekend. He took her to a flower show, for an Italian meal, and to an open-air concert. She liked the vistas of the Heath and the fresh smell the breeze brought, particularly after a light shower. She linked her arm with his, confiding that she much preferred their long walks to Simon's exercises. Sunday brought the final stage of the Tour de France, and she was delighted with the result: Lance Armstrong—an American and a Texan!—won.

In another arena, however, the news was not as good. Bill Jeffries had rung late in the day to report a series of phone calls they'd received, possibly innocuous and unrelated, but all concerning Jenny. He had taken the first, allegedly from a credit card company wanting to extend additional credit to her and asking for her address. He'd told the caller that she didn't need a higher limit.

He'd thought no more about it even when the second call had come, several days later. Prescott University was engaged in a fund-raising campaign, and each graduating class was competing for the highest percentage of participation. Peggy hadn't given any information about Jenny to the caller, simply requesting that the donor contribution card be mailed to their Houston home.

Matt had taken the third call. It was a young woman, purporting to be a friend of Jenny's. Matt had simply said that she'd gone back to London. He didn't know her address. If she wanted it, she'd have to call back and ask his parents.

"I pressed him, Colin," Jeffries said. "He swears he said nothing about you, not your name, your profession, your relationship to Jenny, nothing. Then the fourth call came. It may have been the same person. She sounded friendly, but when I told her that I needed her information so Jenny could contact her, she hung up. I have to confess, I'm suspicious."

"Sir, if someone's asking after her in Houston, she's safer with me," Colin responded. "There is no record of her presence here."

"She hasn't used either of her credit cards," Jeffries noted.

"No, sir. I recommended that they be for emergencies only," Colin said. "I can't tell you how many times a paper trail has led us to the person we're seeking. In Jenny's case, I don't want to give any advantage to an evildoer, however unlikely his existence may be. And sir—thank you for not disclosing this to her." She had too many worries already. She knew he had to hold back during Theo's homework. Some nights their sessions ended with her tears. He would have to find ways to reassure her.

CHAPTER 21

"How did your week go?" asked Dr. Knowles at Colin and Jenny's third therapy session.

"Better than our last appointment," she answered with an apologetic smile. "I really gave you a hard time. I think the medicine has calmed me down some."

"Would you be a bit more specific?"

"Colin discovered all the places I'm ticklish. Will that do? No, I guess not." She glanced at Colin's hands and blushed, remembering. The little exclamations when he saw her completely nude. The pleasure he took from touching her.

"Did you caress him?"

"Yes, as much as I was allowed."

Knowles heard the resentment. "Jenny, this extended activity will enrich your relationship later on. I don't want you to be concerned about being able to satisfy Colin at this time."

"Of course I'm concerned about being able to satisfy him!" she retorted. "He's frustrated, and it's my fault."

"You are not responsible for his frustration, Jenny," Knowles insisted.

"Yes, I am! He touches me, and it's exciting, and then he has to stop. What does that sound like to you?"

"Let me be clear: You are not responsible for *relieving* Colin's frustration. At this point in your therapy, you are responsible only for *your* feelings." Jenny's frown revealed her impatience, but she did not argue aloud. "Now I'd like to discuss one of the issues identified by your description of your attack: anger. Have you ever seen Colin angry?"

"Yes," she answered, squirming in her chair. "He yelled at me because I went out by myself."

"Am I missing something here?" Knowles asked. "Colin, why would that make you angry?"

"I made a series of mistakes. When Scott heard the verdict, he threatened her life, and I didn't disclose it to her. She was still in witness protection, of course, but I didn't mention it even after she returned to London with me. I didn't want her to go out by herself, but I didn't tell her that, either. Instead I tried to make it unnecessary, by shopping with her when we'd been out for dinner, for example. I came home from work one day, and she was gone. When she came in a bit later with a bottle of wine, I couldn't believe she'd taken such a risk for a frivolous reason. It was an overreaction on my part, but I did yell at her."

"Jenny?"

"Talk about going from high to low! I was desolate. It took a couple days and some stern guidance from Simon before we worked it out."

"He advised the two of you?"

"No, he advised me," she said.

Knowles looked at her thoughtfully. "Do you have a support system, my dear?"

"Just the guys. Well, Simon, mainly, but they all keep in touch with me. Esther Hollister's nice—at the bookstore—but she doesn't know anything about my history."

"Jenny," Colin asked, "what was the wine for? You never told me."

She turned to look at him. "A celebration. I'd realized that day that I loved you, and I was planning to tell you over a glass of wine."

He was stunned. "Damn, I'm sorry, Jen. I made a real hash out of it, didn't I?"

"Colin, have there been other times when you were angry at Jenny?"

"Damn," he repeated softly. "Sorry?"

"Other times," Knowles prompted.

"No, but I was close once. After the attack at the courthouse where Sullivan was hurt, she was afraid for the other men and didn't want to be protected any more. Of course that was out of the question."

"What happened?"

"I found a way to make her smile, and that broke the tension. And then I kissed her. I shouldn't have done, but I knew by then that I fancied her, and I'd almost lost her before I'd even had the chance to tell her."

"I remember that," she whispered. "How amazed I was. The hope I felt."

"Tell her now," Knowles said quietly.

Colin pulled his chair closer to her. "In my early years on the Job, I wore a uniform. Uniformed officers are called to deal with all sorts of disturbances, and we all start out wearing a uniform."

She remembered the photo Colin's mother had given her: Colin in his constable's uniform, tall and proud and confident.

"Along with break-ins, burglaries, assaults, and so forth, I saw my share of sudden death. Sometimes it was evident that a death was accidental. Sometimes it wasn't. Even when there was no Who, I wanted to know Why—even before I became a detective, before it was my job to know. And that's when the anger began, anger at the waste, the unnecessary loss of life. The rather macabre humour that coppers develop only masks the horror."

Knowles did not interrupt.

"Later, as a young detective, I was given aspects of a case to investigate. In big cases, the incident room displayed all the avenues of enquiry, but I wasn't involved in the entire picture. I didn't often have much contact with the family of the victim. It wasn't until I became a detective inspector that I played a major role in murder investigations. The families suffer more because so many additional questions are required. Everyone must be looked at, but more questions inflict more pain.

"It's more difficult for the officers as well. The anger becomes more personal. It's anger at a person—or persons—who had the gall to act without considering the consequences for someone else. I was a DI when my father died. Before that time I experienced concern, sometimes deep concern for the families, but I could usually remain detached unless there were children or a woman affected."

He paused for a moment. "After my father died, every case was more difficult, because when I saw a grieving family, I saw myself. No one had killed my father, but the grief was the same, and the loss."

She knew all about grief: It was stubborn. It stayed with you. Just when you thought you had it under control, it flooded you again.

"Then you were found. One of the uniforms on the spot was a rookie, younger than Sullivan, younger than you, Jenny. He thought you were dead. Fortunately you weren't, but there were days at the beginning when it was touch-and-go. Jenny, you were in terrible shape. I saw you suffer, and I thought of my father's suffering. I heard your despair, and I felt my own. You were a witness, and it was my job to interview you, to encourage you to cooperate with us, and to gather all the evidence you could provide. At the same time I wanted to protect you, even from us. I wasn't prepared for the conflict I felt."

"You always looked so tired," she said.

"Many nights I stayed away from the flat where you were. You were recovering, but it was painful for you, and I couldn't watch it. I knew Casey would keep you moving in the right direction."

"Did he ever," she remembered.

"This job means you don't sleep until you get them—the evildoers. When you've got them—charged them—then you rest. You let the victim go." He took a ragged breath. "If you don't get them—if you don't solve it, if you can't fit all the pieces together, and no arrest is made—then you can't let go. The murdered person lives inside you.

"You lived, Jenny, and we charged Scott—but there was something different about you. Early on I had trouble letting go."

"Tell me about the anger," Knowles said, to set him back on track.

"In Jenny's case I felt it when I first saw her in hospital. So broken, so alone. I was angry at the monster who was responsible, even before I knew who he was. When Scott was identified, I was outraged. His upbringing hadn't been different to my own. He was privileged. He had a mandate to care for the less fortunate, and he had disgraced it."

He turned back to her. "Over the years I learnt that I couldn't help the dead, but I believed I could protect the living."

"Colin, what did you feel before the anger? Can you recall?" Knowles asked.

Colin was silent for a long time. "Something akin to fear," he finally said. "I was worried that she hadn't received medical help in time. I feared that our best efforts would fall short, and there would be no justice. I was concerned that other women would die. I wanted to guarantee her safety, but I was afraid that I couldn't."

"So you protected her from the truth," Knowles said, bringing him back to the incident that had triggered Colin's discourse. "And became angry when she went out."

She left her chair and put her arms around Colin.

"Jenny, what would have happened if Colin had said he was afraid for you, instead of losing his temper?"

"I would have told him I loved him on the spot," she answered. "I wouldn't have needed the wine."

"Thank you, Jenny." Knowles sighed. "You'll both forgive me, I hope, if I make a point here? I am, after all, a psychiatrist." He saw Colin's half smile. "Anger's often a secondary emotion. There's usually something—fear, for example—that precedes it. Stick with what comes first, and I promise it will make all the difference."

"Is that our homework for the week?" she asked.

"No, your homework has a physical component. Jenny, would you like to touch Colin more intimately?" She nodded. "Then trade places. This week, Jenny, you are to keep your trousers on. What Colin wears is up to you."

He paused. "There's something else. Jenny, I can't emphasise strongly enough that you are to proceed at your own pace. There is no score card." He leant forward. "Colin, everything Jenny does must be her choice. It's entirely possible that seeing your hands on your belt was a psychological trigger. I don't want that negative visual cue. Jenny, the last time you saw a man's naked body was in a frightening and painful circumstance. I want you to learn not to be afraid of Colin's."

CHAPTER 22

On Tuesday Jenny had lunch with Simon at one of the little cafés in Covent Garden, planning to visit some of the bookstores on Charing Cross Road afterward. She'd told Mr. Hollister that she'd be on the lookout for creative book displays or marketing ideas that could be adapted for the Hampstead shop. "Before we head out, I'd like to use the ladies'," she told Simon.

On her way back, one of the other diners approached her. "Enjoy the food, did you?" he asked, looking at her intently.

"Yes, thank you," she said.

"Are you a frequent customer?"

"It's my first visit." She stepped past him.

"Do you live nearby?"

"No, I don't." He was still staring at her, and she felt a little uncomfortable. When she reached her table, Simon was on his feet. "Let's be going," he said, a hard edge to his voice.

"Simon, he didn't do anything."

"Stay close." He guided her into a little shop and asked the proprietor to show them the back door. They exited on a small alley and mingled with the crowd when they reached the main street. "The tube station next."

No bookstores today, she thought. What will I tell the Hollisters?

They boarded what she thought was the wrong train, and after several stops, changed trains and directions. She was really confused now. If this were the way home, it was the most circuitous route she could imagine. Finally she saw the familiar stop, and they mounted the stairs to the street and turned in the direction of Colin's flat. Simon was punching the buttons on his mobile before she had even locked the door. "Casey here," she heard him say. "Jenny's home and she's fine, but I think she was recognised." There was a pause. "Covent Garden. No, sir, we weren't followed." He rang off.

"I'll make tea," she said. "That should show you how culturally assimilated I've become."

They sipped their tea and nibbled on lemon cakes from Sainsbury's until Colin arrived. "Let's hear it," he said, accepting a quick hug from her.

"A man spoke to me at the restaurant. In Texas people you don't know speak to you—it's not unusual."

"He didn't want to make friends, love. He wanted to see if you had an American accent."

"Anything else?" Colin asked.

"He saw my scar, but of course everyone does. Then Simon said we had to leave, and we did."

"Casey?"

"He'd been watching her in the café. When she went to the ladies', he intercepted her on her way back. I don't know who he was, but I didn't think we should wait to find out."

"Physical description?"

"Five foot nine or ten, approximately eleven stone," Simon said. "Straight hair, parted on the left. Wire-rimmed glasses, thin moustache, narrow, ferret-like face. He was pale, anaemic looking. He wore a white button-down shirt, print tie, and rumpled blue trousers. My guess is he's a reporter. No one else would pay that much attention. He left the café right after we did, but he wasn't able to keep up with us."

She felt the muscles in her stomach tightening. "Should I be afraid?"

"No," Colin answered shortly.

"Can I go to work tomorrow?"

"It shouldn't be a problem, Jenny."

"I'll be off, sir."

"Come here to me, Jen," Colin said when he had closed and locked the door behind Casey.

Her stomach tensed further. "Colin, I want to get off the merry-go-round for a while."

"I'll just hold you then."

CHAPTER 23

Jenny woke often and early. When she went into the kitchen, Colin was already there brewing the tea, and the look on his face told her that his night hadn't been any more peaceful than hers. He turned the newspaper in her direction, and her knees felt weak. The headline read: "Scott Witness Still in London."

"You can't be identified from the description in the article," Colin remarked.

"No, but that reporter pegged Simon, didn't he? 'A rugged-looking individual with short, sandy-coloured hair and military bearing.'"

"Jenny, if this had to happen, I'm glad you were with him and not with me. I've been interviewed by the media, I've testified in numerous cases, and I'm more likely to be recognised. Casey has operated under the radar for a long time."

She folded the newspaper closed. "Colin, I'm sorry about last night. The homework, I mean. I love you. I don't want you to think that I don't."

He moved behind her and leant over to embrace her. "You're under a good deal of stress, Jen. We'll work through it." When she lifted her face for his kiss, her mouth was warm from the tea.

After he left, she began her exercises, an ingrained habit now, but her limbs felt heavy, as if they were pinned to the floor. Whose body is it anyway, she railed at herself. Surely she could get through *these* exercises! She sat up. Everywhere she looked she saw her failure and her fear—Colin's sofa, her bedroom. On her way to change clothes, she closed his bedroom door. He wanted her to be there with him, and she couldn't. It was too much—they loved and desired each other, but she had a monster on her back, and now someone might as well have painted a target on her chest.

Stick it out, Brian would say. She dragged herself to the bookstore. Mr. Hollister had left instructions on the computer table next to the morning newspaper. She hadn't been online very long when she heard the doorbell jingle and Simon's voice. Esther directed him upstairs.

"I'm on late turn today, love. I saw the article—just thought I'd check on you before I go in."

She was hunched forward.

"Stomach bothering you? Stand up and show me where it hurts."

Esther Hollister couldn't hear their voices, but she could see the young policeman rest the flat of his hand on Jenny's stomach. His arm was around her shoulders.

"Tense these muscles and count to ten," he told her. "Then relax to a count of ten. Eventually—if a period of relaxation always follows the period of tension—the tension itself can become a cue for the relief to follow."

"I wish you didn't have to leave."

"You'll be okay, love. I'll see you soon."

"Yes, Simon. Thanks." She watched him go down the stairs and heard his farewell to Esther before he went out. She turned back to the computer screen, but between the newspaper on the corner of the table and the ache in the pit of her stomach, it was slow going. Finally she stopped trying, resting her hands in her lap. Her cowardly hands—afraid to touch Colin where he wanted to be touched. How do you build a relationship when the undertow of fear is so strong?

Mr. Hollister startled her, and she couldn't wipe the tears away quickly enough. "Miss Jeffries, are you all right? We're very happy to have you with us, you know. You mustn't worry if you don't complete my list today. Essie!" he called. "Tea for Miss Jeffries, please." The tea was always hot, so Esther joined them straightaway. "Essie, I think we're working Miss Jeffries too hard," he said.

Esther set the cup next to the computer. "I don't think that's the problem, Reggie. Jenny, would you like to tell us what's upsetting you?"

She looked at their concerned faces. They had daughters, she knew—two daughters and a son. Surely their children had trusted them with confidences! She knew neither Colin nor Simon would want her to disclose anything, but they seemed very far away. She opened the newspaper and pointed to the words beneath the masthead. "That's about me," she said. "I'm the Scott witness. I'm still in London."

"Reggie, close the shop," Esther said. She pulled a chair next to Jenny and took both of her hands in her own. "My poor dear." She waited for her husband to return.

"I'm sorry I didn't tell you the truth before," Jenny said. "I shouldn't be telling you now. Please don't fire me. I really like coming here."

"We'll do nothing of the sort," Mr. Hollister assured her.

"Goodness me, that explains a lot," Esther smiled. "You know more policemen than I have books on the shelves, and they are all so protective of you."

"And you've been so shy about your personal information," Mr. Hollister added. "You've not let your name be recorded anywhere, and you've never given us your address."

"Colin thought it would be best."

"Why, Jenny?"

"Because Colin thinks he's still after me. He was so angry when the verdict was read. There have been incidents, but the police haven't been able to link them to—to—*him*. Oh, you won't tell anyone, will you?"

"Wouldn't think of it," Mr. Hollister said firmly. "Essie, what can we do to help this young lady?"

"People and books, that's where I always turn," she answered. "Jenny, if you feel safe here and you want to continue, you're welcome to come in whenever you like. I also want you to have our home address and phone—if you need us, ring or stop round. We have plenty of space, and we won't pry."

Mr. Hollister wrote their contact information on the back of his business card.

"Reggie, that book about FDR that just came in—can you put your hands on it? I think it might be just the thing for Jenny."

It was downstairs, but Mr. Hollister located it quickly. Jenny's eyes filled when she saw the title: *Freedom From Fear.*

CHAPTER 24

"Difficult week?" Dr. Knowles asked. "I saw the newspaper article."

No one spoke. Jenny was sitting on the sofa, her shoulders slumped, and Colin was beside her, watching her.

"Did it make you feel more vulnerable, Jenny?"

Looking down, she didn't answer.

"Recovery doesn't occur in a vacuum, Jenny."

"I'm not recovering at all," she said in a hollow voice. "I'm more afraid. I feel like the monster is around every corner. I need Colin more than ever, and I'm less capable of responding."

"Something else happened this week then."

"It's not fair!" she burst out. "The monster has had what Colin hasn't, and it's not right! I can't give him what I want to give him!"

"No, it isn't fair," Knowles agreed calmly. "But the monster, as you call him, took it, while Colin doesn't want it until you're ready to give it. Will you tell me about it?"

She remembered how she had felt when she removed his trousers. She had put her hands on the waistband of his undershorts and felt time stop. He had called her name, once, twice. Slowly—oh so slowly—she had eased his shorts down. The forest of dark hair that swirled between his legs made him look menacing, and she had not been able to touch him there. She had been unable to go forward, unable to go back, paralyzed except for her racing heart. "No. Night after night I've hurt him, and I don't want to do it anymore."

All week Colin had fought with his expectations. Jenny's tentative little fingers were so much more exciting than a confident, experienced touch would have been. At times the anticipation had been almost unbearable. Discouragement had followed.

"Jenny, these are exactly the things we need to talk about, the things that frighten or disturb you. Tell me, and let me put it into context for Colin. Did you see him naked this week?"

She nodded and started to cry.

"And what did you think about that?"

"I thought—I thought—it looked like a weapon," she said, her voice failing.

Colin looked at the floor. His eyes took in the beige carpet, Theo's shoes, the tuft of dust behind the leg of his chair. It had been bad enough seeing her reaction; hearing her describe it to Theo was worse. Why this woman? he asked himself. Since his divorce, he'd had several affairs. Those women had been willing to sleep with him. They had been charming and clever. Why hadn't he fallen in love with one of them? Theo's response surprised him, but it didn't make him feel any better.

"Of course you did, my dear," he said gently. "That was your experience with Scott, wasn't it? But tell me—when you saw Colin, did you want to run?"

"No. He was kissing me and whispering my name."

"Were you afraid?"

"Colin, say something," she sobbed.

What could he say? He had said it all, and it had not made a difference.

"What did you think would happen?" Knowles persisted.

"He'd hurt me. He wouldn't mean to, but he would."

"What sort of man is Colin, Jenny?"

"He's wonderful—thoughtful and gentle and strong. He believes in helping people, in protecting them and seeking justice for them. He knows what to do. He's sure of himself. He's loving and generous."

"Jenny, sex is more than two bodies coming together. Our sexuality comes from who we are as human beings. It's directly related to our character. Even now, you respond when Colin touches you because the touches are *his.* Later, when he makes love to you, you'll respond, not just to a set of anatomical parts, but to the whole individual, his values, his personality, his commitment to you. In mathematics they teach that the sum is greater than the total of its parts. That's true in loving relationships, too."

"Dr. Knowles, why does it have to be so hard? I love him, and I want so badly to be able to follow through."

"Are there any other fears you haven't related to me? Fear of pregnancy, for example? Perhaps birth control is a subject you and Colin should address, if you haven't already."

Why? Colin thought. Birth control is for couples who actually make love.

"We did, and Colin said—" She looked at him, but he didn't answer.

"What is our current therapeutic theme?"

She sighed. "I'm in charge of my body."

"That's correct. Therefore I'd like you to be responsible for this issue."

She had gone white. "I'm afraid of going to that kind of doctor," she stammered.

Knowles frowned. "Jenny, you must have had a pelvic examination as part of your medical while you were in hospital."

She looked at Colin.

"Yes, and a forensic examination as well," Colin replied after a moment, "but she was unconscious."

"Have you had one since you left hospital?"

She opened her mouth then closed it without speaking. "Sort of," she finally said.

"Would you explain that, Jenny?"

"I had pain, terrible pain. I hadn't had a period in so long that I thought the monster had gotten me pregnant. Brian held me down, and Simon—he did what he had to do, I guess. Made sure I wasn't miscarrying."

Colin remembered Jenny confessing her pregnancy fears to Knowles. Casey had been present. "He examined you?" he demanded, his detached tone gone. "Jenny, he was out of line!"

Dear God, thought Knowles. That stern-faced young policeman. "How did you feel about what he did?"

"Terrified. And so mad I accused him of being a rapist. I had fought him, you see, him and Brian, and I had lost."

"How did he react?"

"He went ballistic. He was so angry I was sure he was out of control."

"I should have been told," Colin said.

She gave him a rueful smile. "Things happened at the flat that we didn't tell you. Anyway, it was awful, because I was exhausted and afraid and I couldn't get away from him."

"Did he hurt you, Jenny?" Knowles asked.

"No, and that's the amazing thing. He calmed down. He explained the difference between anger and violence—anger being what you feel and violence, what you do. Then he proved by his behavior that they weren't always connected. It was a turning point for me, because after that I was never afraid of him."

"And now you're close," Knowles commented.

Too close, in Colin's view.

"Yes. He taught me a lot during the time we were in the flat. And Colin—" she turned toward him—"that's why I didn't run when you got mad. I waited to see what you'd do."

"Jenny, having heard all this, I'd like to alter my stance on the issue of birth control. I'll make it a recommendation, not a requirement, that you be responsible for the method. It's your body. In this instance, if you choose to trust Colin to protect you, I will as well. You should know, however, that most physicians do not require a pelvic examination prior to providing that sort of medication."

"What's our homework?" she asked.

"What would you like it to be?"

"I want Colin to give me another chance."

CHAPTER 25

On Saturday Colin went into the Yard to catch up on paperwork. Jenny needed a distraction, so she curled up with the book about Franklin Roosevelt that the Hollisters had given her. Colin hadn't been happy about her disclosures to them; in fact, he'd questioned her at length about the information she'd given. Over and over she'd told him that the Hollisters hadn't asked her anything. Their only concern had been her safety. And aside from confessing that she was the Scott witness, she hadn't revealed very much, only that it was Colin's case and that the policemen they'd met had been part of her protection team. She assured him that they recognized the need for discretion. Esther had said, "We'll close the book on this issue. Your secret is safe with us." Colin had finally concluded that no harm had been done, but she had been left with the feeling that she had done something wrong.

Freedom From Fear: A Treatise on the Life of Franklin Delano Roosevelt, the title page read. There was a brief bio of the author, Bernard Alleson, but no photograph. He was born and educated in the northeast. Alleson's was an athletic family, and he had participated in school and community competitions. When he was in his late teens, however, an accident had left him paralyzed below the waist.

"Everyone has a failing of some kind," Alleson wrote in the introduction. "We all must reconcile ourselves to our limitations. The process is simply more pronounced in those individuals with physical handicaps, whose restrictions are evident and extreme." Denial was the first stage, he claimed, in which we either do not accept what has happened to us or do not believe that its effect will be permanent. Bitterness and grief follow denial, but the phase he dubbed "now what" was the one that had spurred him to research and write the book. What happened once you dealt with the fear brought on by your condition? What did your life look like, once you decided to proceed with it?

She set the book down for a moment, angered by Alleson's smooth prose. Was she supposed to accept that she would never heal, that the monster's attack would mark her for the rest of her life? To settle for a life in which love played no part?

Chapter One gave a brief summary of the facts of FDR's life. She skimmed it, remembering the advice of one of her college professors: "Look for the big idea, because it's the anchor for everything else." Chapter Two revealed Alleson's conviction that a historian is called to probe beyond the demonstrable facts of history to the intangibles that, however difficult to illustrate, caused a subject to come alive. Not every brilliant, well-educated, upper class man became successful in political life. Roosevelt had become paralyzed in 1921, yet eleven years later he had been elected President of the United States. How had he done it? The expectations of others had not been the driving force—his family had not wanted him to continue in politics after his illness. "It was a product instead," Alleson wrote, "of Roosevelt's self-concept. He had been indulged as a child, raised to believe that he was capable of great things. It was that mental image of himself, however at odds with his physical reality, that he carried with him and would not alter. Being a patriot, it was that mental image that he transferred to his country, believing always that his nation, no matter how besieged, could respond with greatness."

The witness protection team had believed in her. So had Colin. Did he still? He loved her. Was that the same thing? Dr. Knowles thought he could help. Irrelevant—FDR had believed in *himself.* She needed to believe in herself.

Colin had not returned, and it was time for lunch. She made herself a sandwich and continued her reading. Alleson did not speculate at length about FDR's fears, mentioning only that death would have been the initial fear, surfacing when his illness first struck, when the pain had been at its worst and the diagnosis vague. Over time treatment had promised life but not mobility. His fear of death had then receded, to be replaced by a fear of failure, the fear that he wouldn't have a future worth living. For a man of Roosevelt's stature, lack of a productive life was almost equivalent to death.

During dinner with Colin she was quiet, remembering Dr. Knowles' concern that she feel safe sexually and his recommendation that some fabric remain between her and Colin. After spending most of the day reading a book about a handicapped man, written by a handicapped man, she saw her clothes as evidence of her handicap. The motorcyclist's bullets could have crippled her; her body armor hadn't covered her completely. Instead the monster had crippled her. Not with his fists—her bones and bruises had healed, and she could walk—but with his sexual attack. Had Roosevelt felt like a prisoner in his own body? Had Alleson? Why did she, when she had stood up to the monster in court?

Colin knew she'd been shaken by the newspaper story. He'd been shaken by the last therapy session and what had preceded it. Relationships weren't linear; perhaps they would both benefit from a step back physically. It could ease the crushing disappointment he felt. He put his arms around her but gave her chaste kisses.

- -

On Sunday while Colin studied the newspaper, she delved further into the book about Roosevelt. His fears had clearly not led him to make safety a priority in his life. He had loved the sea and had spent as much time as he could on yachts and naval vessels. He had taken long trips by plane. He had had a car specially engineered so he could drive it. He had learned not to be afraid of his physical body. Wheelchair or not, his exploits proved that even his body was capable of more than people would have expected. His wheelchair had been an accessory, a tool that got him where he needed to go.

Roosevelt first referred to what he called the "Four Freedoms" in a speech he gave to Congress on January 6, 1941. It was Alleson's belief that they were a result of fears that FDR had experienced, fears that he had overcome, and a complete chapter was devoted to each one. Freedom of speech and expression was the first. However illogical, handicapped people were often treated as if their intelligence were deficient also. What had Roosevelt's response been? To run for political office, to meet with leaders of other nations, to give fireside chats to his countrymen, and to communicate his vision for freedom worldwide. Freedom of speech meant freedom to teach and freedom to learn.

Freedom of every person to worship God in his own way was the next cornerstone of Roosevelt's quartet. Spiritual freedom was critical when you were not physically free—FDR chained by his paralysis, millions around the world imprisoned by unjust and repressive political systems. She remembered the Bible story of Paul and Silas, singing in prison, although their feet were in stocks and their bodies bloody from the beatings they had received. Freedom to worship meant the freedom to forgive. Roosevelt had sung hymns, too. His faith may have been shaken, but it had not been destroyed.

FDR had never been poor, but his illness had taught him the difference that having financial resources made. He had received the best medical care available. For the less fortunate, freedom from want meant that their basic needs could be met, for food, shelter, and clothing. For those who were more fortunate, freedom from want meant freedom to give, and Roosevelt had donated large sums of money to construct therapeutic centers to treat others afflicted with his disease.

She took a deep breath. The last freedom of the four was the one that concerned her the most: freedom from fear. In his speech, FDR had been referring to the fear that results from knowing another nation is capable of attacking yours. In his personal life, however, Roosevelt had been less able to defend himself than most men. He must have also been afraid of further physical deterioration. Hitler was on the international scene, yet Roosevelt resisted even the appearance of fright, standing strong first against the Nazi rhetoric, next by establishing an alliance with his British counterpart, Winston Churchill, and last by exercising his right as commander-in-chief to send the American military around the world to make courage visible. Love of country and hatred of evil had motivated him.

She looked up from the book. Freedom from fear meant the freedom to love. You couldn't love somebody—really love them—if you were afraid for your personal safety. Allied soldiers had left their homes and their families and fought for freedom. Not all had returned, but those who did built new lives and taught their children to love peace.

"If a 'whole' man had been in office instead of Roosevelt," Alleson concluded, "someone whose experience of lack of freedom had been less profound, the course of history could have been completely altered." Freedom was not a vague concept for FDR, but a tangible necessity of life. Every day that he put on his leg braces or pushed the wheels on his chair, his commitment to freedom grew, and his legacy was political freedom for millions who, without his resolve, would have been enslaved.

She closed the book, a slim volume full of wisdom she wanted to apply to her life. Colin was waiting, and as they headed toward the Heath, she tried first to describe what she'd read. "The book was all about freedom," she said. "Freedom of speech was critical."

"Yes, the leaders of both our countries used that freedom effectively," he agreed.

"Freedom to worship."

"It's best not to underestimate the importance of that. Faith can move mountains."

"Freedom from want."

She wasn't giving any details, and he didn't ask for any. "Jenny, I'm capable of providing for you. I hope you know that."

The weather was glorious, and the Heath was crowded with people, families having picnics, couples throwing Frisbees, individuals on bicycles. After spending two days indoors reading with artificial light, the sun seemed especially bright to her. A husband and wife passed them, the man with his small son astride his shoulders. The little boy was laughing with each intentional bounce his father made. Above them the sky was a limitless blue, the children's kites as vivid as their parents' smiles. None of them had any obvious handicaps.

"Freedom from fear," she told him. "That was the last freedom I read about."

They stepped aside to let a runner pass, then another. From the top of Parliament Hill they could see a stadium below. The race must finish there, because the ones who went by, sweating heavily and panting, their mouths open, had their eyes focused in that direction. They had conquered the last climb. It was downhill for them all the way now.

"Hitler was a monster, but he was defeated. I'm going to defeat my monster, too."

He was no longer certain that it was possible.

"It's the last big hill I have to overcome." She peered up at him. They weren't even holding hands, but other couples were. One bearded young man was stretched out on a blanket next to a girl. Would they go home and make love to each other later that night? If they could do it, why couldn't she?

He was in no hurry to return to the flat. The public areas of Hampstead masked his growing feeling of estrangement. A couple in love—that was what they were supposed to be—but privacy did not benefit them.

CHAPTER 26

Monday came, Colin went back to the Yard, and Jenny told Esther Hollister how helpful the book about Roosevelt had been. Esther patted her shoulder and bade her keep it. A customer—Jenny had learned to distinguish between potential buyers and those who simply liked to loiter—came in, and Jenny went upstairs to see what computer tasks Mr. Hollister had left for her.

While she worked, she continued to ponder the example of FDR. He was paralyzed: That was a fact. He hadn't overcome his impediments; he had succeeded in spite of them. The author of the book was paralyzed also, but his condition had not kept him from writing a compelling work. She had been raped and brutalized. That was a part of her history she could not change.

Last week when she'd come home from the bookstore and waited for Colin to come through the door, she'd thought she could love him, but her body had betrayed her. Then had come that terrible session with Dr. Knowles when he'd made her say out loud what her reaction had been. It was worse than testifying. And now Colin didn't want to do the homework exercises at all.

That night over omelettes and salad, she tried again to explain to him what she had read. In the witness protection flat they had discussed issues which arose from published material, and they had become closer. "Roosevelt survived a lot of campaigns before he became president. Every speech, every election was a chance to fail."

Colin put his fork down very deliberately. "Damn it, Jenny," he said quietly, shaking his head. "Each one was an opportunity to succeed as well. And he did."

Her eyes widened. He was mad at her because she hadn't succeeded. But she hadn't quit! She tried now to keep the conversation going. "That's true. I was just going to say that. His illness didn't keep him from achieving great things. If he hadn't been president during World War II—"

"And Churchill, Prime Minister," he reminded her automatically.

"Where would we be? Two men with infirmities—didn't you tell me Churchill had a speech impediment?—and neither played it safe. They motivated millions, men on the battlefield and families at home. They gave people hope."

"One way or another, our experiences in life mark us. We have to decide if that mark will be a scar or a star."

That hurt. She sipped her wine and searched for a question that would involve him. "What about God, Colin? Was it an accident? That Roosevelt and Churchill were in office at the right time? That you were in the hospital when I woke up? If Simon had been there then, I would never have made it."

Perhaps not, but she was certainly close to him now. "Goodwyn wouldn't think so," he replied. "He believes that encouragement comes when we need it. He'd probably argue that it's the same for nations."

Nations—that wasn't very personal. She tried again. "I've thought a lot about the Scripture he quoted. Do you remember? 'He has not given us a spirit of fear, but of power, and of love, and of a sound mind.' Love is the key, Colin. FDR used love of country to motivate him. I'm going to use love of Colin."

He looked at her for a long time. "It's been a rough week, Jenny," he finally said.

Not Jen.

Tuesday evening was no better. Colin was distant, offering only minimal conversation during dinner and going to his bedroom afterward, leaving her to do the washing up by herself. She had been unable to engage him, and she had run out of neutral topics. She stood in his doorway. "Colin, the other women you've been with—did you sleep with all of them on the first date?"

He looked up, startled. "No, of course not."

"Did they all ooh and aah when they saw you naked?"

She saw a flash of anger cross his face, and he did not answer.

"Had any of them been raped?"

His jaw tensed. "No."

She didn't know how to reach him. Was she supposed to throw herself at his feet? "Do I need to find somewhere else to live, Colin?"

His answer was not immediately forthcoming. Seeing her fear of his male anatomy and hearing her words to Theo—that one-two punch ate at him. His body was not a weapon, but as long as she thought it was, what hope was there? Jenny's rejection of him was more personal than Vi's had been. But he still wanted Jenny. In his heart he had sworn to love, protect, and honour her. He shook his head slowly.

"I miss you, Colin." She waited by the door, but after a few minutes she realized he wasn't going to say anything. That night she dreamed she and Colin were going sailing. She stepped into the boat first and turned around to watch him board. But he didn't—he held the bow line in his hand for a moment before tossing it onto the deck. The boat drifted slowly away, and he stood on the dock, watching it go.

CHAPTER 27

Jenny did her morning exercises half-heartedly, still thinking about Colin and FDR. Roosevelt had consulted colleagues and advisors, and she would call hers. She phoned Danny first.

"Watch funny films, Sis," he recommended. *"Liar, Liar's* good. Laughter distracts you, relaxes you. You'll be better able to deal with things."

Next, Brian. "Have a backup plan," he said.

Even Hunt. "Take the offensive."

Last, Simon. It was gone one when he called by the bookshop. Hampstead sidewalks were always busy, but it was still possible to find an uncrowded spot on the Heath. They headed there. "The Hollisters know about me," she said.

"Is that wise?"

Exasperated, she shook her head at him. "Colin had the same reaction. I didn't mean to tell them, but the day the article appeared in the newspaper, I was upset. You came to see me, remember? I cried after you left, and that's when I told them who I was. I didn't talk about the attack, and they didn't ask, but now they understand why all my friends are policemen. And they gave me a book about FDR—Simon, there was a whole chapter on freedom from fear! Of course the author was putting it in a global context, peaceful nations fearing hostile, more belligerent ones, but I think it applies to individuals, too. If someone's not armed and not aggressive, I shouldn't be afraid of them."

They found an unoccupied bench. "Were any of the men you served with afraid? What did they do about it? And don't call it 'apprehension.' I'm way past apprehension."

He waited until the woman with the child in the pushchair had gone by. The Heath was popular with all ages, particularly on summer afternoons. Was she focused on fear because of the possible repercussions of the newspaper story, or was her relationship with Sinclair frightening her? "Training comes first," he answered. "You prepare your body for what it has to do. You master the weapons and other equipment."

She nodded for him to continue.

"Practice is next. Going over the elements of a plan builds confidence."

That must be the reasoning behind the homework assignments.

"When an objective is identified, a team is designated. Everyone has a function, but you work as a team. In the best scenario, each man feels responsible for the success of the mission."

"If a mission fails, does each man feel responsible for that, too?"

"Absolutely."

Oh, God. Poor Colin. And it wasn't his fault. But it wasn't her fault either! "Go on."

"Not everyone is equally experienced. In the best teams, individuals complement each other. Usually the team leader is a bit older with some successful ops under his belt."

She smiled wryly to herself. It was an unfortunate choice of words, but it fit. Colin was older. He'd been successful, in and out of marriage, "under his belt." "You've covered before and during. What happens when a mission is over?"

"The after-action report. A debrief. We examine what we did well, what we did poorly, and what we can do differently."

That was what Dr. Knowles did. Reviewed their progress. "Are you ever afraid?"

"Yes, but I'm sent into dangerous places. A little apprehension is healthy—makes me careful, keeps me alert."

"When you were injured—was your mission over?"

"We'd accomplished our objective, but no mission is over until all involved return to base. And no mission is a complete success when men are lost."

"If you'd been injured earlier in the mission, would you have been more afraid?"

"We're taught to put more emphasis on the mission than our individual feelings, but yes, I'd have had some anxiety about my ability to pull my own weight."

"'Anxiety'—that's military understatement," she commented.

"Injuries often occur on a mission. Many times a mission is completed in spite of injuries." He paused. "I'm not sure how this helps you, love."

"Dr. Knowles uses some of the same processes. He explains things—to me, mostly. He gives us assignments. He follows up."

Damn. The bloody newspaper report wasn't behind this conversation. Was he opening doors for her and Sinclair and simultaneously closing them for himself? "Does he tell you what to do?"

"No, he tells us what not to do, but it isn't working. Why am I still afraid?"

"We're trained in advance of an operation. We're not unprepared for what we encounter." He paused. "Is Sinclair pressurising you, Jenny?"

"Not anymore," she said. "He's quit trying."

Bastard. He took her hand and rubbed his thumb over her fingers. "And you haven't."

"No."

"Are you unhappy there?"

"Sometimes." She looked up at him. "Simon, how do you do it? I've never seen you afraid."

He was afraid now. Afraid of what he wanted to do. "Will you be all right for twenty-four hours?" he asked. "I'll call for you at Hollister's tomorrow afternoon."

- -

Colin slammed the door when he came home. "You were with him, weren't you?"

"What?" she stammered.

"I rang the bookshop this afternoon, Jenny. Esther Hollister told me you were out with a police sergeant. It was Casey, wasn't it?"

"We went for a *walk*."

"I don't want to share you with another man, Jenny."

She raised her chin. "Colin, I needed a friend!"

"Sorry," he said after a moment but the closed look hadn't left his eyes.

She heard Simon's voice, counting to make her feet move toward the courtroom. She took a few steps closer to Colin. "I know I've hurt you," she said. "Colin, I'm so sorry. I'm doing everything I can to fix it, but I can't do it by myself." She took another step. She could touch his hand if she reached out for it.

"Jenny, I need some time."

She kept her arms at her sides. "I can give you that. And some space, too." She picked up her handbag and keys and left the flat, wishing he would come after her.

He heard the door shut. When he went to the bay window, there was no sign of her on either side of the street. Then he spotted her sitting on the stoop, leaning against the railing, her head in her hands. Was she crying? He could not tell. What did she expect him to do? Forget how soundly she had rejected him? An hour later when he checked, she was still there.

CHAPTER 28

When Jenny returned to the flat, Colin's bedroom door was closed. No light showed under it. When morning came, she tried to tell if his bed had been slept in. Hers hadn't—she'd been awake most of the night, her journal in her hand, but her list of *Ways To Reach Colin* was blank. He had never shut her out before, and she didn't know how to get through to him.

She made herself a cup of tea, dressed, and went to Hollister's early. The hours dragged until Simon arrived. "All fear isn't equal," he told her as they walked. "There are degrees. Sometimes it's just tension or nervousness, and you can tame it by what you call it."

"My fear's like an iceberg, and I'm the Titanic. It has punched a hole in my hull, and I'm sinking."

He tried another tack. "Fear's not always a bad thing. It can be fuel to motivate you to train harder. If you're not a little afraid, you're not pushing yourself hard enough."

"What exactly are soldiers—or police—afraid of?"

"Failure. We're taught to focus on getting the job done. We're not encouraged to focus on the personal risk, beyond accepting that the work we do is inherently dangerous. There's only ever the mission. And the team. Nothing else."

The bench was occupied. They found a shady spot to sit on the grass. She took his hand, conscious as she did so that Colin would draw inappropriate conclusions from it if he saw it. "When are you most afraid? At the beginning?"

He smiled. "No, when the adrenalin kicks in, it feeds excitement as well as fear."

"Why are you excited?"

"Because I want to do what I've trained to do, not just chat about it or wait in a van or other assault position."

She remembered feeling that combination, but lately the fear had smothered the excitement. "Do excitement and fear always go together?"

"Yes, but there must be a balance. Too much fear, and you're either in the wrong line of work or you're a sick bastard. Too much excitement can lead to irresponsibility. Fear keeps you from doing something reckless."

They watched a cyclist speed by and then swerve suddenly. The bicycle's wheels skidded, losing traction, and the rider went down hard.

Simon helped her to her feet. The young man was still on the ground, leaning forward and grimacing in pain.

"I could take a look, sir," Simon said.

"He has medical training," Jenny offered.

"If you've broken anything, you'll need an ambulance," Simon continued.

The man's teeth were clenched, but he nodded.

"Don't watch him, watch me," she said, taking the man's hand. She heard his sharp intake of breath and knew Simon was examining him.

"Your ankle's sprained."

"If you'll help me up, I can get home then," the young man said. "I'll use my bike as a crutch."

"Ice it the first forty-eight hours, no more than twenty minutes at a time," Simon advised. "Elevate it. It'll reduce the swelling. Wait an hour between ice treatments. It wouldn't hurt to have an x-ray in a couple days if it's still bothering you."

The man tried to smile his thanks.

"Don't worry if bruises appear. Do worry if your pain spreads or your toes become numb. And you'll need some exercises to lessen the chance of reinjury."

"He's big on exercises," she explained.

They watched him go, hobbling next to his machine. Jenny and Simon walked farther into the park. "Was he reckless?" she asked. "I'd like to be reckless—to be able to love someone recklessly, without worrying if I'm going to fall."

"What's happening between you and Sinclair, Jenny?"

She wanted to explain without mentioning body parts. "Imagine that every day when you come home from work, there's a fresh apple pie on the counter. It's still warm, and it smells fantastic. You cut a slice, put it on a plate, and spear a forkful. But you're not allowed to eat it. Each day the scent greets you, but you can't take a bite. Eventually you wouldn't want to come home. You'd start to hate apple pie." She paused. "Colin's the one who comes home, and I'm the apple pie."

He restrained a smile. "How can I help, love?"

"I don't know. You taught me to face things, and I am, but it's intense. Sometimes I wish I could take a break."

"You could come to my flat for a bit," he suggested, trying for a matter-of-fact tone.

"I'd cramp your style."

"No obligation, Jenny. I've a sofa to sleep on."

"You're a gentleman, Simon."

No woman had ever called him that.

"I've thought about going, but if I don't find the solution with Colin, I won't have anything to offer anyone else. I have to see this through."

He had taught her too well.

They turned back toward Hollister's and stopped briefly to let an elderly couple pass by. The grey-haired gentleman was smiling gently at his wife and holding her hand as they walked. Her face was lined with trust.

"Look, Simon," she said. "That's what I want."

"To be old?"

"Yes. To have loved someone for years. To be comfortable and secure in that love. To know it will last because it has."

The despair in her tone disturbed him. He put his arm around her and permitted his lips to rest against her hair. Would her hair smell this good when she was fifty? He thought so.

CHAPTER 29

Jenny hadn't been certain Colin would join her for their next Knowles appointment. He'd been coming home later and later from the Yard, and she was afraid to push him beyond pleasantries. When she tried to tell him about Danny's visit to the bookstore—he'd accepted Esther's offer of a cup of tea, made himself comfortable, and charmed everyone, including the children, with his playful sense of humor—she felt like she was talking to herself.

She'd been afraid that her fear would come between them, and it had. Colin no longer touched her at all. To occupy her time, she started a new list: *Lessons Learned.* Brian was right: She needed a plan. How did other people deal with fear? Churchill hadn't given in. Roosevelt had led a nation. Surely she could love one man!

What would Colin tell her to do? Gather all the information she could. Believe in herself, in what she could be. But she still felt like Jenny Past, not Jenny Future.

Friends were important, Colin's mother had said. Simon was a friend, and he had always encouraged her to accept help. He also believed in preparing yourself mentally—having the right mindset—but she didn't see how that applied. She knew in her mind what she wanted; she just didn't know how to get her body to go along. Simon would also tell her to rely on the strength of her team. How? Dr. Knowles was guiding her with his sessions and assignments, but it wasn't enough.

She looked at her list. Each ingredient was important, but something was missing. And no recipe would cook if the oven shut off.

When they entered Dr. Knowles' consulting room, Colin didn't sit. He walked stiffly to the window and looked out, his body rigid and unyielding.

"What would you like to discuss today?" Knowles asked.

"Helplessness," she answered, her eyes on Colin's back.

"That's one of the most difficult issues we face as human beings," Knowles said, choosing not to confront Colin, "because regardless of our rank and station, we all experience it at some point in our lives. Studies show that victims of trauma often feel helpless long after the event."

"My fear makes me helpless. I was afraid of the monster, afraid in the hospital, and afraid in witness protection, but I conquered those fears. I'm afraid with Colin, and I shouldn't be. I don't want to be."

Knowles glanced at Colin but saw no reaction.

"But the worst fear of all is fear of sex, because none of my other fears hurt anyone else. And I'm more helpless than I've ever been, because I can't conquer this fear by myself."

She saw Colin bow his head and turn slowly in her direction. He did not speak.

"More helpless than when you were alone with Scott?" Knowles asked, still hoping that Colin would participate voluntarily. His anger was palpable.

"Dr. Knowles, somebody removed my clothes when I was unconscious. At first I thought it must have been the two men who worked for the monster, but then I realized that they'd never have stripped me and not raped me. So it must have been the monster himself. He must have savored how helpless I was and anticipated how helpless he'd make me later. He removed my *underwear.* He saw—everything. It makes my skin crawl, thinking about him touching me when I didn't know."

Her voice dropped to a whisper. "Sometimes I wonder—why did he stop kicking me when I was unconscious? When I couldn't feel it anymore? Is anger not satisfying unless you can see that the other person is hurting?"

Colin's eyes narrowed, and his jaw tensed where he had nicked himself shaving. She addressed the blue eyes. "It's fear, not love, that's the problem. Colin, please," she begged. "I didn't mean to hurt you. I want you to need me again!"

"Are you afraid of Casey?" Colin asked in his impersonal policeman's voice.

"Colin, he was my bodyguard, my doctor. He saved my life. He treated my wounds. But if he took his pants off, I'd be afraid."

"How close are you?" The stern tone could not disguise his jealousy.

"Why don't you take out your notebook and record my statement?" she retorted. "Close enough for him to see how much I love Detective Chief Inspector Colin Sinclair, and how much panic and despair I feel because he has given up on me!"

"I haven't given up," Colin said woodenly.

"Dr. Knowles," she said desperately, "why am I still so afraid of this man's body? Why does progress have to be so slow, when I love him so much?"

"Because a monster nearly murdered you," Knowles replied gently. "Being helpless at a critical time arrested your sexual development. We're involved in some psychological CPR here."

"But CPR takes two people, doesn't it? I can't do it by myself! I need mouth-to-mouth!"

Colin recalled suddenly seeing her for the first time, her precious mouth closed around the tube that helped her breathe. He remembered how laboured and painful her solo breaths had been. How she had struggled to walk. How she had looked bleeding behind the courthouse. He saw again the depth of her commitment, to life, to justice, and finally, to him. His wife, Violet, had betrayed him, not this ardent young woman who wore her heart on her sleeve. "Jenny," he said hoarsely.

His face was stricken, but his arms were open. She pressed herself against him and felt his embrace. "Colin—Colin—remember the purple heart watch you gave me? I'm going to earn those purple hearts again. I promise!"

Dr. Knowles waited, relieved. Seeing Colin vulnerable could empower Jenny, and a renewed pledge could strengthen them both.

When Colin took out his handkerchief, she laughed through her tears. They sat down together on Dr. Knowles' sofa, Jenny holding Colin's hand with both of hers.

"What happened this week between the two of you?" Knowles asked.

"I pulled away," Colin answered.

"You didn't want to come tonight, did you?"

"No."

"Why did you then?"

"I love her, Theo. In spite of everything."

"Colin, why did you pull away from her?"

"I was angry that I couldn't change her perspective."

Knowles leant forward. "Think back, Colin. How did you feel before the anger? What feeling came first?"

"I was shocked by her reaction to me in last week's session. I didn't think we could recover."

"Colin, what were you afraid of?" Knowles pressed.

"That she'd never want me," he said in a hollow voice.

She listened carefully to Dr. Knowles. He was seeking information from Colin, not judging him. His voice did not reveal alarm. Did he think she could heal? He had been encouraging at the beginning; would he be now?

As the two men talked, she realized that until this past week, she had never felt unwanted in her relationship with Colin. Now, however, she understood in a small way the hopelessness he felt. How do you keep going when something so basic to your identity is unappreciated? No—denied. She had felt alien, set apart, since the attack. She felt less of a woman because she hadn't experienced the positive side of sex that so many other women had. Had her problem—her rejection—caused Colin to feel less of a man? If so, what she had done was unforgivable. She rubbed Colin's fingers gently, hoping to massage some life into them.

Knowles leant back in his chair. "Crisis in a relationship gives us an opportunity to re-examine our commitment."

She paled, and her fingers tensed involuntarily, pinching Colin's. "Colin, I love you. Please don't send me away."

He kissed her once, gently, on the side of her head. "I'll not do that. I promise."

"Colin, do you understand what has just taken place here?" Knowles asked. “Jenny has proved that she has the ability to cope, not just in an everyday environment but in one that is extremely stressful. It’s a very significant indication of future success, I must say.”

CHAPTER 30

Colin and Jenny spent the weekend getting reacquainted. Friday evening they held each other gently, and she tried to let the sound of his beating heart reassure her.

On Saturday he looked a little less haunted, but they didn't seem able to step into their usual routine. After morning tea—the universal palliative, she called it—she suggested that they have a Sainsbury's shopping spree instead of a walk on the Heath. "Food fortifies you," she said. "At least that's what Brian always said. Let's go without a list and choose whatever is most appealing. What's your comfort food?"

"Roast beef with creamy mash."

She couldn't restrain a laugh. "Potatoes! Why don't you have a paunch?"

"I've been working out quite a bit lately. At the gym."

Ouch. "Do you want to go there today?" she asked carefully.

"No, Jenny. Let's be together today."

- -

She followed Brian's recipe for the potatoes, mashing them with warm cream and melted butter and adding a dash of nutmeg as well as salt and pepper. The smell of cooking beef gradually filled the flat with the warmth of home, but she and Colin had still not addressed any of the issues that hung in the air between them. "Colin, I need some CPR," she said after dinner.

"Sergeant Casey is better qualified in that area, Jenny."

"Oh, Colin, I want *you* to see if my heart's beating, not Simon."

"Has he ever kissed you?"

"Colin, it's not a romantic relationship. It's a coral-clinging-to-the-rock relationship. I respect him. He teaches me things I need to know. That's all."

"You cling to him?"

"This last week I did, metaphorically speaking. I needed all the help I could get."

"You rang him?"

When Colin had interviewed her long ago, she had been the victim. Now she felt like the offender. "I didn't know what else to do, Colin! You had built a wall around yourself."

"What did you tell him?"

"That I had to find a way to deal with my fear. He didn't have to ask what I was afraid of."

"Did he talk to you about sex?"

"No, he talked about *soldiers.* He said that fear of failure was the common thread among most servicemen. He said that a mission can be completed even when people are injured. That gave me hope, Colin—maybe I don't have to be entirely healed to solve this thing."

She saw his slow nod.

"Colin, I'm not going to apologize for trusting him. It's what you wanted me to do, after all. And in witness protection—I was with your policemen twenty-four hours a day. You came and went. Except for brief leaves, they didn't. Now I'm alone much of the time. The Hollisters are nice, but the work isn't compelling. And there's nothing else."

"Fair enough," he concluded. "Have you told Casey you're all right?"

"No, because I'm not."

"What would you have me do?"

"Stop kissing me like I'm your sister!"

Rapid, shallow breaths, heart rate elevated, prognosis for the patient—still guarded.

- -

On Sunday afternoon she asked Colin about Violet.

"Jenny, I don't still love her, and I don't think of her. Why do you want to know about her?"

"Because you've shared things with her that we haven't. Like a bed."

He shifted uncomfortably in his chair. "Youth and sexual attraction go a long way. In our case they concealed a basic difference in values."

"I'm attracted to you."

He smiled briefly. "I know. I know you are."

"Colin, what went wrong?"

"She didn't support my choice of career. I thought she'd adjust to it over time, but I was wrong. Being married to a copper didn't play well on the social scene. I thought having children would settle her, but she didn't want them. Then my father became ill." He sighed.

She was on the sofa, and he was sitting in one of the armchairs nearby, leaning forward, his elbows on his knees. She waited to see if he would continue.

"She wasn't just unsympathetic, she was repelled. Disease, medical treatments, death—none of it's pretty. The 'for better or for worse' vow? She couldn't adhere to the 'for worse' part."

"Colin, is this our 'for worse' part?"

He was silent for a moment. "There's a time for healing. I believe we'll get to the 'for better.'"

"Was she unfaithful to you?"

"It's possible. I don't know. I don't want to know."

Detectives always want to know.

"She remarried as soon as it was legally possible."

He lost his wife and his father at about the same time. That would shut anybody down. "Colin, how did you keep going?"

"Goodwyn. I spoke with Neil Goodwyn."

"I liked him," she remembered.

"He waited until I was ready to talk to him, actually. Then he countered every statement I made with, 'Yes, but God is…'"

"God is what?"

"God is strong enough to withstand my anger. God is merciful enough to forgive my shortcomings. God is loving enough to understand my grief. God is big enough to direct my life. No matter what storms come."

"Even Hurricane Jenny?"

He smiled.

"Does He care enough to heal me, Colin?"

He hesitated only slightly. "I believe so. Jenny, if you can walk, you can dance. And when you do, I want it to be with me."

CHAPTER 31

On Monday Jenny went to Hollister's late, needing some time to reflect on the events of the weekend. She and Colin had made a new start, but their connection was still tenuous. He had not withdrawn his proposal, but he had not referred to it since her disastrous disclosure to Dr. Knowles, and she was afraid to bring it up. Looking back, she wished she had been more careful in her choice of words. The monster's entire body had been a weapon, not just one part. His hands and his feet had caused pain, too, and he had even used the sound in his throat against her. However, what he had done with the part that made him male had been the worst.

The monster. She'd thought her mission against him was over when the trial ended and the verdict was handed down. But Simon had told her that a mission wasn't over until you returned to your base. Her base—where she'd come from—was Houston. She'd gone home, but that hadn't been the solution. Maybe returning to base for her didn't mean a place, but a state of mind where her body was not at war with itself.

In a murder case you couldn't let go until you'd fitted all the pieces together, Colin had said. She hadn't been able to fit all the pieces of her relationship with Colin together, and until she did, the monster would continue to live inside her, affecting her actions and responses. Somehow she needed to exorcise him, to drive the fear away. Fear was crippling, but it was a feeling. She had been terrified of the monster, but she had pushed herself to testify against him. She looked up at the flag Colin had given her, impressed by its bold colors. Roosevelt and Churchill had used bold words. She was capable of bold actions.

Freedom from fear—Roosevelt had coined the phrase. Dr. Knowles hadn't used those words, but that was the goal of the therapy he was providing. He considered lovemaking to be a response to an entire individual, to his intangible qualities as well as his tangible ones. But perhaps humans were never entirely free from fear. She remembered Simon's statement about pushing yourself until you were a little afraid. It must be okay, then, to be a *little* afraid.

FDR had discussed four freedoms, however. Each led to a particular benefit, but together they added up to something more—more than a cessation of conflict, more than the dismissal of danger, more than the removal of persecution—their sum was peace. Peace had been declared, and men had put down their weapons. Perhaps peace was what she needed to seek.

How? She couldn't borrow Dorothy's bewitching shoes and be transformed. Her parents' minister had defined peace as a sense of inner calm despite stormy circumstances. He had implied that healing would bring peace. Based on Colin's behavior this last weekend, if she wanted more than affection, she would have to show him. He had made no move to undress her. She'd have to let go of fear, one breath at a time, one kiss at a time, one touch at a time. She would strive to clothe Colin and herself in peace.

CHAPTER 32

"We're better, Dr. Knowles," Jenny began. "We've talked. We've touched."

"Then the two of you have had a positive week."

Colin wondered what she would choose to report. She'd been freer in her affections since the crisis between them had been resolved. She had exposed him a bit more with each exercise. She had seemed complimented, not threatened, when she excited him.

"Tell me about it!" she exclaimed.

Knowles smiled at her expression for strong agreement. "I think you're meant to tell me."

She blushed and shook her head.

"Jenny, sex is a language. I need to know what you are communicating to Colin when you touch him."

"You want to know what I *say*?"

"Not exactly, no. I want to be sure that whatever you and Colin do together, you do freely. What are you thinking when you're with him?"

"I'm not thinking," she said, coloring again.

"Being aware of what we're feeling is a form of thinking," Knowles explained. "I need to know if fear is still involved."

"At first I was afraid of what he would do. Then I was afraid of his body. It took me a long time to realize that I owe him the same attentiveness and gentleness that he's shown me."

"We are all wounded," Knowles agreed. "The nature of the wound varies, that's all."

"I feel safe with him now, Dr. Knowles. I just don't always feel safe other places."

"Where don't you feel safe?"

"We go out to eat often, and if it's somewhere I haven't been before, I'm uneasy. I want to know where the alternate exits are, if any, and which way out is the quickest. I wonder about the other people in the restaurant. Are they friendly? That kind of thing."

"Jenny, you should feel encouraged. Many victims experience generalised fear—that is, fear of one man that expands to encompass fear of all men. You reversed this process while you were in witness protection, thanks to the support you received from those officers."

"That one man still comes at me, Dr. Knowles."

"In nightmares?"

"Yes. In witness protection I was spoiled—the guys would wake me up if they thought I was having a bad dream. A cup of tea or cocoa in the middle of the night if it was really bad, a little company and some reassuring words when it wasn't. At Colin's there's no one on watch, of course. Sometimes I wish we were sleeping together, because then I wouldn't be alone when the dreams come."

I can grant that wish, Colin thought.

"You can counter that with a purposeful dream," Knowles said, "one you can control. It's called visualisation, using the mind to precede and guide the body. We think of possible courses of action, decide how we feel about them, and then choose what to do. However, creating one positive scenario is not enough. Embellish your mental image. The more specific you can be, the better. All sorts of situations can benefit from this technique, but you can use it to prepare yourself for a more intimate physical relationship with Colin. Where do you want him to touch you? How will his fingers feel on your skin? What will he say? See him in your mind, and watch your body respond. Harness the power of your imagination, evaluate the feelings that are generated, but Jenny—do not act on those feelings yet."

"You want me to think about making love, but not do it."

"More than that—I want you to think it *through*. The pathway to healing is truth. Be honest with yourself. If at any point in your mental exercise you feel even the mildest anxiety, stop the tape, rewind, and begin again."

"But Dr. Knowles—"

"Jenny, there is no risk in patience. Every minute you invest now will pay great dividends later on. I am not suspending your physical exercises, you understand, simply adding an intellectual one."

She frowned. "I don't see how—"

"We all daydream. I'm asking you to set aside some time for a very focussed daydream. Even persons with an established sexual relationship can benefit from an active, healthy fantasy life."

CHAPTER 33

MISSING!

Have you seen our beloved daughter?

Height: 5'2" *Approximate weight: 7 stone*

Generous reward offered for relevant information.

There was a contact number given on the handbill, and the face that looked back at Sinclair was Jenny's.

He had taken the Jubilee line from Finchley Road tube station to Westminster, where he removed the first notice from the wall. On the way to the platform for the District line, he tore down the second. Upon his exit at St. James's, he ripped away the third. It was fraud of the most dangerous kind.

"Sir, they're everywhere," Andrews said when he entered his office at the Yard. "I took down all the ones I saw." He had placed them in a stack on Sinclair's desk. "Where'd they get the snap?"

"Must have been a school photo," Sinclair replied. "Jenny?" he said when she answered her mobile. "Do not leave the flat for any reason. Promise me! I'll ring you back shortly to explain." He put the phone down. "I'll ring Graves and request a meet. Transport Police need to be informed."

"Does Graves know Jenny's in London?" Andrews asked.

"After the article in the Telegraph, he demanded to know her whereabouts." He picked up the phone again and was told by Graves' secretary that he would be available in thirty minutes. "There's danger not only to Jenny, but to anyone who resembles her. Those flyers must come down immediately."

Again he was dialling. "Mother, I'm sending Jenny to you today. She needs a place to hide for a while. Continue your regular activities, and don't advise anyone of her presence. I'll give you more information later." He ended the call, and his mobile rang almost immediately. "Sinclair speaking."

"Casey here, sir. How's Jenny?"

"All right for the moment, but I could do with your help. I want her to go to my mother's, in Kent, but I can't get away, and I don't want her to use public transport."

"I have a car, sir, and I'm not on until late. How far is it?"

"This side of Ashford. No more than three hours' drive."

"I'll collect her within the hour."

"Ring me when you're on the M20, and I'll give you further directions. And thank you, Sergeant."

His next call was to Jenny. He explained as briefly as he could about the bulletins in the tube stations. "Casey's on his way. I want you to go with him, Jenny. Pack quickly. My mother is expecting you."

When she spoke, her voice was unsteady. "Will I be able to see you before I go?"

"It's not possible. Ring me after you arrive. I'll tell the Hollisters you won't be coming in. I love you, Jen."

When Simon arrived, Jenny was glad she'd changed into blue jeans. He drove a jeep, and the inside looked as if it had been under siege. She hadn't known how long Colin wanted her to stay in Kent, so she'd filled one suitcase and one rolling bag. Simon put both of them in the back of the 4x4.

Jenny put on her sunglasses until they were out of the city and thought about how swiftly one's life can change. On Saturday she and Colin had spent a glorious day walking on the Heath and touring Kenwood House just to the north of it. The paintings—by Rembrandt, Turner, Vermeer, and others—and the elegance of the decor made it hard to believe that this mansion had been someone's summer home. It was even more exquisite than the Wallace Collection, and the library, designed by the Scottish architect Robert Adam, was a graceful room, with rounded columns, an ornate curved ceiling, and delicate arches. No studious atmosphere here—light abounded in the vast interior. The classical artists whose works she'd seen had portrayed their subjects on canvases stretched between wooden frames, but this whole room had been Adam's canvas.

After they'd seen the house, she and Colin had picnicked on the grounds until the orchestral concert began in the amphitheatre. It had been a feast for the senses—the house, the meal, the music. Colin's hand in hers as they walked home in the dark. His lips on hers afterward. Now she felt numb.

She heard Simon's voice and turned toward him, listening while he repeated the directions Colin was giving him. "Simon, why would you do this for me?" she asked when he closed his mobile.

"Habits are hard to break, particularly bad ones."

"Simon!"

"Mission isn't over if you're still in harm's way."

They turned off the highway. When she had come with Colin, it had been dark, and she hadn't been able to see the twists and turns through the countryside. She recognized the house, though, when they pulled up in front of it.

Simon paused for a moment before turning off the ignition, taking in the house and the grounds that surrounded it. If Jenny stayed with Sinclair, she would never want for anything.

"I'm so glad you're here safely," Joanne said, coming out of the house and embracing her. "You must be Sergeant Casey."

"Simon, ma'am." He took Jenny's bags out of the jeep.

"You have the Rose again," Joanne said. "Meet me in the kitchen. We'll have lunch."

Simon followed Jenny up the stairs and deposited her bags in the bedroom with the roses. "I can't stay," he said. She wouldn't be needing him. He had some holiday time coming. He'd take it.

CHAPTER 34

In Kent, the danger seemed very far away. With profuse apologies, Colin's mother dashed off to a garden club event not long after lunch. She didn't spend much time at home on weekdays, she explained to Jenny, and Colin had told her she wasn't to alter her regular schedule in any way. She encouraged Jenny to make herself comfortable.

During Joanne's absence, she explored the rooms on the ground floor. She found the TV in a wooden cabinet in the smaller of the two sitting rooms. The conservatory was less formal, cushions on wrought-iron frames instead of upholstered furniture. The use of glass had been maximized, bringing the blue of the sky and the green of the forest into the room, and the pillows on the love seats were a pale teal, as if the outdoor elements had been blended in the interior color scheme.

The library was an elegant space with cool blue wallpaper and an ivory tree pattern. She inspected some of the volumes there, none of which appeared to be recent publications. Prior to her time at Hollister's, she wouldn't have noticed, but these shelves were full of fine or near fine leather-bound editions by all the major British historians: Carlyle, Macaulay, and Gibbon. Churchill was well represented. Shakespeare's complete works were there, as well as those of Dickens. Major poets—Byron, Shelley, Keats, and Tennyson—were included as well as several lesser known ones. Delderfield and Buchan were the only contemporary novelists, and there were no paperback books of any kind.

Finding Shelley was like finding an old friend. Remembering Esther Hollister's declaration that a book needed to be held, she removed one from the shelf and looked around for a place to sit. It was strange that the desk was set away from the wall, she thought, but a closer look revealed that the back was just as attractive as the front, the wood curved and finished with detailed drawings of ferns and other flora. The dark brown leather recliner was slightly worn, and she wondered why, when everything else in the room was in such pristine condition, until she sank into the soft cushions.

Colin phoned every night, a disembodied voice. Simon did not call at all. Everyone seemed far away except for Mr. MacKenna, who had had to wait in the drive Tuesday morning until Joanne woke and spotted his vehicle. Since the bedrooms were upstairs, she hadn't heard his knock. When Jenny came down for her tea, the pot was almost empty, Joanne having filled MacKenna's cup repeatedly. Colin had told her a retired copper would be coming to keep an eye on things.

Jenny found his presence reassuring, because it reminded her of her time in witness protection, although she could leave the house if she wanted to. Sean MacKenna didn't walk with her, trailing a dozen or more yards behind. "Best if I keep my eyes about," he said, and he did. If she took a book with her and propped her feet on the bench in the arbor, he was in the area but not close enough to smell the honeysuckle. When she stopped at the duck pond, she could see his stocky form leaning against a tree, watching and waiting for her to move on. His eyes were never on her, peering instead over her head, around her, making a complete circuit and then beginning again. He rolled his own cigarettes, bending his ruddy face forward when he lit them and smoking them until the ash blackened his fingers. When the butts were cool, he placed them in a handkerchief in his pocket. He kept his beard and mustache neatly trimmed, and in his hands, smoking was a tidy habit.

- -

Colin's weekend in Kent had passed quickly. When he left on Sunday, his mind was heavy with the memory of his conversation with Jenny about Scott. She had pressed him for information, not understanding how someone from a nice family could have so many crime connections.

"He was involved with drugs, Jenny. That subculture is peopled with unsavory characters. Drug raids often yield caches of weapons as well. Dealers and their henchmen are prepared to use them to protect their investment. He could have had contact with any number of persons who were willing to do anything for the right price."

"Did drugs make him a rapist? And a murderer?"

"No, we believe that he was predisposed toward violence against women. We had a psychological profile prepared, so we knew a good deal about him before we knew his specific identity. A profile is an investigative tool, you understand. It can't be used evidentially unless we can root out material to support it."

"What did the profile say?"

"That we were looking for a man in his thirties, possibly late thirties, who had been abused as a child, either by his father or another male authority figure. He would have been angry at his abuser but envious of his power and stature. Somehow sex and violence became inextricably linked. As he grew, he modelled his abuser's behaviour and discovered that violence empowered him. He felt rage at his mother, who likely knew and didn't protect him. His sadism and need to dominate wouldn't have led him to be successful with women in traditional relationships."

She shook her head slowly. "It's hard to believe that a father would do that to his own son."

"We were never able to demonstrate it. Jenny, if Scott had sought help—instead of acting on his impulses—I would have every sympathy for him. When he injured someone else, however, he passed the point of no return. As far as I'm concerned, he deserves everything he gets."

"Is he raping people in prison, do you think?"

"No, it's likely they're raping him. A sort of justice exists behind bars."

"Will he ever stop coming after me?"

"I believe so. Prison has a way of settling a man."

"I want to come home, Colin."

"I know, Jenny." There were flowers in bloom around them and clear skies above. He changed the subject and postponed telling her his decision as long as he could. It would take time for her image on the flyers to fade and for him to be convinced that this incident was a one-off.

- -

Joanne was worried about Jenny. After Colin had left Sunday night, she'd brought her into the kitchen for a cup of tea and tried to comfort her. Jenny had asked about the times she was separated from her husband. Had she ever been afraid?

"Some of the countries where he was posted weren't politically as stable as ours," Joanne admitted, "but most of the time our only real enemies were the climate, the shortages, and the lack of consistent telephone service. There were times when I'm certain I would have been safer somewhere else, but I would never agree to go."

"I'd rather be afraid with him than without him. I couldn't make him understand that." The tea was still too hot even to sip. Maybe she should stir it a few thousand more times.

"When conditions were less than ideal, we made do together. When we missed the children, we reminisced together. And we were never apart for very long. But Jenny—I was never threatened personally."

"How did you stand it? When he died. If you'll forgive my asking."

Joanne gave her a sad smile. "Sometimes death is a release," she said. "He was in such pain. Something better was awaiting him, and there came a time when I had to let him go."

Joanne's tea was almost gone. The milk she added to it must have cooled it. Jenny had not yet adopted that English habit. "You seem happy now. Does grief end?"

Joanne looked at her thoughtfully. Was Jenny grieving? "It eases; it never ends. I miss all the things we would have done together. But I have so many wonderful memories—we raised a family together, we had many years together. And we had time to say good-bye. That's important, I think. Although his death still felt sudden when it came."

"Time to say good-bye," Jenny echoed. The tea was warm in her throat. Good-bye was the last thing she wanted to say, to Colin at least.

"In a way I am still connected to him," Joanne continued. "I sleep on his side of the bed. I eat his favourite foods. I see that his son is happy, happier than he has been in years."

Jenny didn't even know what Colin's favorite foods were. And she'd never slept in his bed.

- -

Daydream, Dr. Knowles had said, and her first daydreams were about Rob. Their lives had been so carefree! It seemed almost blasphemous now that they had referred to final exams and research papers as pressures. And he hadn't included "'til death do us part" in his promise to her. It hadn't occurred to him—to either of them—that death would come between them. Perhaps she should say good-bye to him. She never had—his death had been so sudden, and afterward she had wanted to hold on to him, not let him go. So in her mind she wrote to him, a long letter, and when she finished, she was thankful that there was no notepaper for her tears to soil.

Of course the person who wrote the letter was her younger self, who no longer existed. She should say good-bye to her, too, to the innocent Jenny whose only pains had been growing pains and whose smiles had outnumbered her tears a hundred to one. For some reason this farewell was more difficult. Words were not enough. She wrapped her arms around herself and sobbed for her naiveté and her unmarred skin. Colin did not seem affected by her scars, but they were smaller on the outside than they were on the inside. The pain on the surface was gone.

Charming, gentle, loving Colin. She had dreamed of meeting someone like him—how cruel of life to send him to her when circumstances conspired to keep them apart! He wanted to do things *with* her, not to her. He'd begun to show her how he liked to be touched, and she'd discovered that sex, even her incomplete experience of it, was not all dark and intense. They'd laughed sometimes, and always he'd wanted to be sure that he was giving her pleasure.

Gradually she let her thoughts travel across the miles. If she were with him, what would she do? Kiss him so passionately that it would take his breath away! Then what? If she were in charge, where would she want him to kiss her? Where would she want his fingers to be? When would she stop him? No, this wasn't supposed to be about stopping. She imagined that the breeze she felt, soft on her face and ruffling her hair, was his breath. His fingers were agile enough to undo her buttons and tender enough to make her flesh tingle. He had never hurt her. Hurt—wrong word, wrong thought. She started again, thinking, no, planning each stage. She felt a little more confident each time she saw him in her mind, caressing her, but she didn't know if she could yield completely. No. Yielding implied that something wasn't freely given. Would she ever be able to involve her body? Think it through, Dr. Knowles had said, but some things she'd just have to take on faith. Oh, she wanted *Colin's* arms around her, not her own, and the tears that ran down her cheeks were cleansing ones, tears of longing because something deep inside her had softened and relaxed.

CHAPTER 35

The flyers that appeared the following Tuesday had been reworded. "*Our daughter is still missing,*" they read. *"We are desperate. Please help us!"* The photograph of Jenny was the same, but an arrow pointed to her cheek with the caption, *"Small scar here,"* and another detail suggested that her hair might be shorter. Scott's defence team was the likely source, but none of them acknowledged anything when questioned by police. The contact number led only to an untraceable mobile phone. In addition, they'd been unsuccessful in identifying the individuals who had posted them. You didn't have to be a criminal to accept a quick fifty quid for an easy job like that.

Damn, Sinclair thought. She would not be able to come home at the weekend, and he would have to tell her. But not everything—not that this time bus shelters had been plastered with the bloody things as well as the train and tube stations. Last weekend had been difficult enough. She had been overjoyed to see him, but she had expected that they'd go home together on the Sunday, and when she'd heard him tell MacKenna to report back that evening, she'd known he would be leaving without her. They'd had a real row, Jenny not understanding his caution. He'd felt a right prick saying no, and the fact that he'd been correct in doing so was no consolation. She'd been in tears when he left.

The danger was twofold. Someone could see her and report where, and someone could see her with him. She hadn't left a paper trail anywhere that he knew of, but he could be traced. If a link between them were suspected, she could never come home. For her own good he had to keep her away.

- -

Joanne had been shocked by Colin's news that a second round of circulars had been distributed—MacKenna as well—but Jenny most of all. "Something has to be done," the taciturn MacKenna insisted, and Joanne knew that he expected her to figure out what it would be. She rang her vicar, explained about Jenny, and asked him to call by.

"Jenny, I'd like you to meet Father Rogers. Selwyn, this is my guest,

Jennifer Jeffries. I'm serving tea in the conservatory, Jenny. You'll join us, won't you?"

The table was already set. Sponge cake, fresh strawberries, sugar, clotted cream, all served on china plates. If Father Rogers were fed treats like this everywhere he went, no wonder his cheeks were round and his expression virtually jolly. All he needed was the red suit, and he would have been a perfect Santa.

She shook his outstretched hand and accepted the cup of tea that Joanne poured. While they made small talk, Jenny blew gently on her tea to cool it.

"Jenny, I hope you'll forgive me, but I've told Selwyn a little about you."

"What did you tell him?" The heat she felt spreading from her chest to her face burned more than her tea.

"Your history and the trials that are keeping you and Colin apart. I've wanted so badly to help you, and I've felt so inadequate. Jenny, I trusted him to bury my husband. You can trust him. I'll leave you now."

Jenny watched her go, not knowing which was worse, the shock or the shame. She looked down. Her hands still held the teacup, but she couldn't feel it. If Father Rogers spoke, she didn't hear him. "Are you going to talk to me about God?"

"If you'll allow me, yes. If you prefer, I can help you talk to God."

"I have a psychiatrist. I don't need to talk to God."

Rogers nodded. "A good psychiatrist can accelerate emotional healing. That's a very positive thing to be doing."

"But not sufficient."

"In my view, no. A psychiatrist uses words and feelings. Sometimes God speaks to us with words, but more often he responds with gifts that are more lasting—hope, peace, and love."

"Well, he hasn't sent me any of those!" she said angrily. "I've struggled for months, and the only difference is, now I get to do it all by myself!"

Father Rogers ate another strawberry. "Jennifer, do you believe in God?"

She raised her chin. "I think God would call me Jenny."

"He calls you Beloved," Rogers answered. "Do you believe in Him?"

His gaze was disconcerting. His glasses had no rims, and she felt he could see her far too well. "I guess so. Everyone says I should, because I didn't die."

"That's right. God has power over life and death. He is very powerful—powerful enough to break the chains that bind us to the past, powerful enough to create freedom from fear, powerful enough to bring good out of evil."

"Franklin Roosevelt used that phrase," she said slowly. "Freedom from fear. I read a book about him recently."

"I don't believe it's a coincidence then that I used it today. God is very serious about communicating with us."

"What is He trying to tell me?"

"That it is possible to live a life free from the bondage of fear. Love is the answer. Love God and trust that He loves you. He created you, and He loves you. And when you love someone, you always hope that they'll love you back, don't you?"

Oh, yes. Colin in particular.

"There is a corollary, forgiveness, because love and forgiveness go hand in hand."

She shook her head. "Forgive and forget the monster who attacked me? No!"

"Jenny, I will never, ever ask you to forget. I will encourage you to remember and yet to forgive. Your forgiveness doesn't excuse his behaviour; it doesn't endorse it. It doesn't affect his healing, but it does affect yours. It will remove the power your abuser still has over you and bring you peace."

"I can't do this," she said, unable to restrain the tears. "As Faulkner said, 'The past isn't dead. It's not even past.' He is still trying to kill me. There is no way I can do this."

"None of us can, without God's help. With His help, we can *decide* to do it. That's the first step. The second step is to do it, not once, but many, many times. The greater the offence against us, the longer it may take to forgive."

No kidding. She could not speak. Mercifully, Father Rogers did not stare at her wet cheeks.

"Love is stronger than fear, Jenny. It may mature more slowly, but its roots are deeper and its life longer." He looked up. "God's presence is everywhere, but I always feel it particularly in this room. These wide windows enable us to see His world so clearly, don't you agree?"

"I'm not promising anything," she finally said.

"Of course not," Father Rogers agreed. "That is a commitment you make to God, not to me." He set his plate on the table. "May I pray with you before I go?"

"I don't think I'll live long enough to forgive him."

Rogers smiled. "Then I will pray that you have a long life," he said.

"Will you pray for Colin, too? Joanne's son."

"I know Colin well," Rogers nodded. "I'll pray that the love between you will grow."

- -

It was Saturday, and Colin and Jenny went for a walk. She knew Mr. MacKenna wouldn't follow them; Colin had given him a twenty-four-hour leave. Joanne would not invade their privacy, either in the house or elsewhere. "Colin, I want to come home," she said.

His face was filled with concern. "Mac said you had a rough week."

"I did. It's safe here, I know, but safety isn't everything. We're losing each other."

"Jenny, I can't be certain that all the bulletins have been removed, or that new ones won't be posted."

"Colin, I'll wear dark glasses. I'll bleach my hair. I'll gain weight! September 14 is a week from Tuesday. It will have been one year since—since. Please don't leave me here." They had walked far enough from the house so they could not be seen. She stopped and put her arms around him. "I love you. I miss you," she said.

"This hasn't been easy for me either, Jen."

"How about this? I'll take my rolling bag and walk out to the lane. Someone will come along. I'll hitch a ride. There's a train station in Ashford, isn't there? I'm sure someone would direct me—maybe even a *policeman.* I'll buy a ticket for London and take a cab from the station to Hampstead."

"Mac would stop you, Jenny."

"What if I talked him into coming with me? I could hold a newspaper in front of my face. Or wear a hat with a wide brim. I bet your mother has one. Colin, there are so many ways I could disguise my appearance."

"Jenny, the risk assessment—"

"Colin, I'm less afraid of the monster hurting me than I am of his coming between us." It had been so long since he had held her, really held her. She pressed her body against his. "Tell me you don't want me to come home."

He knelt down in the grass and took her in his arms. "This week," he promised. "If your picture's not posted, I'll collect you this week."

"When?" she panted.

"I'll drive down Wednesday night. We'll leave before first light on Thursday. I'll have to work a regular day on Thursday."

Her smile was dazzling. Perhaps that was why her tears affected him so deeply—because they washed away her smile. She sat up, and he brushed the leaves from her hair and the back of her clothes. "When I scratch my chigger bites, I'll think of you," she teased.

Her sense of humour, in the most unexpected places—God, he had missed her.

CHAPTER 36

Colin was at the wheel of his car, Jenny's bags in the boot. No additional flyers had been posted, and after early morning good-byes, she was on her way back to Hampstead with him. When they arrived at the flat, Colin changed clothes quickly. "I'll see you tonight," he said. "I hope not too late."

She had the entire day ahead of her, and she had promised him that she wouldn't go anywhere. She wrote a letter of thanks to Joanne and then decided to send a note to her own mother, in spite of the possibility that heart failure might result. She surfed the TV channels. She reviewed her Italian. By mid-afternoon she was sleepy, so she made herself a cup of tea, taking it, however, into Colin's bedroom rather than her own. She missed him. She had come back from Kent to be with him, but of course he would gone a lot of the time.

She took her cup back to the kitchen. She was still sleepy, and remembering Joanne's words about sleeping on her husband's side of the bed to feel close to him, she climbed into Colin's bed and rested her head on his pillow.

When Colin came home, the flat was quiet. "Jenny?" he called. There was no response. He took a quick look in her room. Could she have gone out? After her fervent assurances that she wouldn't? He stepped into his bedroom to hang up his coat, and there she was, asleep in his bed, her jeans in a heap on the floor. He reached over and stroked her cheek gently. "Jenny," he smiled, "what are you doing in my bed?"

She sat up slowly. "Missing you." She pushed the covers back.

Her feet were bare; her legs were bare. She had napped in her t-shirt and knickers. He watched her pull on her blue jeans. Damn. It hadn't been an invitation.

He had brought Chinese food for dinner, and she seemed shy and quiet while they ate. She leaned against him while they watched TV, and he reminded himself that Knowles' restrictions were likely still in force and regulated his response to her. They did not have another appointment scheduled. Perhaps they would go later the next week if the tube and train stations remained void of adverts about her.

Jenny lay in bed, frustrated with herself and the events of the evening. Colin had been warm and affectionate but restrained, and she had been unsure about how to proceed. Dr. Knowles had encouraged her to visualize making love to Colin, but he hadn't told her how to make that vision a reality. One of them would have to make the first move, and she wished that he had—but of course he had, weeks ago, and she had shut it down. He couldn't read her mind, and anyway, she was supposed to be responsible for herself. She slipped out of bed.

His door was open. "Colin? Colin, are you awake?" she whispered. She heard a muffled sound. "May I come in?"

He pushed himself up on one elbow, and the sight of his bare chest made her knees feel weak. She had her nightlight in her hand, and she held it out. "Would you plug this in for me? In here?"

"Let me get some trousers on," he said.

She hadn't realized that he slept in the nude. "No, don't do that," she said quickly. "Just show me where the outlet is."

He pointed to the left of the chest of drawers. She knelt down, affixed the light, and then approached the bed. "I've been in a cocoon, and I'm ready to come out. But there are so many butterflies in my stomach—will you help me?"

"Jenny, are you sure about this?"

"Yes. I want you, all of you, and I don't want to hold anything back."

Her nightdress had thin blue straps on each shoulder. He pushed one aside. "You're trembling, Jen."

"I don't care. I love you so much."

He moved the other strap and watched the soft fabric slide to her feet. "Come here to me then." He made room for her beside him.

She did not have to tell him what to do. Kisses, deep kisses, which she returned just as passionately as they were given. Kisses everywhere, his hands everywhere. His fingers between her legs, then grazing her chest.

He cupped her face in his hands. "Are you sure?"

She took a deep breath, the way people do before plunging off a high dive. "Yes. Oh, yes."

He moved on top of her and felt her body tense. Should he pull away? No, her arms were around him, holding him close. He eased into her as gently as he could, whispering her name, once, twice. He heard her fractured breaths abate and felt her lift her knees, and a fierce desire to give her every good thing and to protect her from every bad thing surged inside him, and he didn't give a jot how unrealistic it was.

She had hoped solely for the absence of pain. She heard his voice and relaxed, totally unprepared for the shock of pleasure she felt. What

Colin was doing wasn't violent; he was caressing her. Her physical sensations intensified. She began to move with him, as if they were one body. They were one body. Like the sugar she dissolved in her tea, she didn't know where her skin ended and his began.

Wanting to prolong their closeness, Colin slowed his pace. In the glow from the nightlight she could see his tender smile. He stroked her face and kissed her again. When he increased his tempo, she did as well. He called her name, not in a whisper but in an involuntary outburst, raw enough to tell her how great his need for her had been. And then her tears started—tears unlike any she had shed before: tears of relief, renaissance, revelation. He kissed her wet cheeks and told her he loved her. For the first time since the attack, she forgot about her scars and felt beautiful.

- -

In the half light of dawn, the nightlight flickered, casting shadows across her naked body. She stretched, realizing that the cool shivers on her skin came from the tips of Colin's fingers. They floated over her, barely touching her, smooth gentle strokes up her thighs and across her bottom. The sensations remained for a few seconds even after his fingers had moved on. He kissed her ears and her neck. She rolled onto her back. Some parts of her body were waking up faster than others, but his body was fully awake. Her eyes still closed, she put her arms around his neck and welcomed him in.

- -

When she awoke next, he had showered and gone. Even naked, she felt warm in his bed, and she made no move to get up. She thought about how alive he had made her feel. For a long time she'd only known she was alive because she'd had pain. Then the physical pain had receded, and emotional pain had been the indicator. Finally she had traded fear and trembling for passion. Now she was filled with a sense of well-being. Milan Kundera had described the lightness of being as unbearable, but the lightness she felt now wasn't unbearable at all. It was a weightlessness that spread throughout her, the result of deep burdens removed. Nothing of gravity held her down, and the wings of happiness were beneath her. Why didn't her body lift off the mattress?

CHAPTER 37

Dr. Knowles' first questions to Colin and Jenny centred on the handbill episodes and their response to them.

"My freedom of movement is still significantly curtailed," she answered. "I didn't go back to the bookstore until yesterday, and I was uneasy even then. It's probably paranoid of me, but I feel like people are looking at me everywhere I go."

"Was your time in Kent productive?"

She smiled. She should start a new list: *Dr. Knowles' Cute Adjectives.* "The most productive thing that happened in Kent was my convincing Colin to let me come home."

"And after your return?"

She blushed deeply and looked at her lap. "My body is Colin's now," she whispered. "I gave it to him."

"Good for you," Knowles said softly. "Would you tell me a bit about it? Without disclosing any details you'd like to keep private, of course."

"I missed him so much when we were apart. When I came home, I was nervous, but I wasn't afraid. There's a difference, but I don't know how to explain it. I cried almost the whole time, but I wasn't afraid."

"Why did you cry, my dear?"

"First, because it didn't hurt, and I was so relieved. Then because it felt good, which I never expected. I cried because being so close to him was overwhelming." Her voice broke, and she laughed at herself because she was crying. "I cried because I was happy, and later I cried because it was over."

Neither man could restrain a smile.

"Did we break the rules?"

"No," Knowles said. "It had to be your choice, not mine. If I had given you permission, it would have meant that I was in charge. That was never my intent. Any problem areas?"

Initial tension every time, Colin thought, but it always eased, so he didn't feel bound to report it. There was something, however, that she needed to disclose. He took her hand. "We need to tell him about Tuesday, my love." She'd been tense when he left for work. Reluctant to see him go, but all right. "One year ago Tuesday Jenny was attacked," he said. "I left a bit late for the Yard. About midday Casey rang to tell me she wasn't answering her mobile. I couldn't get through either. I went home."

"I couldn't get up," she explained. "I had cramps in my legs and pains in my chest and stomach. Sharp pains."

All the lights had been on in the flat when he arrived. Midday, and all the lights were on. He'd found her in bed, lying on her side with her knees pulled up. "I wanted to ring for an ambulance. She wouldn't have it."

"No more hospitals," she said. "No more strangers' hands."

"I decided to run her a bath. If it didn't help, an ambulance was still an option." She'd cried when he lowered her into the water, but she'd been able to stretch out her limbs. She'd accepted the glass of wine he brought. And the refill.

"The hot water eased the pain." She hadn't had anything to eat, and the wine had made her tipsy. He'd been sitting on the edge of the tub, and she'd splashed him, first by accident and then on purpose. He'd splashed her back, but her laughter at his sopping shirt had turned to hysterical tears. He'd put his arms around her slippery body and held her. Then he had kissed her. She had responded with a rush of emotion, stripping his clothes away, and he had taken her out of the bath and made love to her, but she had never closed her eyes.

Knowles leant forward, knowing from their pauses that far more had happened than they were telling him.

"Colin put me to bed."

She had cried hard, and her words had broken his heart. "Colin, I wish you'd been my first," she'd said. "In all the ways that matter, I believe I was," he'd replied. He hadn't gone back to the Yard; he hadn't been able to leave her.

"Jenny, tell me what you were feeling," Knowles said.

"I wasn't conscious of feeling anything. Just how badly my body hurt. It was like being blind. So much has happened this last year—the attack was an eternity ago. But on Tuesday, it was a heartbeat ago."

"You remembered your rape. Were you surprised?"

"Shocked is more like it. Why was it so bad? I've been in Colin's arms, unafraid. Don't you see? I've won."

"Your trauma is still alive, my dear. Dormant until something triggers it."

"Why don't I have closure? The monster's in prison!"

"Because there's not an end to the feeling process. Feelings ebb and flow—they change, but they don't stop. Closure is a deceptive concept. How did you feel when you woke?"

"Hung over," she smiled ruefully. "Dazed. But I don't think it was from the alcohol."

"And on Wednesday?"

"About the same. I was happy to be home. I stayed in bed most of the day. Thursday I was better. I went back to Hollister's."

Knowles leant back in his chair. "Jenny, your fear of intercourse was the problem that led you to seek my help. It's evident that together you have resolved that issue, and a new level of intimacy—emotional as well as physical—has been the result. However, I would like to caution you."

"There's more?" she asked.

Knowles smiled. "Your psychological recovery," he said to her, "didn't begin in earnest until you decided to trust someone and accept help. Fear was the inhibitor. It kept you from trusting the protection team for a time, and it kept you from experiencing Colin's love. Fear is a normal reaction to certain events—public speaking, dying, and visiting the dentist are the first three that come to mind—but these fears aren't usually crippling. Fear that results from traumatic events can be diminished, however. Believe it or not, one of these days you will be able to relive the attack without the emotional response. And that brings me to your next assignment."

More sexual homework? Colin wondered. One of Theo's initial therapeutic goals had been for Jenny to experience sexual frustration, and Colin had taken that to mean that he should hold back during the exercises, not attempt to guide her toward her own release. On the weekend he'd finally felt free to show her what all the fuss was about. He hadn't been successful at first. Losing control completely was still frightening to her, and he'd had to encourage her repeatedly with soft words and tender touches. When she had finally let herself go, it had been one of the happiest moments of his life, knowing he had her trust, seeing her joy. Theo's voice brought him back to attention.

"Jenny, before our next session, I'd like you to make two lists for me: one of everything you've been afraid of since reaching adulthood—fear, past tense—and two, everything you're still afraid of—fear, present tense. And Colin, I'm giving you a similar assignment, because fear has had an impact on your life as well. List whatever fears you have. Just present tense. Fear is still the issue that will affect your future together the most. I'll see you in two weeks."

CHAPTER 38

The man's eyes followed Jenny. He was good with faces, always had been, and he'd seen her somewhere before. Something wasn't quite the way he recalled it, but it would come to him in time. It always did. He was an unlikely-looking sort himself. No one paid him any mind, and that gave him the freedom to concentrate on other people's faces.

He waited outside the bakery when she went in. She had no tourist maps or carrier-bags. Her bakery purchase she held in her hand, taking the odd bite as she headed quickly up the High Street.

He walked a ways past her so as not to alarm her, saw the scar, stopped, watched her cross the street, and remembered. The pics that had been posted some weeks back: She'd been the subject. Her hair had been dark in the snap, all dark, not bleached or dyed or whatever they call it like it was now. No matter. It was the same face, and there was money to be made off that face.

She paused, scanning the street behind her, but she didn't notice him. He was outside her field of view.

Had he kept the flyer? Probably. He never threw anything away. Except his wife, and he hadn't had to throw her far, haha.

She passed the fancy hotel near Royal Free. There wasn't another that he knew of between here and Finchley. She must live here. He ambled along behind.

She headed through the residential streets, and she knew where she was going. Her pace never slowed. She turned right, but when he reached the corner, there was no sign of her. No problem. Everything that was anything happened on the High Street. She'd be back, and so would he.

CHAPTER 39

Casey stopped down the pub on his way home from Hampstead. Why did pubs have so much wooden décor? he wondered. Tradition, or a way to hide the stains from the nicotine-soaked air? He sipped his pint and peered through the stale smoke. The dark interior didn't reveal many daytime drinkers, and none of them looked happy, but Jenny had been, today. She'd been relaxed, holding his arm while they walked and regaling him with amusing anecdotes from her work at the bookstore. The dark glasses she wore and the scarf on her hair—attempts to alter her appearance for security reasons—hadn't dimmed her smile.

He hadn't seen her since the drive to Kent. Colin's mother was nice, but as Jenny put it, she "had a life." Sinclair had sent a "dour man" to follow her round but she had been lonely with everyone she knew and loved so far away. When she returned to London, she'd had to endure the anniversary of Scott's attack. Nice to have all that behind her, to see her so lighthearted.

Then it hit him like a fist in the gut: Sinclair's having it off with her. He took a long drink. He should be glad. She's happy, so she must be okay with it, and if anyone deserves to be happy, she does. But there was a lingering ache in his groin. He ordered another pint.

Sinclair had bided his time, brought her back from Texas, and then—got the shove-off. What bloke in his right mind got interested in a girl like that? Someone who was scared every time you wanted to get your leg over? They'd been seeing Knowles, and he wondered what those sessions were like. Did they have to describe everything to him?

He remembered how bruised and battered Jenny had been when he first saw her, how frightened every time he'd had to touch her. Most frustrating patient he'd ever had—impulsive, defiant, always talking back, testing the limits. He'd never met anyone who cried so much. But she had a sense of humour, just quips at first, though later she'd felt safe enough to tease them all. There hadn't been much laughter when he was growing up. His mum had tried, but she was dead worried all the time about earning her crust. SBS humour had been dark, cynical, obscene. It had suited him. His glass was empty. He signalled the barman.

As a medic, his mandate had been, fix it fast. Even minor injuries in the field became serious if not treated quickly. Major injuries could mean death. SFO teamwork was the same. When you finally got the order to go, speed was critical. Lives could be at stake. They practised rapid entry, for Chrissakes! He laughed to himself. Sinclair hadn't got that.

He hadn't been able to fix Jenny fast. He'd wanted to: He'd been impatient with her, with the mission, and with himself. He'd pushed her, to face things, to get on with it, but waiting was an inherent part of every op. Perhaps Sinclair had realised that. If so, she was better off with Sinclair.

Her pain had disturbed him. It had brought to mind his career-ending injury, when he had been angry at the entire friggin' world. The pain hadn't surprised him; he'd been hurt before. Pain masters you for a bit, then you push past it, like everything else. The selection process had been demanding, the training was demanding, and the missions were demanding. He had worked with men who required as much if not more from themselves as they did from you. You pushed past all of it, and it meant something. He'd gone from that to a hospital bed, to Rita telling him he was lucky to be alive. She hadn't understood that life without a mission was not a life. He had gone from something to nothing. So had Jenny. He beckoned the barman.

For him, physical attraction to a particular woman was what motivated him to get to know her. He had had a professional relationship with Jenny, and he had never expected to be attracted to her. Respect had come first. He'd known that you can't walk away from a mission, but until she sent her father home without her, he didn't think that she understood the concept. Then there'd been that black trouser suit at New Year's—and the time she'd been so ill and he'd cut off her nightdress. When you've seen a woman starkers, you don't forget, not if she has a shape like Jenny's. But he usually favoured women with longer legs. And now Jenny was opening hers for Sinclair. Damn! That pint had gone down quickly. He was still thirsty. Easy to remedy that. He raised his hand, and the barman replaced his empty glass with a full one.

Professional relationship. Right. At what point had it become personal? When she and Sullivan were shot? No, before that. When she'd finally trusted him, she'd talked to him about a lot of things. Why hadn't he talked to her? God knows he'd had chances. He should have told her how he felt. But he hadn't; he'd waited to see how she felt about Sinclair. And then it was too late. Better that way—Sinclair had more to offer her, position, land, real money, more than a regular copper could ever make. He needed another pint. It was supplied.

He had only himself to blame. He knew she felt close to him, and he'd never responded to any of her overtures. That walk they'd taken during the last night at the flat—he should have kissed her, given her something to think about while she was in Texas. Instead he'd held back. Completed the mission. Let her go. And after she returned, advised her to get professional help to resolve her problems with Sinclair. What a bloody fool he was!

He had sent Rita away. He should have fought to keep her. He had contained himself with Jenny. He should have fought to win her. When the barman looked his way, he nodded.

Knowles' sessions must have helped. It had not been easy for her to go, but she loved Sinclair, and she had done it more for him than for herself. What had it been like for her, when her trust was finally great enough to let him inside? And what had it been like for him, to have that lovely little body wrapped around him and hold that tender heart in his hands?

What about *his* heart? He worked hard, he played hard, but he had one, in spite of what others might think. Thoughts of Jenny retreated only temporarily. When he saw her, the tissues in his heart ruptured all over again. There were no sutures strong enough. "Another," he called.

He thought again about Sinclair. How had he managed it? Had it been difficult for him, making it good for her? Well, somehow he had done. She had been glowing. And he'd earned it—he'd gone through weeks of therapy with her. Sit in a shrink's office? He wouldn't have wanted any part of that himself, not even for Jenny. Well—maybe for Jenny.

CHAPTER 40

Jenny sighed. She could imagine the headline in tomorrow's newspaper: "Warning: Paper Shortage in Britain Expected; Inveterate List-maker on the Loose."

"Our session will be over before you get to the bottom of my list, Dr. Knowles." She handed him a sheet with one very long column, the things that had caused her to be afraid:

Disappointing my parents
Loss of loved ones
The dark
Being naked
The monster
His thugs
Angry people
Doctors
Policemen
The bandages coming off
The hospital attacker
Injections
Staying in the hospital
Being in witness protection
Separation from my family
Sergeant Casey
Brian
Being touched
Sleeping (because of the bad dreams)
Letting Colin and the other men down
That Danny would die
Hope (It can be a dangerous thing)
That something would happen to the other men
Hunt, sort of
Testifying/the defense attorneys
Going out by myself
Disappointing Colin
Sex
Losing Colin
Strangers
Places I haven't been to
People's curiosity

There were only five items on her list of current fears:

Disappointing my parents
Death of loved ones
The dark
The monster
His thugs

There were also five items which she admitted caused her to be wary, but no longer afraid:

Angry people
Going out by myself
Strangers
New places
People's curiosity

"It's okay," she said. "You can laugh if you want to. I know it's an exhaustive list. And I forgot one fear—telling my mother I streaked my hair."

She was smiling now, but she hadn't been while making those lists, Colin recalled. Theo's assignment had required her to look back, and it hadn't been easy or quick. "I had so few fears before the monster," she'd said. "Nothing really worth mentioning. The typical teenage angst about identity—piece of cake. Post-monster is a different story. Rape destroys you. I still don't feel like I'm a real person." She'd left those concerns off the final inventory.

"This list should empower you," Dr. Knowles said. "You've overcome a great deal. The only items which remain on your current list are specific, rational fears. It is rational to be afraid of the men who abused you, their incarceration notwithstanding."

"I didn't do it by myself. Simon said that most missions are achieved through teamwork, and he's right."

"The entries you listed as being wary of—you may find over time that your uneasiness about them lessens. Colin, I would caution you. As Jenny becomes more independent, you may have to adjust your degree of protectiveness."

She gave him a quick glance. "Feeling safe enabled me to make the progress I did," she said. "I have to confess: It took a lot of people a long time to make me feel that way. The guys had to prove themselves over and over."

"You may always consider safety to be an important part of your relationships, and that's all right," Knowles agreed. "Most persons do, although they take its presence for granted. Beware, however, of giving Scott too much power. When your fear and shame were at their peak, he was in control of your behaviour. At the other end of the spectrum, if you develop an excessive need to be in charge of your environment, that will derive from him as well. A balanced, healthy awareness will fall somewhere in between."

"Awareness"—that was a shrink word if she ever heard one.

"Nightmares were not on your second list," Knowles observed. "Are you no longer experiencing them?"

"They're shorter now, because Colin wakes me up and comforts me." She couldn't help blushing and hoped Dr. Knowles wouldn't require her to elaborate. She didn't sleep nude, although Colin wanted her to, but if the bedclothes came off during the night, the cold she felt triggered the dreams. After one such episode she had understood the comforting nature of sex. Colin's body had been warm, and it had not taken him long to distract her from her distress.

"What factors assisted you most in your recovery?" Knowles asked.

She thought for a moment. "Having people I knew I could depend on, people I could trust, helped a lot. I don't think I could have done it by myself, although I wanted to at first. The guys knew all about me, and it didn't matter." She paused. "Learning to be patient with myself wasn't easy. Some days I felt I'd made progress and some days I didn't. It took me a long time to let go of my fear."

"And your determination, Jenny," Colin added.

She smiled at him. "Yes, and your love was the motivator. That and your faith in our future. And coming here helped."

"In the right environment, healing can occur through self-disclosure," Knowles agreed. "Colin, did you bring a list?"

"I didn't have to write anything down," he said, "because there's only one thing I'm truly afraid of: something happening to Jenny. Her safety has been my primary concern since last September, and it still is."

"Colin, aren't you afraid of losing your mom?"

"I don't see that happening in the immediate future, Jen. As she ages, I'll dread it, but I'm not afraid of grief. My father's death taught me that I can survive it."

She looked at the older man. "Have I done enough, Dr. Knowles? Do we have to keep coming?"

"Yes, my dear."

"But Dr. Knowles—I passed the final exam, in a manner of speaking. Why don't I get the diploma?"

Knowles' eyes were gentle. "Aftershocks of trauma can last a long time, Jenny. Some issues we have not addressed. Others remain unresolved—memory versus reality being one of them—as evidenced by the intensity of your reaction on the anniversary of your attack. I suspect you have a good deal of residual anger at Scott. I would recommend that you continue your therapy, but you may begin to reduce your medication. I would encourage but not require Colin to accompany you."

"So it's *Hasta la vista*—until I see you again—instead of *Adios.*"

"I'm afraid so. I'd like you to consider me a resource. Unpleasant surprises may yet arise. In the meantime, remember that everyone faces limitations in life. Focus on what you can do, and the limitations won't defeat you."

CHAPTER 41

Colin spun round. "Behind me!" he yelled to Jenny, his body shielding her from the big man with the knife. He swung his right forearm wide, meeting the blade in midair. His left foot followed, smashing hard and fast into the knee of the attacker. The thug went down, screaming, losing his grip on the knife.

He was not the only one screaming: Jenny had found her voice.

The second man moved in, a smaller more agile version of the first, his weapon held low, his hand in constant motion. Colin parried his thrusts, but he would not expose Jenny, and when the man lunged forward, Colin did not step aside. He felt the sharp edge bite into his thigh. His left fist connected with the man's right cheek, and the man realised that the odds had changed. His companion was trying unsuccessfully to get to his feet, and their target was not soft. He ran past Colin and Jenny and down the street.

"Down! Stay down!" Colin shouted to the first man, slamming his foot against the flat of his back and pinning him to the ground. "Your scarf, Jenny." She had gone mute, her face taut with horror.

Colin tied the man's hands behind his back. "Urgent police assistance required," he panted into his mobile. He gave the street name and closest cross street. "Hampstead. ABH. Suspect subdued."

"Do you need an ambulance, sir?"

"Yes." Still breathing hard, he ended the call. "It's all right, Jenny." The sweet sound of sirens rent the dark air.

The two officers in the first panda car saw three persons in their headlamps: a tall well-dressed male with one arm around a short dark-haired female, and a heavy-set rumpled individual on the ground. The long-limbed man's clothes were torn, and blood was staining the handkerchief he held to his thigh. The man down was whimpering.

Colin identified himself, gave a brief description of the incident and the assailant who got away, and accepted the first aid that was offered. "Flick knives," he added. "One of them's not too far off." His knees buckled, and Jenny felt his weight on her shoulder.

The ambulance arrived, and a second panda pulled up behind it. "We'll take it from here, sir," Colin was told. "Best if you have your wounds seen to straightaway. This bastard can wait for the next ambulance. We'll catch you up at the hospital later."

"She stays with me," Colin told the ambulance attendant. He had not released his hold on Jenny.

Jenny was by herself. The doctor in casualty had insisted very gently that she wait outside the treatment room while he irrigated, disinfected, and sutured Colin's injuries. She felt sick. Colin was the third person who had been harmed because of her, he was the one she cared about most, and she had been useless. She dialed Simon's number on her mobile. "They had knives," she reported. "I couldn't do anything but scream. Colin did it all. We're at the hospital. Royal Free."

His voice was sharp. "Are you all right? Is Sinclair?"

"I wasn't hurt. Colin kept me behind him all the time. He kicked the first man in the knee."

Primary objective—reduce the odds. Quickly. "How many were there?"

"Two. Colin's getting stitches in his arm and his leg."

Second—accept injuries when necessary to protect the principal. Not bad for a suit.

"He'll be okay, but I'm scared! One of them got away."

Street fighters then. For someone professionally trained, one on two weren't bad odds. "On my way."

The borough detectives arrived before Simon did. Jenny heard them asking at the nurses' station if Mr. Sinclair were available to answer a few questions. The nurse gestured in her direction, and they moved toward her. "Miss—?"

She didn't answer. They looked like carbon copies with their slim faces and physiques, one with paler skin than the other.

"I'm Detective Sergeant Chase, and this is Detective Constable Dodd. We're here to assist you." Chase held out his hand, and Jenny hesitated before taking it. He had ink on his fingers. She had blood on hers.

"Were you injured in any way?" Sergeant Chase's eyes took in everything: her manner of dress, her appearance, her hands clenched in her lap. Dodd had quietly removed a small notebook from an inside pocket of his coat.

She shook her head.

"You've had a frightening experience. Are you up to a little chat?"

"I don't know what I can say," she told them. "You'll have to wait for Colin."

"Did you witness the incident?"

She didn't know which of them had spoken. She was straining to hear what was going on with Colin and the doctor. "Yes," she said slowly.

The treatment room door opened. "You may come through now," the doctor said. She saw Colin sitting on the treatment table, his face gray, with one shirtsleeve cut away and his trouser leg gaping. There were two bandages, one much larger than the other. She moved to Colin's left and uninjured side.

"I'm all right, Jen," he assured her.

"One of the lacerations was rather deep," the doctor said. "We'll be keeping him overnight for observation. Mr. Sinclair, someone will notify you when your room is ready."

She saw Colin nod in greeting and realized she had forgotten all about the two detectives. "Gentlemen, I've been expecting you." He held up his right arm. "This was the work of the suspect you have in custody. He was the initiator and the heavier built of the two men. The suspect who got away from me was in his early thirties, just under six feet tall, weighing between twelve and thirteen stone. He was wearing dark jeans and a black sweatshirt. He had dark brown hair and brown eyes. He needed a shave and a trim. No distinguishing marks, but he'll have left me with one."

Dodd was writing it all down. "Miss, can you confirm this?" Chase asked Jenny.

He'll have scars, she thought, and it doesn't matter. It doesn't matter at all.

"We need to keep her out of it," Colin said.

"We can't, sir," Chase answered. "Miss, can you add anything to this description?"

"Not much. I just watched his hands. They were hairy, and his nails were too long. The knife had a long thin blade. He took it with him."

"Could you identify him if you saw him again?"

"She won't be doing that," Colin insisted. "She's not giving a statement. Mine will have to suffice. And no press."

"And why is that, sir? If I may ask."

"You may not," Colin said firmly.

"Not a random attack, then, sir?"

Colin did not reply.

"The record will have to reflect her name and her refusal to cooperate," Chase persisted.

"She is not refusing. *I* am refusing on her behalf. I'll have my super ring your super about it tomorrow."

Chase paused. "Yes, sir," he conceded. They withdrew.

Colin and Jenny were alone. Their evening had begun as a celebration: She had accepted his formal proposal of marriage, and he'd never felt better. She had healed, physically and psychologically. Scott was at Dartmoor, and the other evildoers were housed at the pleasure of Her Majesty's government as well. The sniper remained at large but was not likely a concern, and there had been no notices with Jenny's snap for almost a month. They had shared a bottle of champagne, and he had taken her to her favourite Italian restaurant for dinner. She had teased him, saying that since she'd be giving up her name, he'd finally found a way to make Inspector Rawson happy. They had been on their way home when he'd sensed movement behind them and heard the unmistakable sound of a blade being released for action.

Casey's knock startled him. The champagne, the rush of adrenalin now dissipated, the painkiller—Colin knew his reflexes were dull.

"Well done, sir," Casey said, his eyes passing quickly over Colin and coming to rest on Jenny. There were smudges of dried blood on her face. She must have wiped her tears with her hands, and no one had thought to clean her up. "What now?" he asked, removing some paper towels from the dispenser, dampening them, and handing them to her.

"Colin has to stay overnight, so I'll be here," she said. "Tomorrow—I don't know." She rubbed her hands and then, at Casey's nod, applied the wet towels to her cheeks.

The nurse was waiting with Colin's gown and wheelchair, and the detectives would want his clothes. Casey knew the procedure. "I'll stay with her while they get you sorted, sir."

"Keep the vultures away," Colin said. "I don't want her involved."

"Those two coppers outside? They're on the boil all right! Not to worry. And we'll find you when you're settled." He left Colin to the nurse's ministrations and found a quiet waiting area. He put his arm around Jenny's shoulders. "Are you sure you're okay, love? Did anybody have a look at you?"

"It wasn't necessary," she whispered. "Simon, I should have been able to help. You tried to teach me self-defense, remember? But I couldn't learn it. I thought they were going to kill us, and I couldn't recall even the first thing to do."

"Sinclair did well, love. You were in good hands."

She looked at him. She hadn't forgotten how forbidding he had seemed during the early days at the flat. Now, however, the strength in his face was like a port in a storm, steadfast, resolute, and unchanging. "He'll want me to go away again, Simon, and I don't know what to do."

He didn't respond right away. "Love—how close were you to his block when the attack occurred?"

The intent of the question hit her hard. Had the men followed them from the High Street or had they been waiting? "Oh, God, Simon, if they know where I live, I'll never be able to go home!"

"One step at a time, love. Assessing the risk always precedes planning."

"Simon, I don't want to run away, but I don't want to put anyone else in jeopardy, either."

"It's early days, love. We'll get him. There are options. Steady on." He rose to his feet. "Sir."

She looked up at Detective Superintendent Graves. "Is Colin in danger because of me? We weren't all the way back to his flat when it happened. And the other detectives don't know—" Her throat was tight.

Graves sat down beside her. "The suspect will be interrogated by someone who knows what questions to ask. Miss Jeffries, I assure you, we are well aware of the complications."

"Do I have to make a statement? Will I have to testify?"

Graves' gaze was steady. "Let us worry about that. We have one man in custody, and we'll be pressing him rather hard for information about his accomplice. When he realises he attacked a police officer, he may choose not to plead his case in court." He stood. "Miss Jeffries, I am concerned about your safety. Do you have a place to go?"

Did he know she lived with Colin? Of course he did. And he didn't want her to go there.

"I'll take care of it, sir," Simon answered for her.

Graves turned. "Ah, the nurse." He nodded shortly at Casey and left them.

"Sergeant Casey?" the nurse inquired. "Mr. Sinclair asked me to direct you to his room."

They walked down a long corridor, took the lift, turned right, and passed the nurses' station. "Here we are," the nurse said finally, pushing the door open for them. It was a private room. Of course—Sinclair had resources.

Colin's eyes were heavy. "Casey, I can't protect her tonight," he said.

"I'll do, sir. I'll stand watch outside."

CHAPTER 42

There were two chairs in Colin's hospital room. Simon took one outside, and Jenny put a blanket around her shoulders and tried to make herself comfortable in the other while she watched him sleep. There was a tightness between his brows now, and she wondered if he were concerned for her, even in rest. That expression had been on his face the first time she'd seen him and many times since. Was it habit, or a manifestation of his subconscious mind?

She saw his fist clench and relax. His wrists were bare. What had happened to his cufflinks? At dinner he'd worn a pair with the Union Jack symbol on them, and she'd teased him about wearing her flag. The champagne had unleashed his charm, and he'd expounded again on the meaning of the three crosses, this time personalizing the analogy of the saints in a way that both pleased and embarrassed her. "My little St. George," he called her. "You've slain more dragons than he ever did. St. Andrew was a witness until death, and you're as loving and courageous as he was. And now I can anoint you St. Patrick, because you have chosen to live in the land where you were abused, as he did."

She'd demurred. "I'm no saint," she'd laughed. And she wasn't—but the flag and the God who had inspired it had journeyed with her through difficult seas. There had been times when it had seemed menacing, with bars holding her in, but on other occasions it had fortified her, keeping the storms at bay. In her mind she saw the flag with its bold colors and thought it had a bold message, too: My arms are open, My love is unending, My heart is yours.

Colin had given her his heart. He had made her hope real. He had gone down on one knee when he proposed to her, making her cry, of course. She had wished for some eloquent response but could only murmur "Yes," and then he had kissed her and she couldn't speak at all. "My mother wants you to have her engagement ring," he'd said later. "She's waiting for me to collect it. Violet never wore it—it wasn't offered to her." They'd decided to wait until it was official before sharing the news with anyone else.

She felt stiff. She stood and stretched. When the nurse came in to check on Colin, Jenny was already standing by the bed, holding his hand. He didn't need the physical contact; she did. The nurse woke him, and Jenny thought what a strange practice it was, disturbing the sleep of patients when rest was what they needed most. Colin was groggy but managed to swallow the medication, smiling when he felt Jenny's lips on his cheek. She sat down again.

"Tea, love?" It was Simon, her rock, her anchor.

"Simon, they would have killed us. When I close my eyes, I see them coming at us."

"I know, love. That's why I'm here. But they didn't succeed, did they?" He bent his head down and rested his cheek briefly against her hair. Sinclair would send her away; he'd have to. He didn't know when he'd see her again.

The tea was hot and sweet, just the way she liked it. "It's my fault."

"It bloody well isn't," The Voice said.

He might put sugar in her cup, but he never sugarcoated anything else. She watched him step outside. She felt safe with him there. She loved him, too, in a way she didn't understand. How many cups of tea had they shared? How many late-night discussions? He had kept her on course so many times when she had thought her soul would break. She went into the hall to thank him. He was leaning back in the chair with his head against the wall, but his eyes were alert. "I'll miss you," she said and went back in.

Her soul—that reminded her of the phrases she'd wanted to quote to Colin, about loving him to the "depth and breadth and height / My soul can reach," as Elizabeth Barrett Browning had written. She could not love him purely—that had been taken from her—but most of the other verses were appropriate. "I love thee with the passion put to use / In my old griefs"—Colin knew what those were. And the poem contained the promise she wanted to make to him: "I love thee with the breath / Smiles, tears, of all my life!—and, if God choose, I shall but love thee better after death."

Death—she had hoped the threat was past, that the monster's anger would abate or his influence wane. She thought ruefully that Inspector Rawson had been right: She did need protection even after the legal process ended. She was still glad that she had not chosen to be anonymous, however. She would have missed so much. But it did seem like a merciless twist of fate for yet another menace to burst forth just when she was on the cusp of an exciting new future.

Everything hinged on how much the bad guys knew. If her association with Colin had been discovered, he would be in danger whether she were present or not. And she could not go to Kent—hazard would follow her like iron filings to a magnet. With morning would come the discussion she dreaded. She didn't want to be separated from this man; yet even as she thought the words, she knew that love would dictate that she go willingly wherever he asked. Choose life, Colin had commanded long ago. And she had chosen it, not once but many times. She had moved forward and she had succeeded, not because she was strong but because those around her were. Simon had taught her to face life head-on, and when the new day dawned, she would. It would not be easy—Colin would be making another proposal to her, one that might keep them apart for who knows how long, when the proposal she wanted to think about was the one that would unite them forever.

Colin woke, feeling stiff and sore, to find her asleep in the hospital chair. She had rung Casey. Was he still outside? Was it feeling for her or loyalty to him as a fellow copper that held him there? It didn't matter now. She had stayed all night. She knew his condition wasn't serious, yet she had kept a vigil by his bed. She was here. She was his. She loved him.

When he had first seen her, her eyes had been closed. They had awakened with pain. He wanted to see the love in them now, but he would not wake her. A few more moments of peace were all he could give her today.

CHAPTER 43

Brighton: seaside city, holiday destination, but Jenny was a refugee, not a vacationer. Colin had wanted her out of Hampstead before Chase and Dodd conducted their follow-on interviews, so she left the same day he came home from the hospital. Sergeant Andrews had taken her by tube to Victoria Station, where he had put her on the train south.

John Ogilvie met her train in Brighton and escorted her to a hotel. He was a detective superintendent, a colleague of Colin's, a tall, lean man with an air of importance and a confident stride. His easygoing manner was deceptive, barely concealing a quick and astute mind. She was sure he noticed her bare ring finger. "Colin tells me you've a bit of a situation and need to disappear for a few weeks. I'm glad he chose Brighton for you—we've got a sizeable population of foreign students here. You'll blend in."

When her luggage was stowed, he gave her a brief tour of the area. There were numerous sights to see, many within walking distance of the hotel. He left her with a map, a tourist guide, and his card. "Your room is in my name," he said. "Feel free to eat either inside or outside the hotel. Browse in the outlet stores, or anywhere else you like, but make cash purchases only. If you need more money, ring me. Colin will wire it to me."

"Are you my handler?"

"Nothing as formal as that."

It was an attractive room, not as nicely furnished as the Hotel La Place but larger and with a sea view. When the door closed behind D/S Ogilvie, she felt more isolated than at any time since the monster's attack. The walls of her room were a deeper blue than Colin's eyes but sufficient to remind her of him. There was a small desk with a straight chair, but she could not write him. Nothing must appear at his flat with her name, her address. Two armchairs with a round table between them looked out over the water, but only one of them would receive any use during her stay. And the bed was a double, with room enough for him beside her, but he would not be there. This trip was a cruel blow, because she knew what she was missing in her separation from him.

The hotel provided a complementary full English breakfast and had a restaurant that served light fare throughout the afternoon and evening, but she ate every meal alone. Her only interaction with people was the courtesy shown to strangers, the cashier at the bookstore already smiling at the next customer before she had stepped away.

It was too cool for any beach activities that involved the water, but the weather was beautiful—not one drop of rain since she'd arrived. She walked along the beach and contemplated the millions of grains of sand beneath her feet. She looked out at the English Channel. At night she couldn't tell where the sea ended and the sky began—it was all dark, dead dark. In contrast, Brighton glowed, like a huge organism with a radioactive substance pulsing through its veins.

Colin kept her apprised of the investigation. The second knifer was in police custody, and both men were being questioned about their employer and the scope of their assignment. They were reticent about the details so far, but Graves had arranged for two interview teams instead of one in the hope that extensive questioning and different approaches would wear them down. Colin minimised the pain from his wounds, admitting only to discomfort. He was well enough for Andrews to drive him to the Yard, he insisted, and yes, he elevated his leg when he got there. He loved her. He missed her.

As the days passed, Jenny tired of her tourist status. She received no genuine smiles, no flashes of recognition as she trekked up and down the streets. The Mexican restaurant where she ate made her homesick for Texas, and the Italian restaurant—although more informal than her favorite in Hampstead—made her ache inside for the happy times she and Colin had shared there. She began to see the people she knew in the people she saw—a woman with her mother's haircut, a man with Simon's mouth, a thin pimply-faced teenager with Colin's eyes. Each time she felt an irrational surge of hunger born out of her longing for contact, some personal contact. Her nightly talks with Colin—and occasional ones with Simon and her family—were all she had.

No one could visit her, Colin said. Not even Hunt, because they were all connected to her and that connection must remain unknown. Talk to God, he suggested, so she did. At first her conversations were full of what Simon would call whingeing—get me out of Brighton, I don't like it here, I miss Colin, I'm lonely—and she was sure that God tired of hearing it. Then she tried to reason with God, explaining over and over why she and Colin should be together. She bargained, promising to do every good thing she could think of if He would just let her go home. God was silent, but the process did relieve some of her tension, and it kept her from thinking she was going crazy. She wasn't talking to herself, after all.

Ogilvie was always relaxed when she saw him. He chided her gently about her impatience, and she wondered why older people weren't even more hurried. Each time he asked only a question or two about her, never writing anything down, but she realized that gradually he was acquiring a wealth of information. Finally she asked him directly: "What do you know about me?"

"Not enough; in this business, never enough," he answered.

He could have been Colin, fifteen years or so into the future, his desire to know having escalated, not moderated.

She did not ask Colin how much longer she'd be exiled. She did ask whether the two men who had attacked them knew where she lived and what her relationship with him was. He answered "yes" to the former and "it's unconfirmed" to the latter question, emphasising that it was essential as a result for them to discover who had sent them. Her life with Colin depended on that.

She had plenty of time to think about him, but it was too painful to daydream about being his wife when her identity had led to his injuries. She had accepted his marriage proposal, but she could not honor it if it put him in danger. She still saw them being attacked, the two men coming at them, Colin bleeding. She still felt her helplessness. In the dark of night she cried about the sacrifice she feared she would have to make. In the daylight she worried about everything else—how long she'd have to be in Brighton; whether she'd have to move to another location; what her future prospects would be. She was surprised when Ogilvie brought her a package. It had his name on it, but the New Scotland Yard return address told her it was from Colin. It contained the blanket he had given her so many months ago. It had warmed her during witness protection, its colors reminding her of the Texas heat.

Her days dragged. She couldn't even take a class. She had asked Ogilvie, thinking that it would be fun to learn more Italian. Perhaps she and Colin could go to Italy and she could impress him with her fluency in the language. Or first aid, a practical skill. She could be useful to someone. Somewhere. Sometime.

Ogilvie had become very still, abandoning his casual manner. "Even if it were possible for you to register under an assumed name, regular contact with the same group of persons would not be wise. And people talk—particularly when they don't know they're not meant to and when they have a subject to discuss like a lovely young woman with an appealing accent, an unusual watch, and—distinguishing marks."

The purple hearts were striking; she probably shouldn't have worn the watch outside the hotel. Frustrated, she'd asked what difference it made now—at least here if danger came, no one else would be hurt.

"We both know someone to whom it would make a significant difference," he had said. "Someone who would be deeply hurt if anything happened to you."

That was true. She was feeling sorry for herself, and she mustn't. Following that talk she didn't strike up a conversation with anyone, lest they ask her to introduce herself. She had no Colin, no Simon, no Esther Hollister. Inspector Rawson had finally gotten his wish—that she would no longer exist as Jennifer Jeffries—because even though she had not lost her name, she couldn't use it and thus was just as anonymous. She wondered if other witnesses felt haunted after their legal obligations had been met. If they visited the same store two days in a row, did they take a different route home the second time? Were they spooked when the sun began to set and shadows dotted the landscape? Did they sit behind securely locked and latched doors and wait to hear if the voices in the corridor stopped or passed by?

Between dusk and dawn time stood still. Colin continued to call every night with words of love and reassurance, and when they hung up she tried to remember what his body had felt like, whether they had really made love or if it had only been a dream. She did not dream in Brighton, not in the daytime or at night. During her waking hours she was watchful, and in the evening she was tired from being on guard all day. Other people's laughter exhausted her, as did D/S Ogilvie's gentle concern. She no longer cried. Grief shared was grief halved, but grieving alone was like falling but never hitting bottom.

She bought a blank journal and spent an entire afternoon wondering why, when she had nothing to enter on the pages. Was she a blank book, too? Brian thought she was a fighter. Simon had called her a soldier. She was a survivor, she knew that much. And a daughter and a sister. What she wanted to be was Colin's wife.

Her parents were appalled by the whole situation. Her mother felt she had been a burden on Colin long enough and begged her to come back to Texas. Unlike Brighton, there would be some familiar faces in Houston, and perhaps she could get a job, put down some roots. Perhaps it would be different this time, she argued silently with Simon. She wouldn't have the same expectations. Several days after she reported those thoughts to Colin, another package arrived via Ogilvie—her British flag, with a message from Colin: Don't give up. Don't give in. Wait for me.

When the pain came early in the morning, she knew what it was but was unprepared to treat it. She'd packed quickly for Brighton, and she hadn't thought she'd be gone long enough to need sanitary napkins or prescription pain medication. She rang Ogilvie and asked him to send a policewoman as soon as he could. The WPC assessed the situation and brought the supplies Jenny needed and the strongest over-the-counter medication available, but she called her Ma'am, and for some reason that hurt. She was only twenty-four! Had her pain aged her? Or was it the contrast between the constable's optimistic face and her despairing one?

"Shall I ask Detective Superintendent Ogilvie to call by later?"

"No. God, no." She didn't want Ogilvie. She wanted Simon, with the medicine that didn't quit and The Voice that wouldn't let her quit either. It hadn't been this bad since that first time in the witness protection flat. Since then she'd been able to treat it early, with meds that knocked out the pain and her too. The WPC had done her best, but the nonprescription pills didn't ease the sharp pangs significantly, and there would be no more help coming.

She went back to bed. She wanted Colin, who called her scars wrinkles and considered her body beautiful in spite of them. When she had first slept in this room, she'd reached out in the dark for him, having become accustomed very quickly to sharing his bed. As the days and then the weeks had passed, her isolation had deepened, and she had stopped expecting to find him next to her.

Now, however, alone and in pain, she cried for him, and the tears she had disciplined herself not to shed would not be withheld. As the knots in her belly twisted, she sobbed his name, but there was no one to hear.

The first time her mobile rang, she was crying too hard to answer it; the second time, too. It was too early for Colin's call. It had to be Ogilvie, but the third time she didn't care that she couldn't be brave anymore in front of him. But it was Colin, and in tortured phrases she asked him all the questions she had suppressed. "How much longer do I have to stay away? If you love me, how can you leave me here? Why can't I see you, for a day, a night, an hour? Why can't I come home? I want to hold you. I want to make love to you. Why did our time together have to be so short? When do I get to have a life? Why does the monster always win? I reached out for happiness, and he slapped my hand."

When her sobs subsided, he did not tell her how thorough and painstaking every police investigation had to be. He did not describe the legal constraints, the rights of accused persons, the endless checking and rechecking of facts that were involved.

He did not tell her how many nights he went to bed with his hands throbbing, because he had pounded them against the shower walls, cursing his inability to help the woman he loved. What use was it, being a copper? Had anyone's life been made better by his work? Vi had left him, and he had had to send Jenny away. He did not tell her how empty his bed seemed, how lifeless his flat was without her.

He told her that he loved her, that he would always love her. He told her that a part of him was missing because he was not with her. "Jenny, I've been to Kent," he said. "I have your ring, your engagement ring. It's waiting for you. *I'm* waiting for you. Progress is being made. I'm confident we'll be reunited soon. I want a future with you, and this is the only way. Jenny, I've seen Goodwyn. He's praying for us. We may be separated from each other, but we're not separated from God. God is big enough for this. *God is!*"

When he finally allowed her to hang up, her stomach still throbbed, but her spirit was soothed. She had been a witness in a court of law, but Colin was a witness in a larger forum. He had tried to strengthen her with a power greater than his own. She wished she had his faith: It was stronger than hers. Then pray to have it, he had said, and she would. Only one question remained: Why hadn't she packed any of his handkerchiefs?

CHAPTER 44

Several nights later, long after the sun had gone down, Colin called with good news. "Jenny, it's over."

"You've arrested someone?"

"Yes, but more than that—it's *all* over. Scott's dead, Jen. He was killed in prison. You can come home for good this time."

Tears of relief and anticipation bubbled over. A new horizon lay ahead of her!

"Ogilvie will take you to the train tomorrow. I'll meet you at Victoria Station."

"Then I'll be in your arms before nightfall! Colin, I was afraid we'd never be able to be together."

"I know, Jen, but there's nothing to hold us back now. Come home and marry me."

When they ended their conversation, Jenny felt her fatigue lift, as if every blood vessel had been infused with a breath of oxygen. She was energized—she would pack tonight.

The monster was dead. It was a stunning report—he had been invincible for so long! Simon would have given her the details she had forgotten to ask Colin. Brian would have said, "Good news, JJ," with quiet satisfaction. Hunt would have reveled in the exposé, and Danny—he would have laughed and winked the way he did before laying down a winning poker hand: "Game over, Sis!"

No more running! No more hiding! She would have to face herself now, but that no longer seemed as difficult as it once had. She could hear Simon's voice: "You're stronger than you think you are, love." The monster had demolished her concept of who she was, but now she realized that the witness protection team had already helped her begin to reshape it. Simon had challenged her to meet his standards and required her to focus on her commitment. Brian had provided thoughtfulness and generosity. Danny had added encouragement and spontaneity. Hunt's outspokenness had tempered her. And Colin—he had had a clear vision of her potential, and with grace and patience he had led her into a loving relationship that was more rewarding than she could have imagined.

If those men had built a real bricks-and-mortar house instead of the one where her spirit dwelt, Simon would have installed the security system and then made certain she knew how to activate it. Brian would have had the foundation inspected and arranged for any structural flaws to be corrected. Danny would have been enthusiastic about the fun she'd have living there, and Hunt would have urged her to sign her name on the dotted line and move in before the ink was dry.

If it were a real house, she would want lots of windows to let the light in, to see the clouds coming, and to watch the rains that cleansed the world and made all things new. She would want Colin to carry her across the threshold.

Mrs. Colin Thomas Dowding Sinclair. Would the minister use all Colin's names when he invited them to recite their vows? Colin would be so elegant and handsome that she wondered if she'd have the breath to repeat them. When the minister asked her to "love, honor, and obey," would it count if Colin received two of those pledges and Simon the other? What would she wear? Something with sleeves, but only her protection team would know why. Danny would play soccer—football—with her brothers in the back yard. Brian would help her mother in the kitchen. She hoped Hunt would exclude the church service from his irreverent commentary. Yes, she wanted them all to be there—even Hunt.

Epilogue

The sun rose, its rays warm enough to burn off the fog by mid-morning. It was a crisp, breezy, glorious day in Brighton, but Jenny hadn't a single regret about leaving it behind. Detective Superintendent Ogilvie brought her a copy of the morning paper to read on the train, and she was amazed to see the monster's epitaph reduced to a single column of ten-point type.

Cecil Scott Latest Dartmoor Death

WILLIAM CECIL CRIGHTON SCOTT, 38, of London, popularly known as the "Carpet Killer," was found dead in his cell, the governor of HMP Dartmoor reported today.

Scott, son of Ambassador Sir Edward Cullen Scott and a member of one of Britain's most prominent families, was convicted of serial murder and rape and sentenced to life imprisonment earlier this year.

Forensic examination revealed that Scott was the victim of a brutal beating. Bruises around the mouth and wrists indicated that he had been forcibly restrained and silenced while the attack took place. Multiple stab wounds were inflicted but none appeared to have penetrated a major artery. Initial findings suggest that he bled to death over time, but a complete postmortem has been scheduled.

A spokesman for the Scott family described their devastation at the news and threatened to call for a public inquiry into the prison service and staff who permitted the atrocity to occur. "At the least Dartmoor officials were incompetent and at worst they were vengeful and sadistic," the spokesman said. Evidently Scott had complained about receiving harsh treatment.

Dartmoor houses a high percentage of black prisoners and has long been considered to have an unusually violent prison population. Scott's death is not the first incident of brutality to occur at the notorious site. Repeated attempts to close it down, however, have proved unsuccessful, various prison officials requesting a last chance for a facility which appears to offer no chance of betterment for the offenders who are confined there.

Scott's death is the second tragedy to befall his family in as many weeks. Maurice Owen Blythe, longtime associate of the family, is being held by police on a variety of felony charges. Neither MPS personnel nor Blythe's solicitor would comment.

An inquiry will be conducted into the circumstances surrounding the decease.

- -

It was a work day for Colin. He was wearing a natty three-piece suit. Jenny was in jeans and a sweater. He was 6'2" tall, easy to spot in the crowded station. She was 5'2". He had short hair; she had long. His eyes were blue, with crow's feet at the corners, and they were combing the throng looking for her. Hers were brown, and her skin was unlined except for a small stripe on one cheek. He carried no luggage. She was overencumbered with two carryon cases and a shopping bag to hold the overflow. His face was anxious with anticipation; hers was radiant when their eyes met. They looked mismatched in every way, but when he put his arms around her, they were both crying.

THE END

ACKNOWLEDGEMENTS

My book is entitled *The Witness* because a number of the main characters are witnesses: Jenny, who recovers from her injuries and trauma and testifies against her attacker in a court of law; Sergeant Simon Casey, whose life illustrates the importance of honor; Detective Chief Inspector Colin Sinclair, who testifies to the power of love; Dr. Theodore Knowles, who believes that healing is possible; and Reverend Neil Goodwyn, who testifies in a spiritual forum.

Writing the book required me to relive my own hurricane trauma and thus was a trial of sorts. Among my expert witnesses were: Dewey Lane, M.D., who gave clear and patient explanations of medical conditions; Marjorie A. Husbands, LPC, who assisted with psychological issues; Jason French-Williams, Solicitor-Advocate, who provided legal advice; Hal and Gulshan Jaffer, who answered odd questions and did a bit of sleuthing for me; Dr. James E. Auer, CDR, USN (Retired), for unfailing support; and John-Edward Alley, for connecting me with invaluable resources in the UK.

From London's Metropolitan Police Service (also known as New Scotland Yard): Phillip Hagon QPM, Commander (Retired), for his astute mind and generous spirit; Bill Tillbrook, Chief Superintendent (Retired) for gracious assistance; Detective Inspector Heather Toulson, for insight into the work of SOIT officers; and DC Clare A. Knowles. From the Specialist Firearms Unit of the Met: PC Gary Willis, "C" Relief, 1999-2005; and PC Ian Chadwick, 1982-2007 (previous service with Her Majesty's Corps of Royal Marines). Last but not least: the two anonymous Metropolitan Police armed officers who did not arrest me for taking pictures of New Scotland Yard in November, 2005 ("suspicious use of camera in sensitive area?"). Any errors, whether intended or not, belong to me and not to any of them.

Among those who read the "transcript" and provided constructive feedback were: my husband, Larry, who for some reason thought it fun to have new chapters read aloud to him and was my biggest cheerleader and best researcher; my son, Jeff, who read Parts One and Two and had to wait three months for me to write the remainder; my son, Paul, who corrected my poker terms; and my daughter-in-law, Jennifer, whose enthusiasm touched me (she stayed up half the night because

AUTHOR'S NOTE

The Witness is written in two languages: British English (including spelling and expressions) for the British characters and American English for the American characters. This was done to emphasize the estrangement of the American protagonist in a country that allegedly spoke the same language and to give added depth to the British characters.

Thus you will note, for example, "realise/recognise" for "realize/recognize" and "colour/honour/neighbour" for "color/honor/neighbor." British English sometimes omits or uses fewer or different prepositions, and their past tenses may be unlike ours: "in hospital" for "in the hospital," "different to" for "different than" and "learnt" for "learned."

she couldn't stop reading).

My publisher, David Dunham of Dunham Books, served as the judge. My thanks to him for his many sustaining rulings from the bench (shepherding a new author through the publication process).

You, the readers, are the jury.

About the Author

Naomi Kryske was educated at Rice University, Houston, Texas. She left Texas when she became a Navy wife. Following her husband, Larry's, retirement from the Navy, she lived on the Mississippi Gulf Coast until Hurricane Katrina caused their relocation to north Texas. *The Witness* is the first of a series of novels set in London, involving the Metropolitan Police, and exploring the themes of trauma and recovery. In 2008 she was awarded a grant from the Melissa English Writing Trust for *The Witness*.

Visit Naomi on the Web at www.naomikryske.com.

COMING SOON, THE SECOND IN
THE WITNESS SERIES:

THE MISSION

Prologue

The Gold Commander at New Scotland Yard could not believe what he saw. His twenty-seven years of experience with London's Metropolitan Police had taught him to maintain outward calm regardless of inner turmoil, but this afternoon he was finding it difficult. His attention had been directed away from the bank of screens he was monitoring in MetOps, covering the policing of the Arms Fair at the London Docklands. On the lower left, screens showed an aeroplane exploding as it flew into a towering skyscraper in New York City. Was the crash intentional? Had someone found a novel way to kill himself? Certainly no capable pilot could miss the World Trade Center! He watched the replay. No, the skies were perfectly clear, and the plane looked too large to be a private craft. Dear God, what was happening in America? Mass murder? He forced himself to concentrate. Then a second plane hit the second tower, and all hell broke loose.

There wasn't an officer in the room who didn't have the same emotional discipline as he, but none of them had dealt with an act of terrorism on this scale. Voices were raised in shock and disbelief. Terse phrases were spit out as individuals attempted to communicate what they were seeing. Frustration erupted as they realised they were powerless to assist their neighbours across the pond in any way. Their brief was to make London safer for its citizens, but loss of innocent life anywhere in the world hit them hard. Britain had been the target of IRA attacks for years, but the landscape of American law enforcement—and her security forces—was now irrevocably altered. Indeed, the entire world had changed in the space of a few minutes, because, for the first time, suicide bombers had operated outside the Middle East, setting a dangerous precedent. More attacks would come, perhaps even in his own country. What could be done to prevent them? What would the likely targets be? Senior officials in the building would be discussing those questions in the very near future, he knew, but each officer needed to be ready to do his part.

The Commissioner of Police was in the air over the mid-Atlantic, on his way to confer with senior NYPD officials. Gold rang the Commissioner's office and was told by his personal assistant that he had been informed of the crisis. Because American air space was now closed, his plane had been forced to turn about and would be returning home.

"The Pentagon, sir," an associate behind him mumbled thickly. "An aeroplane has hit the Pentagon in Washington, D.C."

"That makes three," he responded. "How many more? When will this slaughter in the skies end?" He thought of his wife and children and felt a desperate need to ring them and assure himself of their safety. As quickly as the thought arose, however, he quelled it: Individual needs must be set aside. Seeing to the security of the many must take priority over personal concerns. He had not become a policeman to protect one life at a time; he had always hoped he would prove worthy of a rank high enough to affect the safety and well-being of many more.

By now the visual images would have seared into the minds of all who had seen them. Because of the United Kingdom's close alliance with the United States, London could be the next target. People were spontaneously evacuating high-rise buildings and crowding the streets. To prevent panic, he must supply mental pictures that would reassure them. Uniformed police were a symbol of stability in a country ruled by law. The public looked to the police for protection. They must be seen to be on the Job. He ordered all leaves cancelled and made arrangements for every available officer to report for high visibility duties. He summoned his deputy, whose stricken face had aged him. "Contact our counterparts in Kent and the other neighbouring counties. We'll need manpower from them to assist us."

The news must have got round the demonstrators at the Docklands. The screens showed the mass of people splintering into groups which huddled together briefly before dispersing. Excellent. He could reduce the quantity of officers assigned there and increase the number on London streets. He rang the Silver Commander.

There may have been British citizens on the hijacked planes, but regardless of nationality, every seat had held a human being. When had the passengers known their fate? How had parents controlled their own fears and comforted their children? He was put in mind of his early days on the Job. In his two probationary years he had seen more human tragedy than most experienced in a lifetime. Road accidents, train wrecks, bodies battered beyond recognition. In some cases he'd had to notify the next of kin and watched their desperate disbelief replaced by despair as facts crowded out the last slivers of hope. Some screamed; some went silent. Eventually, determination to carry on, to honour the dead, to see justice done, prevailed.

MetOps was now crowded with officers straining to see the drama being played out on the screens. Gasps and exclamations from them joined his own. One of the World Trade Center towers had collapsed, the ash mixing with dark billowing smoke. Without a doubt British citizens had worked in the World Trade Centers. Many would have been killed along with their American colleagues. The lucky ones had died instantly. Others would carry their fears and scars to the gates of heaven. Still others could be missing under the thousands of tonnes of rubble still being shown. And the loved ones they left behind would be devastated with grief.

He looked about. Not unlike many offices in the World Trade Centers, MetOps was an interior room, artificially lit, located in one of New Scotland Yard's two-tower buildings. Occupants would have no warning of an approaching threat. Mercifully, however, MetOps was on Victoria Block's second floor, an unlikely target for an insidious attack of this sort. Fortunately smoking was not allowed. He could not have tolerated the sight of even a wisp of smoke.

He returned to the screens. "Four," he whispered, his concentration so complete that he was unaware he had spoken aloud. In Pennsylvania a fourth plane had crashed. Still the nightmare continued: A second tower fell, then part of the Pentagon. He felt again the shock, then the grip of despair, and resolved that he would not give in to either. Determination was the order of the day. His mission: take steps to do everything within his considerable power to deliver the best security to Londoners that his force could provide. He knew he'd be on watch indefinitely. He reached for his phone.

PART ONE

SEPTEMBER, 2001

The battle has been joined on many fronts.

— George W. Bush

CHAPTER 1

Jennifer Sinclair's serene September day was shattered by a phone call. It was her husband, Colin, a detective chief inspector with London's Metropolitan Police. He often called during the day, but this time his voice was terse and strained. "Jenny, turn on the telly. Your country's been attacked. New York and other places. We're all on alert here. I don't know when I'll be home. Jenny — remember that evil cannot win. There are more of us fighting it than those participating in it."

"Texas — is Texas okay?"

"So far."

"Colin, I wish you were here!"

"I know. I'll be with you as soon as I can. I love you."

All the news channels were covering the events. Over and over she saw planes flying into buildings, the skies raining flames, smoke, ash, glass, papers, and—*people.* People had jumped to their deaths from the burning towers. She didn't mind the repetitive nature of the reports: It helped the unthinkable to sink in. Terrorists had attacked her country and murdered hundreds, perhaps thousands, of her people. She imagined her nation uttering one great collective scream before the silence of shock muted her.

The memory of her rape resurrected itself with frightening intensity: the terror she had felt, how helpless she had been. But her attacker hadn't known or cared that she was an American, only that she was the right size and sex for his violence. Then when he had discovered she had been found alive, he had sent others to kill her. Colin had placed her in witness protection, but she had endured months of fear until her attacker had been convicted. Would her country face further attacks? The tightness in her chest made it hard to get a breath. Like her country, she had lost her innocence through violent acts on a beautifully clear fall day. And as she had, tomorrow all Americans would wake to a new and frightening world in which the rules of engagement were forever changed.

Over the pounding of her heart, she heard her mobile ring again. This time her hands were shaking when she answered.

"Are you all right, love?" a voice she knew well asked. One of the Met's specialist firearms officers, Sergeant Simon Casey had been in charge of her witness protection team. Everything about him had frightened her at first: his stern expression, his uncompromising manner, even his icy blue eyes, which had dared her not to meet his expectations. Prior to joining the police, he had been a Special Forces operative until an injury required him to retire from military service.

"Simon, what does it mean?"

"Your country's at war. Unless I miss my guess, we'll be in it with you. And I'm in the wrong bloody uniform."

"At war with who? Didn't the terrorist die on the planes?"

"Jenny, someone sent them. It was a complex and coordinated attack. They were well trained and well equipped."

"Simon, I can't stop shaking."

"Breathe. Focus. Like I taught you."

"Is it over? Will there be more?"

"It's too soon to know, but your people will find out who is behind it. Don't panic. You're safe with us."

"Thank you, Simon." She closed her phone. Safe. She had been safe ever since Colin had become a part of her life. He had made sure of it. She returned to the news coverage. She saw again the fireballs when the planes hit their targets. She knew how fragile people's bodies were, how easily skin split open and bones broke. Had their blood burned, those passengers who had flown into eternity? Passengers — my God, there would have been women and children on those planes! What kind of monster planned to murder *children?*

Lines from Longfellow's poem, "The Building of the Ship," flashed through her mind: "Sail on, O Ship of State! / Humanity with all its fears, / With all the hopes of future years, / Is hanging breathless on thy fate!" The British named their warships after courageous qualities: HMS Dauntless, HMS Resolute, and HMS Invincible. Gilbert and Sullivan had poked fun at the practice by placing sailors in one of their operettas on HMS Pinafore, named for a girl's article of clothing, but seamen on the real ships were proud of their legacy and wanted to prove themselves worthy. Now America was like the Titanic, a ship touted as unsinkable but vulnerable nonetheless to an insidious threat.

She shivered. Their flat in Hampstead, a suburb north of London, was difficult to heat, but she suspected she was chilled more by the fear in the air. She made some tea — the British palliative — and dialed her parents' number again, but only the busy signal answered, and she felt lonely and defenseless. In witness protection the officers assigned to her had provided a constant, reassuring presence. PC Danny Sullivan, not much older than her brothers, was an inveterate practical joker who had kept the atmosphere light. Even today he would have found a way to pierce the dread and make her smile. PC Brian Davies, a huge bear of a man whose wife was now one of her closest friends, had been an outstanding cook. Maybe if the flat were filled with the aroma of one of his dishes, she would feel less alone. Even Hunt, the irreverent

PC Alan Hunt, would remind her not to take life too seriously. And, of course, the ginger-haired thirty-something Simon, who had treated her tension with regular doses of exercise and challenged her to face every adversity. She respected his dedication and focus.

"Colin, I want to go home," she said when he called again.

"You'll have to wait for a bit. All planes are grounded in the States, and no international flights are allowed into American air space."

"But I can't reach my family!"

"They'll be all right, Jenny. They are out of the line of fire. Open a bottle of wine. I'll be home before too long. I have something for you. Wait there for me."

It would take at least thirty minutes, she knew, for him to walk to the Embankment Station, take the Edgware branch of the Northern Line to Hampstead Station, and traverse the Hampstead streets that lay between the tube and their home. She washed her face, ran a brush through her hair, and found the corkscrew, all the while wondering what he could be bringing her.

It was an American flag.